IN THE
RED

ALSO BY REGAN C. ASHBAUGH

Downtick

Available from Pocket Books

REGAN C. ASHBAUGH

IN THE
RED

POCKET BOOKS

New York London Toronto Sydney Tokyo Singapore

POCKET BOOKS, a division of Simon & Schuster Inc.
1230 Avenue of the Americas, New York, NY 10020

Ashbaugh, Regan C.
    In the red / Regan C. Ashbaugh
        p.   cm.
    ISBN: 0-671-01890-6
    I. Title.
    PS3551.S3614I6   1999
    813'.54—dc21   98-50122
                                        CIP

First Pocket Books hardcover printing April 1999

10 9 8 7 6 5 4 3 2 1

for Lucas

You will always be my special buddy.
Never forget how much I truly love you.

And finally . . .

To Trevor, his classmates, and the many, many autistic individuals in the great state of Maine. I make you all this promise—I won't stop until the dream becomes a reality. Smile, my friends. We will make it happen!

REGAN

Acknowledgments

ONCE AGAIN, AS I sit contemplating the list of people to whom I am indebted, I am taken *and* honored by its sheer length. So many have helped me in one capacity or another that to list them all is simply not feasible. To those whom I omit, please accept my humblest apologies and know that I will always be appreciative of your efforts. There are, however, a few who deserve to be mentioned by name. Without their tireless support this work would never be of the quality that it is. Consequently, I would like to express my heartfelt thanks to the following individuals: Judy Conley, Steve Gifford, Jim Gribbell, Beau Gros, Greg Hanson, Steve Henderson, Tom Major, Dianne McGrath, Jim Richardson, and Scotty Thomes. You all know the unique part you played in the final outcome. Words are not adequate to express my gratitude.

Finally, there are a handful of individuals without whose dedication and commitment I could never have written this work. It is sobering indeed to realize that grown adults, grappling with all of life's travails, still made the time to help see me through this effort. It is to these special few that I will forever be indebted; not only for their guidance, but for their devotion and friendship as well.

To the City of Portland, Maine, Fire Department—I am profoundly grateful for its assistance, and for a level of cooperation few authors can ever hope to imagine. . . . To Fire Lieutenant Fred LaMontagne, of Bramhall Station's Ladder Six—what can I say, Fred? Your input, friendship, and commitment to the cause were in large part a reason for this ever reaching the light of day. Without your backing, this entire endeavor would probably have remained only a dream. Truly, I cannot thank you enough. . . . To the officers and firefighters of Bramhall Station's Shift Three—I am proud and honored that you allowed me to enter your "family" so unconditionally, for so long a period of time. I only wish I could cook so well. . . . To Deputy Fire Chiefs Donald Brown, Richard Curran, Ronald Thompson, and Reginald Wyman—I am indebted to you all for allowing me on the inside, and to fully understand the enormous responsibility you and your brethren undertake. . . . To Fire Captain Stephen Doyle, and the officers and firefighters of Willard Engine & Ladder Co. #2—I am sincerely grateful for the opportunity and privilege to serve our great community, and for the many invaluable lessons I have learned, not only about myself, but also the true art of fire fighting. . . . To my agent and friend, Charlie Peers—we both know who put us together, and if for no other reason than that, my faith continues to grow. I thank you for standing by me, as well as for your guidance and unwavering friendship. You and I, Charlie, it was meant to be. . . . To Police Detective Daniel Young—once again, Danny, I extend my heartfelt appreciation for your help, your friendship, and your unyielding faith. . . . To my good friend and editor, Tristram Coburn—it's drier in the boat, isn't it, Tris? Thanks for going above and beyond the call of duty. You, my friend, are a class act. . . . And finally, to my best friend and assistant, Jean Gray—words seem superfluous, don't they? Thank you, Jean. A thousand times over, I thank you. Smile. We both know what lies ahead.

REGAN C. ASHBAUGH
August 3, 1998

All creatures kill—there seems to be no exception. But for the whole list man is the only one that kills for fun; he is the only one that kills in malice, the only one that kills for revenge.

—MARK TWAIN
(1835–1910)

A BURNING DESIRE

Book I

Sunday
September 8

THE PHONE CALL came at 2:47 A.M., shattering the oppressively hot and muggy night air in his bedroom like a head-on train collision. It was one of those steamy, sleepless summer evenings every New Yorker dreads, the kind where no one without air-conditioning even bothers with a sheet. Jacob Ferguson jumped from a fitful sleep, peeling his body off the bed. Reaching clumsily for the receiver on his nightstand, he knocked off his alarm clock.

Shit. "Yeah," he moaned as he sat, his brain still in the netherworld from which he'd just been catapulted.

"Jake, it's Don."

Jake knew it was Ederling before he even picked up. At least he hoped so. They'd done this drill a thousand times before. "What's up?" he asked, scratching the hair on the back of his head with his fingernails, instantly aware of the relentless buzzing of a fly against the black night of his bedroom window.

"I think we got another one."

An uneasy silence followed. But Ederling knew that Jake had heard him. He always did. After all, it was the middle of the night. Ederling knew that news just takes longer to filter through the rocks that form in your brain during REM sleep. Especially news like this.

"Jesus."

"It's not pretty, Jake."

"I bet. If it's anything like the last." Jake bent over to retrieve his clock. It had fallen on its numbers and glowed with an eerie, translucent red past its sides through the fabric of his carpet. *Bad omen.* "Where?"

"Mount Kisco."

Jake replaced the clock on his nightstand, asking the question to which he already knew the answer. "Same MO?"

3

"To a T. Victim's as crispy as you'll ever find. Can't tell the sex, but twenty bucks says it's another woman."

"Shhhit," Jake said, wiping away the sweat under his testicles with a sheet. "I hate roasts, Donny. They ruin my appetite for a week."

"Yeah . . . well . . . ever think of a new line of work? Kind of like a dentist hating teeth, don't you think?"

"Funny. What's the address?"

Jake fumbled for the light, holding the receiver between his chin and left shoulder while he jotted down the necessary information. He hung up, stuck the sheet of paper between his teeth, and slipped on the underwear he'd left on the floor when he'd retired for the night just three hours earlier. He sat silently on the edge of his bed, listening meditatively to the fly as it bumped again and again against the darkness of the glass. Jake grabbed for a pillow and felt an odd delight at the prospect of extinguishing this annoying little speck, and bringing silence, once again, to his womb. But there would be enough death to witness tonight. He reached down, opened his screen, and whooshed it away with his hands, watching with satisfaction as it made its way into the muggy night.

Jacob Ferguson had been named chief fire marshal for Westchester County in the spring of 1987. To everyone's surprise, including Jake's, he was chosen over Ederling, even though Ederling had been Westchester County's deputy fire marshal, as Jake liked to say, "since Christ was a corporal." There was a time, long since gone, when the appointment had formed a gaping chasm between the two men. But a lot can happen in twelve years, and Jake's appointment seemed to them now both ephemeral and distant, almost as if in another life. They had since grown as close as brothers.

Jake stood, stretching his neck slowly from side to side. He glanced at his clock again: 2:54 A.M. He lived in Port Chester and figured he could dress, drag a comb through his receding, coffee-colored hair, and make Mount Kisco before 3:30 A.M. He started toward the bathroom and stopped at the foot of his king-size bed. Jake gazed at its unrumpled right side, biting his bottom lip slightly, disillusioned that he was, yet again, fighting off demons. The lining of Jake's heart grew cold at the thought that it might always be like this, that he would never again experience inner peace.

He walked slowly to the tidy side of his bed and gently sat, as if not to wake a sleeping child. Reaching for the pillow with both hands, he held it softly to his face, breathing deeply through his nose. Jake closed his eyes, letting the distant echoes of her scent send him fleetingly to another world, a safer world—one in which he was not alone. He placed the pillow carefully back in its place and covered it with a sheet, as he had done a thousand times before.

"I love you," he whispered.

Jake slipped on a pair of chinos and a T-shirt, hit the light, and shuffled sleepily to the bathroom. A night-light usually served his purposes for midnight jaunts to the toilet. The overhead was for wake-up time. To assist in the process he had wired his radio so that it clicked on when he flipped the wall switch. It seemed louder than usual this morning.

". . . and the Yankees continue their tear through the Eastern Division, finishing a sweep last night of the red-hot . . ." The words continued ringing in his ears as he flipped the radio off manually. Though a Yankee fan, he wasn't interested in baseball right now. He preferred his own thoughts, his private slice of found sanity. It mattered little right then that it was fabricated, because real or imaginary, still, it was quiet and serene. The world Jake was about to enter would be anything but.

He splashed some water on his hair, whisking a brush through it just long enough to look presentable, slapped a glob of Crest on an old, fraying toothbrush, and stared hard at himself as he mindlessly went through the motions. He could see the exhaustion in his eyes; their whites were red, yet almost seemed to blend harmoniously with the golden honey color of his irises. Jake leaned closer, never having noticed that before. When he finished, he leaned against the tiled counter, closed his eyes, and took one long, deep breath.

"Ready?" he asked himself in the mirror.

As ready as you're ever going to be, came the customary response.

It was time.

AS JAKE TURNED the corner to Chiswell Lane, the scene was like hundreds of others he had witnessed before. Legions of flashing red and blue lights punctuated the surrounding trees and homes, inharmoniously fracturing the pure black of night in a macabre effect Jake liked to call Lucifer's Disco.

It was 3:37 A.M. when Jake Ferguson pulled his department-issue, 1998 Crown Victoria behind a yellow, articulated fire truck. He pocketed his keys and, as was his habit, stood silent a moment, eyeing the assembled crowd. He was actually looking beyond the crowd, hoping to see that one solitary face hiding behind a tree, a car, a Dumpster. Fire starters seldom hang with the throng. They prefer to watch, but usually from a distance. The experienced ones know better than to stand inside the lion's den.

It wasn't that Jake necessarily expected to catch anyone, although he was always optimistic. But if there was one quality for which he was known, it was his keen eye and photographic memory. He'd remember a face if he'd seen it at another scene—even if it was two years ago. He walked casually a few houses down one side of the street, then back up the other side, scanning his surroundings, searching for anyone out of the ordinary.

Jake walked back to the trunk of his car and slipped on the working uniform of his profession. He looked like any other firefighter now, with his thick Ranger Firewalker boots, bunker pants, red suspenders, and bunker jacket. The only thing that set him apart from the others were the words CHIEF FIRE MAR-SHAL written in bright yellow on the rise of his helmet and across the back of his jacket. It was unbearably hot, and Jake consequently held his heavy firefighter helmet under his arm.

The captain on the scene was casual in his hello. "Chief," he said, sucking water from a sports bottle as Jake approached from the side of his truck.

"Hey, Rob," Jake responded. "Two bagger, huh?"

"Yeah. She was workin' pretty good when we got here. I called for a second the moment I saw it," the captain said, indicating that he'd immediately requested a second alarm.

Like all fire junkies, Jake had a scanner at home. But he asked anyway. "When was that?"

The captain removed his helmet, wiping sweat from his brow with a dirty, gloved hand. "Call came in about quarter of one, something like that. We probably got here ten, maybe eleven minutes later."

"Were you first in?" Jake asked, unwrapping a lozenge he'd pulled from a pack he always kept in his jacket.

"Yep," the captain responded, shaking away Jake's offer of a lozenge.

Jake raised his left hand silently at a couple of acknowledging firefighters as they walked by. "So that puts you here just about one, right?"

"Close enough."

"You say she was pretty well involved when you got here?"

"I'll say. We had fire showing on both sides of the house."

"Roof?"

"No, but she was smokin' like a bitch. We vented a few holes."

Jake understood the meaning of the captain's last comment. A good working fire creates incredible amounts of smoke and heat. If not given a venue for escape, it makes attacking the fire from inside more difficult, *and* more deadly. Known as *truckies*, ladder companies have but two primary functions at all working fires: search-and-rescue, and ventilation. Jake knew the captain had ordered his ladder personnel to the roof to vent some holes to facilitate the release of both heat and smoke.

And so began the obligatory interrogation of the officer on the scene. The captain had been through this before, albeit not as often as officers in larger towns. But still, enough to make it routine. He could have told Jake everything he wanted to know, but politely let him ask anyway. This fact didn't escape Jake, but there was protocol to follow. They were after a pro, a sick one at that. Both men felt it wise to follow procedure.

"See anybody coming or going?" Jake asked, resting his helmet upside down on the street, pulling a notebook and pen from his jacket pocket.

"Not that I noticed. I'll need to speak to my men when we get back."

"Do that and get back to me, will you, Rob?"

"Sure thing."

Jake scribbled something in his notebook. "Doors locked when you arrived?"

"Yep. Had to force our way in. Nothing out of the ordinary, really."

Jake looked at Rob, his face lit repeatedly red in staccato fashion, like a white ball in a room full of amber strobe lights. "Nothing but the roast in the bed."

The captain sneered at him. "Nice, Jake."

"Sorry. Under a lot of pressure is all."

Jake spotted Ederling as he came out of the house. At six seven, 263 pounds, he was a formidable figure; hard to miss in a crowd. Ederling spotted Jake speaking with the captain in the street and stopped to light a smoke. Someone approached and whispered something in his ear. Ederling nodded and strode across the lawn toward his boss.

"Thanks, Rob," Jake said, indicating he had what he needed. "Call me after you've debriefed your men."

"No sweat," the captain said before disappearing behind his truck.

Jake walked the incline of the front lawn, meeting Ederling halfway between the truck and the house. Fire hoses were haphazardly strewn across the grass, the smell of smoke still thick in the air.

"Hey," Jake said, staring up at the still-smoldering three-story Tudor home. "This is going to get old quick, huh, Don? Anything?"

"Nah. I spoke to the first three men to enter the house. Neighbors told them they thought there were occupants, so they went in for rescue."

Jake shook his head slightly. "Never ceases to amaze me the balls these guys have."

Ederling dug something out of the corner of his right eye with his ring finger. "Yeah, it's a rush I guess. God knows they don't do it for the money."

"So what have we got?"

"Shit, Jake, I don't know what to make out of this guy. I can't figure out what his gig is. I mean . . . I don't know if fire's his thing, or he just torches his scenes to make it more difficult to investigate."

It was quiet a moment. "Let's go see if we can narrow it down," Jake said, nodding his head toward the house. "Origin the same?"

"Yeah, I already told the fire boys the bedroom's ours."

"Good. Let's take a look."

"Time for more fun and games. Did you eat yet?" Ederling asked.

"No. Why?"

"After you see this one, you won't for a while."

It always struck Ederling as odd that Jake was so viscerally repulsed by a burnt body. Fire professionals call them crispy critters or roasts. A bit of gallows humor meant to protect their psyches. It's a defense mechanism used to lessen the burden of constant confrontation with destruction of human life and spirit. It's easier to face the evil that has no name. No fire professional likes to see it, but most can put it out of their minds. Unfortunately, mere euphemisms were not enough to protect Jake from the horror.

For it was the fire that juiced him. Fire is a living creature that eats and breathes—and kills. When Jake was five, growing up in Poughkeepsie, he could remember the conflagration of the three-story apartment building across the street from his. But then again, how could he forget? Thirty-seven years later he still carried vivid memories of that bitter cold January evening and still suffered nightmares at the sound of the screams from the burning man on the third floor before Jake watched him jump to his death. In fact, he could remember it as if it were yesterday, and only Jacob Ferguson knew why.

Jake suffered a love-hate relationship with fire, but from his earliest memories there was nothing else that would ever fascinate him so much. After Poughkeepsie, his future had been preordained. Fire became his obsession—his reason for being. Unfortunately, it was a package deal, for fire brings with it unimaginable suffering. The two are inseparable, like spiders and webs.

Ederling waited at the front door as a couple of firefighters dragged out hoses. He entered the house first, climbing the soggy, burnt carpeting of the steps. Firefighters were overhauling rooms, ripping down plaster, throwing furniture out windows onto the back lawn, searching for that one remaining hot spot, that one ember that could set it all off again.

No one touched the master bedroom. Ederling had arrived at the scene before it was even extinguished and was let in as soon as the commanding officer deemed it safe. A good fire investigator itches to start working the scene. The sooner the better. Several of the rooms in the house showed signs of accelerated fire, but Ederling was only concerned with the master bedroom right now. Unlike the others, it was there that a murder had taken place. After determining that it, also, was a room of origin, Ederling had strung a yellow ribbon across the door marked FIRE SCENE—DO NOT ENTER.

"This one's mine," he'd told a firefighter as he walked away, pointing over his shoulder with a thumb to the room.

Ederling stepped aside and let Jake enter first. Ducking under the yellow ribbon, Jake stood at the doorway for a few moments eyeing the devastation. Fire leaves clear and generally unmistakable evidence of where it started and where it traveled, like skid marks on a highway. Jake reached into his jacket pocket and removed a small, voice-activated tape recorder that he always carried. He organized his thoughts before turning it on.

Jake never worried that he would forget what he'd seen, but at criminal trials, tapes are a must. He had learned too well the difficulty of convincing a jury that he could keep it all in his head. He poked around, slowly at first, making comments into his recorder. Jake knew what lay on the bed and consciously avoided it while scanning every other part of the room first.

The heat of the flames had burned the plaster off the ceiling joists. Jake could see from the scorching of the beams directly above and around the bed that the flames had burned there longest. The others were exposed but not charred. As he soaked in his surroundings, the similarities between this scene and the last were striking. There was no doubt they had a bloodthirsty torch on their hands. If they were lucky, this one wasn't smart.

Jake knew that serial fire starters almost always leave a signature of some kind. It can be something as generic as the type of dwelling, or more specific, such as location of the point of origin, or the accelerant favored for the job. It's almost as if he's saying, *That's right, Mr. Fireman. I did this one, too.* While the casual observer might notice nothing more than ash, embers, and destruction, Jake's seasoned eye could read it like a fingerprint. Nevertheless, he knew that though it might point to a pattern of behavior, unlike fingerprints it doesn't always point to an individual.

Ederling slipped under the ribbon and stood next to his boss. "Looks like he started it in her hair, Jake. Just like the last one," he said, treading toward the bed. He had already removed the fallen plaster.

When Jake finally approached the foot of the bed, his stomach tightened, shriveling as he cast his eyes upon the hapless corpse chained to the charred bedposts. Ederling watched Jake's face grow pensive, almost pinching with pain. Both men stood silently on either side of the bed for a minute or so, each intuitively experiencing the horror and violence of the victim's death. It was a road neither could afford to travel too far.

Jake stared at the body, but his internal video was replaying the man in Poughkeepsie jumping out of his window, his back and hair devoured in flame. It was the screaming Jake couldn't get out of his ears. He could hear it now and couldn't allow himself to think that the person lying in front of him had let out anything more hideous. Tinnitus of the damned.

The heat in the room had caused the moisture in the victim's brain to expand with steam, thus popping the head open similar to the way a hot dog splits when cooked. The body had been burned beyond recognition, resembling a blackened mummy. The ME would tell them its gender, but both men already knew. Jake removed his helmet and ran his fingers through his sweat-soaked hair.

"What the hell is this guy up to?" Ederling asked.

Jake looked up, waiting to catch his eye. "I'm not sure, but two of them gives us a hell of a lot more to go on. Did you get samples?"

"Yeah, I took them from the pillow. Didn't want to touch the body until the ME arrives. Figured he can get us samples from the scalp."

"Where's Sparky?" Jake asked.

"In the car."

Jake glanced up at the burnt ceiling joists with his flashlight. "Did you bring her through yet?"

"No."

"Why don't you bring her in. Let's see if he used accelerants anyplace else but on the bed."

"I was thinking we'd run her after the lab boys go through."

Jake had dropped to his knees, feeling some electric cords that ran along the baseboard. "Get Sparky," he said from under the bed.

Sparky was one of two specially trained fire dogs used by the county, paid for and trained with taxpayer dollars and worth her weight in gold. Ederling treated her as if she were his own. The only difference was that she wasn't fed like a normal domestic animal. She only ate when she worked.

For this reason, Ederling took Sparky to scenes for practice at least once a day. Even if it had been determined to be an accident or the torch had already been arrested. If, on rare occasions, there hadn't been a recent fire conducive to his needs, he'd work her at the office or at home. A typical practice session would last upward of an hour, generally taking place in different rooms of a house or sections of a building.

Jake rose as he heard Ederling leave and squatted beside the bed, staring at eye level at the charred body lying on top. These moments were important to him. They offered him a oneness with the victim, an opportunity to peer inside its soul. He visually tried to ascertain if the victim was male or female, but there was too much damage. Only the ME would be able to tell him for sure. For a brief moment Jake allowed himself to hear its screams but quickly extinguished the thought.

He spoke softly, almost as if whispering in its ear. "I'll get this bastard. I promise."

Jake stood. He could hear Sparky lumbering up the steps as Ederling offered her constant words of encouragement. "That's a girl, Spark. Good girl."

Jake walked to the middle of the room. He wanted to give her room to jump on him. Over time they'd become tight, and it was not unusual for Jake to take her home for a weekend. "Hey, Sparky!" he boomed as she ran toward him, her paws landing on the front of his bunker jacket. He patted her side vigorously and dropped to his knees, letting her lick his sweaty face.

Ederling watched, smiling. Sparky was part of his family. It was as easy for him to live vicariously through her pleasure as it was for him to do so through his three kids.

When the two were finished with their hellos, Jake rose to his feet, patting her once more on the side. "Time to work now, girl. Go on." Sparky kept licking. "Go on, now," he said, laughing. "Donny . . . help me here, will you?"

Ederling pulled her leash lightly. Sparky obeyed the subtle command, jumping to his side. He took her to a corner of the room and leaned down, snapping his fingers along the baseboards.

"Seek, girl. Seek." Snap, snap, snap. "Seek. Come on, seek." Snap, snap, snap. "Seek," snap. "Seek," snap. "Seek," snap, snap.

Ederling worked his way around the room in this fashion, slowly moving her along a few feet at a time. To prevent discouragement, he brought her to the head of the bed, the one spot where he assumed she would have the best opportunity to smell something. He began snapping around the victim's head. Sparky went wild, barking and looking to Ederling.

"Show me," he said while she stuck her nose in the vicinity of the victim's head, barked, sat, and looked up. Ederling was a tough taskmaster, and as close as he'd grown to her, it still never escaped his mind that she was trained for a specific and important job.

"Show me better," he said, and Sparky again stuck her nose in the vicinity of the head and sat down, looking up expectantly, all the while barking madly.

"Good girl!" Ederling said, reaching into a small, zippered carry bag he wore around his waist. He pulled out a couple of Milk-Bone treats and handed them to her, washing her with praise. "Good girl! Good girl!" he said, vigorously patting her side.

The two worked the baseboards and around the furniture first, then worked the room in a crisscrossing pattern, until finally they were done. Jake had watched it all from a far corner, once again dutifully impressed with Ederling's mastery over his dog.

"Nothing else," Ederling said.

Jake smiled. "Good job, Don," he said, noticing Ederling was sweating freely. Bending at the waist, working a dog for over an hour, is harder than it sounds. "Sorry to make you work tonight, but with a maniac like this, we got to make sure we cover every base."

Ederling was smiling at Sparky, feeding her a handful of Milk-Bone treats. "No sweat," he answered. "No pun intended."

"Why don't you put her back and come on up. We need to talk some."

"Come on, Spark," Ederling said as he took her away.

The state medical examiner had arrived during Sparky's act and had used the time to examine the body. He was busy now putting something into a vial. No corpse moves until the ME says so. And when that time came, Jake and Ederling would be the lucky volunteers.

"It's okay to move," the ME said, pulling a latex glove off his hand with a snap.

"What time do you think you can autopsy it?" Jake asked.

The ME looked at Jake's sweaty face. "It's been a hot summer, Jake. Lot's going on. I got three lined up before this one. Probably not until later this afternoon. Three-ish. Something like that."

"Good. We'll be there."

Ederling returned from outside, wiping his face with a towel he'd grabbed from one of the trucks outside. "Hey, Doc," he said, acknowledging the ME.

"Don," the ME said, not looking up as he put something into his black bag.

Jake interrupted, "You know, Donny, we're going to need to do the whole house."

"I know," Ederling said, throwing the towel over his shoulder. "There's no way this place could have gotten so involved so quickly without a little help somewhere along the line."

"Rob said the call came in at twelve forty-five. Hard to tell how long it'd been burning before that. First thing tomorrow—"

"It is tomorrow," Ederling interrupted.

"Right. Well . . . Doc here says it's okay to bag," Jake said, his lips curling in disgust. He knew that burn victims are often in such a state of deterioration, their limbs break off when moved. "Let's get it over with."

Ederling eyed the body. "God, I hate this."

When they'd finished, Jake looked at his watch: 5:32 A.M. The state police crime-scene lab technicians would be arriving shortly. "Why don't we work a few more rooms with Sparky and then try for a bite at the diner when the lab boys get here. Give them a chance to work the place over."

Both men would spend many hours here, meticulously digging every inch of the home. But in this high-profile a murder case, the place would be swarming with police technicians, thus making it more difficult than usual to properly work the scene. Though reluctant, Jake felt it best if they left for an hour or so, then return when they could have the scene to themselves.

"We can interview neighbors when we get back. We'll start with whoever made the call," Jake said.

"If we can find him," Ederling added. "Remember last time? You and I both know who made the call, and it wasn't any neighbor."

"Maybe. We'll see. I'd like to start now, but I doubt people are going to be too fond of us waking them up at five in the morning."

"I was able to speak to some of the neighbors while the fire boys were still fightin' it," Ederling said.

That caught Jake's attention. Every fire investigator knows that spectators are generally more apt to talk while a fire is still burning. "And?" he asked, looking at his friend.

"Spoke to the people next door. The woman says she remembers getting up. Thought she heard screams."

"No shit. What time?"

"I pressed her every which way from Sunday, Jake," Ederling said, shaking his head slightly in disappointment. "She swears she didn't look at a clock. Just can't remember."

"Ffffuck. Wouldn't you know it? Well, we'll learn more in a couple of hours. Thank God it's Sunday. Most everyone will be home. I'd hate to have to call all these people at work, or worse yet, wait until they got home. Do we know who lives here?" Jake asked, pulling a precarious piece of Sheetrock off the wall and watching it fall with a wet thud to the floor.

Ederling checked his notebook. "Clawson. Edward and Roberta Clawson. Ten to one that was Roberta right there," he said, motioning to the bed.

"Where's Mr. Clawson? . . . Let me guess. He's on a business trip?"

"You're a regular Columbo. You ready for this? Seems Mr. Clawson also works for Morson Grayhead in the city. Heads up the"—Ederling looked at his notes—"the Strategic Planning Department. Whatever the hell that is."

Jake felt physically stunned. "You gotta be shitting me? Morson Grayhead? You sure?"

"That's what the neighbors say. What do you want to bet it's no coincidence, Jake?"

"Are you kidding me? I wouldn't take that bet, no matter the odds. We just got ourselves the break we've been looking for. We got to get the name and number of the guy who runs that show and talk to him. Somebody's out to ruin his company."

"At this rate, it won't take long. But why the wives? Why not the employees?"

"Shit, Don, what do I look like, the Shell answer man?"

IT WAS JUST past 6:00 A.M. when Jake and Ederling took a seat in the relative cool of the Mount Kisco Diner, enjoying their respective breakfasts to varying degrees. Jake poked at his pancakes, moving bits and pieces to and fro, somehow thinking a messy plate might help hide a zero tolerance for food.

Don Ederling was sopping up the last of his two soft-boiled eggs with a slice of rye toast. "You gonna eat those?" he asked, pointing to Jake's pancakes with his fork.

Jake sipped a steaming cup of black coffee, waving his meal good-bye with his left hand. They had left Sparky in the car parked just outside their window, and Jake watched her reflectively as she calmly sniffed the glass of the rear window. Sparky was used to the car. It was her second home. But at forty thousand dollars a clip, you just don't lock a fire dog in a hot car with the windows rolled down a quarter of the way. Whenever it was necessary to keep her there for extended periods, they'd leave the car running, the doors locked and the air conditioner on full bore. Jake often thought that all dogs should be so lucky.

Ederling looked at Jake. "I told you you weren't gonna eat for a while."

"Don, what makes someone commit murder?" Jake asked out of the blue, as if not hearing Ederling's comment.

"How do you mean?" he answered, scraping Jake's pancakes onto his plate. "You talking philosophically?"

"No. I mean, what are the basic reasons that would cause one human being to take the life of another?"

Jake was big on this kind of questioning. Always taking it to the lowest common denominator. Always whittling things down to the rawest of basics. Ederling knew that Jake knew them as well as he. "You serious?"

"Yes," Jake answered, eyeing Ederling over the steam of his coffee.

Ederling was quiet for a moment while he shook some Tabasco sauce on his home fries. He stabbed a forkful and gazed up to meet Jake's faraway stare.

"Well, it never seems to change much," Ederling said in a serious tone before taking on his favorite persona. Jake called it the Brooklyn cabbie. Kind of a cross between Archie Bunker and Cliff Clavin. It always made Jake laugh, and he nearly spit out his coffee when Ederling started in.

"You knows, yous got your basic five dere. Yous got de revenge ting and de anger ting. And den dere's dat, ah . . . watchyamacallit? Dat dere love ting. Dere's always de popular profit ting. And last but not least, yous got yours dat dere . . . ah . . . homicidal maniac. You knows? De guy who does it for jollies."

Nothing made Jake laugh harder. No matter the circumstances, he was putty in Ederling's hands when, from left field, he'd become Joey from Brooklyn. Maybe it was the tension of the moment, or the much needed humor, but whatever the reason, coffee was nearly coming out Jake's nose when he spoke. "Stop it," he said, trying to take on a more somber tone. "Come on now, I'm serious."

Ederling laughed at Jake's reaction.

"You and that damned Brooklyn thing," Jake said, shaking his head. "I swear, one of these days you're going to make me choke to death."

"Nah. Yous see, yous got dat dere, ah . . . dat Heimrick ting."

"Would you *please* stop?"

"All right," Ederling said, changing back. "Those are the basics. There's others. Prevention of blackmail, humiliation, and disgrace."

"So which ones do you think we can rule out?" Jake asked, wiping his nose with a napkin.

"Hard to say. On the surface, it doesn't look to be fear driven. With one crispy critter, I suppose we might have considered a love angle, but now with two . . . I'd say no."

Jake motioned for the waitress. "Profit?"

"That's a good question. Maybe a variation on the theme. I mean, both these guys make good money and work on Wall Street. Money could easily be involved, although I'm not sure I'd call it profit driven. Yet."

"Revenge?"

"Couldn't say. I don't think we know enough. Could be, I guess. I mean, either both their husbands did something to really piss someone off, or our boy's not done yet and his real goal is to bring down the whole company. Either way, revenge would fit."

"What if it doesn't have anything to do with the men?" Jake asked. "What if it was directed at the women?"

"Maybe," Ederling responded with a shrug. "But again, if we just had the one, I'd be more inclined to believe it. With two? I doubt it."

"Possible?"

"Of course."

Jake took out his notebook. "Let's go over what we know."

"It ain't much."

"Yeah, well, that'll change. Okay, so let's assume this last one is also a woman. That means we got two women, both married to top executives at Morson Grayhead. They both lived in Westchester County. They were both chained to their beds and burned alive from their hair."

"We don't know this last one was alive . . . *or* that it was a woman."

Jake craned his neck, rubbing its stubble of growth. "Okay, but let's assume. I'll be shocked if she wasn't."

Ederling nodded his head. "I agree."

"Neither home showed apparent signs of B and E, and both were fully involved when the crews arrived."

"Yep, and I'd bet good money that he used lighter fluid on this last one, too."

"We'll find out soon enough," Jake said, jotting down something in his notebook. "Both men were on business trips. That's got to be more than just coincidence, Don. Somehow, some way, our torch knew these guys were gone."

"Yeah, and something else—" Ederling said, stopping short as the waitress brought over the bill, continuing after she'd left. "Both families were empty nesters. Kids were grown and out of the house. You think he knew that? Or is that also a coincidence?"

"I wish I knew," Jake said, reaching into his pants pocket for some bills.

Ederling was studying the check. "Did you order a third coffee?"

"Give me that thing, will you?" Jake said, ripping it from his hands. "You have to be the cheapest fuck I ever met."

"Hey, Mr. Bachelor, I got three kids at home." Ederling knew he'd made a mistake as the words left his mouth.

He didn't mean anything by it and Jake knew it, too. But still, the words shook his soul. Ederling watched as Jake closed his eyes and took a deep breath. Inside, Ederling cursed himself.

"Listen, I'm sorry, Jake. I keep . . ."

"Forget it," Jake said, tossing a ten-dollar bill on the table. "Let's go talk to some neighbors."

JAKE PULLED HIS Crown Victoria behind the last remaining fire truck on Chiswell Lane, popped the trunk, and got out. Ederling left to go to his Bronco, leaving Jake alone with his thoughts. Jake pulled on his boots and bunker pants and leaned with both hands up against the open trunk.

Dammit! It wasn't supposed to be this way. At forty-two, he was supposed to be married, with little rug rats of his own making a mess of the house. It was a snowy Saturday in February 1995 when his life was changed forever.

He and his wife were both due at his brother's house in Rockland County at 2:00 P.M. for his nephew's seventh birthday party. But Danielle had final preparations to make for a big presentation her firm was due to give to what was then NYNEX on Monday and told Jake she'd meet him there.

"Come on, Danny. Just stay here with me," he'd pleaded, squeezing her right buttocks with a warm hand. "We can romp around in bed for a bit and grab some breakfast at that new place in Port Chester. You can do that stuff tomorrow."

"It's really important to me, honey. I just can't relax thinking I may have made that mistake on the slides. What if I don't have enough time tomorrow to fix them?"

"Yeah, but you don't even know for sure that you screwed them up."

"Exactly. That's why I can't relax. This is my chance to shine, hon. If I didn't, then I'll be home in less than an hour. We can romp then, you horny toad."

"Wait! What's that?" Jake asked, laying his ear to her stomach. "It's our baby. He's sayin', 'Hey, Mom, stay and romp with Dad. Once I pop out, you won't have that many more chances.'"

"Stop it," Danielle said, grabbing his head. "You're tickling me. Anyway, it's a she, and she's got more sense than you. She's saying, 'Go check your slides, Mom. Then come spend the weekend with Dad after you're more relaxed.'"

"Come on. Pleeaase."

"Jake, I'm sorry, honey," she said, getting out of bed. "Just let me check and I'll be right home. I promise."

Jake's hand fell off his wife's stomach to the sheets. "All right, all right, go check your slides."

Jake was in the shower when Danielle popped her head in the bathroom. "I'll call you from the office. Love you!"

Those were the last words he would ever hear her say. The knock at the door came not more than thirty minutes later. Jake knew something was terribly wrong the moment he saw the New York state trooper standing at his door.

"Mr. Ferguson?" the trooper asked.

"Yes?" Jake answered nervously.

"Good morning, sir. My name is Trooper . . ."

Apparently a fuel truck had jackknifed on I-287, and Danielle had . . . The rest was just fog. Jake would later learn that Danielle never had a chance, running broadside into the belly of the truck, sending the entire scene into a mushroom cloud of flame and smoke. The police said she died instantly, but Jake had his doubts. They always say that.

"Jake, you all right?" Ederling was asking from the side of the open trunk. "Jake?"

Jake turned his head toward the voice, staring blankly beyond. "What?"

"You okay, buddy?"

"Yeah."

Ederling knew what had happened. It didn't happen often, but he'd seen it before. "Why don't you take a break, man? I can handle this myself."

"Sometimes it really hurts, Don."

"I know."

"She almost stayed home, Don. I could have pushed more."

Ederling walked next to him and sat on the bumper. "Yeah, you could have, but you didn't. And the reason you didn't is because you were a good husband. You cared for Danny and what was important to her."

"Yeah, I know. But . . ."

Ederling felt for his friend. But four years is a long time. He felt as much frustration at these moments as anything else. "But nothing. You can't do this to yourself, Jake. It's killing you. I know it's hard, but you gotta try and move beyond it. There was no way you could have known, man. No way."

"I know."

Ederling had been thinking about doing this for some time. He didn't think there'd be a better chance. "Don't hit me when I tell you this, okay?"

Jake sat down next to Ederling and looked straight ahead.

"Okay?" he asked again.

Jake looked at him, already suspicious. "No promises."

"You need to go on a date."

Jake laughed. "A date? I wouldn't know where to start. I'm so out of the loop I wouldn't even know what clothes to wear."

"Bullshit. I think you're scared of it."

"I'm not scared," Jake said with just enough accentuation on the last word to belie the truth.

"Listen. Do you remember when I told you about Sammy's teacher? You know, that knockout redhead I met at our last parent-teacher night?"

"Oh, no, you don't," Jake said, rising from the trunk and taking a few steps forward.

"Why not? Jake, listen to me. She's bright, funny, has an ass to die for, and lips I'd pay good money to see in action."

Jake turned, visibly uncomfortable. "Come on, Donny, I couldn't even think about it. Really. Thanks just the same, but I can't do it right now."

Ederling reached into his shirt pocket and took out a cigarette. He twisted it in his lips a couple of times, thinking. "Whatever. But if you ask me, Danny's lookin' down on you right now, and her heart's breaking. She'd want you to go on with your life, Jake. Let's say it happened the other way around. Would you want Danny to live the way you are now for the rest of her life?"

There was silence.

Ederling didn't know just how it happened but knew he was at a threshold. He rose to his feet for equal footing. "Would you?"

Jake met his eyes. "Look, Don, let me think about it? All right?"

"Hey, whatever makes you happy," Ederling said, knowing the hook had been set. "I'm just trying to help."

"Well, thanks, but that's about as much help as I can stand right now, okay? My hands are sweating."

"Women will do that to you. Remember?"

Jake reached into the trunk and took out his chief fire marshal badge and hung it from his shirt pocket. "Let's go talk to some of these assholes."

Ederling decided that he'd pushed enough for now. But Jake was sorely mistaken if he thought his partner was going to let it die. "Assholes it is," he said.

S**EVERIN RYBECK HAD** been chairman and chief executive officer of Morson Grayhead for eight years and was widely regarded on Wall Street as the primary force behind his company's steady and dazzling rise to prominence among the Street's few remaining independent financial juggernauts. A firm and unyielding believer in the saying "If it looks great, it's too late," time and again he had rocked the Street with an uncanny knack for acquiring crown jewels at fire-sale prices.

Once or twice a decade the stock markets, and the companies whose revenues and reputations derive from them, find themselves mired in a bear-market funk. Those post-bull-market periods where anything even smelling of stock seems to suffer from an unremitting hangover. Mutual fund sales plummet, initial public offerings slow to a trickle, and prices of publicly traded brokerage houses drop to ten-year lows.

But Severin Rybeck had a nose for fear. Almost alone among Wall Street's power brokers, he thrived on fear. Not the kind engendered from an autocratic management style. On the contrary, his was quite democratic, though of course Severin's word was final. But investor panic? Now *that* was a different story.

There are times in all investors' careers when the markets seem to drop forever. Periods when even the most seasoned and savvy pros begin to wonder if maybe this time it's different. Maybe this time stocks won't stop going down. Maybe this is the next October 1929. That maybe, just maybe, they've been suckered into a horrible myth, led to believe that there's some ethereal, unwritten, universal law that states that hammered stock markets always rebound.

It's times like these when investment professionals begin to drink more, fight with their spouses, and wake in cold sweats in the middle of the night.

The fear becomes omnipresent throughout the Street, clearly visible in people's faces and actions, their buying patterns and work habits. Until finally, most investors and many pros just can't take it anymore and they begin to sell, leading to that final blow-off; that final, panicked rush for cash known on Wall Street as a selling climax.

Oh, how Severin Rybeck relished selling climaxes. As a young trader, he had learned many years ago that the absolute best time to buy is when it hurts—really hurts—when it's just about all you can do to write the ticket. And it was exactly at these times that Severin Rybeck was at his best; when he would sit, burning the midnight oil, scanning financial reports, looking for that next diamond in the rough.

A prominent board member once asked him why he was not taking advantage of the market's recent drubbing to acquire a mutual fund company whose purchase they had previously approved.

"Complacency," he responded glibly. "One of my managing directors just bought a Cessna last weekend. That . . . ladies and gentlemen, is not fear. I'll wait."

And wait he would. But no one doubted his ability and willingness to pull the trigger. And once he zeroed in on a target, you could take that purchase to the bank.

Twice in his eight-year tenure Rybeck had been given the opportunity he sought. On one such occasion he had purchased a well-respected brokerage house for just north of $1 billion dollars, and on a second occasion had purchased a well-known, but undercapitalized, life insurance company for $800 million. Word on the Street was that he had either gone mad or was one of the greatest investors of our time.

Severin Rybeck was at the top of his game. Almost under the dark of night, he had single-handedly created a financial powerhouse capable of developing and distributing virtually any investment or insurance vehicle the country's aging baby boomers would need for the next thirty years.

To some, his vision was viewed as almost mythical. To others, he and Morson Grayhead posed a large and very real threat. The *Wall Street Journal* quoted portions of a speech Rybeck had made at last year's annual shareholders' meeting. Perhaps, more than anything else, this alone caused nonbelievers to sit up and take notice. So simple in it's delivery, so clear in its message.

"Ladies and gentlemen. I have come here today to ask you a simple question," the *Journal* quoted him as saying. "How many of you have ever seen a python eat a pig?"

Severin Rybeck was not one to joke, so all who knew him or his reputation sat in rapt silence, intuitively knowing they were about to be enlightened.

"When a python eats a pig, it is by far the biggest part of the snake. You can't miss it, would you not agree?" At this, an overhead slide projected a twenty-foot python looking as if it had just swallowed a VW Beetle. "You see that protuberance?" he asked, pointing a thin red beam at it from a handheld laser projector. "That is a python who has eaten a baby pig. It is also something else. It is the baby-boomer generation working its way through the American economy. Can anyone here tell me what were the best performing stocks of the 1950s?"

A few hearty souls shouted out incorrect guesses. "Wrong!" Rybeck boomed. "Toy stocks. And why was that? You guessed it. Our beloved baby boomers needed toys."

People began to see the magic of the moment, and you could feel the excitement begin to quietly work its way through the throng.

"And now, ladies and gentlemen," Rybeck continued, "a baby boomer turns fifty every fourteen seconds, and will do so for the next twenty-plus years. Are they concerned with toys? No. That was the eighties," he said with a smile, and had to wait for the laughter to subside. "So, I ask you, what do you think they are concerned with now? Two things. Their health and their retirement. Not only will they buy billions of dollars in insurance premiums, but they will invest unprecedented sums in their 401(k) plans and their IRAs. Ladies and gentlemen, I am proud to tell you that, alone among Wall Street's behemoths, Morson Grayhead and its thirty-eight thousand superbly trained employees worldwide are uniquely poised to offer every investment vehicle they will need as they work their way through the snake. It has been our unwavering goal to be here, strong and ready, and you, our loyal shareholders, are about to reap the rewards of that vision."

The applause was thunderous. Rybeck was hailed a visionary, someone to whom an investor or an employee could hitch his wagon and know deep down he was in for a good ride.

And now, for some inexplicable reason, it appeared that a madman was beginning to shake the foundation of his firm. Everything he'd worked for, all his twenty-hour days, would soon not matter anymore. When word spread, as it certainly would, employee fear—the real kind—would replace it all. For the first time in a long time, Severin Rybeck was frightened. Not for his family, but for his "baby."

JAKE FERGUSON AND Don Ederling arrived Sunday at Severin Rybeck's imposing, Bedford, New York, home shortly after 11:30 A.M. It sat alone on a hill overlooking a small valley on one side and a large reservoir on the other. The stone-pillared, electric gate was of ornate wrought iron, designed in a flowery Victorian style so that when closed both halves spelled the firm's New York Stock Exchange symbol, MGR. It was also manned. Jake noticed the guard's jet-black 9mm Glock semiautomatic as he approached the car.

"May I help you, sir?" the guard asked Jake through his open window, opportunistically using the occasion to scan the inside of Jake's car.

Sensing this was not a time for pleasantries, Jake spoke firmly. "Yes. We have an appointment with Mr. Rybeck. I am Chief Fire Marshal Jacob Ferguson, and this is Deputy Chief Donald Ederling."

The guard was polite but businesslike. "May I see some identification please, gentlemen?"

Jake dutifully reached for his wallet and his ID card while Ederling did the same. Jake attempted to hand the man his wallet.

"Please remove them from your wallets, sirs," the guard said, taking his time in reviewing them once they had done so. "One moment," he said, before taking their IDs with him into his small, stone-walled command post.

Jake peered through the gate, catching a glimpse of at least one other armed guard with a dog on the other side. He was sure there were others.

The outside guard reappeared. "Gentlemen, Mr. Rybeck is expecting you. You will find him in the pool house adjacent to the greenhouse in back. Take this drive here," he said, pointing up the cobblestoned drive through the gates. "As you approach the house, you will see a two-car, porticoed entrance. Take the drive past it, down and to the right. Park by the outdoor pool shed. It should be self-explanatory from there."

"Thank you," Jake said, taking the two IDs back from the still-stoic guard.

Jake waited patiently for the gates to open and drove slowly through, nodding slightly at the guard and the dog on the inside as he passed.

"Jesus Christ," Ederling said. "I wasn't expecting anything like that, were you?"

"No."

Jake felt sure the grounds were monitored with some type of electronic motion detectors, automatic lights, and a very loud alarm system. Was this a man with something to fear, or do hundreds of millions of dollars just make someone ultracautious?

The two men drove up a winding incline that veered sharply off to their right, then back again to the left slightly but steeply. As they came to the top of the rise, Jake let go a long, slow whistle.

"Man, oh, man, would you look at that? Is this guy loaded or what?"

"It's enough to make your dick feel two inches long, huh?" Ederling said, staring at the sprawling home in front of them.

"Hey, speak for yourself."

To call Severin Rybeck's palatial residence a home is like calling a Rolls-Royce a car—technically accurate, but not quite on the mark. It stood solitary on the rise, the late-morning sun casting long, disproportionate shadows down the sweeping front lawn. The house alone seemed to cover two or three acres, and Jake found himself wondering how many rooms a house this size would have. He counted four chimneys.

It was a two-story home, save for the tower housing the front door. That rose a full story or more above the row of second-floor windows and contained a third window extending halfway above the line of the roof. The top was narrowly gabled with a widow's perch at its peak.

The exterior was a combination of hand-cut stone and wood, obviously built when foreign labor, predominantly newly immigrated Italians, could be hired for slave wages. Jake had heard the saying "They don't build things the way they used to" many times. But then again, he thought that sometime this century we stopped paying laborers ten cents a day. In an odd way he thought the Rybeck home conveyed almost an ecclesiastical aura. As the two men approached, Jake eyed its fanciful woodworking and stone carvings and couldn't help but feel that these, combined with the four sequentially lower-gabled roofs, lent the entire structure a mood and ambience of medieval England.

There is an awful lot of money in Westchester County, and both men had seen their share of wealth, but neither could remember anything quite like this. There was wealth and there was *wealth*. Severin Rybeck clearly belonged in the latter.

"I can't get over this place," Ederling said as Jake dutifully pulled his car down the sloping drive toward the pool shed.

"That's a pool shed?" Jake asked. "Christ . . . my *house* isn't that big."

As he spoke, a man in shorts and a white tank top exited the stone building, dragging aqua-blue spiral hoses and a water filter.

"Just a wild guess, mind you," said Ederling, "but I'd say yes."

Jake looked at Ederling with mischievous eyes and smiled. He scanned the structure to his left, pointing it out with his left hand. "That must be it. Let's go have a little talk with the lord of the manor."

They walked side by side in its direction, taking it all in. "You think a guy like this carries a mortgage or just pays cash?"

Jake shook his head. "I can't even begin to imagine. It's got to cost what? Fifty, a hundred mil?"

Ederling giggled, almost embarrassed by the surrounding opulence. "Can you imagine writing a hundred-million-dollar check? I'd shit my pants."

Jake turned suddenly serious. "I want to handle this right, Don. Who do you think should do the talking?"

"I don't know. I was wonderin' about that. A guy like this, you gotta figure he's used to control. Maybe he'd respect you more, seeing as how you got the word *chief* on your badge."

"Maybe," Jake said, bobbing his shoulders. "But we might get more out of him if you spoke, seeing as how he'll view you as a lackey. He might be more cavalier, tossing you aside as not worthy of his time."

"Hey," Ederling said, pretending to be hurt.

"You know what I mean."

"Well, it's your call, boss. It could go either way. Six of one, half dozen of the other if you ask me."

"All right, screw it," Jake said. "I'll do the talking."

Ederling wiped his brow in lampoon fashion. "Good. That way I get to look around." They had reached the door to the pool house and Jake glanced at his friend with an over-my-dead-body look.

Ederling answered the look. "Only joking."

Jake opened the door to the expansive room and felt a rush of humid air hit him, relatively cool by comparison to the developing steam outside. Ederling followed and quietly closed the door behind him. They stood for a few moments watching a tall, tan, athletically built man swimming laps in yellow trunks with what looked like bright pink orchids printed on them. Between splashes, they could make out Rybeck's bald top, and the silver on either side of his head reminded Jake of the shine of mackerel when they're running under the dock.

"Man, I wish I could swim like that," Jake said, feeling self-conscious about the slowly widening tire spreading around his waist.

Ederling whispered to Jake, "I'm assuming that's not the butler."

"Probably a good guess," Jake said, walking to the far end of the pool, placing himself at the head of the lane from which Severin Rybeck would soon kick off for another lap. Ederling continued standing at the pool's long edge, watching Jake kneel at one end as he prepared to tap Rybeck's head with a hand as he approached.

Severin Rybeck was apparently not used to this type of interruption, and Jake was somewhat taken aback by the momentary look of fear in Rybeck's eyes as he gazed up from his watery gym.

"Mr. Rybeck," Jake added quickly. "I'm Chief Fire Marshal Jacob Ferguson. I called you earlier regarding Mrs. Clawson."

"Oh, yes, yes," Rybeck said, pushing off the side of the pool and wriggling on his back to the steps in the corner.

Jake remained where he was while Ederling walked around the pool toward him. Rybeck bounded out of the water and plastered what hair he had to the sides of his head with both hands. He walked to a small glass table, retrieved a large burgundy towel, and quickly dried his face, head, and hands. Jake approached him with Ederling in tow.

"Sorry to interrupt," Jake said.

"Oh, no bother," Rybeck answered, extending a damp hand. "Severin Rybeck, pleased to meet you."

"Yes, sir. I introduced myself at the pool, but maybe we should try it again. I am Jacob Ferguson, Chief Fire Marshal for the County of Westchester, and this is Deputy Fire Marshal Donald Ederling. We work together."

"Partners?" Rybeck asked.

"Something like that."

Rybeck bent to dry off his legs, and Jake could see that he was breathing hard. "You really push yourself in there," he said, beginning with the customary, but dreaded, small talk.

"Gentlemen, in my line of work, you eat lunch or you are lunch. It's one of the few ways I've found to stay physically and mentally sharp. I try to swim a crisp two miles every day."

Ederling whistled. "I'm lucky if I can get out to walk my dog."

"Why's that, Mr. . . . ?"

"Ederling. Don Ederling."

"Why do you say that, Mr. Ederling?" Rybeck asked.

"I have three kids."

Rybeck caught his eye. "That pretty much explains that, don't you think?"

"I'll say. You add kids and the whole picture changes."

Rybeck appeared uneasy as he pulled a towel back and forth across his back with two raised hands, as if somehow the subject of children was unwelcome. Jake also found himself growing uncomfortable with the direction of the conversation and didn't much feel like discussing children right then. He figured the best defense is a good offense. "Mr. Rybeck, we apologize for disturbing your Sunday like this. I'm sure a man in your position relishes his time off."

Rybeck interrupted, "No more than yourself, I'm sure. After all, I'm in here swimming and you're in here working. I respect that." He lifted a forefinger in the air. "Excuse me just one moment," he said, walking over to the glass table and depressing a button on a console lying on top. Rybeck ambled over to a hook on a tiled wall closest to the table and threw on an oversize white polo shirt. He was slipping on a pair of beat-up thongs when an older, white-haired black gentleman dressed in a white tuxedo with a black bow tie appeared through a door closest to the house. Jake guessed him for somewhere around seventy and wondered just how long he had worked for Rybeck.

"I'll be taking my lunch on the veranda, Benjamin," Rybeck said. "And would you please ask Millie to put together two more settings? These two gentlemen are joining me. We'll take iced teas all around."

"Yes, Mr. Rybeck."

"Thank you, Benjamin."

Jake was surprised his jaw didn't break as it hit the floor. He was stunned. *People actually live like this?* It was like a living rerun of a 1940s movie. He half expected Humphrey Bogart to stride out from behind one of the dozen palm trees lining the inside walls of the room. "Thank you, Mr. Rybeck," he began, "but that won't be—"

"Don't be silly," Rybeck said with a wave of his hand. "It's lunchtime, and you have to eat. We can talk and eat at the same time. Might as well kill two birds with one stone."

Jake looked at Ederling, who shrugged his shoulders. "Hey, it's free."

"Well, all right. Thank you for your hospitality, Mr. Rybeck. We've been up since very early this morning and a small bite would hit the spot."

They followed Rybeck out the back of the pool house and down a lushly flowered, manicured stone path to a small, shady patio built around a huge maple and, to Jake's surprise, a waterfall. Though man-made, if Jake didn't know better, he would have sworn it to be the real thing.

What *was* real was that a very sick and deadly madman was on the loose, and for whatever reason, he appeared to have placed Morson Grayhead squarely in the middle of his crosshairs. Jake felt there had been enough pleasantries for one day.

He took a seat across from Rybeck at a relatively large, round glass table and wasted no time getting to the point. "Mr. Rybeck—"

"Severin, please."

"Okay. Thank you . . . Severin. As you know, sir, we have just come from Mr. Clawson's home in Mount Kisco."

Rybeck shook his head with heartfelt commiseration. "I didn't know anything about it until the police called me this morning. Terrible tragedy."

If you only knew. "Yes, it is, sir. Mr. Ederling and I are here to try to get a better handle on just what these two men had in common and whether or not you might have any inkling of who might possibly be responsible for these acts."

Rybeck looked first to Ederling and then fixed his owlish, raisin-colored eyes on Jake. "Why do you ask what the *men* had in common? It's the women he appears to be after, no? That they both happen to be wives of Morson Grayhead executives is true. But to draw conclusions from that is highly speculative,

Mr. Ferguson. *Highly* speculative indeed. Christ . . . you're beginning to sound like the goddamned media."

"What makes you say that it's speculative, sir?" Jake asked.

Rybeck looked at him, eyebrow raised. "What else would it be, Mr. Ferguson? I even heard the possibility mentioned on the radio this morning."

"True enough," Jake responded. "But you yourself just referred to the fact that they also mentioned the possibility of a Morson Grayhead connection."

Rybeck waved him off as if the mere suggestion were preposterous. His mind simply could not lend credence to such obvious media hype. "Ridiculous. You know the press. They'll stop at nothing to sell papers."

Rybeck's retort surprised Jake. The connection certainly appeared more than plausible to him. "I agree. But it would be folly to rule it out, don't you think?"

"You can't believe that, Mr. Ferguson?" Rybeck responded, staring at Jake through squinted eyes. He acted as if he were being told that the sun was blue.

"Right now, sir, we don't know what to believe. That's why we're here. We were hoping that perhaps you might be able to shed some light on the situation."

Rybeck was thinking contemplatively when Benjamin appeared from around the corner wheeling a cloth-covered table cart brimming with various fruits and vegetables, three different cheeses, chicken, tuna and lobster salads, rolls, breads, crackers, and two large, sweating pitchers of iced tea.

As he began to pull china out from under the cart, Rybeck stopped him. "Thank you, Benjamin. That will be all. We'll help ourselves."

"Sir?"

"We'll get it ourselves."

"Very well, sir," and as quickly as he had appeared, Benjamin was gone.

Rybeck rose and strode to the cart, reaching down and grabbing three plates, some napkins, and silverware. He walked them to the table and placed them in a quiet heap.

"Grab what you need, gentlemen."

Jake and Ederling looked at one another. Jake thought Rybeck seemed halfway normal. For a short period, no one spoke, busy as they were filling their plates with various levels of nutrition. Jake felt famished but was embarrassed when he sat down and compared the contents of his plate to that of his host's. He wished now he'd been less greedy.

"Please, eat," Rybeck said, slipping a forkful of tuna-fish salad into his mouth.

They ate and drank, discussing the case periodically between bites. Jake asked the next question. "Mr. Rybeck, we couldn't help but notice that you have taken extraordinary measures to protect your premises. Is there a specific reason for that?"

Rybeck smiled at him. "Mr. Ferguson . . . let me explain something to you. Obviously, I have been successful, and not everyone agrees with my standard of living. Frankly, I don't give a shit what anyone else thinks. I have toiled the better part of a decade to turn Morson Grayhead into the multibillion-dollar Wall Street powerhouse that it is today and have no apologies for the way I live. But there are those among us who would use my wealth and station to their advantage. Do you have any idea how many death threats I receive in a year? How many threats my family receives in one capacity or another? As I'm sure you know, there's no shortage of wackos out there. Simply put, I can afford the peace of mind my security detail provides, and I therefore employ them to the fullest."

"Is there any one person or group of people you fear specifically?" Jake asked.

Rybeck looked them both slowly in the eyes, assuring extended contact so as to drive home his point. "Gentlemen, I don't fear anyone."

Why am I not convinced, Mr. Rybeck? "Certainly, you can see where an outsider might infer otherwise? Armed men and dogs have a funny way of doing that."

Rybeck spoke with a mouthful of tuna. "Let's just say I'm not stupid."

"No argument here," Jake said, thinking it might be time to shake things up a bit. "Severin, I'm going to ask you a favor. List for me, if you would please, the possible reasons why someone might be targeting your executives' wives."

"Jesus, you can't be serious? Where would I even start? The options are endless."

Jake took a bite of his lobster-salad sandwich. "Not really," he said, chewing. "Placate me, just for the hell of it."

Rybeck seemed annoyed, which in turn annoyed Jake. He felt it was time to take control. He leaned forward and turned unexpectedly professional. "Mr. Rybeck, let me remind you, sir, of the seriousness of the situation. From where I sit, someone might well be methodically burning alive the wives of some of your most highly placed employees." Jake almost slipped and mentioned the rapes, but fortuitously caught himself. "I'd like to think that it will stop here, but frankly, I doubt it. Now, we either all work together to stop this madman or your employees and their families could suffer unimaginable pain, and your firm untold damage. The decision is yours, sir. What's it going to be?"

Jake worried for a moment that he might just have turned what little remained of this interview for the worse. Still, he had hit home.

"You know, Mr. Ferguson, not too many people have the opportunity to speak to me in that fashion," Rybeck said, stalling. "I'm smiling because I just came within a hairsbreadth of telling you where to go. But frankly, I'm impressed."

Jake nodded his head, feigning appreciation. *Enough of this bullshit, already. I'm glad you've allowed me to come into your mini-empire and speak to you like a man. Now, can we please get on with the matter at hand?*

Rybeck sat silent for a moment. "Are you telling me that you believe these two burnings are somehow connected with my firm?"

"We're not sure yet," Jake responded. "But it's obviously a possibility."

Rybeck shook his head. "I don't agree with your premise, but I'll work with it just the same to answer your question. Let me think." He tilted his head down toward his tuna fish, thought for a moment, then looked up. "Are you interested in specific people, or more generic scenarios?"

Jake shrugged. "Either. Whichever you think might be most plausible."

"Well . . . generically . . . one has to consider the possibility of revenge. Who and why I can only begin to imagine."

"We'll have you do that later," Jake said.

Rybeck frowned. "I'm not sure I'm cut out for this, gentlemen."

"You're doing just fine."

Jake and Ederling sat expressionless, as if in a game of poker.

"Maybe both men had dealings with the perpetrator and for some reason he feels scorned. Maybe he is killing the wives as a way of making them suffer. You know? If he killed them, it would be over. This way they have to live with their grief."

Jake smiled inside. *Good one, Rybeck. You sure you've never done this before?*

"Keep going. But try to focus on why."

Rybeck took a long sip of iced tea and looked at Jake with a helpless expression. "Isn't that what I've been doing?"

"Yes and no," Jake said, shaking his head and shoulders slightly back and forth. "You've been focusing more on causality. If you can, try now to focus on effect. What they are trying to accomplish?"

Rybeck's eyes lit up. "I see. Don't focus on the motive but on the desired result."

"Exactly."

"Let me think. Hmm . . . Well, like I said earlier, whoever it is could be trying to punish the two men, make them suffer. Or he could be after the wives for that matter. But *suffering* would be the operative word in either case. One just longer than the other."

Jake closed his eyes as thoughts of Danielle passed through his mind. He was most interested in just how many scenarios Rybeck could think of. No matter how Jake looked at it, his own list kept coming up rather short. "Anything else? Think in terms of your firm."

Rybeck was visibly perturbed. He stared silently at Jake, clearly displeased at being made to even think such a thing. "Well . . . let's see. What else? What else?" Rybeck said, annoyingly drumming the fingers of his right hand on the table glass. "Boy, this list is shorter than I thought. Could be a disgruntled investor, I suppose."

"Desired result, remember?" Jake reminded him.

"Oh, yes," Rybeck said while nodding. "I suppose someone could be trying to get back at me for some reason. You don't always make friends in this business, you know?"

"Desired result?"

"Sorry. Well, I guess it's possible that he . . . or she . . . could be trying to . . . you know? To . . ."

Rybeck's face looked drawn and Jake could see he was becoming uncomfortable. There was a long pause, which Jake finally interrupted. "To what?"

"You know?" Rybeck asked impotently again. "Would either one of you like some more iced tea?"

Jake watched him refill his glass. *He can't bring himself to even say it. Sorry, no one gets off easy today.* "To what?" Jake asked again, forcing the issue.

Ederling sat watching the cat-and-mouse game in front of him, suddenly noticing that his heart had kicked up in rhythm. He took a quiet, deep breath and leaned back in his chair. It's a twofer, he thought. Free lunch *and* entertainment.

"Someone could be trying to ruin the firm," Rybeck spit out, almost tripping over his words.

There, that wasn't so bad, was it? The door's open. Push. Push hard. "Why would this ruin the firm, sir?" Jake asked, feigning ignorance.

"Do you have any idea what something like this, left unchecked, could do to employee morale? If this continues, they'll begin leaving in . . ." Rybeck started, then stood, visibly disturbed at the very thought of what he was saying. He walked to the edge of the patio and knelt to smell a patch of roses. "Look, gentlemen, this is very difficult for me. I am a rarity in this business. I have spent my entire career with one firm and have worked myself dogged to witness the success Morson Grayhead enjoys today. Talking about her possible ruin is almost impossible for me to do." Rybeck turned and looked at Ederling. "Certainly you understand, Mr. Ederling? This is like discussing the ruin of one's family. I just can't do it."

There was silence, and even among the excess surrounding him, to Jake's astonishment, he found himself feeling sorry for this man. He glanced at Ederling, who rolled his eyes and mimed playing a violin. Jake took a sip of iced tea, rose, and walked over to his host.

Rybeck was aware of Jake's presence but didn't acknowledge him. He remained lost in his roses, then suddenly spoke. "You know, Mr. Ferguson, when I was a kid growing up in the Bronx, my mother always had cut roses on the kitchen table. Don't ask me where she got them, because to this day, I swear there couldn't have been a rosebush within a half mile of us. But she did. Every damned day. We were poor back then. Dirt poor. Dad worked as a laborer during the day, then as a janitor for a local landlord at night. He worked seven days a week. I hardly even knew him."

Jake didn't know how to respond, so chose the most logical response: silence.

"Look around you, Mr. Ferguson. All of this is bought and paid for, and I have another one in Florida, only larger."

Jesus Christ. Jake could certainly see where some people might not have Severin Rybeck on their Christmas list.

"You know what?" Rybeck asked, suddenly turning his eyes to Jake's. "I'd give it all away tomorrow if they told me I could have my mother and father back. They were all my brothers and I had. They taught us right from wrong, the value of a buck, and the value of hard work. Now they're gone and so is my son."

"You have a son?" Jake asked.

"Yes. He's grown now." Rybeck turned to face Jake. "Morson Grayhead *is* my family, Mr. Ferguson. It's more than I can bear to think that someone may be trying to do her harm. I can look you in the eye and tell you that should that be the case, and should I find out who it is, I will kill him."

Jake stared out over the expanse of the back lawn, noticing four flags in a large putting green on a plateau halfway down. At that moment, the man with everything seemed to have nothing. Jake wondered if Rybeck was close to his son or if he had rebelled and become lost in the fray the way so many wealthy kids are apt to do. It seemed a painful moment, and not knowing the answer, Jake dared not ask.

"What about your wife?" Jake asked instead, quietly annoyed that he felt the need to coddle this extraordinarily wealthy and powerful man. "Certainly you and she are enjoying all that you have?"

"Are you married, Mr. Ferguson?" Rybeck asked.

"No."

"Ever been?"

"Once."

"Has she remarried?"

"No."

"Well, my wife and I have been married for thirty-six years. I got her pregnant when I was a senior at Brown. Academic scholarship, in case you're wondering. You don't know how proud that made my parents. Anyway, Lianne was attending Pembroke, and back then marriage was the only option. Let's just say that from the beginning, ours was not a match made in heaven. She does her thing. I do mine. But a man in my position should have a woman on his arm at some functions. She plays the part in return for her freedom, and all of this," he said with an expansive gesture across the back lawn.

"Mr. Rybeck," Jake said softly, "I know this is difficult for you, sir. But I'm afraid we have no choice. We must discuss why someone might want to bring down your firm, and who else this maniac might go after to accomplish that goal. To do that, we'll need to play through the impact of what has recently transpired. I know it will be hard, but I also know you can do it. You must. It's quite possible that the future of Morson Grayhead and its thousands of employees rests in the balance. This is not a time to go into denial."

"I am *not* in denial, Mr. Ferguson."

"With all due respect, Mr. Rybeck, I don't know what else to call it."

Rybeck turned, his eyes burning into Jake's. Jake could see his face was almost twisted in anguish, but his eyes spoke of a rising, steely determination. Rybeck walked to the table and sat down. "Don't be shy, Mr. Ederling. Please, eat."

Rybeck clasped his hands on the table. If Jake was correct and someone was perpetuating this horror to ruin Rybeck's firm, it would be all he could do to maintain his sanity. "All right, Mr. Ferguson," Rybeck said, breathing deeply, "I am prepared to do whatever is necessary. Where do we start?"

Monday
September 9

E ARLY IN THE afternoon, Jake sat with Ederling at a small, rectangular conference table in a relatively modern interrogation room in the fire marshal's offices in White Plains, New York. Ederling was munching a bag of Oreos, breaking them open and eating the cream side first, while Jake sipped from a plastic bottle of Poland Spring mineral water.

They sat staring at a white eraser board propped up on a wooden tripod in the corner of the room. Scribbled in red and black ink on the board was a flow chart more or less delineating the hierarchy of Morson Grayhead's upper management. At the very top was the word *God* written in red. When viewed as a whole, the montage resembled an octopus, as multiple arrows of various lengths pointed down and away linking the upper chain of command to Severin Rybeck.

Three men answered directly to him. The president and chief operating officer, vice chairman/group chief executive, and the executive vice president/chief financial officer. Jake had boxed their names immediately below the word *God* and connected them with black arrows.

Eight senior vice presidents reported to them. They were written in boxes in a horizontal row directly below and included the sr. vice president/marketing, sr. vice president/strategic planning, sr. vice president/investments, sr. vice president/chief accounting officer, sr. vice president/human resources, sr. vice president/corporate communications & investor relations, sr. vice president/chief information officer, and sr. vice president/general counsel.

Below these were many smaller circles comprising an eclectic mix of executive vice presidents. Included among them were the heads of Retail Sales, Institutional Sales, Corporate Syndicate, Investment Banking, Merchant Banking,

Bond Trading, Equity Trading, Computer Services, Stock Loan, Security, and
Research.

Morson Grayhead was a huge firm, and the list branched out quickly like
a two-year-old chain letter. Though still highly compensated, Jake and Ederling gambled that this latter, lower rung was most likely not the immediate
focus of whoever their murderer was.

One is not enough. Three is a bull's-eye. But two seemingly connected murders puts the investigator in that dreaded gray area—like standing in front of a
wooden sign in the forest pointing to a dozen different trails. Any one of the
arrows fits, but only one of them is right. And, more often than not, he won't
know he's chosen incorrectly until well into his trek. It's a heart-wrenching
waste of time, energy, and resources, so the good ones try to think it through
well before beginning the journey. Jake and Ederling had just about massaged
the thing to death.

"All right," Jake said, standing up and stretching his back. "So we can rule
out the love angle and the homicidal coincidence angle. Even though our torch
is obviously a maniac, there's reasoning to his madness, I think. We both can't
seem to find an appropriate profit angle. So we'll work it as revenge. You
agree?"

"We've got to pick a door, Jake," Ederling said, tossing the last of his
Oreos in his mouth. "That's the most logical one to open, if you ask me."

Jake stood with his right arm pinned to his chest by his left elbow. He
picked mindlessly at his teeth with his left thumbnail. "If it's revenge, the
wives have got to be a proxy, don't you think? It's just too coincidental that
our man could have a gripe with two women whose husbands happen to be
senior management at the same firm."

"Yeah, but still we need to check the basics. To really rule it out, we need
to check for common denominators. You know? Same clubs, organizations,
were they close to each other, maybe sisters?"

"I know, but I bet we'll come up empty. Okay, you run with the connection angle. Find out what you can. Let's waste as little time on it as possible.
See if you can have some answers by this time tomorrow."

"At the latest."

"You ask me, I say the big one's going to be trying to figure out whether
the torch has a bug up his ass for these two specifically or Morson Grayhead
generally. In a selfish kind of way, I wish we had a third to work on. It'd make
it so much easier."

Ederling stood and tossed his wrapper in the trash, spitting in the can after
it. "Somethin' tells me if we don't find the connection soon, you may just get
your wish."

Jake walked to the board and picked up an erasable red marker. He put a large *X* through the senior vice presidents of strategic planning and the senior vice president of investments. "We got eight men and one woman who report to this row here," he said, pointing to the upper three. "Two of their wives are dead." Jake looped the remaining names with a broad oval. "Any of these get hit next, we know we got problems."

"We got problems now."

"Well . . . then bigger problems."

Ederling strode to the far end of the table and sat down, plopping the heels of his black-and-burgundy saddle shoes on the table. "Jake, we're gonna need to speak to the rest. We can't have them out there, doin' their thing, not knowing the possible connection."

"Yeah, but if we go whipping up hysteria behind Rybeck's back, he's going to have an aneurysm. Let's talk to the man and see how he wants us to handle it. It *is* his firm."

"It's the shareholders' firm."

Jake shrugged with an annoyed face. "Whatever."

"Where do all these people live?"

Jake checked his notebook. Actually, he'd remembered all the towns, but hadn't read the list Rybeck had given him thoroughly enough to remember who went where. "Misters Investments and Strategic Planning were Scarsdale and Mount Kisco respectively. They're history." He marked the board with abbreviations for towns and states as he continued. "General counsel, Summit, New Jersey. Chief information officer, Greenwich, Connecticut. Chief accounting officer, New Canaan, Connecticut. Human resources, Franklin Lakes, New Jersey. Communications, Rye, New York. Marketing, Irvington, New York."

"Okay, so Irvington and Rye are in Westchester. How 'bout the big three?"

Jake checked his notes again. "Chief operating officer, Central Park West. Vice chairman, Sea Cliff, Long Island. Chief financial officer, Scarsdale, New York."

Jake had just listed some of the wealthiest towns in the country. "Boy, these guys are really slummin', huh?" Ederling added.

"Hey, they probably make a million a year. Each."

"At least. My mother told me to go to business school. Well, anyway, that gives us three in Westchester."

Jake tilted his head and ran his fingers through his hair several times. "Don, how are we ever going to be able to protect this many people in this many locations? We got three different states and a dozen different towns. It's a logistical nightmare."

"I don't know that we can," Ederling said, putting his feet down and walking to the watercooler in the corner nearest him. The water bubbled as he spoke. "We got to talk to Rybeck and see what he wants to do. I say we get 'em all together, tell them the circumstances, inform local law enforcement, and pray to the heavens we catch this maniac."

Jake agreed. "Call Rybeck. See if we can meet him at home tonight."

"Shit, Jake, the guy probably works until eleven."

"Tell him to change his plans."

SEVERIN RYBECK STOOD in his reading room with both hands resting on either side of a large, maroon-velour-draped window. He picked up his Scotch and water off the sill, twirled it a few times, and took a long, thoughtful swallow. Jake could hear the ice crackling against the sides of the glass as he drank.

This thing was hitting closer to home than Rybeck had originally anticipated. He was not a happy man. "Gentlemen, there must be some other way. If I call together the top dozen executives of my firm and tell them we think that their or their spouses' lives are in danger because they work for Morson Grayhead . . ." He didn't need to continue. The prospects were not heartwarming.

"What are our choices, Severin?" Jake asked. "We've already got two of your top executives' wives murdered. The rest have to be told we think there's a possible connection. How can we live with ourselves if something happens to one of them or their spouses, and they didn't even know it was coming?"

"Mr. Ferguson, we don't know yet that there is a connection to the firm. I mean, you think there might be, but you can't say for sure. Correct?"

Jake glanced at Ederling, who was seated in the sofa's matching chair to his left. He was sipping a Pepsi. Jake heard a voice in his head asking why Ederling always seemed to have something in his mouth. *Must be a Freudian thing.*

Ederling sat upright and spoke. "Mr. Rybeck, we don't know enough yet to rule anything out. But the alternative to full disclosure is not pretty. If you are seriously considering not informing your employees, then I ask you to forget the moral dilemma. The subsequent lawsuit should be enough to give you pause."

Rybeck sipped his Scotch and returned to his contemplative pose. Jake looked at Ederling and shrugged as if to say, "Hey, you tried."

Rybeck spoke firmly to the window. "Can either of you comprehend the magnitude of the decisions I make every day? They affect hundreds, no, thousands of people. Maybe even the markets. And yet, ironically, I can make those without batting an eye. Decisions in which scores of families are left without a primary source of income, whole departments slashed or eliminated. Billions of dollars are at stake. Billions, gentlemen. And it doesn't bother me a wink. You know why? Because my job description is easy. I am charged by my board of directors and my shareholders to do what is right for the long-term health of my company."

The word *billions* didn't even faze Jake. It was a concept beyond his ability to grasp—like death and the afterlife.

"Now," Rybeck continued, "you are asking me to put the welfare of a select few above that of the stability of the firm. It runs counter to everything I have done for almost a decade."

"I can understand your frustration, sir," Jake said from across the room. "But surely, you're not suggesting to keep them in the dark and risk lawsuits, humiliation, and scorn? Not to mention perhaps more tortured and dead victims?"

Rybeck did not remove his gaze from the large elms on his front lawn. "You say that, Mr. Ferguson, as if I am Joseph Goebbels."

Jake found the analogy apt, seeing as how Goebbels had chosen self-immolation rather than Allied capture. "I'm sorry. You've misconstrued my meaning."

"There must be a middle ground, is there not? My three top executives are highly compensated professionals, and I have no doubt they will remain silent if I ask them to. How about just telling them?"

Jake did not expect this fight. Certainly Rybeck would do everything in his power to protect his people? "Again, sir, with all due respect. Like Don said, forgetting the moral aspect of this. I don't see how that exonerates you in the eyes of the law if something were to happen. I mean, it's the next rung of executives who have been hit. Any lawyer out of school could make a damn good case that you had an obligation to inform them."

There was a protracted silence and Jake could feel the early stages of discomfort beginning to settle in. What more could be said? In his mind they were already rehashing it more than necessary. *What's to decide, Severin?* The only response he could envision was full disclosure.

"Gentlemen, I have decided," Rybeck finally said, turning from the window, breaking the uneasy silence. "I will not inform my employees of the situation. The facts are, as yet, too circumstantial, and the ramifications too profound, to risk causing mass hysteria within the firm."

Jake could not believe his ears. "Mr. Rybeck, I implore you to . . ."

Rybeck walked to his desk and leaned on both hands, as if to push home his decisiveness. "My decision is final, Mr. Ferguson."

Jake stood; Ederling followed suit. "Mr. Rybeck, I came here this evening out of respect for you. I have to admit I never thought this would be your decision. I must tell you that I believe it to be a poor one—"

"I don't care what—"

Jake interrupted Rybeck for the first time since they had met. "Let me finish, sir. Please. I do not agree with your decision and I must tell you that I will do what is in my power to circumvent it."

Rybeck's eyes smoldered. "Do not cross me, Ferguson."

"Are you threatening me, *Mr.* Rybeck?" Jake asked indignantly.

Ederling was surprised by the sudden turn of events. It took him a moment to realize what was transpiring. "Whoa, whoa, gentlemen. Come on, both of you. You disagree on an issue. Simple as that. You two are going to need each other as this investigation proceeds. I'm telling you both that it's in no one's best interest to allow personal differences to get in the way of our investigation."

Ederling wasn't sure that either man had heard a word he'd said, staring as they were at each other like two schoolboys fighting over the new girl in town. He put his fingers to his mouth and blew a loud whistle. "Hey! I'm not bullshitting here. Both of you. Look at me." To his surprise, they actually did. "Everyone is under a great deal of pressure right now. Jake, you want to catch this mother in the worst way. Mr. Rybeck, you have a company to protect. Both of those are honorable pursuits, and frankly, I can see both sides. Let's everyone just take a deep breath and see if we can end this on a civil note."

Rybeck sat on the windowsill, drink in hand. He stared at the floor for a bit, then looked up. "I didn't mean to threaten you, Mr. Ferguson. You probably won't believe this, but actually, it's not my style. I was concerned you might inadvertently start a series of events that could prove catastrophic to my company. Once that cat is out of the bag, I fear we may not be able to put it back. I urge you to try to see things my way. The fate of nearly forty thousand employees depends on how we handle this."

Jake was still fuming, but hid it well. Ederling was right. They would need this man. "Mr. Rybeck, you and I both have responsibilities. As a public servant, mine differ from yours. I apologize if I seemed indifferent."

"Apology accepted."

Jake felt flushed with fury that the man sitting on the sill before him would even feel that an apology was in order. If anything, Rybeck owed *him* one. But still, in a Herculean attempt at fairness, Jake tried to view things his way.

"I have to be concerned with the people most at risk, Mr. Rybeck. That is my job."

"Yes, and mine is the mirror image."

"Agreed. But you must have some obligation, I mean on a corporate level, to protect the safety of *all* your employees?"

Rybeck placed his drink on the desk in front of him and turned, placing the palms of his hands on the sill. "That is correct, Mr. Ferguson," he began, speaking to the window. "*If*, and that's the operative word here, *if* I feel they are in danger. There simply isn't enough information at this juncture for me to feel justified in creating panic."

Jake didn't agree but could see his point. *Maybe I'm more paranoid than I should be.* Maybe Rybeck was actually the more together one after all.

"I will say this," Rybeck continued. "And it even hurts to think it . . . but . . . if there should be a third, then I will not stand in your way. I will play it out exactly as you see fit."

"But by then," Jake said, shaking his head, "there will already be at least one more dead body. Can you live with that on your conscience?"

Rybeck rose from the sill and walked to the fireplace, staring silently at a turn-of-the-century portrait of some man in his midsixties, replete with military regalia. "You're assuming, Mr. Ferguson, that even if we do tell them, they will be able to prevent these horrible events from occurring. Has it occurred to you that perhaps, even with forewarning, they will be victimized anyway? They can't all move to Anchorage, Alaska, or hole up in some cave. My people are still going to have to earn paychecks, Mr. Ferguson. And to do that, I will expect them to travel. Their wives are still going to have to sleep."

"Yes, sir, I have thought of that. But at least any decisions they make will have been with forethought of the possible consequences. The playing field just seems more level to me under those circumstances."

"You're forgetting one more thing, Mr. Ferguson," Rybeck said, turning from the mantel. "My employees do not work under a code of silence, sir. They all talk amongst themselves. They are not stupid people. I can't imagine that they will not take appropriate precautions when word spreads that this has happened a second time. I already sent out a memo today urging people to be more diligent in general. At least until such time as the authorities can find the person or people responsible for these murders. Believe me when I tell you, all is not rosy at Morson Grayhead at present. Things are becoming untenable as it is. To then turn around and tell them that we believe there to be a connection when, in fact, we don't know that to be the case . . . I cannot do that now, Mr. Ferguson. I'm sorry. Our stock is already down a full five and a half points since all this began. A full-fledged employee panic could create wholesale selling.

Let's just try it my way and see if this thing dies down. If not . . . then as I've stated, you can call the shots."

"Too bad you can't make money when a stock falls," Ederling interjected for levity.

Rybeck looked across the room at him. "Oh, but you can."

Jake looked up at him. What he knew about finance would fit quite nicely in a thimble. "You can? Could you elaborate some on that?"

Rybeck was matter-of-fact. "Well, there are a handful of ways. Shorting the stock for one. But to make any meaningful money, you'd need a good deal of capital to begin with. The easier way is the option market."

Jake and Ederling caught each other's eyes. Interesting. "Maybe we shouldn't trow da profit ting out so quick," Ederling said to his boss.

Jake smiled. Rybeck had caught his interest. "Mr. Rybeck, would you be kind enough to explain to us just how options work?"

"Sure," he said, sitting down on the other end of the couch from Jake. "It's simple, really."

"So's brain surgery, if you know what you're doing," Ederling interrupted.

Rybeck laughed. "Well, let's see, I haven't explained this in years." He looked to the ceiling for a bit, then fixed his eyes on his two students. "Okay, there are two kinds of options—puts and calls. In essence, they are contracts that allow you to control large blocks of stock for relatively little money." He looked at both men. "With me so far?"

Both men nodded. "So far," Jake said, "but I got a bad feeling it's going to get harder."

Rybeck smiled. "I'll try to keep it in English. Okay . . . a call option gives the owner the right, or option, thus the name, to call from someone an agreed-upon stock at an agreed-upon price. We call it the strike price. It doesn't change. It remains constant throughout the life of the contract. Each contract has an expiration date. It could be March, April, or May, so on and so forth."

"Do all companies have options?" Jake asked.

"No, but many do," Rybeck said, shaking his head. "Certainly your larger ones."

"Do all companies have the same expiration dates?" Ederling asked.

"No. Different companies trade on different cycles. Each cycle has its own expiration months. But all options expire on the third Friday of the month."

"All options expire on the third Friday?" Ederling asked.

"All of them."

Jake pursed his lips. This game was more exact than he'd thought. "Go on," Jake said.

"If an investor buys a call, they want the stock to go up. If they buy a put, they want it to go down. A good way to remember that is this. You call some-one up to put them down. That's a little ditty on the Street. We all learned that way, or at least that's how it was taught when I was trained."

"The Street?" Ederling asked.

"Oh, sorry. That's our nomenclature for Wall Street. Everyone in the industry just calls it the Street."

"Oh."

"So, anyway, if General Motors is trading at fifty dollars a share, and I own, let's say, the December forty-five calls, that means I have the option to call GM stock from someone at forty-five dollars a share. That option will expire the third Friday in December."

"Do you have to wait until December to do something with it?" Jake asked.

"No, you can sell it before then, or you can exercise it anytime."

"Exercise?" Ederling asked.

"Yes, it means you want to actually own the stock. Let's say I want to exer-cise my option. In my scenario, I call GM from someone at forty-five dollars—you don't know who, and you don't care. That's the brokerage house's respon-sibility. Now, I own it at forty-five, and guess what? I'm going to turn around and sell it in the open market at fifty dollars. I just made five dollars a share."

"How much are these things?" Jake asked.

"Depends. In my example, the contract would be worth at least five dollars. It could be more depending on how far out the contract expiration month is. The further out it is, the more time premium the contract will have."

"You lost me," Ederling said.

"Me, too," Jake said.

"It's hard to explain, really. Bottom line is this. All option prices comprise two things: intrinsic value, and time premium. The intrinsic value is the differ-ence between the strike price and the stock price, although the stock may be trading below the strike price. In which case, there is no intrinsic value. Follow me?"

Ederling shook his head in bewilderment.

"Kind of," Jake said. "Keep going."

"Well, just remember this. The farther out a contract's expiration month, the more the same strike price will be worth."

"So a September forty-five will cost less than a December forty-five?" Jake asked.

Rybeck pointed a finger at him. "Exactly."

"Why?" Ederling asked.

"Well, if a contract expires tomorrow, the stock in question is probably not going to move that much between now and then. Consequently, people aren't willing to pay much premium . . . actually, in this case, they wouldn't be willing to pay any. Twenty-four hours is the snap of a finger in my world. But, if the contract expiration is seven or eight months out, a lot can happen in that time. People are willing to pay up for the extra time. That, gentlemen, is known as time premium."

Jake leaned forward. "So, let me get this straight. You mean, I could actually buy a contract that has no intrinsic value?"

Rybeck nodded. "Absolutely. In fact, if you hit it right, you could make a fortune. A stock that is trading below it's strike price, at least with call options, is said to be trading 'out of the money.' In the case of a put, the stock would be trading above its strike price."

Ederling looked at Jake. "You getting all this?"

Jake wiggled his shoulders, indicating he was giving it his best.

"Now, I'm keeping this simple, you understand?" Rybeck continued. "There are so many variations on the theme. You can sell calls as well as buy them, just like you can sell puts instead of buying them. And you can be covered or naked."

Ederling was not amused. "Huh?" he asked, his eyes taking on the glass veneer universally recognized as a sign of complete puzzlement.

Rybeck waved a hand. "All that's for another day. Suffice it to say that I'm always amazed at the number of ways traders can think up to make money."

Jake was fascinated by this newly found fact. "Do you mean to tell me that there might be someone, or more than one person out there, actually making money as Morson Grayhead's stock drops?"

"That's what I'm saying. In fact, I'm sure of it. There are a large number of outstanding calls and puts, called open interest, on our stock," Rybeck said, suddenly looking quizzical. "Why this sudden curiosity in options? You're not suggesting someone's going through all this just to make money on our stock? There's plenty of money to be made on the Street without having to kill a soul. And anyway, wouldn't it just make sense to kill the employees, rather than their wives, and really do damage?"

Jake wasn't sure himself. It seemed like an awful lot of hoops to jump through just to make some money. He was convinced that if there was any validity to a possible profit motive, there had to be more to the story. "We're just fishing right now, Severin," he said. "The more information we have, the better. Please continue."

"Well, it's important to remember that a good trader doesn't care which way the market moves as long as it does so with a vengeance. That, and he also has to hope he's on the right side of the market. And there's also more ways to make money on a dropping stock than just buying options."

Jake raised an eyebrow. It looked as if he and Ederling were in for a crash course in finance. "So what happens when the stock goes down? Say GM goes to forty."

"Well, you're pretty much up shit's creek. You certainly aren't going to exercise your option to buy it at forty-five, when you can buy it in the open market at forty. Right?"

Jake and Ederling looked at each other.

"So, let me see if I've got this straight. If GM keeps going up, say to sixty, then my call option is going to be worth fifteen dollars, right?"

Rybeck smiled. "You're catching on, Mr. Ferguson. At least fifteen. Remember, there could also be some time premium in there."

"If someone wanted to buy the contract, it would only cost fifteen dollars?" Ederling asked.

"Oh, no, no," Rybeck said, chuckling. "Each contract controls one hundred shares of stock, so you have to multiply its value by one hundred."

"Oh, I see," Jake said, as if a lightbulb had just gone off. "I was wondering about that. So, in this case, the contract would be worth fifteen hundred dollars."

"Right."

"All right, so how do puts work? Give me an example there, but this time use your own stock."

"Same way, just the inverse. If I own a put, I want the stock to go down, right? With a put, you have the right to sell, or put, stock to someone at an agreed-upon price by some date."

Ederling shook his head. "You followin' this, Jake?"

"Yeah, I think."

"Good, because I'm gonna need you to explain it to me on the way home."

Jake smiled. "So, go ahead, Severin. Talk to me about puts."

"Well, let's say Morson Grayhead is trading at fifty-three. Say you own a December fifty put. Your contract is out of the money, right? You're not going to sell, or put, your stock to someone at fifty when you can sell it in the open market at fifty-three. Make sense?"

Jake and Ederling looked at each other. Ederling closed his eyes and shook his head. Jake was desperately trying to keep up. "I think."

"Okay, say our stock drops to forty. Now you have the option to sell it, or put it, to someone at fifty. Now it has an intrinsic value of ten, right? So you buy the stock at forty and turn around and sell it to the person who owns the puts at fifty. Quick ten points."

Jake was contemplative. He was obviously thinking this all through, especially as it pertained to the case. "Answer me this, Severin. Is it possible that

I could own a put whose strike price is way far away? Say, a forty, or even a thirty-five?"

Rybeck looked at him. "It's possible. The exchange would have to have created a strike that far out of the money. Strike prices don't go in multiples of five to zero. They generally are within fifteen or twenty points of the stock's current price. It's a bit more complex than that, but that will work for purposes of our conversation. Obviously, if at some time during the option's life, the stock in question has been, let's say, at twenty, then, yes, you would have strike prices of ten, fifteen, and so on."

"So, if Morson Grayhead is at fifty-three, and someone bought, oh, I don't know, let's say, a thirty-five put, it would cost next to nothing, right?"

"That's right. It obviously has no intrinsic value, but there might be a sixteenth, maybe an eighth, time premium."

"An eighth?" Jake asked. "That's twelve dollars and fifty cents for a hundred shares?"

"Technically. It's more accurate to say that you've spent twelve dollars and fifty cents to *control* a hundred shares."

"I see," Jake said with a nod. "So, in theory, I could buy a thousand contracts for twelve hundred and fifty dollars?"

Rybeck nodded. "And, if for some reason, our stock started approaching thirty-five, you can bet that time premium would increase."

"You mean, the closer the stock gets to thirty-five, the more valuable the option becomes?"

"That's right."

"Even though the stock is still trading above the thirty-five strike price and has no intrinsic value?"

"That's correct."

Jake placed his elbows on his knees, holding his hands out in front of him, as if condensing it all into something that made sense. "All right, just for the hell of it, if I knew that Morson Grayhead was going to drop, in theory I could have loaded up on these out-of-the-money puts and make a bundle if the stock started to tank, right?"

"You bet. You could make hundreds of thousands of dollars. Millions, I suppose, depending upon how many contracts you originally bought. Just think about it. If you bought a thousand puts for an eighth, with a strike price of thirty-five, you've spent twelve hundred and fifty dollars, right? Let's say our stock goes to thirty-eight. Those contracts could easily trade at two, three, maybe even four dollars."

Jake whistled aloud. "So, you're telling me that my twelve-hundred-dollar investment is now worth two or three hundred thousand?"

"That's how it works."

"Who would be so stupid to sell someone something like that?" Ederling asked.

Rybeck smiled. "Well, Mr. Ederling, obviously when he sold it, he didn't expect the market to go against him. But in this case, our hypothetical seller was wrong, wasn't he?"

"I'll say. This shit actually happens?" Ederling asked.

"Every day," Rybeck said, his eyes beaming as if he were discussing grandchildren.

"I'll be damned," Ederling continued. "How do you guys do that stuff and still sleep at night?"

"That, Mr. Ederling, is why the trading side of this business is a young man's game. The older ones either lose their nerve with age, can't live with the pressure anymore, or die."

"Jesus, it sounds like a shark tank," Jake added.

Rybeck sat up on the edge of the couch and put his elbows on his knees. "Mr. Ferguson," he said, turning to look at Jake, "I would say you put your finger right on it."

"You like it, huh?" Ederling asked.

"I live for it, sir."

Tuesday
September 10

VIRTUALLY EVERY BROKERAGE firm of any size is armed with battalions of compliance officers whose daily job it is to look for anything out of the ordinary. In the bigger houses, compliance departments are segmented, reporting to a divisional head who reports to the firm-wide vice president in charge of Legal and Compliance.

Reams of computer-generated printouts are thoroughly scanned every day, in search of that one grain of sand in the ointment—that one trade that screams out, "What's wrong with this picture?"

All investors have a trading pattern. Whether it's little old Aunt Mollie who buys one hundred shares of AT&T at a time, or the cowboy who thinks he's got the markets figured out and trades scores of options at a clip. Compliance officers scan their daily runs looking for that one trade, that one foreign blip on the radar screen that sends red flags waving and phone lines buzzing.

On Tuesday morning, the alarms went off in the White Plains branch of Thompson McElvay, one of the nation's largest brokerage firms. The office manager had just finished his weekly sales meeting and was settling in for another day of putting out fires when the divisional compliance officer interrupted his morning coffee.

"Barry, it's Saul."

Saul Bremmer was an institution at Thompson. For some reason, he'd never been promoted above his present post. Some thought maybe he was viewed as too bureaucratic, too by the book. Which, if true, was the ultimate irony. Because in this day and age on the Street, if there's one thing everyone plays by now, it's the book. The Street is fully aware of its self-inflicted black eye and is single-mindedly determined to change it.

The go-go eighties had hardly helped the Street's reputation—with the likes of Boesky, Milken, and Levine; insider trading; junk bonds; federal charges of racketeering, fraud, and money laundering. The very pistons that drive America's capitalistic engines were at risk, eyed ever more suspiciously by the public as well as the government. The Crash of '87 brought it all crumbling down. And this time, as Wall Street rebuilt, the powers that be were determined to do it right.

"Hey, Saul," Barry Rheinhoffer said. "Why does my heart skip a beat every time you call me?"

"I know, I know. Sometimes I feel like the tax man."

"You know, Bremmer, if you came up here and got a real job selling for me, you wouldn't have to suffer like that."

"Barry, what do you know about a client of yours by the name of Warren Parks?"

Barry Rheinhoffer leaned toward his computer, plugging in the last name Parks. "Who's the broker?"

"Ted Wilkinson."

"Parks, Parks . . . shit, Bremmer, we got nearly twenty thousand clients in here. Name doesn't ring a bell. Why?"

"Seems he's a two-bit options trader. You know the kind, ten options here, fifteen there. Been doing it off and on for a few years now."

Options buyers are the market's version of a suicide risk. Invariably they go down in a ball of flames. "There's a miracle," Rheinhoffer said. "Never seen an option player last that long."

"Yeah, well, it seems this one just bought a brand-new pair of brass balls."

"Oh, wait a minute," Rheinhoffer interrupted. "Parks. Now I remember. I signed some tickets for Ted last week. In fact I even called the guy. Wanted to make sure he understood the risks involved before we started entering orders that size. I remember the guy now. So what's up? You got a problem with the Morson puts, right?"

Any broker will tell you that buying options is for losers. They are perfectly legitimate investment tools when used properly, primarily as a hedging technique. But when a client gambles with them and loses, look out. In reality, they are nothing more than Wall Street's version of adult entertainment. As firms are apt to remind their brokers time and again, "Your client loses money trading options, just get out the checkbook." A not so subtle reminder that brokers seldom win option lawsuits, regardless of fault.

"Barry, do you know that over the past month Parks has bought nearly one hundred and fifty puts on Morson Grayhead? I don't need to tell you what's going on over there. What the hell are you doing up there?"

"Now wait just a minute, Saul," Rheinhoffer interrupted defensively. "The guy's been a good client, he's got the money. I spoke to him for twenty minutes and made sure Ted updated the client profile. Don't forget, as much as New York hates to admit it, we're in a risk business."

"Come on, Barry. Buying a thousand shares of IBM is risk. Buying one hundred and fifty puts is nothing more than gambling. Shit, that's not an investment, Barry, that's a roll of the dice. Tell the guy to go to the track or Atlantic City."

"Saul, I'm looking at the guy's account right now. He's got nearly three hundred thousand dollars in there. His activity page shows he bought them anywhere from a steeny to a quarter. If the whole thing goes belly-up, he's not going to lose more than twenty K."

Bremmer was annoyed. He hated these veterans who grew callous to risk. They were few and far between, but every once in a while he'd run into one. Barry Rheinhoffer was notorious for it. But he ran a clean office, had precious few customer complaints, and was profitable as hell. Bremmer wondered who his New York rabbi was.

"Barry, my run shows this guy bought fifty contracts at a steeny over two days last week alone," he said, using Street language for a sixteenth. "These contracts are so far out of the money, Morson would have to practically go under for this guy to make out."

"I don't know, Bremmer, with the shit going on over there, he may end up looking like a genius. The stock's dropping like a kamikaze pilot. He's already made fifty percent on his money."

"Barry, when was the last fire?"

"At Morson?"

"No, at Merrill. Yes, of course at Morson."

The gist of Bremmer's question did not go unnoticed. "What are you trying to say, Saul? You know as well as I do. The first happened a week ago Wednesday. The last one on Sunday."

"Exactly. One woman gets murdered and this guys loads up on Morson Grayhead puts. He didn't know there'd be another because it didn't happen until Sunday morning."

Rheinhoffer closed his eyes and smirked. "Oh, come on, Saul. You're killing me. So now you're telling me we're doing business with Jack the Ripper? No one's that stupid."

"Really?" Bremmer asked condescendingly. "Just what do you know about this Mr. Parks?"

"Don't patronize me, Saul. You already know the answer to that question. What I do know is that he has the money, knows what he's doing, and is aware of the risks. You want me to start sending my clients a morality questionnaire? 'Dear client, have you ever smoked marijuana?' Come on, get real."

"All right, Barry, then why do you think Parks bought so many worthless options?"

"Bremmer, an investment is worthless when it's zero. Right now, those babies are trading three-eighths, bid. That's not worthless in my book."

"All right, so Parks is a genius," Bremmer said impatiently. "But why did he buy them? You must have asked him *that* when you spoke to him."

"Yeah, he had three reasons, actually. Made sense to me. He thinks the market as a whole is toppy. I can't argue with him there. He thinks the Fed's going to raise rates. Probably right there also. And he thinks all this Morson Grayhead shit is just that. He thinks the stock is way overvalued. Can't argue that one either. Hell, it's trading nearly three times book. You have to admit, the man knows his stuff. He may be smarter than all of us."

Bremmer hated these conversations. "Barry, listen to me. This guy's never bought more than twenty options in his life. Now he's practically the entire open interest on that contract. That doesn't strike you as a little odd?"

Rheinhoffer needed to be careful. There was a line he could approach in defense of his broker. He didn't want to cross it. It's always best to have Compliance on your side, but still, he was confident of his position.

"Saul, look, I don't care about the number of contracts as much as I care about dollar volume. Yes, a hundred and fifty seems like a lot, and, yes, it caught my eye. But he's invested less in these than he has in other positions he's taken over the years. And, yes, I actually checked it."

"Well, I know this is going to piss you off, Barry, but there's no way I can let this slide without bringing it to Mussman's attention."

As Thompson's head Legal and Compliance officer, Bruce Mussman carried a great deal of weight. "Oh, that's beautiful, Saul. Why don't we just go and arrest the man? You realize you start hassling him and he walks, right? We can't insult our clients like that."

"I'm not saying anyone's going to hassle him. But I have no choice, Barry. The shit going on over at Morson is the talk of the Street. I let a red flag like this go up without a mention and I just may end up there selling for you. I'm serious, Barry. They would fry my ass."

"Fine," Rheinhoffer said, his annoyance clearly audible. "Talk to Mussman. But I tell you this: anyone starts calling my clients with questions, I want to know about it in advance. Got it?"

"Yeah, I got it."

Rheinhoffer was fed up to here with New York. Often he wondered whose side they were really on. "You know, Saul, every time we make a move out here in the field, you guys go apoplectic. It's getting so that all we can do is sell mutual funds and blue chips. Don't forget that risk *is* our business,

Saul. It's what we do. I got forty-two brokers in here busting their asses every day, walkin' around with bull's-eyes on their backs. It's like investors feel they should never lose money. Someone ought to get the word out. Stocks go up *and* down. I'm here to tell you, if you guys spent one week out here on the front lines with us, you'd walk away with a different perspective."

Bremmer had heard it all a thousand times before. "Look, Barry, don't go getting a bug up your ass over this. You know I have no choice. This whole Morson thing is just too big."

"Yeah, yeah."

JAKE HAD DECIDED to set his alarm an hour early. The trip to Rybeck's pool house and the vision of the sixty-year-old man looking more like Jake's junior had humiliated him into trying to get his sagging body back into shape. He put on a pair of gym shorts and a T-shirt that read WHITE PLAINS FIRE DEPARTMENT. He fumbled blindly on the floor of his closet for his Asics sneakers and finally gave in to his need for light. He flicked on the overhead, grabbed his shoes, and sat on Danielle's side of the bed to lace up. Jake glanced for a moment at her pillow, leaned down to tie his shoes, and rose for battle.

The radio in the bathroom bellowed something about an approaching storm, but Jake was only half-listening, the way you hear Muzak in a mall. He reached under the sink and pulled out a dusty scale Danielle had given him for his thirty-eighth birthday. A remnant of the last time he'd decided he was going to try to do something good for his body. *Two hundred and six pounds! My God, the last time I used it I only weighed in at one ninety-two!*

Jake locked his front door and shoved the key above the sill. He walked mindlessly to the elevator and waited while it climbed the three stories of his co-op complex. He trudged in, hit L, and leaned against the back rail. *I can't believe I'm doing this.* More than once, he considered turning around and snuggling back into bed. *After all, who am I trying to impress?* Jake moaned to himself at the enormity of the battle he was about to wage. He hated dieting. In fact, the mere thought of what lay ahead weighed on his brain like a cinder block. The loneliness and drudgery of counting calories and chewing on carrot sticks like some misplaced rabbit made him wonder if man was supposed to be thin.

The thought of the redhead Ederling had spoken of over the weekend flittered across his brain, and for the first time in years, Jake realized he was lonely for a woman. The elevator doors slowly creaked open. *Maybe I should call her.* Jake walked out of the lobby, eyeing the morning steam lying still in the trees; the suburban equivalent of the rain forest. *This heat wave is brutal.* Ninety-five-plus every day. Whatever storm the weatherman had mentioned couldn't arrive quickly enough. The buzz of ten thousand cicadas broke the early-morning calm as he stood at his complex's front door. Jake was strangely aware of their ubiquitous shrill as he bent at the waist, preparing to exercise for the first time in over four years.

He tried a few halfhearted jumping jacks, leaned against the rail and stretched his calves, went through a few other perfunctory motions he thought were as good as any for the torture that lay ahead.

A mile or so from home, Jake was feeling rather proud of himself. He knew he had to be cautious, careful not to overdo it on this first time out, when from nowhere, a shooting pain began to grip his right side. At first, he tried to ignore it. Then he ran for a short distance with his hands over his head. His mind screamed, *Don't quit!* but his body said otherwise.

A disillusioning reality struck him as he slowed to a crawl. There would be no way he could continue. Not *this* morning. Jake was disappointed in himself, inwardly embarrassed to find the very act of breathing difficult. He began to walk and broke into laughter at the brashness of his earlier goals. He found a chain-link fence and leaned his hands against it, almost in tears. He wasn't sure if they were from the pain or the hilarity of his pitiful attempt to resurrect his lifeless body.

A police officer apparently shared Jake's vision of himself. He pulled his cruiser alongside him. "You okay, fella?" he asked as Jake took turns laughing, holding his sides, and trying to breathe.

Don't ask him for a ride. Whatever you do, don't ask him for a ride. "Yeah," Jake said, looking up in agony. "First time out in years. I'm afraid my body's a little older than I thought."

"Well, don't kill yourself. Bein' in shape's no good if you're six feet under."

Jake watched the cop's parking lights grow hazy in the developing steam above the street as he pulled away. Jake turned and began walking toward home with his hands over his head, inhaling deeply for oxygen, wincing at every breath. As his pulse slowed, the Morson Grayhead case began to take precedence over his questionable survival.

Severin Rybeck had explained a number of trading vehicles the night before, and Jake found himself reviewing them in his mind. Once more, he went over put and call options, trying to get it all straight. "You can buy a put or short a call," Rybeck had said. Surprisingly, Jake found the whole process fascinating. Before last night he never even knew it existed.

It didn't strike him as plausible that someone would go through this much trouble just to make money. On that score Jake agreed with Rybeck. Yet, somehow he couldn't get the thought out of his head. If someone was bent on the firm's destruction, wouldn't it be just that much sweeter if he could profit in the process? Jake reasoned that in the torch's mind, it would be similar to icing on the cake.

He tried to become one with the mind of a man who would do something like this. Every bit of Jake's experience told him that revenge was the driving force behind it all. But the profit angle might just be the avenue he could use to find him. *Always follow the money.* He hoped his hunch was correct, but the fact that two incidents weren't quite enough to set a pattern nagged at his psyche. Jake prayed there wouldn't be another, yet he also knew they'd catch whoever was responsible if there was.

Jake limped to his front door from the elevator, realizing that his efforts next time around would require more forethought and sequentially smaller baby steps. Just owning the motivation wasn't good enough anymore. He unlocked his door, closed it behind him, and walked to the kitchen for a tall glass of orange juice. He had already removed his T-shirt and used it to mop the perspiration still dripping from his brow.

Jake leaned over the sink, watching dejectedly as droplets of sweat ran off his chin, splattering on the stainless steel beneath him. Like the clang of a solitary church bell, they conveyed a certain hollowness as they hit, echoing what he felt inside. He thought he heard something move in the living room and turned to listen closer. Something or someone was in his apartment. Jake could hear the crinkle of a newspaper. *Shit!* He'd left his .357 semiautomatic in the bedroom. It was decision time.

"Okay, asshole," he bluffed. "You got three seconds to get on the floor or I'm coming out firing. One . . ."

"Whoa, Jake, it's me," Ederling said from across the apartment.

Jake entered the living room to eye him. "Jesus Christ, Donny! Don't do that to me. What the *fuck* are you doing in here, anyway?"

"I was in the neighborhood and thought I'd drop by to fill you in on the victims. I checked the sill, found the key, and knew you'd be back. Figured you went out for a bite."

"Well, I didn't."

"No shit," Ederling said, eyeing Jake with mischievous eyes. "What the hell happened to you anyway? You look like you got hit by a truck."

"Worse."

"Do my eyes deceive me, Jake?" Ederling said with a beaming face. "You weren't out trying to jog in this soup, were you?"

Jake gave him a do-you-mind? look. "*Trying* is the operative word. I just about died."

"I don't know, Jake, you might be dead. You check your pulse?"

"Oh . . . okay, Jack La Lanne. I don't see you out there trying to drop a few. People who live in glass houses, Donny, and all that."

"Are you kidding me?" Ederling asked with a chortle. "I won't take out the trash in this weather. Bad for your health, you know?"

"Hey, anytime you want to fill me in on what you learned, you just go right ahead. Don't let my near-death experience stop you."

Ederling ignored his request. "So what the hell's all this about?"

"All what?"

"All what? You come in here lookin' like you just crossed the Mojave Desert on foot, and you ask me 'all what?' "

"You mean the jogging? I just thought it might be time to start to take control of my life again."

Ederling could see a cute little redhead in Jake's future. He decided not to push too hard. Yet. "Any particular reason?"

"Do I need a reason?"

"Easy there, boy. I just thought you might have a reason for putting yourself through such agony. Must be for the fun of it, I guess."

"Look . . . fuck you, okay? What have you got?"

Ederling gave him one last, long look up and down, shaking his head through giggles. "Well, you weren't quite right on the crispy critters. Seems they did both belong to the same civic group. Some hoity-toity organization to prevent blight in Westchester. You know? They're afraid unchecked growth is going to make the place look like Long Island if it's not stopped."

Jake pulled up a dining room chair and sat with its back to his chest. "Yeah. Well, they're right, you know? Everywhere I turn, they're building some piece of shit after another."

"Goes by the name Keep Westchester Green."

"Cute. Now there are some women with far too much time on their hands."

"Maybe. But they took it pretty serious. Seems they were always lobbying some state rep or congressman. They even spoke in front of some legislative subcommittee up in Albany."

"So how do you read it?" Jake asked.

"Seems to me we could be looking at some developer trying to keep the money gates open."

Jake wiped the back of his neck with his T-shirt. "Could be. But why all the histrionics? I mean the fire, the chaining, and the rape? Why not just knock them off and be done with it?"

"We keep coming back to that, don't we?" Ederling asked. "I don't know. Fear can go a long way, Jake. Maybe they're trying to prove a point. You know? Send a message to the other lonely housewives."

Jake ran his fingers through his sopping hair. "All right. Run with this for a while. See if you can find any specific developers they actually thwarted. Maybe someone they've tied up for a while. Someone who's losing big-time bucks with each passing day."

"On it."

"I don't know, Don. I still think it's a red herring."

"Could be. We won't know for sure until I dig some." Ederling attempted to leave. "I'll let you know what I find. What's on your docket?"

"I have to go see Rybeck again. We need more info on how to track some of these option positions. I'm also hoping he can point me to someone at Morson who can give me some insight on any recent firings or terminations. You know? Sloppy ones. People who made threats as they left. Maybe some wackos they quietly terminated who had somehow slipped through their screening process."

"You going into the city?"

"Yeah. Rybeck knows I'm coming."

"That should be fun."

"Different."

"Better you than me. I hate the city. It's a pigsty. It sure as hell ain't like when I was growing up. People used to actually dress up to go in. Not anymore."

Jake looked up at Ederling. "You think I should wear a tie?"

"You're going to see Rybeck? In his office? Yeah, I'd say a tie is in order," Ederling said, walking to the door. "You might want to shower first."

"Thanks anyway. I already took one this week," Jake called out, his head turned. "Just call me tonight."

"Sure thing."

Slam.

Jake walked to the bathroom and stood sideways in front of the mirror. He played various games with the truth, pulling his shorts up over his gut, sucking it in just enough so as not to feel too ashamed. Then, as if to hit home the need for vigilance, he stuck his gut out as far as he could. *Jesus. You're getting older, boy.* But Jake would have the last laugh. Of *that*, Jake was sure.

"MR. RYBECK IS in a meeting at the moment, Mr. Ferguson," Morson Grayhead's executive receptionist said. "Can I get you a cup of coffee, or perhaps some juice?"

"No, thank you," Jake answered, feeling strangely out of place amongst the surrounding corporate opulence.

He sat quietly in the dark green velvet of a large, high-backed, Queen

Anne–looking chair, fidgeting occasionally for a more comfortable position. Once, he caught the receptionist's eyes, followed by an awkward moment when they both smiled at each other with nothing to say. Jake guessed her for around thirty. She was black, with a foreign, exotic look, and a slight British accent that seemed to soften his unease. He could tell she had done this before. He rose and walked to the mahogany-paneled wall, viewing oil paintings of various sizes.

"Are these originals?" he finally asked.

"Yes, sir. That one is a Chagall."

Chagall, he mouthed to the painting, turning his head slightly. The name sounded vaguely familiar. *Should I know that name?* He didn't dare ask. Jake took a few steps farther down, studying the painterly strokes of another artist. This one looked familiar, like someone he should recognize.

Jake took a few steps down the wall and read the signature on the painting in front of him. "Monet, huh?" he said, faking indifferent confidence. As he turned, Jake thought he could see the receptionist's lips break into the slightest of smiles and wondered just how much of an asshole he was making of himself. *Hey, so I don't know my art. Sue me.*

"Yes," she responded politely. "You like him?"

"He's always been one of my favorites," Jake said, wishing like hell he'd kept his mouth shut.

"Really?" she asked, exhibiting enthusiasm for the first time. "You like the impressionists?"

Now you've done it. Try and see if you can pull this off without subjecting yourself to total and complete humiliation. He had turned to say something, God only knows what, when he heard a woman's starched, formal voice break his thoughts.

"Sally," the woman interjected over the intercom. "Mr. Rybeck is finished now. Please show Mr. Ferguson in."

Saved by the bell.

"Mr. Rybeck will see you now, Mr. Ferguson," the receptionist said, standing. "If you would, please follow me. I'll show you to the corporate suites."

The two turned a corner around the wall behind the receptionist area and walked, what seemed to Jake, the length of a hockey rink. They passed a dozen or so paintings along the way, and Jake noticed a marble statue at the end of the hall. *Jesus Christ, it's like a museum.* They stopped just outside two large, carved cherrywood doors with the words SEVERIN RYBECK—CHAIRMAN & CHIEF EXECUTIVE OFFICER etched deeply in gold flake in two lines on the door to the left. Jake wondered what they would do when he retired. Buy new doors? The receptionist pulled open the right door and stood in front of it, smiling as she motioned for Jake to enter.

"Janet will help you," she said, motioning to a woman behind an immaculate desk to the left of yet two more large, wooden doors. "It was a pleasure meeting you."

Jake turned to thank her just in time to watch the huge door swing shut. *Scene two.* He stood, momentarily dumbfounded, before realizing that the woman on the other side of the small anteroom was calling his name.

"Mr. Ferguson," she said a second time, motioning to a dark burgundy, wing-back, Victorian-era sofa. "Please have a seat, sir. I'll tell Mr. Rybeck you're here."

"Mr. Ferguson," Rybeck said, standing at an open door less than two minutes later. "Sorry to have kept you waiting. Please, please, come in." Rybeck extended a firm handshake as Jake approached the door. "Can I get you something to drink? Coffee? Soda? Martini?" he said with a smile.

Jake looked at him.

"Just joking. Please. Make yourself comfortable."

Rybeck stuck his head out the door as Jake scanned the room. "Janet. Please have dining prepare lunch for two." He turned. "You like salmon, Mr. Ferguson?"

"Mr. Rybeck, I didn't know we'd be having . . ."

"Don't be silly. How does salmon sound?"

Jake could get used to this. "I love salmon. Poached if possible," he said, pushing the envelope.

"Poached it is," Rybeck said, turning back toward his secretary. "Poached for Mr. Ferguson. Make mine the usual. We'll dine at twelve-fifteen. Thank you, Janet."

Rybeck closed the door behind him and stood, watching Jake eye the Statue of Liberty and Ellis Island out his corner office. "Awe-inspiring, isn't she?" he asked Jake, referring to Miss Liberty.

Jake turned his gaze. "Yes. She is."

"The 'Lady' was my grandparents' first glimpse of the land of freedom," Rybeck said. "They were two of the millions who climbed that giant flight of steps on Ellis Island. From eastern Russia. She was holding my two-year-old father in her arms when the guards pulled my grandfather out of line. Said he looked like he had diphtheria. From what I can understand, she never saw him again." He gazed forlornly out his window, staring blankly at the island in the harbor. "Unimaginable sacrifice, I would say. Can you imagine that, Mr. Ferguson? If someone just took your spouse away?" Rybeck snapped his fingers. "Just like that?"

Jake did not answer.

"But . . . that was a long time ago. You are here for more immediate concerns. Please," Rybeck said, motioning to four chairs around a table in the corner. He glanced at his watch. "Have a seat. We don't have much time before lunch. Let's make it count."

Jake took a seat nearest the wall. Somehow with all the trappings of wealth and power, Rybeck had never flinched at calling Jake Mr. Ferguson. Jake figured there were probably precious few people Rybeck afforded that respect. "Call me Jake."

Rybeck looked at him. "Sorry?"

"I said, call me Jake."

"A pleasure, Jake," Rybeck said with a smile. "You know . . . Jake, I feel bad about last night. It really isn't my style to jump down someone's throat like that. I hope you didn't take offense. I suppose I was just frightened of what could happen to this company."

Jake had indeed taken offense. Rybeck's deplorable behavior had spoken volumes about the man. But what's done is done, and obviously, he and Severin Rybeck were going to need to work closely with one another.

"No harm, no foul," Jake said. "It's been a trying time for all of us."

Rybeck nodded his head. "Yes, it has." Rybeck rested his elbows on the table, cupping his hands over each other, resting his chin on the heap. "You know, you gentlemen fascinate me. I don't know what it is about you both, but I can't help but be intrigued by what you do for a living."

"It has its moments, but let's be honest," Jake said, waving his hand across the room. "It doesn't exactly pay like this."

"So what brings you here, Jake?"

Time for business. "Well . . . last night you mentioned a good number of facts of which Don and I had previously been unaware. It's an awful lot for a layperson such as myself to soak in. I thought we might revisit it a little . . . just to make sure I understand things more fully."

"Of course," Rybeck answered, feigning renewed interest.

"Also, it would be helpful if I could speak to whomever is in charge of personnel. I need to begin reviewing termination records and dismissals."

"Yes. I'm afraid I couldn't help you much there. As you know, this is a large firm."

"But you can put me in touch with someone who can?"

Rybeck tilted his head slightly as if to say, "I do run the company, Mr. Ferguson." He hesitated to give Jake free rein over it, cautious of the legal exposure. "I want to try and keep this as quiet as possible for now. I've already spoken to Tom Delaman. Most likely, I'll have you start there."

"Tom Delaman?"

"Yes, he heads up our Human Resources Department. Extraordinarily competent. You'll like him. He can point you in the right direction."

"Good," Jake said, not quite finished. "I'd also like to find out how one goes about tracking who owns different options across the Street."

"You mean, who owns the short positions?"

I guess. "Yes."

Rybeck raised a finger. "Ah . . . gotcha. Remember what I taught you about being short. If you're short, you don't own it. Remember?"

This guy actually has a sense of humor. For some reason that surprised Jake. "See what I mean? It'll help to review it."

Actually, Jake didn't need to review it. He remembered most every word Rybeck had said last night. What he was looking for now were the nuances. The little things you don't pick up when you first learn something new.

"So how do you track these things?"

"What things? The options?"

"Yes."

"We call them positions."

Jake nodded, scribbling something in his notebook. "Seems like a huge undertaking to me."

"It is. Billions of shares trade every day across the globe, Jake. And I shudder to think at the number of option contracts just the CBOE handles every day."

"The CBOE?"

"Sorry. The Chicago Board of Options Exchange."

"Oh. Would they be able to help me track different positions?"

"With the appropriate documentation. Yes. Obviously, they're not going to just open their books because of your looks. But our contracts don't trade on the CBOE. They trade on the Philadelphia Exchange."

Jake couldn't figure out if Rybeck was playing with him or just lost in his own world. "Could they help me?"

"Of course. Same rules apply."

Jake felt overwhelmed by the magnitude of the task at hand. It seemed like paving a road with a butter knife. "What about the short positions?"

"Short options?" Rybeck asked.

"No. Short stock positions."

Rybeck clucked his teeth with a flick of his head. *"That . . .* I'm afraid won't be as easy. Primarily because it's not centralized. With the option contracts, you have one source. With a short position, you have scores of brokerage houses. You would need teams of people to perform that task."

Jake looked at Rybeck despairingly. *How am I ever going to do this?*

"Of course, Jake, I can't think of anything more important than what you and your partner are doing right now. I can provide you with as many people as you'll need to do the job. Just tell me what you want to do."

Jake's eyes must have lit up because Rybeck smiled as he saw them. "I'm a businessman, Jake. Not a monster."

Jake just couldn't read this man. A veritable reservoir of human paradoxes, Rybeck could infuriate one minute, bend over backward to please the next. Jake felt he would do well to understand Severin Rybeck more clearly.

"Well, if tracking the shorts is as difficult as you say, then maybe we should start with the options. Could you have someone get back to me with what I'll need to subpoena the Philadelphia Exchange's records?"

"What are you looking for? Specifically, Jake?"

"You're asking me?" Jake asked with a smile. "Hell . . . Severin, I don't know. I suppose I'll know it when I see it. An overlap of some sort would probably catch my eye."

Rybeck angled his head inquisitively. "Overlap?"

"Yeah, you know? Running into the same name in two places. If I see a name come back from Philadelphia that I also happen to have discussed with your personnel people here, that would certainly qualify. It will narrow the field considerably."

"Interesting."

"Hey, it's a shot in the dark. Don's working another angle as we speak. Oh . . . and, Severin . . . there is just one more thing."

"Mr. Rybeck," Janet said, interrupting on the intercom. "Lunch is ready."

Rybeck spoke loudly to the air in the room. "Thank you, Janet. We'll be right out." He looked at Jake. "Lunch is served."

"Just one more thing, Severin. You wouldn't happen to have changed your mind on what we discussed last night, would you? Don and I both think your employees should know."

Rybeck was silent for a moment, staring out the window. "You have no idea how difficult a decision that was for me to make. For now, the answer is still no. You must understand, Jake, my ultimate responsibility is to the shareholders of this company. Indeed, ninety percent of its employees *are* shareholders. I simply can't risk the financial well-being of thousands of people based upon the lurid fantasies of some beat reporter looking to make a name for himself."

Jake hesitated before responding, certain still that Rybeck was making an error in judgment. But, it wasn't Jake's firm. He tried. "Just thought I'd ask."

"I pray I'm right."

"I'm not too big on prayer, sir, but for the sake of your employees and their families, this is one I will be happy to join you in."

T HE TRAIN RIDE home offered Jake a brief but much needed rest. He caught Metro-North's 2:40 P.M. to Port Chester and consequently missed the throngs of commuters who would follow just a few hours behind. He folded the *New York Daily News* and laid it in his lap, leaning his head back against the discolored, industrial-strength vinyl of his seat. His mind focused on the vibration of the wheels as they spun a relaxing, continuous buzz through his brain.

Jake would be home in less than fifty minutes and found himself beset by an internal conflict that pitted the virtues of reviewing what he'd learned of the case so far against his body's subconscious desire for sleep. But like the fear people have of closing their eyes after they've flipped that snooze button to off, Jake didn't dare attempt a nap. He was afraid he'd end up in Stamford.

As if turning the pages of an outline in his head, Jake began reciting the various facets of the case in his mind. There was the obvious—or so it appeared—Morson Grayhead connection. There was the less than obvious Keep Westchester Green connection. Severin Rybeck was unexpectedly loath to allow full disclosure to his employees. Morson Grayhead stock was tumbling, and it was possible someone could be profiting from that. And whoever was responsible for these horrid deaths apparently knew when the men of the house would be away.

Jake again reviewed the killer's MO and a litany of other minutiae that only a fire investigator would know, or care about. The women had been raped, so a man was at least involved in some way. The lab would tell him if the DNA in both cases matched. He expected that it would and found himself wondering if his torch knew that semen remains relatively intact in the womb of a burn victim, or if he mistakenly thought all evidence would be destroyed in the flames.

As a rule, fire marshals are seldom used to investigate murder. Almost always, their sole job is to ascertain the cause and origin of fire. If it turned out to be murder, the case was usually handed over to the local or state police. But Jake's résumé was unique. Prior to joining the county's Fire Marshal's Office, he had worked fire-investigation/arson-homicide with the New York State Police for seven years. He knew the players, the ins and outs; and much to law enforcement's chagrin, after the Clawson death, the New York State public safety commissioner had named Jake the lead investigator on the Morson Grayhead case. The commissioner viscerally knew what the cops had only heard. Not only did Jake Ferguson know fire, but he was a very good investigator. Woe be to the suspect he set in his crosshairs.

Jake pulled out his notebook and turned to a new page. He scribbled the words POSSIBLE SUSPECTS in large, block letters across its top. He jotted down the name Rybeck and followed it with a large question mark. He then listed the present avenues of investigation and then a dozen or more avenues he felt should be pursued: delivery people, gardeners, repairmen, house cleaners, personal trainers, and the like.

As always, the possibilities were endless, the time and manpower short. All murder investigators have their own quirks, their own means of pursuit: individual idiosyncrasies that leave their imprint on an investigation. But some rules are inviolate, no matter the country, no matter the agency. A good investigator always takes the hottest trail and follows it to its logical conclusion. If, as was often the case, it wound up a dead end, then it was back to square one. No passing GO. No two hundred dollars.

The first forty-eight hours of a murder investigation are always the most crucial. After that the leads begin to cool. Jake felt a wistful sense of luck, in that he'd already been given two two-day periods. Jake was pretty sure there'd be more. He hoped like hell that Rybeck was right, but his intuition told him otherwise.

Jake had that feeling in his gut, the one that turned the lining of his stomach into ice. He and Ederling would pursue every angle, but still, he knew the connection lay somehow with the firm. They'd check deliveries and repairmen as any good investigator would, but intuitively, he knew the path to beat led to Wall Street. What he found himself wondering now was whether or not it would lead to Severin Rybeck's office. So unlikely, yet so intriguing.

The train's public-address system crackled to life. "Next stop, Port Chester," came the announcement. "Port Chester. Next stop."

Jake rose and waited for the doors to open. The burst of sticky summer air slapped him in the face as he stepped onto the platform at 3:28 P.M. He trudged slowly down the steps to the parking lot below, careful not to exert more energy than was absolutely necessary. Sometimes, on a hot New York summer day, just breathing makes you sweat. He lived only a short distance from the station, but wished now he'd brought his car. A solid burst of Ford AC would certainly hit the spot. Jake had heard it a thousand times before, but it really is true. It ain't the heat, it's the humidity.

He wore a blue oxford shirt, somewhat worn at the collar, with a twirly-patterned, red-and-blue Jerry Garcia tie his brother had given him for Christmas. He slid open the knot and undid his top button, feeling sympathy for those sorry souls who had to don this crap every day. Jake was aware of the tickle of sweat as it rolled down his ribs and wiggled his torso at the irritatingly wet and clinging shirt.

By the time Jake reached his apartment, his shirt was turning dark blue. Fortunately, he'd thought enough in advance to leave his air conditioner on when he'd left for the day. He stepped through the front door, slamming out the heat behind him. Before reaching the kitchen, Jerry Garcia had been flung unceremoniously on the dining room table and his shirt was coming over his head. Jake poured himself a large, caffeine-free diet Coke and walked quickly to the air conditioner, letting its icy jets attack his body's moisture. He was leaning over it, cooling his face, when his telephone rang.

"Hello?"

"Jesus Christ, Jake," Ederling said. "I thought maybe Rybeck offered you a job or something. I've been trying you since one."

"I just walked in."

"Ever hear of an answering machine?"

"It's broken."

"You could at least answer your pager."

"I forgot it."

"No shit. Listen . . . what are you doing for dinner tonight?"

Jake saw it coming and wasn't sure he felt up to it. "I'm not sure. Why?"

"Abby and the kids want to know if you'd like to join us. Nothing big. I got a few porterhouses on sale at A&P. They're looking mighty tasty."

Jake really was not in the mood for company right now—especially the family type. "I don't know, Don. It's been a hell of a day."

"Come on," Ederling said, hiding his true intentions. "You never want to come and you're always glad when you do. Just for a couple of hours. It'll be fun."

Kids. Jake did like Don's kids. Still, he hated feeling pressured. He closed his eyes. "All right. What time?"

"Whenever. I'm probably gonna throw 'em on about five, five-thirty."

"Okay," Jake said, suckered once again. "I'll be there around five. Want me to bring anything?"

"Yeah, grab a six-pack. Something good. None of that Bud shit."

"I like Bud."

"I know," Ederling said condescendingly. "Try to expand your horizons."

"Bud Light?"

"There's an idea. See you at five."

Ederling had hung up before Jake remembered he'd sworn off the brew. Not while his beer gut still had the upper hand. He stripped to his boxer shorts, plopping down in the BarcaLounger he'd bought on what would have been his anniversary last year. He stared at the dining room table. Visions of papers strewn all over it and Danielle studying for some course flashed into his head. He wasn't happy with his life. Ederling was right. Somehow, after Danielle's death, Jake had put everything on hold, as if someday she'd come back and they could pick up where they'd left off.

Jake's spine tingled, his back and shoulders quivering as he thought of asking Don's redhead for a date. *Where would we go? A movie maybe? They're always safe. You don't have to talk much.* The thought of carrying on a conversation with a woman frightened him. *What should I say? What do I possibly have to share that can kill four or five hours? And that dreaded moment when you walk her to the door!* He shook his head in dread.

He remembered some horrific moments in his earlier days. Times he thought he'd shit his pants. Say what they will, no man asks a woman out on a date without at least a fleeting thought that it will lead to more. Not that they necessarily think they'll end up romping in bed on the first date. But still, the need for acceptance is paramount, and that first kiss usually tells it all. But how does a man know when a woman feels the same way? Jake thought if he tried to be gentlemanly and didn't attempt a kiss, he'd never know if she actually wanted him to. But then again, if he did, and she recoiled . . . The very thought gave him goose bumps.

And that's just what he could remember from his dating years. *Now . . . Christ, it's got to be a thousand times worse now, what with all the viral crap floating around out there.* Jake could see her asking for a blood test before they even kissed. It was so easy with Danielle. The tender moments. The sex. It all seemed like an extension of who he was. But now, the thought of beginning anew with someone he'd never met . . . his stomach began to feel queasy.

But as he looked around his home, it was somehow lacking. On the mantel there were still the Lladro figurines his in-laws had given them, and still sitting on the counter were those little kitchen canisters that looked like hobbit homes. But over the years, his apartment had taken on a starker appearance. It carried an edge about it that screamed "Bachelor!" Something about a feminine touch finished a home, and right now—at best—his was a work in regress.

Jake thought maybe he'd invite her over for dinner. They could bake a quiche or something. Maybe share a bottle of wine. *But that won't work. Not on a first date. Too informal. Too suggestive.* Jake stood and walked to the mantel, staring at a Lladro. He picked up a baseball lying next to it that he'd caught at Yankee Stadium and flipped it up and down in his palm. *But then again, maybe we'd have fun. There's no rule that says a blind date has to be a disaster. Maybe we'd even hit it off.*

A tinge of excitement whirled through him at the thought of female company. Not sex so much, though the thought certainly entered his mind. No, not sex, but the concept of sharing—sharing his fears, his desires, his dreams. He returned the baseball to its spot, pulling off his underwear on his way to the shower. *We'll see. Maybe it's just too soon.*

"UNCLE JAKE'S HERE!" screamed one of Ederling's three boys, rushing off his tricycle toward Jake's car as it pulled to the curb in front of the Ederling home.

Jake had to admit, it was nice having a family he could call his own. Even if they weren't. "Hey, Christopher, you old hound! How'ya doin', buddy?" Jake said, swooping him up in his arms.

"Hi, Uncle Jake," Chris said, hugging him tightly around the neck. "Wanna see my new bike?"

Jake shifted him to his right arm. "Sure. Is that it there? Man, what a cool color! Fire-engine red. My favorite."

"Uh-huh."

"Show me how you ride it."

The other boys ran out of the house. At four, Chris was the youngest. The other two were seven and fraternal twins. "Uncle Jake! Uncle Jake!" they shouted as they ran down the small front lawn.

Jake put Christopher down, picking the other two up in his arms as they simultaneously slammed into his body. "Oooh, man," he grunted. "You guys are gettin' heavy. You must weigh a hundred pounds."

He opened the passenger-seat door and pulled out a six-pack of New Amsterdam. The four of them chummed up the lawn together, Jake entering the house last.

"Hi, Jake. I'm so glad you came," Abigail Ederling said, pecking his cheek.

"Hi, Abby. Been a while. Thanks for the invite," he said, handing her the beer. "Man . . . the kids are growing like weeds."

"I know. Isn't it amazing?"

Don Ederling entered the living room, wiping his hands on a towel. He wore an apron over a pair of blue Nike shorts, a white tank top, and a pair of Birkenstock sandals. "Hey, buddy. What'ya got there?" he asked, stealing a peek at the beer Abby was carrying to the kitchen. "All *right*. New Amsterdam. Now you're talking. For once, we can drink some *real* beer."

Twenty minutes of exhausting mayhem ensued, where Jake was dragged from one spiderweb to the next, one new toy to the other. He was shown forts, monster hiding places, cuts and bruises, and neat new finds.

Ederling had brought out five steaks on a tray along with garlic powder, pepper, and Aunt Molly's powdered butter. If there was one thing Ederling could cook, it was steak. He always timed them just perfect, seven minutes a side. No matter how Jake tried, he always butchered a steak.

Jake took a seat in a plastic lawn chair beside the Weber grill, wishing like hell he could have a beer. The smell of an open grill permeated the air, and Jake found himself actually beginning to relax. There's something special about summer—about not being cooped up inside for months at a time— that lends a special flavor to life. For Jake, even the unremitting heat was better than the cold.

"Here you go," Abby said, walking out onto the back patio, frosty mugs and opened beers in her hands.

"Thanks," Jake said, relieving her of the load and placing them on the cement at his feet. He didn't have the heart to tell her he wasn't drinking. In fact, looking at the mugs, he wasn't so sure that might not be a lie.

"Here," he said, pouring a glass and handing it to Ederling.

"Thanks. Cheers," he said, taking a long swallow. "Aaah, man, that's good." Ederling placed his mug on the tray next to the grill and slapped on the porterhouses.

Jake heard them sizzle, one after another, as they hit the grill. He moved his mug and beer to the opposite side of his chair, hoping to keep Ederling from noticing he wasn't drinking—at least for a while.

The Ederlings lived in a quiet, manicured blue-collar neighborhood in New Rochelle. Somehow, all the wealth, country clubs, and excess had passed New Rochelle by. It was inhabited predominantly by working-class Italians and Irish—the masons, electricians, policemen, and plumbers who served the rest of the county.

The Ederling home was a small, white-clapboard, three-room ranch with a detached, one-car garage. Jake figured it couldn't have been more than eleven hundred square feet. But it was quaint and full of love. Abby and Don Ederling were good parents, reasonable with discipline and punishment, and overwhelmingly magnanimous with affection and praise. The fruits of their labors were obvious. The boys were good children—respectful, caring, and mannered. Jake knew they would make their parents proud. He sure hoped so. They deserved it.

The sweating, ice-cold beer at his side physically pulled Jake toward it. He simply couldn't sit there with it whispering in his ear. "I'm going to try and drop twenty pounds, Don," Jake finally said, hoping that getting it out in the open would end the torture.

"You're not gonna do that drinking New Amsterdam."

"For your information, I haven't touched it. It's sitting right over here." Jake picked up the bottle and showed it to Ederling.

Ederling frowned. "What? You're not drinking? Great. We're in the middle of the biggest case we've worked in years and we can't throw it around over a couple of beers."

"Since when is beer necessary to solve a case?"

"It's not. I just like drinking with you. You know? We lube the old gray matter a bit and ideas just start to flow." Ederling closed the cover to the Weber. "But, hey, I understand. If you gotta lose weight, then you gotta lose weight. I'll just have to break the case myself."

Jake smiled. "Some of us don't need booze to think."

"That's what you think," Ederling said, flipping the steaks with an oversize fork. "Abby!" he called out. "Can you bring Jake a soda? He's dieting."

Abigail poked her head out the sliding-glass window. "You're dieting, Jake? Oh, please see if you can get my husband to join you. They're gonna float him in the Macy's Thanksgiving Day Parade this year."

Ederling cocked his head, looking at her. "Funny," he called out. "I is what I is. Look at it this way. It's just more for you to love."

"Ha!" she said, ducking back inside.

This was how Jake pictured marriage to be. Love, needling, barbecues, kids scurrying across the yard. He felt momentarily lonely, but was surprised to feel himself perking up at the thought of his date. Maybe he *did* have an ulterior motive for coming here this evening. That worked okay, for although Jake didn't know it, Ederling had one for inviting him.

"So, Jake," Ederling asked. "Jogging? Dieting? You have an epiphany or something?"

"No, I told you, it's just time to pull my shit together."

"I'll say," Ederling said with a smile, before booming out, "Chow time!"

"You're an asshole, know that?"

"Hey, can't argue with you there."

The five Ederlings and Jake sat at the patio table, laughing, joking, and eating. They ate steak, corn on the cob, Abby's out-of-this-world salad, and sherbet. Ederling drank beer, Abby and Jake iced tea. The boys drank purple Juicy Juice.

When they were done, Abigail rose to clear the table. "Don't, Abby," Jake said, touching her delicate arm with his hand. "I'll get it."

"You're a guest, Jake Ferguson. You just sit right—"

"No, really. I'll get it, I want to."

She looked at him. "Okay, if you're going to twist my arm like that." She carried in the boys' glasses and yelled out the kitchen window from over the sink, "Okay, guys! Let's get ready for bed. Last one in's a rotten egg!"

Jake sat at the table as the kids all mobbed him, hugging him good-bye. "See you, Uncle Jake!" "Love you!"

When they had gone, Ederling looked at Jake. "Thank God school's started. With two working parents and the kids at home all day, I'll tell you, Jake, it's a scheduling nightmare."

Jake nodded his head. He figured that meant more to a parent than it did to him. They sat silent for a moment, each sipping on his beverage of choice. It seemed a sin to ruin this moment with shoptalk. Both men sensed it, so neither man spoke. Ederling finally broke the silence.

"Jake, now don't blow up, okay?"

Jake had secretly waited for this. *Good. Here it comes.*

"Remember, I told you about that redhead that teaches at Sammy's school?"

"Redhead?" Jake asked, trying his best to pretend he had forgotten.

"You remember. The redhead? We were standin' out by your car before we dug the Clawson scene?"

"Oh, yeah, the redhead," Jake said, acting as if it had just come back to him. "The one with the lips and ass."

"Yeah, that's her."

"Yeah? What about her?"

"Well, matchmaking's not really my bag, Jake."

"Thanks for sharing."

Ederling pulled away from the table, crossing his legs. "I think you'd like her, Jake."

"You do, huh?"

"Yes, I do, Mr. Living Life to the Fullest. So does Abby. We spoke about it, Jake. Abby thinks you guys would really hit it off. She's down-to-earth, funny, and bright. And Abby knows she's not seeing anyone."

"How does Abby know that?"

"She teaches there, Jake, remember?"

"Oh, yeah. So, what am I going to do? Take her class?"

Ederling smirked. "Yes, Jake. That's what we want you to do. It'll be good for you. You'll learn sharing and the alphabet. Jesus, Jake. Call her."

"Call her?"

"Yes, Jake," Ederling said with wide eyes. "Call her. She won't bite. I promise."

Jake felt a stab of anxiety in his gut. He'd hoped this moment would happen, but now—now he'd have to do it or Ederling would forever harangue him for being a wimp. For a brief moment, he found himself worrying that if he didn't call her, Ederling would never again be as empathetic to Danielle's death— never as understanding and willing to listen. Was that what he'd been doing all these years? The sudden realization dazed him. Had he been subconsciously fishing for sympathy? Jake felt small. *Christ, Ferguson. You're pathetic, you know that?*

"What do you say, Jake?"

Jake looked at Ederling. "What?"

"What do you say?"

"What do I say, what?"

"Jesus Christ, Jake, are you listening to me? I said I have her number. But I'm only going to give it to you if you promise me you'll call her."

Jake's hands trembled. Did he have the balls to call a stranger out of the blue and ask her out on a date? He was riddled with second thoughts. A piece of him still felt like the infidel. "I don't know, Donny. I mean, I've never even met the woman. Anyway, redheads were never my thing."

" 'Redheads were never my thing,' " Ederling repeated slowly. "You're helpless, you know that? You haven't been laid in over four years and you're not even willing to pick up the phone."

"Oh . . . that will work," Jake said mockingly. "Hello? Ms. What's Your Name? Hi, I'm Jake Ferguson. Want to hop in the sack?"

Ederling looked at Jake a long time, his eyes revealing an uneasy puzzlement. A part of him understood that Jake was scared. Another part was becoming fed up with his endless self-pity. He didn't want to hurt Jake, but he had to push him off the fence. If it had been anyone but his best friend, Ederling would probably have moved slower.

"You piss me off, you know that?"

Jake's eyes narrowed as his head shot back an inch. "I piss you off?"

"That's what I said. You piss me off."

"Well, I'm sorry you feel that way."

"Jake. I'm your closest friend, right?"

"You were."

"Come on. You know I would never . . . never . . . do something I thought would hurt you. And you know what an angel Abby is. Don't blow this, Jake. I'm telling you, God acts in strange ways."

Jake's voice dripped with spite. "I'll say."

Ederling leaned forward. "Jake, look at me."

They stared at each other for a few moments. Jake finally bulged his eyes. "Yes?"

Ederling reached out his hand, sliding a small, ripped piece of yellow paper toward Jake. He kept his forefinger on it. He was determined not to let it go until he had his promise. "Call her, Jake. Please. Just call her. For me."

Jake wanted that piece of paper. In a strange, sublime way, he knew what Ederling held under his finger could turn his life around. *It all comes down to this? A stupid piece of ripped-up legal pad?* Jake's right leg pumped up and down like a piston as he realized he was digging his fingernails into his palms.

Ederling had asked the closing question. His pitch was over. There was nothing to do now but sit—and wait. He'd sit, staring at Jake, all night if he had to.

Jake brought his hands from his lap and laid his palms flat on the table. Ederling watched his eyes, aware of the move. Jake couldn't help but think of a lion stalking its prey. Ederling knew not to say a word.

"All right," Jake said, reaching across the table.

Ederling grabbed his hand. "Promise? You'll call her, right?"

Jake stared at him. "Yes," he said, attempting to pull his lifeline from under Ederling's fingers.

"Ah," Ederling said, not letting go, tugging Jake's hand slightly. "Say it, Jake."

"Say what?"

"Tell me what color boxers you're going to wear tomorrow. Come on. Say it."

"All right, all right. I'll call her. I promise."

"Mean it?"

"Yes! Can I have it now, please?"

Ederling lifted his finger. "My pleasure."

S EVERIN RYBECK'S LIMOUSINE driver was far more than your run-of-the-mill, well-dressed chauffeur. Ostensibly, his sole function was to drive Rybeck where he needed to go when he wanted to go there. Divorced and childless, the driver also made for one hell of a bodyguard. His given name was Chandler Boutet, but everyone knew him as Chan. He stood six feet one and had a forty-nine-inch chest. Rybeck always felt safe in his presence.

Chan carried a pager as well as a cellular phone and lived in a handsomely furnished, two-bedroom apartment above Rybeck's four-car garage. Chan's keen ability to handle a quarter-million-dollar, bulletproof stretch Lincoln smoothly around turns was the least of his job qualifications. He was highly trained in the martial arts as well as firearms, carried a registered 9mm Glock semiautomatic under his coat, and could throw Rybeck's limo into reverse and whip it around one hundred eighty degrees on a dime.

In his previous career Chan drove foreign dignitaries in and around Washington, D.C., for the Secret Service. Once, in 1980, he had even driven the pope. He didn't miss it in the least. He liked this job much more. It paid well for what it was, and the perks couldn't be beat. Rybeck paid him fifty-two thousand a year plus a Christmas bonus. Chan enjoyed unlimited access to almost all of Rybeck's West View Estate facilities in Bedford and Sunny Banks in West Palm Beach, when there.

Rybeck had been known to enjoy the company of women at his home now and then and didn't mind if Chan did, too. All Rybeck asked was that Chan relay any visitor's name and social security number to the guard on duty an hour prior to arrival. This last item had caused more than one stir in Chan's social life, but usually kept his dates wanting more when he told them why.

71

In fact, Chan couldn't remember the last time a woman had refused the request. He liked to think it was him, but knew that, in reality, it was the intrigue that acted to heighten their curiosity. He didn't mind. It was a good icebreaker, made for great conversation, and truth be told probably got him more overnight guests than Chan could have dreamed of if left to his own devices.

It was shortly after 10:00 P.M. when the limo's car phone rang. Chan picked it up on the first ring. It was not necessary to identify himself or the vehicle. A series of security codes had to be entered before anyone could reach the car, and precious few people knew what they were. Those that did used them sparingly.

"Yes?"

"Hi, Chandler. May I speak with Severin, please?" Royston Craddock asked.

Craddock was Morson Grayhead's vice chairman and, like Rybeck, had climbed its ladder his entire career.

"One moment, Mr. Craddock," Chan said, placing the call on hold and depressing the intercom key. Rybeck sat invisible behind a partition of retractable black glass. "Mr. Rybeck, Mr. Craddock is on the phone, sir."

Severin Rybeck usually used this hour-and-fifteen-minute ride to review proposals, scour profit-and-loss statements, scan annual reports and 10-Q filings and a half dozen newspapers from around the country. This evening, he was half watching CNN, half sipping a Scotch and water he'd poured from the bar opposite him.

"Put him through."

Chan replaced his receiver and punched two buttons, relaying the call to the rear of the car.

"Hi, Roy," Rybeck said dispassionately.

"Hi, Sev. We need to talk."

"I'm like Ross Perot, Roy. All ears."

"I just had Danny, Pete, Veronica, and Stu in my office for over an hour. They're not happy, Sev."

"Why not?" Rybeck asked, flicking the television off.

"It's these burnings. I'm telling you, if we don't do something meaningful soon, we're going to have a mutiny on our hands."

There was a brief silence. "What do you mean, 'mutiny'?"

"They are very uncomfortable with what's going on and how it's being handled, Severin. They—"

"How it's being handled?" Rybeck interrupted with disdain. "What the hell do they want me to do? It's not like we can just go out there and find the maniac, Roy. I'm working as closely with the authorities as I can on this."

"Severin, I know that. I told them that. I think they know it, too."

Rybeck gulped his drink. "Well, what's the problem then? I can't do more than I'm doing."

"Severin, not everyone feels as protected as you. And, with all due respect, they all have better relationships with their spouses than you do with Lianne."

Craddock's comment did not sit well with Rybeck. "Don't ever pull that shit on me again, Roy. To even imply that I don't care . . ."

"That's not what I'm saying, Severin, and you know it. But, as well paid as they are, they're not quite in your income bracket. None of us are. To be honest with you, I'm worried, too. My wife can't even sleep anymore. She's had to seek psychiatric help. You're the only one in the entire firm with round-the-clock security, and frankly, the general consensus is you're too far removed from the day-to-day fear to fully empathize."

"Christ, Roy, what're you telling me? They want more empathy? Fine. I'll start wearing a black armband."

"That's a little cold, don't you think, Severin?"

"Cold, my ass! It's not like I'm enjoying this, Roy."

"Severin, you're not listening to me."

"I've heard *every* word you've said."

"Well, you may have heard it, but it's not sinking in."

Rybeck depressed the speaker button, placed the phone in its cradle, and leaned forward to pour himself another drink. Double Scotch, one ice cube, a lemon rind, no water. This thing was fast becoming a monster with a long and suffocating reach, slowly squeezing his balls. And Severin Rybeck was not used to having *his* balls squeezed. He could see it wouldn't be long before it took on a life of its own, paralyzing his team. Rybeck was not happy. Just when it looked as if they'd reached the summit—just when it looked as if they couldn't be stopped.

"Severin?"

"What?"

"We need to attack this thing head-on. We need outside help. Someone who can help us form a tactical team whose sole purpose is to handle the PR on this, develop some type of prophylactic security measures, and deal with the worries and morale of employees and their spouses."

Rybeck was beginning to feel the squeeze. First Jake and his unreasonable demand to whip up fear, and now this. "Roy, let me ask you a question."

"What?"

"Why do you think someone is doing this?"

Craddock paused before answering. "A thousand reasons, Severin. You can't get inside the head of a maniac like this."

"I'll reword it," Rybeck said, noticing that Chan had just taken the Bedford exit off 684. "Do you think that Steve and Ed were connected?" he asked, referring to the two men whose wives had already met their end. "Or were they part of a larger plan? You think these burnings will continue?"

Craddock didn't speak for some time, obviously giving the question some thought. "I'm not sure. I do know that acting like this thing is somehow going to blow over could backfire in our faces. Especially if there's another one. We have to act under the assumption others will follow. If we're wrong, good. If we're not, then we can look at ourselves in the mirror every morning."

That sounded familiar. "Have you spoken to any of the detectives on this case yet?"

"No."

Good, Rybeck thought. "Answer me this. We don't know that there is a connection with the firm, right? I mean, no one's come up with some master scheme that I haven't been told about yet, have they?"

"No, but everyone is feeling that precautions are in order. I can't say I disagree."

"What are people doing, Roy? I mean, what measures are they taking for protection?"

"I know Pete and Stu have already sent their wives away. Pete's went to their summer home; I think Stu's went to her mother's."

"And the others?"

"Veronica mentioned that her husband doesn't know what to do. He's not really frightened, but feels he doesn't want to be stupid either."

"And Danny?"

"Says his wife's worried, but hasn't decided what to do yet. I think he and the others are looking to you for direction. They know you're working with the authorities, and I think they'd feel a whole lot better if they knew what you know and what you thought. Sheldon left for Chicago this afternoon. He called me from La Guardia. Said his wife refuses to run. He asked if I could arrange some type of surveillance. Two people in the meeting even mentioned that they'd like permission to cancel their upcoming trips until we can all get a handle on this thing."

This is exactly what Rybeck feared. No one was going to cancel any business trips. There was still a business to run. "Cancel their trips? Who said that?"

Royston Craddock felt for his employees and tended to agree with their concerns and assessment of the situation. He wondered why they all went to him and not Rybeck, but could now see clearly why they had. He worried if having access to Rybeck the way he did had numbed him to the dangers of power and the unspoken and inherent fear it creates. This was too important, too personal, to allow Severin to chalk up mental black balls. People's lives were at stake.

"That's not important."

"Bullshit, it's not important! We have a business to run, Roy."

Craddock was becoming angry with his boss. Just how cold could one man be? "Goddamnit, Severin! People are beginning to fear for their lives. Do you understand that? To hell with business trips. I care as much for this firm as you do and you know it, but we have a serious problem here, and people want to know what you plan to do about it. I'm not sure I see where that's so unreasonable."

Royston Craddock and Severin Rybeck had known each other over thirty years. Not only was Craddock the *only* one in the firm with unlimited access to him, but he was also Rybeck's closest friend. They knew an awful lot about each other, not all of which they'd like shared. Alone among Morson Grayhead's executive management team, Craddock could tell Severin Rybeck when he was full of shit.

Rybeck sat quietly, watching the black outlines of the trees whiz by from his air-conditioned view. Craddock knew he was there. He could wait. Rybeck twirled his drink, watching his lone ice cube rotate, not quite making it to the sides. He finally spoke. "I'm at a loss, Roy. I can tell you the authorities don't know shit. They haven't got a clue who might be doing this, or why."

"What did they suggest you do, Sev?" Craddock asked, assuming there had to be more to it than just that. "They must have offered some ideas."

Rybeck had thought this might come up. He was beginning to feel like an ant trying to keep the lid on a boiling lobster pot. If he came clean now and told Roy what they thought, the whole thing would blow open. He'd come this far so that would not happen. He wasn't about to change his mind now. Yet this meeting between Craddock and four of his loyal guard worried him. It seemed possible now that the greater danger lay from within.

"They're not so sure that there will be others. They're thinking that making more out of this than necessary at this point would probably cause undo alarm," Rybeck lied.

Craddock was surprised. "So you're telling me they think we should just sit on our hands and wait?"

"They think that's the best approach for now."

"Jesus Christ, Severin, I can't believe that. Well, for what it's worth, I disagree. At the very least, we should hire an outside agency and provide one, preferably two guards outside everyone's home until this thing is over."

"Everyone's?"

"You know what I mean. The ten remaining executives who have yet to be victimized."

The poignancy of the situation had not yet seeped in. Rybeck only counted seven. "Ten?" he asked.

"Yes, the seven remaining senior vice presidents and Tom, Matthew, and myself. It doesn't look good, Sev, your holing yourself up there in West View surrounded by the Green Berets, and everyone else left to fend for themselves. Look, I may sound self-serving, putting myself on the list, but let's face it. All of us are vulnerable. Except you. I'll tell you this much, Severin. If you don't do this, and something else happens, you are going to have a very difficult time continuing to run this ship. I don't think any of them could ever hold you in the same esteem."

Rybeck's shoulders stiffened. He bridled at threats of any kind. Veiled or not. "What you really mean to say is 'any of us,' right, Roy?"

Unlike the others, Craddock wasn't concerned for his job. He knew Rybeck would never fire him for telling the truth as he saw it, no matter how insubordinate it might seem. He had more money than he'd ever dreamed of, and anyway, half a dozen Wall Street firms would snatch him up in a heartbeat. This was one of those rare moments in business where doing the right thing superseded all else. Consequences be damned. It was nonnegotiable in Craddock's eyes.

"All right, Severin, I'll come right out and say it," Craddock began. "Yes, it's true that I would probably never look at you the same again if you don't act on this. There would forever be a black mark above your name in my book. I know what you're thinking, but with all due respect, I think you're wrong. The firm does not come first here, Severin. Not even close. People's lives rest in the balance."

"You don't know that, Roy."

"True. But unless you know for certain I'm wrong, you'd better pray like hell this guy's done."

"Or what?" Rybeck asked.

"What?"

"You said, I better pray like hell this guy's done. I asked you, 'Or what?' "

"Severin, are you telling me you are seriously considering doing nothing?"

"Or what, Roy?"

"Or may God have mercy on your soul."

Wednesday
September 11

2:13 A.M. SHELDON BORMAN'S wife was every man's ideal. Fifty-two, doctoral candidate in psychology, loving, giving, vivacious, and nobody's fool. At gatherings and corporate functions people sought her out like moths to a porch light. No pissant misogynist with a flare for the gruesome was going to run her out of her house.

"It's exactly what he wants, Shelly," she told her husband the morning he was due to fly to Chicago. "We all start running like cockroaches and he's already won."

Shelly Borman loved his wife, but knew better than anyone how stubborn she could be. "Now, Ginny . . . please don't be pigheaded about this. No one's asking you to leave the country. Just be reasonable. Go see Myrna for a couple of days, just until we get a better handle on what we're dealing with. She'd love to see you, and you know how you love the kids."

"Sheldon, please. Even if I were planning on going to Myrna's this week, I'd cancel my plans. I am not going to play into this psycho's game. Just go to Chicago and come home. Everything will be fine. I have the .45 we bought, and I still remember my lessons. Now please, go. Make some money and come back."

Shelly knew there was no pushing her once she'd taken a stand. Normally he could live with it. This time it worried him. "Okay, but I'm telling you right now, I'm going to see if I can get someone to watch the house for the night."

"Don't be ridiculous, Sheldon. Nothing's going to happen. You're starting to sound like an old maid."

And so it went. But Sheldon Borman was true to his word and had called Craddock to see if the firm could arrange some type of security detail or surveillance. That call, and the four executives entering his office for an unannounced meeting, had precipitated Craddock's conversation with Rybeck.

As is the case in any crisis, different people respond in different ways. In the bizarre case of the Morson Grayhead burnings, some of the wives didn't need to be told to seek safer refuge. Others had to be cajoled. Some weren't sure. Virginia Borman wasn't going anywhere. Or so she thought. She was about to embark on the longest trip of her life.

THE CHAINS WERE thin, the width of the links you hook trout to over the side of a fishing boat. They were tightly wrapped twice around her wrists and ankles, her tender, pale skin protruding through the openings in the links like Play-Doh through a press mold. Her desperate, constant yanking and pulling only tightened the grip, so that in time blood began trickling down her arms.

Virginia Borman thought she knew horror. She was thirty-four when she and Shelly had lost their only daughter in a boating accident in New Hampshire. She knew horror and grief all right; and depression and fear. She knew them better than she could even admit. The pain was insufferable for many years. But that was a pain engendered by the loss of a piece of one's soul.

But this—this was a different kind of pain and horror. She knew that now. This was the kind of horror that rubs the body's DNA deeply against the grain. The kind that wails, "I'm going to die!" The kind that runs counter to every atom that embodies who we are.

She strained her neck, nearly popping her shoulders from their sockets in an attempt to see her captor. He wore a black ski mask and had just finished wrapping a roll of laundry-softener strips around her neck. He was slowly unfurling the roll down her torso, through her outstretched legs, and out to the door of the bedroom. She recognized the box as he worked around the retch she'd just vomited onto her neck. She used it in her dryer. In her wildest dreams, she could not imagine what it was for, though her imagination was little daunted by the task of drumming up possibilities.

Her interloper seemed obsessed, nearly oblivious to her presence, wrapped inside his myopic little world of hate, lust, and revenge. At least one of his sadistic needs had already been met. The rape itself, while mind-numbingly violating, had ended soon enough. Ginny Borman wanted to scream, but the .45 revolver he'd found lying on her nightstand was now pointed directly at her throat. The light in the hall reflected mutedly off the barrel of the gun, and she watched in horror as it slowly moved up and down, in unison with his thrusts.

She was desperate to scream, but more desperate to live. She vomited during the act instead and was smart enough to turn her head, fearful of drowning in her purge of disgust. She thanked God when it was over, and as he shoved a rolled-up pair of socks in her mouth, she prayed for an opportunity to kill this man.

But, oddly, that seemed another lifetime ago. The nightmare was only just beginning for Ginny Borman, and she knew she could not afford a moment's dwelling on the past. Her fight-or-flight instincts pumped adrenaline into her veins and found her brain perilously close to the snapping point. For Ginny was less fortunate than her predecessors. She was all too aware of what was to come. A deep sense of primordial dread thundered against the inside walls of her skull.

Suddenly, it was quiet. He had gone. She was left dangling to her sanity, ripping her chains through her skin. Her heart cracked against her ribs and she closed her eyes, desperately attempting not to vomit again at the sensation of warm semen oozing from her vagina.

Ginny's precarious hold on sanity stemmed from, and focused on, the knowledge that there might just be a way out. For she knew something her maniacal guest did not. The headboard behind her and accompanying bedposts to which she was chained like an animal were a Borman heirloom and had been in Sheldon's family for over a century.

When she and Shelly moved to Rye, one of the posts had broken in the move. Shelly fixed it at the time with Elmer's wood glue. But over the years it had weakened. She had even mentioned to Shelly that he needed to look at it. If she could just pull hard enough to weaken the joint, she might just get herself a weapon. But it was the left bedpost, and she was right-handed.

Ginny could hear footsteps in the hall. She tugged steady and hard, following her efforts with intermittent yanks. She could feel the blood as it ran down her arms, dripping from her elbows. Her heart beat spasmodically as her assailant entered the room, climbed onto the bed, and stood straddling her nude body. Beads of sweat flowed from between her exposed bosom, her eyes bulging with fear, as she watched him remove his penis from his pants yet again. She turned her head in disgust as the warmth of urine struck her torso, splashing onto her face.

The time was near and she knew it. She gaped pop-eyed as he removed a large yellow container of Ronsonol lighter fluid from his back pocket and yanked for her life when he laughed, squirting it at her head. He soaked the pillows, her hair, the wall behind the bed, the headboard, giggling like a little boy. She could hear him breathing deeply and yearned, more than she desired to live, to hurt this man.

And then . . . Yes! She thanked God when it gave. Finally, she knew she had done it. She could sense the angle of the bend in her left elbow growing slowly but unmistakably sharper and knew it was giving way. Time was crucial. She mustn't let him know, but she had to move quickly. The blood pumped through her body like water through a fire hose. She could feel the pressure building in the nuclei of every cell.

He turned, jumped from the bed, and walked away down the hall. She gave the post a final, heavy yank, pulling up and away so as to prevent it from hitting her, but more importantly, to keep it from slamming against the wall as it was set loose. There could be no sound. Nothing could give away her triumph. Ginny had wrapped her hand firmly around the post now, but lay possumlike in her supine position. She had a weapon, but she was hardly free.

Ginny Borman knew she had but one chance to kill this maniac. If she just hurt him . . . she shuddered at the thought. He reentered the room and stood at the left side of the bed, staring at his prize. To her horror, she watched as he reached into his pants pockets, pulling out a silver, flip-top cigarette lighter. She could see it was monogrammed, but the light in the hall behind him cast a silhouette-type darkness that prevented her from making out the letters. He let go a deep, demented snicker as his thumb sent the spark of the flint to the wick.

Now! Ginny brought the bedpost down with lightning speed, sensing an odd panic as it crashed against his skull. She could hear the crack of the oak against bone and knew she had scored a direct hit. She also knew she had just depleted her one chance to live. It was now or never for Ginny Borman. The room fell deathly silent, the only sound her own frenzied breathing. She lay silent, listening for movement, but there was nothing but stillness in the early-morning air of her room. When she heard nothing, she dropped the post by her side and reached over to the chains on her right arm, feeling with the fingers of her left hand how she might set herself free. The sock in her mouth didn't even enter her mind. She needed to escape.

The chains on her left ankle dug deeply into her skin as she twisted and strained her upper body, trying to allow enough give so she could pull her hand through the chains on her right wrist. Please, God, she begged quietly. Come on, come on! her mind screamed. Hurry! Tears of fear streaked down her face as she toiled, her fright and panic only slowing the process.

It was no easy task. For one thing, her wrist was far enough up the bedpost to be next to impossible to reach. But more importantly, the muscles of her lower back were beginning to spasm. She twisted her back, straining wildly to reach. She was fingering the chains when she felt something pop. Instinctively, Ginny's body shot back to the bed, her face grotesquely contorted. The excruciating pain made all the worse by the dizziness and disorientation she suffered from the overpowering fumes all around her.

She had to try. Ginny twisted again, wincing deeply from the torrent of heat shooting through her synapses to her toes. She was determined to die trying. It was her only chance.

"Yooou bitch!" came a deep, guttural cry from the floor below.

Oh, God! No! her brain screamed into the sock. Nooo!

She could hear him moaning. Her eyes grew wild with alarm as she watched him crawl to the door of her room. The outline of his body was crisp against the hall light, while the orange-blue of his lighter's flame cast a macabre glow against his shadow. Without a word or a moment's hesitation, he lowered it to the floor, setting something ablaze that hurled a small but rapid whirl of flames across the floor in her direction.

She watched him as he crawled out of sight, down the hall, and for a fleeting moment felt victorious as the flames approaching the foot of the bed receded from her view. But in seconds, they came flashing into view again, as she realized what was happening.

She realized it was the dryer sheets! Oh, my God, her mind screamed again, as she desperately struggled to free herself. The flames were traveling along the roll of softener. She could feel it burning her pubic hair and the skin of her stomach as it quickly approached her face. Almost in shock, she ripped with her free hand at the oily material he'd wrapped around her neck, pulling it wildly out from under her, shrieking into the sock, desperately trying to shush it all away in a violent flurry of falling ash and jumping flame.

Out of the corner of her right eye she could see a small, flaming ember floating featherlike, down toward the pillow. She rose with animalistic fury, ripping the chains of her right wrist through her skin, but it wouldn't matter. The ensuing fireball saw to that.

The shadow of a man stood silently, leaning against the doorway. He puffed calmly on a cigarette as he watched the writhing ball of flames in front of him. Blood dripped down and off his nose from the gash on top of his skull, and he wondered if he would need stitches. But he would worry about that later. For now, he had earned this view. Too bad he'd shoved a sock in her mouth. He yearned to hear her screams.

T HE CALL CAME to the station house at 2:54 A.M. House fire, occupants possibly trapped. Four men were on duty this night, every one of them lost in sleep, or as lost as you can get while at the station. Firefighters always sleep better at home than while on duty. The mind's never knowing when the tones will ring lends to every moment an imperceptible tension—enough to prevent full relaxation.

And though some slept in the nude at home, none of them did so at the station. They all wore underwear, T-shirts, and socks. Some occasionally slept in their pants, though with the unbearable summer heat, no one did on this night. Within a minute, they had slipped on their boots and bunker pants, slid down the shiny brass pole to the red concrete floor below, and were pulling turnout coats and helmets off their respective locations against their trucks.

The fire department in Rye, New York, is like most others in Westchester County—part full-time, part volunteer. The four men at the station were the drivers and their partners, one of them a fourteen-year veteran, Lieutenant Thomas O'Reilly. When en route to a call, O'Reilly was responsible for telling the driver where to go and how to get there. The volunteers would meet them at the scene.

O'Reilly handed each driver a piece of paper as they climbed into their respective Mack engine and Pierce snorkel, still throwing on their turnout coats. The red beacons atop their apparatus were already twirling as the ignition buttons were pressed and the huge, white doors slid open. The red snorkel went first. The pumper followed suit.

For the same reason one's steps seem to creak more in the middle of the night, frightened neighbors could hear the sirens long before the trucks were even close. This early in the morning, the damp, still air held little to drown them out. The Bormans lived on the water, out on Milton Point, and could not have been farther from the station. The trucks could faintly be heard miles out, growing slowly louder, as terrified onlookers prayed for them to be there now.

On the ride, each firefighter donned his Scott Air-Pak and buttoned his jacket, snapping his Nomex coat collar into place around his neck. As they roared up the street, O'Reilly could see flames jumping from two windows on the second floor. A volunteer met them at the nearest hydrant, prepared to dress it and to attach the four-inch supply line the engine would drop before heading toward the Borman home.

O'Reilly eyed the distance. He could already tell this night was starting out poorly. The engine was equipped with two thousand feet of four-inch line, but the burning house had to be at least twenty-five hundred feet away. He immediately radioed Rye dispatch.

"Engine One to fire alarm."

"Ten-three, Engine One," the dispatcher responded, using the universal ten code for "go ahead."

"Instruct second due engine to complete lay from the hydrant."

"Ten-four, Lieutenant."

O'Reilly knew that they were now heading to a major house fire with nothing more than the five hundred gallons of water they held in their tank. On a good day, that would last four, maybe five minutes. His heart sank as he watched the last of his four-inch couplings thud to the pavement behind them in the glow of the engine's lights. It was hardly ideal, but O'Reilly had no choice. There was a report of trapped occupants. They had to move on.

Armed with an inordinate array of floodlights, headlights, and bright red strobes, the engines caused an insanity of illumination to dance across the night air, clearly revealing waves of thick black smoke billowing from open windows and attic vents. O'Reilly jumped from his truck and rushed up the lawn, eyeing the animal and the best way to attack it. Neighbors had approached him, screaming something about people being inside.

"Are you sure?" O'Reilly asked one of them.

"The cars are here. They must be inside."

"Do they have children in the house?"

"No, they've all moved out."

"Have you been inside before?"

"Yes, many times."

"Where's their bedroom?"

O'Reilly performed a quick, customary but essential perimeter check of the Borman home, then began booming orders to a volunteer and a full-time man.

"Frankie! Beau! Get your masks on. See if you can make it upstairs. There's no kids. Check the master bedroom first. It'll be down the hall on the left."

This is what it's all about, that terrifying moment when a firefighter rushes into a building engulfed in flames, risking his life to save another. Firefighters dream about it in their sleep. Everyone wants the opportunity to save someone from the deadly, hungry claws of the flames. It's a job fraught with peril; the slightest hesitation or miscalculation can cost you your life, or worse yet, someone else's. And yet, every firefighter will tell you the rewards far outweigh the risks. Most don't talk about it. As a fraternity, firefighters are loath to brag, and like love, it's impossible to describe anyway.

"Sammy! Diggy!" O'Reilly yelled. "Follow them in. Keep a hose on 'em! Easy on the water. We're workin' off the tank!"

The senior officer at the scene must keep dispatch fully informed of the situation at any fire. O'Reilly spoke into the mike on the shoulder of his jacket. "Engine One to fire alarm," he said, contacting Rye dispatch. "We've got a working structure fire. Heavy fire showing on floor number two. Fire is doubtful. Strike a second."

"Ten-four," came the dispatcher's response. "Striking second alarm."

Each fire station is divided into companies. The engine company, or hose huggers, do search-and-rescue and battle the blaze from the inside out. The truckies perform search-and-rescue on floors above the flames, cut holes for ventilation, work the roofs, perform aerial ladder rescues, and when appropriate, hit the fire from the outside—even though this latter function is not in their job description.

O'Reilly had sent a man from his ladder company to the roof to begin a vent hole. There has to be an escape for the deadly heat, gas, and smoke. And something needs to lure the fire away from the point of escape. Drawn through the roof, all its energy will focus there, preventing its rushing to a door or window when opened. Although this time, flames were already roaring out open windows—it was already being fed. All the more reason to give the heat and smoke another means of escape.

Frankie and Beau worked the front door while O'Reilly watched the truckie on the roof. A trained firefighter never opens a door in a fire without feeling for heat first. A fire lives for cool, fresh air. Without it, it dies. Air feeds the animal and, like a predator waiting to pounce on its prey, can cause a massive and deadly explosion. The two men knew that with air already being sucked in through the windows, the chances of that were decreased. But still, it's always wise to be safe.

Frankie peeled his glove back, exposing the back of his wrist, running his hand palm-side out across its top, feeling the doorknob in similar fashion. He had learned in training never to feel a metal object with his palm. Both men crouched, shining a flashlight at the bottom of the door, looking for telltale signs of smoke. It's a smoldering building that breathes, the scenes you pull up to with smoke but no visible flame where the danger of a backdraft exists. But instead, thick black smoke seeped from every crevice of the Borman house.

Crashing down a door to a smoldering, breathing building feeds the hungry beast, offering it a blast of life-giving oxygen. The ensuing backdraft could potentially hurl both men twenty feet back on the lawn in a ball of flame and superheated gas; and if their masks melting to their faces didn't kill them, the blast of heat would. But with the fire being fed through the window from the bedroom, they both knew the chance of a backdraft was next to nil. Still, they broke it down slowly, a little at a time. It was that or wait for completion of the vent.

Frankie wedged a haligan between the door and the frame and held the knob with a free hand, while Beau struck it with the hammer end of his ax. Known as the irons, the haligan-ax combination is not always ideal. But in this case the door gave on the third strike. Reflexively, both men stood back and away. Frankie slowly opened the door with the longest reach he had, releasing a mushroom wave of thick black smoke into the night air. Sammy and Diggy approached the steps with hose in hand, holding back its magic.

"Ready?" Beau asked through his mask above the crackling pop of the flames.

Everyone nodded.

"Show time!" he said, turning and entering the house in a crouched position.

Frankie and Beau were now in the world of the surreal. A world no outsider could ever imagine. Their self-contained breathing apparatus caused each breath to echo mechanically in their ears as they vainly attempted to see through the worn and scratched plastic of their masks. But it wouldn't have mattered if someone had painted them over in black. In a working fire the smoke is often so thick, you can't see your hand in front of your face. By instinct, each of them kept a mental note of which way they'd come. Left. Up the stairs. Left again.

The truckie was frantically working on the roof with a chain saw, but it would take him five or six minutes to finish the job. If given its druthers, smoke will travel up. But with no other egress, waves of thick black smoke poured down the steps, meeting the two men head-on as they climbed on their knees toward the upstairs hall.

The carpeting on the stairs was burning rapidly, and Frankie could see that in some spots the stairs were beginning to burn through. In this kind of heat he knew it wouldn't be long before they would no longer offer a viable means of escape. The railing was in flames, and Beau could tell just by feel that the fire had entered the wall to his left, eating away at everything in between, roaring up toward the roof, like smoke up a chimney.

As they approached the landing, both men winced from the intense heat. Sammy and Diggy hit the ceiling and walls above them with short, successive bursts out of their one-and-three-quarter-inch hose from the foyer below, cascading an ember-filled, steaming waterfall onto Frankie's and Beau's helmets and down the backs of their jackets. They were both on their stomachs now, desperately trying to stay low. The heat above would surely sear them like a microwave in seconds if they rose. Stay low, they told themselves. Stay low. An occasional slab of plaster crashed to the floor around them, bringing with it a rush of heat and flame. Periodically they would stop and listen as waves of heat hit the exposed skin of their faces and the backs of their necks.

Having entered the smoke-filled house, Frankie and Beau were in their own worlds now, barely able to communicate, unable to see. Blind and disoriented, they poked around the floorboards, feeling for anything soft, anything that might be flesh. The heat gouged at their earlobes and necks, and they both knew instinctively they only had a short while left.

Frankie grabbed what he thought felt like the foot of a bed and was working his way to its left when he realized he couldn't feel water anymore. He kept wondering where in the hell the engine guys were. He figured the line had kinked somewhere, or worse yet, maybe the fire had forced them out. It's a visceral thing, that moment when a firefighter knows he's got to retreat. What little of Frankie's skin was exposed burned from the heat of the gases in the room's atmosphere. He knew the time was near. For whatever reason or reasons, his backup was missing. Finding someone now was the least of his worries. He knew he had to get out of that room or it would be the last one he ever searched.

But Frankie knew something was terribly wrong. An engine crew would *never* leave two guys unprotected as they searched a burning room. Not now, not ever. It was a shame, too, because if they were there, they could have put the wonders of steam conversion to work. Water converts to seventeen hundred times its volume when it turns to steam, and Frankie knew a good thirty-second blast from an inch-and-three-quarter hose could snuff this room cold. But maybe. Just maybe . . .

"Goddamnit!" he screamed into his mask. "Where are they?" Frankie couldn't imagine why they weren't there. Unless . . . a house fire working like this, in several different locations—the first thing you assume is arson. Firefighters have a saying: "Nice people, one fire." That's what they always want to think. But ask any firefighter who's been shot at while working a blaze—not all people are nice. And not all fires have one point of origin. Frankie thought maybe the engine crew couldn't get away from the hall. He knew that it's an accelerant's vapors that burn, not the accelerant itself. Maybe no matter how much they hit it, falling embers kept reigniting the vapors in the hall. He knew they were operating off the water from just the tank and, consequently, had to be careful how much they applied at any one time. Maybe that's why they couldn't get away and up to the room.

Frankie tried to think. In his rush to get up the stairs he couldn't remember for sure, but he thought he'd seen flames crawling down the hallway toward the foyer where they'd entered. The only thing he could imagine is that the engine boys were busy working that. If his memory was correct, and he'd seen it right, they'd have no choice but to keep knocking that down before it hit the stairwell. If they didn't, and the flames got to those stairs . . . well . . . then he knew he and Beau could kiss it good-bye. You lose the stairwell, you lose the house. Period. They couldn't spare enough water to do anything else. It was the only logical explanation. Not that he needed one right now, because all that really mattered was that without water in the room, he had to get out.

Frankie started to crawl backward, in the direction from which he'd come. He knew no one could be alive in that room. If people were in here, they were long since dead, and he felt sure that if he stayed much longer, he could easily join them. As Frankie began inching out, suddenly and without warning something fell on his back, pinning him to the floor. It was an antique bureau, large and exceedingly heavy.

"Fffuck!" he screamed. He had no leverage. He wasn't on his hands and knees but flat on his stomach. Frankie tried valiantly to free himself, attempting with all his might to push his body up, but he was stuck. Stuck good. The heat was becoming unbearable, and he felt his earlobes begin to sizzle like bacon on a grill. He was in mind-twisting pain and knew soon enough his nerve endings would be burned dead. As long as he could feel the pain, there was still time. But he also knew if someone didn't find him very soon, he would die.

"Help!" Frankie screamed through his mask. "Help!"

For a brief moment he thought of removing his mask and letting the room's hot vapors sear his lungs and trachea. While he knew it might not kill him outright, he thought at least he'd suffocate before the flames engulfed him. As it stood now, his Scott Air-Pak would keep him alive and he would die the most horrid of deaths—from the flames, not the smoke. Frankie was filled with an odd mix of panic and tranquillity, like the feeling a man must experience in his final seconds before the firing squad. Something deep down told him to hang in, even though he knew if they saved him now, his face would never look the same.

Frankie knew it would be a matter of seconds before his bright orange PASS alarm would sound. An acronym for Personal Alert Safety System, a PASS is designed to activate if a firefighter is motionless for thirty seconds straight. Ten times louder than a smoke detector, they help other firefighters find their fallen brother. He tried to reach back to turn it on manually, but it was no use. The massive piece of furniture was lying directly on it, and his position was such that he couldn't tuck his arm underneath. Frankie tried twisting his hips, just enough to give him room to reach between the floor and the bureau, but it was futile.

O'REILLY SEEMED PERPLEXED as he watched Beau come bounding out of the house. Beau looked wildly around, trying to spot Frankie, thinking he was already out. O'Reilly walked toward him. It hadn't yet clicked what was happening.

"Where's Frankie?" O'Reilly asked, thinking maybe he'd missed his exit.

"I thought he was out!" Beau shouted.

O'Reilly began to worry. "I didn't see him come out."

"But I called. I called three times!"

Both men stopped dead in their tracks as the unmistakable screech of Frankie's PASS shattered the air around them.

"Jesus fucking Christ!" O'Reilly boomed.

Everyone knew what the searing sound meant. One of their own was down. Pandemonium ensued. O'Reilly began shouting orders, screaming to his men inside to keep the fire out of the stairwell. He radioed the truckie on the roof, ordering him off to prepare for the rescue of a possibly trapped firefighter.

He had to have a second line. O'Reilly turned to tell Beau, ordering him to lay it. "Beau! Grab a second line!"

But Beau had already redonned his mask and reentered the house. All O'Reilly caught was a glimpse of the back of Beau's turnout coat as he tore back inside. "Shit!" O'Reilly roared. Again he contacted dispatch.

"Engine One to Rye base," he said, short of breath. "Firefighter trapped."

The dispatcher paused, the delay seemingly a week. "Rye base to Engine One. Tommy, please repeat."

"Rye base, repeat. We have a firefighter trapped! Is Harrison en route yet?"

"Affirmative."

"Rye base, we need help here," O'Reilly said, his voice surprisingly professional. "Tell them to move it."

O'Reilly knew it would be a cardinal sin to have his snorkel hit that room.

Five to seven hundred gallons of water a minute thrown into a room that hot would steam anyone inside alive. All the textbooks tell you not to do it, not with men inside. He also knew a rush of water that large would push the heat and gas out the room's door with deadly force, thus sending Beau flying down the stairwell in a murderous cloud of heat and gas. It was moot now, anyway. There was no water.

His mind swirled as he tried to think of the proper way to proceed. But he was not given the luxury of time, for it was the one commodity that was quickly running out. He radioed his snorkel operator before donning his mask. "Dickie!" he yelled into his mike. "Get that bucket to the nearest window! Prepare it for rescue!"

O'Reilly could hear the snorkel moving off the roof and into position as he tightened his mask to his face, preparing to enter the house. "Beau!" he screamed just before rotating his regulator into place. He took one breath, activating his breathing apparatus, and ran inside after him. "Beau!"

He knew Beau could die in there. O'Reilly crouched and crawled up the steps after him, feeling a windowsill against the wall to his left at the landing. There was no use screaming now. No one could hear him. Not with the roar of the flames, his mask, the water from the hose, and the ear-piercing PASS splitting the air for miles around. As he climbed, the heat became nearly unbearable, driving him nearer to the floor with each step, until eventually he lay flat on his stomach, trying desperately to acclimate himself to his surroundings.

THE MEN FROM Harrison were juiced. They were making a mutual aid call to a working structure fire, and that was rare in this neck of the woods. They only had three or four working fires a year, and a mutual aid call was even rarer. The men sat in their speeding engines, thumping their gloved fingers like drumsticks against the inside of their thighs, pumping their legs and feet up and down with nervous rapidity. The big boys in New York, hell, they got these a handful of times a week. But this didn't happen every night here. This one was for real.

The trucks' respective drivers had turned their radios to Rye's primary channel, listening to transmissions from the scene. When they heard Tommy's call to Rye base, the crew's mood changed. They could hear the PASS screeching in the background on his call, and suddenly it wasn't fun anymore. A brother was down. The beast was winning this war. Shit like this just didn't happen here. The elite in the city might see it, but this was Rye, New York. This wasn't supposed to be happening.

O'REILLY CRAWLED ON his stomach over burning carpeting and fallen pictures, furniture, and timbers. One arm was outstretched in front of him, hoping he might feel Beau's feet. He reached out with his other arm, trying desperately to feel a wall, a baseboard, anything that might tell him where he was. O'Reilly was angry Beau had gone back in and was angrier still he felt the responsibility to save him. You have to have your senses about you at times like these. You can't put yourself, and hence others, in danger because you let emotions get in the way. But a brother was down, and even the calmest can crack when the shit hits the fan. It was different now. It was a friend, a father, and most of all, a brother. His rescue had no cost too high. Right now, nothing else mattered.

O'Reilly felt an opening to a doorway lying in the direction of the PASS's alarm and entered, feeling to his left and right. He crawled three feet forward and smashed his head into a wall. He wasn't sure what he'd hit. It could be so many things: a bureau, desk, or chest. He didn't know it at first, but finally realized he'd entered a large closet. O'Reilly knew the engine crew must have been getting close, for he thought he could begin to feel the distinct sensation of steam fill the room.

But the joy he felt knowing that his hose men had somehow made it up the stairs was quickly overcome by the worst imaginable news.

"Lieutenant!" came the panicked voice. "Where's Harrison? I'm almost out of water, Loo!"

"Ssshit!" O'Reilly screamed. He knew now that he was in a lethal race against time. The skin on the back of his neck and ears bubbled as he searched, the heat searing his brain. He knew he had to get out. He figured Frankie was dead by now, but where was Beau? He backed out of the closet, crawling quickly toward the wail of the PASS, when his helmet smashed into something else.

As his gloved hand reached out blindly, trying to feel where he was, his heart leapt with joy at the sensation of a hand touching his face. He'd found someone and he was still alive! O'Reilly grabbed the arm at his face—his grab a primal, silent signal that help had arrived. "Now," it said, "let's get the fuck out of here!" He didn't know if it was Beau or Frankie, but could hear that PASS just a foot or two away. "Beau! Beau . . . is that you?" he screamed, but the PASS was too loud for him to be heard. For a second, O'Reilly imagined it was Frankie he'd grabbed and that Beau had already made it out. The PASS's wail pained his eardrums, but he didn't care if he could never hear again, not if it was Frankie who'd touched him.

O'Reilly thought he heard a loud crash and knew something must have fallen when a wave of heat smacked into his face and down his back. If it wasn't for his Scott, he would have smelled the paint burning on his helmet. He knew he had to get out and felt certain he'd pull one of them out of there alive. They were going to make it, but they'd have to move with lightning speed. And that's harder than it sounds when you're lying on your stomach.

"Lieutenant!" he could hear his pump operator scream through his mike. "I'm out of water, Loo! Get the hell out! Repeat. I'm out of water!"

Jesus! On sheer reflexes, whoever it was who'd touched O'Reilly's face had grabbed one of his boots now. Snakelike, they wound their way toward the door, arms and legs moving in tandem. O'Reilly fumbled for the opening but couldn't find it. In his mind's eye he thought he knew exactly where it was. Firefighters always think they know exactly where they came in. Perhaps it's confidence, perhaps something more Freudian to help block out the fear, but it's a fact.

On this night, O'Reilly had hit it right on, but still, there was no opening! He reached up a couple of feet, feeling in both directions, the heat burning his exposed wrists. He thought he could feel knobs, like the kind you find on a dresser. What the hell are they doing here? he asked himself. He knew there'd been a door here just a minute ago. "Where is that fucking door?" he yelled. O'Reilly knew Harrison had to be getting close. He thought he could hear the wails of their sirens as they sped toward the scene. But he wasn't sure. It was all too jumbled—the roar of the flames, his mask, the fear.

He could hear the faint sound of a fallen brother's Vibralert, a sound-emitting, vibrating mechanism built inside each firefighter's regulator, which, when deployed, indicates that less than five minutes of air remain. Even as its clanking vibration strained to be heard above the wailing of the PASS, O'Reilly knew that it had to be Beau's. He had turned his air off when he went outside, while Frankie's had been on the whole time. If only one Vibralert was sounding, O'Reilly knew it could not be Frankie's. His had no doubt stopped once he'd run out of air, leaving little doubt in the lieutenant's mind that Frankie was now dead. But with Beau's still sounding, at least *he* might still have a chance.

Beau's grip on his boot weakened, then released. He had either just passed out or died. It was too much now. O'Reilly screamed in pain through his mask as he realized the horrible burning sensation on his ears was beginning to lessen. A *very* bad sign. Seconds seemed like weeks. They would both die soon if they didn't get out of that room. Beau's PASS began to shriek through the room now, resonating a mile away over the blackness of night.

O'Reilly reached behind him, squeezing at the thick, black air, desperately trying to tug at the man who had just released his grip. Any hope of the welcoming sensation of steam was now long gone. Without water he knew his hose men would have had no choice but to retreat. They were probably regrouping, preparing to attempt a rescue. He desperately wanted their help, yet secretly wished they would stay away from this room. O'Reilly knew that it had now become every firefighter's worst nightmare—a blazing chamber of death.

The engine crew was no longer available to cool the ceiling's superheated gases with their lifesaving stream of water. In its absence, the gas and smoke reignited without warning, sending the fire roaring down the hallway and into the room, toward its open window and the all-important supply of air. The fire began to roll across the ceiling now, engulfing the room and hall in tidal waves of roaring flames, forcing the engine-crew-turned-rescue-crew to retreat for their lives.

Then he remembered the snorkel. O'Reilly knew the snorkel could never attempt a rescue out the bedroom window. With the flames roaring out toward the endless supply of oxygen, the operator would be lucky if he could get the bucket within fifteen feet of it. After he'd given the order, O'Reilly reasoned that the snorkel's operator would have set the bucket at the window he'd felt on the stair's first landing. If he could only get to the hall, he could make it to the window. He knew he *had* to make it to that window. But he was trapped. He couldn't get out!

O'Reilly knew he couldn't have been but just a few feet from the hall. So close, yet so far. He turned, searching the floor beneath him one last, desperate time, exploring the unmistakable contours of someone's Air-Pak with his hands as he changed his course. Was it Beau, or Frankie? He wasn't sure but assumed it was Beau, because he could clearly make out the Vibralert's mechanical-like buzzing in his ears as he palmed the tank.

"Beau!" O'Reilly called out, trying in vain to drag his body along with him. "Come on, buddy!" he screamed as he tugged. But with the flames rolling overhead and down and around him, it was just too hot—unimaginably hot—making it impossible for him to even sit up for leverage. He pulled and pulled some more, terror striking him as Beau's Vibralert finally turned silent. "Help!" he screamed, hoping someone on the other side might hear. "Help!" Within seconds, O'Reilly could no longer move. His body seemed frozen, as if all his joints had fused together.

Harrison had arrived shortly after O'Reilly entered the Borman home. Every firefighter knows what a PASS sounds like, and they could hear Frankie's the second they killed their sirens. They knew they had a real one on their hands. Just a few minutes before they'd all been asleep, and now they were rushing to help save a downed brother. They only heard one PASS and were unaware of the other two men toiling in the inferno's bowels. But soon, all hell broke loose as one wailing PASS gave way to two . . . then finally . . . three.

No pumping fire engine is ever left unattended at a scene. Someone, known as a driver, has to man the valves, keep an eye on pressure, be the eyes and ears outside. A good firefighter *never* deviates from his given task, and the driver from Rye's task was to watch the truck. While not generally dangerous, it is vitally important. There's too much at stake. Other people's lives depend on it. But it was a near-death experience for him to watch it all from the safety of his truck. Harrison's captain approached to get a read on the situation, immediately noticing that Rye's driver was at once crazed with fury and frustration at the scene unfolding before him.

"Jesus Christ, Captain, we got three men up there!" he screamed in response. "My lieutenant followed one of our men in who was trackin' a PASS on the second floor. Now they're all goin' off. Christ, Captain, get some help up there! They're burnin' alive!"

Though less than twelve minutes had passed since Rye had first pulled up to the scene, it felt like five days. Unlike the crew from Rye, Harrison's captain and his men were not yet lost in the emotions of the moment, were not swimming in irrationality and guilt. New to the scene and more composed, he knew within a matter of seconds that it was doubtful they would save the three men from Rye. His men were looking to him for instructions, eager to help save their brothers, but secretly hoping he would not send them on what was so clearly a mission of death.

Harrison's captain shouted orders to one of his companies while their ladder rose and swiveled into position. He attempted sending men upstairs, but that proved impossible. The heat and flames were too intense, and the steps had burned through a third of the way down. Getting a ladder up to the second-floor hallway wasn't even an option. He wanted so badly to save his brothers, but simply could not see a way.

THE BORMANS' MASTER bedroom had become a raging oven as O'Reilly tried one last time to radio for help. But his gloves were on fire now and he could not key his mike. He knew now it was over and screamed again and again through his mask, the pain unbearable as he realized that his body was literally beginning to boil beneath his gear. He screamed aloud inside his mask, "Oh, God! Please! Please, God! I have to get out!" It all seemed a jumbled mess now. Everything seemed to be spinning around him, yet nothing seemed to move. Beau's PASS was screeching now, as well as Frankie's; their high-pitched waves numbing his eardrums. His own Vibralert began to sound, followed almost immediately by his PASS. He thought of his wife, his children, his men . . . I gotta get to that window! I gotta get . . . I got . . . That was the lieutenant's last thought. The home where Ginny Borman had died so agonizing a death had become the oven of the damned.

THE CAPTAIN FROM Harrison closed his eyes and slowly shook his head, indicating that it was over. They'd lost them. No one else would be sent into the Borman home tonight. No one is going to order their men to commit conscious suicide when it's for sure all who've entered before have perished. Better to live to fight the animal another day, and to bring pride and reason to so horrid an event, and the memories of such honorable and brave men. From here on out, it would be suppression only. Rescue was suddenly out of the question.

Then, in a few moments of lurid reality, as if driving home the sanity of his decision, one by one the PASSes stopped wailing, no doubt engulfed and melted by the flames. It was over seventeen hundred degrees in that room, and not much survives it intact—living or otherwise. When the last PASS subsided, it didn't end abruptly, but rather, its piercing alarm seemed to liquefy into a warble, as if symbolically hanging on for dear life. And then, but for the roar of the flames and the diesel engines . . . there was silence.

No one spoke. The vivid images of what was happening to their colleagues played havoc with the remaining crews' imaginations, sending a collective chill through their numb and tortured psyches. Finally, but too late, hoses were stretched to the room, and grown men sprayed hundreds of gallons of water on the flames as tears streamed freely down their faces. Everyone went through the motions, but the beast had won. They would put it out in due time. It's what they are paid to do. But more than one thought it useless now.

Losing just one civilian victim to the animal is hard enough. But pros learn to shrug it off as best they can. They can't afford to internalize every loss or they'd become screaming maniacs. But to lose a brother—three brothers—*that* you don't see every day. The faint cry of the last PASS alarm, as it slowly succumbed to the ravages of the inferno, would forever ring in the ears of every firefighter at that scene.

Even twenty-year veterans wept. It was a tragedy by any standard. It was downright unbelievable in Rye, New York. When the Rye crew finally finished for the night, they would have to go back to the station and stare at their fallen brothers' unmade beds, the half-read books, and pictures of families taped to their lockers. It would be a long, long time before the station house would again approach anything closely resembling normal. And to a man, they would for-ever ask, "Why was I spared?"

Even those who thought they'd seen it all would attend the department-sponsored Critical Incident Stress Debriefing session, or CISD. A small, trained group of their peers would be present, most likely from New York City, a psychologist or psychiatrist, a medical doctor, a chaplain, and a closed door. There is no rank and no blame in a CISD, just help for those who need it, and especially for those who think they don't.

They would be counseled on signs of post–traumatic stress disorder: night sweats, alcohol or drug abuse, nightmares, loss of appetite, depression, loneliness, and marital stress. The CISD would be an opportunity for every-one to discuss how they felt, voice their anger, rage, and fears. Phone num-bers would be exchanged, and everyone would be encouraged to use them whenever they thought they needed help to get through. Still, some would feel odd, reasoning that firefighters have kept it in for centuries. Others would worry, asking themselves, "What if I'm just not strong enough to do this job?" The simple question had a simple answer—there are none stronger.

A FIRE'S SCENT

Book II

JAKE FERGUSON'S PHONE rang at 4:03 A.M. "What?" he barked, longing for just *one* good night's sleep.

"Jake, it's Don."

Please don't tell me what I think you're going to tell me. "Talk to me."

There was a moment's silence while Ederling took a long breath. "We got another one."

Ederling could hear Jake moving in bed and remained silent, waiting for the shit to hit the fan. "Jesus Christ!" Jake boomed, feeling his insides churn with anger and remorse. He sat on the side of the bed and could sense his intestines tighten. "I'm gonna kill that son of a bitch! I told him there'd be others. I told that motherfucker to do something!"

Ederling knew it would be like this. He was more than a little upset himself, but there was work to be done. "Come on, Jake, get dressed. We got our third one now. We got shit to do." He stopped briefly, dreading his next words. "Oh, and Jake, there's something else."

"What do you mean 'something else'?"

There was no sense holding back. It wasn't as if Jake wouldn't find out. "It's bad, Jake. We lost three of our own."

Jake closed his eyes and hung his head, shaking it slowly from side to side. "Jesus Christ," he said softly. "How did it happen?"

"I'll tell you when you get here. Listen, Jake, I'm there now, and—"

"Where?"

"Rye." Ederling continued, "Listen. This is getting big. There's already crews here from all three networks. Reporters swarmin' all over the place."

Jake held the phone to his shoulder, pulling a pen out of his drawer. "This is un . . . fucking . . . believable. Three men! Which company?"

"Engine and Snorkel One."

Jake wanted to ask which platoon, and if anyone he knew had perished in the flames, but he knew better. Shit, he knew most every firefighter in the county. "Don't tell me names, Donny. I can't deal with it right now."

That worked okay with Ederling. Jake and O'Reilly were tight. Ederling would just as soon not have to inform Jake over the phone anyway. It was going to be hard news to break, especially since Jake was probably thinking the lieutenant wasn't one of them. More than likely, Jake would assume he was directing the scene from the outside. Ederling knew that Jake would not automatically assume O'Reilly had been inside the Borman home and wanted to be there for him when he learned otherwise.

"Where in Rye?" Jake asked.

And so it went, as it had gone a thousand times before. Jake wrote down the address, dressed, and was leaning yet again against the bathroom wall, urinating, when he realized he hadn't looked at Danielle's pillow or even her side of the bed. He thought it strange that in the midst of such death, destruction, and pain, the cocooned caterpillar inside him was turning into a butterfly. Somewhere, deep down, he'd always hoped this rebirth would occur. He just never thought the metamorphosis would happen now. Funny how the important things never seem to happen on our schedule.

Jake followed the exact same procedure he always did: brushing his teeth, dragging a wet comb through his rumpled hair, speaking to himself in the mirror. He walked sluggishly down the hall to the kitchen and zapped a measuring cup full of water in the microwave. He poured himself a large glass of orange juice and popped a small cranberry muffin in his mouth. He wanted to get something in his stomach now, because he knew he wouldn't eat for a while. When the timer rang, Jake poured the water into a travel mug, threw in two heaping tablespoons of instant coffee, and stirred it as he left, closing his door silently behind him.

RYE IS NEXT door to Port Chester, where Jake lived, so he took the back roads to Milton Point. As he turned right off Stuyvesant Avenue toward Long Island Sound, the flashing red and blue lights seemed everywhere. He counted five fire trucks, two ambulances, and four police cars, one of which had blocked the road in front of him.

He showed the officer his identification and drove his Crown Victoria slowly toward the scene, looking in all directions for that lonely, hiding face. He kept thinking that one of these days he'd get lucky. Jake pulled up behind Ederling's red Bronco, got out, and looked around. He was always at such a disadvantage at night, pulling up to every scene with headlights on. Any torch could see him coming a mile away. Just once he wanted to approach in darkness.

He generally liked to keep a low profile upon approaching a fire where death had occurred. The fire marshal was the last line of defense, the one to whom everyone at the scene would turn for direction and guidance. It was important for him to have enough time to himself to assess the situation and to develop a plan of action.

Jake sat on the hood of his car dictating observations into his tape recorder. It wasn't really necessary, but as always, he was trying to think like a jury. Photographic memory or not, he had better have it all in a notebook or on tape. He noted the exact address, the time he arrived at the scene, lighting, personnel, vehicles, and weather conditions. This last one is not always important, but Jake had learned a long time ago that when a case goes to trial, the accuracy of his notes would be called into question. The defense attorney would drop a seed of doubt with the jury by discussing the emotions and mayhem of the moment.

"Surely, Mr. Ferguson, amongst the hysteria, it's possible you didn't notice everything? Wouldn't you say, sir?"

Jake knew that noting the weather was a detail not lost on juries. It tended to lend more credibility to virtually everything else he'd say. A pro at work.

He finished, tucked his tape recorder into his bunker jacket, and walked toward the house, passing Ederling's car. He rapped once on the Bronco's window with his knuckle, smiling as Sparky went berserk. He opened the door and climbed up to the backseat. "Hey, Spark! How are you, girl?"

Sparky bounced madly all over him, yelping and licking his face. Jake enjoyed the camaraderie, the unconditional love and affection. It would be his booster shot before entering earth's best rendition of hell. He played with her, letting Sparky sit in his lap. He had slipped on his gear and was already sweating when he entered Ederling's Bronco. Ederling had left the car running with the air-conditioning on, as usual. Jake was conscious of its soothing feel and realized fairly soon that he was stalling.

"You know what, Spark? I really don't want to go in there tonight. You think I'm afraid, girl? Huh? Do you?" he said smiling, patting her side vigorously. "You do, huh?"

Jake put up his fists, as if boxing, softly slapping the side of her snout with his open hand. "What do you think, girl? You think maybe Uncle Jake wasn't made for this job? You think maybe I've paid my price?"

Jake stared at her. If dogs smile, he thought this was about as close as it got. Sparky panted heavily, a bright sparkle in her eyes.

"So, what do you think I should do, girl? Think Uncle Jake should just turn around and go home?"

Jake jerked up at the flash of a reporter's bulb through the window. They had followed Ederling down the lawn to the car. Ederling opened the door and climbed in the front seat. "What the hell are you *doing* in here?"

"We're just playing, aren't we, girl?" Jake said, smiling in Sparky's face, scratching her behind both ears.

Ederling knew the score. You can't spend more time with someone than any other living soul and not know when something's up. "Jake."

Jake continued playing with the dog.

"Jake!" Ederling said louder as flashes of light exploded through the glass.

Jake moved Sparky aside, leaning back in the seat. "I heard you the first time."

"Listen, Jake, I know this is going to be hard. They were my friends, too. But you see those reporters out there? They think we're in here discussing the case. They'd shit a brick if they thought I was in here trying to help you get up the nerve to enter that house."

Jake was pleasant but firm. "I don't need your help, or anyone else's for that matter, to help me get up some nerve, Don. Sparky just went wild as I passed the car, and I couldn't just walk away from her."

"Right. How'd you get this job anyway?" he asked, half in jest, half in earnest wonderment.

Jake thought of the unspeakable horror he was about to witness, sights that would keep the average person awake for weeks. "Just lucky, I guess."

"Listen, Jake, I might as well tell you now. Tommy was one of them."

Jake dropped his hand from Sparky's neck, his face glazing over with shock. "Oh, Don. Tommy?" he asked, tears welling up in his eyes. "Tell me you're lying, Don."

Ederling sat sideways, his right hand across the front seat's back. He pursed his lips and shook his head. "Sorry, Jake. You had to find out sooner or later."

Jake dropped his head, rubbing his temples with his hands. "Jesus, Don. Has anyone told Bessy yet?" he asked, looking up.

"No, I thought maybe you'd want to go."

Jake nodded. "He was the best, Donny. The best. They just don't make 'em like that anymore."

Ederling spoke softly. "I know. We got to go in, Jake. You ready?"

"I want this motherfucker, Don. I want him in the worst way."

"Horrible as it sounds, Jake, this one will help."

"Who were the other two?"

"Beau and Frankie."

Ederling could see that Jake was fighting back tears and watched helplessly as he wiped his eyes with the thumb and forefinger of his right hand. "Christ, Donny. It just never gets easier, does it?"

"No, but they're all depending on us, Jake. They want him, too."

Jake's sorrow suddenly turned to rage. "Well, I'll tell you what, Don. When we find this fuck, I'm personally going to deliver him to the station house. We'll see if the Rye boys might not like a chance to even the score."

"Come on, Jake, they're waiting for us."

Jake wrapped his hand around the handle on the door. "Wait. Donny?"

"What?" Ederling asked, turning back to look at him.

"Promise me. If we find him, we deliver him to Rye."

Ederling took a long, deep breath. "Come on. Let's go."

The truckies worked in teams of two, overhauling the Borman home. They toiled in silence, grunting occasionally as they ripped down sheets of plaster from the walls and ceilings. There's no greater embarrassment to a fire department than to leave the scene and have the whole thing rekindle itself in their absence. They would search every nook and cranny for that one missed pocket of flame, that one remaining burning ember. And with every tug and yank, their only thought would be to get the hell out of that house.

Jake and Ederling stepped to one side, allowing two firefighters to carry a smoldering sofa out onto the lawn. Jake led the way. This time he didn't need to be told where it started. The top third of the stairs had burned away, so they had to climb a ladder to the upstairs hall.

"Chief," someone said, ripping away a portion of the ceiling as Jake stepped to his feet in the hall. Jake raised his hand. Words seemed sinful now.

Jake reached down and grabbed Ederling's hand, yanking him up the last rung to the hallway. "To the left," Ederling said.

Jake stood at the smoldering doorway, scanning the scene beyond. He immediately noticed the three bumpy, white sheets lying one after the other, almost touching one another. He didn't bother looking at the bed. Twice before, he'd already seen what lay there.

"The ME been here yet?" he asked, talking to the charred bedroom.

"On his way," Ederling said.

The truckies upstairs had stopped overhauling and stood motionless, staring at Jake with their axes over their shoulders. They eyed Jake as he stood outside the yellow police tape, studying the grizzly scene before him with stone-hard eyes. He would exhibit no outward release of emotion. Not now. Not while they eyed him. Jake would cry later, alone, in the privacy of his home.

Jake could feel their eyes upon him, and knew without a word how important his demeanor was. They needed stability now—the cold, calculating mind and methods he would bring to the case. They looked to him for strength and determination. He was the savior—the man who would find the monster who had done this. Like the cavalry charging in to save the day, his upright posture and stoic expression spoke volumes. "Let us have a crack at it now, boys," it said. "We may have lost the battle, but we won't lose the war."

"Hey, Chief," a truckie said softly. Jake turned around. "Find him, okay? Just find him."

"Oh, we'll find him. Make book on it."

The truckie didn't speak. He caught Jake's eyes and looked into them for a moment, just long enough for Jake to see his pain. The firefighter turned, whipped the adze end of his ax into the wall, and pulled, not flinching as a slab of steaming plaster fell on his boots.

"Everyone's pretty choked up, Jake," Ederling said, ducking under the tape, following his boss into the room.

Jake walked to the sheet at the head of the line and knelt, placing his helmet on his knee. He lifted a wet corner, but saw nothing that would identify the victim as his friend. He was charred beyond recognition, and his helmet had melted onto his skull. There was no way to know who was who until the autopsy. Even then, the degree of charring would require a forensic odontologist to identify them via their teeth. Other than the reflexive contraction of his nostrils, Jake showed no response. But inwardly, he simultaneously fought back tears and vomit.

All three men had curled, to varying degrees, into what is known as a pugilistic attitude. This defensive boxing position or, in some cases, a fetal position, is assumed as the larger muscles of the arms and legs contract under the intense heat, thereby pulling them in toward the torso. Similarly, their gloves had burned away, and Jake could see their hands had cupped inward, in clawlike fashion, toward their palms.

Jake knew better than to ask identities. No one would know. He wanted to turn over the body lying in front of him to see if he could read the shield on his helmet, but knew to leave everything as found until the medical examiner arrived. It was just as well. The body would probably break into pieces, and what little remained of the shield would be impossible to read anyway.

Jake followed the same procedure with the other two men. Granted, he would need to view them all, but it wasn't necessary he do it now. It was a show of respect really. These men had paid the ultimate price. It didn't get any more expensive than this. They had died the most horrible of deaths in the performance of their duties, and Jake felt the least he could do was look them in the eyes. They'd all died facedown, so that wasn't possible. But he took solace in the attempt.

"A cryin' shame, huh?" Ederling said. "They were so close to that window."

The two men would later learn that the fire's sucking the air into the room was the probable cause of the advanced rate of burn on the bureau's cabriole legs nearest the door, resulting in their burning through enough to cause it to topple and block the doorway. As the ME would later tell it, O'Reilly had apparently been in the lead, with Beau at his feet. One of the two men had freed Frankie of the fallen dresser, but the ME could tell from an examination of his trachea that he had died prior to burning. The other two had not been so lucky.

Through interviews and crime scene analysis, Jake and Ederling were able to ascertain, with a fair degree of certainty, the sequence of events. The dresser that fell on Frankie lay on the floor, drawers down, which meant that through most of the conflagration's final, horrid moments, it lay closest to the floor. After lifting it up, it was fairly obvious from the indentations on its front that it had fallen on Frankie's air tank. They knew Beau had been the first to reenter the Borman home and also guessed from his position to Frankie that it was he who had lifted it off his back. They could see scratch marks where Beau had dragged it off him, and they also noticed a missing drawer handle, which they later found wedged in Frankie's air tank—probably the reason he couldn't initially pull himself free.

They scanned the body on the bed, removing wet plaster from the burnt torso. Jake and Ederling assumed it was a wife of one of Morson Grayhead's executives, although Jake thought for a moment it could be the lone woman on the firm's executive team. They'd come back to her later. She wasn't going anywhere. Four people had died in this room. Three of them took precedence right now.

The two men stood, staring at the dresser. "That's one hell of a big piece of furniture, Jake," Ederling said. "To move that, a man would have to have stood. At least to his knees."

Jake nodded, knowing how unbearable even knee height could be.

"Either way, he wasn't flat on the floor, Jake. The heat, even this far up," Ederling said, motioning with his hand somewhere between his knees and waist. "Christ, Jake, he must have been burning alive as he was trying to save him."

"How can you ever explain that kind of bravery, Don?" Jake asked solemnly. "The man knew the odds of coming out of here alive were a thousand to one. And yet, he didn't even flinch. The guys say Tommy was screaming his name all the way up the steps."

"Yeah, and Tommy didn't hesitate to follow him. God, do I love these men, Jake. I really do. I'd do just about anything if we could bring them back."

"Jesus." Jake shook his head. "You know by the time Tom got up here, he couldn't see shit, Don. This room had to have been an inferno. It just makes me want to scream."

The two men spent a good deal of time reviewing the possible scenarios surrounding the firefighter's deaths. Finally, they turned their attention to the bed. They were both standing to its left, viewing the charred remains of Ginny Borman, when the ME entered the room.

He stood still for a moment, glancing at the sheets. There's an unspoken grief all professionals feel at the death of a policeman or a firefighter. But especially a firefighter. The overwhelming preponderance of slain policemen are shot. And while clearly a tragedy, somehow the idea of dying in that manner doesn't stack up to the horrors of the beast. More often than not, firefighters die an agonizing death, the way just about everyone fears most of all. If given the choice between death by gunshot or death by fire, you would be hard-pressed to find an eager taker of the latter.

The ME looked at the bed, then to Jake and Ederling. "You going to catch this asshole, or what?"

Jake wasn't happy. "Oh, that's good, Doc. Thanks. We weren't sure we should, but now that you mention it, I guess we'll get working on it."

"This is three now, Jake," the ME said, slipping on a pair of latex gloves. "What the hell are these people doing, at home, alone like this, with a maniac on the loose?"

Jake thought of Rybeck. *That goddamned son of a bitch!* Jake was determined to pay him a visit later this morning. He was going to become Rybeck's worst nightmare. "I don't know, but it's about to change."

"Yeah. Well . . . a little late for these four I'd say."

Jake hardly needed the reminders of the gravity of the situation. "You get up on the wrong side of the bed this morning, Doc?"

The ME was full of trepidation at the task at hand. He spoke as if psychologically removed, lost in thoughts of sorrow. "Yeah," he said, staring at the sheets. "Wrong side of the bed."

The ME worked on the three men under the sheets while Jake and Ederling worked around the body on the bed. Ederling had retrieved several airtight gallon- and pint-size metal containers as well as some quart-size, resealable mason jars from his Bronco and brought them up to the room in a cardboard box. He and Jake would need to carefully select those samples that were to be sent to the lab for analysis, and several containers would be necessary for the task.

Jake's assistant ordered large quantities of containers directly from the manufacturers four times a year. Jake, in a tribute to his professionalism, sent random samples of each new delivery to the lab for analysis. This way, he could ensure they were free from contaminants and thus circumvent some defense lawyer's argument that the evidence contained therein had been hopelessly tainted.

Some people can afford legal counsel that could prove Satan himself was a Boy Scout, and little pissed Jake off more than watching an arsonist walk free. Unlike a bullet, fire, once started, has no single trajectory. It's an indiscriminate killer. He'd been forced more than once at trial to show evidence of this type of thoroughness.

A good investigator is always aware that lab technicians handle thousands of pieces of evidence, in sterile environments, far removed from the scenes of destruction from which they were retrieved. Jake would take great care in selecting and securing the most viable samples for analysis, knowing that virtually all of the liquid accelerant had long since been burned away, and what was left had been deluged with perhaps thousands of gallons of water. You simply aren't grounded in reality if you expect a technician to perform laboratory miracles on an indiscriminate selection of samples. And that's where Sparky came in—to help assure the highest-quality samples.

"This is odd," Ederling said.

Jake had seen it. "The bedpost, right?"

"Yeah, the bedpost. See how her hand is out of the chains on that side?"

"Sure do."

"And the bedpost is layin' right here on the bed beside her," Ederling said, kneeling to take a closer look. "Makes you kind of wonder, doesn't it?"

"Sure does."

"You think somehow maybe she pulled it away when he lit her? You know, superhuman strength?"

Jake shook his head. "I thought that, too. But it wouldn't make sense that her hand is free. She'd hardly have been able to get her hand free of the chains if she were burning alive. Don't you think?"

"Makes sense. But that would mean she would have broken free prior to immolation."

Jake was leaning down, looking at the base of the headboard from which Ginny Borman had pulled the bedpost. "Intriguing thought, isn't it?"

"You think it's possible she was able to get a swipe at the guy before he lit her?"

Jake pursed his lips. "Anything's possible."

Ederling tilted his head. "Okay, so how do you explain that it's just lyin' on the bed? Wouldn't she have her hand wrapped around it?"

Jake stood, placing his arms out and up, as if crucified. "How about this? She somehow pulls it free. We got to have the lab look at that headboard. It's old, maybe it had been screwed or nailed back together or something. Okay, so she pulls free. One of two things happen. She either whacks him right then, or she lays it down, waiting for him to come. But either way, you want to use your free arm to undo the other one, right?"

Ederling thought about the scenarios, going over the scene in his mind. "Hard to believe she'd have freed one hand and not immediately gone for the other."

"Not easy either," Jake said, reaching across his body with his left hand, trying to reach the wrist of his right. "Not with your ankles chained."

"Hmm, so maybe she hit him. Kind of opens up the field a little, don't you think?"

"Possibly. I'll tell you this much, Donny. We run across *anyone* in this investigation wearing a big bandage of some kind, you can bet your ass he's going to the top of my list."

Ederling knew that even with today's extraordinary forensic technology, it still couldn't do everything. Some fires are just too intense. "I wish to God forensics could tell us if there's blood on it."

"Let's run Sparky through and see what we find."

Ederling retrieved Sparky, working the room with her as before. To no one's surprise, Sparky went wild at the head of the bed. The fire had obviously been aided by an accelerant, liberally doused along the pillows, headboard, and wall. And like the others, it was quickly spread through the house by means of torching other rooms. All together, Sparky found traces of accelerant in four of the five upstairs bedrooms.

They were digging through a guest room when the ME came in. "They're okay to move," he said.

Jake and Ederling both knew it would be a sacrilege to move the men themselves, not without offering the honors to their surviving comrades. The truckies were overhauling a room in the back when Jake approached. "ME says they're okay to move, guys. I thought you might want to do it yourselves?"

"Damn right."

Jake and Ederling watched from opposite the bed as five men prepared the thick plastic bags. A fire chaplain had been called, and they all said a prayer on their knees before undertaking the grizzly task of transferring the slain firefighters to their bags.

They carried them soberly down the steps, one bag at a time, each man vying to hold a piece of their brother. As they exited the house, the remaining crews stood, saluting at attention. Hordes of reporters and photographers converged on the lawn. Like vultures, they'd been waiting for this moment.

The captain from Mamaroneck would have none of it. He would not allow the memories of these brave men to become fodder for newspaper sales. "Jesus Christ, folks," he said, motioning for police help. "Come on, back it up. Back it up. Give the men their dignity, will you? How 'bout a little respect. You people know what that is? Come on, back it up. Let's move."

The three men were loaded into a county coroner's van, which would take them to the morgue. Another van sat idly by, waiting patiently for the remains of Ginny Borman. But for her, the bedroom was now empty of corpses.

Jake looked at the ME. "You guys got a run on that DNA yet?" he asked, referring to the two previous semen samples.

The ME didn't look at him. "No."

"Jesus Christ, Doc. What the hell are you guys waiting for?" Jake asked, already knowing the answer.

"Jake, you know better than anyone how backed up we are."

"I don't give a flying hoot's ass how backed up you are. Just push it to the top, okay, Doc?"

"I would if I could, Jake. You have a suspect yet?"

Jake looked down at Ginny, lying gruesomely on the bed. "No, but we're close," he lied.

"Then it doesn't matter yet anyway, does it?"

"Just push it along, Doc."

"I'll try."

"Was she raped?"

"Impossible to say. But, the good news is, for some unknown reason we're slow today. I'll probably cut her as soon as I get back. How's that work with your schedule?"

Jake and Ederling looked at each other. Jake looked at his watch: 8:18 A.M. What Jake really wanted to do was take a train to New York and carve Severin Rybeck a new asshole. Ederling shrugged, as if to say, "I've got nothing pressing."

There was no way they would miss this autopsy. Something had happened here this morning, different from the rest—the bedpost said so. Jake hoped like hell the ME could tell them what it was. But there was one unresolved issue.

"Doc, I got to stop by one of the victim's homes. He and I were friends."

"Wife?"

"Yeah."

"I don't envy you."

Jake had been on the receiving end before. "I don't envy her."

"What time then?" the ME asked.

"Give us a couple of hours. How about eleven?"

The ME was tucking something into his jacket. "I'll block it out. Bag her up. I'll meet you at the morgue at eleven."

"We'll be there."

AUTOPSIES WERE THE worst for Jake. He didn't mind the cold, stainless-steel tables, or the slight angle at which their slabs lay, enabling body fluids to drip through a spout. He wasn't bothered by the freezers in which people were laid with their heads on wooden blocks and their big toes tagged with an accession number like a human antiquity at auction. And he didn't mind the tools of the trade: the needles, scalpels, and circular saw used for cutting the scalp so as to remove the brain. The room itself, though tiled, cold, and sterile, carried no particular angst for Jake.

But the sight of the bodies, so horribly disfigured, so tortured with pain—he could hear their screams for days afterward, almost as if Jake were there during their final, agonizing moments of life. It was always the same. *Poughkeepsie.* It just kept coming back. Over and over and over again. Sometimes the guilt was paralyzing, sedating all that he did, contaminating all that he thought. He felt certain he would die with the horrid cry of the man's screams in his ears.

Jake leaned against the wall he always leaned against, sucking on a menthol lozenge to help ward off the smell. He watched the medical examiner as he spoke into a handheld, voice-activated tape recorder. "Case number nine six, oh eight two three, victim as yet unidentified. The body is sixty-seven inches long and weighs seventy-six pounds. The skin is thoroughly charred, with epidermal splitting visible from the cephalic to the caudal regions. Trauma particularly acute in the posterior region, as the victim was found lying in bed, no doubt helping augment the . . ."

Other than the means and the motive, there was not much new here for Jake. He'd seen it all many times before. Most people who perish in bed suffer greater destruction from the flames than do those found on floors. Body fluids and fats seep into the mattress, thus feeding the fire's hunger. This, and a little lighter fluid to help matters along, had made Ginny Borman one of his worst. It didn't help matters any that this one could have been prevented. Maybe Jake should have forced the issue with Rybeck. He couldn't help but feel now that he was wrong to have backed down.

"Same MO?" the medical examiner asked.

"Looks that way, Doc," Ederling said. "Sparky went wild when she got to the area around her head."

All three men knew this meant that blood and lung specimens would need to be sent to the lab for gas chromatographic and mass spectrophotometric analysis. These tests can analyze and identify the flammable vapors present in the samples and are invaluable in getting a better handle on the torch's preferred means of acceleration. If it turned out to be lighter fluid, it would simply add to the evidence of the case; if something else, an entirely different set of scenarios could arise, not the least of which might be a copycat. This was but one reason why Jake was so determined to get his hands on those DNA results.

The ME showed Jake and Ederling where Ginny had practically ripped the chains of her right wrist down to the bone. The left arm showed no such findings. The three men speculated for a short while, finally determining that it was her right arm she yanked with fury during the blaze, and that her left arm was probably free when the fire started.

The external examination had been completed, and the ME began incising a large Y across the chest, from shoulder joint to shoulder joint, followed by a straight cut down the sternum, continuing down the abdomen and ending in the pubic area. Slowly, methodically, he would check and weigh each organ, laying them on a small-parts dissection table that resembled a steel TV tray with its legs cut halfway off. They would be analyzed for toxins, drugs, and alcohol. Semen samples were taken from her uterus and would also be sent to the state police for analysis.

Jake and Ederling were particularly interested whether she was alive when she burned. "Was she alive, Doc?" Jake asked.

The ME was inconclusive. Her windpipe seemed relatively clean. "Hard to say for sure. You'll have to wait for the lab results."

A quick check of the windpipe usually reveals the answer. People who die in fires generally breathe heavy quantities of smoke before passing out. Soot is inhaled and can be found in the nose, nasal passages, and throat. More often than not people are unconscious by the time flames begin licking their skin. Jake feared that Ginny Borman had not been so lucky. For he knew all too well she was not inhaling when the flames engulfed her, but rather she was screaming, albeit into a sock. Most likely, the sock itself helped keep her throat clean, at least until it burned.

However, the lab technicians would perform two tests to ascertain the answer. The first one would check for traces of carbon monoxide in her lungs. The second checks for carboxyhemoglobin—the level of carbon monoxide present in the red blood cells of the body. Carbon monoxide will adhere to the body's red blood cells at a rate over two hundred times greater than that of oxygen. This level is perhaps the single most important factor in determining whether the fire was ante- or postmortem.

Jake was visibly disappointed. The one thing that might help him through the night was knowing she'd at least escaped the ultimate nightmare.

"My guess?" the ME offered.

"Yes?"

"She was breathing."

"Great," Jake said in disgust. He closed his eyes. "Conscious?"

The ME shook his head. "Can't say."

CHAN PULLED SEVERIN Rybeck's limousine into the circle at the side entrance of Morson Grayhead's headquarters at 7:34 A.M. If the press didn't know whose it was when he first pulled up, they figured it out soon enough when they saw the MG1 license plate. Rybeck could see the press corps swarming toward his car, causing his worst nightmare to blossom in full. "Chan, help me get inside, will you?"

"Sure thing, Mr. Rybeck."

Chan walked behind the limousine, opening Rybeck's door. He tried to shield him as best he could, shoving photographers out of their way.

"Mr. Rybeck!" they seemed to scream in unison. "Is true, sir . . . ?"; "Have the authorities made . . . ?"; "Do you plan on . . . ?"; "Have the board of directors . . . ?"

Rybeck thanked God he had Chan with him. "Please! Make room, make room," Chan ordered. "Step aside, ma'am. Come on, out of the *goddamned* way. Let's move!"

By now, of course, word had spread like a brush fire throughout the firm. The Borman burning had occurred too late to make the morning papers, but the story was prominently broadcast on the local news shows and was the talk of the radio, commuter trains, subways, and bus stops. New Yorkers see just about everything, and even by their standards this was hot stuff.

Chan pushed Rybeck through the revolving glass door first, following in behind him in the next compartment, before holding it, preventing its moving any further. The crowd outside pounded on the glass, flashbulbs bursting, video cameras shooting. "How about some help over here!" Chan yelled as two uniformed guards rushed to his rescue.

"Hold it until I can get Rybeck upstairs," Chan said, fully aware now that his cushy job had just taken a serious turn for the worse. No doubt, he would be earning his money for the foreseeable future. Chan's demeanor took on a sudden, no-nonsense professionalism that Rybeck had never seen before. "This way, please, Mr. Rybeck. *Now*, sir."

Three minutes earlier Severin Rybeck had been reading the *Wall Street Journal* in his limousine. But now he was clearly shaken at the abrupt turn of events. He was staring, almost in shock, at the mob outside the door and turned at the sound of Chan's controlled but firm voice.

"Jesus Christ," Rybeck said, walking quickly toward the far elevator. It would take them directly to Rybeck's floor. It had no other stops.

As Rybeck entered, Chan stood at the door, then faced the doors as they slid closed. Once moving, he turned to his boss. "You okay, Mr. Rybeck?"

Rybeck had obviously been taken off guard. "Yes, I think so. Just a little shaken."

"We'll need to discuss another avenue of departure for this evening, sir. Obviously, we can't keep doing this. I'll talk to security and maintenance. See if we can't arrange to leave via the underground delivery docks."

Rybeck nodded his head.

"I'll call you and let you know what to do, but it looks as though you're going to have a hell of a day. What should I do if you're in a meeting?"

"Interrupt me."

"All right, sir. I will."

It was quiet as the elevator rose to the forty-second floor. Severin Rybeck was quickly beginning to realize the severity of the situation. He thought of the mob outside his building, the endless calls his secretary would field all day from scores of publications, and for the first time, found himself worrying how his colleagues would receive him.

Finally Rybeck spoke. "You know, Chan, I really didn't think there would be another one. I truly believed that the two deaths were not related to the firm."

The elevator rang as it slowed to a stop. Chan stood facing the doors. "I understand, sir."

Rybeck's face had paled and his eyes seemed transfixed, as if haunted with fear and guilt. "You do believe me, don't you, Chan?"

The doors opened. "Here we are, sir. Let me walk you to your office, just to be safe."

Another secretary was standing at the receptionist counter speaking with the woman from whom Jake had learned about the paintings. They turned as the doors opened, staring silently as Chan stepped from the elevator with Rybeck in tow.

Rybeck tried to act calm. "Ladies," he said, hearing no response as he turned the corner to the hallway leading to his office.

They strode quickly down the hall. Rybeck's spine seemed to jump as, one after the other, office doors slammed shut as he approached. Few on this floor planned on being at Morson Grayhead much longer, and they no longer cared about Rybeck's response or any retribution he might seek. So far, three men had lost their wives in excruciating fashion while Severin Rybeck remained tucked safely away on his estate, behind the impregnable defense of his own imperial guard. People's families were being ripped asunder, and to date, the one man they all looked to for leadership had done nothing to stop it.

The show of disrespect and mistrust was not lost on Chandler Boutet. He had come to this floor many times in the past, and it had always been apparent who ran the show, whom everyone looked up to at Morson Grayhead. Chan was filled with a sudden chill as he walked the hall, but continued straight ahead, glancing back over his shoulder every few yards.

Chandler Boutet had wondered on the drive in just what would await them upon arrival. He expected some press, but nothing like the near riot they had just dodged. He had also expected some level of discomfort and fear among Rybeck's employees, but had never envisioned anything like this. Even to a relative outsider such as Chan, there was little doubt now, at least in the eyes of Morson Grayhead's senior management, that the emperor wore no clothes. And now, as Chan tried to ignore the sequential slamming of doors, it was nearly impossible for him to imagine Rybeck's recovering from this. Until this moment, it had not dawned on Chan that he should begin to worry about his job.

Chan opened the large wooden door on the right, walked in, and stood aside for Rybeck to enter. He could see that Rybeck was upset, but wasn't sure if he was frightened or just angry.

"Morning," Rybeck said curtly to his secretary. "We're going to be a hornets' nest today, Janet. Tell the press I'm unavailable for comment," he said, opening the door to his office.

"Mr. Rybeck . . ."

"One minute, Janet.

"Call me," Rybeck said quietly to Chan.

"I will, sir."

"But Mr. Rybeck—" Janet said again.

"Please, Janet! One minute, okay?"

Fine, she thought, find out for yourself. I don't give a shit.

"Oh, and, Chan?"

Chan turned. "Yes, sir?"

"You didn't answer my question."

"What question was that, sir?"

"The one I asked you in the elevator. You do believe me, right?"

Chan hesitated. It was subconscious, but still, just long enough for it to hurt. "Of course, sir."

As Chan walked away, Rybeck watched him, repeating the words he'd just heard. He stepped inside his office and closed the door, leaning his back against it. He breathed deeply, trying to regain his composure. He would need it today. He hung his jacket on a carved rosewood coat hanger and walked to his desk, where three dozen pink slips lay in two neat but distinct piles. Rybeck took a pair of reading glasses from his top drawer and placed them on the end of his nose, thumbing through them.

There were calls from the *Wall Street Journal, Barron's, Investor's Business Daily, Newsweek, Time, Business Week, Fortune, Forbes,* the *New York Times,* the *Daily News,* and the *Post.* He stopped reading when he realized he was holding the media pile. Rybeck stacked them, as if preparing for a hand of poker, and set them down on a corner of his desk. They'd all have to be contacted. He just wasn't sure by whom.

Morson Grayhead needed serious PR help, and now. Rybeck thought of depressing his intercom to have Janet set up a meeting with his senior vice president in charge of Communications and Investor Relations, but stopped short with his finger still on the button. He couldn't remember if *his* wife had been one of the unlucky ones. This thing was clearly out of control.

"Shit," he said, looking up. Royston Craddock sat cross-legged, against the wall at the table Rybeck and Jake had spoken across just the day before. Rybeck recoiled, jumping in shock at the sight of his longtime friend. "Jesus Christ, Roy, you scared the shit out of me," he said, removing his glasses. Then, in almost pathetic oblivion, he asked the ultimate of rhetorical questions: "What the hell are you doing here?"

Craddock stared, weighing Rybeck's reaction with a critical squint. "I just spoke to Shelly. The police had just contacted him, but there weren't any flights from Chicago that early. So I chartered a Learjet for him. They're flying him back to Westchester as we speak."

"Thank you, Roy. How's he holding up?"

"Oh, he's just ducky, Severin. Never better."

Rybeck did not have to be told a battle was brewing. He could see it in Craddock's eyes and could hear it in his voice. The hair on Rybeck's arms stood on end. But as far as he knew, he was still the captain of this ship, and he was damn well not going to act any differently. Fine, Rybeck thought disdainfully. You want curt, I'll give you curt. "Anything else?" he asked sharply.

There was silence.

"Roy," Rybeck began, annoyed at this unwanted disruption. "I don't need to tell you what today's going to be like for all of us. Do you have anything else?" he asked again, this time with a touch more appeasement.

Craddock was unnervingly calm. "No," he said, checking a fingernail. "That's about it, I guess." He didn't move, except for his obsessive picking at a finger with his thumbnail.

Rybeck sat down and stared at him. Rybeck wanted desperately to tell Craddock to leave. He knew the score. But he knew Craddock was just *itching* for a fight. Fine, he thought, sit there. "You can watch me if you'd like," Rybeck said, desperately attempting to avoid confrontation. Intuitively, he knew his whole world was crumbling, and he was loath to expend precious mental energy he would later need.

"Thank you, Severin," Craddock said, looking up. "I think I will."

Rybeck replaced his reading glasses on his nose and began thumbing through his other pile of messages. Lianne had called. That was rare, to say the least. Jake Ferguson had called. Sheldon Borman had called. He dreaded even the *thought* of that conversation. He glanced up above his glasses, catching a severe stare from Craddock.

Rybeck couldn't help but be reminded of a high school game. He'd had enough. "All right, Roy. You win. You want to tell me you told me so? Go ahead. Get it out."

Craddock uncrossed his legs, stretching them out in front of him, placing his hands behind his head. "Is that all you can think about, Severin? That somehow this is all some big game, and you lost? Oh, yeah . . . I told you so, all right."

Rybeck stood, resting his hands on his desk. "Don't fuck with me, Roy. You *know* that is not how I view this."

Craddock's voice dripped with sarcasm. "Really? Then tell me, how *do* you view it? How does it *feel*, Severin? Tell me how it feels to know that Ginny Borman and three firemen are lying in a morgue somewhere, burned alive like some hamburger at a company picnic?"

Rybeck slammed his desk with a fist, sending his neatly placed pile of messages scurrying through the air. "Enough! I will not tolerate your sitting there like some Cheshire cat, throwing this thing back in my face! As if . . . as if, somehow, *I'm* the one responsible."

"Who should we blame, Severin? The authorities for not catching him soon enough? Maybe Ginny for not running away like a mouse? Or how about those poor firemen? They should never have responded to the call, right?"

"What the hell does that mean? Need I remind you, Roy, we only spoke about arranging security details for the employees at ten-thirty last night. Even if I had acted on it immediately, Ginny Borman would still be dead."

Craddock rose, walking slowly toward Rybeck's desk. "Oh, that's true enough, Severin. You keep telling yourself that. But you want to know what I'm thinking? I'm thinking a better man would have done something proactive a long time ago. I should *never* have had to call you and argue . . . and *argue* no less . . . about setting something up. After the second killing, you should have been all over this."

"Roy, even the authorities said we should do nothing. They told me . . ."

Craddock crossed his arms across his chest, watching Rybeck lie to his face. "I spoke with Mr. Ferguson, Severin," he interrupted.

"Good for you. Even they said to . . ." Rybeck met Craddock's eyes, aware now he'd been caught. "You what?"

Craddock placed his hands on his side of the desk and leaned forward. "Hard of hearing in your old age, Severin? I said . . . I spoke with Mr. Ferguson."

Rybeck's heart jumped. "So?"

"So what do you think he told me?" Craddock said, standing back from Rybeck's desk and recrossing his arms.

Rybeck sat down. He could see it coming right between the eyes. "How the hell do I know what he told you? No . . . wait," he said in mocking fashion. "Here, let me pull out my crystal ball. I'll tell you in a second."

Craddock stared at him. "Having fun? Or just stalling?"

Rybeck leaned back in his green leather chair. "There was not enough evidence to support creating panic in this firm," Rybeck said, staring Craddock in the eyes.

"You *knew*, Severin. You lied to me."

"I did *not* lie to you!"

"You killed them, Severin. Oh, you may not have lit the match, but you might as well have. You wantonly put their lives in danger because of some fucked-up, misguided call to duty. Have you spoken to Shelly yet? You ever hear a grown man babble like a lunatic? I have. Just an hour ago. What are you going to tell him when you speak to him? How will you even look him in the eyes? Any of them, for that matter. Let's make no mistake about it, Severin. As far as I'm concerned, you killed Ginny Borman. You're the reason she's no longer with us. You and your freakish obsession with Morson Grayhead."

Any semblance of civility was now long gone. The battle had begun.

There is hardly a more acrimonious confrontation than that between two people who know each other best. The ones closest to you know the hot buttons to push, the words that can ultimately destroy a soul.

Every cell in Rybeck's body told him to attack. "Fuck you, Roy! I have a company to run here. The board and the shareholders have placed that trust in me. In *me*, Roy. Not you. Me. This company employs tens of thousands of people, with billions of dollars in revenues. *Billions*, Roy. With a capital *B.*"

Craddock took a seat in one of the two Renaissance Revival chairs opposite Rybeck. He remained eerily calm, almost as if suppressing a maniacal rage. "Don't stop, Severin. What else do we do? Please. Tell me. I'm only the vice chairman of the whole goddamned thing. But I love learning new things. Please, go on. Tell me, Severin, do we sell stocks?"

Rybeck's eyes squinted with fury. "You insubordinate little shit! You have no idea the pressures related to running this business. Absolutely none! And I'll fill you in on a little secret, Roy. *You* could never do it. Not in a million years."

"That's too bad . . . because I've called an emergency meeting of the board for four o'clock today. I think they might feel a little differently than—"

Rybeck jumped to his feet. "You called a *what?*" he boomed nearly at the top of his lungs. "Only I can do that, Roy. Who do you think you are, calling a . . . ?"

"Relax, Severin. It was easy. Really. I told each one of them about my conversation with Mr. Ferguson. Let's just say I piqued their interest. I think they'd like to hear more. And I'll tell you something else. I'm not sure who I am right now, or what I'll be tomorrow. But I am sure of one thing. This time tomorrow, *you* will not be chairman of Morson Grayhead."

Rybeck's eyes bulged, seething with rage. His face had grown scarlet and swollen, and Craddock could actually see veins throbbing at his temples. "You son of a bitch," Rybeck muttered venomously. "You backstabbing, cocksucking son of a bitch! You take this firm from me, Craddock, and I will kill you."

"Is that a threat?"

"You bet your ass it is."

"You and I both know you don't have the balls."

"Try me."

"You know . . . you really are a prick. All these years I kept looking for the hidden side, the human side, assuming that underneath it all, there lived a caring, compassionate man. Guess that doesn't say much for my intelligence, does it?"

Rybeck glared at Craddock through snake-slit eyes, his words choked with disdain. "Just who are you to talk about my caring? My compassion? You don't know *shit* about me."

Craddock sat disarmingly calm. Rybeck was not used to this blatant level of pompous indignation. No one acted this smug around him. Ever. Confident, yes. Smug, no. Where did this sudden arrogance come from? Only a loaded gun could give an underling so much self-assurance. He half expected Roy to pull a revolver from his coat.

Craddock nodded his head slowly, acknowledging Rybeck's statement as fact. "You're right. I don't."

"Now, you listen to me, and listen to me good, Roy. I want you to cancel that board meeting immediately. No one's going to even *attempt* to wrest control of this firm from me in front of my face. Not while I'm alive."

"I'll be glad to do it behind your back."

"You won't do it at all! Tell them you had your facts wrong."

Craddock played with his nail again, unfazed by Rybeck's orders. He didn't speak for some time, allowing Rybeck to feel as though he may have regained the upper hand. "So, let me get this straight," Craddock began, speaking calmly to his hand. "You knew the authorities wanted to inform our employees, and you did nothing. No, let me change that. You actively fought their request."

"I did no such thing!"

"That's not what that arson investigator told me."

"He's lying."

"I see."

Rybeck rose from his chair and walked to a window, facing the Statue of Liberty. "Do you, Roy?" he asked, staring out at the harbor. "Do you honestly believe I would ignore a request like that? You're not as smart as I thought you were."

"I thought I'd already established that."

Rybeck turned from the window. "Well, it looks as though it's his word against mine then, doesn't it?"

"And his partner's."

"Well, who do you think the board's going to believe, Roy? Severin Rybeck, or some tinhorn fire investigator looking to cover his department's ass?"

Craddock's response was immediate. "Oh, the great Severin Rybeck," he snapped back viperously. "Morson Grayhead's high, grand, exalted, mystic ruler. The man whose shit doesn't stink. Well, maybe it's about time someone told them not to pay attention to that man behind the curtain."

"Cancel the meeting, Roy, or I will do it myself."

"No, you won't."

Rybeck was incredulous. "No, I won't?"

"That's right. No, you won't. They'll want to hear me tell them I was wrong. It loses something coming from you, don't you think? We'll see who wins this afternoon, Severin, but I can tell you this much. You cancel that meeting, and I think you'll look pretty suspicious. What do you think? And there's no way in hell I'll ever back down from my statements. Sounds like three against one to me."

"I'll kill you," Rybeck said, his lips curling with disgust.

"Again with the threats. Is that supposed to scare me? It doesn't become you. Now . . . if you told me you were going to burn my wife alive . . . now *that* would upset me."

"Don't you *dare* imply—"

"Imply?" Craddock asked with incredulity. "I'm not *implying* anything. Go ahead, kill me. You think I give a shit right now? You think my life matters to me right now? We could have prevented Ginny's death, Severin. *And* the firefighters'. Not only could we have, we *should* have. But I, the blind and loyal lackey, went along with Severin Rybeck's stealth campaign for the good of the firm. After the second one, I knew. I *knew* we had a connection. But I didn't push you. Not until it was too late. And now Morson's going to disintegrate from the inside out. It was a tumor, Severin. A vicious, malignant tumor, and I let you ignore it."

"You can stand around and let this firm fall apart if you want," Rybeck seethed, "but I will *not* let it happen."

"That's what it's all about, isn't it, Severin? The firm. It's always been the firm, hasn't it? Nothing else has ever mattered. When your boy needed you most, you abandoned him because he got in the way of your duties. Even after you threw him in the crazy bin, you never went to see him—"

"Now, you wait just a goddamned minute, Roy!" Rybeck burst out.

But Craddock was on a roll. He'd kept quiet long enough. Years of anger seethed from his pores. "Just wasn't convenient, was it, Severin?" he continued, ignoring Rybeck's admonition. "Didn't look good, did it? Scotty needed you, and you dumped him like a hot potato. All because the firm came first. *Your own son!*"

"How *dare* you bring Scotty into this!"

"You couldn't even tell me what he looks like now, could you? You don't even know where the hell he is."

Rybeck shook with rage. "*Get out!* Get out of my office now or so help me . . ."

Craddock rose to leave, walking toward the large wooden doors. "Don't worry, Severin, I'm leaving," he said, turning as he placed his hand on the knob. "But don't get too comfy in here." He looked at a Monet on the wall. "You know, I think when this office is mine, I'm going to hang Mr. Grayhead's portrait there."

JAKE FERGUSON AND Don Ederling were not happy men. Ederling had driven them from the morgue to Morson Grayhead's headquarters in New York and had changed his shoes for the ride. Jake still wore his boots and bunker pants with red suspenders over a blue fire marshal's T-shirt. He had wanted to be dressed like a brother when he broke the news to Tommy's wife. Both men were covered in sweat and ash and reeked of smoke.

"You sure you want to go in *those* things?" Ederling asked Jake, motioning to his bunker pants as they drove down the Hutchinson River Parkway to Morson Grayhead headquarters in New York.

The call for the Borman fire had come early. In actuality, Jake had walked to his cruiser in the dark heat of night and had slipped his bunker pants on over a pair of gym shorts before leaving his parking garage. He wasn't interested in anything right now but facing down Severin Rybeck, and especially not in telling Ederling that he didn't have any other pants.

"Yeah, I'm sure," Jake answered, his tone indicating that it was the least of his concerns.

They parked in the circle outside the revolving doors where Rybeck had been accosted earlier that morning. Jake knew the way and motioned for Ederling to follow him. Two guards stopped them as they approached the executive elevator. "Excuse me, gentlemen, where are you going?"

Jake had expected interference. "To see Severin Rybeck," he answered abruptly, not giving them so much as a glance.

"I don't think so," one of the guards said.

Their paths were blocked now. "You don't think so?" Jake asked, as if to say, *Did I hear you right?* "We dress like this because we got nothing better to do. I am Chief Fire Marshal Jacob Ferguson and this is Deputy Chief Donald Ederling. We have just come from the scene of last night's fire. Now step aside so we can see Rybeck."

Jake was in true form, and Ederling could see the situation quickly deteriorating. He moved in to calm everyone's emotions. "Jake, show the man your ID," he said, reaching into his wallet. Jake sighed, doing likewise. "Gentlemen," Ederling continued, "it is imperative that we speak with Mr. Rybeck immediately."

Jake's emotions notwithstanding, Ederling knew they would see Severin Rybeck, and they would see him now. This was too important. There was too much at stake. But sometimes you have to play the game. Always the calmer of the two, Ederling felt that given the circumstances, his approach might just work better.

One of the guards took their wallets, reading their respective IDs. "One minute, gentlemen," he said, leaving for his desk to call upstairs.

Jake was fuming. A woman had taken the elevator down to the lobby, and Jake watched her exit, leaving its doors wide open. Her eyes filled with fear at the sight of Jake decked out in his fire garb. She knew immediately why he was there. But Jake didn't notice her. All he saw was opportunity, and he took it. He walked past the second guard and directly onto the elevator. "Screw this," Jake said to Ederling, motioning him in with his arms. "Come on, let's go." Jake pushed the only floor button it had.

"Hey! We told you to stay here," the guard yelled, lunging toward the elevator. Ederling followed behind the guard, stepping inside. There was no way the guard was going to pull them off, and he knew it. Especially Ederling. The guard screamed something to his partner at the security desk as the doors began to close.

"I said get off that elevator!" the guard ordered, trying to wedge his way in. Jake shoved him with a boot and waved good-bye, wearing a screw-you smile from ear to ear.

"That was nice," Ederling said as the doors closed.

"Fuck him," Jake said. "I don't have time for some wanna-be cop to cover his ass."

Ederling shook his head, smiling. *How to Win Friends and Influence People*, by Jake Ferguson. Now selling at bookstores near you. You know they'll come after us."

Jake smirked. "Like I care, Don. They'll have to shoot me to stop me from doing this."

"Careful, Jake. Don't go doing something stupid. You have a department to represent."

Jake tilted his head down, looking at Ederling through the tops of his eyes. "There goes that reputation, huh?"

Ederling was concerned by Jake's demeanor. Like it or not, they still needed Severin Rybeck. "Remember, Jake, we still have to work with this guy. As much as it might drive you crazy, he still runs the show. You go in there swinging and we might lose any cooperation we're gonna need to close this thing."

"Donny, don't tell me to be a gentleman. I can't do that. Not after this morning. And anyway, Rybeck may run the show now, but he won't be running it tomorrow."

"You don't know that, Jake. Look, no one's asking you to be a gentleman. Just don't do anything you'll regret later. At least for now. We need him."

"We'll see."

The elevator slowed to a stop and the doors opened. They expected another confrontation and were surprised to find none. Apparently the guards in the lobby and the lone elevator to the executive suite were the first and last line of defense. It was immediately obvious, however, that the guards had called. Jake recognized the black woman behind the receptionist counter. She was standing and visibly frightened. Her wild-eyed stare said it all.

"Hi," Jake said, walking past her. "I brought my friend to see your art collection."

They turned the corner and stormed down the hall, catching curious glances along the way. Jake opened the large wooden door on the right and entered Rybeck's secretarial foyer. "Janet," he said casually. "Is Severin in?"

He didn't wait for a response, but walked directly to Rybeck's office, opened the door, and motioned elegantly for Ederling to go first. Three of his brothers had died today because of the self-righteous asshole he was about to see. Jake really didn't care what anyone else thought. It was time to show a little disrespect.

Janet was expecting them. Normally she would have stood in front of Rybeck's door, or at least put up some kind of a fuss. But it was all crashing down now and somehow it just didn't matter to her anymore. "Mr. Ferguson . . ." was all he heard her say as he followed Ederling into the office.

Rybeck was on a conference call with his general counsel and investor relations VP. He had been forewarned and was expecting them. "Gentlemen," he said into the phone's speaker. "My unannounced guests have arrived. Let's pick up from here after they've left. I'll call you. But stay put. It shouldn't take long."

Jake walked to the front of Rybeck's desk, slapping an open manila envelope onto it. Photographs spilled out and across it, pushing away a neatly stacked pile of papers. "You're right, Rybeck, this won't take long."

Jake's fury was unmistakable. Rybeck stared at him, not sure what it meant or what to do about it. "Mr. Ferguson, just what the hell do you think you're doing? You can't just come barging in here like—"

"Yeah, well, I just did," Jake interrupted. "I'm real sorry to inconvenience you, Severin, but I just thought you might want to take a peek at what Don and I have been doing for the last eight hours. Not that I think you'll give a shit."

Three security personnel rushed into Rybeck's office just as Jake finished speaking. They, too, were not happy. "Okay, assholes, let's go," the lead guard said as the other two approached them. "You're coming with us."

Jake looked at Rybeck. "Is this how it's going to be, Severin? You sitting there watching your goons give us the bum's rush because you don't have the balls to discuss this man to man?"

A guard stood behind Jake. "Come on, asshole," he said, wrapping his large hands around Jake's biceps. "Let's go."

Jake ripped himself free with a rotating turn of his shoulders. "Get your *fucking* hands off of me!"

A larger guard stood behind Ederling, but wisely hadn't touched him yet. Ederling turned with a forefinger in the air. "Don't *even* try it."

Rybeck was standing, looking at his two visitors. At least he still had the authority to have them removed.

"Well?" Jake asked, motioning to the envelope. "You going to look at them or not? I brought them just for you."

"I apologize, Mr. Rybeck," the head guard started. "They forced their way past us at the elevator. Let me call for some backup and we'll have these . . . *gentlemen* removed."

Rybeck looked at the five men opposite his desk, finally catching Jake's eyes. "No. Thank you, Mike. That won't be necessary."

"But, Mr. Rybeck, it will only . . ."

Rybeck thanked God that Jake and Ederling weren't terrorists with guns. He'd have to revamp security when this thing blew over. "No, that won't be necessary. I need to speak to these men. But thank you for your diligence just the same. I can see them to the elevator when we're done."

"Are you sure, sir?"

"Yes. Thank you."

Angry glares were exchanged as the three guards left the room.

"Close the door, will you, Mike? Thanks," Rybeck said as they left, leaving Rybeck and his two visitors alone in his office.

The three men stood silent for some time. Jake was physically shaking and took long, deep breaths in a vain effort to regroup. "Well, Severin," he began, forcing a smile that could kill. "There they are. Why don't you take a peek? I think it'll be good for you. It'll certainly be good for your firm. Because I think after you catch a glimpse of those, you just might start to appreciate the gravity of the situation."

Rybeck sat in his seat. He felt a strange and morbid curiosity for the photos in front of him, but was determined not to look at them now, if for no other reason than to deprive Jake of the satisfaction. The man standing before him was the enemy, in bed with Craddock and his scheming plans.

"I don't need to look at your pictures, Mr. Ferguson. I am fully aware of the horror of what has transpired."

"Really?" Jake leaned over Rybeck's desk and scooped them up as if sweeping a deck of cards off a table. He stood and shuffled them, one after the other at waist height, pulling one from the batch. He leaned on his elbows over Rybeck's desk. "How's the saying go? Oh, yeah. 'Don't sell yourself short.'" He held a picture out in front of him, facing Rybeck. "This one here. This is a beauty, don't you think? Shot it myself. Not bad, huh? See here"—he pointed at something over the picture's top with a finger—"see how her face is all twisted in pain?"

Rybeck peered down his nose contemptuously at the horrid picture of Ginny Borman's charred and tortured face, trying desperately to remain outwardly dispassionate. The distinctive odor of burnt wood and seared flesh was clearly discernible as Jake reached forward, sending waves of bile up Rybeck's throat. He'd done the best he could with what little information they all had, and while in retrospect it was clearly a flawed decision, he wondered if Jake would really have done things any differently if the tables had been turned.

"Good shot, huh?" Jake asked again.

Rybeck looked over the picture into Jake's eyes, his face hot and pinched with annoyance. "What do you want me to say, Mr. Ferguson?"

Jake turned the picture toward himself, holding it toward his face. "Say? Gee, I don't know, Severin. I guess 'I'm sorry' would be a little weak right now, don't you think?" Jake continued in disgust. "You know, I look at this and I can almost hear her screams. How about you?"

Rybeck was quiet, willing to let Jake vent. But he wouldn't stand for this much longer. His patience was wearing thin.

"I can't leave without showing you this one," Jake said as if sharing pictures of a trip to the Grand Canyon. "This one's a beauty. What do you think?" Jake pulled out a shot of O'Reilly's body nearly melted to the floor. "Here's one of the three firefighters. See how he's gripping the man next to him, like he was trying to save him? Now there's one for *Life* magazine if you ask me."

Rybeck was clearly feeling the one-two punch take its toll. First Craddock and his none-too-subtle threat to take his firm away, and now this. He glanced at the photo with an unyielding jaw, his face assuming the look of a dark mask. He took the picture from Jake and placed it facedown on his desk, laying both his palms over it.

Ederling watched the proceedings with a mix of joy and anxiety. There was never a moment's boredom with Jacob Ferguson at the helm. Ederling took a seat, staring at Rybeck's face for reactions. Rybeck seemed to be melting before his eyes, and Ederling couldn't help but wonder when it would become a full-fledged meltdown. The wait was nerve-racking. He knew Jake would push and push some more. He was just aching for a fight.

Rybeck knew it, too, and felt the best approach was as little approach as possible. Something inside told him not to lock horns with Jake Ferguson. Not today. Emotions were too high, and deep inside he feared what he might hear.

"Mr. Ferguson, I am aware of what happened this morning at the Borman household. I want to express my deepest sympathies at the loss of your three colleagues. I am truly sorry."

Jake wiped an imaginary tear from his cheek. "That's touching, Severin. Really, it is. I'll be sure to tell their wives. It'll help them greatly in their time of grief."

"Why *are* you here, Mr. Ferguson?" Rybeck said, leaning forward and clasping his hands on top of his closed legs. "Did you come all the way down here just to play games?"

Jake glared at him, slashing him with his eyes. "Games? You know my definition of games, Severin? My definition is when your own vice chairman calls you to discuss options to prevent this from happening again, and you tell him we suggested you do nothing. Now *that*, Severin . . . is playing games. The only difference is that, in your version, people die."

"I told you when we spoke on Sunday, Mr. Ferguson, that if there should be another, we would do things your way. I am a man of my word. What do you suggest?"

"What do I suggest?" Jake said, rubbing his mouth and chin. "Well, let's see. We could start with your resignation. That'd be a good jumping-off spot. Then maybe we can get someone in that seat who is willing to *do* something to keep his employees from frying at the hands of a maniac."

Rybeck laughed, crossing his arms across his chest. Jake could read body language as well as anyone and knew that as confident as Rybeck tried to sound, he was anything but. Jake was determined to push him to the brink, and beyond, if at all possible. He hoped Rybeck would come after him so he could lay him cold on the floor, but didn't think that likely. The man was too smart for that. Too smart, or too cowardly.

"Something funny?" Jake asked.

Rybeck rose and walked slowly to a window. He placed a foot on the ledge, leaning on a knee. "Thank you for your input, Mr. Ferguson, but I am *not* going to resign. Two nights ago I was explaining the concept of options to you, and now you want to have a say over who runs *my* company."

Jake shook his head. "Oh, no. I wouldn't pretend to know anything about that," he stated emphatically. "I'm just trying to have a say over who *shouldn't* run it."

There followed a long moment of silence as Rybeck watched traffic flow along the lower West Side Highway. "Hindsight is twenty-twenty, Mr. Ferguson. I'm not sure this Monday-morning quarterbacking is going to help anything right now, are you?"

"Monday-morning quarterbacking? Rybeck, I begged you to tell your people. To get them to see the seriousness of the situation. And now six people are dead. Burned alive in the most horrible death imaginable. And Don and I have seen and touched each one of them. I don't call that hindsight. I call that murder."

"Murder, Mr. Ferguson?" Rybeck asked, turning away from his view. "That's a bit harsh, don't you think?"

Jake's face smoldered. "Fuck you, Rybeck. We're running this show now, and you will do what *we* tell you to do."

Ederling watched it all in silence. Here we go, he thought, though it had taken a little longer than he'd imagined.

"No, Mr. Ferguson. Fuck *you*," Rybeck said with arrogance, pointing his finger at Jake. "You and your holier-than-thou attitude. Not to mention your pretentious fantasy that getting everyone in on this would have prevented anything. Morson Grayhead is *my* responsibility, sir. Mine. Not yours. I make the decisions, and those decisions are final. You may have the benefit now of looking this thing in the mirror, but I did not have that advantage when I made my decision."

"Yeah . . . well, I guess we can all agree it was a pretty rotten one at that."

"I did the best I could under the circumstances, Mr. Ferguson. I am as pained by this as anyone, and if you don't believe that, then you can go to hell."

"Okay, Rybeck, so I'm going to hell. But you listen, and you listen good. There will be no more waiting," Jake ordered. "No more stalling. Today. Immediately. You are to call an emergency meeting of your top executives and their wives. Provide day care for those with children if you have to, but get them here *today*. I do not want another night to go by without everyone fully informed of the facts in this case and your plan of action."

"And just what should that be?" Rybeck asked, sitting on the ledge.

"First, you will cancel all business trips. Second, you will offer to provide a twenty-four-hour security detail for any wife whose husband is out of town, and anyone else who wants it. Third, you will offer a safe haven for wives and children until such time as this is over."

Rybeck could feel the walls of Morson Grayhead falling in around him and was more determined than ever to maintain the aura of control. "Really?" he asked indignantly. "Such as?"

Jake smirked. "I don't know, Severin. Figure it out. Rent a resort, the floor of a hotel. Anything. Someplace where they will be confined and can be watched as a group. Preferably out of the country."

Rybeck felt it politically incorrect to comment on how much that would cost. Perhaps this wasn't the time to voice bottom-line concerns. At least not publicly. "Time's a problem. There's been a board meeting called at four today."

"We know," Ederling said.

Rybeck was shocked, staring at Ederling and then into Jake's eyes. "Have *you* been asked to attend?"

"Look, I don't give a shit how you do it, just work it out," Jake said. "But I'm warning you. Have that meeting today. It is nonnegotiable." Jake desperately wanted to take this little encounter to the next level, but knew in his heart that Ederling was right. They needed this man. At least for now. Tomorrow might prove to be a different story, but for now, they had a job to do. "Now let me ask *you* a question. Who would have access to the travel itineraries of your top executives?"

At that moment, Rybeck was not fond of Jake. Yet, in a strange way, he was aware of a growing respect for this fire-fighting-clad man standing before him. "Not many, really. I certainly don't know where they all are at any given time. My people are a busy lot, Mr. Ferguson. Sometimes they're gone two or three weeks out of the month."

"You say 'not many.' Name some who *would* know."

Rybeck dropped his head, scratching its top. "Well, their secretaries for one."

"Yeah, okay, but who would know *everyone's* schedule?"

"I'm not sure. Someone at Executive Travel, I guess. They book all our trips firm-wide."

"Is that in-house?" Jake asked.

"No. It used to be, but we found it more cost effective to sub it out."

"So it's another company?"

"Yes."

"We need their number and a contact person. Somebody high up."

"Are you attending the board meeting, Mr. Ferguson?" Rybeck asked again as he walked toward his intercom to buzz Janet.

"Also, we need to work with someone in personnel," Jake continued, ignoring Rybeck's question for a second time. He was not interested in Rybeck's egocentric concerns, nor was he interested in letting him take control of the meeting. "You said the other day that you'd be willing to supply us people. Well, we need them now. Give us someone with access to all files. Preferably someone who can spend as much time with us as we need."

Rybeck buzzed Janet and asked her to get the name and number Jake wanted at Executive Travel and to call the senior VP of human resources to inform him to expect visitors. "Tell him to clear his calendar until further word from me."

Jake turned to Ederling. "Donny, why don't you take the personnel angle? You know what we're looking for. I'll work Executive Travel. See if we might not dig something up there." Jake turned to speak to Rybeck, who was now standing at his desk. "Severin, where is Executive Travel?"

"They're in this complex on the ground floor."

"Good." Jake tossed the photos back on Rybeck's desk. "We got shit to do. Tell Donny how to get to the personnel department." He looked at his watch as he turned back to Ederling. "Don, I'll meet you at the car at five."

"The car at five," Ederling repeated.

"Unless I finish up sooner," Jake added. "Then I'll hook up with you in personnel. Also, Severin, call your lackeys and tell them not to tow the red Bronco out front. It's Donny's. Okay, let's move."

Rybeck's mind reeled. He knew five o'clock was enough time for Jake to attend the board meeting. Rybeck stopped them as they turned to leave. "You didn't answer my question, Mr. Ferguson."

"Which one was that?"

"Have you been asked to attend the board meeting?"

Jake looked into Rybeck's hunted eyes, seeing fear for the first time. "Only the important part."

"Mr. Ferguson?" Rybeck called as they opened the door.

Jake turned, visibly annoyed. "What?"

Rybeck was holding the stack of pictures out in his hand. "You forgot your photos."

Ederling had left the office and Jake stood with a hand on the knob. "They're yours, Severin. Keep them. I got lots more where those came from. Maybe you can stick 'em in an album or something—you know, for the memories."

MORSON GRAYHEAD'S THIRTEEN-MEMBER board was diverse, an eclectic group embodying captains of industry from varying fields. Included were the chairmen or ex-chairmen of some of the nation's largest automotive, electronics, telecommunications, chemicals, defense, banking, and agribusiness concerns. There was also a smattering of supposedly brilliant minds from the world of academe, an extremely wealthy philanthropist, an ex-president of the United States, and the eccentric but outspoken granddaughter of Cornelius Grayhead, one of the firm's founding fathers.

Put simply, there was no shortage of money or ego in the Morson Grayhead boardroom into which Jake Ferguson apprehensively waited to be summoned. They met on the top floor of Grayhead's Wall Street headquarters, in an ornately furnished, wood-paneled, egg-shaped room. Two tuxedo-clad waiters tended to their every need; each was served, without being asked, his or her favorite nonalcoholic drink, coffee, or bottled water, a trick made possible from records kept on file in computer data banks in the back offices of the Executive Dining Department.

On such short notice, not all members of the board could be present. But in a testament to their dedication, the unparalleled series of events leading up to it, and the serious nature of the accusations leveled against Severin Rybeck, all but three made it. They certainly had more than enough for a quorum, which meant more than enough to decide Severin Rybeck's fate.

Jake sat, still in his bunker pants and boots, wishing now he'd taken the time to change. His feet sweat profusely in his heavy rubber boots, and a warm pool of perspiration caused an irritable itch between the crack of his buttocks and the skin of his scrotum. He wanted desperately to reach in and scratch, but feared that with his luck someone would come for him just as his hand was deeply entrenched in his pants. So, he sat uncomfortably instead, watching the second hand on his watch crawl slowly by in circles, moving slower than a glacier.

It had been a long day indeed. Jake sat, eyes closed, with his hands clasped between his legs and the back of his head leaning against the paneled wall. He was beyond tired, his mind having entered that anxious, buzzing state you encounter after pulling an all-nighter for a college exam. Visions of O'Reilly and his two other brothers scurried through his mind; their charred bodies and anguished souls etched into his retinas. Jake tried to imagine what political squabbling and self-serving positioning was taking place in the adjacent room and felt a dull, empty ache gnawing at his belly. That anyone was doing *anything* other than mourning the death of such brave and selfless men seemed almost blasphemous to him.

But if Jake was anything, he was a realist. He knew the world would continue to turn; people would continue to make love, war, and money, commit suicide and murder, and eat, drink, and sleep. His shoulders felt heavy at the thought of the daunting task ahead of him. He and Ederling still needed to contact the Philadelphia Exchange and see if they could ferret out who, if anyone, was profiting from this nightmare. They would need to scan years of Morson Grayhead's personnel records, dig deeper into the Keep Westchester Green group, and help secure the safety of the remaining executives and their families. Jake felt thankful that the public safety commissioner had put the state police at his service.

He wondered if the people in the adjoining room had any idea what they were up against—not just with Rybeck and his distorted, myopic view of the world, but also with this madman running loose on the streets. Jake thought maybe it would help bring it all home if he passed a couple of choice photos around the table. Reading and hearing about it is one thing, but touching it, breathing it, smelling it, seeing it—*that* was something else altogether. Just how grounded in reality could they really be, what with their limos, diamonds, and power?

This world into which Jake had recently found himself thrust was so different to him, unlike anything else he had experienced to date. So much money and power; enormous bank accounts and even larger egos. Executives dressed smartly in thousand-dollar suits, starched man-tailored shirts, traveling the world in search of a buck; all of it ran counter to who Jake was and what made him feel at ease.

He'd take a Bud and a Yankee game over Scotch on the rocks and golf any day. He found himself wondering how long ago it had probably been since any of them had ventured to the South Bronx to see the Bombers play. The House That Ruth Built, smack-dab in the middle of the urban decay of the greatest city in the world. Now *that* was what life was all about.

Jake smiled slightly as the thought entered his mind. *Of course. Why didn't it occur to me earlier? I'll take Don's redhead to a Yankee game.* They could talk, but still not have to focus exclusively on each other, and just maybe, if he was lucky, she'd be impressed by his knowledge of baseball. Jake hadn't met a woman yet who really knew anything about it. *It'll be perfect.*

"Mr. Ferguson," a tuxedo-clad man said as a large, cherry-colored door opened from the boardroom. "The board will see you now, sir."

Jake was so absorbed with thoughts, his sweaty ass and testicles, and his date with the redhead, he hadn't given himself time to get nervous. He rose, tucking his blue T-shirt into his bunker pants, ran his fingers through his hair a few times, and walked slowly toward the man at the door. He swallowed dryly, feeling the lining of his stomach flutter slightly as he approached their inner sanctum. In his mind he kept thinking, "Why do you give a shit?" Jake didn't know, and it didn't matter. He was nervous.

The door was closed quietly behind him, and Jake found himself standing alone, at the foot of a long, oval cherry table. He thought of a runway and, strangely, pictured red and blue landing lights running down its middle. So many things caught his eye, yet he was unable to focus on any of them. A dozen people sat staring at him, and the last thing he wanted to be caught doing was gaping around the room.

The carpeting was a dark green with some logo or pattern woven throughout. It reminded him of the floor of the U.S. Senate chambers. Crystal sconces adorned the paneled walls, and for a moment Jake thought they were actually lit by candles. Three plates of sliced fruit and assorted cookies on blue and white china were spaced at four-foot intervals down the length of the table. In glancing at the one closest to him, he noticed the letters *MGR* neatly calligraphed in Gothic style on the rise of its edge.

Jake noticed that all but two of the men were either bald or gray, or both. He also noticed that there was but one woman. A stately figure, whose softly curled, shoulder-length, silver hair seemed out of place for a woman of her years. But there was something about her eyes. Without being told, Jake knew she was not *just* the token female. The waiters were nowhere to be found, and Jake could only assume they had sought refuge behind one of two curved, dark, wooden doors on either side of Rybeck. Severin Rybeck sat at the head of the table at the other end of the room, piercing Jake with narrow, speculative eyes.

Jake stood in his worn boots and bunker pants, red suspenders and dirty T-shirt, unsure of himself and completely out of his element. He reeked of smoke. His sweaty, soot-stained, matted hair and gritty fingernails stood in jarring contrast to the genteel civility surrounding him. He felt naked as he stood with his hands crossed timidly at the waist. Including Rybeck and Craddock, twelve pairs of eyes scanned him with varying degrees of curiosity, suspicion, and bewilderment.

Jake might have felt better had he known his attire lent him an air of respectable credibility. He was clearly the man who had seen the effects of the monster up close, who had touched and moved the hapless victims of the murderer's warped and demented deeds. Anything else would not have conjured up the powerful images his current state produced.

Craddock rose and walked over to greet Jake. He shook his hand and began to speak. "Ladies and gentlemen, this is Chief Jacob Ferguson, of the Westchester County Fire Marshal's Office. He has been kind enough to agree to join us here this afternoon. Needless to say, he has been a very busy man, and I know I speak for all of us when I say, 'Thank you, Mr. Ferguson.' "

Jake nodded slightly, not sure whether to smile. Smartly, he opted for stoic impassivity.

"First," Craddock began, "let me say the following. You all know that I have spent my entire thirty-six-year career at this firm. There is no one"—Craddock stared at Rybeck—"in this room who cares more for Morson Grayhead than do I. That is why I want it clear and up front that I do not wish now, nor in the future, to be considered for the post of chairman."

"Oh, that's beautiful, Roy," came Rybeck's scornful retort. "Played to the hilt. You're really something, you know that?"

Grayhead's granddaughter spoke. "That will be all, Severin. We are here for a reason, and right now that reason is to listen to what Mr. Ferguson has to say." She turned to Jake. "Mr. Ferguson, thank you for taking the time to be with us this afternoon. I am sure you have more important issues to attend to. Not all of us were aware that you would be here today"—she looked at Craddock—"but we are anxious to hear your insights on the case and the uncomfortable matter at hand, nonetheless."

"Well, Roy," Rybeck said, "you heard Bernice. Let the man talk."

"With all due respect, Severin," Craddock started, "my purpose here today is to remove you from your post—"

"That's enough, Mr. Craddock!" the ex-president said.

"Mr. President, I beg to differ, sir. We are in receipt of information that calls into question Severin's suitability for office."

"Or so you say, Roy," Rybeck chimed in.

Jake knew Craddock was right and wanted to interrupt, but he also knew deep down that this was not his battle to fight. Yet. He stood silent, eyeing the paintings on the wall above Rybeck's head.

"Yes, Severin. So I say."

"Gentlemen, please!" Bernice pleaded. "Severin, you will have ample opportunity to respond. No one is looking to railroad you out of here."

Jake watched the proceedings with some interest. *Speak for yourself, lady.* He didn't know who this woman was, but he had been right, she clearly carried weight in this room.

"If I may continue, please," Craddock started again. "I believe strongly, Mr. President, that for the good of this firm, someone must lead that charge. If it is to be me, then the only way the actions we take here today can be noted seriously is if I remove all doubt as to my motives. All of you know that Severin and I go way back. Long before any of you sat on this board. Long before Severin or I ever dreamed we would be here today. But, as much as this pains me, there is no doubt in my mind that I am doing the right thing. Morson Grayhead is *not* Severin Rybeck, Mr. President. It is the tens of thousands of fine, hardworking, dedicated individuals who are heading home to their families as we speak. How many of them won't come back tomorrow? I ask each of you to consider the implications of that question. Morson Grayhead is only as good as its employees, and I believe Severin was wrong to *ever* consider placing it, and its fine name, above the safety of those who make it great."

The other members sat in stunned silence. What was taking place before them was tantamount to mutiny. It was highly unusual for someone outside the family ever to witness the inner workings of the Morson Grayhead board, and downright unthinkable to allow them to view a family squabble. But now, not only was this stranger dressed as a firefighter privy to it all, but their vice chairman was committing the unspeakable by waging a campaign against the very man they all so deeply admired. None of them had ever dreamed they would live to see this day.

"Okay, Roy," Bernice interrupted. "Your lack of interest in Severin's post is duly noted. Now, please tell us just what the hell is going on here."

"The facts are simple, really—"

"Using a little poetic license with the word *facts* aren't you, Roy?" Rybeck interrupted.

"Severin! Please!" Bernice thundered. "Enough. You'll have your day in court."

Craddock continued, "I called Severin in his limousine about ten o'clock last night. Several of our senior executives had just left my office. They came to express concern . . ."

Craddock relayed the events of the prior evening as he recalled them, emphasizing that Rybeck had indicated the authorities felt it best to do nothing.

"Is this true, Severin?" the ex-president asked.

Rybeck sat back in his chair with his arms wrapped around his chest. "Somewhat."

Craddock continued, "This morning, Mr. Ferguson was attempting to reach Severin and was put through to me. We spoke for ten minutes or so, and it became obvious to me very quickly that what they were suggesting . . . in fact, what they had *been* suggesting since last Sunday, was full disclosure to our employees and the arrangement of some type of security to assure their safety."

"That is a lie!" Rybeck boomed, rising to his feet.

Jake had had enough bullshit for one afternoon. Though initially intimidated, at that moment he didn't really care what any of them thought. He was damned if he was about to let Rybeck steamroll the truth in pursuit of his own self-absorbed conceit. "If I might, ladies and gentlemen, I think I can add a little something here," Jake started clumsily.

"Please do, Mr. Ferguson," said the ex-president. "I know I for one would like to hear from *someone* who doesn't have a rooster in this fight."

"Thank you, Mr. President," Jake began, pulling a stack of color photos from a pocket on the side of his pants. "Before any of us speak another word, I think it would be useful if we all truly understand the nature of what is taking place here."

Craddock seemed nervous. He knew that what Jake held in his hands could hardly be considered prime-time viewing material. "Mr. Ferguson," he broke in, "I don't think that's—"

"I'm sorry, Mr. Craddock, but I disagree, sir," Jake interrupted, passing two equal stacks to his left and right.

"I'd like to see them," Bernice said.

Jake continued, "I'm concerned this meeting might lose its focus and center on Mr. Rybeck. And while I understand that is your function here, still, I think it's important we not lose sight of what this thing's really about. It's about six people, now all deceased, burned alive in the most horrible death you can imagine. I think it very fitting that we all remind ourselves of that."

A hushed silence hung over the room as board members solemnly passed the photos to one another. Jake could hear quiet sighs and moans as, one after the other, Morson Grayhead's board members bridled at the photos in front of them. Jake let a few minutes pass, allowing the gravity to seep in.

"Those were *real* people, ladies and gentlemen," Jake began with a wave of his hand across the table. "Not unlike you and me. They were married, had children, jobs, families, friends, dreams. Don and I have seen and touched every one of them."

"Who's Don, Mr. Ferguson?" Bernice asked.

"Oh . . . I'm sorry. He's my deputy chief."

Bernice nodded her head in acknowledgment.

"Well, anyway, you might say we have taken this rather personally now, and I can tell you without doubt that what Mr. Craddock is saying is the truth. Donny and I met with Mr. Rybeck for several hours on Sunday and again on Monday night. I met with him alone, here, yesterday afternoon, and pleaded with him to reconsider his position. We were convinced there was a pattern developing and felt it best to be safe rather than sorry. He was concerned what such actions would have on morale and was adamant in his refusal to see our requests through."

All eyes turned to Rybeck. "Is he telling us the truth, Severin?" the lone philanthropist asked.

Rybeck felt his skin crawl and hoped that the twitch he was feeling in his right eye was discernible only to him. "Of course not," he stated emphatically. "Mr. Ferguson here is clearly trying to cover his ass for an obvious oversight made on the part of his department. Neither he nor his partner ever said any such thing to me."

Jake stood with his arms crossed around his chest, staring at the man he once thought he respected. "Are you calling me a liar, Mr. Rybeck?"

"That is *exactly* what I am calling you, sir. You are lying, and you know it. I will not be your fall boy. Not on your life."

Ford's chairman was amused: "Well, well. I don't consider myself a rocket scientist, folks, but it looks to me like someone is not telling us the truth."

Craddock leaned on the table, staring Rybeck down. "I think that's a good assumption, don't you, Severin?"

"Roy, you realize that tomorrow you will be fired, don't you?" Rybeck asserted.

"Enough!" boomed General Dynamics' ex-chairman. "I missed my grandson's first soccer game to be here today, and I'll be damned if I am going to let this thing die on the vine. Now . . . one of you is not telling the truth, and frankly, it has me more than a little upset. I don't know about anyone else, but I've had just about enough of this childish crap."

Jake didn't really care who believed him. He cared about two things only—protecting the remaining employees and their families, and finding the maniac responsible for this mess.

"I am the chairman of this company," a fuming Rybeck interjected. "No one is going to make . . ."

Jake put a stop to it all. He thought this might happen. Maybe his anticipatory skills had been honed by years of watching sleazeball defense attorneys set wanton criminals free to walk the streets, or maybe he'd fine-tuned a way to sell a constantly doubting jury on the credibility of a photographic memory. But whatever the reason, as usual, Jake had thought several moves ahead.

He reached into the side pocket of his pants and pulled his handheld, voice-activated tape recorder up in the air. "Ladies and gentlemen, I think I can solve our little problem," he said. Rybeck's eyes widened in alarm, knowing instantly that he was in trouble. His face grew chalky as the blood in his veins flowed directly to his toes. He could feel sweat dripping down the small of his back.

"I have here, Mr. Rybeck, a tape recording of our conversation yesterday."

"That's illegal!" Rybeck shouted.

"Maybe. But this is not a court of law, sir. As I understand it, this is a hearing of your peers to decide whether or not you are fit, morally and ethically, to continue running this firm. And frankly . . . *sir* . . . if making a horrendously bad decision, one that just cost four innocent people their lives . . . if that doesn't disqualify you, just maybe lying to their faces will."

On the ride in with Ederling, Jake had stopped his tape recorder at the exact spot where he had asked Rybeck one last time over the table in his office to do something for his employees. Jake walked to the middle of the huge board table, laid the recorder on top, hit play, and stood back, inwardly smirking as he watched Rybeck dissolve into his chair.

Jake's voice was clearly distinguishable on the tape. Everyone sat motionless, listening to it intently. "Just one more thing, Severin. You wouldn't happen to have changed your mind on what we discussed last night, would you? Don and I both think your employees should know."

One by one, people's faces turned to Rybeck as his taped voice broke the silence of the room. "You have no idea how difficult a decision that was for me to make. For now, the answer is no. You must understand, Jake, my ultimate responsibility is to the shareholders of this company. Indeed, ninety percent of its employees *are* shareholders. I simply can't risk the financial well-being of thousands of people based upon the lurid fantasies of some beat reporter looking to make a name for himself."

"Just thought I'd ask."

"I pray I'm right."

"I'm not too big on prayer, sir, but for the sake of your employees and their families, this is one I will be happy to join you in."

No one called Jacob Ferguson a liar and got away with it. Especially in a room full of people. "Still say I'm a liar, Mr. Rybeck?"

Rybeck had suffered an ignominious blow. He dropped his head, shaking it slowly from side to side.

"Good," Jake said, picking his tape recorder up off the table. "Just wanted to clear that up."

There was silence in the room. No one asked to hear the tape again. It wasn't necessary. The conversation was clear as day. It was over for Severin Rybeck and his tour as Morson Grayhead's chairman. The board vote was unanimous. Rybeck was dismissed. Effective immediately, his post would be filled by the chief operating officer, until such time as a suitable replacement could be found.

CHANDLER BOUTET DUTIFULLY met Severin Rybeck at the loading docks in the bowels of Morson Grayhead's headquarters. Rybeck was trudging down the steps from one of the docks, noticeably lacking the usual spring in his step. Over the years Chan had noticed that no matter the market conditions or the occasional spate of bad press, Rybeck was the eternal optimist, a man in love with his life's work. He carried about him an energy and youthfulness that, more than once, caused Chan to feel old beyond his years. But not tonight. Rybeck plodded toward the limousine, carrying his jacket over his shoulder, holding his briefcase in his right hand.

Of course, Chan had no idea what had just transpired. "Bad day, sir?" he asked, holding the rear door of the limousine open for his boss.

Rybeck stopped short, looking his chauffeur in the eyes. Chan could see nothing dwelling inside but pain and torment and wondered for a moment if Rybeck had been crying. Chan knew today had probably been a living hell for him. He could sense that just by the way it had started. But still, coming from someone so consistently on, so upbeat, so on top of his game, the degree of Rybeck's dispirited countenance unsettled him.

"Yes, Chan," Rybeck answered with a smile, "it's been a bad day."

"Well, sir, hop in. Make yourself a drink and relax. I'll have you home in no time."

"Thank you," Rybeck said, climbing into the rear of his limo.

Chan closed the door after him, walked around the idling limousine, and drove up the ramp, pulling out into Wall Street's heavy, 6:00 P.M. traffic. This time of night there really was no good way to travel north. He pulled south onto West Street and began the long, slow creep through the tunnel to the East River Drive, eventually hooking up with the FDR. A car had stalled somewhere, and it was a good forty minutes before they were north of 110th Street, and a half hour after that before they reached the Hutchinson River Parkway.

It was almost 7:30 P.M. when Chan finally swung the Lincoln onto 684 North, sure now he would be late for an 8:00 P.M. date. He tried calling her from the car phone, but there was no answer. Oh, well, he thought. There'll be others. The job comes first. But still, Chan was disappointed. This one seemed special.

Severin Rybeck sat motionless on the limousine's handcrafted, maroon leather rear seat. He was beyond dejection. He was crushed. A gaggle of spineless cowards had just ripped his baby from his arms. He wanted to scream, to lash out, to smash and break all that was within his reach. He sat, leaning back with his eyes closed, while the emotional battle raged within his brain. His mind roiled in torment, as if flinching from repeated blows.

Yesterday he was a powerful man with a problem, but still certain it was one within his control. Today he sat staring blankly out the window of his limousine, watching trees whiz by in a blur of green, knowing that tomorrow he'd have nowhere to go, no decisions to make, no meetings to run, no functions to attend. Poof! Just like that, it was all gone.

Rybeck still could not believe that those sons of bitches had taken his company away from him. They had done more than that. They had taken his *life* away from him. In a million years he never dreamt it would end like this. He'd envisioned a hundred different scenarios of how it might end: a mad gunman, a terrorist act, a stroke, a coronary, a car accident. But *this!* It was all too much. Rybeck loathed the thought of waking tomorrow, reading of his demise on the front page of the *Wall Street Journal* and the *New York Times*.

The very thought nauseated him, that *they* were the ones to second-guess his decision—to tell *him* that he was no longer fit to run the greatest house on the Street! He knew that he alone had made it what it was. Not them. He had single-handedly made Morson Grayhead the powerhouse that it was! Rybeck scoffed at the very notion that even one of them had ever steered him in the direction he eventually took the firm. None of them had ever counseled him on what to buy and when to buy it.

Rybeck viewed them all as a frightened pack of lemmings, covering their asses, fearing the legal fallout from inaction. Shit, canning him was the only thing they'd ever done on their own. If it weren't for him and his cutting-edge, prophetic mind, they'd all be nowhere, sitting around pretending to manage some two-bit Wall Street also-ran.

Oh, sure, Rybeck knew they'd have the press believe they were in on every decision, beating the bush with machetes in hand. After all, they were powerful and successful people in their own right. Most of them. But when you got right down to it, they knew precious little about Wall Street's ways, what really makes a good investor tick, the in-your-face, go-for-the-jugular mind-set that separates it from the rest of corporate America.

Rybeck knew the real score. He alone *knew* they had looked to him for every major decision Morson Grayhead ever made. Try as they might to put the proper spin on their role within the firm, he felt in his heart that the whole lot of them combined couldn't match his brilliance, his balls, his keen eye for a deal.

And now, with the snap of a finger, he was out, never to enter Morson Grayhead's doors again. Never to run another board meeting. Never to make another deal. Never to witness, firsthand, the fulfillment of his life's ambition. "Those bastards," he scowled aloud. "Those traitorous cowards! When it really mattered, not one of them stood by my side. Not one!"

His mind worked in overdrive now, filling with resentment and hatred. "Just what do they think they would have done? What decision do they think they would have made?" Yes, he thought, I lied. Yes, I got caught. But Rybeck knew that in the scheme of things, it could not possibly be a good enough reason to shove him out the door like an unwelcome guest. And for them to even imply that he was insensitive! To imply that he cared more for the firm than he did for his own people! The thought drove him wild with fury.

The sheer arrogance galled him. Of course Rybeck felt for his executives and their families. What kind of a monster do they think I am? he thought. In retrospect, yes, he had made the wrong decision. But it could just as easily have gone the other way. When a quarterback throws a risky but winning touchdown pass, no one complains if it works. Rybeck wondered, would any of them have thanked him for saving the firm if another burning hadn't occurred?

Rybeck couldn't escape the demons dancing through his mind. He had been humiliated in front of his peers, beaten senseless in the middle of the ring. He leaned forward and grabbed a bottle of Chivas Regal, pouring himself a double with one ice cube and a lemon rind. He held it between his legs, amazed at the smoothness of the ride and the lack of vibration in the light brown liquid. Rybeck twirled it a bit, just to cool it off, brought it to his lips, and finished half of it in one swallow. He realized he hadn't eaten yet today and grimaced at the burning heat as it oozed its way down his esophagus, splashing into the emptiness of his belly.

Almost immediately, Rybeck could feel the effects of the booze hit his brain and was aware of a slight tingle in the tips of his fingers. He sat, staring into the abyss of his drink, twirling the half-melted ice cube more vigorously now. He wondered, how could he continue to live under these circumstances? What else did he have to live for? There *was* nothing else.

His only child had disowned him years ago. Adrift and without purpose, the last Rybeck had heard, his son had moved somewhere nearby the estate. Craddock had been correct, Rybeck didn't know what his son looked like, nor did he know exactly where he was. Scotty was truly a mess, and Rybeck knew Scotty would forever blame him and his zealous devotion to Morson Grayhead for his own lack of self-worth, and subsequent nervous breakdown—a horrendous withdrawal into an almost childlike fantasy world Severin was loathe to even imagine. But still, he couldn't help but wonder, since when does someone get kicked off a board for being a bad father? And then there was Lianne, nothing more, really, than a distant memory. True, they shared the same home, but she might as well have been a neighbor three houses down.

Rybeck slugged home the last of his drink, leaned forward, and poured another one, not bothering with ice on this go-round. He felt slightly dizzy and knew from experience that another one so quickly would put him over the edge. Good, he thought, I deserve it.

He finished his second drink minutes after it was poured and thought for a moment he might get sick. But the feeling soon passed, replaced by a delightful warmth, a numbing security that enveloped both his body and mind. Rybeck leaned against the door, wearing a smile of malicious delight. His teeming mind raged with fury. I'll show them, he thought. Like a child seeking sympathy after a fall, he thought how fitting an end it would be, how guilty they would all feel. He reached forward, pulled open a small, wood-paneled compartment just to the right of the bar. Even with the fading sunlight and tinted windows, the bluish black steel of the .45 semiautomatic glistened in its case, like a pot of gold at the end of a rainbow.

Safety had always been a preoccupation with Severin Rybeck, and it was not enough for him to know his chauffeur was armed. What if Chan was taken out in a blizzard of lead? What protection would he have then? Rybeck always had a gun somewhere nearby: in his office, in several rooms at home, in Florida, his plane, his helicopter, and his limousine. He wasn't thinking straight now. "You can never be too careful these days, you know?" he mumbled. Rybeck pulled the gun out cautiously, as if somehow Chan would know what he was doing behind the solitude of his black glass partition.

Seemingly engaged in some masochistic foreplay, Rybeck fondled the weapon smoothly, massaging the thought clearly in his mind, bringing the gun ever closer to its ultimate, deadly purpose. He laid it on the leather to his right, reached into his briefcase, and pulled out a laptop computer. His eyelids were heavy, and the struggle to keep them open was somewhat surprising. Rybeck couldn't help but think that one's final moments on earth should somehow be filled more with trepidation and fear rather than resignation and yearning.

But as always, Rybeck's decision had been reached, and as with most he ever made, it was final. Oddly, with it came a warmth of relaxation, a soothing finality that calmed his battered spirits. With his one reason for living now yanked from his grasp, the deed seemed so logical, so obvious.

CHAN DROVE FASTER than usual on this night. He had been divorced twelve years now and was becoming increasingly aware that he was searching for someone to fill the void. He had a date tonight with a woman he had met at the Sea Port a few days earlier. Chan had found her not only sensuously attractive, but lighthearted and funny as well. He was disappointed her first formal encounter with him would begin so inauspiciously and hoped that among her other qualities she was also understanding.

Chan had planned to take her to a dinner theater and was lost in thought of missing his newfound chance when the explosion rocked the inside of the car. He had fired many thousands of rounds in his day and knew what a gunshot sounded like. He knew intuitively that something was terribly wrong. He also knew immediately that there would be no date tonight. He swerved off 684 onto the shoulder of the road, threw the limousine in park, and whipped out of his seat.

At first, Chan hadn't thought of the gun he knew Rybeck had at his disposal, but in the few seconds between the time he got out of the car and opening its rear door, the thought slammed into his brain like someone cracking him over the head with a baseball bat. He feared what he might see when he opened the door, but that certainly didn't slow him down.

A cloud of spent cordite smacked his nostrils the second he opened the door, and Chan knew without looking that his next sight would not be pretty. "Holy shit!" he moaned under his breath, leaning forward to check on his boss. Rybeck sat motionless, his head resting back on the top of his seat, his mouth gaping open. The gun lay at his side, the computer still lay on his lap.

As best Chan could tell, Rybeck had swallowed the shot, spraying blood and gray matter along the entire back of the Lincoln's rear window, the seat, the ceiling, and the window to his right. The shot had smashed into the bulletproof window behind him, leaving in its wake a white crater from which a million cracks spiderwebbed across the glass like rays emanating from the sun.

Chan wasn't sure what to do. With all his training over the years, still, this was something for which he was woefully unprepared. His lips formed a tight line as he rubbed his forehead with the fingers of his left hand. "Christ," he said. He reached in, then pulled his hand back, only to rub his forehead again. Chan held his hands in front of him, moving them rapidly but meaninglessly, helplessly clenching and unclenching his fists. He was at a complete loss.

"Shit!"

Everything Chan had ever learned told him not to touch a thing, but the sheer thought of someone finding his boss like this pained him. Rybeck was a difficult man to understand, but Chan thought he'd come to know him about as well as one could, even though he never let on. Maybe because Chan saw Rybeck's other side, the one he hid so well from the rest of the world. Whatever it was, Chan was certain that Severin Rybeck was misunderstood and often wondered if, deep down, it had ever bothered him. It was too late now. Chandler Boutet would never know.

Anyway, it wasn't as if the police would be looking for a killer. It was obvious what had happened in here tonight. Still, Chan wondered what he should do. He wanted to at least clean Rybeck up, make him presentable to the authorities, but knew that would be a serious mistake. He had to think of his future and knew if he fucked this up, it could hurt him for a long time to come. He closed the door and walked to the other side of the car, opening the door nearest Rybeck. He leaned in and noticed the computer was still on. Words were typed on its screen, and Chan felt certain they most likely did not pertain to finance. He was no psychiatrist, but a man doesn't review profit-and-loss statements as he's preparing to blow his head off.

Chan felt a certain sense that he was somehow invading Rybeck's private world. He knew that these words were probably not meant for his eyes. But then again, if Rybeck was thinking at all, he would have had to assume that Chan would be the first person to find him. Maybe this note *was* meant for him. But it didn't matter either way. Chan knew once the police arrived, he'd never have this kind of access to Rybeck again. With the single exception of pressing the "page down" key with the tip of a pen, he didn't touch a thing. The screen was a mess. Blood trickled down its fluorescent glow in tiny droplets, as if someone had just shaken a red fountain pen over it a few times. Chan leaned in awkwardly and began to read.

My Dearest Scotty,
   As I write you this letter, I am reminded of the time you found a turtle in the pond in back, and how excited you were. Remember? Remember, you came upstairs all out of breath, screaming, "Dad! Dad! Guess what I found?" I remember, Son.

I remember like it was yesterday. But I was busy with some proposal and told you I couldn't be bothered right then. I will never forget the look of disappointment in your eyes. You wanted to share that moment with me in the worst way, and I sent you out of the room alone, dejected and hurt.

It's too late now, and I know that. But, Scotty, I want to tell you that I'm sorry. You were such a good boy. Strong, full of life, caring. I don't know how it happened, but somewhere along the way, I got my priorities screwed up.

My heart aches now when I think that I was never there for your baseball games, your teacher conferences, your school functions. All that is left for me to do now is tell you how much I love you, and that I worry about you so.

You always tried. You tried so hard. When you were younger and your mother told me you were having problems, I guess I became frightened. Scared of you, of my career, scared that you were of my blood. I realize now that I was the worst possible father. I should have been there, but instead, I ran. I ran as fast and as far away as I could.

I don't ask for forgiveness, I know whatever chance I had for redemption has long since come and gone. And I guess I will have to take my chances now with God. But I want you to know, Son, there is something we have never spoken of, and I realize now how serious it was.

Why I did nothing, I cannot say. I guess I just wouldn't believe it. It was too hard to imagine. But I should have rescued you from Josephine and Warren. It was beyond my wildest comprehension that they could have done the things I would later hear. I suppose that by the time I was aware of what was going on, it was just too late.

But I should have been there for you. I should have offered you a shoulder to cry on, an ear to listen to your pain. It all seems like a blur, but I know now how much you needed me, and how unforgivably absent I was. I will forever blame myself for leaving you to fend for yourself. Such a handsome young boy, you couldn't have been more than what? Seven? Eight?

The shame and self-hatred I feel can never be fully described. But if it's pain you want me to feel, then take solace in the fact that it's been with me for years, in my every waking moment.

It's over for me now, and I can only hope God is benevolent and understanding. For if he's not, then I will surely burn in hell for an eternity. Perhaps that's just. You will probably think so. My one regret now is that I was not able to say these words to your face.

I don't know where you are now, or how long it will take the authorities to finally get this note to you. But I trust that they will, and maybe after reading it, you can gather yourself together and go on with your life.

You have a great deal to offer this world, Scotty, and I can only pray that my reaching out has not come too late. I love you, and I will miss you. Good Luck!

All My Love,
Dad

The words seemed to leap off the page and into Chan's heart. For a moment he forgot that Severin Rybeck lay inches from him, soaked in a bath of blood and brain. My God! Chan was shocked to learn what secrets this man must have carried inside him all these years. In all the time he'd known him, Rybeck had only mentioned Scotty once. This letter seemed written by another man, not the one Chan knew. Could it be possible for a man to harbor such deep-rooted feelings for thirty years?

"Jesus Christ," Chan said softly. It was no wonder the man killed himself.

What Chan did not know, could not have known, was the impetus for the event: the emasculating, humiliating push from the height of the mountain, the peak whose air and view had provided Rybeck with his sole reason for living.

Chan rubbed his upper lip and mouth with the fingers of his left hand. "Shit," he said as the thought of a new job flitted through his mind. "What a fucking mess." He breathed deep, closed the door, and walked around to the driver's seat.

"New York State Police. What is your emergency?"

"Yes, I'd like to report a suicide."

"Where, sir?"

"In my car."

"In your car, sir?"

"Yes. In my car."

"Do you know the victim, sir?"

"Yes."

"What is the victim's name, sir?"

Chan had heard better suggestions. He was on a cell phone, which could by itself be overheard by a dozen different scanners. But when dispatch sent out word over the radio that Severin Rybeck had shot himself, Chan could envision droves of news-hungry, scanner-listening media vultures descending upon the scene.

"I'm sorry, ma'am," he said apologetically. "This is not a secured line. I can't give you that information over the phone."

"Sir?"

"You heard me. I can't give you that information over this line."

"Very well, sir. What is your location?"

Chan informed her where he was, got out of the car, and leaned against the trunk, awaiting a cruiser's arrival. He pulled a pack of cigarettes out of his jacket pocket, slapped it once against the butt of his palm, removed one, and lit it, tossing the match to the asphalt below. He tried not to smoke much but never seemed able to completely kick the habit. He didn't feel guilty. Not now. Stress always made Chan want a smoke. He figured this certainly qualified.

Thursday
September 12

BOTH THE MEDICAL examiner and the New York State Police homicide detective assigned to Rybeck's death concurred, and it was officially ruled a suicide shortly after the detective's conversation with Royston Craddock around 9:30 P.M. that night. Rybeck's body was bagged by the county coroner's office and unceremoniously transferred to the county morgue, where it would lie nude in a freezer with two dozen other lifeless bodies, waiting patiently to be placed in their final resting grounds.

Severin Rybeck the man would now speak louder than his words. He was left to meet his maker and attempt to justify his accomplishments, or lack thereof, on earth. Whatever opportunities he had been given to make his world a little better were now gone. Rybeck had just punched his time card for the last time, proving for the ten billionth time that in spite of it all, life marches on. No matter the power, no matter the wealth, when it's all said and done, the grass covers you just as sure—just as thick and green.

At Craddock's request, the New York State Police contacted Jake shortly after 7:30 A.M., informing him of Rybeck's ouster, his suicide, and the letter found on his computer. They agreed to fax it to his office, and Jake held it in his lap now as he sat at his desk, trying to ascertain its meaning. He knew Scotty was Rybeck's son. But *who* was he, and what made him tick? And what, if any, relationship did he have to this case? Who were Josephine and Warren, and what could they possibly have done to Rybeck's son that would cause such fury and dementia? Jake didn't know, but aimed to find out.

Ederling walked in, holding a large Styrofoam cup of iced coffee. "Mornin'," he said, tossing the keys to his Bronco on his desk. Jake had left a copy of the letter on his seat and watched as Ederling picked it up and began to read. "What the hell's this?"

148

"Morning. It seems our friend, Mr. Rybeck, saw fit to swallow a .45 last night. That there is his swan song."

Ederling looked at Jake, raising an eyebrow in a questioning slant. "No shit? He bought it? Seems a little out of character for someone who thought he owned the world."

Jake and Ederling had spoken at length about the board meeting on the drive home yesterday. They both knew it didn't look good for Rybeck. "Yeah, well, he didn't own the world last night," Jake said. "The board gave him the hook. Just couldn't deal with it, I guess."

Ederling sat down and sipped his coffee as he read. When he finished the note, he laid it on his desk and leaned back, clasping his hands behind his head. "Seems there was something else he couldn't deal with either."

"You just never know, do you?" Jake asked. "I mean, here was a guy with more money than God, who lived like Louis the Fourteenth, and he goes and blows his brains out."

Ederling shook his head. "All because he was without a job. Christ, if I won the lottery tomorrow, I'd be out of here in a heartbeat."

"Donny, I'm surprised at you," Jake added with mock amazement. "You mean you wouldn't keep on bagging crispy critters for the sake of society?"

"No, I'd leave that to you. Even though you hate it. It's what you live for . . . though for the life of me, I can't figure out why."

"Just goes to show you, Donny, things are seldom as they seem."

"You got *that* right," Ederling said, sitting up. "Well, we got to get a line on this Scotty."

"Sure do. Seems to me there's one place to start."

Ederling smiled. "Hello, Mrs. Rybeck?"

JAKE AND EDERLING did not know what to expect from Mrs. Lianne Rybeck on their second trip to the West View Estate. Given Rybeck's earlier comments regarding their relationship, they both thought it possible that she would not be distraught at the loss of her husband. But they didn't know what trail the money would take, or whether she would be forced to leave her palatial surroundings. They also thought it possible that Rybeck would not have left her a penny. More than anything, they reasoned, that could prove to be more rousing than her learning of her husband's death. But you just never know. If they had learned one thing in their many years on the job, it was that people are strange.

The two men went through the motions at the front gate, eventually pulling up to the pillared portico as instructed by the guard. They had called beforehand, and a woman was waiting for them outside, trimming a flower-box full of golden magnolias with yellow garden clippers. She wore a pair of white stretch pants and a light blue, long-sleeved Polo shirt rolled up at the sleeves. Her straw planter's hat shaded her aging face, and Jake could see she was wearing sunglasses. He guessed her at around sixty.

He pulled his Crown Victoria to the right and around through the portico facing the direction he'd come, stopping several yards from her. Ederling got out first, eyeing the woman ahead of him. Lianne had stopped trimming and stood, holding her shears at her side in her yellow-and-blue, flower-patterned gardening-gloved hand. The eyes give away so much, but with her sunglasses he really couldn't tell just what mood she was in. Jake closed his door with a firm thud and walked toward the woman he assumed to be Mrs. Severin Rybeck.

"Mrs. Rybeck?" Jake asked.

She nodded in polite acknowledgment.

"Good morning, ma'am. I am Chief Fire Marshal Jacob Ferguson. This here," he said with a slight motion of his right hand, "is Deputy Chief Donald Ederling. We're pleased to meet you."

Lianne smiled slightly. "Likewise, I'm sure."

Jake didn't know whether or not she cared, but kept with formality as a reflex. "Please accept our deepest regrets at the death of your husband, Mrs. Rybeck," he said perfunctorily.

She laid her clippers in the flower box. "It's going to be a beautiful day, gentlemen," she said, looking up toward the baby blue, already hazing sky. "Why don't we take a little walk around the grounds?"

Ederling shrugged slightly. "Works for me," Jake said. They followed her as she walked slowly down the turn of the drive toward the pool house. "This time of year is my favorite," she said, speaking to no one in particular. "Warm, humid, just the way I like it. Everything in full bloom. Thick and lush. Winter is so depressing for me. Everything dies."

Jake glanced at Ederling, then back to Lianne. *This should be fun.* "Not everything," he said, following a few steps behind.

She stopped, letting both men catch up. "True, Mr. Ferguson, but whatever doesn't die sleeps for several months. Nothing blooms, that much is for sure."

"Can't argue with you there, ma'am," Ederling said.

Neither man was in a rush to hurry the conversation along, not that either cared much for the horticultural merits of summer; but watching, listening to people at times like this can reveal a great deal. They were here to dig into Lianne Rybeck's past and dredge up what could well be very painful memories. Knowing whom they were dealing with would help make the transition more effortless when the time finally came. Jake and Ederling soaked in her every movement, her every word. They would move it along when necessary.

"You see those pines?" she asked, motioning to her left. "They were planted with this house when it was first built in 1898. I swear, they have looked exactly like that since the day we moved in."

"When was that, Mrs. Rybeck?" Ederling asked.

"Nineteen sixty-nine," came her immediate response.

Jake's lips turned. That was thirty years ago. It didn't quite fit with what he thought to be the facts. Rybeck had only been chairman of Morson Grayhead for ten years. While he may have been well paid before that, certainly he would not have had the resources to buy an estate of this magnitude prior to his relatively recent success with the firm. Granted, it didn't cost then what it would now, but then again, everyone was also paid in 1969 dollars back then.

Nineteen sixty-nine? That doesn't make any sense. "Ma'am?" he asked.

Lianne stopped and turned toward him. Jake could see she spent a good deal of time in the sun. Her face appeared slightly leathery—so common to sun worshipers—and yet it also seemed delicate, distinguishably tanned to a light caramel hue. Her narrow English nose seemed a perfect fit for West View. Jake desperately wanted to look into her eyes and almost asked her to remove her glasses, but refrained from the intrusion into her privacy.

She repeated herself. "I said we moved here in 1969."

"That was thirty years ago," Jake said, somewhat confused.

"You're good with math, I see, Mr. Ferguson."

One slight rub deserves another. Jake knew immediately that he and Ederling faced a formidable foe. "It's always harder for me when I have to resort to using my toes."

Mrs. Rybeck looked at him, as if sizing him up. "Is that a surprise to you, Mr. Ferguson? The fact that we moved here that long ago?"

"Uh, well, no . . . I mean . . . yes. It's just that your husband . . ."

"He *was* my husband, Mr. Rybeck."

No love lost here. "Excuse me, your ex-husband. It's just that my understanding was that he didn't become chairman of Morson Grayhead until the late eighties."

"That's correct. And? Your point is?"

Jake felt as if he were pulling teeth. "It's just that this is a rather expansive residence. Certainly not your average home." He motioned around with his arms. "I would assume, even then, it cost a pretty penny. I guess I'm wondering how much money your husband made prior to becoming chairman."

"He was always a successful man, Mr. Ferguson."

"Oh, no doubt, ma'am. It's just that . . ."

It was too painful for Ederling to watch. Just ask it, Jake, he thought. "I think what my partner's trying to ask, Mrs. Rybeck," Ederling chimed in, "is how was it possible for your husband to buy this house twenty years before becoming Morson Grayhead's chairman?"

"Is that what you were driving at, Mr. Ferguson?" Lianne asked with the slightest of grins.

"Yes," Jake answered, glancing defeatedly at Ederling.

She bent down to pull a dandelion from the lawn. "That's an easy one. He didn't buy it. I did."

Jake and Ederling both looked at each other. "*You* bought this estate, Mrs. Rybeck?" Jake blurted, immediately regretting his reaction.

"Are you hard of hearing, Mr. Ferguson? It appears that you came in here with a series of preconceived notions. Is that your normal investigative technique?"

What could he say? Jake inferred from Lianne's question exactly what she meant, and she was right. A good reality check is a healthy thing. "You'll have to forgive me, ma'am, if I thought your husband's wealth paid for this. I apologize for my presumption. I guess I just assumed that—"

"Yes," she interrupted. "And we know what happens when you assume, don't we?"

Ederling smiled. Jake wished they could start over again. After a brief silence she spoke again, this time in a softer tone. "I paid thirteen million dollars for this in 1969. It's worth a good deal more than that now, I would suspect."

"I would suspect," Ederling said.

Jake wanted to ask her directly where in the hell she had got that kind of money, especially back then. He chose a more diplomatic detour: "Would you care to explain the circumstances to us?"

She walked slowly down the slope of the lawn, stopping at a rectangular flower bed. "These damn aphids," she said, turning over a rosebush leaf. "I've tried everything, but I just can't get rid of them."

"Seems they like summer, too," Ederling added.

Lianne smiled at him. "Can't say as I blame them," she said, snapping off a dying bud. "Mr. Ferguson, other than idle curiosity, I can't see where learning the circumstances under which I purchased this home could have any bearing on your case. For that matter, I don't see where my husband's suicide does either."

Ah, the case. If ever there was an opening, this was it. "It's not quite that simple, Mrs. Rybeck. Mr. Ederling and I both work in the world of fire. There's usually two reasons people set them: revenge and money. And even then, you would be surprised how often they somehow interconnect. Now, please don't misunderstand, Mrs. Rybeck, it's not that we feel you have any connection to the case. It's just that we seldom go wrong when we follow the money. And we have done nothing but swim in it since all this started. Frankly, I guess you could say that when I hear someone has a good deal of it . . . let's just say it piques my interest."

"That may be so," she began, assuming a posture of superiority. "But I still don't see the connection." She waved her hand. "It doesn't matter. Hell, I don't give a hoot. If you spoke to Severin, then you are probably aware," she said as she ambled toward the putting green, "that he and I were hardly Ozzie and Harriet."

Neither man responded, and she stopped to look at them as if she would refuse to continue if that was news to them. "Yes," Jake answered. "Mr. Rybeck mentioned your marriage was more for show than anything else."

She laughed inwardly. "He was always so astute. Well, when we were both much younger, seniors in college actually, Severin and I had a brief, whirlwind fling. To my horror, I became pregnant." She removed her hat, wiping her forehead with the back of a glove. Jake could see she had pulled her flaxen hair back into a small bun. He figured she must dye her hair, for it was void of gray. "You must remember, gentlemen, this was back when that type of thing was still quite scandalous."

Both men nodded. Boy, how times had changed.

"So, anyway . . . you see, my family is descended from the original Himmertons."

That was a name Jake recognized. Like the Carnegies, the Rockefellers, the Mellons; every American had heard that name. "The *railroad* Himmertons?" he asked.

She nodded gravely.

Ederling let go a slow whistle.

"Exactly right, Mr. Ederling," she said as she crossed the green, removing a hickory-shafted Callaway putter from a bag on a stand at its side. She smacked a half dozen balls down the slope of the green and walked toward them, speaking louder now. "Forget the fact that I was pregnant. Just being involved in any romantic capacity with someone of Severin's stature was an unspeakable sin in my family's eyes."

Jake remembered his conversation with Rybeck on the patio the previous Sunday and thought he knew what she meant, but he'd had enough assuming for one day. "What do you mean by *stature*, ma'am?"

"That's the point," she said, eyeing a ten-footer. "He had none. He was from a lower-income, working-class family in the Bronx. I thought my father was going to have a heart attack. But I wasn't sure if he'd die from cardiac arrest or from humiliation."

Jake and Ederling stood on the edge of the green, watching as her putt traveled up the break and rolled to a stop just inches from the hole. "Nice putt," Ederling said.

"Thank you," she said, looking up. "A friend just gave me this Callaway, and I'm not sure I like it. I'm used to something heavier."

"I'm afraid I don't understand," Jake said. "I mean, it sounds to me like your family would have disinherited you rather than give you the money to buy this house."

Lianne laughed. "Oh, my father did, all right. He never spoke to me again. It was my mother who left me the money. You know the upper crust. They intermarry. Self-perpetuating superiority and all that crap. It's almost incestuous, really. Mom was a Theobald. You know, the banking family from Philadelphia?" Lianne let go another putt and cocked her head, urging it along with a slight push of the hip. It hit the edge of the cup and lipped out eighteen inches to the left.

A budding golfer, Ederling was impressed. "You can putt, Mrs. Rybeck."

"You're kind, but the greens are a little slow this morning. And trust me, with my short game, that's an advantage."

Jake gave Ederling a look.

"Hey," Ederling whispered. "The lady can putt."

Jake rolled his eyes. "So your mother is the one who left you the inheritance to buy all this?"

Lianne was hunched over another ball, remaining quiet as she eyed it. "Yes," she finally answered after her putter swung through the ball. "I was her only daughter, and we were always quite close. I really don't think she and my father had all that great a marriage either. More than anything, deep down, I think she just wanted me to be happy."

"Did she know of the strains in your marriage?" Jake asked.

"No. Thank God," she said, urging her putt on. "She died before things really went to hell in a handbasket."

Curplop.

"*That* was a nice putt," Ederling said.

"You golf, Mr. Ederling?"

"Oh, I'm a weekend warrior. But I don't think I'll ever have your stroke. I putt like a gorilla."

"Here," she said, walking toward him, holding out the Callaway. "This might help your game. It's too light for me, but it could be just what you need."

That putter had to be one hundred and fifty, maybe two hundred dollars. "Oh, no, I couldn't. Thank you anyway, but really, I can't. It'd be too small for me anyway."

"Then give it to your wife. I'm just going to give it to someone else. Please. I want you to have it."

Jake asked another question, and Ederling took the opportunity to snatch the club from her hands. "Thank you," he whispered.

"You're quite welcome. What was that again, Mr. Ferguson?"

"I asked why you bothered staying married when you had the resources to leave?"

"We had a son, Mr. Ferguson," she said, walking back to the bag on the other edge of the green. "A son needs a father."

Some father. Both men knew now was the time. They would never get closer than this. "Was Severin a good father, Mrs. Rybeck?" Jake asked.

She selected another putter and walked in their direction. "Gentlemen," she said, staring at them both, "Severin Rybeck was a lousy father. The word was not in his vocabulary. Maybe because he was always gone, I really don't know. But all I do know is he was no more a father to my son than I am a mother to yours."

"From the very beginning?" Ederling asked. "Or did he grow more distant over time?"

She leaned forward, both hands on her putter. "No. Actually, he was okay in the beginning. Not great, mind you, but okay. He'd help bathe him, read him bedtime stories, that kind of thing."

Jake and Ederling were in the fruited plain now. Jake hoped she would remain this open, but you just never knew when that one spoken word, that one probing question, would shut someone up like a touched clam. "When did it start to go downhill?" he asked.

"Coincidentally, about the time we moved here. He was named head of trading and became starstruck. I think from that moment on really, he could see nothing but the summit. It became his obsession."

"Any guess as to why?" Jake asked.

Mrs. Rybeck shrugged a shoulder. "I have a few. I think he was determined to make his parents proud. He loved them very much. Especially his mother. I also think it drove him wild that *I* was the one who bought this house. He became obsessed with proving that he could have done it himself, even if he didn't have to."

Jake needed clarification. "You mean, even though it was paid for, he wanted to be able to say he could have afforded it himself?"

"Precisely."

"Did he succeed?"

Lianne chuckled. "Yes, he did. That's what Florida was all about. You know about Florida, right?"

Both men nodded acknowledgment.

Jake knew from the New York State Police that she had not yet been shown the suicide letter. He could afford to play dumb for now. "What is your son's name?"

Mrs. Rybeck seemed to hesitate. "Scott Woodrow Theobald Rybeck. Everyone just *called* him Scotty."

"Called?" Ederling asked.

"Excuse me?"

"You said everyone just called him Scotty. Why past tense?"

There followed a long pause. Lianne walked to the hole in which she had just sunk her putt, reached down, and pulled out her ball. Jake could hear a slight breeze rustle through the pines and found himself focusing on its cooling sound rather than the unsettling silence on the green. He felt somewhat guilty playing this misleading game, but needed her unfettered thoughts. No one is more protective than a mother, and the less she was aware they knew, the better. At least for now. And anyway, they really didn't know much.

Lianne eyed a putt toward the farthest hole, down and away from the break this time. Both men watched in silence as the ball scooted four feet to the left. Ederling thought the miss rather telling.

"You don't know about Scotty?" she finally asked, looking up at them both.

"No," Jake said. "Your husband never mentioned him. Should we?"

They were clearly cutting to the quick now. She stood silent, removed her glasses and a glove, and wiped her eyes with her thumb and forefinger. Both men were silent. To speak now could forever close the floodgates. It doesn't take much.

"Scotty was the love of my life, gentlemen. I lived and breathed for that boy. He was so angelic. So handsome, smart, and full of life. I can remember just standing on that veranda," she said, motioning to a stone landing jutting out from the house above. "Just watching him play. He was so curious. There was nothing he wouldn't try."

As if golf seemed disgracefully superfluous now, she walked in silence over to her bag, pushed her putter in lightly, and walked down the green. "Let's walk, shall we?"

Both men broke into a slight jog, catching up to her just beyond the lower lip of the green. What they needed here was a probing question. Something to grease the skids.

"What happened?" Jake asked.

"Scotty worshiped his father," she began, walking to her left toward a tall row of sycamores. "He wanted so desperately to be loved by him, to be accepted by him. But Severin was possessed. Focused beyond all reason on

Morson Grayhead and his goddamned career. Scotty was probably around nine when Severin just stopped taking any interest in him at all. I mean *none*. No parent-teacher conferences, no baseball games, no father-son activities. If Scotty had died, I swear Severin wouldn't even have known it. And quite frankly, I can't say with certainty whether he would have cared."

"I'm sorry," Ederling said.

"That's all history now, I suppose. I tried to speak with Severin, but he was beyond saving. He would leave at six in the morning and not come home until well past ten. Sometimes midnight. He worked weekends and was always on the road."

"Why didn't you leave then?" Jake asked.

"This was my mother's gift to me, Mr. Ferguson. I couldn't walk on her grave by leaving it. I decided the best thing to do was to pretend as if Severin did not exist. Scotty and I talked about it. He understood, or so he said. I felt trapped. I loved him so much, but he was going to live without a father whether we stayed here or left. We opted to stay."

"I see," Jake responded. "Why didn't you just file for a divorce? Make Severin leave?"

"Good question, Mr. Ferguson. It was about this time that I took ill. Deathly ill. Somehow I contracted Hodgkin's disease, and nearly died. Its survival rate is quite high if properly treated, but I ignored it too long. By the time I underwent treatment, it took me almost a year to get back to normal. I very nearly didn't make it."

Jake could see this one coming. "Who cared for Scotty?"

Another long pause ensued. "You see these flower beds here," Lianne said, walking to a neatly manicured row of delicate yellow flowers. She knelt, playing with one in her hand. "These are called fluttermills. Some people call them Ozark sundrops. You can look and look and never see them out East. They're native to Oklahoma, I think. I always felt this section of the property needed something. For so long it was nothing more than long stretches of burnt grass. I thought it needed some life, so I once spent an entire summer out here. Kind of made it my project. I planted them myself. What do you think?"

"Nice," Ederling answered.

"Very," said Jake, desperately wishing to move forward.

More silence. They were painfully close now. Intuitively, both men knew it. They needed to probe carefully, not choking off the budding flower of truth and cleansing so aching to be free. But a long-buried secret can sometimes die in the light of day. Without communicating it, Jake and Ederling both knew it was vitally important to let it blossom at its own speed. They could wait. They had all day. Just an occasional, slight push was all that was needed now.

Lianne stood and walked a short way down the flower bed, kneeling over to smell a white rose, as if its soothing aroma somehow helped shield her from the memories. "It pained me so to not be there for him. To not be able to be his mother. I wanted so much to be there for my precious Scotty."

"Did something happen, Mrs. Rybeck?" Jake asked softly.

Lianne brought her right hand to her trembling mouth, staring deeply into the bed of roses and flowers. Her left arm crossed her bosom, clutching her elbow tightly to her side. The moment had arrived, the one Jake and Ederling had waited for. And, with the feeling you have as you cross the peak of the roller-coaster ride, just before beginning that gut-wrenching descent, they waited nervously for the free fall to begin.

It was obviously painful for Lianne, and Jake and Ederling both felt sorry for her. But an apparent madman was on the loose, and both men knew that, above all else, he *had* to be stopped. In the web of this hidden, sordid tale, the past had somehow become maniacally interwoven with the here and now, and unfortunately for Lianne Rybeck, the only way they could think to catch him was to revisit it.

"We hired a couple," she began timidly through a saliva bubble forming on her lips. "They seemed so nice, so caring. I thought having a man around the house would be good for Scotty. You know? Take him fishing, to baseball games, that sort of thing. God knows Severin wouldn't give him the time of day."

She wept openly now, removing her sunglasses and holding the tips of her fingers to her eyes. It was uncomfortable. Jake hardly knew this woman, yet she was clearly in need of consoling. He felt like offering a shoulder, wrapping his arm around her and telling her everything was going to be all right. But he didn't dare.

For a brief period Jake thought she might withdraw, shrivel up into her protective cocoon, never to reemerge. If she slammed shut now, they might never get the full story. Both men remained quiet, not wanting to appear cold or too self-focused, but they couldn't risk letting her psyche retreat. The risks were too large, the societal downside too unimaginable.

"Did they hurt Scotty?" Ederling asked.

That was all it took. "Yes! Yes!" she sobbed, ripping up a handful of flowers, throwing them through the air in vengeful anger. "Yes, they hurt him! Goddamn them! I pray, every day I pray they rot in hell. Especially her. And Severin can join them."

So it was out. The boulder had been pushed down the hill. All that was left now was to see how far it would roll.

"I knew something was wrong," Lianne continued weakly. "I could see Scotty beginning to withdraw. I tried to get him to speak with me, but I realize now how frightened he must have been. How frightened and confused. Scared of her and her threats, and scared of me being near death. He was just a little boy, left to fend for himself with those *monsters*. He never had a chance." She wept, her voice trailing off into a sob. "Never a chance."

Jake stepped over to her and touched her lightly on the shoulder. Maybe if she needed someone, anyone, she could read his sign. She turned slowly, her bloodshot, agonized eyes pleading with him for help. She grabbed him, as if clinging to a floating log in the rapids of a great and tumultuous river, darkening his light green shirt with her sobs and saliva. Slowly, Jake placed his arms around her, patting her back softly. Ederling looked in his eyes while Jake just shook his head.

For a long period no one spoke. Jake wasn't worried now that she would not continue. Pandora's box was open. What everyone needed now was just a little time to let the stench dissipate in the air.

"It's okay, ma'am," Jake finally said. "I reacted the same way when my wife died."

In time, she broke away, dabbing her eyes with balled tissue. She eyed Jake, her look emoting an unspoken bond between two people who have experienced unspeakable pain. "I'm sorry, Mr. Ferguson."

Jake waved a hand. "That was a long time ago, Mrs. Rybeck."

Ederling was surprised by Jake's admission. He had never heard Jake speak to anyone but him about Danny's death. Ever. Ederling thought that perhaps Jake was moving beyond it, that maybe there was hope for him after all. Even in the emotional turmoil surrounding him, Ederling couldn't help but wonder if Jake had called the redhead yet. He made a mental note to ask him on the drive back.

Lianne closed her eyes before continuing, as if the names were too painful to remember, even through time's haze. "I can picture them both as if they were standing here now," she said. "The Parks. Warren and Josephine Parks." Her body shook. Jake could see an almost visible repulsion fill the lines of her face. "Despicable human beings. I can't even think of them without feeling rage. Shortly after the fire, Warren left. It wasn't until sometime later, when I was much better, that I began to figure it all out. But by then I'm afraid the damage was done."

Jake and Ederling were both paralyzed, stunned to the point of shock. They both looked at each other, standing as if shot and waiting to fall. "The fire?" Jake asked, practically incredulous that they were learning of this only now. "What fire?"

"You don't know?" she asked, her eyes scanning Jake with quizzical uncertainty. "Years ago," she began, pointing to a spot on the property southwest of where they stood. "There used to be a separate guest quarters over by the large pines I showed you. It burned to the ground early one January morning. I think it was 1970, maybe '71. The firemen found Josephine inside, burned beyond recognition. I can only hope she died a long, slow, painful death."

Jake and Ederling stood motionless, listening to her relay the story. They could hardly believe their ears. It was almost too much. Something terrible had happened to the son of the chairman of the company whose executives' wives were systematically being burned alive, and they find out now the woman who was responsible had died in a similar manner. Why hadn't Severin said anything? Was it just too long ago for him to make any connection? It didn't matter now. They had hit the mother lode. And though they both knew a good deal of digging still remained, at least now they knew where to mark the X.

Jake couldn't help but wonder if either of the Rybecks had ever made a connection in their head. In the worst way he wanted to ask, but didn't want to risk putting her on the defensive. They might still need her. And he could only guess how angry she would be when she was eventually shown the suicide note. She would certainly realize then that both men had already seen it before their "fact-finding" visit here today.

"Did you ever learn what caused the fire?" Ederling asked.

She answered calmly, seemingly oblivious to the possible connection to this case. "Faulty wiring in the electric heater, I believe. Something like that."

Jake had seen that one before. Any arsonist worth his salt can make a fire look like an accident—especially an electrical fire. Jake knew that recent research suggested that while electrical fires do occur, they do so with far less regularity than was previously believed to be the case. An untrained, tired, or lazy fire investigator can make a cursory visual inspection of the point of origin and easily mislabel an accelerated fire as electrical in nature.

He knew it was just a dream, but still, Jake wished like hell he could get his hands on that heater. He knew a copper conductor discolors in a fire, but also knew that scraping the conductor's surface could tell him the source of the heat. They generally turn cherry red in the heat of a blaze, but only on the outside if the source was external. It would be uniformly discolored throughout if the source was internal. His sixth sense whispered in his ear that it was a good bet the conductor on that heater was copper-colored underneath.

A lot had changed in twenty-five years, both technologically and procedurally. It was too long ago for him to know who it might have been, but he couldn't help but wonder if the investigator at that time was any good or if he'd had any lingering doubts. Jake would have to check the microfiche to find his name. If he wasn't already dead, maybe he could tell him something. Jake did some quick math in his head. He guessed whoever held his post back then was

probably forty to fifty. Something in that range. That would put him somewhere around sixty-five to seventy-five today. It was possible. He'd have to follow it up. Maybe there'd be something about the case that had stuck in the
investigator's memory.

Lianne had a strange look in her eyes. Jake could see that something
strange had just clicked. "What is it, Mrs. Rybeck?"

"Oh, nothing. It's not important."

Jake had heard that before, too. Enough to know that it was often not the
case. "Go on. Please."

"Well . . . it's just that I remember the day after the fire, after all the firemen and investigators had left. I remember I saw Warren putting that heater
in the trunk of his car."

Jake and Ederling caught each other's eyes. "Are you sure, ma'am?"
Ederling asked.

"Oh, yes," she said, nodding her head vigorously. "I'm *very* sure. I remember thinking how strange it was. How warped and melted it looked. I
remember thinking he must have wanted it as some kind of memento, although
I couldn't figure out for the life of me why a man would want a keepsake of the
cause of his wife's death."

"Did you report it to anyone?" Jake asked.

"No. I guess I didn't think it was that important. Odd, but not important."

"Do you know where Mr. Parks is now, Mrs. Rybeck?" Jake asked.

"No, I don't. I even hired a private investigator to find him. I wanted to
press child abuse charges. But he left no trail."

Jake moved cautiously, aware they were not yet out of the emotional
woods. "I know this is difficult, Mrs. Rybeck, but what did Mr. and Mrs.
Parks do to Scotty?"

She held her hands over her mouth, her eyes staring straight ahead in a
catatonic trance. "Josephine was emotionally abusive. Always telling Scotty
how useless he was, how his father was right to ignore him, that he would
never amount to anything. They brainwashed him into thinking he was
nothing, then offered him hope through their own twisted religious beliefs."

"Twisted?" Jake asked, bewildered. "In what way?"

"The Parks claimed to be devil worshipers, Mr. Ferguson. I don't know if
they really believed in it or just used it as a means to satisfy their cruel and per-
verse natures. But Scotty was impressionable. And with their almost unlimited
access to him, he made an easy mark. Scotty became a willing devotee, partici-
pating in satanic rituals, sacrifices, the works. Scotty was never the same after
they finished with him. I got him professional help, but I'm afraid the scars
from his father, the deep-seated inferiority, ran too deep. He seemed to go

downhill quickly after that." Lianne paused, pushing back tears, as if the very thought seared her insides. "He suffered some type of breakdown. No one ever did adequately explain it . . . or certainly not to my satisfaction. But he seemed to regress back to early childhood, as if somehow, living in his earlier years would protect him. He was fifteen when we had him institutionalized for the first time. There would be many more to follow. Severin was the only person capable of saving him at the time. I was incapacitated, but he wasn't. He should have known. He should have cared." Tears streamed from her eyes. "I never forgave him."

"I'm sorry, Mrs. Rybeck. It must be a horrible burden to live with," Jake said.

"Yes," she said, removing her sunglasses and looking him in the eyes. "Well, we all have our crosses to bear, don't we, Mr. Ferguson?"

Jake nodded slightly. *If you only knew.* "Mrs. Rybeck, do you know where Scotty is? Have you heard from him recently?"

Her eyes narrowed. "Why? You don't think Scotty has anything to do with these burnings, do you? He's been through enough, Mr. Ferguson. Please. I beg you. Just leave him alone."

Jake toyed with the idea of listing the many reasons why they would want to talk to her son—not the least of which was that, right now, he made for one hell of a suspect. "We just want to speak with him, Mrs. Rybeck. We have no choice but to pursue every angle. Do you know where Scotty is?"

Lianne had betrayed her son once before. She would never do it again. Not if she could prevent it. "No," she lied. "I have no idea where he is."

Both men thought she might be lying, but you can't prove a negative. "If you should happen to hear from him," Jake said, handing her his card, "please let me know. It's important, Mrs. Rybeck."

She took the card and stuffed it in a back pocket without looking at it. "I will."

Jake inwardly frowned. There it was again, that sixth sense. *Why am I not convinced?*

EDERLING WAITED UNTIL they had left the compound before speaking. He thought maybe he was being a touch paranoid, but still wasn't sure just how powerful any listening devices on the grounds might be. If the technology exists for the CIA to listen to conversations in an enclosed room a half mile away . . . with all the money that surrounded them, he just thought it wise to play it safe. "She's lying, Jake. She knows where Scotty is," he said as the guardhouse grew smaller in the rearview mirror.

"I know."

"You think it's him?"

They had spent over two hours at West View, and Jake's stomach growled from hunger. He was thinking of food as he slowed at a four-way stop, turning left onto Route 22. "Donny, this whole thing has me confused now. We're starting to get more moving parts than an F-16, and right now I'm not sure which way is up."

Ederling rolled down his window, spitting forcefully to the moving ground below. "I know," he said, rolling the window back up. "Usually, you follow the money, you catch your perp. But this, Jake . . . this whole thing is drowning in dough. All these people got more cash than they know what to do with. It just can't be the money."

"Maybe. But in this whole equation, who's the one person not rolling in it?"

"Well, I'm guessing she keeps Scotty supplied with what he needs. Parks is the one name I can think of."

"Yesiree, Don. Just for kicks, let's run Mr. Warren Parks through NCIC, also VICAP. You never know what might turn up."

The National Crime Information Computer and Violent Criminal Apprehension Program are central-clearinghouse computer data banks run by the FBI. If someone's been up to no good, and the cops have become involved in any way, one of them has it on file.

"We also need a psychological assessment of who we're dealing with here, Don. This thing's gotten too complicated. When we get back, I want you to contact Quantico. See if you can get ISU to work us up a profile on our torch."

The FBI's Investigative Support Unit is part of the larger National Center for the Analysis of Violent Crime at the Academy in Quantico, Virginia. Among ISU's many departments is the Arson and Bombing Investigative Services Subunit. They offer special services to law enforcement, from crime analysis to description of offender characteristics, known as profiles. They also offer helpful insights into investigative strategy and interviewing techniques, search-warrant information, prosecutive strategy, and help in expert-witness testimony.

Jake had used them on more than one occasion. ISU can be helpful in narrowing the number of most-probable suspects, refocusing an investigation that's dying on the vine, or reducing investigative man-hours. Both he and Ederling were all for anything that would help cut back their hours. Not that they were lazy, but even *they* needed to sleep.

"I also think we'd be smart to follow through on who might be making out on the demise of Grayhead's stock," Jake said. "Something keeps telling me we shouldn't drop that angle just yet."

"You're the man," Ederling said. "You want to run Scotty, too?"

Jake looked at his friend. "You bet your ass."

J AKE AND EDERLING caught a quick drive-through lunch at Roy Rogers, wolfing it down on their way back to the office. Both men carried their large colas in with them and placed them on their desks as they settled in for a day's work on the phones. Jake had been through enough arson investigations to already know much of what ISU might have to offer a greener professional.

In cases such as this it is not uncommon for investigators to turn to the FBI's ISU. If the shit really hit the fan, Jake knew that he could always turn to the Bureau of Alcohol, Tobacco, and Firearms. But even then, the ATF's services were more of a scene-by-scene consultative nature. For the most part, cases like the one in which Jake found himself embroiled are handled the hard way— interjurisdictional cooperation, all sides gumshoeing it every inch of the way. And maybe it was Jake's ego, or just his confidence in himself and his team, but whatever the cause, Jake knew he and his people could go this one alone. Still, he thought a cursory review of the FBI's findings might prove helpful.

He swiveled in his chair, opened a crammed file cabinet, and thumbed through his dog-eared, alphabetized Pendaflex folders. Jake knew he kept a copy of ISU's Arson Criminal Investigative Analysis somewhere in there. He looked first under the *C*'s, then the *A*'s, and finally hit pay dirt with the *I*'s. He pulled out a file entitled *"The Serial Firesetter,"* with the Department of Justice, Federal Bureau of Investigation seal on the front and laid it on his desk. It was a relatively thin photocopy, one he'd kept from a conference he'd attended in Quantico a few years back. Jake creased the title page over and began reading.

A few minutes passed as he flipped pages, glancing at various chapter titles and subheadings. He didn't bother reading the text, but knew he'd pulled out the right report when he saw covered subjects as varied as Geography of Arson, NCAVC Arson Analysis Requirements, Temporal Analysis, Criminal Investigative Analysis Program, Uses of Criminal Profiling, and Crime Scene Assessment.

"Donny, come here for a second, will you?" Jake said, looking up.

Ederling walked over and stood behind him. "What'ya got?"

"Remember when you played football? How every once in a while your coach would make both lines block and tackle until you puked? No plays, no films. Just the basics."

"Don't make me think about it. I hated those practices. It was usually punishment for some game we should have won but somehow fucked up."

"Well, I think it's time *we* got back to basics. I just pulled out this ISU arson analysis and thought it might not hurt either one of us to review it. Here, follow me," Jake said, walking over to a round table in the corner of the office. He slid the report across the table to Ederling, tapping his forefinger on the top part of a page. "Read that."

Ederling's eyes moved back and forth as he read to himself for a moment. "Yeah? So what?" he asked, not comprehending its importance. "This is Arson Investigation 101, Jake."

"I know, but placate me. Sometimes we tend to get too wrapped up in the larger picture. I think this will help us. It lists a motive-based offender analysis, right?"

Ederling glanced down at the paper in front of him. "Yeah."

"We already think we know those, right?" Jake asked, crossing the calves of his legs over the corner of the table.

"Right."

"Read them to me anyway."

Ederling gave him a we-don't-have-anything-better-to-do? look, then found his spot on the page. "It lists six motives most commonly linked to arson: crime concealment, profit, extremism, vandalism, excitement, and revenge. They've subgrouped four categories under revenge: individual, group, institution, and society in general."

"What else?" Jake asked.

"They list two other motive considerations." Ederling leaned back in his chair, pulling the sheet of paper onto his lap. "Power: 'the ability or capacity to exercise control over another person.' "

"Or a fire department," Jake interjected. "Sometimes they feel powerful just calling them out of bed in the middle of the night. It gives them a hard-on to look at all those flashing lights and all that apparatus, knowing it's all because of them."

"Right. It's the same thing if you ask me. It's still power over someone or a group of people."

"Okay, go on. What else?"

"Then they list pyromania. They say it's 'a diagnosis in search of a disorder. An irresistible impulse or an impulse not resisted.' "

Jake sipped his soda. "They list characteristics there?"

Ederling turned the page over, scanning for an answer. "Why do I get the sense you already know the answers to all these questions?"

"Lighten up. This isn't going to kill us."

"You're telling *me* to lighten up? Shit, Jake, I couldn't pull a needle out of your ass with a tractor. Hey, that reminds me. You call that redhead yet?"

Jake hesitated. "No."

Ederling eyed him disapprovingly. "You promised, Jake."

"Donny . . . I'll call her. Promise. I want to. Really, I do. But it would help if I could find the time to brush my teeth."

Ederling looked at Jake with disbelieving eyes while Jake parried back, serving up a read-the-paper look. "All right, all right," Ederling said. "Yes, they list characteristics under two categories: the organized arsonist, and the disorganized arsonist."

"Do they list crime-scene indicators?"

"Yes. But we already know our guy's organized."

"I know. But this will clarify things for us. I think it will get us back on track."

"Well, it says here that indicators of an organized arsonist are the device used, preparation for the act, ignition location, severity of the fire planned, effort required for access, and unlimited mobility."

"Any behavioral characteristics?"

The analysis was in outline form, and the list ended halfway through the second page. Ederling lifted the sheet to see if it continued before reading, " 'A conscious indifference to society, egocentric, manipulative, methodical and cunning, lives some distance from the scene, and has a chameleon personality.' "

Jake dropped his legs to the floor, laying both forearms across the table, cupping his soda in both hands. "All right, what about the disorganized arsonist?"

"Disorganized," Ederling repeated, tucking the previous sheet under his thumb. "Disorganized arsonist. Says here that indicators are 'impulsive, open flame, random targets, use of whatever accelerants are available, severity of fire unplanned, crime scene readily accessible, and limited mobility.' "

"And the behavior?"

" 'Loner, feels rejected.' " Ederling stopped at that and looked at Jake, catching a broad smile across his partner's face. " 'Has few friends, lacks cunning, sets fires near home, nocturnal, may abuse alcohol or drugs.' "

"We're almost done, Don. What's it say about spatial analysis?"

Ederling turned a few pages. "Let's see, spatial analysis, spatial analysis. Here we go. Spatial analysis. It says that 'serial arsonists who set fires within the same geographic area are said to form a cluster of activity. Finding the geographic center often reveals where the offender lives, works, or frequents. A cluster center that moves often indicates the offender has either changed residence or workplace. If the cluster center does not significantly move, the offender likely has not changed job or residence.' "

"This case is odd, Donny. I mean, we clearly have the markings of an organized arsonist. His preparation is pronounced, the ignition location is always the same, and the severity of the fires is clearly planned."

"Tell me something I don't know."

"Okay, how about this for starters. The behavioral characteristics aren't in sync. I mean, our scene indicators clearly point to an organized individual. We seem to have a cluster. They're always the same, always thought out. But if it's Scotty, I have to believe his behavioral characteristics are exactly the opposite. I think we can safely assume he's no egomaniac. He fits the disorganized profile much better. No friends, feels rejected, loner. The two just don't jibe. Something doesn't fit. The entire MO seems to fit Warren much better."

Ederling laid the report down on the table. "Yeah, but arson appears to be the means, not the end in this case, Jake. There's more to this picture than just fire. There's the rapes, the immolation, the possible attempt to bring Morson Grayhead down. This circle's much wider than that."

Jake needed something of Scotty's for DNA comparison. He wished he could just ask Lianne for a lock of his baby hair, but knew that even *if* she complied, it would prove futile without a follicle. It's the hair follicle from which DNA results can be obtained. Hair clippings are useless. "Donny, make a note to call Mrs. Rybeck and see if she has a brush or a comb. Something that would have Scotty's hair in it. I'll call the ME and see if we can move those DNA test results up."

"She's not going to give us anything of his, Jake. You saw how she protected that boy. We'll be pissing in the wind."

"Maybe, maybe not. Tell her it just might exonerate him. Make her sweat it out. It'd be a shame if we arrested him and she had the evidence that could free her son. Maybe she'll see the light."

"Okay, but why on earth would she still have a brush of his? He hasn't lived there in years."

Jake shrugged slightly. "You just never know, Don. Mothers save the strangest things."

"Just for the hell of it, let's assume she has one," Ederling said, playing along, "and by the way, I think we got a better chance of winning the lottery. But if I call and ask her for a brush or comb, and she refuses, seems to me we just gave her a heads up what to throw out. Wouldn't you rather get a warrant and search the premises ourselves?"

"And do what, Don? Confiscate every brush and comb we find? How will we possibly know whose is whose? No, I don't want to make it acrimonious. Not unless we have to. Anyway, if she does have one tucked away, it's probably in a box somewhere in the attic. We'd be days in there. We might luck out, Don. Maybe she'll swallow the exoneration thing. Just try it. We have nothing to lose."

"Done," Ederling said, scribbling something in his notebook.

"So what have we got?" Jake asked, rising from his chair and walking to a map of Westchester County pinned on the wall behind the table. He pointed to three bright red thumbtacks they had previously stuck in the locations of the three fires to date. "We got Scarsdale, Mount Kisco, and now Rye. That's a pretty tight circle, wouldn't you say?"

Ederling did a half-nod, half-shake of his head, moving his shoulders back and forth. "Kind of. Mount Kisco is a little off the beaten path."

"True. But it's a shitload closer than Hoboken." Jake circled a finger in the vicinity between the three tacks. "What do you want to bet our man lives somewhere in here?"

"I don't know, Jake. The spatial thing doesn't work for me here. I mean, this isn't just some thrill seeker. These cases are related."

"Maybe. But he also hasn't hit anyone in Jersey or New York. I agree the spatial analysis viewpoint needs to be considered differently, but still, I think it fits."

After their meeting with Lianne Rybeck, Jake now thought they knew whom they might be looking for. He wasn't ready to make an arrest yet, but knew the suspect list had just narrowed considerably. "Check the local post offices, Don. See if you can find a Warren Parks or a Scotty Rybeck. I got a good feeling about this. In the meantime, I'm going to get in touch with a friend in Philadelphia. If we're lucky, I think we can get him to do the legwork at the Exchange."

"Okay," Ederling said with an intonation indicating he had plenty of work to do. "I'll be back to you as soon as I can. Oh, and, Jake . . ."

"What?"

"Don't forget to call the redhead."

Jake rolled his eyes. "Just start checking."

A BURNING PASSION

Book III

J AKE HAD ATTENDED many conferences over the years. They were useful on a number of fronts, not least of which was the ability they afforded him to network. He had befriended a counterpart in Philadelphia over the past few years and now drummed through the *M*'s in his Rolodex, searching for his card. He figured he would have to leave a message and was pleasantly surprised when he found him in.

"Jake Ferguson. How the hell are ya, old buddy?" Cesar Machigonne asked.

"Holding my own, Cesar. How are things in the big city?"

"Oh, you know how it goes, Jake. Never ends."

"Tell me about it. Look, Cesar . . . I figure you know I'm not calling to check on the weather down there."

"No shit?" Machigonne asked with mock surprise.

"Listen, I'm in a hell of a mess up here. I got some psycho torching the wives of the top executives at one of the largest brokerage houses on Wall Street. I need your help."

Cesar let go a whistle. "The Grayhead thing's yours? I've been reading about that one. Man, now *that's* messy."

"*Messy* ain't the word for it. This thing's so tangled I'd rather reconstruct a scrambled egg."

"Ouch. What d'ya need, Jake? Just say the word."

"Is the Philadelphia Exchange in your jurisdiction?"

"Sure is. I was down there just last week."

"I'm trying to track down a money angle—"

"There's a surprise," Machigonne interrupted.

"Right. So, anyway, Morson Grayhead's options trade on the Philadelphia Exchange, and I was hoping rather than jump through all the hoops having our DA call your DA, the court route, and all that crap, it might be quicker if you could subpoena their records for me."

"That's it? Shit, Jake, that's a snap. I can have that done by tomorrow."

Jake had worried he might have to run all the paperwork himself. He was relieved Cesar could do it so quickly, and even more so that it was apparently not a big deal. Not that Cesar would have told him if it was. "That's beautiful, Cesar. You're a good man."

"Tell that to my wife."

Jake laughed. "Listen, the way it works is this. They won't have a record of every individual who owns those things. I just need a list of all the financial institutions that have positions in them. I can handle the rest from here."

"I thought you were going to ask me something big. Consider it done. When do you need them?"

"Yesterday," they both answered in unison.

"Overnight them, right?" Machigonne asked.

"Same day if possible."

Jake thanked his colleague, reminding him not to hesitate if he ever needed the favor returned. That's how it works. He pressed the cradle down with his finger and dialed Morson Grayhead in New York. Jake wouldn't know the new chairman if he bumped into him in an elevator, but he did know Royston Craddock.

"Jake, a pleasure to hear your voice," Craddock said. "The State Police contacted you, I assume?"

"Yes."

"A damn shame, huh? I never thought Severin would end it like that."

Jake was hardly full of remorse. "Yeah, well, life's full of surprises, isn't it? You just never know what makes someone tick. Do your employees know yet?"

"No, not yet. Or, at least, not officially. I'm sure they've all heard about it one way or another by now. I've scheduled a meeting this afternoon to discuss the proper way to deliver the news on a corporate level. We want to put the best spin possible on it. Any suggestions?"

Death was part of Jake's job. There is never an easy way to say it. "Not really, Roy. Honesty is your best bet. I guess if I could tell you one thing, it would be not to lie. Trust me. It's not worth it."

"All right. That's good advice. Thank you," Craddock said, genuinely appreciative. "You know, I was going to call you, but as you might imagine, it's been somewhat of a madhouse down here. I wanted to thank you for your help yesterday. I know it was a difficult position to put you in."

"Not really. It was the right thing to do."

"I hope you aren't feeling any guilt about Severin's suicide. It really had nothing to do with you."

Jake thought back to the meeting and his tape recorder and wasn't sure he agreed. But he didn't really care. "Mr. Craddock, I'd feel guilty if I'd pulled the trigger. But I didn't. Guilt is the last thing I'm feeling right now."

Craddock seemed relieved. "Good, that makes me feel better. So, what can I do for you?"

"I need two things, Roy. First, I'm assuming that by now Morson Grayhead is taking proactive steps to assure your remaining employees' and their families' safety."

"Absolutely. Although at this point, I'm afraid it's a bit late. Most everyone has vacated their residences by now. Some have gone to live with family. Others have left on vacation. I think a few have gone to their summer homes. We are working with a national security firm as we speak, arranging protection for each one of them, regardless of location. If they want it, of course."

"Of course. Has anyone refused?" Jake asked.

"Don't know yet. We're still working out the specs. It's become a logistical nightmare. We've got people as far away as New Mexico. I'll tell you, if your boy meant to wreak havoc at this firm, he's certainly done that."

Jake scribbled concentric circles on his desk calendar. "Roy, I need a list of everyone's whereabouts. I need to inform my counterparts of the possible danger in their jurisdictions and what to look for in case something should happen."

"I'll speak to our security people and have them fax it to you."

Cooperation! This is how it should have been from the very beginning. It was a welcome change, to say the least. "Thank you."

"No problem. You said there were two things. What else do you need?"

"I need your help, Roy. Severin promised me the manpower I needed to track down the owners of your firm's options. I'm having the Philadelphia Exchange send up records of all the financial institutions that have positions in them. What I need is help in tracking down individual owners. Can your people do that?"

"Absolutely. Under the auspices of your office, of course. It may take a little while, though. With all that's been going on, the open interest on some of them has grown exponentially."

Rybeck had explained that term, but Jake wanted to hear it again. "Explain open interest again for me, please."

"Open interest," Craddock repeated. "That's the number of contracts outstanding on any given strike price and expiration date on a given stock option series."

Jake still wasn't sure he understood the concept as clearly as he'd like, but it didn't matter—not as long as he didn't have to track them down. "Oh . . . well, as long as you can get me a list of owners, and preferably the date they were purchased. I'm not so sure we have much interest in people who have taken positions subsequent to the Borman fire."

"I understand. You're looking for front-runners."

Jake scratched his head. "Sounds right . . . I think. What's a front-runner?"

"In our business, Jake, a front-runner is someone who has taken a position ahead of publicly disseminated news. Insider trading and all that."

Insider trading. That was one term Jake was familiar with. "Well, I'll tell you this much. If our man's been buying options ahead of his burnings, I think we may have just given the definition new meaning."

"You get me those files, Jake, and we'll get you a list of people that own them. I'll make sure we put as many people on it as it takes. This is beyond business. It's personal."

Tell me about it. "I understand the feeling. I'll call you when I have them. Can you send up a courier when they arrive?"

"Absolutely."

"Thank you, Roy. You'll be hearing from me."

Jake and Ederling were cooking now. Jake always felt energized when an investigation began to gel. There was that extra spurt of adrenaline in his veins when all the digging, research, and interviews began to form the outline of a picture. Jake looked over at Donny and could see he was working the phone as aggressively as he. Something was about to break. He could feel it.

The woman in charge at Executive Travel had been out of town yesterday when Jake visited their offices, but had called his office while he and Ederling were out. He looked at the number his secretary had left on a pink message slip and noticed it ended in 6148. *Must be a direct line.* Jake dialed it, sipping the last of his soda, slurping it to the last drop.

"I teach my kids not to do that," Ederling said, cupping his hand over the receiver.

"Sorry."

Jake was aware of a slight quiver in his belly as he listened to the phone ring. She picked up on the third ring. "Good afternoon, Lisa Shuman speaking. May I help you?"

This was his lucky day. He was getting through to everyone. *Sometimes it just all comes together.* "Good afternoon, Ms. Shuman. My name is Jake Ferguson. I am the chief fire marshal for Westchester County. I stopped by your office yesterday, but they informed me you were away on business."

"Yes, Mr. Ferguson. We had a district meeting in Boston. I called you first thing this morning when I got in, but you were out. What seems to be the problem?"

Jake always preferred these types of discussions in person, but that wasn't possible right now. Not unless he wanted to blow the rest of the day making the trip. He didn't dare. He was on a roll.

"I have some questions for you pertaining to the Morson Grayhead case. Do you have a few moments?"

Jake could sense her unease. "Yes," she answered warily.

"Good. First, let me begin by saying that the nature of our conversation today could be sensitive and may very well be a matter of life and death. I don't wish to alarm you, ma'am . . . but I do need to stress the need for absolute secrecy. Understood?"

Those are words few people ever hear. They certainly got her attention. "Of course, Mr. Ferguson. You have my word that whatever we discuss stays between the two of us."

"Good. Ms. Shuman, as you are no doubt aware, someone has been murdering the wives of Morson Grayhead's top executives—"

"Oh, I know, it's tragic. It's all so horrible."

"Ms. Shuman, who handles travel arrangements for Morson Grayhead's top executives? Are they just serviced at random when they call in, or are they handled separately?"

"Oh, no," she said, obvious pride in her voice. "Morson Grayhead's executives are handled exclusively by a team of two. It was part of our contract. The two of them arrange every detail of every trip for twenty-four, maybe twenty-five executives."

"What do you mean by 'every detail'?"

"We're talking about an extraordinarily busy group of people, Mr. Ferguson. They travel the world over. I figure we've got half of them on the road at any given time. And as you probably know, they never travel in groups larger than two, so that only acts to increase the workload."

That was news to Jake. "Why is that?"

"Oh, it's precautionary, really. You know? In case the plane goes down."

I'll be damned. "Oh."

"So, anyway, there are car rentals, limousines, private charters, hotel reservations, special needs. You know? Kosher meals, low fat, low salt. That type of thing. One of them is a paraplegic, and as you might imagine, that requires a great deal of special arrangement. We are responsible for all passport and visa requirements, foreign-currency conversions, cargo-transport needs. The list is quite extensive, really."

Jesus Christ. I thought you were just a corporate travel service. Jake was surprised at the length of her list. He didn't travel much, and when he did, it always entailed hopping a coach seat and grabbing a taxi when he landed. Like so much in life, you just don't know what you don't know. "Two people do all of that?"

"Yes, sir. And they do it quite well, if I do say so myself."

"Are their terminals linked? I mean, are they capable of knowing what the other has booked?"

"Oh, yes. That's a necessity for obvious reasons. Illness, vacations, coffee breaks. Each one has to have the capability of covering for the other in their absence."

"Can you tell me their names, Ms. Shuman?"

"Of course. Warren started his vacation on Monday. Betty Herman has taken his place while he's out. The other is Missy Ringdorf."

Bells and whistles screamed in Jake's head. His stomach tightened as he sat up on the edge of his chair, snapping his fingers for Donny to listen up. "Warren?" he asked, looking up at Ederling. "What is Warren's last name, Ms. Shuman?"

"Josephs. Warren Josephs."

Josephs? At first Jake felt a numbing disappointment, but then the connection kicked in. *Could it be possible?* He repeated the words in his head. *Josephs. Josephs. Josephine? It just couldn't be.* He believed in luck, both good and bad, but couldn't allow himself to think he would be *this* lucky. "How long will Mr. Josephs be out?"

"Two weeks."

"Ms. Shuman, I remind you again, ma'am, you *must* keep the contents of this conversation private. I simply can't stress to you how important it is that you not repeat this to anyone."

"I understand, Mr. Ferguson."

I hope so. One false move could send Warren Josephs on a one-way sightseeing trip to Brazil. "Let me ask you this, Ms. Shuman. When you hire, do you fingerprint or photograph your employees?"

"We don't fingerprint, but we do drug-test and photograph."

Ederling sat crossways on the edge of Jake's desk now, listening intently to his side of the conversation. "You photograph? Do you have a copy of Mr. Josephs on file that we might have? Perhaps a negative?"

Lisa Shuman was not sure what was going on, but knew this conversation had just taken a threatening turn for the worse. As if snapping out of a coma, she was suddenly aware of the serious nature of Jake's questions and their horrible, inconceivable implications. Without warning or explanation, her willingness to cooperate was abruptly replaced by fear.

She stuttered a little at first. "Mr. Ferguson," she answered slowly, "I think you need to speak to my superior, sir. I don't know the answer to your question, nor do I think I have the authority to release it if I did." She wanted desperately now to get Jake off the phone. "I can transfer you to him if you'd like."

Shit! Jake was painfully aware that he'd lost her now. He knew he'd pushed her too hard, jumping all over this Josephs thing too quickly. If anyone could conduct a good interview, it was Jake, and now, without thinking about it, he had just broken every rule in the book. *Slow down, boy. It will come.* He berated himself for not requesting everyone's picture and made a mental note never to make this mistake again. *Oh, well. All good-luck streaks eventually come to an end.*

"Yes, please," Jake said. "I would appreciate that. What is his name?"

"Frank Warrington. Would you like me to connect you?"

"Please."

Jake jotted down Warrington's name, informing Ederling of what had just transpired while Muzak played in his ear. Ederling was in the middle of a question when Jake stopped him with a forefinger in the air.

"Yes, my name is Jake Ferguson. I am the . . ."

Jake relayed the pertinent information to the secretary on the other line, eventually requesting to speak to Warrington. He knew his streak was dead for sure when she informed him that Warrington was in Chicago and would not be returning until Friday. Jake explained the nature of his previous conversation and the purpose of his call, telling the secretary it was a law enforcement emergency and could she please try to contact Warrington. Friday was too late.

She took Jake's name and number, promising to attempt to locate her boss and have him call as soon as possible. Jake asked if anyone else was available who was authorized to make the decision he needed, but was informed the entire executive staff was holed up in Chicago.

"All right then, please have Mr. Warrington call me immediately, ma'am. It's urgent."

"I understand, sir. I promise."

"Thank you," Jake said, hanging up. "Dammit! We were *this* close," he said to Ederling, holding his thumb and forefinger a half inch apart.

"What happened?" Ederling asked.

Jake picked the corner of an eye with his pinkie finger. "Oh, I had a brain fart and pushed some gal too hard. She got cold feet and pushed me on up the line. All the bigwigs are in Chicago and won't be back until Friday."

"Did I hear you right? Did she say they have photographs?"

"Yep, and they drug-test, too."

"Too bad we can't get DNA from urine."

"I know we're close, Don. I can feel it. I don't know what this guy's angle is, but I know he's involved. In one capacity or another, this Warren asshole's as dirty as mud. We get our hands on him, and I know we can break this case wide open."

"Why don't we just go down and pick him up?"

"He's on vacation. Won't be back for a couple of weeks."

"That's convenient," Ederling said, scooting off Jake's desk and walking over to his to pick something up.

"Yeah, it's convenient all right. I wanted to ask her where the guy lives. But you know if she gets a bug up her butt over some picture, there ain't no way she's going to give me his address."

"Safe bet." Ederling tossed a piece of paper on Jake's desk. "We got two Parks. No Rybecks."

Jake seemed lost in thought. "Something else."

"What?"

"If this *is* our Warren, he's got a new last name. Seems he changed it to Josephs."

Ederling squinted his eyes slightly, trying to make the connection. Finally it clicked. "As in Josephine?"

"As in. Be sure to check the name Josephs with post offices, too."

"Man, do we have shit to do."

There's an understatement. "About fucking time."

JAKE OPENED THE door to his co-op at 7:12 P.M. He unbuttoned his shirt and slung it over a chair, walking directly to his air conditioner. On the ride home the weatherman said a front would be moving through sometime this evening, bringing with it torrential rains, possibly hail, and lightning. What was more important, however, was that behind it was a good, old-fashioned Canadian express. *Thank God for Canada.* With it would come a cooler, drier air mass. Not that Jake felt it necessary for the weatherman to tell anyone it would be less humid. *Shit, the rain forest isn't this muggy.*

He leaned with his hands on the air conditioner, counting the days backward on his fingers. This heat wave had started on Friday but seemed as if it had lasted for weeks. Usually they went three, sometimes four days, then moved on. He couldn't remember one this long or this brutal and wondered if maybe there wasn't something to this global warming everyone was screaming about.

Jake kicked off his loafers and lay down on the couch, his mouth gaping in a wide, almost painful yawn. He and Ederling had been burning the candle at both ends for over two weeks, and he could feel his body screaming for rest. Even warring armies sleep. He crossed his arms across his chest and closed his eyes.

THE BEACH WHERE Jake and the redhead lay in the tropical, afternoon sun was of a fine black sand, similar in texture to table salt. They were both nude, side by side on a large, green beach towel in the pattern of a hundred-dollar bill. Jake was sitting up, rubbing lotion over the hair of his legs, listening calmly as two-foot waves slapped methodically on the wet sand of the shore just a few yards away.

For the first time in a long time Jake felt relaxed, at peace with himself and his life. He scanned the length of the small, hidden beach in both directions but could see no one, only aging palm trees angled at thirty degrees, spreading lazily over their private little sanctuary. Glancing down, he gazed at his sleeping partner as she lay on her back, her long, flowing red hair lying in a disheveled bundle around her head. It seemed to glow in the midafternoon sun, and he found himself thinking how seductive he found it.

Her breasts hung leisurely to either side as they glistened with sweat and oil in the sun's warm rays. Though she was in her midforties, they still exuded a certain firmness, a fleshy buoyancy of which he felt sure he would never tire. Jake watched her nipples move silently up and down with each breath and was aware of a sudden warmth in his groin. He smiled slightly at the sensation of his penis rising slowly off the towel. He toyed with the idea of waking her by rubbing oil on her thighs, but found watching her sleep almost as enticing.

Jake's head hung between his knees as he scanned Morson Grayhead's annual report. Oddly, it was in braille, and he found himself realizing he had no idea how to read it. That's when he felt the touch of her fingers on his hip, just at the bend of his thigh. He looked in her direction, regarding her with longing eyes as she walked her fingers slowly toward his pubic hair.

She rose to her knees and knelt behind him, pressing her breasts firmly against his back. Reaching around his ribs with both arms, she softly fondled his scrotum, cupping his testicles lightly in her hands. Unhurriedly, as if in slow motion, she slid one hand up his shaft, squeezing it firmly with an oily palm, gliding slowly up and down its head.

The sensation shot through him almost immediately. His back stiffened. Jake placed his palms on the towel as she began to work him just the way he liked. She knew how to please him about as well as he knew how to please himself, and within a minute he was lost in a thundering, yearning lust for release. He worked his hips, moving his pelvis up and down, picking up pace at the heightening sensation in his loins. It was then Jake heard the voice for the first time.

Reluctantly, Jake yanked his brain from its lustful realm, opening his eyes to listen more clearly. He heard it again—a faint and distant cry from somewhere offshore. He peered through his sunglasses to the water beyond and stared agape at a small fishing vessel awash in flame, smoke billowing from its cabin. A woman was standing on the stern screaming for help.

"I can't swim!" Jake could hear her yell. "Help me! I can't swim!"

"Honey, stop," he said, grabbing her wrists with both hands. "Someone's in trouble out there."

But she would have none of it. She meant to please and would not be stopped. "Stop! Someone's in trouble out there," he said again, thrashing his body to get free. "Stop! I mean it!

"I'll be right there!" Jake screamed. "Just hang on!" But the redhead clung to him doggedly. "Goddamnit! Let go!" he boomed, wrestling to free himself. "I said, let go!" He fought to his feet, dragging her through the sand. She clung to his ankles like a dog to a bone as he desperately tried to free himself from the maniacal, self-absorbed clutches of the woman Jake thought he knew.

He watched in horror as the woman on the boat screamed impotently for help. The flames of the beast began to lick her hair, and Jake could see her flailing madly at the yellow and orange about her head.

"Jump!" Jake yelled, now dragging his human ball and chain through the surf. "Jump! I'll come get you!" He could hear a bell ringing somewhere in the distance and watched in terror as a speeding fireboat approached, too late now to save the woman covered in flames, her arms and torso thrashing violently in the air.

"Let go of me!" he screamed again, fiercely twisting his torso, leaning down and shoving the ball of his palm at her skull. "Can't you see? She's burning alive! She's going to die!"

JAKE THREW ONE last punch before being mercilessly jettisoned from his private hell. He flailed in the air in a last-ditch attempt to wrestle free, sending himself smashing to the floor. He jerked to his knees, shaking his head, unsure what had just happened or where he was. In one of those rare but wonderful moments, Jake realized it was all a dream and only then became aware that he was covered in sweat. He scrunched a palm over his eyebrows and eyes, shaking off his nightmare. Then his phone rang.

"Jesus," he said, crawling to his feet, rushing to answer it. He picked up just as his answering machine kicked in. "Hello? 'Hi. I'm not in right now . . .' Hang on, hang on," Jake said as he heard his taped voice come over the line. Jake stretched the phone cord over to the answering machine, punched OFF, and started again, aware now that his heart was practically thumping out of his chest. "Sorry about that."

"Mr. Ferguson?" came a voice Jake did not recognize.

"Speaking."

"My name is Frank Warrington, Mr. Ferguson, calling you from Chicago. I'm sorry to bother you at home, but my secretary tells me you have urgent police business you need to discuss with me."

Jake was still lost in his dream. *Man, those things can seem real. Frank Warrington*, he repeated to himself. *Frank Warrington. Oh, yeah, Frank Warrington.* He remembered now. *I'm not exactly a cop. But you're close enough.* "Yes," Jake said, eschewing explanation. "Thank you for calling, Mr. Warrington."

Warrington seemed somewhat curt. "What seems to be the problem, Mr. Ferguson?"

Jake could hear the annoyance. He was in no mood for attitudes. Not now. *Don't even try being short with me, asshole.* "Mr. Warrington, I am heading the investigation into the Morson Grayhead burnings, sir. I'm sure you're aware of them."

"Yes."

"Well, before I start, Mr. Warrington, it is extremely important you understand that whatever we discuss must stay between you and me. I can't stress enough the need for absolute secrecy. The viability of the case may hang in the balance. Can you do that, sir?"

"That depends on what we talk about, Mr. Ferguson."

Okay, that's it. I don't have time for this bullshit. Let's see just how quick this boy really is. "If you'd like, sir, I can have the Illinois State Police deliver a subpoena to your hotel room. We can get to know each other much better then. I need your assistance, Mr. Warrington, and need to know you can keep this between us. It's your call. I really don't care either way."

Jake knew what he'd just said was a crock of shit. Even if he did have a subpoena delivered, which he could no doubt do, it would certainly not insure Warrington's keeping tight-lipped. And from a legal standpoint, there wasn't much of a threat in his words either. But Jake figured Warrington didn't know the difference, and anyway, it sure sounded menacing.

"I'm sorry to be short. It's been a long day," Warrington said apologetically. "My secretary mentioned something about a photograph. What is it exactly that you need?"

Much better. "Between us, and only us now, right?"

"Yes, Mr. Ferguson. This conversation stays between us. You have my word."

"Good. My understanding is that you employ someone by the name of Warren Josephs. Is that correct, sir?"

"Yes, it is."

"I need his address and a photograph of him as soon as possible. Sooner if you can."

"That's it?"

"That's it."

"Did you try Lisa Shuman at the office? She can do that for you, Mr. Ferguson."

I don't think so. "I spoke to her, Mr. Warrington, and frankly, she got cold feet. She would not authorize anything and pushed me on up to you."

Jake could hear Warrington sigh. "The office is closed now, Mr. Ferguson. I can have a photograph and his address mailed to you first thing tomorrow."

If Warrington mailed it tomorrow, Jake knew he would not receive it until Saturday. It was too long a wait. "I need it sooner than that, sir. Rather than mail it, can you have it sent by courier?"

"Of course."

"Good. Let me give you the address."

After Jake hung up, he walked to the kitchen. He put a handful of ice cubes in a glass and poured himself a large glass of water. The Regulator clock on the kitchen wall read 8:24 P.M. Jake leaned back against the counter, taking deep breaths, thinking back to his dream. Some people pay attention to their nocturnal jaunts, others don't. And though his memory did not always cooperate, Jake always dissected them when it did. For reasons he thought all too obvious, this one lingered vividly in his mind.

He closed his eyes and yawned, trying to piece together its different meanings. The hundred-dollar-bill beach towel was obvious, as was Morson Grayhead's annual report being in braille. The burning woman on the boat seemed pretty clear, too—her burning alive just far enough away so that Jake was unable to be of help. He wasn't so sure about the beach, though he thought it might mean he needed a vacation.

But the buxom redhead . . . what the hell was that all about? Yes, some sex would be nice. He found himself yearning more and more for a woman's touch—her feel, her voice, her smell. But her unwillingness to release his penis—his inability to shake her when he needed to be free? *What did that mean? Am I subconsciously afraid I won't like Don's redhead and won't be able to shake her after I've let her into my life?* Jake chuckled to himself. *Yeah, that would happen. Just as soon as people stop setting fires.*

The vision of her full, firm breasts glistening under the sun's rays remained powerfully strong in his mind's eye. Her healthy mound of strawberry-blond pubic hair, feminine thighs, and the feel of her hands as they stroked his penis . . . these he could still clearly see and feel with a reality as if she were standing with him right now.

Jake had known for a long time that he had no life. He didn't need Donny to tell him that what little he had, sucked. Hell, *he* was the one living it—if that was the proper term for it. He knew now more than ever there was more to it than chasing pyromaniacs around the four corners of the country. At forty-two, and sagging a bit around the waist, Jake knew all too well life sure as hell wasn't going to come to him.

He carried his glass of water down the hall to his bedroom and opened his closet door. He started poking through the pockets of his pants and shirts, trying to remember which clothes he had worn to the Ederlings' just a couple nights ago. Jake had made up his mind now. It was time. He would call the red-head and let the chips fall where they may. All he needed now was that slip of paper.

Jake came away from the closet empty-handed, worrying that perhaps he had inadvertently tossed the slip in the trash. He was standing in the hall, thinking, when he stepped inside his bathroom and started rummaging through his hamper. *It damn well better be here.* If it wasn't, he was going to have to call Donny for the number, and Jake would just as soon make this call without anyone else's knowledge.

He flicked on the light, just in time to catch the 8:30 news on his radio. The lead story was something about congressional bickering over the omnibus spending bill currently being debated in the House. Jake pulled out underwear and socks from his overstuffed hamper, wishing that for once those bastards in Washington would put the good of the country before their own embarrassingly obvious self-interest. There was a day when one served in political office much as one serves in the military during war. It was a duty born of love of country, whose term was fulfilled and vacated, left for yet another proud and giving American to try to leave his mark.

The modern political process frustrated Jake like little else. His temples burned with tension as he spotted the Big Dog shorts he'd worn that night lying at the bottom of his hamper. He was filled with a peculiar mix of anxiety and anticipation as he pulled the scrap of yellow legal paper from a back pocket. He was turning to leave just as the Morson Grayhead story aired.

"Authorities still appear stumped as to possible suspects in the recent spate of murders haunting Morson Grayhead, one of New York's premier investment banking firms. Executives at the firm were unavailable for comment, but unnamed sources tell WCBS News that representatives from the Westchester County Fire Marshal's Office have revisited recently deceased chairman Severin Rybeck's Bedford, New York, West View Estate as recently as today."

Shit. Jake hadn't even thought about that. He hated getting blindsided. It hadn't dawned on him that someone at the Rybeck residence could be reporting to the media. The options were endless. So many people worked at West View, and any one of them could be the snitch: gardeners, butlers, maids, pool cleaners, chauffeurs, and security personnel. He wondered if the media was paying someone to supply information and knew he'd have to discuss alternative approaches going forward with Ederling.

"The reason for their visit was not immediately clear," the newsman continued, "while several calls to the Rybeck estate were referred to the public relations firm Morson Grayhead has hired to guide it through this difficult time. Meanwhile, in a related story, the funeral for Severin Rybeck has been set for . . ."

Jake hit the light and walked back up the hall. He already knew the date of Severin's funeral and had arranged with a police photographer to videotape the proceedings. On a whim, he thought it wouldn't hurt to get a shot of all the faces to attend. Sometimes it's the little things that count.

Taking a seat at the dining room table, Jake unfolded the sheet of paper Ederling had given him, staring through it as his mind wandered. It was at this very table, over a Friday-night dinner, that he and Danny had decided to start a family. She had secretly been charting her body temperature and informed him that, from everything she could tell, it looked as if the time was ripe.

They made love for hours that night, fondling and exploring each other, experimenting, pushing to the edge of release, only to pull back from the brink. It was an exquisite evening for them both. Jake's heart shriveled at the thought that he might never again experience such intimacy with another living being. The very concept seemed blasphemous, yet deep down, he knew it was time to try to live again.

Jake walked to the phone on the kitchen wall, pulling the handset to the dining room table. He held it in his lap, his thumb on the dial-tone button, looking at the seven numbers and name in front of him. He had lived for so long in his defensive, walled cocoon, the idea that he might step out into the light of day scared him. As with a forty-year prisoner whose sentence has been served, the thought of walking away from the bars that had bound him—protected him for so long—was at once exhilarating and frightening.

For a brief moment he thought of Ederling, of how hard he would laugh if he could see Jake now. Sweat trickled slowly from his armpits as beads of perspiration gathered on his brow. He wiped his forehead with the back of a hand, standing so as to expand his diaphragm. Jake took a couple of deep breaths, playing again and again the forthcoming conversation in his mind.

"Jesus Christ, Jake," he said. "She's not going to bite you." He took one last, long, deep breath and dialed the number. He almost depressed the dial-tone button with the first ring, but something told him this was his one chance to escape, to have a life again.

"Hello?" Her voice seemed airy, feminine and relaxed.

"Um . . . hi," Jake began tentatively. "Is this Valerie Medforth?"

"Who's calling?" came the wary response.

"My name is Jacob Ferguson. You don't know me, but I believe we have mutual friends. Do you know the Ederlings from New Rochelle?"

There was a slight pause. "Yes, I know the Ederlings."

"Well . . . um . . . I work with Don. I feel kind of awkward saying this, but he and his wife have been trying to get me to call you for some time." Jake suddenly felt three feet tall. "Listen, am I interrupting anything? If I am, please tell me. I can call another time."

Her response was almost immediate. "Oh, no . . . I was just grading some papers."

Jake noticed and took it as a good sign, allowing himself to relax ever so slightly. He wanted desperately to sound confident, to make her feel he was sure of himself. He had a nagging feeling he was being woefully unsuccessful. It had been so long since he'd done this. Jake was more than rusty, he was corroded shut. "Well, I don't know if they've mentioned me to you or not, but—"

"Now that I think of it, Abby has mentioned your name to me. Aren't you the man in charge of the Morson Grayhead investigation?"

Well, at least I'm not going in cold. "Yes. That's me. For better or worse."

"I hope you catch whoever's doing it."

"Thank you. God knows we're trying." Jake wasn't sure if what she'd just said worked in his favor or against it, but painfully forged ahead just the same. However, Valerie Medforth was immediately intrigued by the man on the other end of her phone. She could have saved him a lot of torment, but wanted him to go through the motions anyhow. She thought it would tell her a good deal about the man.

"Well, I don't know exactly how to say this . . . but I was wondering if maybe you would like to . . . you know . . . maybe go out sometime," he finally spilled out, almost tripping over the last four words. Jake half expected a declination and thought it would be less painful if he helped grease the skids himself. "Please don't feel obligated," he said, feigning indifference. "You won't hurt my feelings if you say no," he lied.

Valerie could tell he was nervous and found it kind of cute in its own way. "I think I would like that," she answered coyly. "Did you have a particular night in mind?"

Oh, my God. Just like that? Jake was taken aback. No small talk, no convincing—not that he would have tried. It was that easy. He had just gotten himself a date. "Really?" Jake asked, perhaps a touch too excited. "Well, gee, I . . . I was thinking . . ."

He was suddenly worried about asking her to a Yankee game. *How uncouth is that?* But he hadn't thought of anything else. In fact, for some reason, he hadn't even thought the conversation would get this far. Jake wished now that he had thought it out some more. *Relax. Just relax. She asked when, not what. Just keep your cool.* Somewhere in the back of his mind, something told him that he was actually having fun. Although he secretly prayed it got more enjoyable than this.

"Well, I know this is short notice, but I was wondering if you weren't doing anything tomorrow night, maybe we could grab a bite to eat or something."

"Oh, *tomorrow* night," Valerie responded, her intonation conveying that "I'd love to, but I can't" response. "I'm doing my hair tomorrow night."

"Oh . . . well . . ." *Doing your hair? What does that mean? Isn't that kind of a slight?* "Um . . . okay . . . well, how about . . ."

Valerie listened to him squirm, reminding herself that men never grow up. "I'm joking. Tomorrow night sounds fine. What time?"

Jake's head was spinning. He thought maybe he could use some lessons or something. He hoped she was enjoying herself, because this was killing him. "Well, how does seven o'clock sound?"

"Seven is good. Do you know where I live?"

"No."

"You know the McDonald's on Route . . . ?"

Jake jotted down her address on the back of the scrap of paper in front of him, said good-bye, and placed his thumb on the button. His spine quivered, shaking his shoulders and torso, shooting tingles of electricity down his extremities. He felt alive, worthy of fun again. Jake stood, his mouth locked in a radiant smile, and punched a fist in the air.

"Yes!" he shouted with clenched teeth, pulling his arm back as if calling a runner out at third. "Happy days are here again . . ."

Jake whistled the tune as he walked the phone to the cradle on the wall. For the first time in years—in fact, for the first time since he could remember—he felt light on his feet. Jake whistled all the way down the hall as he entered his room, thinking how lucky he was to be alive.

Friday
September 13

S THE WEATHERMAN had promised, the previous evening's storm had ushered in much more bearable weather. Jake felt perky on this cool and dry morning, his voice mimicking the intoxication of his spirit. "Gooood morning," he said with a smile to a seated Ederling as he entered the Westchester County Fire Marshal's Office.

Ederling observed Jake silently, watching as he hung his windbreaker over the back of his chair and peeled off the plastic top to his steaming hot coffee. Jake sat down, picking up his phone messages, whistling something quietly under his breath. Ederling couldn't quite believe his eyes. Jake's whole demeanor spoke of a youthful, carefree spirit. This was like the Jake of old.

"Aren't we Mr. Happy Genes this morning," Ederling said, not sure what the hell was going on.

Jake sipped his coffee, steam blurring his view as he looked up at Ederling over its rim. Jake quickly raised and lowered his eyebrows in silent acknowledgment. "Beautiful day, huh?"

"All right," Ederling asked, almost annoyed. "What the fuck's up with you? You finally get laid, or what?"

Jake clicked his tongue in mock irritation. "Hey, is that all you think about? What? A guy can't be in a good mood?"

"Sure. Just about anyone but you. You've been sulking in here for so many years, you look like you just spent the night with the Dallas Cowboy Cheerleaders."

Jake was rather pleased with himself. Now that he'd succeeded, he didn't mind sharing the news. "Well, for your information, Mr. Cynic . . . I got myself a date tonight."

"Get out," Ederling said, truly shocked at the news. "You're shittin' me."

"Nope. I'm picking Valerie up tonight at seven. Was thinking maybe dinner and bowling."

Ederling laughed. "Bowling? Yeah, that'll work. You'll have her wrapped right around your little finger."

"What's wrong with that?" Jake asked, suddenly thinking maybe he really didn't have any idea what the hell he was doing.

"Let me get this straight. You're going to take Valerie Medforth bowling?"

"I was thinking about it, yeah."

"Hey, whatever," Ederling said with a shrug of his shoulders. "I already got a wife."

"Oh, fuck you. I think dinner and bowling sounds like a good first date. It's lighthearted and fun. Everyone likes bowling."

"Jake, Valerie's a classy woman. She's smart, educated. I can't imagine she's going to think bowling is fun."

"So what? You saying classy gals don't like to have fun?"

"No. I'm just saying your gut doesn't hang over your belt far enough to fit in at a bowling alley."

Jake was self-conscious now. "Well, if I take her to a movie, we'll sit for two and a half hours and not say a word to each other. I want to get to know her. Not to mention that then I have to worry about whether I should put my arm around her or not. I hate that shit. It makes me queasy just thinking about it. So, what would you do?"

"I don't know. Something more sophisticated, I guess. You know, go out for a couple of drinks afterwards. Maybe one of those coffeehouses popping up all over the place."

Jake sat quiet for a bit, thinking about what Ederling had just said. *Maybe I should do that. Maybe he's right, bowling is too blue-collar.* Jake was a little peeved. Here he was about to go on his first date since Danny had died, and Ederling was already filling him with self-doubt. "Shit," Jake said in frustration. "Now I don't know what to do. Thanks for your support."

Ederling looked at him. He could sense that Jake was truly hurt. "You're right, Jake. I'm sorry. This is a big night for you. I shouldn't be such a spoilsport. I guess I'm thinking bachelors and dates . . . hell, it's like saying bachelors and dirty laundry. It goes with the territory. I forgot this is more than a date for you. I should have kept my big mouth shut." Ederling saw Jake watching him with agreeing eyes. He felt guilty now. "Look, you want to take the woman bowling, take her bowling. What the hell do I know? Maybe you guys will have the time of your lives."

"I'll think about it."

"Well, whatever you do, have a good time. I'm proud of you."

"Thanks, Dad."

"Hey," Ederling responded only half-jokingly. "Go ahead and laugh, but I'm here to tell you, there were times that's who I thought I was. It'll be good for you to get out. You deserve it."

"I still don't see anything wrong with bowling."

"Then take her bowling. Shit, if she likes you, Jake, she'll watch you change your car oil."

Jake's secretary walked into the office. "Jake, I have a courier package here for you. It's from Executive Travel in New York."

"Thanks, Cis," he said, motioning to the table in the corner. "Just lay it there."

"Also . . . Lianne Rybeck called," she said, turning to leave. "Said she couldn't find any combs or brushes of her son's."

"Thanks."

"There's a surprise," Ederling said, before motioning to the courier package. "What's that?"

Jake rose and walked toward the table. "I'm hoping it's the picture and address of Warren Parks, or Josephs, or whatever the hell he's calling himself now."

"Good. Let's get some surveillance on the fucker. I want to see if he's got a bandage on his head."

Jake opened the envelope, holding the picture of Warren Parks in his hands. "Looks mild-mannered enough," he said, handing it to Ederling.

"Yeah, that's what they said about Son of Sam. 'So quiet. Such a nice neighbor.' It's the mild-mannered ones you worry about."

"No shit, huh? Hmmm," Jake said as he read Parks's employment records.

"What?"

"Says here he lives in New Jersey."

"Where?"

"Englewood Cliffs."

Jake rose and walked to his desk. He dialed the New York State Police CID. He and Ederling needed surveillance, and the Criminal Investigation Division was the obvious place to turn. The switchboard operator put him through.

"CID, Henderson."

"Jimmy, it's Jake."

"Hey, Jake. What's up? Anything yet?"

"Well . . . maybe. That's why I'm calling. We got a possible lead, Jim. I'm not sure yet whether he's our guy or just involved up to his elbows, but I know he's dirty. I need the works. Photographs, when he leaves, when he arrives, where he goes. When you're done, I want to know what he gargles with. Can you set that up for us?"

"Sure thing, Jake. What's your timetable?"

"The sooner the better."

"I'll get to work on it. Give me a couple of hours. Where's he live?"

Jake told him Parks's address, making it doubly clear that he wanted to be informed anytime, anyplace, if they saw him on the move. "I don't care if I'm getting my gallbladder removed. Just make sure I know when he's mobile."

"Done."

"One last thing."

"What?"

"If he has any type of gauze or bandage on his head, take him in. Anything that might look as though he's recently taken some kind of a blow. Maybe wearing a cast. Don't question him. Just hold him until we can get there. It doesn't have to be big. Even a visible welt will do."

"We can do that."

"Thanks, Jimmy. I owe you."

"Hey, I want this son of a bitch."

"That makes two of us."

Ederling was reading Parks's employment records when Jake walked back to the table and sat across from him. "What do you say we take a little ride to Lianne's place? See if this is our man," Ederling said.

"Sounds good."

"I THINK IT'S time we turn up the heat on Mrs. Lianne Rybeck," Jake said as he drove his Crown Victoria up Route 22 toward the Cross River Reservoir and the Rybeck mansion.

"What do you have in mind?" Ederling asked.

"I'm not sure. Let me ask you something, Don. If you knew one of your kids was doing something like this, would you protect him or turn him in?"

Ederling looked at Jake. "Man, that's a tough one. I remember listening to G. Gordon Liddy just after they caught that Unabomber asshole. He was all pissed off at the guy's brother for snitching on him. He was saying stuff like, 'You just don't rat out family.' Simple as that. He doesn't think it matters what they've done, family is sacred. But I don't know if I'd agree, even if it was my own kid. I mean, if I thought one of my kids was doing this, you gotta figure he'd be in desperate need of help. I guess I'd want to see if I could get him the psychiatric care he needed. You know? Medication, counseling, something. I couldn't live with myself knowing I was letting it go on."

"You should be a politician."

"Why?"

"Because that was a great response, but it didn't come close to answering my question. Would you turn him in or not?"

Ederling stared through the windshield, pained by the thought. "Would *I?*"

Jake looked at him. "Is there someone else in the car?"

Ederling was silent for a while. "I don't know, Jake. On the one hand, I can't imagine putting myself and my family through the humiliation. But on the other . . ."

Jake waited for a moment. "Well?"

"I just don't know that I can answer that," Ederling finally answered, clearly torn at the very prospect of such a dilemma. "I know this much, though. I sure as hell would make it stop."

"You think the average parent would tell the authorities?"

"Shit, I don't know. It takes all kinds. But, yeah . . . I think your average parent would at the very least make it stop. Some might tell the authorities. But one way or another, they would put an end to it."

"What about Lianne?"

Ederling thought for a moment. "Lianne. No, I'd say she's a bit different. I think people with that kind of money don't take kindly to outside intervention. Someone like that would probably try to take care of it herself."

"But you think she'd do something?"

"Oh, yeah. Definitely. She'd *definitely* do something."

"No, I mean other than just try and protect Scotty from arrest."

"I know what you mean. I think she'd do something to put an end to it, but I'd make book it wouldn't involve us. Why? Where's that little brain of yours headed, Jake?"

"I've been thinking, Donny," Jake said, swinging his car onto Upper Hook Road. "It just seems to me we got a lot of shit up in the air right now. We think Parks is dirty, but we don't know for sure. We think Scotty could also be dirty, but we don't know that either. We think Lianne knows Scotty's whereabouts, but we can't prove that . . . yet. I don't know what it is, but something's not right with this case. I just got a weird feeling about this one."

"I know. There's a lot of unanswered questions right now, but it'll come together. It always does."

"Almost always. What if we speed things up a bit? What do we have to lose if we make her sweat a little? Make her think Scotty's our primary suspect?"

"And?" Ederling asked, looking at Jake's profile. "Then what?"

Jake turned, catching Ederling's eyes. "I think if we play our cards right, we just might get her to lead us right to Scotty."

"You want to set up surveillance on her?"

"Maybe. If we need to. Actually, I was thinking something simpler than that."

"Like?"

"Like we subpoena her phone records," Jake said with a slight smile. "Follow me on this, all right? The authorities hit you over your head with news that they think one of your sons is doing something like this. They come and visit you, tell you of their concerns. Tell you they think you know where he is, and that they're going to become his worst nightmare. Now, you're loaded, like Lianne, and used to things your own way, right? You don't want to involve the authorities. You can't believe they could even *think* such a thing. You're not even sure you can believe your ears. But you figure they must know things you don't, and you sure as hell want to protect your son." Jake turned to look at Ederling, making sure to drive his point home. "*Nothing* is more important. Nothing else even matters. You agree?"

"You bet."

"You feel like you failed him once. And there is no way you're going to let it happen again. So what's the first thing you'd do after they leave?"

"Oh . . . you're a sly one you are, Jake. You think it could possibly be that simple?"

"I don't see why not. I mean, you're either going to go see him, or call him, right?"

"Absolutely. If I knew where he was."

"Well, that's the sixty-four-thousand-dollar question, isn't it? But let's assume we're right and she does know where he is. I say we subpoena her phone records, see who's the first person she calls after we leave. Ten to one it's Scotty. I think we can get her to lead us right to him, and she'll never even know it."

Jake slowed his cruiser, pulling up to the Rybeck guardhouse for the fourth time in six days. "Good idea, Jake. I like it," Ederling said as Jake rolled down his window. "Guess that's why you make the big bucks."

They were waved through after a perfunctory stop. "No, Don," Jake said, motioning forward with his chin. "*This*, is big bucks."

"No shit, huh? Makes me feel like a gerbil on a spinning wheel."

"Yeah . . . well, don't get too depressed. This woman has more money than you and I can both imagine. Doesn't look to me like it's helped her much. Just ask yourself, would you trade places with her?"

Ederling smiled. "No, but I'd trade bank accounts."

BOTH MEN SCAMPERED slowly down the incline of the sloping back lawn, watching Lianne Rybeck off in the distance, eyeing a thirty-foot putt. "How about miniature golf?" Jake asked.

"What?" Ederling asked, not following the connection.

"You don't like the bowling idea, so what do you think about miniature golf?"

Lianne Rybeck had caught their approach out of the corner of her eye and waved at them both as they approached. "Jake," Ederling said, politely waving back, "*anything's* better than bowling."

Jake smiled casually at Lianne Rybeck as they came closer. "I didn't know you were so stuck up," he whispered to Ederling.

"Hey, I didn't know you don't know how to date."

"We'll see."

"Gentlemen," Lianne said with an extended hand, walking toward the apron of the green. "Absolutely beautiful out, isn't it?"

"I thought you liked it warm and muggy," Ederling said, taking her hand.

"Oh, I do, Mr. Ederling, I do. But even a fish jumps out of the water now and then."

True enough. "Mrs. Rybeck," Jake said with a smile as he took her hand. He knew this meeting would be more brief than the last. They were here for two reasons only. To show Lianne Warren Parks's picture, and to plant the seed of doubt. He figured the sooner they got down to it, the more off guard they would put her. In a strange way Jake felt sorry for Lianne Rybeck, but he would still have bet she was lying to them. Unless she proved him wrong, he viewed her now as an adversary. Strangely, he hoped he was right, because if they did need her help after this, Lianne would never again give them the time of day.

"We apologize for interrupting your day like this, Mrs. Rybeck," Jake began. "We'll only be a few minutes."

"I'm disappointed, Mr. Ferguson. Won't you stay for some tea or coffee? I'd enjoy the company."

Let's see how you feel in a few minutes. "Mrs. Rybeck, we brought a picture with us and would like you to tell us if it looks familiar. Will you do that for us?"

"Of course. Who is it?"

"Why don't you look at it first?" Jake said, pulling the photo out of a manila folder and handing it to her. "Does this man look familiar to you at all?"

Lianne Rybeck took the black-and-white photo from his outstretched hand, holding it at waist level. Both Jake and Ederling observed her reaction carefully, surprised when there was none. Almost none. Her face remained stoic, but both men clearly noticed the breath catch in her throat. Lianne's shoulders stiffened slightly as she stood deathly still. It seemed to Jake that she did not breathe for the better part of thirty seconds, as if determining a proper reaction.

"No," she said, finally handing it back. "I'm afraid I've never seen him before. Sorry. Should I have?"

Jake was sure that she was lying. *Why? Why would this woman lie about the one man on earth she claims to want to find more than peace of mind itself? What strange and twisted web have Don and I walked into?* He didn't know, but would die trying to find out. It was time to upset the status quo. Jake always liked to interview people with a false sense of security and that subtle touch of arrogance. They crack so easily under pressure. "You seem flushed, Mrs. Rybeck. Are you sure, ma'am?"

Lianne turned and took a few steps toward a ball, assuming a putting stance. "I said I've never seen him before, Mr. Ferguson," she responded a bit too emphatically.

The tiny white ball traveled the length of the first level, pushing far to the right at the break in the green, rolling to a stop a good nine feet from the hole.

"Perhaps you shouldn't putt when you're upset, Mrs. Rybeck. It seems to disturb your game," Ederling said.

"I am *not* upset, Mr. Ederling," Lianne said, suddenly feeling under attack, regarding each man now as if a hyena on a hunt. "What makes you say that?" she asked, hastily throwing up every wall of defense she could now summon.

She tried desperately to hide it, but Jake could tell it was all Lianne could do not to scream. She was emotionally vulnerable. *The best time to strike.* "Let's cut to the chase, shall we, Mrs. Rybeck?"

She looked Jake in the eyes, her face firm as stone. "Let's."

"Mrs. Rybeck, we have reason to believe your son is responsible for the Morson Grayhead murders," Jake said, pausing for effect. "Frankly, ma'am, we also think you know where he is. Do you care to tell us the truth, or are you going to continue to stand by your statement of yesterday?"

Lianne's eyes sharpened as her voice grew taught. "Just who the hell do you think you are?" she asked indignantly. "Both of you. Coming to *my* home, accusing *my* son of the most heinous of crimes, and accusing *me* of lying? I want you both out of here. Now."

"But, Mrs. Rybeck—" Jake interrupted, not really expecting the chance to finish.

"I told you to leave. Now!"

The bait was cast. "All right, Mrs. Rybeck, we're leaving," Jake said. "But if you *are* in touch with Scotty, tell him we'll find him. One way or another, ma'am . . . we'll find him." Jake stared into her scorching eyes. *Good thing looks can't kill.* "If he's innocent, one vial of his blood will clear him. You can save us all a lot of grief. The decision is yours, Mrs. Rybeck. Make it good." He turned, adding one last thought for her to chew on. "Oh . . . and Mrs. Rybeck. If Scotty *is* guilty, then I'm afraid that could make you an accessory to murder. Good day, ma'am."

Jake and Ederling could feel her eyes burning holes into their backs as they walked back up the lawn. Ederling whispered straight ahead, "So . . . I guess this means we're not having coffee, huh?"

ALL HER ADULT life Lianne Rybeck had fought for her son. When she'd contracted Hodgkin's and lay near death in bed, it wasn't the thought of dying that frightened her. In fact, at times she would just as soon have been freed of her misery. But the notion that she might leave her innocent darling to fend for himself in such a cruel and uncertain world, with no father to speak of . . . there were times Lianne felt certain she was losing her sanity.

Her mind had twisted in a sea of emotions during those long, lonely days. Guilt would replace fear, only to have the fear grip her again, seizing her like a cold fist wrapping itself around her heart. For days on end she would lie in the soft prison of her bed, praying she would survive if only to insure her son's continued well-being and survival. Not long after Lianne recovered enough to become somewhat ambulatory, it became all too obvious that something was terribly wrong with her son.

Lianne would subtly pry, sometimes coaxing Scotty to draw pictures of his thoughts. She colored with him on the bedroom floor, feigning interest in her own works of art, all the while scanning his drawings out of the corner of an eye. What began to emerge were the frightening, horrifying images of a boy possessed: an innocent, ignored little boy who had somehow been pushed over the other side in her absence.

"Scotty, honey," Lianne asked quietly one day, staring in horror at the drawings spewing forth from his mind, her heart thumping wildly somewhere in her throat. "What is that, sweetie? Tell Mommy. What is that a drawing of?"

He was quiet, almost catatonic, scribbling away, sometimes breaking his Crayolas as he pushed down with all his childhood strength in fury and anger. "Nothing," Scotty said, remaining fixated on his work. "Just blood, I guess."

"Blood, honey? Why blood? Why did you draw a picture of blood on that goat, sweetheart?"

"Josephine makes me do it."

Lianne panicked. "What, Scotty?" she asked, her throat closing in spasms. "What? What did Josephine make you do?"

"Mommy?" Scotty asked, staring at his mother with eyes she did not recognize. "Does Lucifer love you, too?"

In time, there would be scores of drawings, each one depicting a child's version of hate and dementia. Scene after scene of sacrifice, pain, and torture were followed by yet more of blindfolded, naked bodies, fire and chains. Lianne lacked the strength to fight the battle alone, although God knows she tried. Severin was so deeply lost in his myopia, he avoided the issues by saying what she really needed was rest. Each night she would cry herself to sleep in the lonely warmth of her bed.

Lianne called the police, built a team of New York's top child psychiatrists, spent virtually every waking moment with her son, but it was too late. He was gone. She thought she would die and even toyed with the thought of killing herself and taking Scotty with her, rather than live the nightmare life that would surely ensue.

"Oh, God," she wailed on her knees at night. "My baby! My baby! What have they done to my baby?"

And now these two men had the unmitigated gall to come to her house and tell her they thought Scotty was responsible for these horrific deaths. Lianne thought that it just couldn't be true. She loved him so much. They had to have been mistaken. From early on, Scotty had always been so vulnerable, so in need of help and love. She kept asking herself the same two questions: "Scotty just couldn't do such a thing—could he?" and "What could possibly have turned him into that kind of an animal?"

Yes, he was troubled. Scotty had long been troubled. Even Severin couldn't ignore it after a while. It was Severin who had finally suggested they put Scotty away for a while. "We can't help him anymore, Lianne," he had said. "Maybe an environment of professionals can help him. We can't do anything more."

"*We* can't do any more?" Lianne responded with near psychotic rage. "*We* can't do any more, Severin? You haven't done a *damn* thing for that boy! *I'm* the one who's pulled everything out of him. *I'm* the one who noticed we had a problem to begin with. Remember, Severin, you didn't even believe me at first. God forbid you would spend any time with him to find out."

"Now, Lianne," Severin said as if she were overreacting.

"Don't you *dare* patronize me, you son of a bitch! The only reason you want him gone is to get him out of your way. So help me, if it's the last thing I ever do, you'll pay for this, Severin. So help me God, you'll pay for this. You and everyone else responsible."

Lianne had long worried that they might have to institutionalize Scotty. The day they left him at the sanitarium . . . it was her worst nightmare come true. Tears streamed freely down her face as she sat beside her husband in the back of his limousine. Lianne kept turning around, staring out the car's rear window, trying to catch a final glimpse of her son, her hand outstretched toward the rear window, as if she were somehow trying to hold him one last time.

The picture was still burned into her mind: Scotty standing there confused and afraid, waving good-bye to his mother, sandwiched between two antiseptic-looking, white-clad attendants. Her soul died that day. Lianne knew in her heart that she would never again be the same.

"Damn you, Severin!" she spoke skyward with hatred. "You son of a bitch. You goddamned selfish prima donna. Why couldn't you have been there for me? For Scotty?" When the family faced the worst crisis it would ever see, Lianne would never understand how he could ever have been so selfish. So isolated. So uncaring. How could Severin have placed the firm over his own son? His own flesh and blood? The minute crisis invaded his life, he went running for the hills, rather than having the backbone to face it.

"Rot in hell, you bastard," she said quietly under her breath as she stood, leaning against her putter. "Burn. Burn, you son of a bitch. Burn like the victims of the monster you helped create."

Lianne stopped breathing, aware now of what she had just said. She worried that the authorities knew something definitive. That they knew something she did not. She felt certain that they wouldn't just arrive making accusations on a whim. Something must have led them to believe Scotty was involved. What Lianne didn't know was what that "something" was.

The thought that she had been blind to what was happening—that she had somehow missed the obvious connection—sent her reeling. Would a better mother have already put two and two together? Had she just not wanted to see it, choosing denial over reality? Would another have intuitively known, or would they, too, have needed the slap across the face that Jake and Ederling had just so painfully delivered?

Her putter dropped to the green at her feet as Lianne pulled on her cheeks with the fingers of both hands. "My God," she said softly. "It can't be. It just can't be." She wondered if the pain would ever end. Suddenly, Lianne Rybeck did not want to live anymore. *What for?* To what purpose could her continued existence on this earth possibly lead? But she knew she wouldn't do it. Lianne knew the answer to that question. She was trapped. Someone had to look out for Scotty. Someone had to pay his bills, his mortgage, buy his food. Without her, she knew he would surely die or, worse yet, spend his remaining years in a mental asylum—alone, with no one in the world to care about what happened to him.

All this was true. But Lianne could not help but worry that maybe, somehow, Scotty was involved. The thought that her beloved son could be responsible for the deaths of six people sent tremors up her spine. Lianne's brain swam with a torrent of terrifying and unthinkable thoughts. If it *was* Scotty, she had to stop him. As much as she adored her son, she could not allow such heinous killing to continue. But she wondered how Warren fell into the picture, and how the authorities found him so quickly. The mere thought that he might somehow be entangled once again with Scotty sent her mind into near apoplectic shock.

It was never supposed to be like this. Lianne wished now that Warren had died with that filthy bitch Josephine. It took everything she had not to spit on the picture Jake had showed her. She worried now that perhaps she *had* let on. As hard as Lianne had tried not to, there lurked an uneasy feeling that Jake and Ederling had noticed her inner angst, her desire to erupt. But she couldn't allow them to get too close, or else her whole terrible secret could implode. She knew they must never find out. *Never.* Or her life's only treasure would surely be left helpless and alone, abandoned, left to struggle through life with what little abilities Scotty still possessed. Lianne would never allow it to happen. Not as long as she still breathed.

But still, Lianne had to know if Scotty was involved, and only one person on earth knew for sure. Her son would never lie to her. Suddenly, Lianne began to run toward the house, sprinting faster than she could ever remember. She fell to her knees as the soles of her sneakers slipped on the grass. She nearly ran over herself as she crawled crablike to her feet. She just had to know.

JAKE DIDN'T EVEN bother driving back to his office, heading instead directly to the district attorney's office in downtown White Plains. He was confident in his plan; he could feel it in his gut. Every ounce of experience told him that Lianne Rybeck had probably already placed her ill-fated call. He and Ederling parked in the subterranean garage and took an elevator to the fifth-floor office of Irena Wojanowski.

Wojanowski was a no-nonsense attorney. Known to harbor an intuitive killer instinct, her reputation preceded her in any case she tried. Behind her back she was dubbed the Terminator, and many a foe had learned the hard way of her brutal ability and willingness to crush an opponent's windpipe once her boot was on his neck. More than assertive, she carried a self-confidence bordering on arrogance, and in a man's world, any number thought her a bitch.

Even though she and Jake were on the same side, still, he seldom looked forward to a Wojanowski grilling. He always got what he needed, but usually not without the third degree. In fact, Jake couldn't understand why she still held her post. He knew she had bigger plans and figured it only a matter of time before she ran for governor, or Congress. He was surprised she hadn't done it by now. But Jake knew she was nobody's fool, and if Wojanowski hadn't run yet, you could bet she had a damn good reason.

Generally, Jake did not need to see the DA to get a subpoena. Usually an office clerk or legal underling performed the task. But on a case this big, he was not surprised that she wanted to be kept directly informed. After a brief wait in a small anteroom, both men were led into her office by a young, eager-looking law clerk. Jake had never seen him before and guessed him for mid to late twenties.

"Ms. Wojanowski will see you now," he said, rising from his chair behind a computer terminal and spreading open her doors.

"How come every time we come here, I feel like I'm entering the Roman Colosseum?" Ederling whispered to Jake as they rose to enter.

"No shit, huh?"

Wojanowski had walked from behind her cluttered desk and was standing in the middle of her office when Jake and Ederling walked in. She smiled, extending a hand as Jake approached.

He had called from his car. She was expecting them. "Jake, good to see you again. Don, how are you?"

Ederling smiled. "Irena," Jake said, taking her hand. "Thank you for seeing us on such short notice. Donny and I seem to have stepped into a beehive with this Morson Grayhead thing, and we're hoping you can help us to not get stung."

"What do you have?" Wojanowski asked, motioning to two chairs in front of her desk.

Jake pulled a notebook out of his windbreaker, walked over to a chair, and sat down. Ederling followed suit while Wojanowski walked around her desk, resting her large frame in a green leather chair. Jake really didn't need his notebook, but had learned from experience that it looked good.

"You'll have to tell us how much detail you want, Irena, but the bottom line is this. Don and I both agree that Lianne Rybeck is somehow involved in this case. We're not sure yet just how, but she is definitely not a disinterested observer."

Wojanowski weighed Jake's remarks with a critical squint. "I would think not, Jake. Her husband just killed himself over the damn thing."

"Well, it's not what it looks like, Irena. I think it's safe to say she doesn't give a shit about that."

"Really?" she said, her voice implying disbelief. "Care to fill me in?"

Jake explained the history behind Lianne and Severin's marriage, what had happened to Scotty, the deadly fire that had killed Josephine, and that he and Ederling both believed Lianne knew where Scotty was and had recognized Warren's photograph when they showed it to her.

"Why do you think she's lying?" Wojanowski asked.

"We're not sure yet. We find the reason for that, I think we break this whole thing wide open," Jake responded.

Wojanowski waved a hand. "No, that's not what I meant. I don't mean her motive for lying. I mean, what causes you to think she *is* lying. Has she said something you know to be untrue or done something illegal?"

Jake was grateful he wasn't seeking a search warrant. He knew this was his weak link. You can't just walk into a judge's chambers, tell him you think someone looks suspicious, then expect him to sign a warrant to search his records. Subpoenas are a hell of a lot easier to get your hands on. Only the DA has to sign off on them, and their office is always on your side.

"No," Jake answered.

Wojanowski was visibly disappointed. "Nothing?"

"Not exactly."

"Jake, don't make me pull teeth here," she said with a twinge of annoyance. "Sounds to me like you're no further along than when you started. If you've got something, then let's hear it. It seems like heat and this Morson Grayhead thing are synonymous, and right now, I'm getting more of it than you can imagine. The entire metropolitan press corps has pitched camp squarely up my asshole, gentlemen. I can't even walk to my car in peace. You guys have got to get me something on this case. Give me crumbs. Something. *Anything.*"

"There is no case," Jake reminded her. "Yet. That's why we're here."

Her eyes widened. "No shit. You said you thought you were onto something. What makes you say that? You've got to have something for me."

"Well . . . yes and no," Jake said as his pager buzzed his waist. He pulled it off his belt, recognizing the number from the medical examiner's office.

Wojanowski rolled her eyes in disgust. "Christ. That's beautiful, Jake. 'Yes and no.' Placate me here, okay? Take a guess. Which one would you say you're leaning toward? The yes, or the no?"

"Definitely yes."

"Why?"

"Experience, I guess. You interview enough people, you pretty much get a feel when they're not telling you the truth. Both Donny and I noticed it when she told us she didn't know where Scotty was. And we both caught it again when she said she didn't recognize the photo. She stopped breathing when she looked at it, Irena. It was pretty obvious."

"That one really stood out, if you ask me," Ederling added.

Wojanowski looked at Ederling, then back to Jake. "That's it? A feel? Nothing more concrete? Based upon what you've told me, that just doesn't make sense. I would think she would want this Parks guy more than anything else in the world. Why on earth would she lie to you about something like that? Ever think it's possible, gentlemen, that your sixth sense isn't right on this one?"

Both men shook their heads. "No," Jake said emphatically. "We know she's lying. We just don't know why."

Wojanowski pulled up to her desk, placed her elbows on its shiny mahogany grain, and rested her chin on the backs of her hands. She breathed deeply before speaking. "All right, what do you need?"

Jake pulled himself up to the edge of his chair, resting his elbows on his knees. He stared across Wojanowski's desk, looking into her eyes. "We need a grand jury subpoena for Lianne Rybeck's phone records dating back to November of last year."

"November?" she asked, opening a drawer for the subpoena form. "Why November?"

"Because mothers always speak to their children during the holidays. It might help us spot a pattern if we can see who she called on or around Thanksgiving or Christmas."

"Okay, November it is. What's her phone number?"

Jake told her and watched as she filled it in, finishing her task by stamping it with the raised seal of the County of Westchester. Jake reached halfway across her desk as she held it out to him. He eyed the subpoena, pulling slightly on the form, only to raise his eyes to hers when it did not release.

"Get me *something*, Jake. I can't go another week with nothing for the press. They've become more than problematic. They're a goddamned nightmare."

I know, I know. It will look bad come election time. "If our hunch is right, Irena, you're about to be pleasantly surprised."

"Good," she said, releasing the subpoena to his grasp. "Let's hope so. For the sake of us both."

As they left her office, Jake stopped to call the ME's office. "You mind?" he asked the young clerk, pointing to the phone.

"Be my guest. Dial nine first."

Jake dialed the number from memory, scanning paperwork from the various different caseloads piled on the clerk's L-shaped desk as he waited for the medical examiner to pick up his call.

"Hi, Jake," the ME said after a few minutes. "Thanks for getting back to me so quickly."

Jake hoped to hell the ME finally had those DNA results. "Look, Doc, if you have what I think you have, I apologize for making you wait."

"Yeah, I have it all right. Just got the finished analysis on my desk a half hour ago."

"Thank God," Jake said, feeling certain now that the Morson Grayhead case was about to break the sound barrier. He could feel it picking up speed and viscerally knew it was about to break wide open. "What are we dealing with?"

"As you know, Jake, the results don't tell us much without a comparative sample."

Thanks for sharing, Doc. "I know, I know. Just tell me who we're dealing with here."

"No surprises, I should think. It's definitely a white male."

"You sure?"

"No doubt."

"Thanks, Doc." The ME was right. Having a DNA test result with nothing to compare it to was like holding a piece of a jigsaw puzzle without the rest of the puzzle on the table. But Jake was sure the missing pieces would arrive soon enough. In the meantime, at least he was relieved to hear that he and Ederling had not spent the last few days hacking deeply into the wrong forest. "Stick tight, Doc. We'll get you comparisons soon enough. But when we do, you got to move them for me. No way we can wait this long next time."

"I understand. You get me some comparisons, and I'll move them to the top of the list. Don't ask me how, but I'll do it."

"You're the man, Doc."

"Just get me those comparisons."

Jake hung up, thinking the ME's last comment was easier said than done. Getting his hands on a subpoena was the easy part. Getting them on a search warrant would be substantially more difficult, especially when one's case is primarily circumstantial. But getting a judge to sign off on an *intrusive* search warrant—one in which the suspect is made to supply hair and blood samples—your case had better be pretty damn good. And while Jake could smell the stench all around him, he knew that he and Ederling had yet to find the room full of rotting garbage. Their case was getting better, but was still a long, long way from "pretty damn good."

It was a five-minute drive to the Fire Marshal's Office, and for the first time all day Jake noticed the beginnings of butterflies forming in his stomach. It was nearly 1:00 P.M., and he realized that in less than six hours he would be going on his first date in years. The thought began to frighten him a little, but he'd had enough clumsy-bachelor bashing for one day, so kept his thoughts to himself.

"Want to grab a bite somewhere?" he asked Ederling, pulling out of the parking garage.

"Yeah, I'm starved."

"Shit, Don, you're always starved."

"No, I mean it," Ederling said, rubbing his stomach. "I'm really hungry. It was like the Keystone Kops at my house this morning and I didn't even grab a bagel. I need something."

"We wouldn't want you to blow away."

"Hey, I know. How about some Kentucky Fried?" Ederling asked as they drove by a red-and-white bucket tilting in the air. "We haven't done that in a while."

Jake looked at him. "Come on, Don, what the fuck am I going to eat there? It's hardly a dieter's paradise."

"They got that skinless stuff," Ederling said, looking at Jake.

"Right, and those world-famous fat-free mashed potatoes and gravy. Why don't we grab some Chinese takeout and go back to the office? I want to get this subpoena working."

Jake's dieting was really getting to Ederling. He didn't care that Jake did it, but they were practically chained to one another, and so naturally, it affected him, too. And if there was one thing Ederling liked, it was his food. "All right," he said with the voice of a young boy who's just been told to go to bed. "Jesus Christ, Jake, just because you're dieting doesn't mean I should have to."

"All right, all right," Jake said with lighthearted disgust. "Jesus, Don, I feel like I'm with my nephew." Jake whipped his Crown Victoria in a U-turn. "We'll drive through. Get whatever artery-clogging shit you want."

"It's chicken, Jake. It's good for you."

"Right."

"No, I'm serious. Chicken's not bad."

Jake shook his head as they pulled into the drive-through lane. "Broiled maybe. I'm not sure I'd exactly call this diet food."

"Whatever," Ederling said, leaning over, looking past Jake at the order board. "I'm not on a diet. I don't give a shit."

JAKE AND EDERLING walked into their office, each placing a bag with his meal on his desk. Jake pulled out a diet Coke, two white Chinese take-out boxes, one filled with steamed white rice, the other with a broccoli-and-chicken combination. Ederling pulled out a container of mashed potatoes, gravy, a biscuit, and four Extra Crispy breasts.

Ederling dug in voraciously as Jake picked up his phone to call his contact at Bell Atlantic. "Hi, Janice. It's Jake," he said, anxious to see what Lianne's phone records would reveal.

"Jacob Ferguson," she said with genuine sentiment. "To what do I owe this pleasure?"

Like all good investigators, Jake had a solid stable of contacts at various government agencies and corporations around the tristate area. With a few phone calls he could get just about anything he needed, from the owner of a certain license plate from DMV, to someone's name from the Social Security Administration. "I apologize for hitting you out of the blue like this, Janice, but I've got a grand jury subpoena here that needs immediate attention. You think it'd be possible for you to work free long enough to get me some phone records? It's important."

"Important, huh? You ever call me with a request that wasn't?"

Jake laughed. "No, I guess you got me there. But this is the Morson Grayhead case. It's more urgent than most."

"Oh, that's right, I forgot. That one *would* be yours, wouldn't it?"

"What can I say? Some people have all the luck."

"When are you coming in?" Corporate policy was clear on this. No records issued without a stamped subpoena *in hand*.

"Listen, Janice, I'm up to my eyeballs in alligators. You mind if I just fax it to you like last time? I can get the original in the mail today."

Janice could see that one coming. "Jake, you're not asking me to do this again, are you? You know I can lose my job if I don't have the original on my desk."

Jake had worked with Janice many times and knew that she trusted him implicitly. In the end, he'd get what he wanted, but he also knew it would probably cost him—especially when he asked her for his next favor. "I know," Jake said, his voice betraying his feelings of guilt. "But I really need it, Janice. There's just too much at stake here." He paused before asking the big one. "Oh . . . I also need something else."

"You're killing me, Jake. You need a reel search, don't you?"

"I need it desperately, Janice," Jake answered in a sheepish voice. "The call I'm most interested in was probably made this morning."

Jake knew there are two drawbacks to a subpoenaed billing search. The first is that a calling record is really nothing more than a copy of a customer's monthly bill and therefore only lists long distance or collect calls. The second is that it only lists calls made up to the printing of the last bill. Consequently, the one call he most wanted to check, the one he hoped Lianne had made after they left her this morning, would not be listed.

To find that, he'd have to order a file reel search. This is performed manually and is therefore time-consuming. And at $225 a pop, they're not cheap either. But you have to do what you have to do, and right now, Jake had no choice. *If* Lianne had called someone after they left, he had to find out whom.

Even then, he doubted a file reel search would show them anything if the call Lianne had placed was local. But sometimes lines are full and calls get rerouted through different trunks. He might just luck out. It wouldn't be the first time. In either event, if Janice was true to form, Jake would find out soon enough every long-distance call Lianne Rybeck had made since November. Jake found himself hoping once again that Scotty didn't live close by.

Janice sighed. "So you want me to order a reel search without a subpoena in-house?"

No sense lying. It is what it is. "Yes. Yesterday if possible. I know I'm pushing, Janice, but I really need your help."

"All right, Jake. I just hope your office is hiring if I get the boot. This one's going to cost you."

Jake had wondered when that was coming. She never missed a chance to help out those less fortunate than herself. "I figured as much. It's worth every penny. Just name your price."

Janice paused momentarily, as if deciding what the risk was worth. "A hundred," she finally said, thinking that a reasonable sum for both parties concerned.

"A hundred clams?" Jake asked, hiding his relief. He had thought she might really slam him on this one. "Man, I need a new contact."

"Hey, times are tough."

"I forgot what a tough bargain you drive. What's the address again?"

"The Brooklyn Heights School for Developmentally Disabled Children. Twenty-three North . . . ," she began, reciting to Jake for the hundredth time the address of her favorite charity. Jake never felt bad writing the checks. The cause was good and he always felt it unique that she made him send donations to a cash-strapped organization in return for corporate favors she could easily have done for free. Jake thought it was a nice touch, but worried how problematic it would be if Janice ever did get caught. Still, though it went unsaid, he didn't worry enough to keep from asking. Some things take precedence.

"I'm going to have to see this place someday," Jake said.

"You should. They do God's work, Jake."

"I can believe it."

"All right, fax me the subpoena and give me a half hour. I'll have the records faxed back to you by two."

"I really mean it, Janice, thank you. You're a saint."

"Yeah, yeah, just don't go making this a habit, Jake. The school needs a new computer, and I'm not sure you can afford to buy them one."

File reel searches can take up to a week. Jake couldn't wait that long. "When can I have the reel search?"

Jake could hear Janice breathe deeply on the other end of the line. "Give me till Monday. I'll see what I can do."

Jake knew it was as good as done. "Thanks again, Janice. I owe you."

"Oh, you owe me, all right. I think you just earned yourself a seat during the school's telethon."

"Count me in."

Jake hung up the phone and sat, staring at his hand on the receiver. "What'd she hit you for this time?" Ederling asked through a mouthful of fried chicken.

"A C-note."

"A hundred bucks?" Little pieces of chicken flew out Ederling's mouth as he let go a long whistle. "Man, she must really love that school."

"She does. You ask me, I got off easy. She had me by the balls on this one." Jake opened a container and shoveled rice onto a Styrofoam plate with a fork. He poured some broccoli and chicken on his rice, taking a mouthful before speaking. Jake knew that getting a grand jury subpoena from Wojanowski was one thing, but getting a judge to sign off on a search warrant was going to be another matter altogether. "You know, Donny, I don't think we've got enough for a search warrant. I think a judge is going to tell us to walk."

Ederling ripped off another piece of chicken, chewing while he thought. "I know," he said after a swallow. "I've been worried about that, too. Let's see what Mrs. Rybeck's records show, then decide how to tackle it. No sense borrowing trouble until we have more facts."

Jake had budgeted ten thousand dollars last year for his department to purchase a computer link to Bell Atlantic. Known as Fast-Trac, in a matter of seconds it could tell him the name and address of most any number, business or personal, in the Bell Atlantic system. When Lianne's records finally came, all he'd have to do was enter numbers in the computer. The only customers who would not appear were those with unlisted numbers or those outside the Bell Atlantic system. It wasn't ideal, but was a hell of a lot better than the alternative.

Jake finished the last of his diet Coke, tossing the empty in a recycling bin near the door. He wrapped up the remnants of his meal, threw them in his wastebasket, and went to the men's room to brush his teeth and wash his face. When he returned, the fax machine in the corner of the office was spewing forth its sixth sheet of paper. He walked over, picked up the pile lying in the bin, and began scanning Lianne Rybeck's telephone billing records.

Apparently Lianne liked her telephone. There were scores of calls, many to every corner of the globe. Jake noticed a dozen or so calls to London, a handful to Paris and Rome, two each to Hong Kong, Sydney, Tel Aviv, and Prague. There were numerous calls to Toronto and Montreal, and several each to California, Texas, Florida, and Pennsylvania. Most, however, were to the tristate area, equally dispersed between Connecticut and New York, with a few made to New Jersey.

Jake had to assume that some of them were made by Severin, though obviously, the exact number would never be known. He was busy counting the many calls he would be unable to trace via Fast-Trac when his secretary entered the office. "Mail call," she said as she had a thousand times before, dumping a stack of envelopes on Jake's desk. She took one off the pile and walked it over to him. "Thought you might want to see this one, Jake. It's kind of unique."

Jake looked up from Lianne's phone bill, staring at the white envelope Cissy held in her hand. "What the hell? *Unique* fits. This just come in?"

"Yep. Just sorted it."

Jake motioned to a table next to the fax machine. "Lay it there, will you, Cis? Oh, and get me a pair of latex gloves. Donny, come here a sec. You'll want to see this."

Ederling walked over, wiping his hands on a napkin. "What'ya got?"

Jake pointed to the envelope. "Oh, boy," Ederling said in a knowing voice. "Let the games begin."

"You think?" Jake asked, looking at him.

"Do I think? Shit, Jake . . . just look at it."

The address on the envelope resembled a ransom note. Every letter was a different font and size and had been meticulously clipped from an assortment of newspapers and magazines. They were neatly glued in place, then covered with a wide band of clear packaging tape. Both men stood quiet, staring at this newest addition of excitement to their lives.

"Here you go, Jake," his secretary said, walking back into the office, handing him a pair of soft-white latex gloves.

"Thanks, Cis," he said, taking the gloves. "You want to stick around for this? Should be interesting." He didn't mind inviting her. She loved the investigative part of his job, and Jake knew her mouth was a steel door.

"Really?" she asked with excitement. "I'd love to."

"Have a seat," Jake said, motioning to the round table in the opposite corner of the room.

Ederling and Cissy both pulled up chairs at the table. Jake followed suit. He placed the envelope facedown on the table, took out a small Swiss army knife from his pants pocket, and placed it on the table next to the envelope. He stared at Donny with curious eyes as he pulled on a pair of gloves.

"Any chance it's a letter bomb?" Ederling asked.

For a moment Jake had thought of that, but decided it was too thin. Judging from its thickness, or lack thereof, it probably only contained one sheet of paper. "Nah, impossible. Too thin." Jake held the envelope down by a corner with a gloved forefinger, sliding the small blade under the flap. "Any guesses?" he asked, stopping in midmotion.

"I got a fin that says it's our Morson Grayhead boy," Ederling said.

"Cis?" Jake asked, staring at his secretary.

She giggled nervously. "I can't believe you guys are betting on this thing. All right, Don's guess sounds good to me."

Jake continued sliding his blade through the envelope. "That makes three of us."

There was silence as Jake pulled the one sheet of white paper from the envelope. He noticed his heart was pumping. You just never know. It could be any number of things, from a death threat to information on yet another murder. Ederling knew it, too, and with a wife and kids at home, he had more to lose. Jake opened it, held it up, then brought it down a few inches as he looked at his rapt audience.

"Never a dull moment, huh?"

Ederling made a face. "Jesus, Jake, just read the friggin' letter, will ya?"

"Okay, okay. Christ, Donny, I swear, sometimes you have the patience of a rattlesnake."

"Yeah, well, this is one of those times."

Jake was quiet, his face turning somber as he read it first to himself. Ederling was visibly perturbed. "Jake, you going to read it out loud, or what?"

Jake turned the letter around for them to see. It looked just like a dozen other ransom letters you see on television, and as on the outside of the envelope, each sentence began with a bold capital letter. Jake turned it back toward him and began to read aloud.

" 'Dear Mr. Fire Marshal,

Jake be Nimble,
Jake be Quick,
Jake jump over the Candle Stick.

Time is a Ticking,
Matches are Burning,
So tell me, Jake,
What are you Learning?

Think you're close to Revealing,
The Monster who burns for Pain and Healing?
Things are seldom as they Appear,
Get too close, and you'll know FEAR.

My advice is to look in a Mirror,
The day of Judgment is drawing NEAR.' "

Jake looked up, only to see the blood drain from his secretary's face. She was staring at him saucer-eyed, fully aware of the not-so-implicit threat in the rhyme her boss had just read. Jake took a deep breath, pretending its contents didn't bother him.

He was surprised by Cissy's reaction. "You okay, Cis? Want some water?"

She shook her head, wondering how Jake could remain so calm. Up until a few moments ago, she thought she liked this investigative stuff. But now, she wasn't so sure. This seemed to cross a line. "How did he know to send this to you?" she asked.

Jake shrugged halfheartedly, as if it didn't matter. "The papers I guess. The guy'd have to live in a cave not to have read about this case." Jake thought for a moment. The murders were bad enough, but now this madman was taunting . . . no . . . threatening him. "Well, Donny," he said, folding the letter neatly and replacing it in the envelope, "what do you think?"

In a million years, Ederling would never have shared his first true thoughts with Jake. He was torn between anger and relief that the letter had not mentioned him or his family. He was quiet for a spell, sorting through his thoughts and emotions. "Well . . . obviously, we'll get it printed, but you and I both know that's gonna be a waste of time."

Jake folded his hands on top of his head and exhaled deeply as he stared at the ceiling. He hated when shit like this happened, that moment in an investigation when the villain becomes emboldened, just arrogant enough to think that threatening Jake would somehow turn him away. It did not happen often, thank God, but this wasn't the first time. Jake was only a man, and of course it made him nervous. But he was also the boss, the one people looked to for direction and focus, and he never thought it appropriate to reveal fear. Inner strength must prevail.

"Yep," Jake said, drawing out the word. "*Now* it's personal. Our boy just made his first big mistake." Jake rose and walked to his desk, pulling out a Ziploc bag from a drawer. He bagged the envelope and handed it to Cissy. "Get this printed, will you, Cis?"

"Sure thing," she said, still visibly shaken.

"And take the rest of the day off."

"You sure, Jake?"

"You bet. Go enjoy your kids."

She thanked him as she closed the door, leaving Jake and Ederling alone in the office.

"You all right?" Ederling asked.

"Me? Shit, I'm fine," Jake lied. "I want this motherfucker in the worst way, Donny. I'll die nailing this son of a bitch."

"That makes two of us. Where do you want to start?"

Jake sat back down at the table, extending his legs out in front of him. "Let me ask you a question, Don. When someone puts something like this together, what do you think is left over?"

"A whole mess of cut-up publications."

"Right. And where do you think they put them?"

There was no doubt Jake was good, but still, it seemed too obvious. "In the trash?" Ederling asked in an unsure voice, thinking he must have missed something.

"In the trash is right. Get on the horn and find out when they pick up the trash in . . . what is it again? Oh, yeah, Englewood Cliffs. I want to go through every scrap of garbage that asshole's thrown out this week. We find the right cut-up publications, I think we may just have enough for our intrusive search warrant."

"On it."

Jake walked back to the fax machine, picked up the remaining five pages of Lianne Rybeck's billing records, and began entering numbers, one at a time, into the Fast-Trac computer. He copied down in his notebook every name and address as it appeared, finding himself thinking once again of his upcoming date.

He was still excited, but somehow now, a good deal of the fun had been taken out of it. Jake was resentful that on the eve of his biggest night in years, fate would intervene to give him cause for more angst. He worried that perhaps it was selfish to even follow through when there was a chance he could actually put Valerie in danger and found himself wondering whether he should tell her. But upon reflection, that seemed about as good a way to kill his chances for revival as was humanly possible.

With all that had just happened, or was about to happen, Jake was starting to feel the beginnings of a true anxiety attack. His heart pumped spasmodically, his palms grew clammy, and his stomach felt as if someone were wringing out a wet dishcloth. He desperately needed fresh air.

"Donny, I'm going to take a quick walk. I'll be right back."

Ederling was on the phone with New Jersey information, but hung up when he heard Jake's words. "You sure you're okay?"

"Yeah, I'm fine. Just need a little fresh air is all. I got to figure out what the hell I'm going to do besides bowling."

Jake's brief walk turned into the better part of forty-five minutes. When he returned to the office, Ederling was entering numbers into Fast-Trac and recording their respective owners on a yellow legal pad. It had been a long day, and Jake felt they'd both benefit if they knocked off early and got a fresh start on Monday.

Normally, when an investigation began to gel, they would work at least a half day on Saturday. But too much was hanging in the air, too many questions that would not be answered until Monday at the earliest. Jake figured from then on they'd both be moving at full speed and thought it best they attack with clear heads and rested bodies.

"Anything?" Jake asked, tossing some papers into his briefcase.

"Nothing yet."

Jake did want to know the Englewood Cliffs garbage schedule. "When's trash pickup?"

"Next one's Monday."

"I think I'll go myself and wait for the truck to come. Did you find out when?"

"Hard to say, exactly. DPW told me Parks's neighborhood is probably early to mid morning."

"All right then, I'll get there early."

The two men walked to the parking lot together. Ederling leaned over the roof of his car, his keys dangling from a finger. He was happy for his friend. "Listen, call me, will ya? I want to know how it goes tonight."

"I will."

"You nervous?"

Jake had opened his car door and stood leaning both elbows on it. "A little."

"You'll do great. I'm sure of it. Hey . . . and listen, if you want to take her bowling, take her bowling. Don't listen to me. I'm sure you guys will have a blast."

Jake smiled. "We'll see."

"Just be yourself."

Like a miler running solo, it's hardest to gauge yourself when you're going it alone. Jake wondered now if he hadn't made a mistake by not making it a double date with Ederling and his wife. A partner keeps you in check, helps give you something to measure yourself by. He wasn't sure he knew just who the hell he was anymore. "I'll try."

"Hey, that's all you can do, right?"

LIANNE RYBECK HAD made at least two dozen calls to Warren Parks since late morning when Jake and Ederling had left her. Fear and uncertainty began to melt into unmitigated panic as time and again she heard nothing but his answering machine. Since their visit, she had done nothing but toss different scenarios around in her head, like so many Ping-Pong balls in a lottery game. She did not know just what the hell was going on, but was sure now it was horrific in its proportions and most likely did involve her son. Whatever was up, Lianne intuitively knew that Warren was at the heart of it. She was about to place the phone on its receiver for what seemed the hundredth time that day when Parks picked up the line.

"Hello?"

Lianne was startled. It took a few moments to respond. "Hello, Warren."

There was a pause on the other end. It spoke to her of paranoia and distrust. For reasons known only to them, Warren immediately recognized her voice. "Hello, Lianne. . . . Look . . . I don't know what game you're playing, but I'm not in the mood. If it's warm and fuzzies you're looking for, find someone else."

"Well, get in the mood," she answered forcefully. "We need to talk. And anyway, you and I both know that I know too much."

"What do you want?" Warren asked impatiently.

Lianne spoke calmly but with firm resolve. "I'm your meal ticket, Warren. Remember? Don't even think of playing coy with me."

There was stone silence on the other end of the line. This time, Warren didn't break it. She knew that would get his attention. "Now, you listen to me very carefully, Warren. I am only going to say this once. If I find out you've been in contact with my son, so help me God, I will kill you."

Warren spoke more calmly, as if suddenly determining the upper hand was now his. "I wondered when you might call."

"Well, you don't need to wonder anymore, do you?"

"Good thing, too. I was losing sleep."

"A pair of fire investigators were here today, Warren. Guess what they showed me?"

"No?" he said mockingly. "Those perverts."

"They showed me a picture of you, Warren," she said, thinking that bit of news just might help erase some of his smugness.

"Yeah? So what?"

"They think you're somehow involved in the Morson Grayhead murders and wanted to know if I recognized you."

"Did you?"

"I'd never seen you before in my life."

"That was a smart move, Lianne. Good to see you can still think on your feet."

"You know what? I think they're right."

"You do, huh? Well, guess what, Lianne? I don't give a shit what you think."

"I didn't think you would. But be careful, Warren . . . my memory just might come back."

"Now, that would be most unfortunate, wouldn't it, Lianne? I don't think you really want to do that, do you?"

A mother's fury raged through Lianne's veins. The mere thought that this sociopathic monster would dare enter Scotty's life again incensed her. "You listen to me, you son of a bitch," she ordered with deep-rooted hatred. "Stay away from my son. Do you understand me? Stay away from him or I swear to God . . ."

"What?" Warren asked, suddenly buoyed. "Or what? You going to blow the lid off the whole thing?" He laughed aloud, ridiculing her forceful pretense. "I don't think so, Lianne. Who's going to care for your precious little nut case once they've slammed the bars on you? He'd surely die out there on his own, and you know it. He wouldn't stand a chance."

"Don't push me, Warren, or I'll take you down with me. I swear I will."

"You're full of shit, Lianne. As they say in the male world, you just don't have the balls, my dear."

Lianne Rybeck would never allow this demented little shit to take over her son's life again. Warren was dangerously close to pushing her too far. "Warren, you don't have any idea just how big my balls are. I warn you, *don't* cross me. Don't even *think* I won't crush you like a bug."

"You're cute when you threaten, you know that?"

"I'm not threatening you, Warren. I'm promising you."

Warren's voice suddenly turned menacingly cold, demonically detached from the person she'd just been speaking with. "Oh, no, Lianne. Perhaps it is *you* who should be careful. You mess with me, and I guarantee you, you're toast."

Lianne's throat closed. It *was* him. "It's you, isn't it? You're the monster behind all this?"

"What? You don't really think I'm *that* stupid, do you? I would have thought the years would have made you wiser. Apparently I was wrong."

Lianne knew Warren's twisted, calculating mind. She knew now he'd covered his tracks. Was he somehow manipulating her son? Had he, unbeknownst to her, dug his talons once again into Scotty's back? Worse yet, had he somehow engineered some plot to frame Scotty for his own deeds? If he had, the further she pushed, the more certain Scotty's arrest and incarceration would be. The thought that her life's treasure would be victimized yet again, vilified, manacled, perhaps put to death . . . Her blood ran cold.

She did not know just who was responsible for what, but knew one thing for sure—Warren Parks could *not* be trusted. While it was nearly impossible for her to believe, still, if it was Scotty, she would need to go to him, rescue him from those who would do him harm. Clearly, he would need to be stopped.

But Lianne knew all too well how powerful the dollar can be. She could arrange his incarceration discreetly, behind the scenes, away from the vulturous, prying eyes of the press. She could see to it that Scotty was safe, warm, and provided for in humanitarian fashion. A foreign country perhaps. The thought of her helpless, disenfranchised son behind bars in a federal penitentiary becoming love fodder for groups of violent, demeaning men . . . the mere thought nearly sent her over the edge. It would never happen. Not while she still lived.

"Are you seeing my son?" she asked forthrightly.

"No," Warren answered, feigning tears. "He dumped me for a younger man. I was heartbroken."

This man was so sick. How could she have let him control her life for so many years? She would get to the bottom of this and protect her son. But once that was done—once her deepest fear in life had been tended to—she swore her final living act would be to rip Warren's heart from his chest.

"If it's the last thing I ever do, Warren, I am going to watch you die. And I will be spitting in your face."

"You listen to me, Lianne. One peep out of you and your whole little world comes crashing down. Don't even *think* of fucking with me. I'm the only friend your son ever had. Without me, he'd be—"

"You *bastard!*" Lianne screamed into the phone. "How *dare* you say such a thing. Don't tell me you are his friend. You know how much I love him. You know he was my reason for living."

"That's not quite how I saw it when I was there in your private little acre of hell. Seemed to me that you and that wacko husband of yours couldn't give him the time of day. There was a kid who never had a chance. All that money, and he was doomed from the time he plopped out. Go figure, huh?"

Lianne shook violently, unable to control her rage. "I nearly died, Warren. You know that. Scotty was the only thing that kept me alive. He is the reason I am alive today."

"Oh, isn't that cute," Warren said with mock charm. "Here, let me get out my violin. I got news for you, Lianne. Scotty was fucked-up by the time we got there. His father, if that's what you want to call him, had scared that boy so bad, he'd have followed a snake home if he thought it had smiled at him. The damage was done long before we got there. We gave the boy something to latch onto. A belief to call his own. Someone he could trust. Someone who believed in him."

Like swipes of a razor to her heart, Warren's every syllable ripped her open. Tears streamed down her face at the realization that her best had simply not been good enough. A boy needs a father, and it's better to have none at all than one who shuns the young man's very existence. Lianne spit on Severin's grave.

She was spent. Every ounce of energy, every wall of defense, every lie she had told herself for so many years—like sand castles at high tide, they all disintegrated on the spot. She prayed desperately for the nightmare to end. "Please, Warren," she implored. "Please leave Scotty alone. I'm begging you. Just let him be."

"Aaah, the true Lianne comes forth. So fragile. So sad. Don't you worry about your little Scotty, Lianne. At least he has a friend."

Her heart bled at the thought of friendship so cruel, so one-sided, so wantonly parasitic. How often had Warren hurt him, if not physically, then certainly mentally? How often had Scotty's heart been broken, only to try to please this madman harder the next time around. How often was he told hurtful, deceptive lies? Lianne had long since lost control of her one meaningful jewel, her one reason for clinging so tenaciously to life. She felt an overwhelming sense of helplessness, of knowing now that it was all happening again.

"Good-bye, Warren," she said softly before hanging up.

Lianne sobbed uncontrollably on the edge of her bed, tears streaming out her eyes, dripping to the hardwood floor below, as her body heaved and swayed in unrestrained anguish. Like a wolf howling at the moon, she wailed aloud, the moans wafting past her door into the hallway beyond. When finally her body could take no more, she curled into a ball and lay on the comforter of her bed, squeezing her pillow close to her. She would cry like that for many hours to come. The staff heard her cries and called a doctor. He incorrectly assumed it was grief over Severin's loss and prescribed a light sedative. Though they remained silent, those who had worked for Lianne the longest knew nothing could be further from the truth.

JAKE TURNED THE key to his co-op at 4:26 P.M. What had started as the happiest day of his widowed life was ending in a twisted eddy of anxiety and emotion. A part of him wished now that he could just crawl into his bed with a good book, read for a while, then sleep for twelve straight hours. For a brief moment he thought of calling Valerie and canceling their evening out, but feared how long he would remain holed up in his insular world if he didn't follow through. He was debating whether he should eat or wait for the date when his phone rang.

"Hello?"

"Jake, it's Pete."

He'd forgotten he'd put eyes on Parks. "Yeah, Pete, what'ya got?"

"Thought you'd like to know, stakeout just reported that your man came home five minutes ago."

"Any marks?"

"No, nothing noticeable."

"Shit. All right, thanks, Pete. Let me know the second he leaves that house. He goes mobile, I want to know. I'll be out tonight, so you'll have to page me. You got the number, right?"

"Yeah. One other thing. Seems he had someone with him."

"Really? Man or woman?"

"Man."

"Hmmm. All right, thanks. Keep me apprised."

"Will do."

"Oh, Pete," Jake said, fearful his CID contact had already hung up.

"What?"

"Listen, Monday's trash day. I need to get my hands on his garbage. I know it's probably too soon to mention it, but just make a note. I plan on being there early, but if for any reason I'm not, make sure your boys know to grab it off the truck."

"Sure thing."

"Off the *truck*, okay?" Jake asked to make sure Pete understood. "The last thing we need is inadmissible evidence."

Jake knew a taxpayer's garbage is private property until such time as it is loaded onto a municipal vehicle. He also knew trash could technically be taken if the cans were sitting over the property line, but didn't want to risk his case on the unknown memory of an Englewood Cliffs sanitation engineer. Not that it would necessarily be better or worse than anyone else's, but when you lift a thousand cans and bags a day, it's a rare judge who will believe someone is capable of remembering a particular can and its exact location. Jake thought it better to play it safe.

"Got it. Off the truck," Pete answered.

"And not from the garbageman's hands either. I mean, off the truck."

"Jake, relax. We've done this before."

"Okay, okay. Sorry." Jake realized he was pushing too hard. He needed rest. "I'm just uptight is all. I want this guy bad."

"No problem," Pete answered calmly. "You're in a big boat."

"Thanks."

Jake hung up and looked at his watch. He still had a couple of hours before he needed to leave to pick up Valerie. He figured forty-five minutes, an hour max, to shower, shave, and pick out his clothes. He was thinking cords and a beige Aran Isle sweater over a pink, oxford shirt. He wasn't quite sure whether he should wear a tie. *Maybe a jog will clear my mind. I'll see how I feel when I get back.*

Jake stripped, throwing his clothes on the bed, and dressed in shorts, a blue fire marshal's sweatshirt, and Asics Gels. He stretched briefly prior to heading out and, before he realized it, was already beyond the point he had reached just a few mornings ago. Maybe because it wasn't 5:00 A.M., or maybe because his adrenaline was pumping overtime, but whatever the reason, Jake found this jaunt less taxing than his last. Not that his previous experience would have been difficult to improve upon.

He returned to his co-op, soaking wet and gasping for air, just after 5:30 P.M. He was relieved he had given himself an hour to regroup, figuring it would take that long for his pulse to return to normal. Still, Jake was pleased with himself. The jog was brutal, but he had done it, and without stopping once. He pulled a dish towel off the refrigerator handle and wiped his face and neck as he sat on the edge of the sofa, head down in the towel, eventually reaching down to unlace his sneakers. He pulled off his wet, heavy sweatshirt and tossed it toward the entrance to the hall.

Jake sat for some time on the couch, almost unable to move. He was curious if his efforts were paying off and picked up his sweatshirt as he headed toward the bathroom, dropping it, his shorts, and jockstrap in the hamper before stepping on his scale. Jake watched himself sweat in the mirror, afraid to look down. What if all his suffering and sacrifice had been for naught? What if it hadn't even moved? He held his breath as he glanced at the digital numbers at his feet, heartened to see that he had dropped five pounds. He knew some of it was water loss, and that things would probably move more slowly from here on out. But still, five pounds is five pounds. He smiled, pleased with himself. At least a few things were going his way.

JAKE HAD ONLY one car, and his department-issue Crown Victoria cruiser was it. As he pulled to the curb in front of Valerie Medforth's apartment, he found himself feeling self-conscious about it. Jake worried now that perhaps it was too authoritarian for a first date, if maybe it would provoke an unwanted, subliminal tension.

Though unmarked on the outside, the car was clearly law-enforcement-related. The three antennae on the trunk and roof saw to that. And if for some reason that wasn't quite enough from the outside, the scanner, radio, microphone, and detachable, red-beacon flasher on the inside left no doubt. Jake wished now he had borrowed Don's Bronco.

Valerie lived on Bedford Road in Pleasantville. Jake instinctively straightened his Jerry Garcia tie, remembering his first burning death years ago, not more than half a mile from where he now sat. He thought momentarily of sharing the memory with Valerie before laughing at the idea and slapping himself back into reality. He checked his teeth, tossed a couple of wintergreen Tic-Tacs in his mouth, and ambled up the brick walk to her front door.

Jake felt calmer than he had anticipated and wondered if he had been better at this as a younger man than he remembered. It didn't matter now. He took a deep breath, exhaled, and pressed the button marked #5, MEDFORTH. Jake looked at his watch: 7:02 P.M. He waited patiently, deciding only then that he really didn't care what anyone else thought. He was going to take her bowling. If she was so stuck-up as not to be able to enjoy something so casual and lighthearted, Jake figured he probably didn't want to see her again anyway.

His pulse quickened as he heard a door shut and then footsteps on the stairs. He felt like a contestant on the old *Dating Game*, waiting for his pick to walk from behind the barrier. "Jacob Ferguson," he could hear the announcer say. "You and your lovely date will be traveling in your very own police cruiser to the romantic lanes of . . ." He saw Valerie's hand on the railing as she hit the last landing and smiled through the glass of the outside door as she turned the last flight of stairs.

Her hair seemed a cinnamon-strawberry blend and was fluffy and full on the top and sides, as if she had run her fingers through it a few times. It was cropped shorter in the back and yet stood away from her scalp. Its soft, bouncy style lent her an air of casual sophistication.

Oh, boy. Donny was right. She is stunning. Jake's palms began to sweat. He wiped his right hand thoroughly on his cords as she strode quickly toward the door, thinking it only had to appear dry long enough to shake her hand.

She opened the door and stepped down to the landing. "Hi," Valerie said, her white teeth glowing in an animated smile.

Jake couldn't explain it, but he felt immediately comfortable. Perhaps it was her spirited smile that set him at ease. "Hi. I'm Jake Ferguson."

"I'm Valerie Medforth," she said, extending a hand.

He shook it firmly. The lighting was not direct, but the penetrating robin's-egg blue of her eyes caught him nonetheless. "Nice to meet you, Valerie."

"Nice to meet you, too, Jake."

"Thanks for agreeing to go out on such short notice. I'm glad you weren't busy." Although, for the life of him, Jake could not understand why she wasn't. He figured a woman like this would be busy every weekend night.

"I am, too."

"Shall we?" Jake asked, waving his left arm down the walk. "That's us right there," he said, falling in beside her. "The white, police-looking car."

"They let you drive them when you're not on duty?"

"It's the only one I have."

"Really?" she asked, climbing in as he opened her door.

He liked her already. He was excited. *This will be fun.* Jake closed her door and whistled to himself as he crossed behind his cruiser and climbed in next to her. He had learned from his mother not to ask a date what she would like to do. "Have the evening planned," she told him. "A woman likes that."

He turned his head toward her, putting his cruiser in gear. She wore khaki pants, a pleated, white blouse buttoned to her neck, over which she wore a camel-colored, tweed Norfolk jacket with leather patches on the elbows. She looked pretty in a relaxed way. But what he really noticed was her perfume. It had been a long time since he had smelled that in his car. He tried to place it, but he'd been out of the loop too long.

"You hungry?" he asked.

"I could stand a bite."

"You like Chinese?"

She looked at him with a demure smile. "I love Chinese. Did Don tell you that?"

"Nope. It's just that I'm on a diet, and it's great diet food."

"Oh, a man after my own heart. I swear, my life is nothing but one perpetual diet. Don't you hate it?"

"I don't know if *hate*'s the right word," he said as he pulled his cruiser onto Bedford Road. "I'll tell you this much though. I'd rather get a root canal."

Valerie laughed. "Want to splurge? Just this once?"

Was it just wishful thinking, or did her question intimate that they would see each other again? "You're not going to be a bad influence on me, are you? Don't do this to me."

"All right," she said with an air of indifference, as if it were just an idea.

Jake looked at her. "What did you have in mind?"

"What's that?" she asked, pointing at his scanner.

Jake told her, using the opportunity to explain the other gadgets in his car. She seemed genuinely interested, and he was now secretly glad he'd driven it.

"Do you carry a gun?"

Jake looked at her. "Sometimes. I always keep one in the car, but don't usually wear it unless I'm going somewhere specifically to make an arrest."

"Really? That sounds so exciting. What exactly do you do? The newspapers say you're a fire marshal. I don't know exactly what that is, but you're not a policeman, right?"

"Right. Although I do have arrest authority. My actual job title is chief . . ." Jake explained his professional responsibilities and the nature of his job as best he could without boring her to death, thrilled that she truly seemed to care.

And so it went for the next two and a half hours, never that awkward moment of silence or a moment when he wondered if she was having a good time.

They ate themselves silly at a new Indian restaurant in White Plains. Jake was pleased to see she felt confident enough with who she was to fill herself and then some. Before he'd met Danielle, he could remember many a date eating like a bird when a perfunctory once-over with his eyes was proof of a significantly different lifestyle. It was a small touch, but he liked it just the same.

Not until they were bowling did Jake notice her breasts. She had removed her jacket for mobility and rolled her sleeves halfway up her arms. When she would turn just right, the fluorescent lights above would cast them in an alluring silhouette against the white cotton of her blouse. Something stirred inside him.

It certainly wasn't that they were large. Jake never did find that a particular turn-on. In fact, as he eyed them several more times throughout the evening, he thought her bust perhaps even a touch smaller than average. But it wasn't their size as much as their shape that caught his eye. She had to be in her midthirties, and yet strangely, and for reasons Jake could not adequately comprehend, they stirred memories of his first lover—an eighteen-year-old high school senior he'd felt certain he would marry.

Jake sat at the scorer's table, Bud Light in hand, and watched as she let go a ball. He realized for the first time all night that he was thinking purely of sex. He stripped her nude with his eyes, envisioning most every act of sex or sensuality the *Kama Sutra* ever thought to mention, and maybe a few it did not. He was aware of an almost animal drive welling up from within and was actually taken aback by its force.

It bothered him that he could sexualize her like that, turn the vision of this fun and lovely woman into nothing more than a pornographic fantasy. But he found her charming and attractive, and like it or not, sex is part of the equation—especially Jake's equation. It wasn't as though he'd had a great deal of it over the last several years. In fact, now that he thought of it, it wasn't as though he'd had any at all. He was only human, relatively healthy and young. Four years is a long time.

Jake had always been a gentleman with women and knew that would never change. And though some men may vehemently deny its existence, even those most gentlemanly on the outside share a darker, primal inside. They guard and hide it with an almost obsessive cloak of secrecy, but it is just as real and just as disturbing as in the most wretched of the gender. He found himself thinking for the thousandth time that if women could read men's minds, there would be no more babies.

Watch your testosterone. You're not a teenager anymore. Let's just see how this thing goes. Take your time. Don't screw it up. She'll let you know if she's interested. He couldn't help but wonder whether she would, and if she did, how long it would take.

Jake was truly enjoying himself. Much more so than he had anticipated. Valerie was funny, bright, energetic, outgoing, and he couldn't help but notice an occasional stare of the men at the bowling alley. Most confident men like that. He had never doubted the veracity of Don's description of her and couldn't help but feel that he had hit this one right on the head. There was certainly no denying Valerie Medforth's femininity, and yet, to Jake, her outward appearance seemed a smaller part of her overall appeal. She was a confident woman, sincere and easygoing—someone with whom Jake intuitively knew he could quickly learn to start anew.

"All right!" he cheered, watching the last of her pins finally topple to the floor.

She jumped up and down, obviously excited, and turned to face him wearing an ear-to-ear grin. "How 'bout them apples?" she asked, grabbing her beer as she approached the table.

Suddenly Jake's face turned solemn. "Damn."

"What?"

"My pager just went off."

"What's that mean?"

"I don't know for sure, but I'd be willing to place a bet," he said, perturbed that he couldn't let the evening conclude on its own terms. "Let me just make a call. I'll be right back."

He left, walking toward the public telephones near the rest rooms, and dialed Pete's number on his pager. "Hey, Pete. What's up?"

"Your man's mobile, Jake."

"Talk to me."

"He's alone and on foot. Walked to some watering hole called the Bird's Nest. You know it?"

"No. Where is it?"

Jake jotted down the address and thanked Pete. "I'm on my way. If there's a change of status, call me in the cruiser."

"Roger."

Jake hung up and laid his palms on the stainless-steel shelf below the phone bank, resting his head against the rough black steel of the phone. *Shit.* What was it about this job that could make him literally walk away from the best thing to happen to him in years? He wondered how healthy it was to put the job before all else, but knew it didn't matter. At this point he would sell his mother to catch this son of a bitch. *Valerie will just have to wait. Hopefully, she'll understand.*

"Valerie," he said when he returned, sitting on a chair as he untied his bowling shoes. "I'm really sorry, but we have to go."

"Ohhhh, Jake," Valerie said in genuine disappointment. "Really? Why?"

At least she seemed upset. *Maybe this thing will go somewhere.* "It's the Morson Grayhead case. My suspect is mobile."

"Let me go with you. It'll be fun."

He looked up at her. "Valerie, I wish I could let you do that. I really do. I'm having a great time. But I just can't. I'm sorry."

"Why not?"

"For one thing, it could be dangerous."

"So what?"

"So what? You could get hurt," Jake said, slipping on a loafer.

"I can handle myself, Jake. I have a black belt in karate."

Jake eyed her suspiciously. "You do not."

"Want to bet?"

"Are you shitting me? You have a black belt in karate?"

"Why is that so hard to believe? Because I'm a woman?"

Jake was quiet for a moment, thinking at first the answer was no. "No, it's just that . . ." Upon reflection, he thought indeed that probably was the only reason. "Get out. You really have a black belt?"

"Sure do."

"I'll be damned."

"So, I can go?"

Jake didn't want to tell her about the letter. He was afraid he would scare her away. "No, I'm sorry. It's an official investigation, Val. I just can't risk you getting involved."

"I might even be able to help," she added demurely.

Jake finished tying his shoes. "You think so, huh? Just how do you think you might do that?"

"Well," she said slowly, thinking, "where is he?"

"In a bar."

"Are you going to tell him who you are, or are you going undercover?"

She's a smart one. "No. It's covert. I want to talk with him when his guard is down. Hopefully just grab a stool next to him. If I'm lucky, maybe he'll have a few pops in him."

"You see. Right there, I can help you fit in more. You know, you'll be far less suspicious if you walk in there with a date."

He couldn't argue with her there. Jake wasn't sure if she really wanted to be with him or just found the excitement of the hunt intoxicating. In either event, he was loath to push her away. He looked at her in silence for a few moments. He knew he shouldn't, but it wasn't as if they were meeting Warren in a dark alley. He wanted to in the worst way, but every professional instinct told him that he just couldn't take the risk.

"Listen, Valerie, I don't think I could find the words to tell you how disappointed I am about this. I'm really enjoying myself. But I just can't. I'm sorry. Please try and understand."

She sat down next to him and placed a hand on his thigh. "Please take me with you."

Jake could feel his insides melting. "How do I know you won't say something that could screw up the whole investigation?"

She knew she had him. "I won't say a word. Just, 'Hi, how are you?'—that type of thing. Please, Jake. I like being with you."

That sealed it. Loneliness creates its own weaknesses. Jake stared down the alley. He was quiet for a long time. *I can't believe I'm doing this.* "Okay," he finally said. "But I want you running at the first sign of trouble, got that?"

"Got it."

"And don't say a word. Promise?"

"Promise."

What am I doing? Fuck it. I am the boss. "All right, let's go. He won't stay there all night."

Valerie watched Jake attach the red, magnetic strobe to the roof of his car and flick a switch to the right of his steering wheel. An electric energy filled her as the trees and cars around them shone intermittently in flashing red.

"Ready?" he asked, flipping on the audible-siren switch. "Buckle up."

Jake cruised at about eighty miles per hour, slowing only when traffic dictated. He took 287 West over the Tappan Zee Bridge and hooked up with Route 9W before connecting to the Palisades Parkway. Most everyone has experienced the unnerving anxiety of seeing alternating headlights, or wigwags, in their rearview mirror, but few civilians experience it from the other side of the dash. Valerie's heart hammered against her chest, as one car after the other changed lanes to clear their way. As it does with most law enforcement professionals, it juiced her.

For the most part, Valerie remained quiet the majority of the trip, only breaking their silence to answer an occasional question or pose one of her own. With someone else, at another time, Jake might have been more self-conscious with the lack of conversation, but he knew she was enjoying herself. And anyway, when the siren is roaring, the inside of a cruiser is hardly conducive to conversation.

At one point she turned to him, speaking louder than normal so as to be heard over the siren's wail. "This man you're going to see. Is he the one responsible for the Morson Grayhead murders?"

Jake glanced at her. "We're not sure yet. We think there's a good chance."

"Why do you think that?"

"Oh, different things Donny and I have discovered in the course of the investigation."

"Like?"

"I'd tell you, but then I'd have to kill you," Jake said, staring straight ahead, finally smiling as he turned to look at her.

She smiled back. "Is it a secret?"

"For now. There's a lot we don't know yet. I think things will start to become more clear on Monday."

"Why Monday?"

Without too much detail, Jake explained the various avenues they were pursuing: the Philadelphia Exchange, phone records, DNA analysis, and intrusive search warrants. He did not mention Lianne Rybeck's name once, nor did he say anything about semen or the rapes. Only a select few law enforcement officers, and the murderer, knew about that. Jake wanted to keep it that way.

Some time passed as Valerie watched Jake pass cars as if they were standing still. Finally she turned to him. "Have you seen the bodies?"

"Which ones?"

"You know, the Morson Grayhead wives."

Jake did not like to think about it. It was the first thing she'd said all night that annoyed him. "Yes. I've seen them."

"Have you *touched* them?"

Jake wasn't sure where her mind was going, but hoped like hell his answers would not turn her off. He thought of changing the subject, but for some reason felt that leaving a question like that unanswered—just hanging out there unresolved—was probably not a good idea. Not at this point in the relationship. If his line of work was going to be a problem, he would just as soon find out about it now.

"Yes. I've touched them."

Valerie was quiet, staring out her window. Jake had that strange sense that she wanted to ask him a question, but didn't have the courage. He finally prompted it. "Why did you want to know that?"

"I guess I'm wondering how a man gets into a line of work like this. I don't think I could do it."

"That's okay. I can't either."

She eyed him skeptically. "I don't understand."

Jake left her comment unanswered, wishing he knew her well enough to talk about Poughkeepsie. All his life, he had kept that horrible night inside him. Like an undetected tumor, it had mutated and grown, haunting his every day for almost forty years. Danny was the only person he had ever told, and he had always believed she would probably be the last.

Mercifully, traffic was light and they made it to the Englewood Cliffs exit in under an hour. Jake figured that, by now, Parks had either left the bar or his tongue was well oiled. But he hadn't gotten a call, so assumed Parks was still in the Bird's Nest. He killed his lights and siren as he exited the Palisades, taking Route 505 West, and slowed to a crawl, shining his floodlight on cross-street signs.

"Here it is," he said, turning left on Hudson Street. He could see the glow on his right from a neon Miller sign illuminating a window of a small, clapboarded neighborhood bar. He pulled his cruiser under an aging elm whose roots were breaking through the nearby concrete walk.

Jake wanted to speak with his CID tail and knew they would be somewhere nearby. He opened his door and placed a foot on the curb. "Stay here," he said, looking at Valerie. "I need to speak with someone. I'll be right back."

"Where're you going?" she asked, a little apprehensive.

He turned to her. "We've obviously been keeping eyes on him, Val. That's how we know he's here. I just want to check in with them. That's all. You know? Let them know we're going in, find out what he's wearing, that kind of thing. It'll only take a sec. I promise. Just stay put. I'll be right back."

Jake closed the door and stood with his back to the door of his cruiser, scanning up and down the street. Other than for an occasional picture in the paper, the New York State Police CID surveillance team wasn't sure what Jake looked like. But they recognized the fire marshal's cruiser the moment it pulled up. Jake saw headlights turn quickly on, then off, and started toward the unmarked, dark brown Ford LTD a few cars down on the opposite side of the street.

The passenger-side cop was rolling down his window as Jake approached. "Jake Ferguson?"

"In the flesh," Jake said, leaning on the cruiser's window ledge. "Thanks for the call."

"That was quick."

"Traffic was light."

"Who's in the cruiser?" the driver asked, nodding his chin toward Jake's car. Jake looked toward his cruiser. "Long story. What do we have?"

The cop in the passenger seat did the rest of the talking. "Went in about an hour ago. Still there as best we can tell."

"Clothing?"

"Jeans and a green flannel shirt."

"Alone?"

"Yep."

"On foot?"

The cop nodded.

"All right. Tell you what," Jake said, looking at his watch. "Give me forty-five minutes. If I'm not out, why don't you come in and take a look?"

"Will do. Good luck."

Jake stood and smacked an open palm twice against the door. "Thanks."

The street was poorly lit, and Jake made a mental note of his surroundings as he walked back toward his cruiser. Just in case, he wanted to be sure he noted avenues of egress: alleyways, side streets, that sort of thing. He tucked in his shirt as he crossed the street, noticing the black shadow of Valerie's head through the rear window of his cruiser.

He opened the door and climbed inside. "All set," he said to Valerie as he reached into his glove compartment, pulling out his holstered Smith & Wesson, Model 65 Military & Police .357 magnum. Jake liked it better than their other six models in the .357 line.

For the first time all evening, Jake saw consternation on Valerie's face as he pulled the gun out in front of her. She frowned, as if in a sudden realization that this was no game. Jake reminded himself this was exactly why he didn't want to do what he was doing. This was the essence of the game: real life and deadly serious. The last thing he needed to be worrying about now was a third party's emotional stability. He had to know that she would not be a liability.

"Can you do this?" he asked, giving her one last out.

Valerie looked at him with determined eyes. "Just watch me."

"You sure?"

"Yes."

Something wasn't right. "What is it then, Val? Something's bothering you."

"I guess I'm just concerned he might recognize you. That *Daily News* photo was pretty prominent yesterday."

Jake remained silent for a moment. "I know." He stared down the dimly lit street through the windshield. "I've thought about that, but it's a chance I have to take. I may not get another opportunity like this. Anyway, not everyone reads the *News.*"

Valerie stared at Jake. "I hope he's not one of them."

"Me, too. . . . Okay. Remember our deal. Speak only if spoken to, all right?"

"All right."

"Any trouble, you head straight for the door. No heroics. Deal?"

"Deal."

Jake checked the magnum's chamber, unsnapped its holster, and stuck it under his belt in the small of his back. "Okay, let's go."

"Jake?"

His legs were already out the door. "What?"

"You think you'll need that?"

"I hope not. Come on."

Jake looked into her face as they stood in front of the door. "You okay?"

"Yeah, I'm fine."

"Good," he said, slipping his arm around her waist. "Sorry, but if we're going to do this for appearances, then we better look the part."

She smiled at him. "I was hoping you'd do that."

Jake thought he'd digest that one later. "Just smile and follow my lead."

He opened the door and escorted her in, chuckling at something he pretended she said. Valerie entered first, followed by Jake with a hand on her waist. The smell of stale beer and tobacco smoke hit her nostrils as she took a few steps inside. She stopped, letting Jake step up even with her. Jake casually scanned the darkness of the pub as Valerie snuggled next to him, whispering something meaningless into his ear. His energies now were focused on the search—the search for a face resembling the photo Warrington had sent him.

In a matter of seconds Jake had soaked it all in. It was a relatively small neighborhood bar, like a thousand others of its kind throughout the tristate region. Eight wooden booths alternately faced four aging, Formica tables along the wall on the left. A handful of beat-up chairs surrounded three cheap, round tables in the middle of the room, haphazardly adorned with colored-glass candles. To the right, a barkeep dried a martini glass with a dish towel, eyeing the two ersatz lovers from behind a rectangular bar against the wall.

A pair of Molson Golden lights hung from a dingy, tin-cut ceiling in the rear of the bar, illuminating the worn green baize of a lone pool table. Jake nudged Valerie lightly toward the bar as he spotted a man in jeans and a green flannel shirt leaning over a jukebox in the far corner. Jake laid a twenty-dollar bill on the lacquered counter and ordered a Budweiser, Miller Lite, and a pack of Marlboros. He left a two-dollar tip for a six-dollar bill, handed Valerie her Miller, and walked her toward the pool table as the room filled with Sinatra belting out a somewhat scratchy rendition of "New York, New York."

"I'm surprised you smoke," Valerie said quietly as they walked in the direction of the music.

Jake didn't want to explain his reasoning, not in such close proximity. "I don't. Usually."

When they reached the back, Valerie sat on a stool below a shelf against the wall. Jake set down his Bud next to her drink, walked up to the pool table, and laid two quarters along its edge. "Playing anyone?" he asked, staring Warren Parks in the eyes.

"Just lonely old me," Parks said through a lit cigarette in the corner of his mouth.

"Care to play?"

Warren was leaning over, preparing to break. "I am playing."

Jake looked at the balls racked in a tight triangle on the table. "You haven't broken yet." He laid a ten-dollar bill on the edge of the table. "I just thought you might want a little competition. You a gambling man?"

Parks looked at the bill, then at Jake. "I've been known to take my chances."

This could be good. Booze, pool, and money. I just might learn a little something. "Well, whad'ya say? Pool's no fun alone."

"Who says?"

"Have it your way," Jake said, reaching down for his money.

Parks laid his palm over Jake's hand. "You're on." Parks reached into his pants, placing another ten on top of Jake's.

Jake unwrapped his Marlboros and laid them on the shelf behind Valerie. He put one, unlit, in his mouth and ambled around the table a bit, scanning its lie and quirks. He grabbed a cue off the rack against the wall, rolled it along the table, and casually approached his prey. "Got a light, by any chance?"

"No."

Mind games. The man is walking around with a half-smoked butt hanging from his mouth and says he doesn't have a light. Jake wanted to point out the inconsistency, but took the obvious slight in stride. "Shoot for break?"

"Be my guest."

It had been a while since Jake had played, but in his college days he'd been known to make a buck or two at the tables. Jake actually felt a touch nervous and hoped that pool was a bit like riding a bike. He worried that maybe he'd lost the magic touch. Jake ran the web of his left hand back and forth on a cylindrical block of chalk and walked to the table, twisting the tip of his stick aggressively in a small, worn cube of blue chalk. He placed the cue ball carefully on the green felt of the table and spread his three left fingers widely just behind and to its left.

Jake laid his cue in the groove between his thumb and forefinger, slid it smoothly back and forth twice, then gently made contact, watching as the white ball rebounded off the far bumper and rolled back toward him, stopping only a few inches from the bumper at his waist. He knew he'd hit a good shot. *Beat that.*

Parks watched in silence, rubbing his stick with a cube of blue chalk. Jake marked his spot with a slight rub of a cube against the felt of the bumper and stepped away from the table. Parks seemed to wince slightly as he rubbed the top of his head, then placed his cigarette in an ashtray on a stool and ambled slowly to the foot of the table. He lined up his shot, taking more time than Jake, and eventually sent his ball sailing smoothly down the expanse of green. Jake's Marlboro hung from his mouth, still unlit, as he watched Warren's ball roll to a stop just inside his own mark.

Without a word from either man, Parks picked up the ball and laid it at a slight angle from the rack. He cubed his stick economically and lined up his shot, breaking the rack cleanly with the solid crack of a man who could obviously play pool. Jake knew immediately he was in trouble. He also realized soon enough that there would be precious little discussion during the match, so decided early on to take it seriously while he played. There'd be time for banter later. He watched Warren run his first four shots, inexplicably missing a relatively easy bank into a side pocket on his fifth. It was ever so subtle, but Jake could see the miss disturbed him.

Parks pulled up a stool to Valerie's right, smiling perfunctorily as he sat. Remembering Jake's admonition, save for the slightest of turns at one corner of her lips, she consciously kept her face a block of stone. Jake walked casually around the table, eyeing his best opportunity and what kind of leave it would offer his opponent. He could play mind games, too, and decided a change of pace about now would be just the thing.

Jake knew the Morson Grayhead fires had been started with lighter fluid and desperately wanted to see what kind of lighter Parks used. "I'm going to go get a light for this thing before I eat it," he said, hoping the threat of delay would force Parks to respond with an offer of a light.

Parks rolled his eyes instead. "Are you kidding me? Now?"

"Hey," Jake said, walking toward the bar, "I asked you for a light, but you said you don't have one."

Valerie wasn't sure exactly what was up, but knew enough to understand Jake's cigarette charade was for a reason. He obviously wanted Parks to give him a light, and he didn't even smoke. Unlike Jake, she did, or used to anyway. This was her chance to prove her worth. She reached behind her casually for Jake's Marlboros and removed one, placing it in her mouth.

"You and I both know you're just playing with him," she said. "Now, how about that light?"

Jake leaned sideways against the bar, waiting for the bartender to finish pouring a patron a draft, watching Valerie and Parks talk from afar. Inside, he winced. *Careful. Careful.* He figured Parks must have said something to her. *Come on, baby. Just don't fuck it up.* He could see she had a cigarette in her mouth and knew in an instant what she was doing. *Oh, she's too good.* He was glad now that he'd brought her. *Just remember that lighter, Val. Remember that lighter.*

Valerie stared into Warren's bullish, seaweed-brown eyes. She noticed that his left was esotropic, pointing in slightly toward his nose. He did not respond at first, seemingly staring through her baby blues. He reached into his shirt pocket, pulled out a monogrammed Zippo lighter, and finally spoke.

"Honey, I'll light your fire anytime," he said, striking the flint with his right hand.

Her blood ran cold at his comment as she eyed the flame illuminating his hand. "Thanks," she said, inhaling deeply, aware of the hole his eyes were drilling into her. It wasn't just for Jake. She needed a cigarette. The toxins in the smoke hit her brain like a sledgehammer. She found herself fighting off dizziness, aware that he was still staring at her hair.

"Like what you see?" she finally asked, forcing herself to make contact with his eyes again. Like the viewing monitor at the end of an endoscope, the eyes give away so much. His seemed frighteningly detached.

"Your hair. It's beautiful. My favorite color: flame red."

She twisted awkwardly on her stool, praying Jake would hurry it up. "Why is that your favorite?"

"Reminds me of someone, that's all."

"Who?"

"It doesn't matter anymore. She's dead now."

"Family?"

Parks hesitated. "Yeah, family."

"All right," Jake said, catching Valerie's eyes as he approached the table with a lit cigarette between his fingers. "That's better. Sorry about that."

"Now, you gonna play pool, or what?" Parks asked impatiently.

Jake stood, staring at Valerie. "Honey, why didn't you tell me you had a light?"

"I didn't," she answered with a broad smile. "Your sneaky opponent here's been holding back on you."

"He has?" Jake asked, looking at Parks. "I'm hurt." Jake kept his right foot on the floor as he sat on the edge of the table, aiming his first shot for the near corner. "Three in the corner," he said, tapping the corner of the table with his stick. He dropped the shot, maintaining his position as he watched the cue ball roll out into the middle of the table.

"What can I say?" Parks responded with a guarded smile. "I'm a sucker for a pretty lady. Especially one with flame-red hair."

What the hell had they been talking about? Jake tried to act casual and leaned down, eyeing a cross-table bank shot of the five ball. "What's so special about flame-red hair?" he asked, a paragon of fake disinterest.

Warren tilted his head, feeling the top with his fingers. "Just shoot."

"That . . . I can do. Although you may be sorry you suggested it." Jake patted the side pocket closest to him. "Five ball here." He dropped his shot neatly, sending the cue ball careening down toward the foot of the table, leaving himself a perfect bank into the far corner.

Jake was circling the table, eyeing his options. "Hurt your head?"

Warren brought his hands down to his lap. "No, why?"

Jake smirked slightly, shrugging his shoulders. "I don't know. You keep rubbing it."

"Just a habit."

Right. Jake continued with the questions. "You live around here?" he asked, squinting as smoke curled up his face from the cigarette hanging from his mouth.

"Do you?"

Jake had to be careful here, or he could easily find himself trapped in a lie. "No."

"What the hell are you doin' here? People don't exactly come to this dive from out of town."

"You didn't answer *my* question," Jake responded, stalling for time.

Warren stared at Jake. "Who wants to know?"

Jake bent at the knees to view the angle on a shot. "Sorry, my name's Tom." He stood up. "That's Melanie," he said, pointing in Valerie's direction with his cue stick.

"Melanie, huh?" Parks said, raising his Heineken at Valerie. "Nice to meet you, Melanie."

Valerie nodded.

"And you?" Jake asked.

"Mel."

"Okay . . . *Mel*, catch a load of this." Jake could feel the old magic coming back. Though he'd left himself a perfect bank of the eleven ball, he thought it was time for something a little different. He hadn't tried jumping a ball in twenty years, but thought now was as good a time as any. "Seven in the far corner," he said, angling his stick down at the bottom of the cue ball.

Parks and Valerie both watched Jake's stretched body as he held his stick, dartlike, in his right hand. He practiced his stab a few times, finally sending the ball flying over the fourteen, solidly connecting with the seven. It popped once and rolled toward the pocket, quicker than Jake would have liked.

"Come on, baby, be home," Jake urged with a slight twist of his hips. "Hello," he said with clenched fist as it clattered slowly in the corner, eventually dropping from view.

Jake had walked around to their side of the table. Valerie rose from her stool and gave him a loud peck on the lips. "I love it when you do that."

Jake smiled. "We're not out of the woods yet."

"Nice shot," Parks said, rising from his stool to get another beer.

"Thank you."

Jake watched Warren walk toward the bar, waiting for him to get far enough away to be out of earshot. Jake turned toward Valerie, leaned down, and gave her a longer, more meaningful kiss. Nothing too serious; just enough to get his point across. He'd caught every sign she'd thrown him and wasn't about to let them go unanswered. Even here.

"What the hell were you guys talking about?"

"He scares me, Jake. You know what he said to me? I asked him for a light . . . you did want to see his lighter, right?"

"Yeah."

"I thought so."

"And?"

"A monogrammed Zippo. Initials WP."

Jake kissed her quickly on the cheek. If for nothing else but that, the trip had already been worthwhile. "You're hired," he said with a smile.

But Valerie wasn't finished. She had to share her fear. "So, I ask him for a light, and he stares at me like I got three eyes or something. Then he says, 'Honey, I'll light your fire anytime.' Said he's a sucker for gals with flame-red hair. The guy gives me the creeps, Jake."

"Just hang in there. You're doing great. Stay cool, though. I hoped he wouldn't recognize me, and he hasn't. So I'm going to pick up the pace a bit."

"Pick up the pace? Hell, you couldn't play any better. You're good, you know that?"

"Thanks," he said, smiling at her eyes. "But I don't mean the game. I mean the conversation. Just don't get complacent on me. Things could get funky."

"Oh, boy."

"You can wait in the car if you want."

"Are you kidding me? I wouldn't miss this for the world. Here he comes."

Jake leaned backward, his elbows resting on the shelf.

"Am I up?" Parks asked, setting his beer down next to Jake.

"No. We've just been talking. I'd rather you be here."

Parks was upset. "Jesus Christ. Let's go already."

Jake looked at his watch. "Hey, what's the rush? We got all night."

"Maybe you got all night. I got to be somewhere at twelve."

Thank you. "Oops. I'll hurry it up, then."

"Please."

"Where the hell you going at midnight?" Jake asked, lining up his next shot.

"What are you, my mother?"

"Thirteen over here," Jake said, grabbing the near corner with his fingers. "I just wish you could hang around longer. I need the cash." Jake looked up at Parks as his shot dropped. "Sure you can't stay for another?"

"We'll see."

Jake had tied the match and proceeded to drop his next shot. He missed the following one, however, leaving Warren an easy shot into a corner pocket. Jake waited for Parks to drop it, then turned up the heat.

"So what's with the flame-red-hair thing? Your mother have red hair?"

"No."

"Your wife?"

Parks looked at him. "You ask a lot of questions, you know that?"

"Hey, I'm just out to have a good time. Just makin' conversation, that's all."

"I don't come here for conversation. And, yes . . . my wife had red hair."

"Had?"

"Yes, *had*. She's dead."

"I'm sorry."

"Yeah, well, life sucks," Parks said, lining up at cross-table bank. "It was a long time ago. Twelve here." He took his shot.

"How'd she die?" Jake added, watching the shot drop.

"She was murdered."

How much of this is bullshit? Jake looked into Warren's eyes, feigning disbelief. "Your wife was murdered?"

Warren sighed. "Yep, burnt like toast in a fire."

"Arson?"

"Yep."

A good deal of talking was going on. Jake knew that was rare for a pool game between strangers, but also knew it was only because he kept acting as the catalyst. He didn't want to push too hard, too fast, so decided to let Warren's last statement hang in the air for a while. He also wanted to see if Parks would follow up his statement of his own accord.

But Jake found it more than interesting that Parks would discuss the events for which he was most likely responsible, even if it did happen a quarter of a century ago. Something about it didn't sit right with Jake. When people carry that kind of secret around with them, they seldom talk about it, even tangentially—especially to strangers. Maybe, just maybe, Jake thought, Warren Parks did not murder his wife.

Parks stood, staring at Jake, taking a swig of his beer. His eyes seemed to be glued to Jake. "Do I know you?" he suddenly asked.

Careful now. Jake felt slightly ill at ease. "Me? I don't think so."

"You sure we haven't met before? It's been bothering me since you put your money down."

"Not that I know of. You don't look familiar to me."

Parks continued staring at Jake, his eyes casting a distrustful glare. "I know I've seen you somewhere before. No matter. I'll think of it."

"Good luck."

Parks circled the table. "I don't forget a face."

Jake shrugged, smiling slightly.

The table was getting thin, and Jake could see that unless Parks choked, he had a good shot at ending the game. Jake waited for Parks to drop his next shot, then asked, "What do you do for work?"

"I'm a travel agent," Parks said, bending over to check a shot. "You?"

Jake had thought about his response and almost changed it after Parks mentioned that he recognized him. He'd no doubt seen his picture in the paper, and Jake was hesitant to mention anything that might jolt his memory. But Jake had read the papers, too. The Morson Grayhead story was huge news in the tristate area. You couldn't pick up a paper without one related headline or another staring you in the face. But unless there'd been a recent picture of which Jake was unaware, the only one he'd seen of himself was the same one the press always used—the media's file shot with him in his turnout gear, his helmet on. It would be a stretch for Parks to make the connection.

But then again, even if Parks had, Jake thought it wouldn't be the end of the world if the man did finally realize his opponent's identity. Jake desperately wanted to shake things up. "I'm a firefighter."

Parks was positioned for his shot, about to strike the cue ball, when he stopped short, standing erect. He eyed Jake dubiously, feeling true unease for the first time. "So, you're a hero, huh? Where?"

Jake thought of naming some locale off the beaten track, someplace that would not be viewed as a threat. *What the hell.* "White Plains," he said, naming Westchester County's largest city. Parks leaned with his palms on his cue stick. He stared at Jake for a while in silence. Jake returned the gaze.

"Is that a problem?" Jake finally asked.

"You're a fireman in White Plains? Ever seen someone burn alive?"

"Oh, God," Valerie said with disgust. "What kind of question is that?"

"Alive?" Jake asked, finding the question more than curious. "No. But I've seen my share of fatalities."

"Well, it ain't pretty. Trust me."

"Why do you say that?" Jake asked. "You saw your wife burn to death?"

"Sure did."

"Oh, man, that must have been horrible. I'm so sorry."

Parks shrugged. "Like anything, I s'pose. You learn to live with it."

The time was now. Jake went for the jugular. "You know, you mention your wife burning in a fire. Makes me think of these Morson Grayhead burnings we got going on up where I am. What do you think would make someone do something like that anyway? I mean, how fucked-up is that?"

Parks knelt. "Ten, side pocket." He dropped his cross-table bank with ease. "Sick stuff if you ask me." He chalked his stick. "Makes you wonder, doesn't it?"

"Sure does."

"There's a sick boy. He doesn't just burn 'em, he has his way with 'em first. That is one sick pup. I hope they fry him when they find him."

Bingo! The first slip of the tongue, and Valerie had heard every word. The authorities had not released any information about the rapes. The media may have been all over this story as if they were a wet suit, but to the best of Jake's knowledge they had been kept completely in the dark on that fact. Few people knew that information, and unless Parks was directly involved, Jake couldn't see how he could possibly be one of them. "He's been raping them?" Jake asked with astonishment. "The papers I read didn't say anything about that. Where'd you hear that?"

Jake eyed his opponent like a hawk now, reading his eyes and body language. If his last question had unnerved Parks, he certainly wasn't giving it away.

"I read it somewhere."

The front door to the bar opened and Jake looked over, watching his two CID trails enter. They glanced around, noticing Jake at the pool table. They moseyed up to the bar and took up stools closest to the pool table.

"Time for a refill," Jake said. "Need another?" he asked Valerie.

"Yeah, thanks. Know what? I'll go with you."

"All right. We'll be back," Jake said to Parks. "No cheating."

Valerie scooted off her stool and put her arm around Jake as they walked toward the bar. Jake leaned on the bar, staring straight ahead. "Everything okay?" one of the cops asked.

Jake motioned for the bartender, turning his head ever so slightly. "Yeah, thanks," Jake whispered.

The bartender stood in front of Jake, wiping his hands on his apron. "What'll it be?"

The second state cop turned his eyes casually toward Parks. "We got trouble."

The other two men turned toward the pool table, but Parks was nowhere to be found. Jake turned, looking hurriedly around the bar. Nothing. "Check the bathrooms," he said, hurrying off his stool. He walked quickly to the front door and stepped outside, looking up and down the deserted, dimly lit street. He was beginning to have that bad feeling in his gut. Jake scampered back inside, meeting up with one of the two CID men at the end of the bar. "Anything?"

The CID man shook his head. "Nothing."

"Shit!" Jake pulled out his badge and shoved it past an ordering patron, toward the bartender's face. "Emergency police business. Is there a back exit?" The bartender didn't answer at first, giving him a who-do-you-think-*you*-are? look. Jake grabbed him by his shirt. "Where's the back exit!"

He stared at Jake wide-eyed. "Down the hallway behind the—"

"Hey! Back here!" the two men heard the other state cop scream from the direction of the rest rooms.

They darted toward his voice, catching up with him in the alleyway behind the pub. The three men stood confused in the blackness, looking in both directions, not one of them with a flashlight. "Dammit! You two. That way," Jake said, pointing down the alley toward Route 505. "I'll try over here."

Jake jogged down the alley to his right, trying desperately to peek into the numerous nooks and crannies used for trash cans and bins. His eyes adjusted gradually to the lack of light, and eventually he slowed to a walk, perspiring and out of breath. There were so many trash cans, fences, yards, and gates, Jake didn't know where to start. Inside, a voice whispered not to even try, but he moved some cans anyway, poking around trash bins and looking over fences, knowing in his heart that Parks was long gone. He stopped, listening for telltale signs: scampering feet, heavy breathing, something falling, or a dog barking in the distance. But for a siren somewhere far off in the night, Jake could hear nothing. It was as silent as the night was black.

He stumbled on something and looked down at his feet. It was a purse, light tan with a brass buckle on the side. Odd, he thought, it looked just like Valerie's. Jake picked it up and carried it with him on his trek, until it finally became obvious he was wasting his time. He placed the straps of the purse around his neck and reluctantly walked slowly back toward the pub, still attuned to anything out of the ordinary.

The other two men met him a quarter of the way down his side of the alley. "Nothing," one of them said. "Not so much as a cat."

"Shit!" Jake thundered, slamming an open palm against the clapboard siding of the bar. "All right," he said, regaining composure. "We lost him. Go back and keep an eye on his place. I'm not sure why he split. Maybe he recognized me, maybe not. If we're lucky, he'll go home. I want to know the second you spot him. But *do not* detain him. Got it?"

No one was going to take in Parks but Jake or Ederling. As good as the New York State Police were, put together they didn't know as much about the Morson Grayhead case as the two of them. If anyone was going to nab Warren Parks, it would be one of them. Jake wanted to be sure they heard every comment, every off-the-cuff remark, every arrogant utterance. Only *they* would know the meaning or relevance of certain comments, and you could make book that if Parks said them at all, he would only say them once.

Jake followed the two men into the bar and was surprised to find Valerie standing in a small crowd gathering at the doorway. He'd forgotten about her. "Jake?" she said.

"Hey, you okay?"

Her eyes lit up. "Oh, my purse! I can't believe you found it. I was so worried."

"This is yours?"

"Yeah, I think so."

"Was your wallet in it?"

"Yes."

"Check for it," he said, handing her the purse.

He watched as she opened it, rifling through her belongings. Jake felt a prickling sensation crawl up his spine as she looked up at him, her face stricken with fear. "It's gone, Jake," she said, rummaging through it again. "Oh my God, it's not here!"

He kicked himself now for bringing her. How could he have been so love struck? He was better than that. "It's okay, Val. You're safe."

"Does he have it?"

"Probably."

Her face was etched in desperation. "Oh, God, Jake. It has everything in it: my driver's license, credit cards. He'll find out where I live."

He already knows. This was no friendly, sandlot softball game. This was World Series hardball, and Valerie was suddenly standing in the batter's box. Tears began to stream down her face as she realized the enormity of what had just transpired. She trembled visibly. Jake took her in his arms, holding her tightly to his chest.

"It'll be okay," Jake whispered. "I promise." He took her by the shoulders. "Look at me." She stared at him with frightened eyes. "No one's going to touch you. I promise I'll keep you safe. You have my word, okay?"

Valerie forced a smile. She knew Jake meant what he said, and also knew it was important to him. As worried as Valerie had become, Jake was more so. Though he would never speak it, his sixth sense kept asking him, just how important would her detail be to the other men assigned to her protection? Would it be viewed as just another boring assignment, or would they truly understand that she could burn to death if they took it lightly? The authorities had three men on Parks tonight. *They* were serious enough, and look how screwed up *it* had become.

"Well . . . you can't stay alone tonight," Jake said. "Is there someplace else I can take you?"

Valerie paused, desperately trying to think of someone she could call this late on a Friday night.

"Is there a friend or neighbor you can call?" Jake asked. "Maybe a relative?" She was thinking when he interrupted her thoughts. "I have an extra room at my place. You're welcome to it . . . if you want. Whatever makes you feel most comfortable."

She looked up at him. "Could I, Jake? Just for tonight?"

This whole mess was his fault. Jake thought now that he should never have let her come with him. And even if he did, he kept asking himself why he had ever let her enter the bar. "Of course," he said, feeling a smidgen better that he at least had something he could offer to ease Valerie's fear.

Jake had to find out who this Warren fellow was. He knew from the Executive Travel information that he was Warren Josephs. He sure as hell looked like him. But was he also Lianne's Warren Parks? Jake didn't know, but he sure as hell aimed to find out. Jake detoured toward the pool table once he and Valerie had reentered the bar and, with a finger down its neck, picked up one of Warren's empty beer bottles. He glanced at the table, surprised to find both ten-dollar bills still lying there. Jake picked them up and shoved them into his pocket.

"Here, open your purse," he said to Valerie, holding out the beer bottle with his finger. Jake placed the bottle in her purse and zipped it for her. "Don't lose it," he said with a smile.

As they walked past the bartender, Jake pulled out a ten and tossed it on the counter. "Sorry for the inconvenience."

He opened his cruiser door for Valerie, closing it as she slid in. He walked around the front, pulled out his .357, and crawled in, placing his weapon in the glove compartment. The two sat in silence for a moment, staring out the windshield. Eventually, Jake looked at Valerie. "I'm sorry. I feel like hell about this."

Valerie touched his shoulder. "Don't, Jake. You told me it could be dangerous."

That he had. Jake worried that perhaps all that had happened over the last twenty minutes might have ruined whatever budding relationship was beginning to bloom between them. "I hope you'll still want to see me again. I'm afraid all this may scare you off."

She looked at him and smiled. "Oh, don't worry about that, Jake Ferguson. I think I'm hooked."

He smiled back. "So am I."

IT WAS AFTER one o'clock in the morning when Jake pushed open the door to his co-op, letting Valerie enter first. He worried what his place looked like. He was trying to recall how he had left it when he remembered today was Friday. Or at least it was the last time he'd been here. Friday was cleaning-lady day—when she decided to come. Lately, she'd been on-again, off-again. He reached in with his left hand and flicked on the hall and dining-room lights.

"It's not much," Jake said, praying it had been cleaned. "But it's home."

Valerie looked around his apartment. It had that lived-in look but thankfully was tidy and clean. She'd seen some bachelor pads that were embarrassingly dirty. She knew instantly that she would sleep comfortably here. "It's nice," she said, walking into the living room.

"Thanks."

Jake locked the door behind him. When he turned, Valerie was standing by a bookshelf, holding a picture of him and Danny in her hands. They had gone on a skiing vacation with friends in Aspen the winter before she died, and someone had snapped a shot just before they unloaded the ski lift. They were laughing, obviously in love, and having fun. He opted for silence, wondering if it was good or bad that he hadn't had the opportunity to do a walk-through before he brought Valerie here. If given his druthers, Jake would have preferred to put some things away, mementos of his past he would rather not reveal so early in the relationship. But he decided it was probably good. *What you see is what you get.*

"Can I get you something?" Jake called out from the kitchen.

"What are you having?" she called back.

"I know this sounds crazy at this hour," he said, poking his head out from inside the kitchen with a smile, "but I could use a cup of coffee."

Valerie was standing at Jake's mantel, eyeing the Lladro figurine. "Coffee would be great. There's no way I'm going to sleep for a while anyway."

He ducked back in the kitchen. "How do you take it?"

"Cream and sugar."

Jake brought out some crackers and cheese on a plate and laid a knife on the coffee table in front of the couch. He suddenly felt nervous. A few hours ago he was hopelessly single, and now it was almost one-thirty in the morning, and his first date in many years was standing in his living room, about to spend the night. It wasn't that he was particularly thinking of sex. In fact, with all that had happened, Jake doubted seriously it was even a remote possibility. That was just fine with him. This whole thing had moved very, very quickly, and he would just as soon have time to regroup. He was certain Valerie felt the same way. Still, Jake knew it would be odd going to bed with a single, attractive woman lying in his guest bed right next door. It had been four years since Danny had slept here, and more years than he could remember since a woman other than she had spent a night under his roof.

Jake sat, reclining in his BarcaLounger, consciously avoiding the couch. He was thinking too much, reasoning that there was something territorial about the recliner in a man's apartment. Like Archie Bunker's TV chair—even though it isn't labeled, it's an unspoken thing. He knew if he sat on the couch, Valerie might think that his chair was off-limits and thus feel obligated to sit on the sofa herself. Jake thought that carried with it implications he would like to avoid for now. And if he did sit on the couch, and she eventually did choose his chair, he hoped to avoid her suffering even a subliminal or unconscious hesitation. The last thing he wanted now was to cause Valerie any unnecessary discomfort. She had been through enough for one night.

He watched her as she guided herself on a tour of his belongings and pictures. "It'll be a few minutes. There's some crackers and cheese here, if you're hungry."

She plopped down heavily on the sofa, sighing as her body sank. "Man," she said with exhaustion. "What a night. I can't believe you do that kind of thing for a living."

Jake smiled, remaining quiet.

Valerie leaned over and helped herself to a slice of white cheddar and a Triscuit. She held them on a napkin in her lap as she leaned back, resting her head against the back of the couch. The room was quiet for some time before Jake finally spoke.

"Guest bedroom's down the hall on the right. Sheets are clean. There're towels and toiletries in the bureau. There's a new toothbrush in the medicine cabinet. You should have most everything you need."

She looked at him, chewing her snack. "Want one?"

"No, thanks."

"Tell me about the case, Jake. Who was that guy, and why do you think he could be the one?"

Jake never discussed his cases with outsiders. Never. But suddenly, Valerie wasn't an outsider anymore. Parks had her wallet and consequently her address. Jake figured it was safe to assume she was now involved and cursed himself for the hundredth time that night for allowing it to happen. He did not speak for a while, trying to weigh how much information was too much and just what Valerie now had a right to know.

"I'm in a tough position here, Val. I know things that I simply can't tell you. Yet, at the same time, there are some things I think you need to know. Please understand if I don't tell you everything. This is just one of those times where the less you know, the better off you'll be. One thing I can tell you for sure is that you cannot repeat any of what you heard tonight to anyone. And I mean, *no one*. Especially the rapes. Okay?"

"I understand." She nodded her head slightly. "But I'm not just a disinterested observer anymore, Jake."

"I know."

"Well, then tell me this. Do you think he'll come after me?"

This was no time to act casual. Valerie would probably never have something else as frightening as this happen to her again in her life. Jake certainly hoped not. He pulled the lever at the side of his chair and sat up. He rested his elbows on his knees and stared at her, steepling his fingers under his nose, tapping them against his upper lip.

"I can't say for sure, Valerie. I think we have to operate under that assumption until we catch him."

"But I heard you tell those men in the alley not to detain him if they spotted him. That doesn't sound to me like you're trying too hard to arrest him."

Jake explained why he told them that: the need for arresting-officer continuity in an apprehension, if for no other reason than to insure the best chance for prosecution.

He rose to get the coffee, bringing back two large, red, fire-hydrant coffee mugs. He set hers down on an old copy of *Firehouse* magazine and leaned back in his chair with his mug in his lap.

"Cute," Valerie said, picking hers up with both hands.

"I thought you'd like them."

They were both quiet for a while, the only sound the ticking from the Regulator clock and an occasional slurp from a mug. Jake tried to imagine what was going through her mind, but found the terrain too depressing. She had removed her shoes, and he watched her stare at her wiggling stockinged toes.

"Were you ever married?" he asked out of the blue.

"Yes. Years ago. Biggest mistake of my life."

"Why?"

"Oh . . . you know how it goes. Lonely, scared high-school senior falls in love with the first guy to treat her like a real woman. I guess I talked myself into overlooking the booze. I didn't learn about his proclivity toward the use of fists until it was too late."

"He beat you?"

"Many times," she said, nodding her head. Valerie was silent for some time, her face betraying the pain she felt at the memories. "You know, spousal abuse is a strange thing," she finally began. "I know that women always say the first time their husband ever did that to them, they'd be gone. We all say that until it actually happens. But then he comes crawling back, promising you the world, telling you how sorry he is, and that it will never, ever happen again." She looked at him. "I hated men for a long time after that."

Jake frowned. "We're not all like that, Val."

"I know."

Jake sipped his coffee. "Go on. I'd like to hear about it."

She waved a hand. "Nah, it's boring."

"Says who?"

She sipped her coffee before starting again. "Well, I can remember being so scared. I didn't want to admit that I could have made such a terrible mistake. I didn't even want to think it could actually be happening to me. It was a fluke, I kept telling myself. I kept thinking that he didn't really beat me *that* bad. Certainly not the way those other women get it. Yes, it was more than a slap, but he didn't really hit me, or I'd be unconscious, right? I prayed that I'd be lucky, that maybe it wouldn't even show."

"What'd you do?"

"I started taking karate. I swore if he ever came at me again, I'd drop him to his knees."

Jake smiled. "That's why you got your black belt?"

"That's it."

"I'll be damned."

"So just watch yourself, mister," she said with a mischievous smile.

"Thanks for the warning. I guess I better switch to plan B. So, whatever happened to him?"

"I really don't know," she said with a shrug. "Last I knew, he'd boozed himself out of a job and right into jail."

"How old were you?"

"Nineteen."

"Ouch."

"I told you it was the biggest mistake of my life."

Jake hoped losing her purse to that maniac wouldn't top it. "Let's hope so, huh?"

Valerie put a hand to her mouth, trying to hide a deep, almost painful yawn. It was nearly two in the morning, and her adrenaline rush was quickly being replaced by exhaustion.

"Tired?" Jake asked, sitting forward on the edge of his chair.

She nodded her head. "Man, suddenly I can't keep my eyes open."

"You're crashing."

"What?"

"Crashing. It's common in law enforcement. Firefighters, too. You have moments where there's massive spurts of adrenaline, but the downside to that is what you're experiencing right now. I've always called it crashing. I don't know if it has a real name." Jake rose from his chair, placing his mug on the coffee table. "Come on, I'll show you to your room."

"Thanks," she said, standing a bit wobbly.

He walked ahead of her down the hall and flicked on the light to her room. Valerie followed behind him. "Sleep as long as you'd like. You were great tonight, Val. You earned it."

She kissed the tip of her forefinger and placed it on his lips. "Thank you, Jake. I really appreciate it."

It felt good to be needed again. "Don't mention it. Sleep tight."

Saturday
September 14

IF SHE WAS anything, Lianne Rybeck was a survivor. Despite all outward appearances, her life had been nothing but a seemingly endless chain of disappointments and nightmares. Those looking in from the outside might have thought they would give anything to trade places with her—that is, until they had stepped into her shoes. Only then would they see the desperation and pain, the torment and anguish. Only then could they possibly realize the private hell that had become Lianne Rybeck's life.

She had spent the last quarter century protecting her son, and now, just when the seas were roughest, she'd be damned if she was going to jettison him like unwanted cargo. Warren may have hung up the phone yesterday thinking he still held all the cards, but he had another thing coming if he was so naive as to assume Lianne would just crawl into a hole and disappear.

Scotty was her last remaining connection to life, her *only* interest in staying alive. No one would ever harm him again—not the system, not the police, and especially not Warren. Rage and fury boiled inside her. It was not enough that Warren had stuck his talons into her back and kept them there for so many years. It was not enough that he continued to bleed her, as if some mutated leech. Now, for some inexplicable reason, he had decided he needed more. Warren had decided to become the puppet master once again.

Lianne knew what she had to do. In fact, it was nonnegotiable. She would kill him before she'd let someone so demented, so self-absorbed and parasitic, touch the life of her precious one again. She would *not* let it happen a second time—not while she still lived—not if she could stop it. And that was exactly what Lianne intended to do.

The sedative the doctor had given her wore off shortly after three in the morning. She spent the next few hours lying in bed, curled up in a ball, hugging her pillow as if it were her life raft in a raging sea. Lianne stared at the red, luminous digits of her alarm clock, fighting off grogginess from whatever tranquilizer had coursed through her veins during the evening. In her mind, she envisioned making Warren scream, punishing him over and over again in countless hours of pain and torture.

Granted, she had fallen apart on the phone when she spoke to him. The sudden, unbearable reality of reinvolvement with Warren was almost too much for her to take. Almost. But a mother's wrath is not to be taken lightly, and if Warren Parks was counting Lianne out, he was making a big and very real mistake. She would see him squirm. If it was the last action she ever took on earth, she would watch him die. Lianne knew now that it had to be done and knew also that she was the only human on earth who could do it.

She waited, watching the digits of her clock melt, one into the next— each seemingly an hour's wait, each one taking longer than the last. At times she wanted to reach out and shake it, certain that it had somehow broken under her unwavering stare. Lianne simultaneously marveled and cursed at the passing of time, its relentless consistency and relative duration. There had been times in her life she prayed for time to slow down, and others, such as now, when she could not will it to move fast enough.

It seemed like days, but in time the glowing digits of her clock read 7:00 A.M. Lianne climbed slowly out of the safety of her warm cocoon, sitting for a short while on the edge of her bed. She rubbed her eyes, rose, and walked to her purse hanging on the back of a Chippendale chair. She removed her checkbook and keys, tossed them on the bed, and walked to her armoire. She dressed quickly in a Nike sweatsuit, put on her socks and sneakers, picked up her checkbook and keys on the way out, and treaded gingerly down the back steps of the hall into the kitchen.

There was a time, not that many hours ago, when Lianne could not have imagined stepping foot into the world without a shower and a splash of makeup. She thought for a moment that, after yesterday's emotional episode, if she was seen unkempt and in disarray, her help might think she was beginning to crack. But the worry quickly passed, for Lianne knew that nothing could be further from the truth. There would be no shower this morning. Not now. She was obsessed, of a single mind, with a laserlike purpose. She did not care what she looked like, nor did she care what others might think. Lianne had done this once before, and though she had never dreamed she would have to do it again, it was painfully obvious there was still unfinished work to be done.

The Rybecks' cook of many years was standing at a large island in the middle of the modern, renovated kitchen. She was chopping scallions with a large Henkel knife and stopped, looking up when she heard Lianne enter the kitchen from the rear entrance. "Mrs. Rybeck. Good morning, ma'am," she said, laying down the knife and wiping her hands on an apron. "We were all so worried about you yesterday. Are you feeling better this morning, ma'am?"

Lianne walked toward the coffeemaker on the counter and poured herself a large, steaming cup. "Yes, Millie, I am. Thank you for asking."

Millie could not remember the last time she had seen Lianne look so disheveled. Things in the Rybeck household were definitely changing, and more quickly than she could keep track. "Can I get you something to eat?"

Lianne turned to leave. "No, thank you, Millie. Maybe later."

"If you wish. It's nice to see you up and about again," she said, the last half of the sentence tailing off as her boss disappeared behind two white, swinging doors.

The morning was cool, promising to be a perfect New York, late-summer day. Lianne grabbed her gardening hat off a hook against the mudroom wall and left, closing the door softly behind her. She walked with more confidence now, her gait almost quick. She stared at the four-car garage in front of her as she passed underneath the portico and down the slight incline of the cobble-stoned drive.

Lianne approached the door to the right of the stone structure, turning the knob first before taking out her keys. She unlocked it, closed and locked it behind her, and climbed the squeaky wooden steps to Chandler Boutet's apartment on the second floor. She wasn't sure just what he'd been up to the last few days, but knew she had not asked him to leave. Besides the West View Estate, she and Severin shared precious little in their lives, and limousines were no exception. Lianne had her own, of course, replete with her own driver, and had just assumed that Chan had begun making other arrangements for employment. She only hoped it was not too late.

She rang the buzzer to Chan's door and stood impatiently, waiting for him to answer. There was no response. She buzzed again, placing her ear to his door, listening for movement. Eventually she heard someone call out from inside. Thank God, Lianne thought. She stood back, trying her best to appear calm and dispassionate.

Not only was it very early for someone to be ringing his doorbell, but given that his apartment was on the grounds of one of the most closely guarded homes in Westchester County, visitors in general were few and far between—especially the unannounced variety.

Chan wore a pair of flannel pajama bottoms and a wrinkled, white chamois shirt. "Mrs. Rybeck," he said, blinking with surprise as he opened the door. Lianne had never been here before, and he could only assume she had come to tell him the inevitable. "Please, come in."

"Thank you, Chandler."

"Chan, please."

"Okay," she said with a slight smile. "Thank you, Chan."

He had begun packing, and half-filled boxes lay strewn throughout the various rooms of his place. As is so often the case when you move, it provides that rare opportunity to go through years of accumulated crap. Chan's anticipated move was no different, and piles of papers and clothes covered every seat and chair.

"Here," he said, picking up a pile of shirts from a cushion on his couch. "Have a seat."

"No, thank you. I think I'll stand."

Chan braced for what was to come. "Okay, what can I do for you?" he asked, figuring he already knew the answer.

Lianne strolled casually around the living/dining room of his small but quaint, two-room apartment. She noticed a half-empty bottle of Johnnie Walker Black on the table, two glasses, and a bra strung over a chair. "Oh, I'm sorry, Chan. I didn't realize I was interrupting anything."

Christ, lady, he thought, it's seven in the morning. If Lianne was going to let him go, Chan wanted to hear it now and get it over with. He followed the direction of her stare, noticed the bra, and smiled. "Oh, that. She's just a friend. Don't worry, she's out like a light. I'm afraid we played a bit too hard last night."

Lianne looked at him. "You don't look so good."

"Let's just say I'm proud of myself for making it to the door. Anyway, if you don't mind me saying so, neither do you. No offense."

"None taken."

Chan was anxious to get his hanging over with. "So, what's up?"

"Are you sure she's asleep?"

He smiled. "Trust me."

"I'd like to, Chan, but you should know, I don't trust anyone. Please close her door."

Chan walked down the hall and quietly closed the door to his room, also closing the hall door as he reentered the living room. All right, he thought, it's not *that* big a secret. Do it already. "Dead to the world," he said, referring to his guest as he stood in front of the table. "What's up?"

"Chan, did Severin ever mention our son to you?"

He was quiet for a moment, nodding his head ever so slightly. Her question seemed to come from left field. "Yes," he finally said with a small shrug. "Once. Scotty, right?"

"Right."

They were off to a strange start. Chan figured this could prove interesting. "Why?"

Lianne took a sip of her coffee. "I need your help, Chan. I know your background, and think—"

"What background is that?"

"Your Secret Service history."

Chan nodded.

"So, anyway . . . I think you are uniquely qualified to provide the services I seek. I am prepared to pay you twice whatever salary Severin was paying you."

The good things in life always seem to come out of the blue. "What kind of services might you be referring to, Mrs. Rybeck?"

"Have a seat, Chan. I'm going to tell you a story that may surprise you."

He walked toward the kitchen. "Okay. Mind if I put on some coffee first?"

"I'm sorry. I didn't think to bring you any."

"No problem," he said from his small, open kitchen. He returned, sat down on the edge of a rocker, and clasped his hands between his knees. He looked at her, anxious to hear what this was all about. "Okay, shoot."

Lianne started from the beginning, skipping unnecessary details for brevity's sake. She hardly knew this man, yet in what brief encounters they'd had along the way, she was always impressed with his professionalism and demeanor. She knew she was taking a chance, but also knew she needed help. Lianne figured Chan was about as close to Severin as one could get and hoped he'd feel some sense of obligation. She also wasn't stupid and thought the promise of a hundred thousand dollars would not hurt her cause any either.

With relative speed, she relayed the story of Scotty's upbringing, her battle with Hodgkin's, Josephine and Warren, and the despicable role they played in her son's eventual fall from normalcy. She left out details of Severin's lapses in fatherhood, fearing she might sound bitter and thus turn Chan off. Lianne thought the story was powerful enough without it. She also studiously avoided telling him anything about her ultimate plans. That was best left unsaid. By the time she had finished, tears were trickling slowly down Lianne's cheeks.

Chan was quiet, staring into her haunted eyes. For the life of him, he could not understand why she was telling him this. "Jesus, Mrs. Rybeck, I'm so sorry. That's a horrible story. I never had any idea."

Lianne wiped away tears with a sleeve.

"But why me?" Chan asked. "I mean, why are you telling *me?*"

Lianne took the seat Chan had cleared for her, leaning forward, staring him firmly in the eyes. "I need you to follow Warren, Chan. Tell me everything he does, everywhere he goes. I want a dossier on this man that would make the CIA jealous."

"Why don't you just call the police?"

She shook her head. "No," she said emphatically. "I want to handle this my way, in my own time. I can't tell you why, but I ask you to trust me. The police cannot be involved. Not yet. You're either in, or you're out, Chan. Either way is fine with me. But if you don't accept my offer, then I have no choice but to ask you to vacate the estate by Friday."

Chan did not know Lianne well, but always assumed beneath the aged-debutante veneer, she knew how to play hardball. He knew now he was right. "How do I get paid?"

"Half now, half when you're finished."

"Mrs. Rybeck, your husband paid me fifty thousand a year, plus a Christmas bonus. It won't be cheap."

Lianne laughed. "I think I can handle it." She pulled out her checkbook. "Here," she said, scribbling something on a check. "Here's a check for fifty-five thousand dollars. There'll be another one just like it when I get my final report."

She ripped out the check and proffered it from an extended hand. Chan looked at her, then the check. That little slip of paper could save him an awful lot of trouble, and what was better still was that he knew it was good. It wasn't as if she were asking him to do anything illegal. He didn't know just exactly *what* was on her agenda, but that really wasn't his concern, not as long as he did his job and stayed on the straight and narrow. He might even have a little fun. He hadn't done anything even remotely resembling cloak-and-dagger for years.

"Can I stay here?"

"Please."

"What's your time frame?"

"Yesterday."

He leaned forward, plucked the check from her insistent hand, whistling aloud as he read it. "All you want me to do is find out where he goes, and what he does with his sorry ass, right?"

"That's it," Lianne said, her stony face etched with an eerie grimness. "Every minute of every day."

He stared at her for a few seconds. "You got yourself a deal," he said, folding the check and stuffing it in his shirt pocket. "Where does he live?"

"I have his phone number. He lives somewhere in New Jersey. It shouldn't be too difficult a task."

Chan nodded slightly. "We'll find out, won't we?"

"I want everything, Chan. I mean, *everything*. You'll have to earn this money."

"Mrs. Rybeck . . . for a hundred K, you'll be surprised how hard I can work."

Lianne rose. "I'm counting on it. Good luck and have a good day," she said, walking toward the door. "Oh, and Chan?"

"What?"

"Get some sleep."

"Later. Right now, it looks like I have a job to do."

Lianne smiled. "A can-do attitude. I like that."

THE RED DIGITS on Jake's alarm clock glowed 6:36 A.M. when he awoke from an unbearable need to urinate. He had been pushing hard and felt almost drugged as he peeled his sheet and blanket aside before lumbering out of bed for the bathroom. He gave the toilet a quick, perfunctory glance and finished his task with his eyes closed, one hand leaning against the wall. Jake almost fell asleep just standing there and stumbled back toward his bedroom, remembering only then, as he eyed the closed door to the guest room, that Valerie lay sleeping in the bed next door.

His heart picked up a couple of beats. Though its ending was far from ideal, the night before had seemed so comfortable, so natural and relaxed. No doubt, the evening's events had pushed them closer together than they could ever have hoped to get in a half dozen dates. But now the night was through, and he found himself worrying what the morning would bring.

Jake remembered many a wild night in his college days, boozing and screwing, only to have the morning bring a sober dose of reality, as if someone had thrown a bucket of ice-cold water in his face. People respond differently to the morning. Some like it, others don't. Jake had always been a morning person and wondered now if Valerie was, too. He couldn't help but worry she might somehow blame him for suddenly finding herself in harm's way. A recurrent fear kept flashing through his brain. He worried that she would awaken, dress, and leave without so much as a good-bye. The thought disturbed him.

Jake crawled back into the comforting warmth of his bed and tried in vain to go back to sleep. God knew he needed it. But the thought kept sneaking through his head, tugging at his innards. He could not seem to let it go. He tossed and turned for the better part of an hour, finally sitting on the edge of his bed, frustrated at the futility of the attempt. He heard the bathroom door close and the toilet flush a few moments later. The swoosh was muffled at first, then louder as Valerie opened the door.

She was up, though Jake wasn't sure it was for good. He hadn't heard her go back to her room, and he quickly pulled on a pair of cotton pajama bottoms, threw on his robe, and walked quietly toward the kitchen, noticing her door was still shut. He didn't know if she had gone back to bed, was out and about, or if his worst thoughts had just been played out. Jake tried to act casual as he walked out of the hall, looking about his apartment, but there was no Valerie. He felt like a jealous high schooler as he went immediately to the front door to check if the dead bolt was still locked. *I'll be damned. She's still here.*

Maybe it would be okay. The knowledge that she had not yet abandoned him put a spring in his gait. He entered the kitchen and began making a pot of coffee, trying to understand the meaning and cause behind his deep-seated worry that Valerie would walk out on him. Was it some Freudian thing, some subliminal slight or fear he felt from losing Danny so suddenly? Or was it even more far-reaching than that? First Danny and now, after one night, Valerie was possibly at risk. Jake wondered if somehow his love life was cursed, doomed to failure from the start. He reminded himself not to borrow trouble—just to deal with whatever happened *when* it happened. He knew that it probably wasn't going to be what he'd envisioned anyway and told himself to just let fate take its course, with a good bit of caution thrown in.

Jake hardly knew this woman sleeping in his guest room and was taken by how head over heels he had fallen for her. He was amused at the irony. Twelve hours ago he was dreading the thought of having to pick her up, and now, as he prepared to start another day, she was all he could think about. It couldn't be love at first sight. He always thought that was so much bunk and didn't believe in it any more than he did the tooth fairy. But still, Jake had to admit, there was something special about Valerie Medforth.

Jake knew the chances were great that he had been more lonely than he thought, more desperate for female companionship than he had fully realized. And suddenly, at the snap of his fingers, here was someone with whom he felt comfortable, and whom he very much wanted to get to know better. And as Providence would have it, she was sleeping under his roof.

But he was tentative, mindful, and not a little afraid, that he might unwittingly latch onto her quicker and more fervently than would be healthy for either of them. No matter what his heart said, Jake was determined to take it slowly. The last thing in the world he wanted to do was scare her away.

The coffee began to drip as he unlocked the door to grab his *New York Times*. Jake was thirsty and figured it must have been from the beer the night before. *So much for the diet.* He tossed the paper on the dining room table and poured himself a large glass of orange juice. As he waited for the coffee to finish, Jake sat at the table and unfolded the *Times* in front of him. Scanning the headlines first, he lazily browsed items of interest. The largest by far described the special prosecutor the attorney general had appointed to investigate allegations of campaign finance illegalities in the White House. On the far right there was an article about the president and his inexplicable ability to deflect blame for years of unseemly behavior. In the center was another describing how the Israelis and Palestinians were at it again, this time in the town of Hebron. *Some things never change.*

Then Jake saw it. In the lower left was an article about the Rybecks entitled "Money, Power, and Greed; Rybecks Share Sordid Past." Jake knew this promised to be good. He poured himself a cup of steaming hot coffee, sat down, and began to read, generally impressed with the reporter's grasp and recounting of the facts. Lianne was obviously unavailable for comment, and as he would have expected, some things were missing. But nonetheless, Jake thought the reporter had clearly done his homework.

Unnamed sources told of Severin's failings as a father and the apparent toll it took on Scotty. Somehow the reporter had discovered many of the seamier facts of the Rybecks' rocky marriage, as well as Lianne's wealth, the 1971 fire that had killed Josephine, and Scotty's institutionalization. There was nothing of importance in the article Jake did not already know, except for one thing: a single snippet of information he thought just might turn the whole investigation around.

For what Jake and Ederling did *not* know was that Scotty had changed his name. The article detailed how he wanted nothing to do with his father, and apparently that included carrying his name. Like Hawthorne's Hester Prynne, Scotty wanted nothing more than to remove the label and the attendant shame he felt it carried. As a consequence, in 1983 he took legal action and changed Rybeck to his mother's maiden name of Himmerton.

Jake felt chagrined that a reporter had found a piece of information that he and Ederling had missed. But over the years, it had happened before, and he figured it would probably happen again. By definition, his scope needed to be significantly broader than the reporter's. You can only do so much at a time. Still, he figured a little ass-covering wasn't out of line here and decided if it came up in his travels, he'd just say that he and Donny were already aware of it. Jake knew he had probably made enemies along the way, though he wasn't certain just who they were. That's what scared him. You never know what someone may use to try to bring you down, and sometimes it doesn't take much. Political climates are finicky, especially in a case as highly charged as this.

He rose, poured himself a second cup of coffee, and checked the phone book before reaching for the wall phone to call Ederling. He had kids. Jake knew he'd be up. Ederling answered on the third ring. "Hello?"

"Don, it's Jake. Am I interrupting anything?"

"I wish. Hey, I'm glad you called. How did it go?"

"What?"

"What?" Ederling repeated sarcastically. "Your date, asshole."

"Oh, that."

"Yeah, *that*. Remember? The most important thing to happen in your sorry life in years?"

There wasn't time now. Anyway, Valerie was still there. "Later," Jake said, dismissing the question. "Listen, Don, did you read the *Times* yet this morning?"

Ederling laughed. "I have three kids, Jake. You're joking, right?"

"There's an article on the front page about the Rybecks. I'll give you three guesses what we missed."

"Lianne's really a transvestite."

"Funny. Guess what name Scotty uses."

"Guess what name Scotty uses," Ederling repeated, trying to think. There were a few moments of silence before he spoke again. "You're shitting me?"

"Nope."

"Himmerton?"

"Yep."

"Damn. It's so obvious. How could we have missed it?"

"I don't know, but if anyone asks—"

"We knew it all along."

"Great minds think alike," Jake said with a smile. "So, listen, we need to see if the post office lists any Himmertons."

"Gee, Jake, it's Saturday. We may be shit out of luck. You check the phone book?"

"Yeah, nothing. The post office will be open."

"The counter maybe, but I doubt there'll be any management types . . . you know? Someone who can make a decision. Listen, I'll try, but we may have to wait till Monday."

Why should this be any different? "Well, see what you can do," Jake said. "I'm going to the office to run through the microfiche. I need to read up on that fire."

"Which fire?"

"Josephine's."

"Oh. Any particular reason?"

Jake had pulled the cord over to the table and was sitting sideways on a chair. He looked up and saw Valerie standing at the entrance to the hallway. She was wearing a pair of old, gray sweats and a red-and-black flannel shirt. Her hair looked a little disheveled, but not all that much different from last night. He figured it was the kind of cut she could just run her fingers through a couple of times and at least look presentable enough.

"Hi," he whispered, holding his palm over the receiver. "Coffee's in the kitchen."

She smiled. "Thanks."

Jake put the receiver back to his ear. "What was that?" he asked Ederling.

"Is someone there?" Ederling asked, his intonation expressing incredulity.

Jake was quiet.

"You dog. And on the first date, no less. Now I'm jealous. Must have been dat dere, ah, bowling ting dat reeled her right in. See? I told ya. Bowling works every time."

"Yeah, must've been," Jake responded with a broad smile. "Look, I have to go. Work the post office. I'll call you from the office."

"From the office, my ass."

"Bye," Jake said mischievously before depressing the dial-tone button.

Valerie was leaning against the kitchen counter. "Who was that?"

"That was Don. I just read an article in the *Times*, and there was something in there about the case we need to check up on."

Valerie wanted to ask Jake if he had told Ederling that she spent the night, but decided to let it go. "Can I read it?"

Jake turned the paper over to the front page. "Starts right here," he said, tapping the article with a finger. "You sleep okay?"

She poured herself a cup of coffee. "Like a baby. Where's the sugar?"

"Oh, it's in a mason jar in the cabinet to your right."

Jake watched her as she reached up. Sex may have seemed like too much for him last night, but it sure didn't sound too bad right now. This gentleman routine could be hell sometimes. He sat quiet, sipping his coffee, waiting for her to join him at the table. She climbed up on the chair closest to Jake and sat, curling her legs up underneath her. Jake wondered how she could sit like that. His legs would have split wide open.

"That was some night," Valerie said.

"I'll say. How you holding up?"

"Fine," she said, pursing her lips. "Things never seem quite as bleak in the light of day. But I guess I do have to cancel my credit cards and stuff, huh?"

"Yeah, I was going to mention that. It's probably not a bad idea."

"God, I hate doing that," Valerie said with a frown. "It's such a royal pain in the butt."

"No argument here." Jake rose to get another coffee. "So, have you decided what you're going to do?"

Valerie nodded, holding her coffee to her lips with both hands. "Yeah, I think I'm just going to go back home. I can't stay here forever."

You're welcome to try. "Don't feel you have to leave on my account. Stay as long as you'd like."

Her eyes twinkled as she looked at him. "Thank you, Jake. That's very nice of you. Actually, I wouldn't mind staying over again, just not under these circumstances."

"I'd like that," he said, approaching her from the kitchen. Jake took his seat. "So, how do you want to handle it?" He didn't want to frighten her, but at least for now, he thought protection was not a bad idea. They had talked about it last night, but he wanted to see if she mentioned it again this morning.

"How do you mean?"

"I mean, do you just want to go back alone?"

Valerie closed her eyes. "I wish I hadn't forgotten my purse."

"We both do, Val, but that's water under the bridge. We got to move forward from here."

"You really think I need protection?"

"Honestly? I can't say you *need* it, but it sure as hell would make sense. At least for a short while. We can reevaluate in a few days. Anyway, Donny and I are getting close. Who knows? Maybe we'll have an arrest by then."

Valerie's eyes lit up. "You think?"

"If we're lucky. Monday's going to be a big day. I think we'll know a lot more than we do now."

"Do I have to give you an answer right now?"

Jake shrugged. "Do you want to leave now?"

She was quiet for a while. "I can't believe I'm saying this, but I like being with you. I'm in no rush, really."

Jake smiled, clearly pleased with her comment. "Sounds good to me."

"Tell you what I could do, though. I could stand a bite to eat. Got any eggs? I make a mean omelette."

Jake had begun to feel the beginnings of the jitters and decided he'd had enough coffee for the time being. He rose from his chair and walked his coffee cup over to the kitchen sink. He walked in her direction and stood on the carpeting by her chair. "I got a better idea. Let's go out. There's a great diner in Port Chester."

"Jake?" Valerie said, looking up at him.

"Yeah?"

She reached out and grabbed an end to one of the ties of his robe, pulling him gently toward her. Jake took two steps nearer and stood with his arms at his sides, careful not to appear the aggressor in any way. Valerie rose, pulling him closer.

She stroked his sideburns gently with the backs of her fingers. "Do we have to leave so soon?"

He eyed her with open fondness. "Not necessarily. Do you have something else in mind?"

She wrapped her arms around him, Jake finally following suit. Valerie wasn't small, but still stood several inches below him. She gazed knowingly up into his eyes, pressing her body close to his. Jake dropped one hand slowly to the soft curve of her buttocks, squeezing slightly as he raised his other hand to the back of her head. They kissed slowly, softly, almost tentatively at first, exploring each other's lips, acclimating to one another's kiss. Valerie arched her neck sensually as Jake ran his tongue down across her throat and neck, sucking her delicate skin softly along the way.

"We'll think of something," she whispered.

Jake wasn't sure how far she wanted this to go and felt self-conscious at the realization that the crotch of his pajamas was beginning to bulge outward. Valerie could feel it rub against her and pushed him from her softly, staring up at him with smoldering eyes. She smiled at him provocatively, her mouth uniquely suggestive. It formed a knowing, longing grin, the kind that melts a man's soul.

"Come on," she said quietly, taking his hand, tugging him gently toward the hall.

A heated sensation of sexual arousal filled Jake's belly and loins, spreading quickly to every nerve ending in his body as they walked hand in hand down the hall. He was among the living once again. "Hey, I've got an idea," he said.

WARREN PARKS DROVE slowly past Valerie's Bedford Road apartment several times. He wanted to give the neighborhood a thorough visual scrub before parking his Mazda and searching more exhaustively on foot. He drove by once, looking only at cars: their makes and occupants. He especially had a keen interest in anything that might house a team: a Bell Atlantic truck, a moving van, an ice cream truck, anything that could fit several people at once.

He knew there was a good chance the police would be scouring the area, though he wasn't sure they were that smart. Warren's second go-round was devoted exclusively to pedestrians. He was looking for anyone just hanging out: someone sitting on a stoop, leaning against a tree, or performing a task, such as a painter, window washer, or meter reader.

Warren was making his third drive through within the hour, scanning for faces he'd seen earlier, looking for anyone who hadn't moved enough to really belong. As he drove, his thoughts drifted to the night before. Once he had finally made the mental connection, he had sprinted from that bar faster than he ever thought possible.

The Borman fire in Rye had occurred too early in the morning for it to make the Wednesday edition, but on Thursday the *Daily News* had run a good-sized picture of Jake as he exited Donny's Bronco at the scene Wednesday morning. Warren was disappointed in himself that he hadn't noticed it earlier, but it wasn't until the discussion moved toward firefighters and the Morson Grayhead murders that it finally clicked. He hadn't been sure, but could not afford to take the chance. In this game, one mistake could mean lethal injection.

He knew he'd already said too much and had already been thinking of a way out when, fortuitously, Jake and his nice little redhead had approached the bar together. Warren saw his opportunity and took it, grabbing Valerie's purse off the stool and ripping her wallet from it just before scaling a chain-link fence, running through backyards in a shortcut to his apartment. If it was Jake, then the authorities were already on to him, and purse snatching would be the least of his worries. If it wasn't, then he'd return it intact. No harm, no foul.

But if Warren's intuition was right, and Jake had entered the bar to see what he could secretly weasel out of him, then that only meant one thing: they'd been tailing him. When Warren had reached his apartment last night, he hadn't even bothered going inside. But he was fortunate. His tail was still busy toiling in the alleyway behind the bar. He hopped in his Mazda and hightailed it out as fast as his wheels would take him, watching his rearview mirror for many, many miles. If they were onto him, the question Warren kept asking himself now was, what should he do about it?

Warren spent the night in a flea-bag motel on Central Avenue somewhere in Yonkers, trying to think his way out of this mess. Maybe he was just paranoid. But if that wasn't Jake Ferguson who had entered his life, then the man had a twin, whether he knew it or not. Warren spread Valerie's belongings out over the bed, half expecting to see a badge or a gun, something that would identify her as a cop. But there was nothing remotely close—no business card, notebook, police ID, badge, gun. Nothing. As best he could tell, this Valerie Medforth was a teacher. At least her union card said so.

Could he possibly have been wrong? Maybe it wasn't Jake Ferguson. He knew one way to find out. Warren picked up the phone and dialed the bar.

"Bird's Nest."

"Patrick, it's Warren."

"Warren! Jesus Christ, man. What the hell did you do? This place was swarming with cops."

Warren knew his intuition was right. They were onto him. "Look, I just wanted to say I'm sorry if I hurt business tonight. There's been a horrible misunderstanding. I'll explain everything when this whole mess gets cleared up."

"Hurt business? Shit, we haven't had live entertainment here since the seventies. Just watch your ass, man."

"Will do."

So, the hunt was on. "Okay, Mr. Jacob Ferguson," Warren said aloud as he hung up. "You want to play hardball? You're on."

His mind raced in a sequence. If the authorities had tailed him, then obviously they knew where he lived. No doubt, they also knew where he worked, which meant they had surely made the travel connection by now. Warren wondered if they had enough for a search warrant and worried they might already have been inside his apartment.

If they had, he kept asking himself what they could have found. What did he have in his apartment that might possibly link him to the Morson Grayhead case? He knew they would undoubtedly search his PC files and certainly find he was linked to the mainframe at work. But so what? What about his trash? No, he'd taken it out on the way to the bar. But Warren worried about that one. If they had a warrant, they would unquestionably search his trash. No matter that it was now in a pile with that of a dozen other residents. He felt certain they would go through it bag by bag—piece by piece if they had to. That could be problematic—at least until they found Scotty's print on the note he'd sent Jake. Warren prayed that then the focus of their investigation would change course, taking the heat off him.

"Dammit!" he cursed aloud, wishing now he'd just kept his mouth shut. Josephine had always told him silence was golden. He had to admit she was right on that score. Warren never thought much of love, but as he thought back on his relationship with Josephine, he figured he was about as much in love with her as was possible—at least for him.

It was true that what had initially attracted him to her was her money, but as time passed, he actually began to have feelings for her. But Lianne had snuffed all that out, right in front of his eyes. They hadn't been married but a year, and everything Josephine was set to inherit was still tied up in trusts. As it turned out, Warren was never to see a penny of her family's small fortune.

Lianne had not only taken from him the one person in his life for whom he cared, but more importantly—much more importantly—she had taken away his due. She had robbed him of his pot of gold at the end of the rainbow! Warren decided right then and there to let Lianne go unpunished—at least by the law. He would make her pay, quite literally, and for the rest of her life. From that day forward, Warren Parks decided he might very well be able to use Lianne Rybeck to his advantage. And in a big way.

BANKING THE FIRE

Book IV

WARREN'S EYES WATCHED every movement on Valerie's street: little kids playing, grandmothers strolling babies down the sidewalks. There was no visible sign of surveillance—*visible* being the operative word. Her street seemed to him as normal as any other in Westchester on such a beautiful, sunny late-summer day. If the cops *were* here, and they were looking for him, then they were a hell of a lot better than Warren was giving them credit for. There were no trucks, no occupied cars, no people hanging out on phone poles, ladders, or roofs.

He decided to make one more slow walk through, this time focusing on buildings. Warren searched long and hard for anyone standing or sitting at a window, for the glare of sun in the lens of a binoculars or a venetian blind pried open. He could find nothing. If he wasn't safe on this street, then they were very good indeed.

Warren knew from the rabid media reports that Jake had been named the lead investigator on the Morson Grayhead case. The letter was meant as a ruse, something to upset Jake's status quo. But with Scotty's prints on it, it was also more than that, meant to serve a much larger purpose in his overall plan. Scotty just didn't know it . . . yet. But if Jake wanted to mess around with his life, Warren would be all too happy to follow through with the letter's threat.

And now as he casually scrutinized Valerie's street, he was struck by his desire. Fire and sex were quickly becoming an uncontrollable compulsion for Warren. He wanted revenge. Prior to their *chance* encounter at the Bird's Nest, Jake was just doing a job. But now he had invaded Warren's privacy, inserting himself into his life under false pretenses. Warren was furious. Time and again, he asked himself just who this asshole thought he was. He would show Jake that he was far from some lapdog Jake could manipulate for political gain. What do I look like, Warren thought, an idiot you can toy with like a child? "Oh, Mr. Fire Marshal," he whispered, "I underestimated you. But then again, you have underestimated me. We shall see who comes out the victor now."

Warren walked slowly up one side of Valerie's street, looking into cars, gazing at windows and stoops. When he reached the end, he crossed and did the same thing on the other side. Convinced that to search further was folly, he glided up Valerie's walk, stopping at the front door to her complex. He examined the mailboxes in the wall to his left and found #5 MEDFORTH. Warren pushed her buzzer and waited, pushing again when there was no response.

He glanced casually around and behind him, making sure one last time. The door was secured with a York lock. Warren reached into his pocket and pulled out his lock-picking set. At least his stint in prison had not gone completely for naught. If you can call eighteen years behind bars a stint. Scotty had been smart to steal the set for him, though it really wasn't necessary. They can be purchased through a dozen different catalogs. Still, it was the only wise thing Scotty had ever done in his life. Warren chuckled at what an idiot Lianne's kid was. He could not *wait* to get rid of him. The very sight of Scotty's face was beginning to nauseate Warren, but he could not sacrifice him just yet—soon, but not quite yet. There was unfinished work to be done.

Warren inserted his picks and finished his task in under twenty seconds. When he heard the lock click, he pushed slightly and stopped, looked around one last time, and opened the door with ease. He was in. Closing the door behind him, Warren gazed out at the street beyond through its glass window. There was no movement. Nothing to catch his eye. No one was rushing toward him. Nothing had changed. Just your typical middle-class neighborhood enjoying a beautiful Saturday morning.

Warren climbed the wooden stairs, noticing apartment numbers as he went. Valerie's was at the end of a hall on the second floor. Good, he thought. Rear access. He had to be careful now. No sight-seeing. No delay. Warren walked toward her door, careful to notice any nosy observers. He snuggled up to her door and entered in the same fashion he had downstairs. If the cops were staking it out, it was now he stood the best chance of capture. It hadn't escaped him that they might even be inside.

He stepped in quickly and closed the door behind him, standing with his back to it, listening for footsteps, movement, breathing—anything that might give away that he was not alone. Valerie's apartment was airy, painted white with pastel trim. Everything about it spoke of femininity, from the stuffed animals on the mantel of the now-defunct fireplace to the pink throw rugs on her wooden floors. Warren remained motionless, eyeing every inch of her place before moving again. He turned, gazed out her peephole down the hall, and, seeing no one, began a slow, casual stroll through Valerie Medforth's life.

He walked quietly to her bedroom, taken by the excitement he felt in just knowing this was where she could meet her end. Bedposts and everything. It was perfect. Warren had not yet decided Valerie's fate. She sure was a pretty little thing, and it would be fun writing the last chapter of her life. But Warren was not in this for fun. At least he hadn't been when it all started. He suddenly felt apprehensive that the inclination was just hitting him now.

There is an unspoken rule that you don't mess with the heat. If Valerie was a cop, which he aimed to find out before leaving her place today, then taking her out would be tantamount to a death wish. And if she wasn't, as he suspected, if she was nothing more than Jake's two-bit schoolhouse whore, her termination would still change the rules overnight. At that point, Warren *knew* that, for Jake, it would no longer be business, it would be personal. Warren wasn't sure he wanted to cross that line just yet.

Yet viscerally, he knew it would all be coming to an end soon enough. If they were watching him, then they were watching Scotty, and that was exactly how he'd planned it. It was important he not make any mistakes now. If Warren played his cards right, he could put Scotty out to slaughter, cash in his chips, and be long gone to South America before the cops even knew what hit them. But he needed to make sure he kept as many back doors open as possible. If for no other reason than to knock Jake off-balance for a day, to buy some time for a successful escape, Warren had to consider Valerie a viable option. In his mind, he thought he would be foolish not to consider it.

He approached her bureau and carefully checked every drawer, but there was nothing of interest. Nothing that interested *him* anyway. He moved aside underwear and bras, socks and T-shirts. There were letters and small mementos of her past: a pressed rose from some special occasion, deodorant blocks, and a diaphragm. Warren smiled, mumbling under his breath, "You won't be needing *that* anymore, my love."

Her closet was neat but boring. There were Reebok sneakers, a couple of pairs of different-colored pumps, one pair of high heels, and a pair of worn, furry slippers that looked like sheep. There was an assortment of hanging skirts and blouses, but nothing out of the ordinary—nothing that stood out, screaming, "Hey, look at me!" Warren could see she had a nice wardrobe and kept thinking he might find something slinky, something that showed a darker, sleazier side. He imagined finding a whip in the corner, or maybe some kind of leather-studded dominatrix getup, but he was to be disappointed. If she liked her sex, she apparently liked it conventional. He'd hoped to see and touch her kinkier side. Ms. Medforth, he thought, you don't know unconventional.

It quickly became obvious that Valerie Medforth was no cop. He had been right. She was indeed a teacher. A neat pile of papers sat on her kitchen table. Warren picked up the top one, reading something about a trip her class had recently taken to city hall. He laid it on the table, scanning the varied aspects of Valerie's life. There were notes from children in her class stuck to her refrigerator door and tacked to her kitchen corkboard. She had even framed and hung two paintings she apparently found worthwhile. Warren thought they looked like shit, not to mention stupid. But, hey, to each his own.

He walked slowly to the door leading to her back porch, making a mental note of the lock. He opened it and looked around thoroughly before stepping out. She'd actually made it look nice. Viny plants hung from the rafters, while others grew over glazed pots lying on the peeling paint of the aging two-by-sixes of the floor. She even had a gas grill in the corner. Stairs led down to the ground below, and Warren stuck his head over the edge, trying to get a sense how traversable this route would be. He thought this would be easy. Like fishing in a barrel.

He'd seen enough. It was perfect. Not only was she no cop, she was the teacher to a horde of precious little snots. Oh, how their lives would be turned upside down if there ever came the day that school officials had to try to explain why their beloved instructor now resembled a forgotten hamburger patty on a July Fourth picnic grill. But that wouldn't be the best of it—icing on the cake maybe, but surely not the best. No, what made Valerie Medforth superspecial, what made the prospect of her death all the more appealing, was that to Warren's eyes she belonged to Jake.

Warren was both moved and disturbed by his desire. For a moment, he allowed himself to dream, to envision it all taking place. Tell me, Mr. Fire Marshal, he thought. How do you like someone poking their head in where it doesn't belong? Warren laughed quietly. "Take *that*, asshole."

VALERIE STOOD BEHIND Jake, kneading his shoulders with her fingers as he sat in front of the microfiche screen in the file room of the Fire Marshal's Office. She craned her head over his shoulder, trying to read the report in front of him.

"What is it *exactly* you're looking for?"

"I'm not sure yet," Jake responded as he leaned forward.

"Does it have to do with Parks?"

"Maybe. This fire happened on the Rybeck estate nearly thirty years ago. If it *was* Parks we met last night, then it was his wife who died in the fire."

Valerie was surprised. She hadn't read the recent *Times* article. "Someone died in a fire at the Rybecks'?"

"Yep, and somehow I got a feeling it's not unrelated to this case. All I'm doing now is seeing if I can find a connection, or something that doesn't fit."

"Such as?"

Jake scrolled, stopping when he came upon the section describing the then fire marshal's explanation as to the cause of the blaze. He put a finger in the air, pausing the conversation. He read for a few minutes, scrolling it back and reading it again.

"What is it?"

"Interesting. Mrs. Rybeck specifically told Donny and me what the fire marshal ruled as a cause of the fire. She was pretty clear about it. But it says here the cause was something else altogether."

"It's not what she told you?"

"Not even close."

"Why do you think she would lie to you?"

Jake shook his head, wheeling his chair sideways. He looked up into Valerie's eyes, recalling for the first time in years the emotions he'd had toward Danny at the realization he was falling in love. A feeling raced through him that was disarmingly similar. He felt off-balance. Surprised really. Hell, he'd known her for less than twenty-four hours. How could it be possible that he could fall so deeply, so quickly, for someone he barely knew? Jake wasn't sure he could believe his feelings. He didn't trust himself. *I'm just lonelier than I thought. Go slow, boy. Go slow. Let's see how you feel once the novelty's worn off.*

"I can't say for sure," Jake said, answering Valerie's question. "This isn't the first time she's lied to us, either. I know she's hiding something. I just don't know what it is." He smiled. "Yet."

"You think it's possible she could be involved?"

"Oh, she's involved all right." He placed his hand above his eyes. "Right up to here. But I don't think she has anything to do with the murders, if that's what you mean."

"What makes you say that?"

"I can't tell you."

"You can't, or you won't?"

Jake looked at her. "Don't be mean."

"Sorry. It's just so fascinating, that's all. I guess I want to know everything about the case so I can help you figure it out."

"I'd like that, too, Valerie, but I just can't. You understand, don't you?"

Valerie was disappointed, but she respected his professionalism. "I guess. But why not? Don't you trust me?"

"It's not that. It's just that . . ."

"Just what?"

Jake turned his head. "You're not being fair, Valerie. This case is too important to screw up. It's not that I think you would *purposely* say anything. It's just that people's tongues slip all the time and they never even realize it. Look what Parks did last night. It's for your own protection, believe me. You can't say what you don't know. It's just one of the rules I operate by."

"I understand," she said with frustration. "I just like being a part of your life."

"You are. Like it or not." Jake rose, walked to a phone, and dialed Donny's number. "Don, it's Jake. Find anything?"

"No luck, Jake. We got to wait until Monday."

"Shit. All right, thanks for trying. See you Monday."

"Hold on there, cowboy. Are you so you can talk, or what?"

"No."

"Still? Jesus Christ, Jake."

"See you Monday."

"Sorry," Jake said, looking at Valerie. "I have to make one more call." He dialed the State Police crime lab. "Art, it's Jake Ferguson. Anything on that letter we sent up yesterday?"

"Yeah, believe it or not. I got the report here somewhere." Jake could hear papers shuffling. "Here it is. Got a real nice right thumb."

The trooper was right. Jake couldn't believe it. It seemed almost *too* good to be true. "And?"

"Well, it's good and bad."

Jake frowned. "What do you mean, good *and* bad?"

"I lifted it this morning myself. First thing I did was run it through AFIS. It came up identical to a set taken from a robbery in Ossining."

"Whose are they?"

"That's the bad part, Jake. No match."

AFIS, or the Automated Fingerprint Identification System, is a computerized fingerprint data bank capable of cross-referencing thousands of prints per second. It's usually regionalized, with smaller or less populated states often pooling resources and funds by connecting to the same database. New York is neither small nor sparsely populated and therefore has its own. Normally, AFIS will choose a half dozen or so sets most closely resembling those entered, but from there it's still left to the technician and his expertise to make the definitive, final match. Jake had never heard of a set in the computer that weren't identified.

His eyes squinted. "No match? What do you mean, 'no match'? What the hell's an unidentified print doing in AFIS?"

"Yeah, that caught my eye, too, so I pulled the records. Guess where they came from?"

"I don't know, Art. Disneyland?"

"A locksmith in Ossining. Someone apparently broke into his shop last June and took a lock-picking set. No cash or valuables. Just the set. I guess they picked up a couple of good prints at the scene. The responding detective thought it might be the harbinger of an impending robbery spree and entered it in the computer on a whim."

Jake whistled. That sure explained a lot. It never ceased to amaze him the forethought and professionalism his fellow law enforcement colleagues showed every day. If the public only knew. "Now *that* guy was thinking. So, let me get this straight," Jake began, casually turning his back to Valerie. "You mean to tell me whoever stole it can get into just about any lock in the country?"

"I suppose, if he knows what he's doing."

"Art, if you had to guess, where do you think someone would learn how to pick locks?" Jake already thought he knew the answer to the question, but wanted justification for his thoughts.

"Christ, Jake, any number of places; the street and the slammer are two that come immediately to mind."

Jake was not surprised by Art's response. "Okay. Thanks, Art. Let me know if you find out anything else."

"Always."

Jake almost forgot the beer bottle. "Oh, Art!" he called out, fearing he'd hung up.

"What?"

"I got a beer bottle I need you to print for me. I'll bring it by after lunch. I need it ASAP."

"Why should this one be different?"

Jake hung up the phone. "Hmmm," he said, staring at his hand still holding the receiver.

"What?" Valerie asked.

Jake was quiet.

"I know, I know. You can't tell me, right?"

Jake hated doing this to her. He wanted nothing more than to share his thoughts on the case with someone other than Ederling. And that she was a woman made it especially appealing. Jake always trusted their intuition. But he had already made one mistake involving Valerie, and no way in hell was he going to make another. She would just have to get used to it.

He smiled. "You're catching on."

"Oh, you're no fun," Valerie said in mock childishness.

"True. But I'm a hell of an investigator."

"*That*, I can believe. You just don't know how exciting all this is to an outsider. I'm loving it."

"Actually, I do. But unfortunately, that's just what you are. Sorry."

Valerie sat in his chair, thinking for a moment. "So . . . that call. It sounded important. What are you going to do now?"

"Get *lunch*."

Valerie looked at him with probing eyes. "Get *lunch?* That's it? Don't you at least want to speak with Mrs. Rybeck?"

"Yes," Jake answered, flicking off the microfiche machine. "But she's not going anywhere. Don and I will speak to her on Monday. Right now, I'm famished, and I also need a break. I don't want to think about this case again until Monday."

"So that's how you guys do it? You just stop working?"

"That's how we do it. What do you think? I'm a robot?"

"I never really thought about it before. I guess even investigators need a life, too, huh?"

Jake nodded. "You bet we do. *Especially* investigators."

She looked at him conspiratorially. "Want to make it a little funky?"

"What do you mean?"

"Come here a sec," she said, curling a finger.

Jake's back stiffened slightly. "Here?"

Valerie's longing eyes spoke volumes, and Jake wanted nothing more than to fulfill his years of desire right then and there. But he could also smell a career buster from a mile away. He smiled, shaking his head. "Oh, you're too much."

"Thank you. I'll take that as a compliment."

Jake grabbed her hands lightly. "Not here, Val." He pecked her cheek. "I can't."

"Oh, come on," she teased, egging him on. "It'll be fun."

"I don't doubt it for a moment," he said, taking her hand in his. "Let's go. I know a motel not two blocks from here. Now *there's* where we can have some fun."

WITH THE EXCEPTION of his stint as Severin Rybeck's limousine driver, Chandler Boutet had spent his entire professional career in the Secret Service. He had protected both presidents and popes, dignitaries and children, and had chauffeured and protected some of this century's most influential and powerful figures. But as age crept up on him, and Chan found himself less agile than he had once been, he was moved out of the field, eventually becoming head of the New York regional office. He had played integral roles in the breaking of billion-dollar counterfeiting rings, and international money-laundering operations.

Chan had put in his twenty years, and then some, and truth be told, he enjoyed every minute of it. The job wasn't the greatest paying, but it was more than enough to meet his needs. He traveled the world over, enjoyed numerous intangible perks, and there was always a whiff of danger and excitement, certainly enough to keep his wanderlust satisfied.

It wasn't until a friend had casually mentioned the Rybeck opportunity that Chan even considered leaving the Service. As with so much in life, timing is everything. The divorce his wife had sought had recently gone through, and for the first time in his life Chan found himself wondering just what it was all about. It had all happened so fast. He interviewed with Severin on a Friday afternoon, more out of curiosity than anything else, and was offered the job the following Tuesday. By the next Monday Chan was liveried and driving Severin Rybeck everywhere he went.

Over the years Chan had harvested myriad contacts throughout the intelligence community, and he knew exactly which ones he could turn to for help. For a hundred thousand dollars, you could bet he was going to use every last one of them. He'd performed his share of favors in his career, and now it was payback time.

Chan sat now a few cars down the road opposite Warren's apartment in a four-wheel-drive Jeep Cherokee, spying it through binoculars. He poured himself a cup of coffee from a thermos and leaned his head back against the seat . . . watching . . . waiting patiently for something, anything, to happen. There was no way he was going to give Lianne Rybeck a reason not to make good on the other fifty grand. When Chan was through using his contacts on Mr. Warren Parks, she'd know what kind of toilet paper he used.

But alone, Chan knew he would be at an extreme disadvantage. Single-man, round-the-clock surveillance is an oxymoron. You have to eat, sleep, and go to the bathroom. Immediately following Lianne's visit, he had contacted three colleagues, all ex-Service. He knew one was unemployed, another wrote children's books, of all things, and the last freelanced as a security consultant to corporate America. Chan offered them each two hundred dollars a day. Cash. Eight-hour shifts. No manual labor. Just sit, watch, and follow. He figured he'd give it up to a week if necessary, then reevaluate. It was the cost of doing business.

Within hours of setting up camp outside Warren's Englewood Cliffs apartment, Chan had company. He turned at the sound of a knuckle rapping on his window and smiled at his old colleague, motioning him inside. "Sammy, you old dog," he said, extending a hand. "How goes the battle?"

"Chan, you old whoretamer. Good to see you, man," Sam Broadman said as he climbed into the Jeep next to his friend. "That was some piece of tough luck, that Rybeck thing, huh? I was sorry to hear it."

"Hey, what are you gonna do, right?"

"So, how'd you land this gig?"

"Don't even ask. You bring the radios?"

"Yep." Broadman laid a small cardboard box between them, pulling out two portables. "Right here. Newly charged."

"Good. We'll need 'em. We could be here awhile."

By definition, surveillance is brutal work. Emotionally draining and dull, it's akin to staring at a spot on a wall for hours at a clip. In time it can take on meditative qualities, and is one reason why coffee and a partner are essential tools of the trade—absolute necessities to assure ultimate success. The simple basics of day-to-day life, such as toileting and sleep, become exponentially more difficult, so that eventually even a moderately long detail can seem to last for years.

His guest settled in, staring out the windshield. "So, what do we got?"

"Bird lives in that nest right there," Chan said, pointing with his binoculars. "The gray three-story with the big oak out front. Top floor."

"Got a photo?" Broadman asked, his hand held out.

"No picture," Chan said with a shake of his head.

Chan had stopped to talk with Lianne one more time before heading out on his new occupation. She didn't have a picture, but had just seen the photograph Jake had shown her. Her description was good enough for government work, at least until Chan could pursue other avenues.

Broadman was almost incredulous. *"Nothing?"*

"For now. I'm working on it, Sammy. Target's about fifty, Caucasian, salt-and-pepper. Stands about five eleven. No facial hair. Drives a green Mazda."

"Eyes?"

"Brown."

"Well, I guess we can consider ourselves lucky, huh? At least he doesn't look like ten million other white men in America."

Chan looked at him. "I told you, I'm working on it."

Broadman pulled out a cigarette, dropped his head, and cupped his hands as he lit it, speaking through the corner of his mouth. "You didn't happen to notice the two guys sitting in the brown Caprice, did you?"

"Yep, they were here when I arrived. Haven't moved in over three hours. Got cop written all over them."

The two New York State CID cops had been staked out in front of Warren's apartment building since Jake had sent them back from the Bird's Nest Friday night. By the time they searched the alley, got back into their car, and drove back to Warren's, he had already left. They missed him by less than a minute.

"What do you think?" Broadman asked.

"They got New York plates. I'm having them run now. Ten to one they're state cops."

"Hmmm. What do you want to do?"

"Give me one of those, will you?" Chan said, motioning to his friend's smoke. Broadman forced out a cigarette with a flick of his forefinger to the bottom of the pack. Chan lit it, exhaling as he spoke. "I'm not sure, but I can tell you this guy doesn't need four baby-sitters. If we don't get some movement by tomorrow night, I'm opting out of this game. There's a hell of a lot more useful shit I can be doing with my time than watching some nest that's already covered."

"Got a scanner with you?" Broadman asked.

"Not here. I didn't know we'd have company."

"What's this guy's gig anyway? I get nervous when I don't know who I'm sittin' on. For all we know, he's got rocket launchers in there."

Chan held the binoculars to his eyes. "Don't know. Don't care."

"You plan on going in?"

"Depends."

"On what?"

What could Chan say? On whether or not I learn enough just sitting here to earn another fifty thousand dollars? "Two things. How long we sit without any action, and our friends down the street."

Chan was loath to break the law, but by the same token, fifty grand was a lot of money to leave on the table. He was sorely tempted to break into Warren's place. But as bad as he wanted the money, he wanted to avoid jail even more. Twenty years in law enforcement just doesn't lend itself to a criminal mind. His contacts were varied and many, and Chan felt certain they would be more than enough to ultimately do this job well.

"Well, I got news for you. Those cops aren't going anywhere."

"I know," Chan said. "Which is exactly why we should be doing something else."

"Shit, Chan, you've only been watching the place a few hours. Your charge was to stay on it, right?"

"Right."

"Then we should stay on it. You want to boogie for greener pastures, be my guest. I'll stick through the night."

"Well, we'll see. I had no idea the heat had an interest in our boy. It definitely changes things. But we should be able to use that to our advantage. If the cops are targeting him, then that means they're talking. And if they're talking, we should be listening. We need a scanner."

Broadman shook his head. "Yeah, but they'll be on a tac channel. Not just any scanner will do."

Chan smirked his lips, looking at Sam with surprise. "What do you think, I bought my scanner at Sears?"

"Well, if you can follow a tac channel, then go get the damn thing."

"I'll hang through the night. Then we'll see."

Broadman knew exactly what Chan was talking about. There was so much that could be done outside of just sitting on Warren's street, not least of which was contacting his connections at Social Security and DMV. Once Chan found Warren's social security number, it would be but a hop, skip, and a jump to whoever filed his W-2s, and hence, his employer. There were also credit card purchases, records from the Medical Information Bureau, and criminal background checks to review.

The list of possible avenues to be searched was lengthy, but two problems stood in their way. Not all of them could be pursued from a car, and it was also a weekend. Monday morning could not come fast enough for Chandler Boutet. Its early rays of the sun would cast a broad and telling floodlight onto Warren Parks's secret life.

There was silence for a while. "Who you working for, anyway?" Broadman finally asked.

"Lianne Rybeck."

"*Lianne Rybeck?*" Broadman asked with astonishment. "What's she pay? Minimum wage?"

"Yeah. Just about."

"My ass."

Chan felt it important he not tell Broadman about the money she was paying him. He thought it strange how, overnight, he'd gone from unemployed livery to highly paid sleuth. A six-figure paycheck is a damn good wage, especially for a week's work. It's funny how the tides can turn. What stared Chan in the face now was the age-old dilemma between management and labor. He had just lost a damn good job and the last thing he needed now was salary negotiations.

Chan had thought enough to bring a blanket and pillow and lay curled up in a ball in the backseat of the Jeep. "Wake me if there's movement," he said.

JAKE'S DAY WAS busier than he had planned. He and Valerie drove to the local State Police crime lab, where he left her in the lobby reading a wrinkled copy of the *New York Post* someone had left behind. He had bagged Warren's beer bottle in a Ziploc bag and brought it in to the State Police evidence technician he'd just spoken to a few hours earlier. As Art went to work, the two men spent the next forty-five minutes discussing various facets of the case.

The clock on the dash of Jake's cruiser read 3:17 P.M. when he and Valerie finally crawled inside. Jake breathed deep and looked at his newfound friend. She looked tired. It had been a long night, and both of them had gotten precious little sleep. Jake was physically exhausted and desperately needed to close his eyes. At his suggestion they both went back to his co-op for a nap. This time they shared his bed.

Sleep did not come easily for Valerie. She dozed intermittently but eventually tired of the effort, choosing to lie quietly next to Jake instead. She eyed the ceiling of Jake's bedroom, following a crack extending from somewhere near the middle to the corner above the door. The lights were off and the bedroom was practically dark, but Valerie's eyes had been open so long they had fully acclimated to the poor lighting in the room. She turned her head quietly, looking at Jake's digital clock: 8:27 P.M.

She studied the crack, staring into it more than at it. Just what was it about Jake that enthralled her so? Valerie was surprised how quickly she had fallen for him. It wasn't as though she had made some secret pact with herself never to allow something like this to happen. She just never thought it would. Single, and thirty-four, it seemed her most vibrant years were slipping slowly away, forever lost to some unforgiving time trap whose door only swung in one direction.

Her dreams were not so far removed from those of millions of other women the world over. Valerie wanted a man who would be her best friend and cheerleader; someone with whom she could share life's victories and defeats. She wanted love and romance, flowers on her birthday, and a warm body to snuggle with on cold winter nights. But more than that, what she really wanted was a family.

As the years went by, there seemed times when Valerie's internal clock ticked so loudly she felt certain others could hear it. And while on the whole, men seemed to lack understanding in so many ways, there never seemed to be one who needed further clarification on that score. Single woman, midthirties, and childless—at times she felt it must have seemed as though she were screaming the word *BABY!* out loud.

Valerie was far from naive and knew she was attractive. But somehow, now, that seemed more a liability than an asset. Men were drawn to her like a magnet, though almost always, their thinly veiled reasons became all too obvious, all too soon. Why was it, she wondered, that all the available men in her age group seemed to come with so much baggage? They were either divorced, bitter and horny, or had children of their own. Not that the latter was grounds for instant disqualification, but she still had hopes of starting fresh, as she'd dreamed of the first time.

But Valerie was only human and felt no shame that at times she had taken a chance. It always annoyed her that when men slept around, somehow society labeled them as studs—but God forbid a woman should do that! The slut/stud conundrum never seemed quite fair. But her mother had taught her well, and like it or not, it had been indelibly etched in her brain. In spite of her upbringing, over the years she had thrown fate to the wind with an occasional lover, hoping he might be the one with whom she could begin anew. But like clockwork, disillusionment and pain almost always seemed to follow.

Something was different about Jake, however. Valerie wasn't sure just what it was, but knew she felt secure and sheltered in his presence. Maybe it was the power of the emotions evoked by the events of the night before, or maybe it was just kismet. Maybe she saw a father figure in his unselfish willingness to step forward and protect her. She would probably never know, and in her mind it didn't really matter. What Valerie did know, what her heart and womb told her, was that she wanted him inside her, to experience their becoming one.

It wasn't like her to open up to a man so quickly, so unconditionally, but there was no doubt it was different when Jake entered her for the first time. There was no hint of the silent praying and wishful thinking that sex always seemed to bring. Even as Valerie helped guide him inside her, she was aware that those fears were missing, replaced instead by a spiritual oneness, a degree of safety and trust she didn't think she had ever experienced. When they made love, Valerie was more attuned to an emotional sense of joy and fulfillment than she was to any physical sense of warmth and lust.

As she lay in Jake's bed, she felt at peace, no disappointment in her actions. On the contrary, for the first time in a long time, Valerie felt safe. Like Jake, she, too, had seemingly spent an eternity alone. The very act of allowing him inside her, of wrapping her arms tightly around a man she could trust, seemed to renew in her a lost sense of womanhood. She had sexual needs of course, and the release caused even her toes to tingle, but Jake's lovemaking seemed to transcend the physical; it carried with it an emotional cleansing as well.

Fatigue pulled at every nerve of her body, and yet there was a reason Valerie Medforth could not sleep. She was torn between a fearful cognizance that perhaps she had found the one, and an inner sadness at the realization that all was not well in Jacob Ferguson's world. It wasn't until she lay beside him on Danny's side of the bed that Valerie had any inkling of the depth of the problem that bubbled just below his steady veneer. Jake had done something that surprised her and, perhaps for that very reason, pierced her heart just that much deeper.

Valerie's cough woke him. Jake opened his eyes and turned to find her lying on her back, staring at the ceiling. He rolled over, placing a hand lightly on her stomach. "Hi," he said, a bit groggy.

"Hi."

"You thinking?"

"Yeah."

He was quiet for a moment, judging the best response. "Try not to worry about it, Val." He propped himself up on a couple of pillows. "It'll be okay. I promise."

"No, Jake, that's not what I'm thinking about."

He rolled over on his side, resting his head on his left hand. "Then what?"

Valerie already knew the answer to the question she was about to ask. Don's wife had told her Jake and Danny's story. And though it was selfish and insensitive, still, for reasons she did not fully understand, it bothered her that in his heart, Jake had not put Danny fully to rest. That morning, when they'd made love the first time, Valerie thought it strange that he led her to the guest room and not his own, but it was painfully clear now. She had never been intimate with a man who'd lost his wife, and as she lay in bed, she thought maybe that's just the way it was. Maybe a piece of his heart would always bleed.

And then this evening, when she did crawl into *his* bed, Jake had done something else that caused her angst. "Jake, why'd you put that pillow in the closet when I laid my head on it? How come I had to bring one in from the guest room?"

Jake sighed deeply and rolled over on his back, placing his hands under his head. "I know, Val, I know," he finally said after a moment of silence. "I knew I'd made a mistake the second I did it. I almost didn't ask you to. Guess I'm just afraid to lose Danny completely."

Valerie didn't want to hurt Jake. It struck her as more than odd how quickly the two of them had gelled. They were only just getting to know one another. But that said, this man whose bed she now shared was special. In her eyes he was brave, loyal, and honorable, and those qualities went a long way in Valerie's book. More than anything, she wanted to appear understanding and empathetic to his loss. But one undeniable fact kept ringing in her ears. Danny was dead and had been for years. She had been taken from Jake's life forever, and as premature as her death had been, as painful as it must have been for him, the simple fact was that Danny was never coming back.

Whoever the next man in her life would be, Valerie wanted much more from the relationship than to play the part of emotional spackling putty, filling the hole of loneliness in a lovelorn man's heart. As she lay in bed, contemplating the nuances of Jake's psyche, it became obvious to her this was one issue that would not just go away. If Valerie was going to allow Jake to become a meaningful part of her life—not just a sexual companion, but an emotional and spiritual partner as well—then he was going to need to come to closure with Danny's death. It was early yet, but Valerie knew if their relationship had any chance of moving forward, this was a stumbling block they would need to remove.

She spoke softly, hesitantly at first. "Jake . . . I can only imagine how painful Danny's loss was." She paused for effect. "But you *have* lost her completely. I know how this will sound, and please don't be angry at me, but Danny is dead, Jake. I don't know, maybe it's too painful for you to hear. Maybe you don't even want to hear it, but she's not coming back. Not now, not ever. I guess I'm just afraid. Scared that we won't be able to move forward until you can get past her."

Jake knew it was coming. Valerie's words stung him. He didn't bother interjecting that while Valerie may have thought he had lost Danny completely, he still cherished her memory. He closed his eyes, trying to govern his breathing. He was quiet for a long time. Though Jake tried to squelch it, when he did finally speak, his voice was laced ever so slightly with a tinge of reproach. "I know Danny's dead, Val. I don't need *you* to tell me that."

"I see," she said, her own voice subtly indignant. "But you still don't want my smell on her pillow, right? Is that how it's going to be, Jake? You're only going to let me in just so far? Every time I get too close, you're going to throw up the 'do not enter' sign? Look . . . maybe this whole thing's moved too fast. I don't think you're ready to let go of her. Maybe you don't want to."

What could Jake say? It wasn't as if Valerie were making it all up. She was probably even right. Maybe he wasn't ready for this. What Jake did know was that he liked Valerie Medforth very much. This early in the game he'd be foolhardy to use the word *love*, though it had disquietly crossed his mind. Jake thought that maybe it was the sex, but something told him to look deeper than that. He'd decided she was special long before they became intimate.

Jake knew he couldn't have it both ways. Valerie was wise to see the invisible umbilical cord connecting him to Danny. And yet, what Jake didn't see was that it was also tied in a knot, slowly starving him of life's vigor and energy. It was an all-or-nothing proposition. If they were ever to blossom as a couple from here, he knew he would have to reach a resolution. In love, gray just doesn't cut it.

"Valerie, I don't know what I want or what I'm ready for. I know I like being with you. Isn't that good enough for now? It's all happened so fast, Val. Maybe I just need a little time to adjust. I don't know where it goes from here, but then . . . neither do you. Can't we just enjoy each other for a while?"

Valerie wasn't lying when she said she was afraid. She was afraid all right: afraid to anger him, to hurt him, to scare him off, and most of all, afraid to have it end as quickly as it had begun. "Look, Jake, I'm not trying to push you," she said, sitting up against the wall. "I know we just met, and don't ask me to explain it, but I'm very fond of you. But I can't allow myself to fall for you, not if I'm just going to be your rebound catch. We'll both end up getting hurt. And I can't put myself through that, Jake. I'm too fragile right now."

Jake rolled over on his side, staring Valerie in the eyes. "Well, I don't know about you, but I'm sure enjoying this conversation."

She looked down at him. "Don't make me feel guilty, Jake."

"Who said anything about guilt? I know you're right. I guess I didn't realize it, but I'm scared, too." Whatever emotional bonds he had loosely attached to her, Jake knew now he would have to untie them, or he risked losing her forever. He hated giving her the out, but could see no other choice. "So, what do you want to do?" he finally asked, fearing her response.

Valerie hugged her knees to her chest. "I don't know. Maybe I should go home for the night."

Jake didn't like the idea. "You sure?"

"No," she said, resting her chin on her knees. "But I need some time to think."

"You want me to set up some police protection for you?"

Valerie looked at him. "Would you, please? I think I'd like that."

Jake sat up, trying his best to act casual. He feared he would never see her again. "Consider it done. Come on, get dressed. I'll take you back and stay until a detail arrives."

THERE WAS AN open spot directly in front when Jake pulled his cruiser up to Valerie's Pleasantville apartment at 9:23 P.M. Jake got out and waited for Valerie before escorting her silently to her door.

"Want me to come in with you?" Jake asked. "Just to check things out?"

"Yes, if you don't mind."

She unlocked the door and the two of them climbed the flight of stairs to her hallway, neither one speaking, both lost in thought. Valerie fumbled with her keys, finally unlocking the door to her apartment.

"Here, let me go first," Jake said.

"How long will it take for the police to set up surveillance?" she asked, following him in and flicking on a light.

Jake looked at his watch. "Well, let's see. I called a half hour ago. Shouldn't take that long, I wouldn't think. Maybe an hour or two to set it up. I'll stick around until they're in place." He caught himself and looked at her. "That is . . . if you want me to."

"Oh, stop it. . . . Want some coffee?"

"Coffee would be great. Thanks."

Valerie walked to the kitchen, pulling out mugs and a filter, pouring water from the pot into the coffeemaker sitting on her counter. She pulled out two spoons and some sugar from a cabinet and turned to set them on the kitchen table. "Oh, my God," she said, the glass sugar container shattering as it dropped to the floor.

Jake had taken a seat on the sofa in the living room. "What?" he asked, jumping to his feet. "Valerie, what is it?"

Valerie stood in the middle of her kitchen, holding both hands to her mouth. "What is it, Valerie?" Jake asked, more desperate now as he joined her.

"My papers," she said, pointing. "Someone's been here, Jake."

Jake looked at the table. "How do you know?"

Valerie began to shake, tears welling up in her eyes. "They're not together, Jake. I was grading them, waiting for you to come last night. The last thing I did when you rang my buzzer . . . I picked them up and stacked them neatly in one pile. Someone's picked this one up," she said, holding out the paper Warren had scanned.

"Maybe you just missed it."

"No!" she screamed. "They were all together, Jake. I know it."

Jake wasn't sure how much credence to place in her observation. Paranoia can reek havoc on the mind. "I'm sure there's a simple explanation, Val. Maybe the wind blew it."

"What wind, Jake?" she asked in distress, waving her hand across the kitchen. "What wind? Do you see any open windows?"

Jake looked around, moving blinds and curtains to make sure. Valerie was right. They were all closed. He walked back toward her and took her hands. "All right, I'll have it printed. In the meantime, let's just walk around and see if anything else seems out of place, okay?"

She nodded her head, visibly shaken.

"Come on," Jake said, holding out his hand. "We'll look together."

They walked hand in hand around the kitchen and living room, both quiet as Valerie eyed every inch of her place. She pulled him slightly toward her bedroom, stopping at the door. "I'm frightened, Jake. Can you just take a look before I go in?"

"Of course. Wait here." Jake left her at the doorway, entering her room for the first time, looking under the bed, behind a chair, and in the closet. "Nothing."

Valerie entered reluctantly, her arms wrapped tightly around her chest. She stood still in the middle of her room, scanning her belongings. Jake stood by the bed. "Check your drawers."

She walked timidly to her bureau, opening her top drawer. In an immediate panic, her eyes seemed to bulge from their sockets. "Oh, Jake," she said, her voice faltering. "Oh, God."

"What?" He walked toward her, putting his arm around her waist as he looked into her drawer. "What is it?"

"Jake, I always fold my underwear a certain way. I know this sounds silly, but I always put my flowered panties on the bottom and my white ones on top. And look, they're not neat at all. I never put my underwear away like this. Never."

Jake looked at the pile of panties. They all looked pretty much the same to him. He wished his drawers looked that neat. "You sure?"

She stared at him with hunted eyes. "I'm positive, Jake. One hundred percent positive. This is *not* how I left this drawer!"

That's all he had to hear. "Okay, that's it. You're staying with me. No ifs, ands, or buts. Start getting your stuff together. We're outta here. Only touch what you need to wear and use. Nothing else, understand?"

Valerie did not respond.

"Understand?"

"Yes," she said, nodding.

"Where's your luggage?"

Valerie stood petrified, staring at the open drawer. "Oh, God, Jake, he's been here, hasn't he?"

Jake clapped his hands twice. "Come on, Val, I mean it now. Let's go. Get your stuff."

Sunday
September 15

BROADMAN AND CHAN had been taking turns eyeing Warren's apartment building, trying desperately not to sleep, when Chan's replacement arrived just past 5:00 P.M., Saturday. Dan Shackling slid into the back of the Jeep wearing a broad smile, shaking both friends' hands and slapping them collegially on the back. The three men joked and talked, trading barbs and snippets of each others' lives, killing half an hour recounting old war stories and snafus only ex-Service personnel could enjoy.

When Chan finally left for West View in Sam's car, it was 5:36 P.M. He was hoping to shower and grab some shut-eye and his scanner, telling his colleagues he would return for the graveyard shift sometime around 2:00 A.M. The two men sat in the Jeep, passing the hours in thirty-minute shifts. The shadows of the trees lining Warren's street grew longer as the afternoon sun gave way to dusk, eventually melting into the blackness of the asphalt as its warming rays dipped slowly out of sight.

Midnight came and went, the minutes ticking by like cold molasses dripping off a spoon. It was dull—very dull. Nothing had come in or out of that building but an old lady walking her dog and an obese young man who lived on the first floor. Broadman was grateful Chan had thought enough to bring a blanket and pillow and lay curled uncomfortably in the back seat, tossing and turning with nerve-racking frequency, pulling the blanket tightly around him in a fruitless, almost anxiety-provoking attempt at sleep.

Shackling sat still, smoking a cigarette, staring at Warren's apartment, feeling oddly uncomfortable himself as he listened to Sam's incessant squirming from behind. He blew smoke rings while keeping his eyes fixed on Warren's apartment.

"Christ, Sammy, what the hell are you doin' back there?" he finally asked in exasperation, glancing in the rearview mirror.

Broadman was none too happy. "Just wait till you try sleeping back here. I was more comfortable in boot camp."

"Why don't you try sittin' up?" Shackling suggested. "Prop yourself up against the door or something. You're drivin' me nuts."

Broadman didn't move, his face half-buried in the pillow Chan had brought. He wore a watch but didn't bother moving to look. "What time you got?" he asked, his smothered voice barely audible from in front.

"What?"

"What time you got?"

"Almost two."

"Thank God," Broadman said, relieved. "Chan should be here soon. Maybe I can go home and get some real sleep."

"Good. Go now."

Broadman sat up, rubbing his scalp with the tips of his fingers. "No way. I'm not leaving 'til he comes. Tell you what I do need to do, though. I have to pinch a loaf the size of a Chevy. Hand me that toilet paper up front there, will you?"

Shackling reached down to the floor on the passenger side, handing Broadman a roll. "Just do it away from the car, okay? Last thing we need is to be sloshing around in your shit."

"Yeah, yeah . . . there's a park a block down the street," Broadman said as he opened the door. "I'll be back in a flash."

Broadman crawled quietly from the car, closing his door silently behind him. Shackling watched in the rearview mirror as Broadman's silhouette grew smaller in the yellow glow from the incandescent streetlamps lining Warren's street. He alternately stared at Warren's place and Broadman's progress until he saw Broadman cross the street a block or so down the road, eventually falling out of sight.

Shackling reached into his shirt pocket and pulled out a flip-top box of Camel Lights, swearing aloud when he found it empty. "Shit." He was leaning over the front seat, rummaging through his small black travel bag, looking for a new pack, when his back stiffened at the sound of a knuckle wrapping softly on the passenger-side window.

Shackling was startled, but immediately relaxed, assuming at first it was Chan. He turned, stared at the stranger out his window, and lifted his chin ever so slightly, acknowledging his presence. It sure as hell wasn't Chan. "What's up?" he asked, reaching to the door, rolling down the window just enough to hear.

Warren smiled. He'd pegged the car up ahead as cops in a heartbeat. But he desperately needed to get into his apartment and decided the Jeep just didn't fit a law enforcement MO. Warren felt confident that whoever it was sitting in it, he was no cop. "Hi," he said. "I'm sorry to bother you, but you wouldn't happen to have a smoke I could bum, would you?"

Shackling was immediately on guard. The man fit the description of their target. "No."

"Oh, come on, man, just one. I can see a pack lyin' right there." Warren could also see Shackling's gun.

"It's empty."

"Just one?" Warren asked with puppy-dog eyes.

"I said *no*," Shackling insisted, more forcefully this time. "It starts with an *n* and ends with an *o*. Look it up."

Warren stared at him through the partially open window, their eyes dueling in the dim lights of the street. "Fuckin' asshole," he chided before turning away.

Shackling was pissed off. He mulled over what had just happened in his mind. I'm sitting here, minding my own business, he thought, and this jerk walks up to me out of the blue and wants to bum a smoke. I said no. Not once, but twice. And now he has the balls to call me a fucking asshole to my face? Shackling figured they'd see who the asshole really was. He opened his door just a crack, knowing it was a mistake the second he did it. He knew he shouldn't, but he'd been out of action too long—his mind had stopped thinking for that split second. When on surveillance, nothing supersedes your target—certainly not some dickhead calling you names through the window of your car.

He took a step from the Jeep, turning to look over the roof. "What was that?" Shackling asked just in time to watch Warren open the passenger-side door. He grabbed the roof of the Jeep with his left hand, and whipped himself back into the Jeep. "Hey, just who the hell do you . . . ?"

Warren had already grabbed Shackling's gun off the front seat and sat, aiming it directly at his face with both hands. "Don't even move," came the menacing reply as Shackling turned, staring down the glinting muzzle of his Glock 9mm semiautomatic.

"What do you want?" Shackling asked, stopping dead in his tracks.

"Not so fast," Warren added, motioning to the steering wheel with a slight flick of the gun. "First things first. Put your hands on the wheel. Slowly now. Very slowly. You don't want to make me jump."

Shackling stared at him, thinking if he could stall just long enough, Sammy would make it back. He didn't move, hoping that the cops up the street might see what was happening, but knew there were too many cars between them.

"What do you think, I'm stupid?" Warren asked. "You think I didn't see your friend there take off down the street? That I just happened to mosey along when you were all alone? Yeah, that's what happened. Now . . . I'm going to ask you one last time. Put your hands on the steering wheel or I will blow a hole the size of a grapefruit out the other side of your brain. Don't even *think* I will hesitate to blow you away. Trust me. You have exactly three seconds. One . . ."

There was something about this man's voice and eyes. Shackling had seen it before. It was almost visceral, intangible. Warren's thoughts and actions betrayed a certain detachment from reality. Shackling could feel it, almost taste it. He slowly laid both hands on the top arch of the steering wheel. "Happy?"

"Oh, very. You're a smart man."

"I'll ask *you* again. What do you want?"

Warren leaned now against the passenger-side door. "Two things. First, tell me who you're working for."

"Don't know. Next."

"Is that so?"

"Yes, that's so."

"What are those?" Warren asked with a point of the gun.

Shackling looked down at the handcuffs on the seat between them, then back up at Warren. "You tell me."

"Don't push me, asshole. Put them on. Through the steering wheel."

No way Shackling was going to do that. The very thought ran counter to everything he'd ever learned. "No," he said in a firm voice.

Warren spoke with deadly earnest. "Put them on now, or you're history. Do I make myself clear? I have nothing to lose, now . . . *don't* push me." He spoke the last three words very slowly as he thrust the gun closer to Shackling's face. He could see his captor was jumpy; nervous but not scared. "Now!" Warren boomed.

Shackling picked the cuffs up off the seat, sliding one over his wrist and closing it slowly shut. He hesitated to follow through, knowing that he was about two seconds away from being this man's prisoner. Once he ran that chain through the steering wheel and attached it to his other wrist, any chance he had of escape or retaliation would be gone. Whatever it was this intruder wanted, it would be his for the taking then. If Shackling could only stall long enough for Sammy to show. He glanced for a second in the rearview mirror, hoping to see his partner crossing the street or walking up the sidewalk.

"What are you looking for? Your better half? Don't hold your breath, pal. He won't be coming back," Warren lied. "Look, I don't have time for this bullshit. Now, put the fucking handcuffs on!"

Shackling stared down the black hole of the muzzle pointed directly in his face. He could not see a way out of this one. Did this psycho really have the balls to shoot him? Was it all an act? Did Shackling dare feel lucky enough to try to find out? Dammit! he thought. How could I have been so stupid? Warren's arms were extended straight out. Something told Shackling not to push his luck. Slowly, dejectedly, he slid the cuffs through the wheel and closed his eyes, attaching them to his other wrist.

"Bad move," Warren said, shaking his head with a smile. It was the moment he'd been hoping he would see. He tossed the gun to the floor and opened his door, reaching to the curb below and behind him. "Now, I got a little surprise for you. He pulled up a squeeze can of Ronsonol lighter fluid. "You've seen this before, right?"

Shackling didn't bother to answer. His heart began to race. He eyed Warren, then the Ronsonol with a half-cocked head, his eyes squinting as likely scenarios raced through his mind. None of them were good. Like Chan and Broadman, Shackling had no idea they were following a madman, certainly not the one responsible for the Morson Grayhead murders. If he had known, he would have put it together immediately. But as it stood, Shackling's mind still had difficulty envisioning his captor would burn him alive.

"Ever in Nam?" Warren asked.

Silence.

Warren turned his head, staring at his captive's eyes. "I asked you if you were ever in Nam?"

"Yes."

"When?"

"'Sixty-seven through '68."

"Ah, those were good years, huh? Ever see a napalm attack?"

Shackling eyed Warren's every move, watching him massage the can of lighter fluid as if it were a much sought after Christmas present. "No," he answered softly, knowing he was in serious trouble. Panic began to overtake him. "Just tell me what you want," Shackling said, his voice taking on a more pleading tone. "Anything. Anything at all, it's yours."

Warren smiled as he flipped up the plastic spigot. "I got what I want. And *you're* it."

Shackling could see it coming now. "*Please* don't do this," he begged. His wrists began to bleed as he yanked relentlessly on the chain between the steering wheel. He tried compassion. "Come on, man, I've got a wife and family. Please don't do this! I'm begging you. Don't do this to me." Warren stared at him for a few seconds, just long enough for Shackling to think maybe he had a chance. "Come on. Whad'ya say? Just let me go, and I'm outta here. I've never seen you before."

Warren laughed. "So let me get this straight. You want me to let you go, and you'll take off and never tell anyone you saw me? Is that right?"

Shackling's eyes begged for mercy. He shook his head vigorously. "I swear to God. You have my word."

Warren stepped out of the car and glanced up the street to see if the cops ahead of them were still seated in their car. They were on the same side of the road as Chan's Jeep, but a good six or seven cars away—enough for the activity behind them to go unnoticed. Warren knew that would soon change. He certainly hoped so.

"You want me to let you go?"

Shackling nodded. "Please?"

Warren mocked him, "Yeah, that'll happen." He leaned in through the open door with a smile. "You guys kill me, you know that? Where do they dredge you morons up, anyway? He sprayed the fluid on the seat next to Shackling, then along his thighs and groin.

Shackling cried now, aware that he was about to die the most horrible of deaths. "Oh, God!" he pleaded. "Please don't!"

"It's you or me, pal. Guess who loses?" Warren struck a match and tossed it on the seat before depressing the lock switch, closing the door quietly after him.

Lighter fluid's combustibility is nothing near that of gasoline's, and consequently it burns more slowly. Gasoline ignites at the rate of forty feet per second and would have fully engulfed the car in one second flat. But Warren's choice of accelerant seemed to feed the flames slowly, allowing Shackling to watch in horror as they voraciously licked the fabric of the seat, crawling toward him as if in a slow-motion film. In reality, it all happened with deadly speed.

"*Nooo!*" Shackling screamed at the top of his lungs. "You son of a bitch! *No!*"

Warren ducked beside the orange glow of the Jeep, glancing around him furtively, making sure he'd not been spotted. The cops obviously hadn't noticed anything up to now, but he knew that was about to change. Warren knew he should leave but couldn't deny himself one last look.

He stared through the window as Shackling struggled, desperately trying to escape the murderous flames. Warren watched with amusement, and some surprise, as Shackling threw his body up on the dash before sliding off, his face now on the opposite side of the steering wheel. For a moment he wondered if Shackling might actually succeed in ripping it off its base, but his fears were unwarranted.

Shackling kicked wildly at the windshield, as if somehow that might help his escape. His hair caught fire as he stared the ever-growing flames on the seat directly in the eyes. His legs and groin were in flames now, and Warren could see him violently shake his head, flailing the air in shrieks of pain with his last breaths of life.

Warren was counting on Shackling's histrionics to be the very thing that would distract the cops and thus clear a path for him to get to his apartment. Warren tapped the car door twice with an open palm. "Thanks, buddy," he said with a wink of an eye. "I owe you one." Warren scampered away on his hands and knees, staying on the curb, close to the line of cars, and thus out of sight. Time was of the essence now. If the cops weren't running in his direction at that very moment, he knew they would be in a second or two.

Shackling's screams of agony were clearly audible through the glass and steel of his enclosed oven as Warren scampered three cars down and sat on the asphalt of the street between the grill of a minivan and a Le Sabre, leaning against the latter's bumper and license plate. He lit a cigarette and inhaled deeply, waiting for all hell to break loose. It took longer than he thought. Or maybe it just seemed that way. In either event, as Warren sat with his cigarette in his mouth, he could clearly see shadows of the cars and trees thrown fuzzily against the now orange hue of the buildings on his street.

Warren sat with his hands behind his head, listening to the tortured wails from inside the Jeep just a few cars away. He tried to picture the scene inside and felt cheated that he couldn't watch. But there was more important work to be done. His freedom rested in the balance. He waited now for the more important elements of his plan to come together. He could hear Broadman hollering something as he ran up the sidewalk, his feet hitting the concrete with surprising strength and speed. Warren could also hear the cops as they ran down the street toward the blazing car, yelling something to each other. The ruse had worked. However fleetingly, he was now free to enter his home.

At first, Warren had thought of torching just any old car on the block, but wasn't sure that would be enough to lure *both* cops from their appointed task. One maybe, but probably not both. But he knew for sure they would respond to screams. What cop wouldn't? He had to have screams. It was the *only* thing Warren felt certain would give him the window of opportunity he needed. After all, his passport was in that apartment, and no one was going to deny him his much deserved day in the sun—not Jake Ferguson, and certainly not two bored, nowhere cops eating doughnuts in front of his house. And if some innocent sucker had to roast in the process—well, it was a price someone had to pay.

Warren eyed the street for the darkest spot and quickly crossed, careful not to stop or look. He wanted to get out of view before people began peering out windows or exiting their homes. In a matter of seconds he was bounding up the steps to his apartment, climbing two at a time. He heard a door open on the landing below and made a mental note as he listened to footsteps creak slowly down the stairs. It was probably old Mrs. Reardon. Warren's apartment was closest to the street and did not offer access to the rear fire escape. Mrs. Reardon's did. If he hurried, he could get what he needed and use her apartment for escape while it was still empty.

Warren opened his door and hurriedly scampered through his apartment, fortuitously illuminated from the orange glow of flames roaring in the Jeep below. He wasted no time on clothes, personal belongings, or toiletries, grabbing only his passport, an ATM card, and his airline tickets from the rolltop desk in the corner of his room. Warren would have plenty of money later. The only thing he needed now was his ticket out.

He left his bedroom and walked through the hall to his living room, standing still in its eerie silence, watching shadows dance on the walls from the conflagration below. He closed his eyes, trying to drown out the ruckus and hollering from the street. He needed to think. What else did he need that he could only get here? He tried to imagine what else would act to insure that his well-crafted plan not be disrupted. This was his one chance. He would never be back.

Satisfied that he had all he needed, he walked to the kitchen and grabbed a plastic container of red lamp oil from under the sink. Warren poured some oil under and on the drapes of his living room, poured a line across its floor, and finished the bottle off on the cushions of a 1920s English two-seater sofa in the middle of his dining room. He scurried frantically now, sure that time was running out.

He stood by the sofa, eyeing the belongings of his life for the last time. His plans had not included it ending this way, but in life, you do what you have to do. Warren flicked his lighter, pressing his mind one last time for anything he may have missed, doused the flame, and ran to the bathroom. He opened the medicine cabinet and pulled out two prescription bottles, one of Xanax, the other of Pepcid. Warren's life was hell without his Pepcid. He never seemed to be without heartburn. He shoved the dark brown, plastic bottles in his pockets and looked around. That was it. He was sure of it. He didn't even stop to think now. Warren grabbed a throw pillow off the sofa, picked it up, and lit the corner with his lighter.

His heart beat quickly as he watched the flames slowly crawl up its sides as he held it in his hand. He released it, letting it drop on the puddle of oil he'd let soak into the cushions. The oil caught fire easily and thoroughly. Warren watched the flames travel the thin pool of oil down the sofa, across the floor to the first puddle of oil under a floor-length curtain in his living room. The flames engulfed the curtain, traveling swiftly in an upward arch, climbing ever higher toward the ceiling, feeding off it, as if a living, breathing entity.

Warren smiled and walked slowly backward, watching his baby—his creation—devour all in its path. As he reached the door, he stared trancelike at the burning pillars surrounding his windows, reaching relentlessly upward, licking the darkening white of the ceiling. He turned and left, making sure to lock his door behind him. No sense making entry any easier than necessary. This was one building Warren wanted to burn to the ground.

He thought it fortuitous that Mrs. Reardon had left the building, feeling certain she would never have made it out alive otherwise. She always smiled and said hello, offered him coffee, cookies, and milk. As for the others, well, they were nothing but a bunch of self-absorbed, whining automatons. Warren didn't care if they never came out alive. But Mrs. Reardon was different. In his own way, he kind of liked her.

He bounded down the steps to Mrs. Reardon's floor in leaping strides, descending them three at a clip, slowing as he came to the landing, careful to check that no one was in the hall. Warren looked about, but it was empty. The various tenants were either not at home this evening or out gawking at the fire. Free entertainment of this magnitude doesn't come along often.

He strode quickly to her door, noticing that it had not been fully closed. Good old Mrs. Reardon, he thought. Warren could always count on her. He could picture her outside on the street, her hair up in curlers, the way it always seemed to be. Without seeing her, Warren knew she was wearing her beat-up, fluffy, pink slippers, and her ripped, age-worn, yellow robe. He could envision her standing there, her hands to her mouth as she watched the inferno roll in gaseous balls within Chan's Jeep.

"Oh, my," he could hear her say in her crisp Queens accent. She had always been good to him. Warren was happy she'd made it out.

A strange sense of excitement filled him as he poked his head inside. The knowledge that an as yet undiscovered inferno raged in an apartment above, that complete pandemonium and virtual destruction would soon ensue— something about the fact that only he knew this secret fanned Warren's inner need for power and control. Something about it fed his unyielding belief in the ultimate infallibility of his being, the preordained success of his plans.

"Hello? Mrs. Reardon?" he called out, hearing nothing. "Mrs. Reardon?" There was silence. She was gone.

He entered her apartment, locking her door behind him, and walked directly to the door in the rear of her kitchen. The very kitchen in which he had sat two dozen times before, eating cookies and sipping coffee, feigning interest in local gossip from his lonely, nosy neighbor. Warren unlocked the door and hit the steps running, sliding his hand on the rail as he bolted down, stopping for a moment once he hit the grass of the small, untended backyard below. Warren could smell the thick, acrid smoke in the air, not certain from which blaze it came. He could hear a distant wail of sirens piercing the still night air as fire apparatus sped to the scene. Warren giggled at the surprise he knew they were in for: responding to a car fire, only to find the apartment building across the street fully involved upon arrival. Talk about a wake-up call.

Warren knew that once they pulled up to the scene, they'd have no choice but to tackle the building first. The Jeep would just have to wait. He couldn't help but think what a strange job being a firefighter must be. One minute you're lost in sleep, and in seconds, you're up, dressed, and out, speeding to a scene where it is expected that you will risk life and limb in an effort to save strangers you will, in most cases, never meet again. Zero to sixty in a few moments, yanking helpless, unsuspecting civilians out from under the voracious, indiscriminate clutches of the beast. In an odd way, Warren respected them, though he wished tonight they'd sleep in. But he knew that was not to be. He knew they were like the sun—they always showed up.

Warren knew it would be only a matter of minutes, if not seconds, before people began surrounding the building, rushing at it from all angles, desperately trying to save its occupants from the hungry, growing flames. The time had come—further delay could prove harmful to his health. He took off behind the garage, in a jog at first, breaking into a full-fledged sprint as he heard the sirens growing louder in the night. There was little doubt that everyone had noticed it by now. Warren's apartment was alive with flames. His one regret, his Achilles' heel, was his trash. He thought for a moment of trying to sift through it, but thought better of it. The idea floated through his mind that he could set the garage on fire, but there simply wasn't time. Some things must be left to fate.

He grabbed on to the limb of an aging maple and pulled himself up to a rickety wooden fence, pausing just long enough to get his bearings and pick a place to land. Warren pounced into a flower bed, then ran across the grass of the backyard, aware of the bark of a dog in the yard next door. He crossed a street, ran down a driveway that emptied into the alleyway from which he had escaped the Bird's Nest just the night before.

Sweat dripped from Warren's forehead as he slowed to a walk, approaching his waiting Mazda. His breathing was labored and his heart thumped with frightening rapidity against his chest. He tried his best now to appear casual, as if this were just any other night in a normal guy's life.

Granted, it was late, but you never know who might step forward to bear witness against you, or from where they may come. Warren knew he was not the only one who suffered from insomnia. Before, he had been nothing but a dark blur running through backyards. But now, as he put the key in the door of his Mazda, if anyone was watching, there was a car to link him to. He needed to take measures not to give cause for doubt or wonder.

The engine of his Mazda turned over, louder than he would have liked, but quickly dropped to a purr as he let it idle for a moment, gathering his composure. Warren felt safe back here in the alley, but knew he had to leave. Momentarily, he would pull his car out into the real world and knew he would need every ounce of himself for the work that lay ahead. First, he needed to get to Westchester. The Palisades to the Tappan Zee Bridge was the quickest, most logical route.

SAM BROADMAN LEANED against a tree, smoking a cigarette, torn with guilt and grief. He'd left his friend for a few minutes only to have Shackling's screams hearken him back to a neighborhood version of World War III. Upon arriving at the scene, he had tried valiantly, but in vain, to open the door to Chan's Jeep. Not that it mattered, for it was immediately obvious that even a successful attempt would have proven useless. By the time Broadman arrived, his friend was fully engulfed in flame, writhing and screaming in unimaginable, mind-searing pain. Broadman could still hear the screams of his friend echoing in his ears and felt genuinely frightened they might never leave.

The flames swiftly devoured everything in the car, filling it quickly with thick, black smoke. There was nothing he could do. The horrible deed had been done. His friend was dead. Broadman ran to the house closest to the car and pressed the buzzer long and hard, letting up only as he saw a few people drift onto the sidewalk. He ran down the walk to one of them, screaming something about the fire department.

But the mind is an extremely potent force, capable of unleashing inexplicable strength and courage, or of dislodging any semblance of rational behavior and thought in times of crisis. Broadman learned about his the hard way. Without warning, he began to chuckle. It surprised him as much, if not more, than those around him. He wasn't sure why, and he knew it was frightfully wrong, but still, he could not help himself. Try as he might, he could not stop. In all his years in the Service, Broadman had never witnessed anything like this. All his training, all his experience, and now he sat on a stoop, nearly buckled over, tears streaming down his cheeks. The chuckle quickly metamorphosed into fits of unrestrained laughter, his body racked with uncontrollable spasms—undoubtedly his mind's defense mechanism against snapping altogether.

Broadman's psyche was practically ripped asunder, throwing him into intermittent fits of laughter and tears. He had urinated in his pants, though he didn't realize it at first. When he did, he didn't seem to care. Broadman was aware of what was happening around him, but in an odd way his mind had somehow removed him from the scene. All he could hear were Shackling's screams; all he could think about was his unbearable, unimaginable pain. And all Broadman could do was laugh.

Warren had yet to set his apartment ablaze, and the fully engulfed Jeep was the focus of everyone's attention. That was, until Broadman began to laugh. A bystander noticed one of the cops speaking into a portable radio and approached him, pointing in Broadman's direction, informing him of the man's strange behavior. And strange it was. Enough to warrant questioning.

The state policeman approached Broadman slowly, identifying himself and showing him his badge. They talked for a short while, the cop trying to read the sanity of the man in front of him. Broadman babbled incoherently, intermixing something about friends, the Service, taking a dump. Before long it became clear that Broadman was in shock, certainly not laughing at anything he thought to be funny. The police brought him back to the cruiser, sat him sideways in the front seat, and wrapped him in a blanket, handing him a cup of coffee from a thermos before calling an ambulance.

It was then that someone noticed the fire in Warren's apartment building, and people began scurrying to and fro in a scene of unrehearsed chaos. Broadman thought of Chan. He had to call Chan. He looked around, but no cops were in the car, nor were they anywhere near it. They had left him unattended, no doubt to assist occupants in need as they escaped, terrified and dazed, from the swelling blaze. Broadman knew Chan had taken his Saab and quickly punched his own car-phone number into the telephone on the dash. This was no time to swim in his own emotional slush. He had to regroup.

"Chan, it's Sam. We got big-time problems here."

"You don't sound good, Sam. Talk to me."

"Danny's dead, Chan." Broadman's voice betrayed his inner torment. "Burned alive in your Jeep like an animal."

Chan couldn't believe his ears. "Danny's *dead?* Are you sure?"

"Oh, I'm sure. Look, this place is a goddamned mess, Chan. There's fire everywhere. The target's building is going up in flames as we speak, and the fire department's not even here yet."

"Did you see who did it?"

"No."

Chan had to think fast. This thing was personal now. "All right, where are you?"

"In a State Police car. You know, our friends up the street?"

"What the hell are you doing in their cruiser?"

"Don't ask."

Chan wondered what that meant. Sammy didn't sound right. "What do you mean, don't ask? Listen, are you okay?"

Broadman answered in a tired, almost wistful voice, "I've been better."

Chan needed Sam to stay with him now emotionally. Don't go losing it on me now, he thought. "Look, Sam, don't go sour on me now. I need you, all right?"

Silence.

"All right?" Chan asked more firmly.

"I'm listening."

"Have they arrested you?"

"No."

"Can you leave?"

Broadman looked around. "Yeah, I think so. They're all busy with the apartment building."

"Well, Jesus Christ, Sammy! Get the fuck out of there. Now. Get out now. You have the keys to Danny's car?"

"No, he had them."

"All right, just walk away, Sammy. Can you get to Stephens Avenue?"

"Is that the one we face if we're sitting in your Jeep?"

"That's it."

"Shit, yeah. I'm looking at it."

"Good. Go there now. Don't get picked up, all right? Remember your training. Dig deep. When you get to Stephens, just keep moving toward the Palisades. I'll be there in a couple of minutes."

"Stephens toward the Palisades. Roger." Broadman hung up the phone, left the blanket on the front seat of the cruiser, and walked quickly down Warren's street. He turned the corner, took one last glance at the mayhem he was leaving behind, and broke into a full sprint, fleeing as fast as his legs would take him.

It was 2:02 A.M. Chan had been only a few minutes from Warren's street when he got the call from Broadman. The last thing he wanted was to be made by the cops and had planned on coming in from the other side. He needed to get to Stephens now, but knew Warren's street was out of the question. Intuitively Chan hung a right before coming upon his road, praying it was a through street to Stephens.

He drove over a small crest and noticed the lights of a larger street as he came over the top. Chan stopped at an intersection and noticed a small sign on a phone pole that read Stephens Avenue. All right, he thought, at least something is working my way. He looked in both directions, trying to compute distance in his mind, figuring Broadman had had enough time to make it this far. Guessing, he decided to turn right. Chan drove slowly, looking on both sides of Stephens, but he could see nothing. Nothing but fire engines roaring toward him in his rearview mirror.

But apparently Sammy was thinking. He had seen Chan's headlights and had taken refuge in someone's hedge. He came out, waving his hands only after he recognized his own car slowly approaching. Chan was startled at first, smiling as he saw his friend. He pulled over to the side of the road, letting Broadman climb in.

"God, am I glad to see you," Broadman said, leaning his head back on the passenger seat. "Just get the hell out of here."

"Way ahead of you."

Chan looked at his passenger. He was a mess, both physically and emotionally. Whatever Broadman had been through had not been pleasant. "Christ, Sammy, what the hell happened back there?"

Broadman sat quietly, rubbing his temples with the fingers of both hands. He could still hear Shackling's screams. "It was horrible, Chan. I'm sorry. I think I snapped."

"What do you mean, you're sorry?"

"I don't know what got into me, Chan. I started to laugh and I couldn't stop."

Chan looked at him. "What do you mean?"

"I mean, I started to laugh."

"Nice."

Broadman was in no mood for bullshit. "Hey, fuck you, okay? It wasn't like that, and you know it."

"Is that what drew the cops to you?"

"Yeah, I think."

Chan felt a momentary flash of anger. What the hell kind of professional does that? he thought. Maybe he didn't know Broadman as well as he thought. But it was moot now. Chan just hoped he could count on him if the going got rough again. "What the hell were you thinking?"

"I don't know, man. I just couldn't take it. It was too much for me to watch Danny burning like that, and I couldn't do a *damn* thing to save him. My mind just went."

Chan didn't like to hear it, but he understood nonetheless. "I'm sure it was brutal, Sammy. Who knows how I would have reacted." Chan didn't tell his friend, but he felt certain it would have been different. "You're sure it was Dan?"

"Yeah, I'm sure."

"What happened?"

"I went to the park down the road to take a shit. I was only gone a few minutes. I swear. Next thing I know, I hear screamin' coming from the direction of your Jeep. I didn't think much of it at first. But they weren't the kind of screams you hear every day. They weren't like some domestic squabble. Something was big-time wrong, and I knew it."

Chan listened intently, keeping his eyes on the road, making sure to drive the speed limit. He hoped one of Sam's rear lights wasn't out. "Go on."

"I didn't even finish wiping. I mean, I know somethin' really bad's going down. So, I pull my pants up and run out of the park. I could see a ball of orange in one of the cars on the street, but wasn't sure whose it was. It was close to the Jeep. I knew that much. I started to run, and as I got closer, I could see it was the Jeep. Christ, Chan, I've never run so fast in my life. I must've gotten there in six seconds."

"Had it exploded?"

"No. Just the inside was on fire. I tried to open the door, but it was locked. Danny was . . ." It was clearly difficult for Broadman to continue. His voice broke as he tried to talk. "He was screaming, Chan. Screaming like I've *never* heard before." Broadman turned quiet, staring blankly out the passenger-side window.

"It's okay, man. It's okay. Just breathe deep." Chan looked at him. Broadman was crying now. "Was Dan on fire?" he asked gently.

Broadman could only nod his head.

Chan slammed the steering wheel. The money didn't matter now. "Shit! That cocksucking son of a bitch. You and I, Sam. We're going to catch this bastard, and when we do, I'm going to *personally* shove his dick down his throat."

Broadman looked at Chan, his face lit occasionally by the light of an intermittent streetlamp. "Chan, what the hell is going on here? Who is this guy, and why are we following him? This ain't no tit detail anymore, my friend. This baby's as real as they come."

Chan began to explain. "Lianne Rybeck asked me to follow him."

"That much I know," Broadman interrupted curtly. "You already told me that. I want to know why, Chan."

Chan relayed the story of Warren and Josephine as best he could remember from his early-morning conversation with Lianne. The only thing he left out was the hundred thousand dollars.

Broadman was quiet, ruminating on what he'd just heard. "So, do you think she wants to kill him?" he finally asked.

"I haven't given it a lot of thought."

Broadman stared at him with disbelieving eyes. "Bullshit."

"All right, all right, so the thought crossed my mind. Hey, do you blame her? I'd want to kill him, too. Anyway, it's none of my business."

"Yeah, well, maybe it wasn't . . . but it is now, isn't it?"

Chan looked at his passenger. "It is at that, Sam. It is at that."

Something didn't sit right with Broadman. Something was definitely wrong with this picture. "Okay, but why now? Why thirty years after the fact? There's something she's not telling you, Chan. She's not showing you all her cards."

"I can't answer those questions," Chan said, shaking his head. "But I'm going to find out."

"You know, the cops are going to trace your plates back to you, Chan. Like it or not, you're up to your eyeballs in this thing."

"I know. How long before you think they come looking for me?"

"Hard to say. I can tell you this much, you won't be driving that Jeep again. There's a good chance they'll think you're Dan, at least until they can make him. That probably gives you a day or so."

"He was that bad?"

"Christ, Chan, you don't even have a clue. The only way they'll make him is with his teeth."

"That works okay with me. I need the time."

They drove in silence for a while, hooking up to the Palisades North. Chan wanted to avoid being stopped, so studiously kept Sam's Saab at sixty-five miles per hour. Chan and Broadman both smoked cigarettes, each flicking ashes out partially open windows. They hadn't been on the Palisades more than a few minutes when a green Mazda came whizzing by.

"Hey, Sam, you see that?"

Broadman was busy looking out his window, lost in his own private hell. "See what?"

"The green Mazda that just passed us."

Broadman looked out the windshield, noticing the car. "Yeah, what about it?"

"Doesn't our man drive a green Mazda?"

Broadman hesitated before answering, thinking that they just couldn't be this lucky. But then again, all of this had only happened a short while ago. And, if for some reason Warren had chosen to escape to Westchester County, this was the quickest way to go. It wasn't as if there were a half dozen alternatives.

"Yeah, he does. But there's got to be thousands of them, Chan."

"Maybe. But at two-thirty in the morning, driving away from Englewood Cliffs, just like us? How many of them do you think are doing that?"

"Remember the plate?"

"RR something," Chan said.

"It's an RR plate!" Broadman yelled with squinted eyes, craning his neck for a better look. They glanced at each other, their eyes lighting up simultaneously at the sudden realization that they had serendipitously come across their man. "Shit, Chan, whatever you do, don't lose that car."

"Oh, Sam, please make it him," Chan pleaded. "If there's a God, please make it him."

WHAT HAD STARTED as a call for a routine car fire turned into one hell of a night for the Englewood Cliffs Fire Department. Granted, dispatch had relayed the report of a man trapped, but if that was indeed the case, they knew that he was long since dead. Upon turning the corner to Warren's street, the three men on the responding E-One pumper could clearly see the dancing glow of the fireball engulfing the interior of Chan's Jeep. It radiated an incandescent orange hue against all that surrounded it, like a hundred thousand candles burning within the same small radius.

The fire that raged inside Warren's apartment was not immediately recognizable as they made the turn, nor did it become apparent as they drove closer to the Jeep. Its luminescence seemed lost in the radiance of the flames most obvious to the expecting eye. The call said a car fire, and as the engine raced down the street, that is exactly what they saw.

As the engine approached, each man eyed what lay ahead, already sizing up the level of danger and required tasks in his mind. No big deal. They'd have it out in five minutes, just like a hundred times before. Rarely does a car's gas tank explode. That phenomenon is mostly Hollywood myth—the type of thing that makes for profitable cinematography. Still, for other reasons, car fires can be tricky. True, dispatch had said this one apparently contained a body, but that would ultimately be the ME's problem. It wasn't until the driver stopped his truck that he noticed people screaming, incongruously pointing up, *away* from the Jeep.

"Holy shit!" he said, hardly believing his eyes. "Lieutenant!" he yelled into his shoulder mike, kneeling at the hydrant. "Across the street, Lieutenant! She's roaring!"

The lieutenant had also been collared by the crowd. He was already directing his attention to the building when he heard the driver's message on his transmitter. This was going to be a long night. One thing was for sure, the Jeep would have to wait. Whoever had fried in there tonight wasn't going anywhere. But across the street, living people were at risk. The lieutenant contacted dispatch, requesting a second-alarm, mutual-aid call from Fort Lee. Warren's street was beginning to resemble Beirut. They were going to need serious help on this one. But precious minutes were lost before the truckies would arrive, and by the time the roof was finally vented, the situation inside Warren's apartment had deteriorated to a deadly degree.

Firefighters don't get paid much. But then again, they're a special breed—the money is irrelevant. And what little they do get paid, on this night they earned every penny . . . and then some. It took almost thirty-five minutes for the blaze to be brought under control, and another two hours or so to overhaul the areas damaged by the flames. Miraculously, no one in the building died, though a couple of firefighters did have to carry an elderly, deaf man suffering from smoke inhalation to safety, from a rear apartment on the bottom floor.

ENGLEWOOD CLIFFS IS far removed from Jake's jurisdiction, and unlike the Morson Grayhead burnings, this one was not immediately attributable to that case. Though neither of the New York state troopers watching Warren's apartment knew just exactly what had transpired on this night, they also didn't need a degree in nuclear physics to know that something was amiss. It was just too coincidental that their target's nest happened to burn while they were sitting there watching it. But Warren's street had gone from a paragon of tranquillity to a hair-raising inferno in a matter of minutes, and there was hardly a shortage of activities to keep them both busy. It wasn't until shortly after 3:00 A.M. that one of them finally contacted a superior. He, in turn, called Jake.

Early-morning calls are always brutal. No law enforcement professional looks forward to them. But this one, being the first in over four years with a woman at his side, was especially difficult for Jake. For the first time in years he felt needed and safe, sleeping soundly with his back to Valerie's, lost in that deep, blissful sleep only a woman's presence and smell can bring.

He and Valerie had enjoyed a surprisingly relaxed evening together. Nothing special really. Casual, laid-back—carryout Chinese, a bottle of chardonnay, and some much needed talk. The lengthy nap they had taken in the afternoon had rejuvenated them both, although more so Jake. They lounged on his sofa for hours, Valerie laying her head in his lap. She pushed him to talk about his feelings, his pain, his dreams. At first he was reticent, feeling awkward as the focus of conversation. But a few glasses of wine works wonders on the mind . . . and tongue. In time, they were discussing Jake, Danny, her death, his four-year hiatus from life, his decision to rejoin it, and Ederling's role in the process.

It wasn't until sometime after midnight that they had actually gone to bed. Jake knew it was put-up-or-shut-up time and had something he needed to prove, to himself as well as to Valerie. They were undressing in Jake's bedroom, preparing for bed, Jake pulling on a pair of worn, cotton pajama bottoms, Valerie a pink, flannel nightgown she'd grabbed from her apartment. Valerie crawled in first, pulling the sheets and blankets tightly to her neck.

Her head sunk into the pillow. It was obviously not the same one she'd been sleeping on the past twenty-four hours. Jake stood at the foot of the bed, watching her smile. She reached back with her arms, squeezing both sides of it with her hands. "This is Danny's, isn't it?"

Jake smiled and nodded.

Valerie's heart melted. "Oh, Jake . . . you didn't have to do that," she said, sitting up.

"Yes, I did. Your hair looks nice on it."

She pulled it out from behind her, holding it tightly to her chest with both arms. "Jake," she started, tears welling in her eyes. "You're so sweet. Thank you. I don't know what to say."

"Say you'll stay here with me."

"Come here," she said, holding her arms out open in front of her. "I want you to hold me."

JAKE WAS RELIVING the events of a few hours ago in his mind as he drove up Stephens Avenue, envisioning Valerie's smile, her sense of acceptance and belonging as he held her body close to his. The smell of smoke hung acrid in the air as he pulled his cruiser onto Warren's street, stopping twenty feet behind an idling pumper, careful not to drive over the two-inch fire hose still lying across the wet pavement. This time, unlike at a thousand other similar scenes to which he had been called, Jake did not bother to look around. Nor did he take his usual stroll. He knew who had started this calamity and seriously doubted that he was anywhere close to the vicinity.

If the scene of Warren's two fires were his jurisdiction, Jake would have put on his turnout coat with the words FIRE MARSHAL printed in yellow on the back. But it wasn't, and therefore, out of respect for his Bergen County colleague, he opted only to slip on his bunker pants and rubber boots. He knew he would be doing some crawling around in water and ash and wanted a modicum of protection. He palmed his helmet for a moment, replacing it upon second thought.

Jake was very aware that he had entered another marshal's scene and studiously avoided wearing anything that read FIRE MARSHAL.

Yes, this was Jake's case, but two arson fires and a murder had occurred here. Jake knew his counterpart would be taking it as seriously as would he if they had occurred in Westchester. He tried to put himself in his colleague's shoes, envisioning how he would feel if someone he barely knew came upon a scene in his jurisdiction decked out to the hilt in a fire marshal's turnout gear. This was hardly the time for territorial infighting. And anyway, technically, Jake was just an observer, though he knew a good deal of cooperation would soon ensue between them. He slammed his trunk closed and walked toward Warren's apartment building, careful not to trip over any of the half dozen fire hoses strewn across the street.

Approaching him, smoking a cigarette, was a similarly clad man, William Kelton, Jake's counterpart for Bergen County, New Jersey. They'd met a few times over the years, primarily at tristate association functions and conferences, though they had worked together on a case six years previous. "Hey, Jake. How ya holding up?" Kelton asked, his hand extended for a shake.

Jake took it, squeezing firmly. "Never better, Bill. Never better."

"No shit?" his counterpart asked sarcastically. "Well, that's about to change."

"Listen, Bill, I want to thank you for holding the scene for me."

Kelton flicked his butt into a puddle of water on the street. "No problem. I've taken a look around, particularly the room of origin. But when the cops told me whose apartment it was, and why they'd been watching it, I figured you'd want to see it intact."

"Sure do."

"This Morson Grayhead thing is the case from hell, huh?"

Jake looked at him. "Somehow, I envision hell as better than this."

Kelton laughed. "All I can say is better you than me."

"Thanks. So what do we have?"

"We got a roast in the Jeep over there," Kelton said, pointing down the street toward the burned-out heap that had been Chan's Jeep.

Here we go. It just never ends. "Any idea who?"

Kelton pulled out another smoke, lighting it with a match in a cupped hand. "You kidding me?" he asked, shaking the match before flicking it to the wet asphalt. "I've only seen one other that bad. Wait until you see it. Anyway, I haven't been able to get close enough. The locks were seared shut. The extrication crew's working it now. Should have it open shortly."

I can't wait. "Did we lose anyone in the building?"

"No. Thank God. Apparently, the boys here were in top form."

"What else is new?"

In a very real sense, people who fight the beast were Jake's only genuine heroes. Everyone fears fire, but few truly understand its destructive powers, its ability to literally transform everything about one's life into a living hell. It is a rare person indeed who is willing to take it on eye to eye. The risks are huge. One blunder can change the quality, or length, of a firefighter's life forever. Jake was always in awe that they did it daily, without hesitation.

"You might be interested to hear this, though," Kelton said, smoke from his cigarette wafting out of his mouth into the night air.

Jake looked at his colleague. "Mind if I bum one of those?"

"I didn't know you smoked," Kelton said, shaking out a cigarette from his pack.

"I don't." Jake took it, feeling the accompanying uneasiness at having to also bum a light. "Thanks," he said, taking a long drag. *I can't believe I'm smoking. I need a break.* "Okay, shoot."

"The Jeep is registered to a Chandler Boutet. Name ring a bell at all?"

Jake looked at him. "No. Should it?"

"Want to guess where he lives?"

Jake looked skyward for a moment. He was in no mood for games and Kelton sensed it.

"Try Severin Rybeck's West View Estate."

Jake looked up at him through the smoke of his cigarette, his eyes squinting in disbelief. "Rybeck?"

"Yeah. Seems he was Rybeck's limousine driver."

Severin Rybeck's limousine driver? This case is getting weirder by the minute. "What the hell is Severin Rybeck's chauffeur doing sitting outside Warren's home?" Jake mused.

"Hey, it's your case. You tell me."

Jake took a last drag on his cigarette, looked at it, and flicked it to the ground. *This is the last habit I need to pick up.* He heard a generator kick in, followed by the unmistakable popping and pinging of steel as the Jaws of Life began extracting metal from Chan's Jeep. "Show me the Jeep."

The two men walked across the street and down a few cars, passing firefighters gathering their hoses along the way. The windows of the Jeep had shattered, uniformly bursting out and to the ground from the intensity of the heat. Flames were roaring from the Jeep when the pumper had arrived, curling up and toward each other, meeting in a massive ball of flame above the middle of the roof. Since Warren's apartment building had obviously taken first priority, the blaze within the Jeep had only been extinguished relatively recently. It was still smoldering as the two men approached.

Three firefighters stood by the driver's-side door. One was kneeling on the pavement, wrestling with the Jaws in gloved hands, wearing protective goggles and ear guards below the rim of his helmet, while the other two made intermittent attempts at prying the door open. The machine is almost always carried on a ladder or rescue truck and is connected by compression hoses to a separate, gas-powered generator. When operating, its hydraulics perform their powerful task in relative quiet. By far, the generator emits the most noise, a cacophonous roar that simultaneously conveys both power and trouble. Jake poked inside a pocket of his bunker pants for a small container that held the wax ear guards he always carried.

Jake reached up toward the windshield lying on the hood, swiping it with a finger. There are many types of glass, from aluminosilicate and borosilicate to single-phase and soda lime. How it reacts in a blaze, and the level of soot adhering to its interior, can be powerful clues to a well-trained arson investigator. As temperatures increase, the molecular activity of glass increases proportionately. The hotter the fire, the greater this activity will be, thereby inhibiting the amount of soot allowed to accumulate on the glass.

A "slow burner," such as the kind caused by a smoldering cigarette on the seat of a car, doesn't heat the glass as quickly and therefore leaves a sooty film, removable to the touch. An intense heat, such as the kind you find in accelerated fires, heats the glass much more quickly, thereby disallowing the attachment of smoke to its surface. Jake checked his finger. Not surprisingly, it was nearly clean.

Kelton watched Jake perform his task. It was always a pleasure to watch another professional at work. "Definitely arson," Kelton said, nearly inaudible over the din of the generator.

Jake raised his head slightly, in an I-didn't-catch-that motion, pulling out one of his formed, protective wax balls. "Say again," he hollered over the noise.

Kelton stepped forward, closer to Jake's ear. "I said, it's definitely arson."

Jake looked inside, noting that the unfortunate victim's arms were still handcuffed to the melted steering-wheel column. "One would think, huh?" he said, walking to the passenger side of the Jeep. He could see the charred body lying grotesquely across the burnt, glistening rise of the transmission in the middle of the floor. Jake poked his head in the window for a better look, snapping it back as the stench of burnt flesh hit his nostrils. "Jesus Christ," he said, whipping his head out of the open window. "*God*, I hate that!" he croaked in disgust, fighting back nausea.

Kelton had joined him. "I told you."

Jake didn't bother to explain, but he was willing to bet it bothered him more than it did his friend. "You see the cuffs?"

Kelton stared at the unidentifiable body, its face frozen in a perpetual, incinerated scream. He nodded his head. "Yep. Whoever it is never had a chance."

Jake took a few steps away from the Jeep, consciously attempting long, deep breaths. *Who is this person?* Whoever it was, he or she was burned beyond any hope of recognition. Jake couldn't even tell if it was a man or a woman. Could it be Scotty? Stranger yet, could it possibly be Warren? If it was this Boutet fellow, just what the hell was *he* doing here, and what did he know or see that would have led to such a painful and horrifying end?

The nature of this burning concerned Jake, differing from the others in so many important aspects. He knew that either a second torch was on the loose or that the one they were after had just changed his MO, using fire now more as a weapon for self-preservation than simply a means of getting his rocks off. If there was a second torch, then it could be Warren, Scotty, or even Lianne inside that Jeep. What Jake needed to know now was whether one of his suspects had just become a roast.

In any event, it was definitely Boutet's Jeep. In and of itself, that raised an eyebrow. Jake wasn't sure just what role Lianne played in all this, but intuitively felt it was far deeper than she had let on. His patience was running thin for her clandestine, private games. People were dying. Seven at last count. Jake knew he would be visiting West View once more. It was time to turn up the heat on the confident and secretive Mrs. Lianne Rybeck.

A large, black Chevrolet Caprice Classic sat idling a few cars away. Jake could see a man sitting inside, illuminated by the inside lights, apparently writing something in a notebook. Kelton followed Jake to the curb. Jake stood next to his colleague, pointing in the car's direction. "That the ME?" he asked loudly.

"Yeah. He's waiting for these guys to finish so he can get inside."

"Mind if we have a little chat with him?" Jake asked. "I need this autopsy yesterday."

Kelton laughed. "This should be rich."

"Why?"

"You'll see."

Jake didn't like surprises. "Can you help me out?"

"Count on it."

The ME happened to look up, obviously lost in thought, and watched as the two fire marshals approached his car. If he didn't know better, he would have mistaken them for a couple of firefighters. But he recognized Kelton, and anyway, firefighters don't usually seek out the medical examiner. That unpleasant duty is usually left to fire marshals or the cops. He closed his notebook, clicked his pen shut, and shoved it in his shirt pocket, clearing his front passenger seat of papers and an empty McDonald's coffee cup as he waited for his visitors to arrive.

Jake walked to the passenger-side door, rapping twice on the window with a knuckle. He opened the door as the ME motioned him inside. "Mind if we join you, Doc?"

"Please, come in."

True to form, Jake started toward the rear door. This was Kelton's jurisdiction. He stopped only when Kelton told him to take the front. After all, this was Jake's case. Jake placed a dirty rubber boot on the floor of the car and slid in, Kelton doing likewise in the rear.

"Charlie," Kelton said by way of a hello as he closed his door.

"Bill."

"Charlie, meet Jake Ferguson," Kelton said from the back. "Westchester County's chief fire marshal. Jake, meet Dr. Charles T. Morehouse *the third*," Kelton said, placing mocking emphasis on the last two words.

Jake extended a hand. "Pleasure to meet you, Doc."

"So you're the unlucky bastard who got stuck with the Morson Grayhead case, huh?"

Interesting approach. "That's me."

"What a mess that thing is."

"Tell me about it."

"Getting close?"

"Yes. Very. Tell you what I need, though, Doc."

"Let me guess," Morehouse interrupted with a smile, glancing at Kelton in the rearview mirror. "You want to know who the roast is, right?"

"Well, that's half of it. The other half is I needed to know about fifteen minutes ago."

Kelton lit a cigarette. "Any chance you can move this autopsy to the top of the list, Doc?"

"Not unless you throw that cigarette out," Morehouse said disdainfully. "You know I hate those things."

"All right, all right. Sorry." Kelton opened the door and flicked it a good ten feet away. "There. So, what do you say, Charlie? This one's big and getting bigger. Jake here could use your help."

Morehouse turned, looking at Kelton directly for the first time. "They're all big, Bill, you know that. Just ask any homicide investigator whose case it is."

"True enough, Charlie. But even you can't argue the fact that they don't come much bigger than this."

Jake was loath to interrupt. He didn't know Dr. Morehouse and would probably do more harm than good. Anyway, as it was, Kelton was doing as good a job advocating for him as he could possibly have done for himself.

Morehouse stared at Jake for a moment. Jake returned the glare. "What do you hope to find, Mr. Ferguson?" he finally asked. "I got six bodies lying in the freezer back at the morgue. Each one a supposed priority. Don't misunderstand me, I guess I just need to know why *this* one is so important to your case."

Jake opened his mouth as if to speak, stopping to motion to Morehouse's window. Morehouse turned, rolling down the window at the sight of a fire captain standing by his door. "What's up?"

"Door's open, Doc. Thought you'd like to know."

"Thank you, Captain. I'll be right there. Please inform your men *not* to touch the body."

"Will do, sir."

Morehouse scrunched his face with his thumb and fingers, rubbing the corners of his eyes. "I got a headache already. Bill, hand me that bag in the back there, will you?"

Kelton laid the bag on the front seat between the two men. Morehouse rifled through, opening a container of Advil, popping two in his mouth, dry. "Well, Mr. Ferguson, you heard the man. I'm on. Tell me what makes this one so special. You have about ten seconds."

"This stays here, right?"

"Of course."

"My department has narrowed it down to two suspects, Doc. And both of them keep bringing us back to the Rybecks. You tell me who the roast is, or more importantly who it's not, and I guarantee you we'll close this case within forty-eight hours."

Morehouse looked at Jake. "You're that close?"

"Yes. We're that close." Jake was a good enough salesman to know that further discussion would be tantamount to losing his chance. He closed his mouth and waited.

Silence hung uncomfortably in the air of the car, all three men sitting quietly, aware of what was at stake. Whoever spoke next would be the loser. Morehouse finally turned to Kelton and said, "He's good, this one is." Kelton shrugged his shoulders, not uttering a word. Morehouse stared out the windshield, studying the chaos of the scene in front of him, his face alternately illuminated by the red beacons flashing from atop the engines lining the street. Morehouse took a long, deep breath, exhaling as if it were his last. "All right, Mr. Ferguson. When do you need it by?"

Jake had succeeded. He owed Kelton for this one and would no doubt have him send a nice bottle of Chivas along to Morehouse as well. With a body this crisp, an autopsy could only tell him so much, such as whether the victim burned alive. Beyond that, there would be little Jake could learn, except one important thing—the decedent's identity. He knew that would prove more difficult.

Maybe they'd luck out and would find dog tags or an inscribed bracelet, assuming of course they survived the intense heat. But it was more likely Morehouse would need the services of a forensic odonatologist. When a body is this far gone, the teeth are usually your last hope. He would need to contact Lianne to find out the name of Scotty's dentist. Even in cases where records are to be used exclusively for identification, dentists are usually reluctant to provide medical records without written authorization from family or a court order.

Jake's mind tore through his options and the various steps he needed to take to secure the necessary records. The upside was that he was really only interested in two men. The downside was that he wasn't sure how quickly he could make all the pieces come together. Jake had done this many times before and figured he could have the court order, and Scotty's records, by noon. He would contact Executive Travel to see whom Warren had listed as next of kin on his employment application and from there could probably hunt someone down who could give him the name of his dentist. Chandler Boutet would be more difficult. The one person of whom Jake was aware who might have that information had blown his head off, and Jake seriously doubted Lianne would be privy to it, much less care. At least Mr. Boutet's identification was not as important—or so he hoped.

Jake and Kelton stood by the ME's car, watching him walk toward the Jeep, holding his bag at his side. "Interesting guy," Jake said.

Kelton's head was tilted down, as he lit yet another smoke. "I warned you," he said, looking up from the top of his eyes.

"Christ, you'd think *I* was the enemy."

Kelton smiled. "Hey, you got what you needed. Nothing else matters, right? The guy *is* busy . . . and he's very good."

Jake was quiet for a bit. "Show me the apartment."

The two men walked slowly toward the building, Kelton inquiring about specifics of the case. As intimately involved as Jake felt with the mayhem surrounding him, still, the entire scene was Kelton's. Like Jake, he now had a murder in his jurisdiction, and although it was clearly linked, however tangentially, to the Morson Grayhead case, he had every right to know what the hell was going on.

They stopped in the middle of the street, not wanting to discuss its more sensitive aspects within the walled confines of the apartment building. Jake bummed another cigarette, and the two men stood, casually smoking amidst the turmoil around them, as Jake outlined what he and Ederling had discovered so far.

"I still don't understand," Kelton said. "If it's this Warren guy, where's the motive? Scotty, I guess I can understand, as far as one can understand something like this. But Warren? Something doesn't fit."

"Welcome to my world," Jake said. "Tomorrow's a big day. We'll know more then."

"What makes you say that?"

Jake explained the various pieces of information he was expecting sometime on Monday: the file reel search his Bell Atlantic contact was sending, the records he'd subpoenaed from the Philadelphia Exchange, Warren's trash, his expected confrontation with Lianne, and the report on the prints from the beer bottle. Ironically, Jake still didn't know if the man with whom he'd played pool just two nights ago was indeed the real Warren Parks. A lot of pieces to this puzzle were missing, and he hoped like hell that tomorrow would be the beginning of the end.

"Man, *you* are going to be busy," Kelton said through his cigarette. "Let me know if I can be of any help."

"Tell you what. Where's the trash in this building?"

Kelton could read Jake's mind. "Don't take it, Jake. You still don't have enough. Shit, a good defense lawyer could even make the case that you set the fire so you could get your hands on it."

Sometimes the system drove Jake crazy. All the rules, rights, and laws— sometimes it seemed law enforcement had all the cards stacked against them. Jake knew his colleague was right, but needed to hear him explain his reasoning. He played devil's advocate just for the hell of it.

"Placate me on this, Bill. The building was torched, right?"

Kelton nodded his head.

"So, that makes the area a crime scene, right?"

"Yes and no," Kelton said, bowing his shoulders up and down. "The trash is kept in the garage and it's a separate building from the apartment. If you didn't have enough to take it a few hours ago, I don't see how a fire in some guy's apartment gives you enough now. Even if the apartment happens to be Parks's. Not unless you can prove that he set it, and that isn't going to happen. I'm telling you, Jake, you search that garbage now, a judge is going to throw anything you might find in it right out of court. Just wait until tomorrow morning. Not every apartment in there is ruined. Someone will be taking out the trash. Shit, I'll even get it for you."

"Seriously?" Jake asked, truly surprised. He hadn't even thought of asking Kelton to do it. "That would be great, Bill. I've already requested State Police help with that, but if you're willing, you're on."

"I'm serious."

"Thanks, Bill. As you can see, time is not my friend right now."

"Consider it done. I'll snatch it right off the truck. Every last bag. I can even bring it up, if you want. We can go through it together."

"That is music to my ears. I can't tell you how much I wasn't looking forward to that trip. I owe you."

"Not really. If it's Parks, I want him, too."

The two men climbed the stairs to Warren's apartment building, Kelton acknowledging a couple of firefighters on the climb. They were mostly finished, though one was still ripping down plaster from a wall in the hallway.

"Nice job, guys," Kelton said.

"Thanks, Chief."

When they reached the top floor, Jake was thankful he was not as winded as his counterpart. He knew he needed to nip this cigarette thing right now. "Room of origin appears to be in here," Kelton said, walking into Warren's living room. When overhauling a dwelling fire, firefighters will usually empty the affected rooms of couches and chairs, or anything else that smolders and can rekindle. Thankfully, Kelton had arrived early enough to keep the room intact. He walked over to the remains of Warren's couch and pointed down the floor toward the windows. "Trailer goes from here to that window there. Then across the floor to the window nearest the kitchen."

Anything arranged in such a way as to facilitate fire traveling from one location to another is known as a trailer. It can be gasoline-soaked towels tied together, accelerant-soaked newspaper, or accelerant splashed across the floor. Liquid accelerant is most often accompanied by distinct burn patterns, known as puddling. Puddle look-alikes are often created by drapes or clothing burning on the floor and, to the untrained eye, can be mistaken for an accelerant's use. But in most cases, a fire investigator can quickly tell the difference.

Kelton knelt at a puddle under a window, directly below where a drape had hung only a few hours ago. "You can see right here," he said, pointing at the floor with a ballpoint pen, "where the accelerant seeped through the floorboards, burning up from between."

In many cases, hundreds of gallons of water are used to extinguish a blaze. In other cases, not so much. But in almost all cases, accelerant puddles tend to hold small pools of freestanding water. Kelton had cleared this particular one with a broom. Jake knelt at its edge, illuminating it with his flashlight. He could clearly see where the grooves of Warren's hardwood floors had burned from the inside up. What was more, he could see the burn was deeper at the puddle's perimeter than at its center—another tell-tale sign.

It's an accelerant's vapors that burn, not the accelerant itself. The unique pattern was immediately evident to Jake. Like hundreds of times before, Jake could see where the pool of liquid had acted as an insulating barrier between the vapors above it and the hardwood floor below. It had burned down and inward from its upper surface, away from the perimeter, thereby leaving a burn pattern deeper at the edges than at the more insulated center. It is there that the liquid is at its greatest depth, therefore providing the most protection from the flames.

Jake looked around the apartment, at the destruction that was once Warren's life. *What is it about this guy and fire?* For the first time since the investigation began, he started to place Warren at the top of his list. Prior to this morning's events, he wasn't really sure, and he didn't know a hell of a lot more now. Yes, it was possible that Scotty had done all this, and, yes, it could be Warren who lay charbroiled in the Jeep just below. But something in Jake's gut told him otherwise.

Jake and Kelton were on their knees, sifting through layers of debris, when their focus was interrupted. "Mr. Ferguson," the ME said, standing in the doorway. "I think you just got a break."

Jake rose, walking toward him. "Talk to me."

"Our roast was wearing this ring." The ME handed it to him.

Jake took it, turning it over in his hands. It was a gold college ring from Rutgers University. Though disfigured, he could still make out a 19 on one side and a 71 on the other. Inscribed on the inside were the words "To DS, Love KT." Jake was ecstatic, though it would be one more thing to do tomorrow. Rutgers could tell him who graduated in 1971 with the initials DS. That would be the easy part. Determining his connection to the case would be a different matter altogether. Nineteen seventy-one was too long ago for it to be Scotty. But still, the initials weren't CB, WP, or WJ for that matter. Jake figured that was both good and bad. At least he felt pretty sure who the victim was not. But it also meant his man was still on the loose, whoever that was. He didn't know Chandler Boutet, but that was about to change, and fast.

"What's it say?" Kelton asked.

"It's a Rutgers University graduation ring, dated 1971. It reads, 'To DS, Love KT.' "

"DS? Who's that? Mean anything to you?"

Jake frowned. "Nope."

"Oh, man," Kelton said through a sardonic chuckle. "This is one for the record books."

CHANDLER BOUTET HAD followed Warren's green Mazda off the Palisades, across the Tappan Zee Bridge, and down the Saw Mill River Parkway to an old, flea-ridden motel in Yonkers, set back from the road. The sign outside read, "Rooms by the Hour—$24.50 a Night." Chan pulled Sam's Saab to the curb, leaving it idling, but killing his lights.

"Now what?" Sam asked.

"Now we do it all over again," Chan said. "You stay here and watch this guy like a hawk. I'm calling a cab. I have to find out just what the hell is going on."

"Where you going?"

"I think a little chat with Lianne Rybeck is in order."

Sam looked at his watch. "At three-thirty in the morning? She'll be dead to the world."

"Well, then, she'll just have to get up, won't she?"

"Oh, man," Sam snickered. "She's gonna love you."

"Yeah, well, the feeling is mutual," Chan said, picking up Sam's car phone to call a taxi.

They sat for a while in silence. "How you feeling?" Chan finally asked, still worried about Sam's emotional state.

"I'm doin' all right."

Sam's response did not instill confidence. "You sure? We can work out something else if you're not up to it."

Sam looked at his friend. "I'm up to it. I want this son of a bitch."

Chan thought it might be best if Sam had the opportunity to let it out, to perform their own private stress-debriefing session right there in the car. "You want to talk about it?"

Sam laid his head back against the seat, exhaling deeply through pursed lips. "I don't know, Chan. What's to talk about? I mean, I've known Dan . . . or I knew him . . . however the fuck I'm supposed to say that now . . . for over twenty years. Shit, I was the best man at his wedding, for Christ's sake. I'm the godfather to his oldest son. And now . . . just like that"—Sam snapped his fingers—"he's gone. If I hadn't left him, he'd still be alive."

Chan's back was pressed against the driver's-side door. He could tell Sam needed to talk. Chan breathed deeply, not particularly enamored at the thought of playing shrink right then. When he spoke, he was more concerned for the overall success of his objective than he was for Sammy's mental health. But at the moment, the two were inescapably intertwined.

"You can't do that to yourself, Sammy. Look at me," Chan said, demanding Sam's full attention. "You can't blame yourself. It'll kill you. You had no way of knowing."

Sam's hands were clasped in his lap. He was clearly holding back tears. "Who's going to tell Kathryn? I'd rather die than be the one to deliver this news."

Chan had worried about that, too. "We'll tell her together."

Sam's head nodded slightly. "I can still hear him, Chan. I've never heard screams like that. I don't think I'll ever get them out of my head."

Sam wouldn't be the first human to witness something traumatic and never quite recover. Call it shell shock, post–traumatic stress disorder, or just the brain's natural defense when the eyes observe one of life's occasional unbearable horrors—the undeniable fact is that the country's Veterans hospitals and city streets are littered with those whose minds never quite made it back.

Chan didn't think now was the appropriate time to bring it up, but he was certain when this was all over, Sam would need professional help. Left unchecked, trauma such as that which Sam had witnessed can become cancerous, seeping into the psyche, slowly dissipating one's sanity, maybe even the will to live. Chan had seen it before. He prayed like hell he wouldn't have to see it again.

The problem was, right now, Chan needed Sam. Like it or not, both of them were up to their eyeballs in this mess. It wasn't as if Chan could give him the night off. He didn't even think that would be healthy. Sam needed to get in the saddle again. Though, secretly, Chan hoped it wouldn't do more harm than good.

"You'll be all right, Sammy. I promise," Chan lied. "It'll just take time."

Sam rubbed his forehead with his thumb and fingers and began hitting it slowly with the ball of his hand. "Time," he said with eyes that almost pleaded. "How much time?"

"I don't know, Sam. As long as it takes, I guess."

"Why don't we just go kill the motherfucker? Let's take an eye for an eye right now and be done with it. That'll help me get over it."

The thought had crossed Chan's mind. "You know we can't do that, Sam. Besides, it'll be better to watch him rot in jail."

Sam spoke quietly. "Says who?"

The thought struck Chan that Sam might try something stupid in his absence. He wasn't sure just how rationally Sam's brain was functioning. "Now, listen to me, Sam. I have to go. Promise me you'll stay right here unless he moves. You can't go doing anything crazy."

There was silence.

"Sam?"

"What?"

"Did you hear me? I have to know you're not going to go after this guy."

"Yeah, I heard ya," Sam said, annoyed.

"Promise me, Sam."

"All right, all right, I promise. But I'll tell you this much. That son of a bitch comes after me, I won't hesitate to blow him away."

"He comes after you, then all bets are off. Just don't go after *him*."

"Don't worry. I won't go mowing the bastard down. Even though I should."

Chan was quiet for a moment. "You sure you can do this? It's too important, Sam. You can't go screwing it up."

"This thing's personal now, Chan. Believe me, I can do it."

"You sure?"

"Yes, I'm sure." Sam answered like a schoolkid shooing away an annoying mother. "Now get the fuck out of here already, will you? You're making me nervous."

There was a moment's silence as Chan sized up Sam with his eyes. "Okay. This asshole sneezes, I want to know about it."

Sam nodded.

Chan jotted something down on the back of a napkin. "Here's my pager number. Use it, all right? He takes a shit, I want to know."

"Don't worry. He moves, you'll know about it."

Some time passed in silence, each man lost in his respective world, Chan thinking through his upcoming confrontation with Lianne, Sam still trying to dislodge Shackling's screams from his ears. Chan opened his door as an orange cab pulled up next to the Saab. He put one foot on the pavement and turned, looking into Sam's eyes.

"Sammy?"

"What?"

"This guy's for real. Watch yourself, okay?"

Sam smiled. "Count on it."

Chan left Sam alone in the darkness of the car, opened the door to the cab, and crawled in. Sam watched him. Chan smiled, the back of his hand pressed against the window, his thumb up in the air. Sam returned the gesture as Chan's face was quickly whisked from view.

"WHERE'S YOUR JEEP, Chan?" the West View guard asked as the taxi pulled to a stop in front of Lianne's wrought-iron gate.

"Don't ask. You got an extra set of keys to the pool house? I lost mine."

"Tough night, huh?" the guard said, opening the gates to the estate.

"You could say that."

The cabbie drove up the incline of the cobblestone drive, looping his beat-up Impala around in front of the four-car garage. "Nice digs," he said.

"Thanks," Chan said, eyeing the total on the meter, handing the driver two twenties. "Keep the change."

"Hey . . . thanks, bud."

Chan stood watching as the cab drove away, not moving as it looped over the crest of the lawn and down to the right and out of sight. He stood motionless in the cool, dark night, taking deep breaths through his mouth, exhaling slowly through his nose. The sweet aroma of dozens of different flowers permeated the jet-black night. At that moment, the thought of Lianne and her stupid flowers annoyed the hell out of him. As Chan stood, staring at the mansion, there seemed to him a glaring incongruity in West View's forced tranquillity and bogus calm. The inevitable comparison to what had transpired earlier that morning stunned him almost physically. He listened to the trees rustle in the cool, early-morning breeze and could hear the screaming of a nighthawk from somewhere above.

Nothing moved. All was calm in Lianne Rybeck's protected little world, while Dan Shackling was dead, literally burned to a crisp, now lying in a plastic bag in some freezer—a John Doe victim in a no-name morgue. *Goddamn* you, Lianne, Chan thought. Just who was this Warren Parks? Who was this madman she had so slyly interposed into his otherwise mundane life? What did she know that she had not bothered to tell him, and why had she kept him in the dark? There were questions to be answered all right, and if Lianne Rybeck thought she could just curl up into her nice, warm bed and forget all about it, she was sadly mistaken.

Chan was not so simple as to think she would take kindly to being rousted out of bed before the roosters woke. But he also didn't give a shit. He worried that what he was about to do would probably ruin his chances for his other fifty-thousand-dollar check. But a close friend of his had been brutally, horrifically murdered on a stakeout—a stakeout for which he had been hired by Chan, and for which Chan felt personally responsible. He hated to kiss the remaining cash good-bye, but right now, he could see little choice.

Lianne had led him to believe it would be a relatively benign assignment. There was never mention of any inherent, deadly danger. Chan's naïveté gnawed at him. In retrospect, he could not believe how quickly Lianne's money had sucked him in; he felt shame over how gullible he had been to think she would pay him so highly for a job that appeared so routine. Chan shuddered to think that maybe this was so, that maybe, somehow, *he* might be responsible. But, if in fact Lianne was privy to something clandestinely sinister, she should damn well have made that clear from the start.

Burning alive is generally not a threat you put on your radar screen while performing surveillance, or most other tasks, for that matter. If there was something unique about Warren Parks and the threat he posed, Chan felt it only reasonable to assume Lianne would have come forward with that information of her own accord. There are some questions you just don't think to ask.

Chan had always had full rein of the Rybecks' estates, or most parts of them anyway, both here and in Florida. The only structure on the West View grounds to which Chan did not have keys was the mansion itself. Consequently, he could enter the pool house any day, anytime, which he always thought odd, since the mansion was easily accessible from it. Chan never did know if it was an oversight or Severin's sneaky way of saying that he trusted him. As fate would have it, he would never find out. Not that it mattered now. But for the first time he was secretly grateful.

He walked quickly but quietly down the slope of the lawn, barely capable of seeing his hand in front of his face. There was no moon on this night. Chan knew the yard by heart, where he could walk safely and where the motion detectors would pick him up. He came to the pool house door, the same one Jake and Ederling had entered a week ago, took out the keys the guard had given him, and fumbled for some time, trying to find the right one. Eventually he succeeded, turning the key and slowly pushing the door open to an unwelcome squeak, one he had never noticed before. It's funny how everything seems thunderous in the dead of night.

Chan stepped inside and closed the door tightly behind him, keeping the knob turned until it would move no more. A slight chlorine odor tickled his nostrils as he stepped quickly around the mirrorlike stillness of the rectangular pool. His heart beat faster as he approached the door leading to a hallway that connected the pool house to the mansion's billiards room. It was pitch-black and he wished now his flashlight had not also been in his Jeep. Chan groped his way around the room, hitting his thigh once against the corner of a table before finally making his way to a set of carpeted, circular stairs, which lead to a landing with two dark, mahogany doors.

Beyond these lay the inner sanctum, the private Rybeck world replete with all its power and money, all its secrets and private hells. It had been years since Chan had come this way, and when he did, he was not paying attention through which door Severin had taken him. He tried envisioning the layout of the mansion in his mind, assuming one door would lead him toward the kitchen, the other toward the study. He took the door to the right, hoping he would not end up in the former.

Chan was virtually blind, feeling his way up the wooden stairs with the toes of his shoes. He counted twelve steps, came to a landing, and opened a door to an expansive room, through which even the dark of night seemed to shed light on his new world. He knew immediately he was in Severin's study. From here he knew the way. Chan had been in here many times before, though he had always come from the portico entrance. He stood still for a moment, letting his eyes adjust to the different shade of black. The room was dark, but somehow a strange, almost translucent light seeped through the windows, illuminating the room's contents. Chan could see the walls of books, Severin's desk, the leather sofas, and the door on the opposite side of the room he needed to take to get to the hallway.

Once in the hallway, the trip down the chandeliered foyer to the split, spiraled staircase was easy. He took them two at a time, aware now there would be no turning back—not that he would have or even wanted to. But Chan had learned years ago not to act when his emotions were running high, and somewhere in the back of his mind, he hoped he wasn't making a horrible mistake. After all, fifty grand is an awful lot of money to throw away. He reached the upstairs hallway and shook his head, disappointed that the thought had even crossed his mind. He owed Dan at least this much.

Chan knew the Rybecks did not sleep together and walked down the hallway, away from Severin's room. What he did not know was which room was Lianne's, or if there was anyone else sleeping in the mansion. The last thing he wanted was to give some unsuspecting guest a heart attack. But Lianne . . . now, *she* was a different story. Chan hoped he scared her half to death. At least when she recovered, she would still be alive, which was more than he could say for some people tonight.

Mercifully, a crystal night-light was plugged into the wall of the hallway, so his travels were finally unimpeded. He walked slowly, stopping at each door, squinting his eyes, trying to make out a lump on the bed or the telltale sounds of sleep. At the end of the hall he came to a closed door. He knew this one had to be it. Chan stood at it for a few seconds, breathing slowly through his nose, willing to let Providence take its course. Some things are just the right thing to do—consequences be damned. If Chan ever knew anything in his life, he knew this was one of those times.

The door was not fully closed. He cupped his hand around it, pushed it open slowly, and poked his head inside the room. He could clearly hear the sound of slumber, that unmistakable snort and snore of someone lost deeply in sleep. A delicate, immediately recognizable fragrance of perfume wafted up his nose. He had found her. Chan was suddenly filled with a mix of angst and rage. He dragged an open palm across the darkened wall, finally flicking on the overhead light, stepped into the room, and slammed the door behind him.

His temples pulsated with anger as he stood, watching Lianne physically jump from her sleep. Chan watched with pleasure as she flailed madly in the air. As if her life were at stake, she slammed her back against the headrest, her eyes widening with alarm, seemingly gorged with horror as they slowly focused on her unannounced guest. Her throat constricted as she gasped in fear.

"Hello, Lianne," Chan said casually but firmly, making no effort to lower his voice. "Did I wake you?"

She sat up, holding her blankets tightly to her chest. Lianne was *not* happy. "Jesus Christ, Chandler! What the hell are you doing here? What time is it? You nearly scared me to death."

"But you're still alive, aren't you?"

The reality of the moment seemed to hit her. Lianne was incensed. "What are you doing in my bedroom?" she asked with open disdain, her face alternating between outright panic and utter contempt.

Chan responded with equal disgust. "The one place you never expected to see a man, right, Lianne?"

"Don't be insolent with me, Chandler. I won't tolerate it."

"You won't *tolerate* it?" he asked with mocking laughter. "Oh, that's a good one, Lianne." Chan took a menacing step forward. "*You* are in no position to make demands."

"Goddamn you! What are you doing in my bedroom?"

"I'll tell you what I'm doing in your bedroom, Lianne. I came here to tell you that one of my best friends was burned alive tonight. Fried to a crisp, inside *my* Jeep, watching *your* Mr. Parks. I just thought you might like to know that."

Lianne continued, unmindful of his words, "Who the hell do you think you are? Coming into my house, my bedroom . . . uninvited, in the middle of the night? Don't you know who I am? Get out. *Now!*"

It seemed incomprehensible to Chan that Lianne could possibly be this cold. Chan moved to the side of her bed. "I don't give a shit *who* you are. Did you hear what I just said to you?" he asked, disbelieving that this would be her only reaction.

"Yes. I heard you. Now get out of my house!"

"So that's it, huh? I tell you one of my best friends was burned alive and all you have to say is 'Get out of my house'?"

Lianne reached for her telephone on the nightstand. "I'm calling the police."

"Here," Chan said, picking up the phone. "Let me call them for you. I think they'll be quite interested to hear just what the hell is going on, don't you think? Which would you prefer? Nine one one or the duty sergeant?"

"Now, you listen to me, young man," Lianne began, clearly taken aback by Chan's offensive stance. "I will not allow you to do this to me. Do you understand? This is *my* house. *My* bedroom. And *you* are trespassing. Now get out!"

Chan was in no mood for diplomacy. He didn't care what happened from here on. Let the police come, he thought. Maybe then he could get some answers. Chan stood with his knees touching her bed, towering over the object of his rage. "No!" he boomed, his face betraying a perilous hold on his darker instincts. "*You* listen to me, you pretentious bitch! You're lucky I don't rip your goddamned lungs out through your nose. Don't *even* ask me to leave here again, or I swear you will regret it. Who do you think you are? Huh? You think your millions give you the right to play tiddlywinks with people's lives? That man had a family, goddamnit. And now he's lying in some morgue thanks to you. Don't you *dare* order me out of your house without at least telling me why."

Lianne moved to the farthest side of her bed. "You have until three, and then I'm going to start screaming," she threatened, only now understanding her vulnerable position.

"I'm afraid it won't be quite that simple, Lianne. Go ahead. Scream if you want. But I'm not leaving here until I get some answers. You think that's so unreasonable, Lianne?"

She stared at him sharply, her eyes narrow slits of contempt. She was quiet. "What kind of answers?" she asked conciliatorily.

"Well . . . for starters, maybe you can explain why you didn't tell me that Parks was dangerous. I had no idea the man was a murderer, Lianne. Did you?"

She stared at him.

"Did you!" Chan bellowed.

Lianne was quiet. It wasn't supposed to be like this. "I had my suspicions," she finally admitted.

"You had your *suspicions?*" Chan asked mockingly. "I think we can safely say your suspicions were correct. For God's sake, why didn't you tell me? Don't you think that's something I should have known?"

Guilt and fear suddenly replaced her rage. She had never dreamt something this horrible would happen. "I wasn't sure, Chandler. I just wasn't sure."

"Well, now you are."

"Yes. Now I am. I am truly sorry about your friend."

"Tell that to his wife and kids."

Lianne closed her eyes. It all seemed as though it would never stop. She kept asking herself, when would she ever be rid of this malignant killing machine? She knew for sure it was Warren now. She knew in her heart that her plan was justified. It was all too much. "I'm sorry, Chandler. I never meant you harm. I don't know what you want me to say. I will be happy to pay his widow and children a tidy sum for their loss."

"Oh, that's beautiful, Lianne. Just beautiful. Money solves it all, doesn't it?"

"I'm sorry, Chandler. What more can I say?"

The tension and hatred in the room, so tangible and pervasive just seconds ago, seemed to drop a notch. Chan wasn't going to get anywhere screaming and threatening Lianne all night. One part of him wanted to kill her, but his more rational side told him Lianne was his only hope at getting to the bottom of this mess. "Is Parks connected to the Morson Grayhead murders?"

"Yes. I think so."

Chan dropped his head in his hands, rubbing his temples with his fingers. "Jesus Christ, Lianne. Why on earth didn't you tell me that? Do you have *any* idea how differently we would have approached this thing had we only known?"

Tears welled up in her eyes. Warren Parks had to die. Lianne needed to make sure that it happened. The world would be a better place without his presence. She wondered now if it was possible to recruit Chan toward that cause. "He's a monster, Chandler."

"A *monster*, Lianne?" he asked, his eyes opening wider. "That's an understatement." Chan turned and looked at her, his rage slowly replaced by empathy and confusion. He believed her when she said she meant no harm. She was clearly in over her head. Chan whipped himself emotionally for not having asked more questions. Again, he was disturbed that he had been so smitten by the money that he had forgotten everything he was ever trained for. "Are you planning on killing him?" Chan asked point-blank.

Lianne looked at him, a lone tear sliding down her left cheek. She was obviously frightened and upset. She closed her eyes, releasing tears down both cheeks. She wanted desperately to answer, to beg Chan for his help. Lianne feared Warren might be too much for her alone, that he would see through her petty little schemes and crush her before her work was done. She didn't care for her own safety, but she could not stand another beat of her heart if she felt that Scotty would forever live under his maniacal rule. And there was only one way she could think to insure that it would never happen again.

"Chandler, there are so many things you do not know," Lianne began. "So much pain, so much history. I admit I left some things out when I approached you yesterday morning. I admit I did not tell you everything. Yes, I left out some of it because I thought you wouldn't help me if you knew. But I swear to you. I swear on my mother's grave . . . I never thought something like this would happen."

"You didn't answer my question."

This was Lianne's moment of truth. If she told him and he thwarted her, she would never die in peace. "Yes, Chandler, yes. Okay? I *am* going to kill him." The words spurted out so fast, they were spoken before Lianne could even think to take them back. She needed to press on, to beg for whatever help she could get. "Please help me, Chandler. *Please?* I beg you. You've seen what an animal he is. The police can't stop him, but I can. I have something he wants very, very much."

Chan squinted his eyes, cocking his head ever so slightly. "What's that?"

"Money, Chandler. That's what he wants."

"Money?" Chan asked, his question harboring a certain incredulity. "That's what this is all about? Money?"

"Does that surprise you? There's only two things that make the world go round, and I can assure you the other one he does not want from me."

Chan's heart grew heavy. It's always the same, he thought. Sex and money. He wondered if the human race would ever grow up. But then again, Chan reminded himself to look at the mess he had allowed himself to get in. He certainly couldn't say it was not because of money. "If you're asking me to kill him, Lianne . . . I can't do that. I'm sorry, but I just can't. Not premeditatedly."

"Even after tonight?"

Chan had to admit the thought *was* appealing. But you can't spend one hundred thousand dollars in prison, and anyway, the very thought ran counter to everything he was, everything Chan stood for and believed in so profoundly. "Yes," he said, exhaling deeply. "Even after tonight. That's what courts are for."

Lianne waved a hand, indicating Chan was not following her line of thinking. "I'm not asking *you* to kill him, Chandler. *I* will do that. I *want* to kill him. I just need you to either lead me to him or lead him to me. That's all you have to do. No one will ever know. I promise you that much, Chandler. I will take it to my grave. I don't care what happens to me. Don't you know that? They can throw me in the chair for all I care. I will die with a smile on my face knowing that wretched animal no longer walks this planet."

Chan cursed in silence. This was different from what he had anticipated. Once again, fact is stranger than fiction. Chan faced a sticky question. Is it the same thing if you knowingly lead someone to his grave, even if you know you aren't the one who is going to pull the trigger? If God is the punishing type, just whom does he blame in a situation like that? The man who wraps the noose around the victim's neck, or the man who pulls the lever?

It wasn't that Chan gave two shits about Warren Parks, the man. In fact, a private part of him wished Lianne success. And he had to admit his faith in the court system dwindled a little more every day. But could Chan live with himself if he knowingly led Warren to his death? Would God forgive him for so malevolent an act, no matter the justification? He wondered if it would have been wrong for someone to have murdered Adolf Hitler and found himself asking just when is it acceptable to partake in the murder of another human being?

Chan sat on the edge of Lianne's bed and sighed deeply. A few minutes ago he wanted to kill her, and now he was actually considering assisting her in murder. "Look, Lianne, I don't know what the hell is going on here, but I think it's high time I did, don't you? Why don't we start over. Tell me what this is all about. From the beginning."

Lianne wiped her eyes with a sheet. She knew she needed to tell Chan everything, but feared the final outcome. If, for any number of reasons her mind could imagine, Chan did not like what he heard, she might not only lose any chance of his help but could well risk arrest. And the thought of incarceration without her final victory was more than she could bear.

"Okay . . . Chan. If I tell you everything, what assurance do I have that it will stay in this room?"

Chan shrugged. "Just my word, I guess."

Lianne stared firmly into his eyes. "Are you telling me I have your word that what you are about to hear will stay between us, and only us?"

"Well . . . I mean, within reason. It's not like you killed someone."

Lianne raised her eyebrows. "What makes you so sure?"

Chan's eyes narrowed. "You've lost me, Lianne," he said, rubbing his forehead. "What kind of question is that?"

"Look," Lianne said, losing her nerve. "Maybe we shouldn't do this. It might be better for both of us if we just went our separate ways."

"Maybe we shouldn't do what? I don't understand, Lianne. What the *hell* are you talking about?"

"I don't think you are emotionally prepared to hear what I have to say, Chan. And I know for sure it hasn't even crossed your mind."

"What? What hasn't crossed my mind? Jesus Christ, Lianne, if you have something to say, then say it. I need to know what's going on. If it's my word you want, then you have it."

There was something about the moment. Call it trust, or maybe even total capitulation—whatever it was, Lianne knew the time had come. "Chan, what would you say if I told you that I *have* killed someone?"

Chan's back stiffened. He stared at her in silence for several seconds. "Depends . . . I guess."

"On what?"

"On whether it was in self-defense. Something like that."

"How about in the defense of my son?"

"That works. Maybe."

"Do you remember yesterday when I told you about Warren and Josephine and their effect on Scotty?"

"Yes."

"Do you remember how I told you that Josephine died in a fire on the West View grounds?"

Chan could only guess where the hell she was going with this one. She couldn't possibly be preparing to tell him what had just entered his mind. Chan just nodded.

"Who do you think started that fire, Chan?"

When it rains, it pours, he thought. "You can't be serious, Lianne?" He turned, curling his right leg up to the bed. "Was she alive? I mean, was she already dead?"

"Oh, she was very much alive, Chan."

In a million years he would never have thought what he'd just heard even remotely possible. "I can't believe this, Lianne. Are you telling me you murdered Warren's wife?"

Lianne nodded her head slowly. "That's *exactly* what I'm telling you. And I have never regretted it. Not even once."

Chan stood up off the bed, walking to a window. He placed a hand to either side, staring at the early light of dawn. "But how?" he asked, speaking away from her. "I mean . . . you can't just burn someone alive and have it go undetected."

She shrugged this off.

"Hell, Lianne . . . she's not going to just stand there and let you immolate her. And if you knocked her out beforehand, or somehow forcibly detained her, certainly the investigating officers would have noticed. At the very least the autopsy would have shown something."

"Autopsy?" Lianne asked under a knowing laugh. "Chan, do you have any idea what money can buy? Even a clue?"

"Jesus Christ," he said in exasperation, turning from the window. Chan could not believe his ears. "You're telling me you bought off the medical examiner? I don't believe you."

Lianne shrugged her shoulders again. "That's up to you, Chan. I really don't care if you believe me or not. You asked me to tell you everything. I'm telling you everything."

"Well . . . lucky me."

"Yes. Lucky you."

"And you expect me not to go to the authorities with this? That's not fair, Lianne."

"You gave me your word, Chan. If you're telling me now that it's no good, then I guess I took my chances and lost, didn't I? You'll do what you have to do, just like I did twenty years ago. I only ask you this much. Don't turn me in until I've finished the job."

This whole mess certainly made more sense now. Chan ran his fingers through his hair, wondering how he could possibly keep a secret like this and live with himself. "Oh, Lianne . . . I wish you hadn't told me this."

"You should have taken the out when I gave it to you."

Chan was confused. Even for him, this night was becoming too much. He sank slowly to the floor under the window, laying his legs out flat in front of him. He needed rest. "How did you do it? Kill her, I mean."

"That was the easy part," Lianne said with a nonchalant wave of her hand. "I smothered a throw pillow with a bottle of ether and held it over her face while she slept."

"She didn't wake up?"

"She fought me for a moment, but not for very long. The witch didn't even know what hit her."

"But why, Lianne? Why kill her? Why not just turn her in to the police?"

Lianne laughed. "Turn her in to the police? And do what? Drag my son through months, maybe years of depositions and trials, not to mention an unbearable media circus? Don't be a fool, Chan. The Rybecks and the Himmertons are high-profile families. It would have been a nightmare. I would rather have died than do that to Scotty. No, Chan . . . Josephine was evil, through and through. She and her sick husband took my baby from me. There is no cop, no judge, no jury, that could *ever* exact the appropriate revenge. Scotty suffered enough, Chan. I did what I had to do."

"So you decided to be judge and jury?"

"Damn right I did," Lianne answered a bit defensively. She wasn't sure but that a response like that meant she was going to lose him. But she had already decided. If that was the case, then so be it. "And I would do it again. And again. I don't trust the courts, Chan. The law is not designed for victims. Be honest with yourself. Look deep inside. Are you telling me you really believe the legal system will deal with Warren the way he *should* be dealt with? Do you *really* have that much faith in the system?"

Chan sat quietly. He had to admit there were times he wished they'd bring back public hangings. The world is full of evil souls, and Chan had seen his share. Some people just don't deserve to live. And Lianne was right about something else, too. Chan did harbor more than his share of doubt in the legal system's ultimate ability to parcel out justice.

He was torn. On the one hand Chan intuitively knew that retribution was not a decision society can leave up to the aggrieved. He worried what kind of nation we would have if victims were allowed to exact their own revenge. There would surely be anarchy. It would be the Wild West all over again. On the other hand, he desperately wanted to see justice carried out in this case. With what had happened to Shackling tonight, it would come close to killing *him* if it didn't.

"Well?" Lianne asked. "Do you? Do you have that much faith in a system that can let O. J. Simpson walk the streets a free man?"

The O.J. trial still pissed him off. "I don't know, Lianne. I have to think this one through."

"What's to think about, Chan? Warren's a monster and you know it. The world will be a better place without him."

Chan's mind churned in a sea of emotions, not the least of which was rising anger at Lianne's self-appointed omnipotence. "Look, we don't even know for sure that Warren did this tonight."

"Oh, there's a twist," Lianne said with sarcasm. "That's not exactly the position you asserted when you came barging in here fifteen minutes ago, was it? *Now* you're not sure? Don't make me laugh. You know it's him, Chan. And so do I."

"Maybe. But it still doesn't work for me, Lianne. I mean, Jesus . . . after tonight, you'd think I have more reason to want to see him dead than you. I can't help you kill a man out of some thirty-year-old grudge. I'm sorry, Lianne, but that's just not good enough for me. The damage to your son has long since been done. My suggestion to you would be, get over it and get on with your life."

"Get on with my life?" she asked resentfully. "Get on with my *life!* Scotty *is* my life, Chan. I have no other reason for wanting to live. And look at your friend tonight. That isn't a good enough reason to want him dead? Just what kind of man are you, anyway?"

Lianne was pushing it now. Just because Chan did not want to participate in murder was hardly cause to question his character. He pointed a finger at her. "Now wait just a goddamned minute," he said, his voice growing louder. "Don't even *think* you can question my integrity."

"Then help me, Chan," Lianne begged with pleading eyes. "Help me do what's right. The courts will find him legally insane. You *know* that! He might even walk someday if he can show them he's changed. They'll study him and feed him drugs. The system has a short memory, and he is very, *very* clever. I know him, Chan. I know what makes him tick, how sick he is inside. And even if he does get better, let's say they find some miracle drug. Does that change the heinous nature of his deeds? Will that bring your friend back? Tell me you could live with yourself if he walked?"

Lianne was right there. Chan probably couldn't live with himself. He would definitely have difficulty swallowing Warren's release. But a thirty-year grudge? He wished like hell she had more immediate grievances. "But why now? Why haven't you done something about this before? My God, Lianne, thirty years is a very long time."

Only then did it dawn on her. "Don't you know?"

"Know what?"

"About Warren and Scotty?"

Chan was bewildered. Warren and Scotty? he thought. Just what the hell was Lianne talking about? "What do you mean, 'Warren and Scotty'? What about them?"

Lianne leaned back against the headboard. It all made sense now. No wonder he was having such trouble seeing the light. "Warren has latched onto Scotty again, Chan," she began, speaking to the ceiling. "He has planted himself firmly in the middle of my son's life. Scotty is not a bad boy. Honestly he's not. He's just simple, is all. Easily conned and manipulated. He's trusting, but lacks the intellectual wherewithal to see right from wrong. He's so desperate for love and belonging, he'd ride the back of a scorpion if he thought it had befriended him. Warren can see it all. He's using him for something, I just don't know what."

"What the hell does that mean?"

Lianne sighed. She knew this part would be most difficult for Chan to hear.

Somehow, over the years, he and Severin had actually become tight. But still, he needed to know. She told him of her husband's failings as a father, how he blatantly ignored Scotty, even as he desperately reached out for love and acceptance. Lianne explained Severin's obsession with Morson Grayhead and his inferiority complex about money, who had it in the family and who did not. Chan sat surprisingly still, listening more stoically than she would have anticipated.

Chan stared at Lianne, the light overhead unsympathetically revealing the lines of her face. "I always thought it strange he didn't talk about his family," he said when she had finished. "I knew the firm was his life, but I just figured it was because Scotty was grown and had moved away." Actually, Chan had gotten an inkling the night Severin decided to blow his head off, but decided to leave out the fact that he'd read the suicide note.

"Not quite."

"So, this is more than just some old grudge? You're trying to protect Scotty from Warren right now? Is that correct?"

Lianne nodded. "Yes."

"But how do you know it has to do with money?" Chan asked. "I mean, you haven't seen him in decades. How can you be so sure?"

Ah . . . *finally*, Lianne thought. Here it is. This was the other part of the deep, dark Rybeck secret she once thought she would always be able to keep to herself. Only Scotty knew, and not through actions of her own. It was a strange feeling for Lianne to reveal it to such a relative stranger. "Because," she began cautiously, staring deep within Chan's eyes, "because, Chandler . . . Warren knows I killed his wife. He watched me do it."

Chan's face took on a look of puzzlement. "I don't understand. What do you mean, he watched you do it?"

"He knows it was me. It's a long story, but he saw me. I didn't know it at the time, of course, but he saw me."

"How do you know?"

"He called me two years ago. He described my actions that night to a T. There was no doubt he'd seen it all. I don't know how, and I don't really care. But he terrorized me, Chan. He started making threats, telling me how vulnerable Scotty would be if I went to jail. He's been blackmailing me ever since. I pay him ten thousand dollars a month and have since the day he called me."

"Well . . . I mean, shit, Lianne. You *did* kill his wife."

"Oh, there's more to it than that, Chan. This is one *very* slick man."

"I'm listening."

Lianne was more than embarrassed by what she was about to tell Chan.

She possessed more than her share of pride. After all, she was a Himmerton. Her mind flirted with the concepts of money, power, and polished civility, realizing now what a bunch of horseshit it all really was. If people only knew the silence money can buy, the twisted arms and veiled threats. The only difference is the truly wealthy hire others to do their dirty work.

"As you know," Lianne continued, "Severin and I were hardly what you might term *intimate*. It happened shortly after I was recovering from my illness, but before I put it all together about the two of them and Scotty."

Lianne had Chan's attention now. Oddly, it struck him that this was like listening to *The Shadow* on the radio, a mysterious voice relaying tales of intrigue and horror in the dark. "What happened?"

"Chan . . . Warren and I became lovers," she said, letting the words hang in the air as if waiting for their toxic presence to dissipate. "Words can't describe how loathsome I feel, how repugnant it is for me to even say that. But unfortunately, it's true."

Chan could only assume she was making half this up. He figured you couldn't even put this shit in a novel. Chan let go a long breath. "Jesus Christ, Lianne! You've got to be kidding me."

"I wish I were. *God* . . . I wish I were. I would give anything . . . *anything* . . . to make it not so. But I was in my prime years, Chan. I was lonely, frightened, and, yes, lustful. I needed companionship, and he was so handsome and virile. He didn't love Josephine. Never did. Oh, he may have thought he did, in his own strange sort of way. But the truth is, Warren only married her for her money. But they had to wait until her twenty-fifth birthday before she would have access to the family trust funds. He was just biding his time, bedding everything that walked in the interim. That was fine with me. I was using him every bit as much as he was me. But now . . . now I know he blames me for taking his pot of gold away."

"Yeah, but of the two, certainly he must have considered you the larger catch."

Lianne laughed. "*Me?* He would have given his left arm if he even thought he had a chance. That's probably why he didn't intervene. But I was married, remember? Anyway, he knew hell would freeze over first."

"Hmmm . . . makes sense. Boy, this guy's a real charmer."

"Oh, he's a charmer all right. Why he waited so many years to finally cash in, I can only imagine."

"Bet I know. Ten to one he was holed up in the slammer somewhere. An opportunist like that, asocial as they come. He would've dug into you as quickly as possible if he'd had the chance. Just think, Lianne, how it must have killed him to have to wait. The years of rage building up in his head. No wonder the guy's obsessed."

Lianne pursed her lips. She'd never thought of that before. "You really think he's been in jail?"

"I'd bet good money on it."

"There's something else."

Nothing would surprise Chan now. "What?"

"Without my knowledge, he told my son."

"Told him what? About the affair, or your murdering Josephine?"

"Josephine. Anyway, he approached me about it one day—"

"Who approached you?"

"Scotty. I tried to lie to him, but I'm afraid that's never been something I've done very well." Lianne looked Chan in the eyes. "I *can* do it, you understand? I just don't think I'm very good at it. Anyway, Scotty knows me too well. He knew I wasn't telling him the truth. He pushed me and pushed me. I just couldn't keep up the farce. Not to my own son. Certainly not after all he'd been through. I couldn't bring myself to do it. He's a good boy, Chan. I really mean that. In his heart, Scotty means well. But he understood, like I knew he would. It wasn't easy, believe me. We hugged and cried. But now I fear Warren is holding it over Scotty's head, threatening to have me put away for life, maybe even executed. Who knows what garbage he's been feeding him."

Chan dropped his head, shaking it slowly in disbelief. He couldn't have dreamed of something as wild as this. "I just can't believe all this, Lianne. You'll pardon me if I come up for air."

"I know it sounds insane."

"So . . . what are you saying?" Chan asked with cocked head, trying to figure exactly where all this was leading. "Are you thinking maybe Scotty's somehow involved in the murders?"

"I don't know. That's why I wanted you to follow Warren." Lianne pulled her knees up to her chest, resting her chin on them. "But I never had any idea it would end like this. I am truly sorry."

Chan nodded in a self-absorbed fashion. He believed her. Lianne was nothing more than a frightened, protective mother, trying desperately to do something . . . anything . . . to save her son. And he also had to agree with her assessment. She *was* in over her head. Dan Shackling was a testimony to that.

"It doesn't matter now anyway," Lianne continued. "Warren's gone. God only knows where he is."

There was silence for a long time as Chan thought through his options. If he told her that he knew Warren's whereabouts, he feared he would become inextricably involved. He knew Lianne would beg him to take her to the motel and probably offer to pay him anything he wanted. For a fleeting moment Chan thought of a price, wondering what he could do with all that money. He laughed inwardly at himself and the workings of the human mind. Sometimes life is just too weird.

But one fact kept reverberating through his head. One that he could not ignore. Warren had brutally murdered his best friend, taking Shackling from his family—and him—in the prime of his life. It was visceral, primordial really, Chan's desire to see Warren executed. He finally decided what he would do; Chan broke the tranquillity of the room.

He looked up, speaking softly. "I know where he is."

Lianne's eyes lit up. "You know where he is? Right now?"

"Yes. Right now," he said, nodding. "I have eyes on him as we speak."

Now it was Lianne who was confused. "But how could that be?"

"Simple. I was driving back to Warren's street to take up the graveyard shift when one of my guys called me. He told me about all that had happened, so I picked him up at a predetermined site. It's not worth going into the details. Suffice it say we needed to get out of there. Warren must have been leaving Englewood Cliffs about the same time, because we weren't on the Palisades more than a couple of minutes when we saw a green Mazda pass us. The plates matched, so we followed it. I took a cab here. My other friend is sitting in a car watching him right now."

"I knew you were good, Chan. Oh, please, take me to him. *Please*, Chan. I beg you. Take me to him."

Chan shook his head. "I can't do that, Lianne," he said with pressed lips. "That would involve my friend, and I won't do that to him. He's been through enough already, believe me." Chan didn't bother telling her that it was more than likely Sam would want to join her. "I'll tell you what I can do, though. I can think of something you have that just might bring him here."

"What's that?"

Not so quick, Chan thought. If he was going to partake in this in any capacity, he was going to make *Lianne* do the thinking. He rose and walked back to the side of her bed. Chan sat down, looking into her eyes. "Let me ask you this. What do you have that he needs right now?"

"Money?" Lianne asked quickly.

"No, you've paid him plenty of that. Right now, he needs something else. Something more basic. What else, Lianne? Think now."

Chan could see that Lianne's eyes were closed, obviously lost in thought. She finally looked up, abandoning her efforts. "I don't know, Chan. I just can't think."

She needed more information. She wasn't privy to all the events of earlier this morning. "All right, try this," Chan added as a hint. "What if I told you that Warren burned his apartment building, and that the police were already onto him when I set up my stakeout? Does that help any?"

"The police were staking him out? How do you know?"

"Trust me, I know."

"Does Warren know it?"

"Does he know it?" Chan asked with astonishment. Maybe she wasn't quite as smart as he gave her credit for. "Oh, I think you can safely say he knows it."

"Chan, please," Lianne said, desperate to move on. "Just tell me. I don't feel like playing games right now."

Chan turned very serious. "Neither do I, Lianne. But if and when this thing is done, I've got to know I can live with myself. If you want me to help you come face-to-face with the man you want to murder, then you are going to have to think it up yourself. I will not do it for you. Now think. Come on, it's not that hard."

"What difference does it make? If you're not going to tell me where he is, how the hell am I going to reach him?"

"I'll place the call. You can talk to him once he's on. That's as far as I'll go."

"Really? You would do that?"

Chan closed his eyes and nodded.

"All right then, you're on. Let's see. He knows the police are onto him, right?"

"Sure does."

Lianne made several guesses, Chan shaking his head at each one. She was clearly frustrated, not pleased at being forced to earn it this way. She'd already paid her dues. "I don't know," she said, her voice acquiescent, almost as if stabbing in the dark. "He's going to have to get away somehow. But—"

"Ah," Chan said with a finger in the air, stopping her thoughts in their tracks. "Stay there."

"Where? Getting away?"

Chan looked at her, not speaking, his eyes saying it all. She stared back, her mind working in overdrive. "Think now," Chan finally said.

She was quiet, formulating the connection in her mind. "Well, I don't know much about police work, but I have to think he can't use the airports, right?" she asked, looking at him for direction.

"You could make that assumption."

"So, he can't use the airports," she repeated to herself, looking up at the ceiling. She spoke more to herself now than to Chan. "Let's see. Bus . . . car . . .

train . . . boat. Can't use a plane . . ." She looked at him, her eyes widening with the sudden realization. Her face almost beamed with glee. "Oh, my God! The plane? Of course. How could I have been so stupid? The jet. I can offer him our plane."

Chan was quiet, letting her piece it all together.

"But he's not stupid," she said, the elation in her face suddenly transforming into a frown of doubt. "He would *never* fall for that. He'd know it's a trap."

Chan pursed his lips, nodding his shoulders back and forth. "Maybe. Maybe not. Reverse it now. What does he have that you want?"

She knew the answer to that one. "Scotty."

Chan smiled. "Sounds to me like you two have the makings of a horse trade. I would think you could find a way to convince him that's a trade you'd be willing to make."

Lianne's eyes narrowed, apparently seeing problems with the plan. "Yes, but how do I get him to come here? He's not just going to—"

"I don't know, Lianne." Chan had already done more than he felt comfortable with. If Lianne wanted to murder another living being, she was going to have to do the rest by herself. "You're smart. Figure it out."

JAKE HOPED THAT Sunday would be a down day. He and Ederling had been pushing the case hard, coming up for air only rarely. As it was, he and Valerie had not gone to bed until sometime after midnight, so that by the time he finally drove onto Warren's street he was working on only about three hours' sleep. The early-morning call saw to that. It was true what Jake had told Valerie. He was not a robot. Like anyone else, he needed sleep and some semblance of a life. *All work and no play makes Jake a dull boy.*

Unlike hundreds of other scenes he had worked in the past, the one to which he'd driven this morning offered little that he needed to investigate. It was clearly arson, and he was willing to bet his job that he knew who'd started it. It was more of the same, really—the one exception being the body in the Jeep. But it was Sunday, and Jake was determined to take at least a little time off. All the case's players would still be there in the morning.

He left Warren's apartment sometime shortly before 7:00 A.M., after he and Kelton had arranged a time to meet tomorrow in Jake's Westchester offices to search Warren's trash. Jake had spent over two hours at the scene of the two fires and in that time only offered his colleague one suggestion—to station a cop on the trash, just to be sure it was not disturbed. Kelton was a pro. He didn't need direction to do his job well.

As Jake drove his cruiser north on the Palisades, he was secretly grateful that he couldn't do much else today. He knew it was certainly possible for him to contact Rutgers Security—university police departments operate seven days a week. But he also knew it could wait. Whoever this DS was, he was as dead as they come and would be for a long time. Jake knew he was getting close. He could feel it in his bones. Tomorrow would work just fine. For now, Jake had a life he was going to try to resume living.

He was in no particular rush and found his thoughts turning to Valerie as he headed home, driving the speed limit in the far right lane. What a whirl-wind of circumstances. Thirty-six hours ago he had actually debated blowing her off, and now he couldn't wait to crawl into bed next to her, to soak in her warmth as he caught up on some desperately needed sleep. A part of him felt vulnerable and afraid. A lot had happened in the last day and a half, and Jake couldn't help but wonder if it was simply loneliness and lust, or something more meaningful—something more lasting than that.

Jake decided not to worry about it. *Only the test of time will tell.* But he was absolutely sure of one thing. He was determined not to let this case get in the way of the best thing to happen to him in many years. The emotions he was now experiencing were new to him. Jake reasoned that he must have felt them with Danny also, but he couldn't really remember. And even if he had, that was a different place and a different time—he was not the same man now. Maybe better, maybe worse, but different nonetheless.

If his and Valerie's relationship was destined for more fertile ground, no way in hell was he going to jeopardize it. The case would still be there, he reminded himself, even if Valerie was not. One could easily get away, while the other he couldn't shake even if he tried. Something told Jake he was at a critical juncture in his life. He couldn't afford to screw it up. Take care of yourself, he kept repeating in his head. *Just take care of yourself.*

Jake pulled into his complex's three-story garage, toying with different activities the two of them might enjoy together once they were finally up and out. He knew of a great brunch spot—buffet style, all you can eat. Bloody Marys, mimosa's, champagne, every cut of meat and type of omelette you could imagine, Danish, fruit, cheese, bagels and lox. Jake's stomach grumbled just thinking about it. He was famished, and right now his diet was the least of his concerns. It was also unique because they had poetry readings and music on Sundays. He'd heard about it sometime ago and, at least prior to Valerie, had always thought the idea pretty stupid. But now with a woman in his life, sud-denly the concept had taken on appeal. *Try and explain that one.*

Jake stepped into his elevator, slumping in the corner. It was not until it began to move that the degree of his fatigue really hit him. He could barely keep his eyes open and relished the thought of sleep. He slipped his key into the lock and entered his co-op. It was mostly dark, though the early morn-ing's rays gamely attempted to shine through the drawn shades. He dumped his jacket on a chair, swallowed a large glass of orange juice, slipped off his shoes, and walked down the hall to his bedroom. He noticed the door was open as he approached, almost giddy at the thought of holding Valerie tightly in his arms. Only then, as he stood disbelieving in his doorway, did Jake realize she was gone.

AT CHAN'S REQUEST, Lianne Rybeck lent him her black Mercedes 450 SEL. He explained to her that every good stakeout needs at least two cars, and she was more than happy to oblige. He gave her Sam's cell phone number and left instructions that she was to contact him in either Sam's Saab or the Mercedes once she had finalized her plan of action. He did, however, make it clear that she was to give him no details, other than that she was ready. Chan didn't want to know, and he especially didn't want whatever it was broadcast over unsecured phone lines. He could not tell her what Warren would do or where he would go, but did make Lianne one promise— wherever Warren went, if it was at all possible, Chan would see to it that she would speak to him when she was ready to make her move.

Chan had now long since parked the Mercedes and rejoined Sam, having just spent the entire day next to his friend in the seat of his Saab. He finished the last of a Whopper with cheese and looked at his watch: 5:27 P.M. Warren's early-morning expedition must have exhausted him, because throughout the remainder of the day a slow trickle of vehicles had been in and out of the motel's drive, and not one of them was a Mazda. At one point Chan began to worry that perhaps they had somehow missed it, or that maybe Sam had momentarily dozed while he had met with Lianne. He even went so far as to approach the motel, only to return to Sam's Saab after he spotted the Mazda parked quietly in a spot behind the building.

"How long are we gonna wait?" Sam finally asked him, after glancing at his watch for the thousandth time that day.

It was Sam's thirty-minute stretch. Chan had reclined the passenger seat back fully, trying to grab a few minutes' rest. "As long as it takes, Sammy. He can't stay in there forever."

"Must just seem that way."

Chan lay with his eyes closed, his arms crossed at his chest. "He'll show, and when he does, we'll be right here."

"How do we know he's even still in there?"

"Where else would he be? He's not going to set out on foot."

"Why not?" Sam asked. "He knows he's in a marked car. Maybe he cut through the back or something."

Chan hated stakeouts as much as the next guy and had to admit that

Sam's words gave him cause for concern. He certainly did not feel like sitting in Sam's Saab indefinitely, waiting for someone who might never show up. Maybe a quick check just to make sure wouldn't be such a bad idea. But how? Chan's mind flipped through his various options, weighing the pros and cons of each. He and Sam discussed it for the better part of a half hour, finally deciding on their plan. But first they would wait for dusk.

Once the sun began to set behind the trees, Chan and Sam decided it was time. Sam was an avid fisherman and always kept his tackle box in his trunk. He retrieved the box, brought it inside the car, and handed Chan a large serrated knife. "You got ten minutes," Sam said. "Then I'm coming looking for you."

"I'll be back long before then."

"Good. I'll be here. Don't get caught."

Chan slipped out of the Saab and walked quietly up the drive to the back of the motel, scanning all around him with trained, wide-angle eyes. He walked to the far side of Warren's Mazda and stood casually for a moment, looking in all directions, then suddenly dropped out of sight. It was dark now, but Warren had proven himself a formidable foe, someone Chan was loath to confront. At least under these circumstances. He finished the job quickly and walked immediately around the motel to the registration office. It was time now for the second part of their plan.

The man behind the counter sat in a rocker, smoking a cigar, watching duckpin bowling on public access TV. He was thin, an unhealthy weight. Chan figured he was a drinker. His wrinkled and leathery face wore a three-day-old, gray mat of stubble, and over the years his dark eyes had sunk deeply into their sockets. Chan wondered what stories he could tell. "You got a guy checked in here with a green Mazda?"

The man glanced at Chan, then back at the TV. He was obviously annoyed, not happy that someone had interrupted his show. "Maybe. Who wants to know?"

If Warren was no longer holed up in the motel, Chan felt certain that what he was about to say would clarify matters quickly—one way or the other. "Well, if you do, someone's slashed his tires. I just thought you'd want to know."

"Shhhit," the man said, rising from his chair. "You sure?"

"I think. I was just cutting through from a trip to the store and saw them. I could be wrong, but they look slashed to me. Who knows? Anyway, I thought you'd want to check it out."

The man was standing behind the counter now, flipping through registration slips. "Yeah, thanks. Like I need this shit."

"Sorry," Chan said, stepping out of the office.

"Any problems?" Sam asked as Chan slid into the seat next to him.

"Smooth as ice. Shouldn't be long now."

Fifteen minutes came and went, then a half hour, then forty-five minutes. Nothing—no AAA vans, no tow trucks, no tire service vehicles, no cabs. Nothing.

Chan looked at his watch: 8:16 P.M. He scratched the back of his neck. "I don't like this. You'd think someone would have come by now."

"I know. I'm getting a bad feeling myself. What now?"

"Okay, why don't you go up?" Chan suggested, watching a red Volvo pull into the drive. "Same routine. Innocent stroll, just happened to see the tires. If the guy couldn't reach Warren, he should say something to that effect."

"You don't think he's gonna get a little bit suspicious?"

Chan looked at Sam. "You got a better idea?"

"All right," Sam said, shrugging his shoulders. "I'll be back in five."

He walked up the drive and around in back, just in time to see someone pull something from his car, throw it in the newly arrived Volvo, and get in the passenger-side seat. Lighting was poor, but the man seemed to fit Warren's description. If it is Warren, he's mobile now, Sam thought. And to top it off, all Sam could think was that he was a couple of hundred yards from his car without a portable radio. He wanted to turn and run, but worried they would see him in their headlights as they turned down the drive. Sam moved crisply in a half-jog, half-walk gait, right up to the point when he could see his shadow lengthening on the pavement in front of him from the Volvo's lights at his back.

He slowed to a casual walk as the Volvo whizzed past and watched as it stopped at the end of the drive, its left blinker flashing, waiting for its chance to pull out onto Central Avenue. Once the car made the turn, Sam broke into a run, approaching his Saab at a full sprint, pointing wildly ahead of him. He literally jumped into the driver's seat, turned the ignition, and whipped his car in a U-turn from its space.

"Jesus Christ, Sam. What the hell's going on?" Chan asked as he gripped the armrest of the door, aware that his heart was suddenly pumping wildly in his chest.

"You see that Volvo that just came out of there?"

"Yeah," Chan said, watching Lianne's parked Mercedes fall from view.

"Our bird's in it."

"No shit. Good eyes, Sammy."

Sam looked in his rearview mirror, craning his neck as he turned to check to his left before switching lanes. "Yeah, I'll tell you this, another thirty seconds and I would have missed him."

"Well, it worked."

"Luckily. Write this down before I forget. License plate reads HIMR-TON. Whatever the hell that means."

"HIMRTON," Chan said, grabbing a pen from his shirt and writing it down on a Burger King napkin. He put his pen back in his pocket and slapped his hands, rubbing them together as if preparing for a job. "All right, Sammy! Just like old times," he said with a smile before breaking into Willie Nelson's lyrics. " 'On the road again . . .' "

Monday
September 16

I HOPE YOU DON'T mind my saying so," Ederling said to Jake as he stared at his friend from across his desk, "but you look like shit."

Jake sat staring, the steam from a cup of coffee on his desk rising, then dissipating in front of his face. Ederling was right in his assessment. Jake did look just this side of a used tire. He'd spent many hours on Sunday, pacing his living room, wanting desperately to track Valerie down, but knew in his heart that she apparently needed space. And then there was that dreaded sixth sense that had tormented him until well past 3:00 A.M. this morning; that little voice that kept nagging at him, whispering that something just wasn't right.

"Thanks," Jake responded before explaining to Ederling what had occurred. He knew in his heart that she would not just leave like that. He prayed he was right. "I just can't figure it out. Something had to have happened."

"So?" Ederling said, glancing over some paperwork. "She got cold feet. She'll call."

Jake shook his head. "Nah, Donny, you just don't understand. There was something special between us."

"I don't get it, Jake. I mean, Christ . . . you only met her on Friday. How special could it possibly be?"

Jake sipped his coffee, looking up at Ederling. "That's the whole point, Don. It wouldn't happen like that again in a million years. I'm telling you, she wouldn't just have left. I *know* it."

Ederling looked at Jake for a while. "You don't think you're reaching just a little bit here, buddy?"

Jake snipped at him, his voice clearly agitated. "No, Don, I don't think I'm reaching, okay? I know how it sounds, but I'm telling you, *something* is wrong."

Ederling found himself wondering what the hell had happened this weekend. It was the strangest thing he had ever seen. "Okay, okay, I'm sorry. The whole thing just sounds pretty weird if you ask me. Especially for a woman you just met."

"Trust me."

Ederling felt that he could if this whole thing had to do with anything but a woman. He remained silent, aware that this was a subject too close to Jake's heart. "So today's the day, my man," he said, changing subjects. "We're gonna have more shit coming at us than we can shake a stick at."

The phone rang. Jake jumped, almost too fast, grabbing it on the first ring. "Jake Ferguson."

Ederling watched him, hoping it was Valerie. He needed Jake's full attention today. "Okay, thanks. I owe you," he heard Jake say as he laid the receiver lightly in its cradle.

"Who was that?"

"Our file reel search is on the way. Janice is faxing it to us now."

"*All right,*" Ederling said with excitement. "Let the games begin."

Both men rose and walked over to the fax machine as it clicked on. They stood side by side as the computer-generated print began appearing in front of them. They watched as the paper rolled slowly out, falling into the basket underneath.

Ederling laid a hand across Jake's back. "Listen, Jake, I don't mean to sound so cold. If you're telling me there was something special between you two, then I believe you. And if you're right, then she'll call. Trust your gut. Don't let demons of self-doubt start playing in your head. You don't need that right now."

Jake looked up at him. "Thanks, Don, I appreciate it. I just wish I knew what the hell happened."

"You'll find out. She won't leave you hanging. Not if she's as special as you say. If she does, then she's not, right?"

Jake wished it were that easy. "Right."

"Okay, let's see what we got," Ederling said, grabbing the sheet of paper out of the basket and walking it to the Bell Atlantic Fast-Trac computer.

"We left the estate at eleven-eighteen," Jake said. "Check the first call made after that."

Ederling ran his finger over the sheet of paper. "Okay, I got it. Jesus, whoever it is, she must have called him two dozen times. Here goes nothin'." He punched in the number and depressed the enter key. In a matter of seconds, the name and address of a Warren Josephs appeared on the screen. Ederling let go a long whistle. "Holy shit."

Jake looked up. "What?"

"You're not gonna believe this."

"Who is it?" Jake asked, walking toward him.

"Take a look," Ederling said, stepping to one side.

Jake scanned the computer, his eyes widening like saucers at the sight. "Well, I'll be damned. I don't believe it."

The two men stood looking at each other. Neither one would ever have guessed this. Lianne Rybeck was up to her eyeballs in this mess, though Jake and Ederling still weren't sure in what capacity. But they were determined to find out.

"West View?" Ederling asked.

"Is there a choice?"

WHEN THE TWO men were buckled in his cruiser, Jake flipped on his wig-wags, stuck his red, magnetic beacon on top of his roof, and took off, faster than he should, down Bryant Avenue racing toward 287 East. From there he hooked up with 684 North and made it to the Cross River Road exit in under twenty minutes.

The morning was clear and quiet with only an occasional, feathery finger cloud dotting an otherwise perfectly clear, baby-blue sky. It was only 9:39 A.M., but Jake could already tell it was going to be warm—not unbearable as it had been the previous week, but certainly enough for a relaxing day at the beach. He decided to come in from the north this morning and drove along the northern ridge of the reservoir, glancing periodically at the reflection of the sky and trees on its glassy surface. A slight mist still hung in spots over the mirrorlike water, and Jake found himself wishing he were on it, lying peacefully in a boat, Budweiser in hand, distantly listening to the world pass him by.

"Nice, huh?" Ederling said, staring out his window.

"I'll say."

Ederling looked at his friend. "Still worrying about Valerie?"

"Something's wrong, Donny. I can feel it."

"It'll work out, Jake. I'm sure of it."

Jake took a deep breath. "I hope so."

"We're almost there," Ederling said, staring at Jake's profile as he sped toward Lianne's West View Estate. "You ready?"

"All set."

"Good. Let's do it."

JAKE AND EDERLING were not surprised at the lukewarm reception they received by the guards at the gate on this visit to West View. Lianne had apparently informed them that they would most likely show, and that unless they were carrying a search warrant, they were to be turned away.

"I'm sorry, sir," the guard said. "But I have specific instructions from Mrs. Rybeck not to allow you to enter the grounds."

Jake was beyond miffed. He was furious. "You're *sorry?*" He read the name off the badge the guard was wearing on his chest. "Look, Mr. . . . Brigger. My partner and I are *not* playing games here. Mrs. Rybeck may not have bothered to tell you this, but she is in serious trouble. I guarantee you, if we have to come back with a court order, she will be leaving with us. I would suggest, *sir*, that you call her again and ask that she reconsider her position. We will *not* be happy if we have to come back."

The inside guard with the attack dog had joined the fray and stood back a few feet from the action, his canine sitting at his side. "What's the problem?" he asked his partner.

The second guard turned to look at him. "Rich, I need to speak with you for a second."

The two guards walked away from Jake and Ederling's earshot, speaking softly back and forth. Jake noticed the dogless guard walk into the guardhouse and pick up the phone. He stood with his back to Jake's cruiser, and both Jake and Ederling knew he was calling Lianne.

Jake turned to Ederling. "If they don't let us in, I'm running the thing."

"Down boy. Don't go doing something stupid this late in the game."

The gates began to open as the first guard walked up to Jake's car. "Mrs. Rybeck will see you now," he said businesslike, as if nothing out of the ordinary had just happened.

Jake put his cruiser in drive. "Smart move."

He parked in front of the Rybecks' four-car garage and walked with Ederling down the incline, toward the stone steps leading to the veranda on which they had dined with Severin Rybeck eight days ago. Descending the steps, they could see Lianne sitting alone at the table, eating a bowl of berries with cream.

"You know, Donny," Jake said, "I'm really starting to hate this bitch."

Ederling smiled.

As he approached, Jake noticed an elegant food cart standing off to one side of the table. It was covered with a finely laced white linen, atop which sat a pot of coffee, a glass carafe of grapefruit juice, and two sterling-silver, engraved pots with lids. Jake assumed they contained the fruit.

The *New York Times* lay spread out on the table in front of a seated Lianne. She must have heard their footsteps on the flagstone, for Jake watched her eyes glance up as she sipped her coffee. She did not offer acknowledgment, nor did she keep up eye contact as they continued their approach. Both men came upon the table and stood awkwardly, momentarily silent as Lianne continued reading, ignoring their presence.

Jake walked over to the food cart, reached underneath as he had seen Severin Rybeck do last Sunday, and pulled out two china coffee cups. "Coffee, Don?"

"Please."

Jake poured them each a cup and pulled up a chair, placing his coffee down on the table as he and Ederling both took seats. Jake recalled the last time they were here, remembering that they had hardly won Lianne's heartfelt affection. Still, he was surprised by the blatantly cold shoulder. People usually found it in themselves to afford him some degree of civility, even if they had to dig deep. Like any law enforcement officer, Jake figured it probably had everything to do with the fact that he possessed the power to ruin one's whole day, and then some, if he wanted to. He wondered if it was her money that filled her with such insolence, or if she was actually frightened, delaying the inevitable as long as he would allow.

Jake sipped his coffee for a while, watching the top of her head as she read the paper. He looked at Ederling, who mimed ripping something from his throat with two fingers. Jake knew what it meant. There would be no more messing around. It was go-for-the-jugular time.

"Mrs. Rybeck, you may be a little too comfortable speaking with us here on your own grounds," Jake began. "Perhaps we might all get more accomplished if we took you down to headquarters for questioning."

She looked up from her paper. "This is private property, Mr. Ferguson. *My* property. You should show some gratitude that I have even allowed you to step on it."

"Oh, I *am* grateful, Mrs. Rybeck," Jake said, looking at Ederling. "You grateful, Don?"

Ederling was sipping his coffee. His eyes widened as he put it down. "Oh . . . very."

Lianne's eyes had resumed scanning a page. "What is it you want, gentlemen?" she asked without looking up.

That was his cue. Jake was on. "Tell us your relationship to Warren Parks, Mrs. Rybeck." He turned his stare toward Lianne. She was looking up now. "Got your attention, I see?"

"Mr. Ferguson, I do not *have* a relationship with Mr. Parks. And for the life of me, I can't figure out why you would bother coming all the way out here to ask me such a ridiculous question."

"Are you sure, Mrs. Rybeck?"

Lianne looked at Ederling, then at Jake. "Yes. I am one hundred percent sure."

Jake pursed his lips, nodding his head slightly. "Is that why you dialed his number over two dozen times immediately after we left here last Friday?"

Both Jake and Ederling were eyeing her for the subliminal now, the slightest flit of fear in the eye, a swallow of the throat, a shift in the chair. Whatever it was she was anticipating they had come here to ask her, this was obviously not it. Lianne remained silent, glancing back down at her paper. "I don't know what you're talking about," she finally answered.

If in doubt, lie, right, Lianne? "So, let me get this straight. You don't have any idea what we're talking about?" Jake asked coyly.

"That's right. Not a clue."

"You'll pardon me, Mrs. Rybeck," Jake said, reaching inside his notebook, pulling out the fax he'd been sent earlier that morning, "but Mr. Ederling and I find that very difficult to believe." He unfolded the paper and set it down across the table, laying it out over her *Times.* "In fact, we think it's safe to say that you're lying to us. Now, I keep asking myself one question. Why you would do that? Feel like helping me out?" Jake sat quietly, as if somehow hoping the silence might entice her to talk. For some reason, Wojanowski's words came to his mind. "Give me *crumbs*, Mrs. Rybeck," he finally said. "I'm hungry right now."

He could see her eyes scanning the computer run. "I did not make these calls," she said, handing Jake back the sheet of paper without looking up.

"You didn't?" he asked in disbelief.

"You heard me."

"This *is* your phone number, correct?"

"Do you want me to spell it out for you, Mr. Ferguson?"

Jake had had enough—enough disrespect, enough of the games, enough bullshit. He reached over and ripped the *Times* out from under her nose. Lianne stared up at him with eyes of contempt. "Mrs. Rybeck, I don't think you fully understand, ma'am. You are about this close to being arrested," he said with his thumb and forefinger a half inch apart. "Do *not* mess with me, or I will become the worst virus you have ever had. Am I making myself clear?"

Lianne spoke softly, returning his stare. "Sorry, someone's already beaten you to it."

"What are you hiding, Mrs. Rybeck? Why won't you help us catch this maniac?"

Lianne placed her elbows on the table, resting her chin on the back of her cupped hands. She wondered if Jake would ever fully understand the irony of that question. "Do you have a warrant for my arrest?"

"Should we?"

"Answer my question, Mr. Ferguson."

"No. Not yet."

"I see. Then, tell me this. Do you have a search warrant?"

What makes her so goddamned unflappable? If I didn't know better, I'd think she didn't care. Jake shook his head, anticipating what would come next.

Lianne stared into Jake's eyes, her mocking superiority nearly sending him over the edge. "Then I would say you are shit out of luck, wouldn't you, Mr. Ferguson? Now . . . please leave. You know the way out."

Jake stood, staring at her. "One last question before we go. Who is Chandler Boutet?"

Jake and Ederling could both see that question had somehow hit home. "He was Severin's limousine driver. Why?"

"Does he know Mr. Parks?" Ederling asked.

"How the hell do I know? Why don't you ask him?"

"We'd like to. Do you know how he can be reached?"

Lianne shook her head. "Sorry."

"Do you have any idea why his Jeep was parked outside Warren's apartment?" Jake asked.

She curled her lips and shook her head. "No," she answered curtly. "You said one more question, Mr. Ferguson. That's four if my math is correct. Now, I'll ask you for the second time. Please leave my property before I have you removed."

Jake gave her a long, unfriendly stare. "Don't worry. We're leaving, Mrs. Rybeck."

"Good. Oh, and if you do come back," she added as an afterthought, "don't plan on getting through those gates unless you have a warrant."

"Oh, we'll be back, Mrs. Rybeck," Jake said, his temples throbbing with anger. "You can count on that."

"Good. I'll be waiting."

Jake placed his palms on the frosted glass of the table and leaned across it, speaking directly into Lianne's eyes. "But when you see us next, Mrs. Rybeck, it won't be to talk."

JAKE WAS FURIOUS as he drove his cruiser down Lianne's driveway, not even bothering to acknowledge the guards as he pulled out. This whole thing was starting to get the better of him. He was tired of pushing on a string and hoped like hell something would come of all that he and Ederling were expecting to receive today. Jake felt stymied, unable to break the heavy cloak of secrecy blanketing the darkest core of the case.

He had not anticipated Lianne's antagonism. It wasn't that Jake expected her to just open up, assisting them at every turn, but he had not bargained on the level of animosity and the degree of noncooperation they had just suffered. He exited the huge wrought-iron gates of Lianne's estate and drove up Route 121, suddenly aware of the onset of a massive, almost debilitating tension headache.

Just what the hell is going on here? Jake and Ederling were both faced with myriad confusing facts that, at least on the surface, seemed to defy all logic. Jake's mind spun with the seemingly endless list. *Lianne obviously knows Warren Parks, though she's taking great pains to deny it. Why was Severin's limousine driver's Jeep sitting outside Warren's apartment? Better yet, why was it torched? Who was DS, and what was his connection to the case? And where the hell is Scotty? Was it his prints the State Police had found on the letter sent to Jake?* There was no shortage of unanswered questions, though Jake knew from experience that would soon change. Breaking a case is similar to spring-cleaning a room—it often gets messier before the job is complete.

What is the underlying thread that Don and I are missing? Lianne is not a stupid woman. She has to know that we will indeed come back, and probably take her with us. Why would she risk that? Why would she almost invite it? Every action Lianne took this morning almost seemed designed to alienate and offend. Jake could only assume she knew something they did not—something that made his threats inconsequential in her mind. *But what? What could make a person so immune to the imminent threat of arrest and incarceration?*

Jake figured it could only be one of two things. Lianne was either confident that she could make most any bail or, worse yet, was planning something herself and thus merely stalling for time. Something was afoot—something he and Ederling had either missed or of which they were completely in the dark. Jake even wondered now if arresting Lianne Rybeck would, in fact, be the most prudent course of action—assuming they actually had enough evidence to do so. And of that, he had serious doubts.

Perhaps it would be better to put a set of eyes on her and watch her every move, see where she went and with whom she met. Jake knew she was smart, but he also knew he could run rings around her procedurally. But he reasoned she couldn't be *that* smart, or she would never have called Warren from her home phone. If Jake played his cards right, he might just be able to leverage Mrs. Lianne Rybeck for his own gain, and if he was *really* lucky, perhaps right up to closure on the case.

Jake could hardly contain his fury. "Can you fucking believe that bitch?" he asked Ederling, turning left onto Cross River Road.

"*That* is one confident lady."

"Yeah, *too* confident."

Jake picked up the phone, punching in the speed-dial number to his office. "Hey, Cis. What's up?" Quite a bit, his secretary told him. He had received a UPS package from Philadelphia, as well as a phone call from the State Police lab. "Good. Anything else?" he asked, secretly hoping that Valerie had called.

"Nope. That's it."

Ederling knew why he asked and could hear the disappointment in his voice. "All right, do me a favor, will you?" Jake asked. Time was an issue. "Call Royston Craddock at Morson Grayhead and ask him for his fax number. Open the UPS package and fax the contents to him personally. Make it clear on the cover sheet that it is for his eyes *only*. Got it?"

"Got it. Anything else?"

"Yeah, give me the number of the crime lab."

Cissy left for a moment, retrieved it from somewhere in the office, and recited it to him. "When are you coming back?"

"We're on our way now. Should be there in half an hour."

Jake pushed the END button on his phone and dialed the number to the lab. "The Philadelphia Exchange stuff come?" Ederling asked as Jake waited for a ring.

"Yes. If we're lucky, maybe we can learn something."

Ederling stared out his window, soaking in the beauty that is northern Westchester. "Why am I not excited?"

Jake wasn't either. "You never know," he said as someone picked up the phone on the third ring.

"Lab, Spellman speaking."

"Art, it's Jake. You called?"

"Oh, hi, Jake. Yeah, as a matter of fact, I did. We got a make on those prints off the beer bottle you dropped by on Saturday."

"And?"

"Does the name Warren Parks mean anything to you?"

The first real, court-qualified connection! "Sure does."

"Well, that's your boy."

Jake put his palm over the phone. "Prints were Warren's," he said to Ederling. "Social?" he asked Art, jotting down Warren's social security number in his notebook. "Okay, Art, thanks. Good work."

"That's why we make the big bucks."

Jake speed-dialed his office again. "Hi, Cis. Me again. Listen, I need you to run a triple I for me." He gave her Warren's name and social security number and told her to call him as soon as she received a response.

A triple I is an acronym for the FBI's Interstate Identification Index. Part of the larger National Crime Information Computer (NCIC) data bank, it is used by criminal justice agencies to retrieve identifying data on individuals with criminal records. If the person in question is on file, NCIC will teletype a return message to the inquiring agency listing the Index record and the location of databases storing the criminal-history records of that individual. If the record is housed within the FBI's computer, it, too, will be sent. If the FBI does not house the information sought, then it becomes necessary to contact the proper state's Bureau of Identification. The record is then sent to the inquiring agency via the National Law Enforcement Telecommunications System, or NLETS.

Triple I is a computerized, on-line system designed for efficiency of response, as well as ultimately freeing up the FBI's own Identification Division, and usually furnishes information to the inquiring agency within seconds of the request. The database currently contains records for over 10 million people who were either born in 1956 or later or whose first arrest occurred on or after July 1, 1974.

The FBI encourages its use for a number of reasons, not least of which is that it is by far the most convenient, time-saving, and highly effective way of ascertaining additional information about an individual's criminal history. Jake knew it would tell him what, if any, aliases Warren had used, scars, tattoos or other identifying marks, and additional dates of birth or social security numbers, as well as any jail time Warren may have served.

"You think he's got a rap sheet?" Ederling asked.

Jake shrugged. Right now, nothing would surprise him, whether he did or didn't. "We'll find out."

Jake dialed the number for Morson Grayhead in New York, asking to speak with Royston Craddock. "Good morning, Mr. Craddock. This is Jake Ferguson."

"Jake! How are you? I've been thinking about you, young man. Any leads on the case yet?"

Young man? There's something he didn't hear every day. He wasn't sure whether he liked it or not. "Between you and me, Mr. Craddock, we're getting very close, sir."

"I suppose it wouldn't be very professional for me to ask who your suspects are, would it?"

"Probably not."

"I didn't think so. I just want whoever it is caught so I can begin to pull this ship around. The headhunters have been circling this place like vultures in the desert. It's been a difficult time here, Jake, as I'm sure you can appreciate."

It's always the firm first. A few days ago Craddock was trying to get Severin ousted for just this type of myopia. *What is it about that place?* "Yes, I can," Jake said, noticing the blatant absence in Craddock's response of any interest in bringing the perpetrator to justice. Jake was disappointed. He thought Craddock was different. "I'm assuming you are also interested in seeing that justice is done," Jake said, hoping he might hear something at least *approaching* human sympathy.

"Oh, of course, Jake, of course," Craddock answered, somewhat embarrassed. "That is paramount. Absolutely no question about it. Seeing this person caught and brought to justice supersedes all else. Please pardon me if I seemed cold or rude. I assure you that is not the case. It's just that . . . well, frankly . . . it's just that I am only one man. I can't do anything to bring those poor people back. But I can save Morson Grayhead. I guess I'm just trying to focus my energies on that which I can change. Please accept my apologies if I appeared indifferent."

That was the Craddock Jake thought he knew. Somehow he felt better knowing the man's heart was in the right place. *Apology accepted.* "With any luck, maybe you'll be able to put this behind you sooner rather than later. Keep your fingers crossed."

"That sounds good, Jake. I will. We could use a break around here."

Royston Craddock would probably make more money this year than Jake would earn in a lifetime. Jake was ashamed to admit it, but deep down, he really didn't care what happened to Morson Grayhead. "It must be difficult," Jake said, feigning empathy.

"So," Craddock said with an uplifted voice, "I'm assuming you think I can help in some way, or you wouldn't be calling. I know how busy you must be. Did you get the records from Philadelphia?"

"Well, yes, as a matter of fact. That's why I'm calling. If you haven't gotten a fax from my secretary yet, you will."

"She just called."

"Good. Mr. Craddock, I can't tell you how quickly we need that information. If at all possible, could you please attend to it at your earliest possible opportunity?"

"As soon as it comes, I will look at it and see how big a job it appears to be. Whatever it takes is what it will get. Nothing will be spared."

"Can you do it today?"

"I already have a team waiting. You get me the fax and we'll be running within the half hour."

"That's great news. Thank you."

"No, Jake. Thank you," Craddock said with sincerity.

"You're welcome. How long do you think it will take?"

"Hard to say really, especially without seeing the computer run. I can't imagine it's going to be that big a deal, though. Our stock is generally not a big mover. Consequently our open interest tends to be low relative to other, more volatile companies."

Open interest. There's that term again. Craddock had explained it to him once before. "Open interest? That's the number of contracts outstanding, right?" Jake asked, pretty sure he had it right.

"Very good, Jake. I'm impressed."

"Don't be. It's the only thing I've learned about Wall Street so far."

"That doesn't surprise me. It's a strange place."

No shit.

"But listen, Jake. If you want my opinion, your problems aren't going to come from our end, they're going to come from the different houses we contact."

Jake didn't like open-ended problems. "How so?"

"Well . . . once we request information from the respective houses on the list, we can't do any more. How fast they respond is up to them."

This was a can of worms Jake hadn't thought of. Just how Machiavellian were Wall Street competitors? He may not have learned much, but he'd learned enough to know it was *not* a business for the faint of heart. But still, he could not imagine they would delay specifically to prolong the investigation, to help fatten their own bottom line or help their chances of landing some big catch from Morson Grayhead. *They're still Americans, are they not? They could not possibly be that cold. Could they?* Jake wondered if he was being naive.

Jake didn't know how to respond. "What are you saying, Mr. Craddock? You're not implying that they would delay on purpose, are you?"

"Oh, God, no. I'm not saying that at all. I would be shocked if that happened. We are all competitors, Jake, but this . . . well, this whole thing has crossed a line. I know these people. It could easily have been them, and they all know it. No, all I'm saying is that once we ask, we can't control turnaround time."

Jake looked at his watch. "Try this. How about telling them the police expect answers by two o'clock? Is that logistically feasible?"

"Very. This is not that difficult, Jake. It's all computerized. All their option departments have to do is punch in some information and they should be able to bring it up in a matter of minutes."

That's all Jake needed to hear. "Fine. Any house doesn't respond in a reasonable time period, call my office. We'll want to know, okay?"

"We can do that."

"So you'll call me as you get responses from around the Street?"

"Up to you. We can give it to you all at once or give it to you as they come in to us."

"Let's do the latter, if that's not a problem."

"No problem at all. Consider it done."

"Okay. Just call the office. If I'm not there, ask to speak to Cissy. She's my assistant. You can give her the names and numbers."

"Numbers?" Craddock asked. "What kind of numbers?"

"Anything you can get. Socials, phone numbers, which contracts, how many, purchase dates. Pay particular attention to those purchased prior to the first burning."

"You happen to have that date handy?" Craddock asked. Jake told him. "Okay, will do."

"Also, look for any open interest of size belonging to one individual or entity. If someone's doing this for money, they're not going to own just a handful of those things."

"I agree," Craddock said, sounding confident, almost raring to go. "We're ready on this end."

"Good. Happy hunting."

HELL HATH
NO FURY . . .

Book V

I N THE WAKE of the burnings and subsequent corporate mayhem, Morson Grayhead's stock had plummeted from a mid-August high of nearly sixty-four dollars a share to a closing low of forty-eight on Friday. If there is one thing traders and professional investors can't tolerate, it's uncertainty, and right now Morson Grayhead had plenty to go around. Royston Craddock was right about one thing. Wall Street's executive head-hunting corps was circling the firm, madly trying to lasso their fair share of rats fleeing a burning ship. No one on the Street was sure if or when there would be another murder, and if there was, to what degree it would speed up an already accelerated process. But, judging from the stock's recent fall, it didn't appear as though anyone felt like experiencing it firsthand.

Warren Parks was very much aware of the stock's travails. In fact, by his calculations, he had already turned an eighteen-thousand-dollar investment into over three hundred thousand dollars. Not bad for a few nights' work. He had purchased the April fifty-five puts—in essence betting that the stock price would drop. Every point drop under fifty-five was fifteen thousand dollars in his pocket. But Warren had spent many years alone in a cell, enough to learn the ins and outs of Wall Street's ways and had consequently played it smart. The April expiration date was far enough out to warrant an excessive buildup of time premium in the contracts. So much so that, by the time the stock broke below fifty dollars a share on Wednesday, he was actually making closer to twenty-five thousand a point. But three hundred thousand–plus lying on paper in some brokerage account was a far cry from having it sitting in cash in an off-shore bank. Warren needed to make one more trade—the most important of his life.

Warren was well aware that options have a next-day settlement, meaning that once bought, they must be paid for by the next business day. Conversely, once sold, the brokerage house must make proceeds available in the same time frame. Warren knew if he could just hang on long enough to close out his position and settle the trade, he could have his three-hundred-thousand-dollar option settlement, and the remaining cash in his Thompson McElvay account, wired via Fed funds to his Cayman Island bank on Tuesday. And for Warren, Fed funds were the magic words. They meant no waiting for the check to clear—over six hundred thousand in total, real-time, on-line, and most important of all, spendable. All he'd need to do then was get out of Dodge. He hadn't yet decided how problematic that might be, but did know one thing: no one was going to stand in his way.

Warren knew the authorities were onto him. But what did that mean? Obviously, if the authorities had enough for an arrest warrant, Jake would have done so Friday night. But Jake didn't. Warren knew they were only fishing, hoping against hope they might trip him up, get something, anything, they might later be able to use against him. At least they *were* fishing until he had opened his big mouth. He worried that he had mentioned the rapes to Jake, and though he didn't know it Friday night, apparently that was privileged information.

It was also true that a very dead body was now lying in a Jeep outside his apartment. But still, that didn't tell the cops anything specific, even if they did harbor pet theories. If only he'd been able to get his hands on that trash.

Warren knew from here on out he could not afford the slightest slip. The most insignificant, minor infraction could easily land him in jail again—perhaps for the rest of his life. He would rather die than let that happen. There could be absolutely *no* transgressions: no littering, no jaywalking, no speeding. For the remaining hours he had left in the United States, Warren Parks would have to give new meaning to the term *squeaky-clean*.

Okay, he thought, so I knew about the rapes. Still, he wasn't sure that would be enough to charge him with the murders. Show me the proof, boys, he kept telling himself. Prove it was me. Warren knew they couldn't. In fact, as far as he could tell, about the only thing they had on him for sure was purse snatching, and that was hardly enough to go checking every international passenger's passport.

Warren thought of all this and more as he lay in bed in Scotty's sparsely furnished guest room, the morning sun shining brightly through the open slats of the venetian blinds. He yawned, rubbing sleep from his eyes, trying to ignore the little knot growing ever so steadily in his stomach. His flight to St. Barts was due to depart at 10:10 A.M. the next morning, and he knew the next twenty-four hours were going to prove the most important, *and* most difficult, of his life. Warren kept reminding himself that he only had to wait another twenty-four measly hours. One thousand four hundred and forty lousy minutes.

But Warren's work was far from done. First, he needed to sell his Morson Grayhead position. He'd already decided not to inform Thompson McElvay of his intent to wire the money out until tomorrow morning. No branch manager wants to lose that kind of account, and Warren didn't feel like drawing attention to himself any sooner than necessary. He knew they wouldn't like it, but what could they do? After all, it was his money. And in Warren's mind, he had earned every penny.

Two things clung unnervingly to his psyche: Lianne Rybeck, and his trash. Lianne was a loose cannon whose fate he wrestled with as he stared at the popcorn stucco of Scotty's ceiling. Of all the people on earth, she alone knew it all, or most of it anyway. Certainly enough to cause Warren problems. Whether or not she would was another question. But he knew something, too—something he was certain she would rather die than have let out of the bag. Lianne had been his cash cow since he was released from prison, and the only thing that bothered Warren was that he hadn't been able to squeeze her sooner. He'd love to be rid of her, but time was running short. In his mind he didn't dare take the chance. So many things could go wrong, and he knew he would be lucky if he'd thought of half of them. As much as Warren hated the idea, he saw little option but to let her live. If only she knew how lucky she was.

But his trash was a different story. It was the one truly remaining loose end. He wished like hell he'd burned the magazine scraps from the letter he'd written Jake and kicked himself time and again for missing so obvious a flaw. He worried that it was always the little things. Warren wasn't sure if the cops would even think to look, but knew better than to underestimate them. Sometimes even *they* can't help but stumble upon a clue.

It was with some consternation that Warren considered just how that meddling Jake Ferguson had come waltzing unannounced right into his face. He'd read about this fire marshal from Westchester County and did not come away feeling warm and fuzzy. Ferguson could present problems if left to his own devices too long. Warren figured his plane was leaving just about as late as was feasible. Any longer, and it was a crapshoot just who would end up the winner.

But even if the authorities did find the clippings in his trash, would that prove enough to issue a warrant for his arrest? After all, Warren had thought enough to hand the note to an unsuspecting Scotty. It was Scotty's prints they would find on it, not his. And if his plan went off without a hitch, Scotty would be securely locked behind bars by this time tomorrow—at least long enough to confuse matters and act as a smoke screen while he taxied down the tarmac at JFK.

There was much to be done, and little room for error. All his waiting and studying, all his years of planning, came down to less than one day. Warren closed his eyes, allowing himself to dream what a new life would be like as a relatively rich man in Brazil with six hundred thousand dollars in cash. Brazil has no extradition treaty with the United States and seemed an excellent and logical choice. Warren only hoped he hadn't missed anything. As he lay on his back smiling, hands cupped under his head, he was surprised by a light rap on the door.

Warren's heart stopped for a moment. "Yeah."

"Good morning, Warren," Scotty said, pushing the door open with a foot, carrying a tray in his hands. "I brought you some muffins and orange juice. Freshly squeezed, just the way you like."

If Warren was quintessentially type A, Scotty was his mirror image. He was passive to a fault, and like a child, completely unaware of the human species' ability to lie, cheat, and harm. It had never once dawned on him that he was being used. In Scotty's eyes, Warren Parks was the best friend he ever had.

Scotty wore a pair of cutoff chinos, Sperry Top-Siders, and a plain white T-shirt with several yellow stains on one side. He had shaved this morning, and his dimpled cheeks had a clean, almost delicate appearance.

Warren fluffed his pillows against the wall, sitting up like a surprised mom on Mother's Day. "Why, thank you, Scotty. That was very nice of you."

Scotty's face grew into a broad smile, the kind a son wears after receiving the all-important "atta boy" from his dad. "You see here," he said, pointing at the muffins after laying the tray down on the bed to Warren's side. "I cut and toasted them for you. I hope they're not too dark."

Warren could not wait to get rid of this moron. He eyed the muffins, frowning slightly. "They're a little dark, but they'll be okay. Thanks anyway, Scotty. I appreciate it."

Scotty frowned and wiped away a long wisp of nutmeg-brown hair. He reached down for the tray. "Here, let me do them again," he said hurriedly, desperate to please. "I have more. I'll do them right this time."

"No, no," Warren said, waving Scotty off with a hand. "They're fine. Really."

"You sure?"

"Positive."

Scotty sat Indian-style on the floor, watching Warren eat. He was so happy to have his only friend staying at his house. Warren chewed, chasing the muffin down with a swig of juice. He looked at Scotty, so serene and clueless, just eyeing him as he would a puppy at a pet store. "What?" Warren finally asked.

Scotty smiled, exposing a portion of his white, Chiclet-like teeth. "Oh, nothing," he said coyly.

"Don't give me that," Warren said knowingly, playing his part to the hilt. "You've got something up your sleeve. Don't you, you sly little bugger?"

"I have a surprise for you."

"Really?" Warren asked through a full mouth. "Well, don't just sit there. Show it to me."

"Can't."

"What do you mean, you can't? How am I going to be surprised if I can't see it?"

"Oh, you can see it, I just can't bring it to you."

"Too big?"

Scotty's camel-colored eyes seemed to glisten with excitement. "Yep, too big."

"What the hell did you buy, Scotty? A new car? What do you mean, it's 'too big'?"

"You'll see."

Warren closed his eyes and breathed deeply. He opened them, painting a forced smile on his face. "So when can I see it?"

"Can I show it to you now?" Scotty asked as he stood. "Please?"

"Sure." Warren only had to put up with this a few more hours. "Where is it?"

"In the basement."

"The basement?" The faintest tug of fear gripped Warren's heart. "What the hell is it, Scotty?"

Scotty was clearly excited now. "That's for me to know and you to find out."

I'm thrilled, Warren thought. He slid the tray over and swung his legs out of bed. "Okay," he said as he got out. "I'm yours. You're not going to make me close my eyes, are you? I'll kill myself on the stairs."

Scotty chuckled. "No," he answered as a five-year-old might when asked a ridiculous, leading question from a parent. "Well, maybe. But only when we get down there."

"I'll follow you."

Scotty scampered joyfully into the hall. "Come on."

They stood at the top of the stairs, Warren waiting for Scotty to lead the way. Warren had to admit he was interested. Maybe it was something expensive. After all, thanks to Mommy Dearest, Scotty never did want for cash. Warren followed him down the stairs, frowning as he heard the unmistakable sound of chains rattle from somewhere beyond. He was suddenly filled with fear, concerned at just what the hell Scotty had done.

Scotty took his hand. "Close your eyes."

Warren was annoyed with all this childish crap. His throat began to constrict slightly. "Scotty, I don't have time for this shit," he said, losing patience. "What do you have down here?"

Scotty was clearly hurt, hanging his head as if reprimanded. "Come on, Warren. Close your eyes. *Please?* You'll like it. I promise."

Warren took a deep breath. He prayed it was a dog. "All right, all right."

Scotty took Warren by the hand, leading him carefully through a door toward the boiler in back. "Okay. Open them."

Warren stood, staring in horror at what he saw. Valerie stared back at him, her face ashen, her bloodshot eyes darting maniacally about. She was chained at both feet to the pipes of the boiler, and Warren could see blood oozing from the bones of her ankles. Warren continued to stare, literally lost for words.

"I found her when I went to Jake's apartment. When you told me about her. I knew you liked her, so I brought her for you."

Warren turned to Scotty, his face pulsating with rage. "Are you out of your fucking mind?" he boomed. "You mindless cretin! Do you have any idea what you've done?"

Scotty cowered, the dumplinglike tire around his waist heaving in and out as tears burst from his eyes. "I'm sorry, Warren," he blubbered. "I'm sorry. I thought you'd like it."

"Like it? Like it!" Warren raged, running his fingers through his hair. "Jesus Christ, Scotty." Warren turned wildly in half circles, trying desperately to think of his alternatives. "I take my eyes off you for one weekend . . . one *lousy* weekend, and you kidnap the fire marshal's old lady?"

Valerie lay on a dirty wool blanket that Scotty had thoughtfully laid for her at the base of the furnace. She struggled with her chains, moaning something through the electrical tape wrapped tightly around her mouth. "Shut up, you fucking whore!" Warren screamed, kicking her in the head with the heel of his foot. Her head slammed into the corner of the boiler's steel casing, breaking the flesh on her already pounding skull. Blood dripped from the back of Valerie's scalp as her head shot down. She didn't realize she was bleeding as she curled up into a ball, huddling against another possible onslaught.

Warren's fury was uncontrolled. He reached down and grabbed an ironing board, whipping it across the room, sending it smashing into Scotty's washing machine. "Have you gone stark raving mad?" he screamed, ripping one of Scotty's drawings off a wall. "What the hell are we going to do with this bitch? Huh?" Warren poked the side of his head violently. "Did you think of *that?* Huh, Einstein? Did you even bother to think of that?"

Warren grabbed a hammer off a shelf. "Here. Kill her. *Now!* You have to kill her, Scotty. Do it!"

Valerie remained huddled in a ball, frightened now for her life. If she could only break free, she knew she could probably lay both these maniacs flat. But not with her legs shackled, not in this predicament.

Scotty was near babbling now. "But, Warren, I . . . I don't want to . . ."

"You don't want? You don't *want?*" The hammer which Warren had flung stuck halfway out of the wall. "*Shit!* All right, I gotta think. Think, Warren. *Think.*" He stopped in midmotion, as if zapped with a stun gun. Warren still had to stick with his plan. He *had* to liquidate his options. "What time is it?"

Scotty was frightened, never intending to bring such wrath down upon himself. "Time?"

"Yes, you moron! What time is it?"

"Almost eleven," Scotty said, looking at his watch.

What was done was done. Warren could not very well wish Valerie away. He took a long, deep breath, trying with all his might to regroup. "All right. Watch her, Scotty. You understand that? Watch her. I have to make a call. I'll be right back."

Warren left, bounding up the steps to the kitchen as perspiration dripped from his brow. He slowed when he got to the phone on the wall, dialing his broker's number by heart. "Come on, come on," he said frantically, egging the phone on. "Yeah, Ted, it's Warren. Listen, I think I've ridden this Morson Grayhead fiasco about as long as I should."

"What a mess, huh? Talk about blood money."

Warren was a chameleon, able to change at the flick of a switch if the circumstances called for it. "Yeah, I feel almost guilty. That's the kind of luck you don't wish for, right?"

"Christ, I'll say. I don't know whether to be happy for you or not. I mean . . . you just hate to hear stuff like that, you know?"

"Yeah, I know. Hey, but what are you gonna do? I'm not giving it back. You can bet on that."

"Hell, a trade like that? It's a once-in-a-lifetime thing, Warren. You made a bloody fortune."

"Yeah, well, liquidate the position, will you? I think I'm going to take my money and go home."

"Okay. As soon as the stock opens."

His broker's words stung Warren. "What do you mean? It's not trading yet?"

"Not yet. There's an order imbalance. The Exchange has delayed opening."

"The options aren't trading?" Warren asked, his heart beginning to palpitate now.

"No. They never do. Not while the stock's closed."

Warren dropped his head in the palm of his hand, rubbing his forehead with his fingers. He couldn't believe his misfortune. Not only did he have his nemesis's old lady in chains downstairs, but now he couldn't even liquidate his winnings. He was almost worried sick at the prospect of what else could possibly go wrong. All these years of planning, and now events out of his control were beginning to dictate the final outcome. Warren felt as though he were struggling to maintain his sanity. "Well, when's it going to open?"

"You're asking me? Five minutes from now. Five hours from now. Maybe tomorrow. Who knows?"

"Tomorrow?" Warren asked disjointedly. This was definitely a bad omen. "You're joking, right?"

"Sort of. I've seen it before, though."

"Any idea what the news is?"

"Not a clue. I sure hope it's not another burning."

Warren almost screamed his response. "It's not . . . I mean . . ." Careful, boy, careful now, he reminded himself. "I mean, I just pray that's not the case."

"Hope you're right."

Warren's plan was falling apart in front of his eyes. His mind began to speed in concentric circles, unable even to comprehend the possibility that it might all go bust. "Okay, the second that stock opens, I want you to liquidate that position. Got that?"

"Got it. Any particular price, or do you just want out at the market?"

"Make it a market order. Just get me out."

"The whole position?"

"Yes, the whole thing."

"Okay," his broker said, repeating Warren's order for his own protection. "So you want me to sell one hundred and fifty Morson Grayhead, April fifty-five puts at the market when the stock opens, right?"

"Right."

"Consider it done."

"I'm not at home now, so I'll call you later."

"Give me a number where I can reach you in case there's a problem."

Warren prayed that there damn well better not be a problem. He'd lose his mind if he couldn't pull this off. "I'm on the road. I'll call you."

Warren hung up and stood motionless for a few moments, his hand still squeezing the phone. He was so close and yet seemed to be inching further away with each passing minute. He had to think. Warren had spent years of his life hatching this scheme, and he'd be damned if he was going to let a few last-minute fireworks screw the whole thing up. He wanted desperately to go for a walk, but didn't dare show his face in public. For now, pacing the linoleum kitchen floor would have to do.

Warren's heart hammered mercilessly against his chest. He closed his eyes, alternating between deep breathing and wiggling his arms at his sides in an effort to relax his shoulders. His nostrils flared as he became aware that his breath was coming raw in his throat. Warren rubbed his temples slowly but firmly with his fingers, staring at the toaster oven Scotty had used to prepare his muffins just a short while ago. There had to be a way out of this mess. Warren was sure that if only he could think hard enough, he could find a way to use Scotty's fiasco to his advantage.

But how? He poured himself a glass of water and sat at the kitchen table, staring at a wall outlet, thinking it all through. Warren had hoped to lay this whole mess squarely at Scotty's front door. There was clearly motive and he was about as loosely wound as a cat's yarn spool. And certainly once the police identified his prints on Jake's note and found all the press clippings Warren had stuffed in his dresser drawer, Warren had no doubt they would nail Scotty to the wall. But now, just as he could smell it, that overgrown kindergartner had shoved a rake handle through his spokes. Warren was furious with himself for ever letting Scotty out of his sight.

His mind worked overtime. He stopped breathing, staring almost meditatively at the wall, and then suddenly it hit him. Of course, he thought. It was almost too good to be true. Why hadn't he thought of it sooner? Scotty, in his simple, inexplicable little world, had inadvertently handed Warren his coup de grâce without even knowing it. What better circumstances could Warren possibly hope for? All he had to do was call the authorities, anonymously finger Scotty, and have them find Jake's girl chained to the boiler right in his very own basement. They would surely fry him then. As surely as hens lay eggs, the DA would make every conceivable human effort to see him sentenced to death.

But still, he had to do something about Valerie. She had seen him. She knew who he was. There was no question she would have to die, and he had to find a way to make Scotty do it. In a thousand lifetimes, Warren could not imagine that Scotty could hold up under the pressure of a police interrogation. He would melt into a heap of blubber, collapsing under the bright lights and intimidation. Scotty would squeal louder than a stuck pig, forever banging his head against a wall, bewailing how horrible a person he had become, how difficult it is to remember. Once the cops heard that, anything else he had to say would hardly make a difference. They'd nail him with the whole thing, regardless of the remainder of his story. He could plead innocence on the Morson Grayhead murders all he wanted. The authorities would surely attempt to pin the entire debacle on him. Case closed, Warren thought. Brazil, here I come.

Maybe everything was going to be all right, after all. Scotty had actually done Warren a favor, though its eventual purpose would be far different from what Scotty had originally planned. As for Morson Grayhead—Warren would just have to have faith. He had to trust that fate would see him through safely to his just and much deserved reward. Warren could not imagine that the stock would not open today. The Exchange might delay opening a few hours, maybe even most of the day. But they would surely resume trading sometime before today's close. As long as he could liquidate his position, Warren didn't care if it happened five minutes after the market opened or five minutes before it closed. It just had to happen today.

He rose from the table and walked to the top of the stairs. "Scotty!" he boomed. "Scotty! Come here!"

"Coming!" came the faint reply from somewhere in the bowels of the basement.

Some time passed. Warren could hear nothing. "Scotty!" he yelled down the basement steps again. "Come up here!"

Scotty appeared a few seconds later, winded, standing at the top of the stairs. He was frightened, the human version of a dog with its tail between its legs. "Hi, Warren."

Warren had taken a seat at the kitchen table. "Scotty, have a seat, will you please?" he said casually, motioning to a chair with a free hand.

Scotty sat, his arms wrapped tightly around his chest. His face was red. He had obviously been crying. "Warren, I'm real sorry—"

"That's why I called you up here," Warren interrupted. "I've been thinking about what you did. You know something, Scotty? That was the nicest thing anybody's ever done for me." Warren smiled, waiting for Scotty to show some sign of relaxing. "I know I got angry, and I feel really bad about that. I still want to be your friend. Can you forgive me for being so mean and selfish? I'm very sorry."

Scotty looked at him skeptically. "You mean it?"

"Yes. Very much. Will you accept my apology?"

Scotty eyed him pensively. "Did you mean those bad things you said down there?"

"No, Scotty, you know that." Warren hung his head in fake shame. "You know what a temper I have. Would you be my friend again? *Please?*"

"Oh, Warren," Scotty said with a beaming face. "You bet I can. You really, really scared me."

"I know."

"You really like her?"

It was one of the hardest acting roles Warren could ever remember performing. He hated this idiot sitting across from him and wanted more than he could admit to rip his heart out of his chest. "I like her very much, Scotty. More than I can say."

"Oh, thank you, Warren. That makes me so happy. I wanted to show you how much you mean to me."

"Well . . . you did that." Warren looked up at Scotty, his face revealing a certain unease. "Just one question, though. How'd you get her here? No one saw you, did they?"

"Oh, no," Scotty said, shaking his head vigorously. "No one saw me. I was real smart about it."

Warren cringed inside. "Tell me," he said, hoping he would not be terrified at what he heard. For a fleeting moment he envisioned an infantry of ninja SWAT killers circling Scotty's house. "Tell me how you did it."

"Well . . . it was kind of a mistake," Scotty said with the faintest of smiles. "I was watchin' Jake's place just like you asked. I looked around, but it was early. There was no one anywhere. So, I go to the door. You know? I was thinking maybe it'd be unlocked, I could take a look around. I remember you tellin' me he wouldn't be there. So I was just standin' there, about to touch the knob, when she opened it up. I think she was getting the paper. She scared me, Warren. I mean, I almost pissed myself."

"Boy, I bet," Warren said, feigning commiseration. In reality, he wasn't sure he could stand to hear the rest. "Then what did you do?"

"It really threw me at first. I had to think so fast, you know?" Scotty looked toward the floor. "I'm not too good at that. I thought she was going to scream. Next thing I know, I push her. I pushed her hard. I was so scared." Scotty's voice trailed off as he spoke, as if he was afraid that what he was about to say would anger his friend. "Anyway, I must've got her off-balance or something, 'cause next thing I know, she's falling." Scotty drew silent, looking up at Warren with fear in his eyes.

"Yeah?" Warren asked anxiously. "And?"

"I didn't mean to, Warren," Scotty said, withdrawing from the table. "I'm really sorry. It was a mistake."

"What?" Warren asked, his patience thinning by the second. "What was a mistake?"

"Well . . . she hit her head," Scotty said in a faint voice.

"What?"

"I said she hit her head."

Warren didn't seem to understand. "So?"

"She hit it pretty bad, Warren. Right at the corner, you know? Where the baseboards meet? But I remembered how much you liked her. I think I ended up doin' pretty good."

"Oh, you did, Scotty. You did. But how'd you know it was her?"

"Her hair. I could tell by her hair. It's so red, just like you said."

Warren nodded. "So, what happened next? Was she moving?"

"No," Scotty said as he shook his head. "So now I'm scared. You know? I mean, she's bleeding and all, and I never meant to hurt her. Never."

"But how did you get her here?"

"I looked around and found a bedspread in a closet. I just rolled her up inside it and flipped it over my shoulder like I was taking it out to get cleaned or somethin'. I felt a little weird. Like an actor or something. I think I kind of liked it, though. Is that bad?"

"Bad?" Warren asked with a grin. "Shit, no . . . you sly dog. Well, I'll be damned. I'm really surprised, Scotty. I never would have thought you had it in you."

Scotty smiled, full of pride. "Maybe you two can get married, you know? Like Josephine. I don't like it when you pay for your dates. Anyway, I think she likes you."

Oh, man, Warren thought, how dark is this kid's cave? "Did she tell you that?"

"Well, no . . . she didn't use those words. She really didn't say much of anything."

"She was unconscious, Scotty."

"No, no. I mean when she finally woke up downstairs. I think I saw it in her eyes. They looked filled with excitement."

Warren thought *excitement* was probably the wrong word. *Absolute horror* was probably more like it. "So that was it? You just picked her up and brought her here?"

"Yeah. Are you proud of me?"

"Just like that? Did you clean up the blood?"

"Yep. Every drop."

Warren simply could not bring himself to believe that Scotty had pulled it off without a hitch. "And that was it?"

"That's it."

"You sure?"

Scotty nodded. "Yeah, I'm sure."

Warren didn't know whether he could trust Scotty. He knew he could trust him morally, as a friend, if that's what you could call him. Warren knew Scotty would never turn on him. But it was Scotty's mental capabilities and perception of reality that alarmed Warren. Scotty was so removed from life's dangers and the way things really worked, Warren figured only the devil knew what had really happened at Jake's place. But, no one had yet burst down their door, automatic rifles cocked at the ready. Warren thought that maybe it did *really* happen the way Scotty said. Whatever the truth, the fact remained Valerie was down there now, just begging to be used as a pawn in Warren's larger scheme. He chuckled inwardly, thinking that he couldn't have planned it better himself. And it certainly didn't matter now anyway. Valerie Medforth was as good as dead.

"I don't believe it," Warren said, unable to comprehend that Scotty had apparently really pulled it off. Warren couldn't help but ask himself if wonders would never cease. "Thank you, Scotty. You have no idea how special she could have been to me. She could have made me very happy."

Warren almost felt a tug at his heart, but there was no room for emotions right now. It excited him that Scotty had brought this pretty little creature into his life. He'd have some fun before this night was through. He toyed with the idea of playing with her now. He still had many hours to kill and could feel the beginning warmth of an erection just imagining the enjoyment he could have with a chained woman in the twilight hours of her life. Maybe later, he thought. No, *definitely* later. But right now there was business to tend to. There was still the thorny issue of Valerie's death. Warren knew he faced the sales job of his life.

"So . . . listen," he said to a proud and beaming Scotty. "I want you to know how happy I am, Scotty. That was really, really nice, your bringing her to me like that and all. But I think we have a little problem. I'm not sure, mind you, but I think so."

Scotty's eyes narrowed with concern. "A problem? What kind of problem, Warren?"

Warren scratched the top of his head. "Well . . . now don't take this wrong, okay?"

"Okay."

"Well, it's just that you kind of took her against her will. Know what I mean? It wasn't exactly her idea to come here, was it?"

"No," Scotty said, his chagrined voice conveying disappointment. "But I didn't mean to hurt her. Anyway, after you guys talk and stuff, I don't think she's gonna be mad. You're nice. She'll like you."

Warren exhaled deeply, rubbing his hand across his mouth. "Well, that's the problem, Scotty. Did you know the police can arrest you for taking someone like that?"

"Like Valerie?"

Warren took a long breath. "No, not like Valerie." He was digging deep now, trying desperately to remain calm. "I mean the *way* you took her. Just stealing her like that. The police get real mad about that. They call it kidnapping. You know? You've seen it in the movies before."

"Yeah . . . but we don't want money or nothin'. She's just . . . I don't know . . . kind of like a wife, you know? You can talk to her. She can be like . . . like your special friend. You won't have to buy girls no more. I don't like it when you do that."

"I know, Scotty, you already said that."

"Well, it's true."

"Look, Scotty . . . I know *you* look at it that way. And I look at it that way, too. But I don't think the police are going to agree. I think if they find her, they're going to be really pissed off at me."

Scotty became visibly agitated by that statement. "*You?* Why would they be mad at you? You didn't do anything."

"It's the rules, Scotty. I mean, you got her for *me*, right?"

"Yeah."

Warren couldn't believe he was actually having this conversation. It seemed to him as though he were playing a bit part in a bad B movie. He couldn't wish his plane to leave fast enough. "Well, it's the person you get the wife for that always gets in trouble. Don't ask me why, but that's how it always happens. At least here in America. I think they do it different in Canada, but I'm not really sure."

Scotty was confused, not sure what it all meant. "So, what happens? I mean, if the police get mad at you, then what do they do? You're not gonna get in trouble, right?"

"Oh, big trouble," Warren said through slit eyes. "That's why I got so mad. They would actually put me in jail."

"No!" Scotty was worried for his friend now. "Jail? You mean like the places my parents used to put me in?"

"Well . . . kind of. I know I wouldn't be able to get out. We'd never see each other again."

Scotty sat with his forearms on the kitchen table. He was staring down at his feet. "Gee, Warren, I'm really, really sorry. I never knew that. What are we going to do? I don't ever want to get you in trouble."

Warren leaned forward, as if confiding his deepest secret to Scotty. "You know I would never lie to you, right?"

"I know that," Scotty said through a childish laugh. "You're my only friend."

"I think this will be hard for you to hear, Scotty. But it's the only way out of this. I really mean it. I'm counting on you. I don't want to get in trouble either."

"What, Warren?" Scotty said, looking up. "What's going to be hard for me to hear?"

"You want to help me, right?"

"Yes. You're my friend. Just tell me how to make it better."

"There is one way." Warren feigned tears, wiping his eyes with the back of his hands. "I feel really bad saying this, Scotty. But if you don't do this, I think it's possible that I won't ever see you again. Not outside of jail, anyway. I don't think I could live without you in my life."

"Do what, Warren?" Scotty asked, desperate to make it all right. "*Anything*. Just tell me."

"Okay, but you have to promise you won't let me down."

Scotty nodded his head.

"Promise?"

"I promise."

That was the clincher. Warren knew he had him. The man would jump off a cliff if he promised you he would. "Well . . . I know this will be hard to hear, but think of *me*, okay, Scotty?"

"Okay."

Warren leaned forward, staring Scotty in the eyes. "You need to kill her," he whispered.

Scotty's brows furled, his face contorting with repulsion. "Oh, Warren, please . . . *please* don't make me do that. She's *so* pretty. Can't we just take her back? Don't make me hurt her."

Warren stared firmly into Scotty's eyes, shaking his head slowly. This part was crucial. He had to win Scotty over. "You don't have to *hurt* her, Scotty. You can just put a pillow over her face until she doesn't breathe anymore. That doesn't hurt at all."

Scotty's eyes lit up, as if he'd just thought of a great way out. "Maybe the police won't find out. I mean, no one knows we have her, right? It'll just be our little secret. If we keep her down there, everything will be okay."

"Scotty, look at me," Warren said with paternal forcefulness. "Listen to what I'm telling you now. The police will take me away forever if they find out. We just can't risk it."

"Then let's just take her back."

Warren closed his eyes and exhaled deeply. "If we take her back, Scotty, she'll go straight to the police. She'll tell them that you took her, and the first place they'll come is right here."

"But why? You mean even if we *return* her?"

"Yes, Scotty. Even if we return her. I would never lie to you, Scotty. You *have* to kill her. It's the only way I can stay your friend."

Scotty rose slowly, his shoulders slumped in dejection.

"Where you going?"

"Downstairs," Scotty said, turning toward Warren before stepping down the first stair to the basement.

Warren didn't want her dead just yet. He still envisioned an evening of fun and games. It excited him, his unique opportunity to make this flaming beauty scream and squeal. He would have his fill of her, and then some, before her heart stopped beating. "Oh, no, Scotty, not yet. It has to be at a special time. If you do it at the time I tell you, the Gehenna spirits can take her directly to Lucifer. He will thank you then. You will hold a special place in his heart."

Scotty didn't seem to care. His mind could only think of the sadness he felt. He didn't want to kill Valerie, but he couldn't bear the thought of losing Warren as a friend. Scotty would be nobody without him. "I'm not going to do it now. I'm just going to chain her back to the boiler."

His words hit Warren's ears like an ice pick shoved through his eardrums. "What did you say?"

"I'm going to chain her back to the boiler."

Warren rose from his chair, his heart skipping beats. "What do you mean you're 'going to chain her *back* to the boiler'? Isn't she chained already?"

"She was," Scotty said, slowly shaking his head. "But you were so mad, and she was bleeding. I undid the chains so she could—"

"You *what?*" Warren yelled, shoving his way past Scotty, bounding down the steps three at a time.

Warren's sudden change in demeanor frightened Scotty. He wondered what he had done wrong now. "I thought you didn't like seeing her that way!" he called after Warren, following him down into the basement.

Warren hit the cement floor with a thud, making the turn quickly, his feet sliding out from underneath him. He pushed his body forward, unable to regain his footing as he scrambled on all fours toward the back of the basement. Valerie was gone!

"Scotty! Scotty!" he screamed at an earsplitting pitch, thrashing about the basement, overturning anything that might hide her.

Scotty could hear the clamor of Warren tossing his belongings to and fro. He took the final step to the cement, knowing that something was terribly wrong. He walked slowly toward the direction of the noise and stood bashfully by the dryer, not daring to get too close. Scotty didn't answer, but rather just stood, watching his friend seemingly lose his mind. Somehow, he knew he'd screwed up again.

Warren was busy throwing boxes and overturning plywood sheets lying sideways against a wall. He looked up at Scotty with wild, murderous eyes. His hair hung in strings across his forehead, covering the whites of his eyes. He dragged his dusty hands across the base of his jaw, stopping when his palms came together. That was when Warren saw it. The bulkhead door was open. The bitch had escaped!

Scotty stood shaking, the warm sensation of urine trickling uncomfortably down his pants leg. He knew this was different now. He was terrified—fearful of his own safety. He had never seen his friend so insane. "I know she's here," Scotty said, the words quivering in the air. "I told her I'd be right back and not to go anywhere."

Warren's eyes seemed to rip Scotty's heart from his chest. "She's gone!" he screamed. "Do you understand what that means? She is *gone!*" Scotty took a few steps backward as Warren began his approach. "Do you have any idea what the *fuck* you have done to me? Come here," he said with deadly venom.

Scotty spoke in a low, frightened voice. He was slow, but he was hardly without his own survival instinct. "No," he said, taking a few steps back.

Warren's eyes bulged wildly, the veins of his throat noticeably pulsating. A string of saliva had lodged on his chin. "I said, come here!"

Tears spurt from Scotty's eyes. "What are you going to do to me?" he asked, his torso beginning to shake uncontrollably.

"I am going to tear your fucking heart out through your mouth, you stupid, motherfucking son of a bitch! Now. I said . . . *come here!*"

CHAN AND SAM sat quietly in the Saab, wishing like hell they had that second car. As it stood now, they could not get food or drink, and defecating was eventually going to prove problematic indeed—at least until nightfall. If either one could wait that long. They both hoped something would happen, and quickly. It was Chan's thirty-minute shift to watch. Sam lay fully reclined in the passenger seat, his eyes closed, half in and out of a very fitful sleep.

Chan looked at his watch, fighting off an unforgiving yawn. He and Sam had been staring at inanimate objects too long. He knew something would soon have to give. Chan was sitting forward, his eyes beginning to play tricks on him. He arched his back as he thought of the '61 Yankees, trying to name every player at every position. When that proved easier than he'd thought, he pushed himself further, seeing if he could remember their numbers.

He watched quietly, fighting off dementia, wondering if the huge pines lining Scotty's drive really were beginning to jump on the lawn in front of him. He rested his chin on the back of his hands as they lay on the steering wheel. Chan knew he could never give it up. He owed Shackling that much. His stomach nearly hit the roof of his mouth when the Saab's car phone rang, its dull chime shattering the quiet of the car out of all proportion to its true volume.

Sam clamored to a sitting position as Chan picked it up on the second ring. "Yeah?"

"Chan?" came Lianne's shy, hesitant voice.

"You got me. What's up?"

"I'm ready. I'd like to speak to Warren, please. When you can arrange it."

"Our location's changed. He's not where he was yesterday. It's a residential neighborhood. Some condo complex. You'll have to give me some time. I'll get back to you when I've got the number."

Lianne had already heard enough. She knew where they were. "Is it in Lewisboro?"

"Why do you ask?"

"It is, isn't it?" Lianne asked, her voice growing more firm. "Chan, don't bullshit me. I have to know. Is it in Lewisboro?"

"Are we in Lewisboro?" Chan asked Sam, placing his palm over the phone. Sam shrugged with a don't-ask-me look.

"I'm not sure, Lianne. We really weren't paying that much attention."

"When you followed him, did you go through Pound Ridge?"

"I think I remember seeing a sign, now that you mention it. Why?"

"You know where he is, don't you?"

Sam eyed Chan, anxious to ascertain the gist of his conversation. Chan returned his look, showing his teeth in a stretched mouth, indicating things were getting interesting. "No, should I?"

"You haven't figured it out yet?"

"Lianne, what the hell are you saying?"

"He's at Scotty's, Chan. That poisonous sack of filth is with my son."

Chan laid his hand over the receiver again. "She thinks this is Scotty's place," he said, motioning ahead with a flick of his chin. "What's it look like?" he asked her.

"It's a condo complex, dark gray shingles, two stories, shoved back in the woods. It borders the game preserve. That's it, isn't it?"

Lianne was either telepathic or she had hit it right on. "Okay, so he's here. Does that change your plans?"

"No, it only gives them more urgency. Don't bother with the number. I have it." She hung up.

Chan sat for a moment before realizing he was listening to a dial tone. Wait a minute, he thought. Just like that he'd been pushed out of the picture? Chan didn't think so. There was still the minor issue of payment, and he wanted to be sure he got it before Lianne landed her ass in jail. Because if she did, Chan felt fairly certain she would not be coming out. Not before she died. He wanted to call her back right then, but hesitated with Sam sitting in the seat next to him. His blood boiled. Lianne had what she wanted, now he wanted his. He'd lived up to his end of the bargain. Now it was Lianne's turn to ante up.

He placed his hand over the receiver again and turned to Sam, not letting on that Lianne had already hung up. "Sammy, I hate to ask you to do this, but I have to speak to Lianne about something private. I'm sorry, but trust me. You don't want to know about it. You've been through enough already."

Sam looked at him, his eyes narrowing slightly. "You want me to leave?" he finally asked as Chan's wish took a moment to register.

Chan's face grew apologetic. "Could you? I'm sorry. But it's just for one minute. Believe me, the less you know about this, the better."

Sam shrugged. "Sure thing," he said, opening his door. "Let me know when it's safe."

Chan watched Sam lean against the passenger-side door as he quietly punched in the Rybeck family phone number. Lianne's voice sounded hurried and full of angst. "Hello?"

"Hi, it's me."

"Yes?"

"Lianne, I know you have more important things on your mind right now, but we need to talk."

"About what?"

Chan spoke in low, almost whispered tones. "About money."

"So you want to get paid for your efforts, do you?"

And someone else's, he thought. There was one more fatherless family in the world right now. "Look, if you're going to do what I think you're going to do . . . and don't say a word. I don't even want to know. But if you are, then I've got to get it now."

"Why?"

"*Why?* Lianne, I don't know what you've got planned, but it seems to me you could get arrested."

Lianne laughed. "No one's going to arrest me, Chan. Don't you worry about that."

Chan scratched his head. "Well, I hope you're right. But just the same, I'd feel better if we got it out of the way."

"You would, huh?"

She wasn't making this any easier. "Am I missing something, Lianne? You do plan on following through with your end of the bargain, right? I did everything you asked of me."

"Yes, you did, Chan. And then some. Don't you worry. I always keep my promises."

"Good. That's what I thought. So how do you want to handle this?"

"If you're right, and they do arrest me, any check I write you is going to be stopped."

Chan hadn't even thought of that. "Okay? So?"

"So, give me your bank account number, and I'll have it wired."

A bank account number? Chan couldn't imagine how the hell he was going to find that sitting in Sammy's Saab. "Lianne, I don't have that with me now."

"Where is your checkbook?"

"In my apartment. On my dresser."

"Fine. That's all I need. Consider it done, Chan."

It seemed almost too easy. He had a weird feeling about this. If she was planning on sacrificing herself, why would she ever bother to pay him? If the tables were turned, he didn't think he would. But there was little he could do about it now. Lianne held every card in the deck. "That's it?"

"That's it. Easy, huh?"

"Yeah," Chan said, thinking it was a bit too easy. He wanted to ask her when she planned on doing it, but even he knew that would be gauche. She was either going to do it or she wasn't. The term *blood money* floated through his head. "Thank you, Lianne. It's been a pleasure doing business with you."

"Thank *you*, Chan. The feeling is mutual."

"Lianne," he called out, afraid she'd hung up.

She sounded detached, almost as if she had reached some sort of final resolution in her mind. "Yes?"

"Good luck."

Lianne chuckled slightly. "Say a little prayer."

Chan hung up, feeling a slight tug at his conscience. When Judgment Day came, he wondered which one of them would have needed prayer most.

SCOTTY HIMMERTON'S CONDOMINIUM complex abutted the expansive and beautiful Ward Pound Ridge Reservation, a game preserve comprising several hundred acres of unspoiled woods and ponds. For a moment Valerie considered heading toward the street, screaming at the top of her lungs, but quickly thought better of it. It was a Monday, and everyone would be at work. And if she were to yell loud enough to be heard by neighbors, she would most certainly be heard by her two captors. And though temporarily free, she wasn't exactly mobile. Valerie's feet and hands were still shackled in handcuffs, so she was forced to shuffle her legs in painful, eight-inch strides, like those of a felon being transferred from one facility to another.

Frustration boiled inside her as she hobbled up the rocky incline behind Scotty's home. Her mind screamed *RUN!* but her body could only move so quickly. More than once Valerie toppled to her face, desperately laboring to hurry out of sight. Fear and panic enveloped her pounding brain as she scooted pathetically forward, hurriedly peering behind her with increasing frequency. Valerie's insufferable immobility transcended the surreal, transforming itself to near madness as blood streamed down her feet, the flesh ripping from her ankles with each forward thrust.

How long did she have before Warren realized Scotty's mindless mistake? Two minutes? One? Maybe less? The open woods can be unforgiving, even to those not nearly as handicapped. But for Valerie, every inch was earned the hard way, desperately clawing and grasping in an effort to save her life, always aware that to stop, to even falter, could easily mean death. She bent and turned, ducked and twisted, with frightening rapidity, frantically thrashing her way through the mass of vines, twigs, and fallen logs. Valerie's face soon glistened with perspiration as she worked her way slowly into the dense and tricky woods, occasionally raising her arms to wipe her eyes on the shoulder of her T-shirt. Nothing would stop her. *Nothing.* If she couldn't move fast enough to escape the madmen she was certain now chased her, she was going to die trying.

A sporadic branch would catch on her face, an arm, her chest, gouging her deeply, stinging her skin painfully as she tore herself free. The minutes ticked by, each one seemingly a week, as she stumbled farther into the woods. Valerie continued, tumbling to the ground again and again, each time rising to her feet as quickly as she fell, maniacally bent on survival. Sweat now dripped freely from her hair and face as she turned with horrified eyes, half expecting to see one or both of her captors giving chase. But Valerie was alone. For now.

She was eventually stymied, arriving at the base of a long, rocky hill. She froze, terrified by its size. It seemed impossible that she could climb it, not that it was particularly large. But in her condition, a school-yard jungle gym would be problematic. There had to be a better way. In a frenzied attempt to find an easier route, she maneuvered several yards to her right, only to see both the hill's angle and height increase.

Valerie stumbled back to her left, a nausea of exhaustion forming in her gut. Her diaphragm sucked the skin of her abdomen tightly against her ribs as her lungs begged in vain for more oxygen. She was beginning to push her body to its limit, and it was beginning to fight back. *STOP!* it begged her. She feared she could not go on. Not like this. Not at this pace. Her head pounded in step with the beat of her heart, as if someone had struck her a blow with a crowbar. But there was no choice. Her stomach churned in an early, telltale sign of heaving. She looked up, valiantly fighting back vomit as she eyed the climb in front of her.

But she couldn't lift her legs! "Dammit," she mumbled. She *had* to get over that hill. Valerie knew one thing for sure, a feeling emanating from deep within her genes: she would rather die attempting to climb this hill than at the hands of the two maniacs who now chased her. She hooked her handcuffs over the root stub of what had once been a small tree growing out of the side of the hill and pulled herself up with every ounce of strength and energy she had. Blood spurted from her wrists as the stainless steel tore through her skin, splashing tiny droplets of crimson on her face. Valerie looked down, hanging her head between her arms, desperately trying to find a foothold on which to place a toe. Finally, and not without great effort and pain, she was able to raise herself a good three feet. Okay, she told herself, you can do this.

On any other day, under any other circumstance, she would have conquered this monster in two minutes flat. But not today. Not with her feet and hands shackled. It was a slow, arduous task, akin to moving a mountain with a spoon. One improbable, agonizing yard at a time, Valerie yanked and tugged, moaned and cried—gallantly, miraculously inching her way up the small hill's face. Occasionally she would crane her neck, peering through the woods behind her with hunted eyes. Inexplicably, her tormentors were nowhere to be seen. It seemed impossible that she might actually make it. Valerie dared not give her mind the thought, fearful of emotional and physical collapse.

In time, she clambered over the top of the hill, lying facedown in the leaves and dirt of the small plateau on top. Her body heaved for air. Leaves and dirt were sucked into her mouth as she lay watching with her cheek to the ground, her lungs gasping for oxygen. She turned her face to look outward, in the direction from which she had come, and for the first time, if only for a minute, allowed her body to stop. Valerie's heart thundered relentlessly against her chest, the blood pulsing through her veins a deafening roar as it whooshed through her eardrums. She listened for the crackle of twigs and leaves underfoot but heard nothing—nothing but the sound of her own body, her own mind, clinging tenuously to sanity, perhaps even to life itself.

Valerie had to stop. To push farther was folly. She would certainly pass out, if not die, and then where would she be? A few minutes passed in relative silence, and for the first time since her escape, she allowed herself to think. She sat up and scooted back against a tree, away and out of view from any possible pursuers. Valerie could feel something trickle down the back of her neck and wasn't sure if it was blood from her wound or simply perspiration. It didn't matter now. Pull it together, she kept telling herself. If her martial arts training had taught her anything, it was that panic only restricts the body's ability to function. Adrenaline is a good thing—fight or flight, and all that. But too much becomes debilitating, stopping the body and the mind dead in their tracks.

She looked behind her, aware now she heard the unmistakable sound of moving water. Nothing had ever sounded quite so dear to her. Behind her, a small brook meandered down the steep terrain, toward the cliff she had just climbed, no doubt cascading down its face farther afield than she had in her haste, attempted to look. Valerie crawled on her elbows and knees toward the brook, almost diving on her chest as she threw her face into the crisp, cleansing water of a small pool. The invigorating sensation sent tingles down her spine. She rubbed the top of her head with water, splashing its rejuvenating feel over the back and sides of her neck. She cupped her hands and drank ravenously.

For a moment, all she did was lie with her head in the water, occasionally lifting it to breathe and toss her hair like a wet sheepdog. Valerie had not been allowed to visit a bathroom in over twenty-four hours, and her sweatpants reeked of urine and feces. She wanted to rip them off, but knew she needed some protection against her skin. She took a few brave steps into the water, its flowing, icy cold stinging the lacerations around her ankles. Valerie winced, looking skyward with closed eyes, viciously gritting her teeth.

She pulled her sweatpants down around her ankles, patting her wounds softly with the wet cloth. Valerie squatted and reached up underneath her, vigorously rubbing her behind with her fingers, scraping away dried feces with her fingernails. The water felt so kind and cleansing. It was cold, but still she thought she could easily lie down in it and go to sleep. She splashed water over the inseam of her pants, scraping away at the fouled areas as best she could with rocks and twigs, rubbing the cloth forcefully between her palms. Valerie had almost lost herself in her task as she desperately tried to regain some sense of her humanity. Her heart stopped at the sound of a snapping twig.

Immediately Valerie rose to her feet, her sweatpants still crumpled around her ankles. She twisted her body, eyeing every inch of the forest about her with panicked, darting eyes. She turned her body, her feet slipping on a large, mossy rock, and fell painfully backward, her legs flying out from underneath her. The sight of the man as he approached was the most terrifying moment of Valerie's life. She stumbled backward, splashing water in front of her, scraping her buttocks and back against the rocks as she pushed madly away with her slippery, stockinged feet.

If Valerie thought she was terrified, she should have been in her trespasser's shoes. A wealthy graduate student in literature at SUNY Purchase, he had intended this morning's trek to be a walk with nature, an attempt to clear his mind and hopefully overcome the writer's block that had begun dogging him the past few weeks. He wore brown Hi-Tec hiking boots over red, wool socks, and a pair of beige shorts. To Valerie's paranoid eyes, his mirrored sunglasses lent him a menacing, frightful look. Yet as terrified as she was, he was twice so.

Her unannounced visitor stopped suddenly and stood at the edge of the brook, some yards upstream from Valerie. He stared at this torn and bleeding, almost animal-like creature, half-naked in the water in front of him. If he lacked for writing material a few minutes ago, his mind was jolted into fertile ground now. "Oh, my God," he said in shock. "Are you okay?" he asked tentatively, taking a step toward her.

Valerie tried desperately to relax, but her mind was far from rational. She could only assume he was with them. As he approached, she scampered farther back, still on her rear in the water.

He could see she was manacled. "I'm not going to hurt you," he said with an outstretched hand, taking a few more timid steps in her direction. "Please. Let me help you."

Valerie stood and pulled up her pants, staring at him with quizzical, distrusting eyes.

He advanced slowly, stepping into the brook, extending his arm a little farther. "Please?"

"Oh, God!" she exclaimed, rushing toward him, stumbling over rocks, nearly falling to her knees. He caught her fall, pulling her to her feet tenderly. "Oh, thank you. Oh, *God*, thank you," she nearly blubbered. Valerie was clearly petrified, her body shaking, her eyes glancing about wildly as if an animal on the run.

"What happened? Who did this to you?"

"Please! We must get out of here. There's no time. Oh, *please!* They're after me! We have to run. Hurry! Please!"

This whole scene stunned him, jolting him as if from a wistful daydream. "Who's after you?" he asked, taking Valerie's shoulders and looking into her eyes.

"Oh, God, please! Take me out of here! I can't run! We have to go *now.*"

His carefree foray into the woods had been startlingly interrupted, but it did not take long for him to put two and two together. He feared for his own safety now. He had few doubts that whoever would do something like this to another human being would not hesitate to do him harm also. And if they were after her, that meant they would soon be after him. At least in one respect, it was Valerie's lucky day. Unbeknownst to her, she had traveled at an angle, cutting across the lower corner of the reservation. "All right. We're not far from my car. I'm going to pick you up, okay?"

Tears streamed down Valerie's face. "Okay," she said, practically mumbling the words.

He was tall, around six feet two, and wore a red T-shirt, the front of which read THE MORE HAIR I LOSE, THE MORE HEAD I GET. It fit snugly around his massive chest, exposing large, well-developed biceps. He leaned down and cupped an arm under her knees, lifting Valerie effortlessly off her feet. He held her in his arms, the way a groom might carry a new bride across the threshold. "I can't carry you like this. My arms won't take it. I'm going to have to put you over my shoulders. It won't be comfortable, but it'll work."

"I don't care. Let's just go."

He lifted her to his shoulders, wrapping Valerie's wet body around his neck and shoulders, and stepped out of the brook, back onto dry land. "Okay," he said, scanning the woods. "Let's get the hell out of here."

He followed the brook as closely as he could for some minutes, eventually cutting down a path to their right. Valerie closed her eyes and placed her battered and bleeding head tightly to his shoulder, sensing the vibrations through his upper torso as his feet pounded the ground below them. They were only a half mile from his car, but it seemed to Valerie as though he carried her for hours. The two didn't speak a word until they came upon a small road near Gilmore Pond. She could tell by the sudden smoothness of the ride that they had reached some type of clearing.

Her savior's breathing was labored, and she could feel the moisture of his T-shirt warming the bruises and cuts of her cheek. She opened her eyes when he slowed to a walk, praising the heavens at the sight of a dark green Nissan Maxima almost within her reach.

"Can you stand?" he asked.

Valerie felt embarrassed, his asking her that after so strenuous and heroic a feat. She nodded her head and he knelt, placing her softly to her feet. "Stay there," he said, reaching into his shorts pocket and pulling out a set of keys. He unlocked the passenger-side door, opened it, and softly slid his hand around her waist, guiding her toward the seat.

"Here . . . sit down," he said, tenderly shuffling her into his car. She winced in pain with each move. He made sure she was in safely, closed the door tightly after her, and whipped around the front of his car to the driver's seat. He immediately dialed the New York State Police.

"Yes, my name is Roger Keene," he said hurriedly and out of breath. "I have found a woman in the Pound Ridge Reservation, handcuffed at her hands and feet."

"Is she alive, sir?"

He looked at Valerie and smiled. "Oh . . . I'm sorry. Yes. Very much so. She was hysterical, claiming that someone was chasing her. Please, send help immediately. I think she's going to need medical attention."

"Where are you presently, sir?"

"On a residential road near Gilmore Pond. I don't know the name, but I'm not staying here anyway. I don't know who these people are, where they are, or whether or not they're armed. But I'm leaving now for Boutonville. I'll meet the cruiser there. I am in a dark green Maxima, New York license PD five, two two eight. Please hurry," he said before hanging up.

Keene looked at Valerie. "You okay?"

She sat with her head resting back against the seat. "Yeah," she said, her body suddenly breaking into a head-to-toe quiver. "Just a little cold."

Keene turned on the heat, did a three-point turn, and began the ten-minute drive to Boutonville. He was more than curious and desperately wanted to ask her what had happened, but thought better of it as he drove away in silence. He thought maybe the less he knew, the better, though he had no doubt he would be dragged, however unwittingly, smack into the storm of the trial—if there ever was one.

Valerie turned her head toward him. "Your name's Roger?"

"Yes," he said, eyeing her with a reassuring smile.

She spoke softly, her voice betraying her complete physical and emotional exhaustion. "Hi, Roger. I'm Valerie."

"Hi, Valerie." Keene was quiet for a moment, then tried a little humor. "You know, Valerie, we have to stop meeting like this."

She turned toward him. Her smile was weak, but grateful. At least she was safe. She had made it, though she would forever ask herself how. Valerie yearned to speak to Jake, to hear his soothing voice and tell him she was okay. She could not hold him close to her ragged and torn body soon enough. "Roger, could I ask you a favor?"

"Sure."

"Can you make a call for me?"

"Of course. Name it."

"I need you to call the Westchester County Fire Marshal's Office. Ask to speak to a Jake Ferguson."

JAKE HAD ALREADY chased down Valerie's mother by phone, only to be told she had no idea where her daughter was. He had just hung up after trying Valerie's apartment for the third time that morning and sat despondently, resting his elbows on the large desk-mat calendar that lay atop his desk. He turned to Ederling. "She's not there," he said, his eyes revealing discord and worry. Somehow Jake knew, if he had never taken her to that bar Friday night, she would still be with him now. "I got a bad feeling about this, Donny. I'm going to call the school. What's the name again?"

"Franklin Roosevelt Elementary."

Jake called information, hung up, and dialed the number. He did not explain who he was, only that he wanted to speak with Valerie Medforth. "Ms. Medforth is not in today, sir. Would you like to leave a message?"

Not in? "Did she call in sick?"

"May I ask who's calling?"

Jake then informed the woman who he was and was told that not only had Valerie not come in, she had not even contacted the school. "It's very unlike her, Mr. Ferguson. Frankly, we're a little concerned. You don't happen to know where she might be, do you?"

This definitely did not bode well. Something was terribly wrong. "No, but if I hear from her, I'll be certain to contact you. Have you called the police?"

"Yes. I believe the principal spoke to them earlier this morning."

"Did they say anything?"

"No, not that I'm aware. To the best of my knowledge it was news to them."

"Do you know if they checked her apartment?"

"Yes. She wasn't there."

"Okay, thank you for your time," Jake said. "I'll see what I can do from this end. If I learn anything, I'll call."

Ederling was looking at Jake when he hung up. "That didn't sound so good. What's up?"

Jake's forehead was lined with worry. "She hasn't shown up and hasn't called. Something's happened, Donny. I know it."

Maybe Jake is right, Ederling thought. Maybe something had happened to her. For the first time, he began to worry some himself. "She didn't call?"

"No."

"What do you want to do? You don't think . . . ?"

Ederling did not have to finish his sentence. The thought that Warren had somehow gotten his hands on Valerie had long since lodged itself into Jake's brain. Though how he could have lured her from his apartment . . . it just didn't make any sense. After all, she had earned a black belt.

"What do you want to do?" Ederling asked.

Jake sat silent, thinking it through. "I'm not sure. What can we do? The only thing I can think is to request an attempt to locate on the computer."

That was a reasonable course of action. Unlike the data link with NCIC that can be used on a national basis, an "attempt to locate" is used primarily on a local jurisdictional level. "You think that will help?" Ederling asked.

"Can't hurt."

Jake was walking toward the Teletype machine when Cissy interrupted on the intercom. "Jake, a Mr. Kelton's here to see you. He says you're expecting him."

Damn! Jake had forgotten all about Kelton and Warren's trash. "Okay, thanks, Cis," he said, looking at his watch: 10:01 A.M. "Tell him I'll be just a minute."

Jake was disturbed by the news he'd just learned from Valerie's school. It didn't make any sense. If there had been foul play, nothing inside his apartment had indicated it. But then again, he knew that if it wasn't foul play, she would certainly have gone to work, or at the very least called in.

When Jake was done at the Teletype, he depressed his intercom button. "Okay, Cis, send Mr. Kelton in, will you? Thanks."

A moment later, Bill Kelton walked into the office wearing a pair of dark blue Dockers, black sneakers, and a red cardigan, sleeves pushed halfway up his forearms, with the words BERGEN COUNTY FIRE MARSHAL'S OFFICE embroidered in black on the left breast. He carried a box of doughnuts in his left hand, and a cardboard container with two large coffees in his right.

Jake walked toward his visitor, still troubled by Valerie's sudden disappearance. There was nothing else he could do for now. Other duties called. "Bill," he said with a forced smile. "Right on time. Any trouble?"

Kelton shook his head. "A layup. Got every last bag the second they were on the truck. They're in a van out front."

In actuality, Kelton and his men had not taken them off the truck in front of Warren's apartment. But Jake already knew this. He fully understood Kelton's poetic license. As is most often the case when the police need someone's trash, Kelton had already spoken to the sanitation crew long before they came upon Warren's building. The crew was instructed to be sure they pulled up with an empty bin. That way, Kelton could be sure that everything he took from the truck would have come only from Warren's building. The crew filled up and drove away, meeting up with Kelton and his deputy at a preordained spot, a few blocks away.

"Good. Oh, I'm sorry," Jake said, motioning toward Ederling. "Bill Kelton, this is Don Ederling. Bill's the chief marshal for Bergen County, Don." The two shook hands, exchanging pleasantries. Jake slapped his hands and rubbed them together. "Well, what are we waiting for? Let's get started."

The three men walked to the parking lot in the front of the building, Jake and Ederling waiting while Kelton inserted a key into the padlock securing the rear doors of the van. He swung them open and Jake let go a long whistle as he gazed inside. There was trash in every conceivable type of container: large black and green trash bags, smaller, white kitchen bags, brown shopping bags, fruit produce bags, and a couple of plastic containers similar to what you might see mail sitting in at the post office. Jake was secretly glad that Warren didn't live in a larger apartment complex. As it was, he figured there were probably forty, maybe forty-five bags of trash in there.

Ederling looked at him. "This should be fun."

"What's with the containers?" Jake asked Kelton, referring to the postal-like carts.

Kelton pulled himself up inside, resting his hand on one. "These?"

"Yeah."

"Stuff that was loose. No home."

Jake was hoping there'd be less than that. *Please don't let us find anything in those.* He knew that even if they did find magazines and newspapers that had been clipped, and even if the missing sections ended up matching those used in the note sent to Jake, if they couldn't be labeled as anyone's in particular, they would prove useless in court. Just finding the cutout publications was a far cry from linking Warren directly to the Morson Grayhead murders. In fact, Jake didn't think it would even give him enough to have a warrant issued for his arrest. Still, they would prove to be one more arrow in his quiver, one more piece of circumstantial evidence that could be used at trial.

"That's more than I'd hoped," Jake said with a frown.

"I know," Kelton added. "I was thinking the same thing as we put it in here. You ready?"

Jake and Ederling nodded, and Kelton handed them each two bags, jumping off the van with three of his own. In ten minutes the van was empty, every last bag stuffed haphazardly into Jake's office. Earlier that morning, in anticipation of Kelton's visit, Jake had parked a large, gray trash container on wheels against the wall near the table in the corner of his office. He wondered now if it was large enough.

"How do you want to work this, Jake?" Kelton asked.

Jake motioned to the gray trash bin, handing each man a pair of latex gloves. "Let's look through the loose trash first. No sense digging through all these if it's in there."

"Makes sense," Kelton said.

"If it's not," Jake continued, "then let's just each take a bag. Look for mail or publications first. That should tell us whose it is. Let's try to be neat. Keep as much inside your respective bags as possible. Once you're sure it's not Warren's, put everything back and place it in that container. When we've finally narrowed it down to just Warren's, we'll dump it out a bag at a time on the table. How's that sound?"

Both men nodded.

"Good luck," Jake said.

The process went smoothly. Many hands make light work, and in less than half an hour they had completely finished the loose trash. Nothing. Then they began searching individual bags, in most cases quickly able to ascertain whose it was—or more importantly, whose it was not. Jake knew that this was the part of an investigation the public never sees—the excruciatingly slow grind, the attention to detail, the almost complete submersion into the minutiae of a suspect's life. Like raking a lawn by hand, one careful leaf at a time.

Jake's biggest fear was that they might find them in one of the smaller produce bags, such as the kind one might use to line the receptacle in the bathroom. If they found the cutouts there, but they were among a sea of Q-Tips, Kleenex, and empty toilet paper rolls, it would hardly prove to be a coup. The cutouts would have to be with mail, something that could identify from whose apartment it came. People don't normally carry out the tiny bags. Rather, they usually put them all in larger bags for convenience. As Jake had assumed, most of the smaller bags of that type had been carried out wrapped within larger bags. *Maybe we'll luck out.*

It was shortly before 11:00 A.M. when Ederling found them. "This one's his," he said, digging slowly through a white, plastic garbage bag. Both men looked up at him with anticipation, half expecting to hear the words, *"Found 'em!"* But no such luck. Jake began to wonder if this whole thing was nothing more than an exercise in frustration. Ederling continued digging, apparently finding nothing much of interest. Jake heard the phone ring twice and had already turned his attention to another bag when Ederling finally spoke the words. "Well, well, well. What have we here?"

"You got 'em?" Jake asked, his voice filled with excitement.

Ederling was quiet for a moment, digging farther inside the bag. At one point, his head seemed halfway stuck inside. "Sure do," he finally said.

Jake clenched his fists. "Yes! It's about time." He removed his bag from the table, as Kelton followed suit. "Pour it out. Let's have a look. Slowly now, don't spill anything."

The three men were pulling out publications that had been clipped, placing them individually in large Baggies, when Cissy burst into the office. She looked excited, as if something big had just occurred. "Cis, what is it?" Jake asked.

"It's Royston Craddock. He's waiting."

Jake rose from the table. "Sorry, guys. Give me two minutes." He took a seat behind his desk and punched a blinking light on his console. "Good morning, Mr. Craddock. That was quick. You find something?"

Jake could hear enthusiasm in Craddock's voice. "Hello again, Jake. Since I received your fax, our people have been all *over* this thing. I think we may have lucked out."

Jake looked at Ederling, raising his eyebrows. He picked up a pen off his desk and reached for something to write on. "Let's hear it."

"Well, it turns out the largest Morson Grayhead position by far is located in the White Plains branch of Thompson McElvay. Ever hear of them?"

It was one of the nation's largest. "Sure."

"Well, their records show they have a client who owns one hundred and fifty Morson Grayhead puts. April fifty-fives."

I actually understand that. "You got the purchase dates?"

"Sure do. They were all bought prior to the first burning. I can give you the specifics if you'd like."

Later. Time is critical now. "This client got a name?"

"Does the name Warren Josephs ring a bell to you?" There was silence on Jake's end of the phone. "Jake?" Craddock asked, not certain he was still on the line.

"I'm here," he said, clenching a fist in the air. "Spell that name for me, please." Craddock repeated it, but Jake was only half-listening. He put his hand over the receiver. "We got him, Donny. It's Warren."

"You get that?" Craddock asked.

"Got it. Listen, Mr. Craddock, for what it's worth, I think you were right. We may have just found our boy. But I must ask you to keep that between us. Please, sir."

"Of course, Jake. When will you know?"

"Very soon, Mr. Craddock. I think we'll know very soon. The second we learn anything, I'll call you. I promise. Tell your people, good work. I think they can stop for now. If we need them further, I'll be in touch."

"So, that's it?" Craddock asked, his voice betraying a certain disappointment.

"Yes, for now. Listen, I'm sorry to do this, but we have a lot of work on this end. I'll call you as soon as we know anything. Thank you, Mr. Craddock. I really mean that. Thank you very, very much."

"Listen, Jake, if it helps bring this madman to justice, we'll do it until hell freezes over."

"I don't think that will be necessary." Jake stood and hung up, reaching on top of his filing cabinet for the Yellow Pages.

"Wha'd he say?" Ederling asked.

Jake was thumbing through the Investment Advisers section, dragging his finger down a page. "It's definitely him, Don. This guy bought one hundred and fifty puts *prior* to the first burning."

Kelton chimed in, "You mentioned the name Warren. Is that the same guy whose apartment we investigated yesterday?"

"The very same one, Bill," Jake said, finding the number and laying the Yellow Pages down on his desk. "This guy's dog meat and he doesn't even know it yet."

Jake dialed the number to the White Plains office of Thompson McElvay, asking to speak to the office manager. He had to wait a bit, but finally got him on the line. "Barry Rheinhoffer speaking. May I help you?"

"Yes, Mr. Rheinhoffer, my name is Jake Ferguson. I am the chief fire marshal for Westchester County."

If you lived in the tristate area, you'd have had to live in a cave not to know who Jake Ferguson was by now. Rheinhoffer had a bad feeling about this call. "Yes, Mr. Ferguson. How may I help you?"

"I understand your office has a client by the name of Warren Josephs. Is that correct, sir?"

Normally Rheinhoffer would have had to look it up, but his conversation a few days ago with Saul Bremmer of Legal and Compliance was still wedged firmly in his brain. Intuitively, Rheinhoffer knew where this conversation was going. Bremmer had warned him about this. In his mind, Rheinhoffer wondered if he had just kissed a twenty-two-year career good-bye. "Yes, we do. Is there a problem, Mr. Ferguson?"

Jake avoided the question. "Can you tell me what's in his account?"

"I can, Mr. Ferguson. But I won't. I have no way of knowing who you really are." A little voice kept whispering in Rheinhoffer's head that this call was for real. Rheinhoffer knew in his heart that Jake was who he said he was, and worse yet, why he was calling. "Look, Mr. Ferguson, I'd be lying if I said I didn't know who you are and what case you're working on. I'm assuming this call has to do with the Morson Grayhead mess?"

"Yes."

Rheinhoffer wanted to help, but had to be careful how he proceeded. People take their money very seriously. "I want to help you, Mr. Ferguson. In the worst way, believe me. But I don't have any proof you are who you say you are. Our clients' holdings are confidential information, sir. I can't just go giving it out to every Tom, Dick, and Harry who calls in telling me they're so-and-so."

Jake hadn't anticipated this problem. He needed to make sure he had the right man. "Well, we have a slight problem then, don't we? Any suggestions?"

It was quiet on Rheinhoffer's end of the line while his mind ticked, trying to think of a way out.

"Tell you what," Jake finally said. "My office is listed in the phone book. Hang up and look up the number, then call me back. If I'm here, maybe you can see what you can do."

"Good idea. That will also give me time to check with the broker on the account. You know? See if Josephs has been in contact with us. I can probably delay some things—"

"What kind of things?"

"Money transfers and the like. But if Mr. Josephs wants to liquidate his position, I'm afraid I'll have no choice. And to keep his money frozen, you'll need to get me something more official. Court documents, or at the very least, come in personally with some form of official identification."

"All I need is no money transfers, Mr. Rheinhoffer. We keep the money here, we keep him here."

"I understand that, Mr. Ferguson. I will do everything I can. You must realize that this is a highly unusual request. Are you telling me you think Mr. Josephs is involved?"

Jake could feel frustration welling up inside him. He was in no mood for explanations. On the other hand, he realized the man did have a business to run. "I'm sorry, Mr. Rheinhoffer, but I can't answer that. I hope you understand. Tell me this, though. If I get you official paperwork, can you freeze his account right away?"

"Absolutely. Immediately."

"Okay, consider it done." Jake looked at his watch. "I'll have them to you in less than an hour. If not me, then one of my associates will bring it to you in person. In the meantime, if at all possible, I want you to delay all activity in that account. This is urgent police business, Mr. Rheinhoffer. See what you can do to delay Mr. Josephs if he should call before we get to you. And *please* . . . call me as soon as possible if that should occur."

"Hang up. I'll be right back to you."

"Fair enough," Jake said. "But I just want to make sure I've got this straight. If we bring you something official, you'll freeze the account, right?"

"By all means."

"Good. We'll be there." Jake hung up.

"What gives?" Ederling asked from across the room. "The guy's not cooperating?"

Jake waited by his desk, expecting to hear from Rheinhoffer any minute. "Not really. But I can't blame him. He has no idea who I really am, and he does have clients to protect. He's going to look up our number in the phone book and call me."

Ederling smirked. "That works. I guess."

"Donny, while we're waiting, tell Cissy what we got. Tell her to get on the horn. We need a court order to freeze Warren's accounts. Have her send Freddy down. As soon as he's got it, let us know."

"Done," Ederling said, getting up from the table.

Jake sat at his desk, looking at Kelton. "Just another boring day at the office, huh, Bill?"

Kelton smiled. "When it rains, it pours."

"We are this close to nailing this scumbag," Jake said, holding two fingers a quarter inch apart. "*This* close."

"Hang in there, buddy," Kelton said with a thumbs-up. "We'll get him."

Jake sat forward as he heard the phone ring. He wanted to get it himself, but thought it would sound more official if someone else picked it up. "Jake," Cissy said on the intercom, "there's a Mr. Rheinhoffer on line two for you."

"Thank you," he said, punching the blinking button on his console as he picked up his phone. For this call, Jake did away with his more casual style. "County Fire Marshal's Office, Jacob Ferguson speaking. May I help you?"

Rheinhoffer was on speakerphone now. "Okay, so you're for real. I'm sorry to have done that to you, Mr. Ferguson. You have no idea the scams people try to pull over on us. I'm afraid we have no choice but to be vigilant. Our clients expect it of us."

"I understand."

"I have a Ted Wilkinson here with me. He is Mr. Josephs's broker. I think you'll want to hear what he has to say."

"Good morning, Mr. Wilkinson," Jake said. "Sorry to interrupt your day like this."

"No problem, Mr. Ferguson. How can I help you?"

"Your boss says you've got something to say. Let's hear it."

"Well, it could be nothing," Wilkinson began. "It just struck me as funny is all. Mr. Josephs called me an hour or so ago. He wanted to liquidate his Morson Grayhead puts."

"Is that so?" Jake asked.

"One hundred and fifty of them," Rheinhoffer added. "April fifty-fives."

"Did you sell them?" Jake asked Wilkinson.

"No. I couldn't. The opening's been delayed."

"English, gentlemen," Jake said. "I don't know your world."

Rheinhoffer spoke. "What that means, Mr. Ferguson, is that for some reason the Exchange has delayed trading in Morson Grayhead stock. It's not currently trading. If the stock doesn't trade, the options don't trade either."

Interesting. Maybe Warren's plan isn't going to go so smoothly after all. "I'll be damned. What might cause such a thing?"

"Oh, any number of things," Rheinhoffer answered. "News pending or an order imbalance are the most common."

"Order imbalance?"

"You know? Too many buyers, or too many sellers. The specialist on the floor can't open the stock until he can find a price where there is some equilibrium."

"Hmm," Jake mused. "Did Mr. Josephs appear upset about it, Mr. Wilkinson?"

"The delay? Yes, a little. I mean, he wasn't screaming or yelling, or anything. But he did say something that caught my ear."

"What's that?"

"We were discussing what the reasons might be for the delay. He asked me what I thought, and I told him that there appeared to be an order imbalance." Wilkinson muffled a cough with his hand. "So, anyway . . . I mentioned that I hoped it wasn't another burning, and he immediately answered, 'It's not.' He caught himself and clarified, but I remember thinking what a strange comment that was."

Jake knew now they had Warren right where it hurt the most. Kill the deal—the purpose for his madness—and Jake knew he would begin to fall apart. "Okay, thank you, Mr. Wilkinson. I appreciate it. Listen, is it possible, Mr. Rheinhoffer, that if he calls again, you can have him connected directly to you?"

"Way ahead of you," Rheinhoffer said. "I've already left instructions with our staff that if Mr. Josephs should call, he is to be switched to me only."

"Good. Is Mr. Wilkinson still there with you, Mr. Rheinhoffer?" Jake asked.

"Yes."

"Well, I'll need to speak to you alone for a moment, if that's okay?"

Jake listened as the two men said something to one another. He was not quite able to make it out and really didn't care. "Good-bye, Mr. Ferguson," Wilkinson said. "Hope I was of some kind of help."

"Thank you, Mr. Wilkinson. You were a great help." Their line was quiet for a few seconds before Jake could hear the sound of a closing door. "Are you alone, Mr. Rheinhoffer?"

"Yes."

"Could you please tell me the value of Mr. Josephs's account?"

Jake could hear Rheinhoffer punching buttons on his computer keyboard. "As of last night, the total account value, including his puts, was over six hundred thousand."

Six hundred K for a scumbag like this? Is there no justice in this world? "Talk to me about this money-wiring process. Who does it? Where is it done? What does it take to make it happen?"

"It's fairly simple. We enter instructions to our mainframe in New York from this office. Once we receive instructions from the client, it's really nothing more than entering some information and pressing a few buttons."

"Just like that?" Jake asked.

"Just like that."

"Is it unusual to receive such a request?"

"Oh, no. I'd say, on average, we get a half dozen requests a day. Give or take."

The words "instructions from the client" hung in Jake's ears. He didn't know the money world well, but if his intuition was correct, they may just have found a way to snag Warren. "You mentioned receiving instructions from the client, Mr. Rheinhoffer. Could you elaborate on that a bit for me?"

"Well, for obvious reasons, we just can't wire our clients' money out to some unknown bank on the basis of a phone call. We need written instructions from the client"—Rheinhoffer stopped in midsentence, finally realizing where Jake was going—"to proceed with any action of that type. Mr. Ferguson, are you thinking what I think you're thinking?"

"Now you know why I wanted you alone. Six hundred grand is quite a lure, don't you think?"

"It is in my book, and I don't exactly flip burgers for a living."

Jake was sure he'd found the angle. "Mr. Rheinhoffer, I want you to do something for me."

There was silence.

"If Josephs calls, tell him Wilkinson went home sick. Went to a client meeting . . . whatever works. Make him think the stock has opened, and that you can liquidate his position if he asks. If . . . and this is important, Mr. Rheinhoffer . . . *if* he requests to wire money, act as if it's no different than a dozen other client requests you've handled today. Tell him what you just told me. That he will need to come in if he wants to complete the wire."

"That's not far off the mark actually, Mr. Ferguson."

"Yes, but you are not going to do it. If, for any reason, he should come in prior to our getting there, you *must* stall him, Mr. Rheinhoffer. Tell him your system's down, bank holiday, just think of something."

"I couldn't wire the funds today anyway. Certainly not all of them."

Jake didn't understand. "Why not?"

"Because he hasn't sold his options yet. Even if the stock opens, and even if we really did sell his puts, option trades settle next day."

"What's that mean?" Jake asked.

"What it means is that the soonest those proceeds would be good funds would be tomorrow."

"Good funds?"

"Yes, you know? Free to wire."

"Oh. When would you need his instructions?"

"Today, tomorrow, whenever. It really doesn't matter as long as it's before we enter his request to wire."

Tomorrow? Jake couldn't help but wonder if Warren could wait that long. "Okay, see if you can get him to come in today. Think of something. Do the requests cross your desk?"

"Every last one. I sign off on all of them."

"No responsibility there, huh?" asked Jake tongue in cheek.

"Tell me about it."

Jake thought for a moment. "Okay, here's what you tell him. Tell him you're going to be out tomorrow and therefore won't be able to sign his request unless he brings it in today. I'm going to have your building surrounded. He calls you to set up a time, I want to know about it."

"I can do that. You want me just to call your office?"

"Yes, immediately."

"Easy enough."

"Good. Now listen . . . you won't see these men, Mr. Rheinhoffer, but trust me, they'll be there." Rheinhoffer was cooperating now. Jake figured he might as well take advantage of it. "What are the chances that I could see a copy of Josephs's statements for the last year or so?"

Rheinhoffer was nobody's fool. He'd already thought this thing all the way through. "Josephs has a Capital Asset Account, Mr. Ferguson. That means he gets a detailed year-end statement delineating every activity that has occurred in his account over the past year. All trades, dividends, withdrawals, deposits. Everything. I have a copy of it right in front of me."

"Can you fax that to me?"

"Officially, not without a signed release from the client."

"We can't very well do that now, can we, Mr. Rheinhoffer?"

"No, we can't. Tell you what, though. You get me the court order and I'll be glad to personally hand it to whoever delivers it."

Jake had had it up to his eyeballs with the legal shenanigans. He needed to see that statement *now*. "But that could take up to an hour, Mr. Rheinhoffer. I don't have that long."

Rheinhoffer wanted to help. He was well aware that this entire Morson Grayhead fiasco could easily have befallen Thompson McElvay. "I'll make you a deal. Get to work on that court order. In the meantime, I might be able to get you a fax. But I need something from you, Mr. Ferguson, okay? Actually, two things."

Jake didn't like the sound of that. This was hardly the time for bartering. "I'm listening."

"You didn't get it here. Understand? Use it for whatever reasons you need, but you are only to show the original in court. Not the fax. Agreed?"

"Agreed."

"We're talking my job here, Mr. Ferguson. There can be no middle ground. Deal?"

"Deal," Jake said, wondering about the other half of the equation. "What's the second thing?"

"If you take Mr. Josephs into custody, I do *not* want it done in my office. That type of thing's not good for business."

"All right. You're on."

"I need your word, Mr. Ferguson."

Jesus. "You have my word."

"Good. When do you want it?"

"How about immediately?"

"I'll do it right now. What's your fax number?"

Jake told him, thanked him, and hung up. He was walking toward the fax machine when Ederling came back into the office. Jake leaned against a long, low filing cabinet, his hands resting backward on top. "It's definitely him, Donny. He's got one hundred and fifty Morson Grayhead puts in his account, and he tried to sell them this morning."

Ederling sat back down at the table across from Kelton. "Glad you came?" he asked him.

Kelton was bagging clippings with a latex-gloved hand. "Hey, I'm loving it. Maybe if I stick around long enough, I can see you guys cuff him."

Jake smiled. "This is as close as we've been on this thing, Bill. You should come more often." Everyone laughed as Jake looked at Ederling. "You know, Don, if he tried to sell them, that means he's on the move. Whatever he's got planned, it's high noon in his book."

The three men spoke for a bit as they waited for Rheinhoffer's fax to come. Jake rose to his feet when he heard the fax machine kick in. He watched as paper slowly spewed forth. The fax would eventually be eleven pages long. Warren had been a busy boy. Jake picked the pages up one at a time as they floated into the bin, glancing over the details of his account.

"Donny, come here," Jake said with an excited voice. "You're not going to believe this."

Ederling looked at Kelton as he rose. "I love this job." He walked across the room to Jake's side. "Whad'ya got?"

"Take a look at this." Jake handed him a page, pointing at a series of deposits drawn off the First Nations Bank of New York.

Ederling read it for a moment, the full weight of what he saw not immediately sinking in. "You gotta be kidding me. That's Lianne's bank."

"Some coincidence, huh?"

Kelton rose. "Oh, you guys can't do this to me. I have to see this."

"Be my guest," Ederling said, handing him the page as he approached. "It's right here," he said, pointing.

Kelton read it, his face breaking into a slight grin. "No shit? Well, shiver me timbers. That's ten thousand a month. How long you think that's been goin' on?"

"At least all of last year," Jake said. "What do you want to bet it's been even longer than that?"

Ederling shook his head. "I wouldn't even take that bet. You *know* this has been going on for a while. So what do you make out of it, Jake?"

Jake scratched the side of his head. "I'm not sure. Why would you pay someone ten grand a month?"

"Sounds like blackmail to me," Ederling said.

"I second that," Kelton said.

Jake frowned. It still didn't make any sense. There was something they didn't know. "But why? What could Warren possibly have over Lianne Rybeck?"

"I don't know, but I say we find out," Ederling said.

Jake walked to his desk and picked up the phone to call Lianne. He heard another call come in as his rang several times, before he finally hung up. A strange feeling began to tug at his gut. There was still a large piece of this puzzle they had yet to discover. Jake had no sooner placed the phone in its cradle than Cissy barged into the office. "Jake! It's Valerie," she said in a hurried voice. "She's on the phone."

Jake practically jumped out of his shoes. "Valerie? Where the hell is she?"

Cissy stood by the open door, her right hand on the knob. "She didn't say, but she doesn't sound right."

Kelton turned to Ederling, trying to make sense of the sudden chaos. "What the hell's going on?"

Ederling explained quickly, not wanting to miss Jake's end of the conversation. He watched as Jake picked up his phone, again punching the blinking button on his console. "Hello? Valerie?" he asked quickly, his voice barely restrained. "Oh, thank *God* you called. Where the hell are you?"

There was silence in the room as Ederling, Kelton, and Cissy all listened, watching Jake sit sideways on his desk. Their only means of determining just what had happened to Valerie was through his face and eyes. They watched intently as it grew tight, deep lines forming on his brow. Jake's lips seemed to turn ever so slightly, registering a disdain bordering on hatred. Ederling looked at Cissy, who returned the stare, lifting her shoulders in a subtle, puzzled shrug.

"All right. At least you're out of there," Jake said on the phone. "I'm on my way now. Tell them to take you to Northern Westchester. I'll be there in twenty minutes."

Jake hung up and grabbed something out of his top drawer. "Northern Westchester?" Ederling asked. "You mean the hospital?"

Jake was moving quickly, obviously not planning on sticking around to explain. "Yeah, the hospital."

"Jake," Ederling said, attempting to slow him down just long enough to fill them in. "Whoa, whoa, Jake. You can't just leave, man. At least give us the Cliffs Notes version. Is she okay?"

Jake stopped in the middle of the office. "Look, Donny, there isn't time now. She's shaken up but I think she'll be fine. That son of a bitch Warren and his sidekick, Scotty, kidnapped her. I'll fill you in on the details later."

Ederling's eyes grew wide. "They *what?*"

"You heard me," Jake said, moving toward the door. He stopped, almost as an afterthought. "Listen, Donny, do me a favor. Get those clippings to the lab ASAP. See if the prints match those we got from the beer bottle. I have to go. I'll call from the hospital." He turned to Cissy. "Cis, can you give us a minute alone, please?"

"Sure thing," she said, closing the door.

Jake waited until it was shut firmly and turned his gaze to Kelton. "Bill, I'm sorry about this. Please accept my apologies. Don will fill you in." Jake turned to Ederling. "Donny, let's get an APB on this cocksucker. Use the Teletype. You know the routine. I hope they find him first, because if I do, I'm going to kill the son of a bitch with my bare hands." He took a long breath, as if to regroup. "Valerie said she was in some condo complex up north. The guy that found her told her to tell me she was in the Pound Ridge Reservation. Get on the phone to the post offices around there. See if you can find a Himmerton. You find it, page me. We're gonna nail this bastard. Also, don't forget that court order to freeze Warren's account. It's in the White Plains branch of Thompson McElvay. When Freddy brings it back, deliver it in person."

"But the guy's expecting *you*, Jake."

"I'll call him from the car. Just make sure it gets done. Yesterday. Ask to speak to a Barry Rheinhoffer. He's the manager. Also, we need the office surrounded. Warren has to go there in person if he wants his money. I have to go, I'll call you."

"Hey, Jake," Ederling called out as he was stepping through the door.

Jake poked his head back inside. "What?"

"I'm glad for you, buddy. Tell Val I said hello."

Jake smiled. "Thanks. We're almost there, Donny. See you."

"Yeah. Almost there."

WARREN PARKS KNEW he had problems. A short while ago he could not think of a reason good enough to prevent his getting on tomorrow's flight. But with Valerie's escape, that had all changed. The phone rang endlessly as he had made quick work of Scotty, beating him ruthlessly with his fists and feet, and anything else he could get his hands on. In a perfect world he would certainly have killed him where he stood. Only two things stopped him. The first was that he didn't have time to mess around. The second was that he needed Scotty's help to find Valerie.

Scotty hung limply, as if a Raggedy Andy doll, as Warren held him up by his T-shirt. Scotty's head rattled violently about with each shake of Warren's merciless rage. All the while, there was the ring of that damn phone. Warren thought it would never stop. "Now, you listen to me, you brainless piece of dog shit! Get your ass outside now and find her. Search the road, every bush, behind every house. She's still manacled, she can't have gone far." Warren practically dragged Scotty out the bulkhead door, making every effort to slam him into walls and corners.

When they reached the top, Warren grabbed Scotty by his ears, holding his face two inches from his own. "You take the right side, I'll take the left. Don't even bother coming back here without her or I swear to God I'll kill you. You got that?" Warren kicked Scotty viciously in the rear, sending him flying to his knees on the grass. "Now *go!* Get the *fuck* out of here."

Warren stood, watching Scotty limp away and out of sight. His mind raced furiously, desperately trying to think like Valerie. He looked to the woods in front of him, momentarily considering giving them a once-over, but decided she wouldn't have been that crazy. She would most certainly have gone for a phone. The thought of one made him realize that Scotty's had been ringing forever. No one lets a phone ring that long. *No one.* Not unless they're desperate.

That one thought made him wonder. He knew it couldn't be the police. They sure as hell weren't going to bother calling. They'd just bust down the door with a battalion of men. And if Warren was right, and Valerie had gotten to a phone, he only had a few minutes . . . at most. Then who else? Every bodily function seemed to freeze as the thought came crashing into his brain. He knew then that it could only be Lianne. Only she would be so crazed about her son. In the ultimate of ironies, it immediately came to him that only *she* could save him. Warren bolted down the bulkhead, charging to the steps leading up to the kitchen. Warren yanked himself furiously up the handrail, taking huge, three-step strides, hitting the phone on the wall in seconds.

"What!" he yelled.

"Warren?" Lianne said with an irritating calm. "I was just getting ready to hang up."

"Fuck you, Lianne."

"Tch, tch, tch. So angry, Warren. Always so angry. I have a deal to make with you."

Come on, come on, he urged her silently. "Good. I've got one for you. What's yours?"

"No, yours first. I like surprises."

Warren had no time for games. He *had* to go. "I need your plane, Lianne."

His words frightened her. She wondered how he could possibly have known. Once again, Warren seemed two steps ahead of her. Lianne worried now that she had become so maniacally bent that she had missed the fact that the snake had actually planned it this way. It was too late now. She did not bother telling him that *her* deal involved the plane, too.

"You do, huh?" she asked. "What do I get in return?"

"What do you want?"

"I want my son back. It doesn't matter how close he lives to me, Warren, and you know it. You control that boy's *mind*, and now I want you out of it."

"Fine. Done. When do you want him?"

Fine? Done? As Chan had felt not that long ago, she found herself troubled at just how easy it had been. Just like that, the deal was struck. Lianne kept asking herself exactly what this sociopath had planned. She had never dreamt it would happen like this. It seemed far too easy. "I want him now, Warren. But I also want something else."

"What?"

"I want you to disown him in front of my eyes. I want to hear you tell him what scum you are, and that *I* am his one true friend."

Warren scoffed at the suggestion. There was *no* way he would do that before he got on that plane. Warren looked at the clock on the wall. Several minutes had passed. He *had* to get out of there. "I do that, Lianne . . . and he doesn't come with me. He's going to stay with you."

"That's the idea."

"No way!" Warren said firmly. "Not before that plane is off the ground. Once I hand him over to you and get on that plane alone, what assurances do I have you're not going to have it surrounded by cops?"

"You have my word."

Warren may have been born at night, but it wasn't last night. "Oh . . . *please*. What do you think? I'm an idiot like your boy there? He comes with me, or the deal's off."

Fine. Lianne really didn't care. Warren was never going to see that plane anyway. She hesitated for a moment for effect. "All right, Warren, we'll do it your way. I just want my boy back."

"Yeah, yeah. Look, I gotta go. I'll bring him by now. Just get that plane ready, you understand? And no bullshit, or this kid will never speak to you again. I can promise you that."

Lianne was not pleased with Warren's flippant approach. "Don't 'yeah, yeah' me, you son of a bitch. This is not some game you can play if you're in the mood. You do what *I* say, or you can rot in jail for the rest of your miserable life."

"Threats now? I won't be the only one, Lianne. There's no statute of limitations on murder, remember?"

Lianne had done nothing but think of this moment since Chan took her Mercedes yesterday morning. There was no way she was going to let on that she didn't care about that anymore. She felt it vital that he still consider her vulnerable. Predators are never more assailable than when they think they have you down.

We'll see, she thought, leaving his threat unanswered. "I'll inform the guards. Be here within the hour."

"Oh, it will be sooner than that."

"Good. The sooner you're out of his life, the better."

Warren hung up the phone and ran outside. "Scotty!" he yelled. "Scotty, come here!" Warren looked for him as he walked down the brick walk, craning his neck down the right side of the street. "Jesus Christ," he mumbled. "How did I ever get tied up with this idiot?" Warren ran his fingers through his hair. "Scotty! I found her! Let's go!" He saw Scotty limp out from behind a fence, looking sheepishly in his direction. "Come on!" Warren said, waving Scotty in with his right hand. "Come on! Run!" As Scotty broke into a pathetic jog, Warren dragged a hand across his mouth, looking down the street for cops. "Jesus Christ."

Scotty limped up the walk, keeping his distance from Warren. "You found her?"

"Well, not exactly. Your mother called. Valerie took a cab there. Come on, get your keys. We got to go pick her up."

Scotty was confused. "Then why did she leave?"

"Scotty . . . *please*. Just get your keys. I'll explain it in the car. Hurry. She's not going to wait long."

Scotty stared at him, not budging an inch. "I don't think I want her to be with you, Warren. You're mean."

"Scotty," Warren said slowly. "Where are your keys?"

Scotty wrapped his arms around his chest and shook his head. "I'm not going to tell you."

Warren's eyes bulged with rage. He wanted desperately to kill Scotty now, to rip the life from his useless body one joint at a time. If Warren didn't need him to insure his escape, he would certainly have murdered him and found his keys himself. He knew for sure that Scotty had no clue just how lucky he was.

It was all Warren could do to maintain a semblance of composure. "Come on now, Scotty. You know how much she means to me. That's why I got so damn mad. I thought I would never see her again."

Scotty eyed him suspiciously. "Warren?"

"What?"

"You promise you won't hit me anymore? I don't like that. It hurts me."

"I promise, Scotty. I won't hit you anymore. Come on, please? Please get your keys." Scotty did not answer right away, the wait seeming interminable to Warren. He thought his heart was going to beat through his ribs. "Scotty?"

"Okay," he finally said, walking toward the front door. "But I'm going to tell Valerie what you did to me."

Warren closed his eyes and bobbed his head slightly. "Whatever. Come on, Scotty, we have to go now."

Warren followed behind Scotty, watching him limp slowly up the steps and into his condo. Come on, come on, his mind urged. Move! Warren bobbed his torso up and down with each slow and endless step, egging Scotty on telepathically. A restive itchiness clawed at his synapses as he plodded slowly behind, begging Scotty to move faster, the way you do when stuck behind an octogenarian driving ten miles under the speed limit.

Finally, Warren couldn't take it anymore. "Scotty, we have to go, man!" he said in veiled disgust, thinking he would explode. "Just tell me where they are, and *I'll* get them." Scotty told him, and Warren bolted toward Scotty's room, yelling behind him, "Get in the car, Scotty. I'll be right there."

As it was, Warren retrieved the keys and was sitting in the Volvo's driver's seat before Scotty even made it into the garage. Warren turned the ignition, hit the automatic garage-door opener, and rolled down the window. "Please, Scotty," he said with as pleasant a firmness as he could muster. "Move it!"

Scotty finally opened the door and lumbered in, sitting down slowly . . . painfully . . . as if he had been shot in the buttocks. Warren waited for him to close his door and whipped the car into drive, bouncing it violently at the base of the driveway as he made his turn. He depressed the garage door opener and took off down the road, mindful to gain speed quickly, but careful not to draw too much attention to himself by squealing his tires. The less people saw, the better.

ON THEIR DRIVE to the estate, Warren stopped at a Texaco station. He knew it would be his last chance at a phone before reaching Lianne's estate. "I have to make a call, Scotty," he said as he pulled in. "Stay here. I'll be right back." Warren got out, closed his door, and dialed the 800 number for the

White Plains Thompson McElvay office. He fidgeted nervously, eyeing the road ahead and behind him for police while waiting for the switchboard operator to connect him to his broker, Wilkinson. It seemed to be taking longer than normal. The delay concerned him. Rheinhoffer finally answered the phone.

"Barry Rheinhoffer speaking. May I help you?"

Warren wondered who the hell Barry Rheinhoffer was. But the name did ring a bell. He wondered if he had seen it on office correspondence before. "I'm afraid there's been a mistake," Warren said.

"Who are you trying to reach?"

"Ted Wilkinson. I must have inadvertently been put through to you."

"No mistake," Rheinhoffer assured him, his voice calm and relaxed. "Mr. Wilkinson had a lunch presentation to give across town this morning. I'm covering for him in his absence. I'm the office manager. Is there something I might help you with, Mr. . . . ?"

"Josephs."

"What can I do for you, Mr. Josephs?" Rheinhoffer asked casually.

"Is Morson Grayhead trading?"

Rheinhoffer depressed the symbol on his keyboard for the sound effect. "Well, let's see. Morson Grayhead. Yep. Just opened a few minutes ago. Forty-five and an eighth bid. Quarter offer. Are you looking to buy it? Because if you are, I'd wait. The thing's sinking like a lead balloon."

Warren's head turned, his eyes darting about like an escaped convict. "No, I need to liquidate my puts."

"Oh, so you're the lucky man with the Morson Grayhead puts. Good luck hitting one like that again."

"No shit, huh? Listen, I'm in kind of a rush. If I give you instructions, can you wire the money out for me?"

"The whole thing?" Rheinhoffer asked with disappointment.

"Yes. Every last cent."

"Has there been a problem of some kind, Mr. Josephs? Something I might be able to help with? We always hate to lose clients of your stature."

Christ, Rheinhoffer, Warren wanted to scream, just do it! Why did everything seem to be moving in slow motion? "No, no problem. I just need the money. I'm in kind of a bind."

"Will you be closing your account, sir?"

"Yes, please. Here," Warren said, taking out his wallet for the wiring instructions. "Let me give you the instructions now while I have you on the phone."

"I'm awfully sorry, Mr. Josephs, but I can't take wire instructions over the phone. You'll need to come in to sign an LOA."

Warren could not believe what he was hearing. "What do you mean, you can't do it over the phone? And what the hell's an LOA?"

"Oh, I'm sorry. That's our nomenclature for letter of approval."

"Are you serious?"

"Very," Rheinhoffer answered sternly. "I apologize for any inconvenience. It's standard procedure in the industry. It's for your own protection, sir. I'm sure you understand."

Warren began to panic now. He seemed to lose his balance, leaning against the clear Plexiglas of the phone booth. His mind roiled in a cloudy tailspin, unable to comprehend the chaos that was taking place around him. All these years, all his planning, and fate was thwarting him now at every turn. Just when victory hung under his nose, just when Warren was about to take his bite of the forbidden fruit, his reward was being irrevocably, heartlessly snatched from his grasp.

"Understand? You're sure I'll *understand?* That is *my* money, Mr. Rheinhoffer. *Mine!* Do you understand that?"

"Oh, yes, sir. I understand that clearly," Rheinhoffer said, enjoying, even savoring, this moment. "And I will be happy to wire it wherever you like, if you would just be good enough to give us a signed LOA. It only takes a minute."

"Are you telling me you will not wire my money out unless I come in?"

"That's correct, sir. The firm is very clear on that. I'm afraid it's nonnegotiable."

"Can I fax you the instructions?" Warren asked.

"Well, yes . . . we can begin the process via a fax. But the actual wire can only be acted upon in your presence."

That wasn't actually true, but Rheinhoffer assumed Warren wouldn't know it. And while it was true that a fax wouldn't work, Warren could easily have mailed the LOA in. But Rheinhoffer didn't know Warren's time frame and sure as hell wasn't going to give him that out.

"Jesus Christ! What kind of a boiler shop are you running down there?"

"Excuse me, sir?"

Warren dug deep, sucking in a lungful of air. He wanted to reach through the phone and rip Rheinhoffer's trachea out with his fingers, but knew he would need the man's help if he was ever to see his money. "I'm sorry, Mr. Rheinhoffer. I didn't mean to explode like that. It's just been a difficult time for me. That's all. Please accept my apologies."

"No problem, Mr. Josephs. I understand how frustrating this must be for you. When can you come in?"

Come in? Warren thought. He knew that he could never risk going to that office. It was fortuitous at the very least that he had not been arrested yet. Warren remained quiet, thinking things through.

"Mr. Josephs? You still with me?"

"Yeah, I'm here. I'm thinking."

"I understand, sir. Take your time. But a word of caution, though. It'll have to be sometime today. I need to sign off on all our wire transfers and will be away on business the rest of the week. I'm afraid today is the only opportunity I will have to sign off on your LOA."

Warren was devastated. He was having trouble maintaining his hold on reality. "I can't believe this," he said in desperation. He looked at his watch: 11:48 A.M. "All right. I can be there before one. Is that okay?"

"Certainly, sir. Whatever is convenient for you. As long as it's before three. I'll be gone after that. My screen indicates that you entered an order earlier this morning to liquidate your entire Morson Grayhead option position. Is that correct?"

"Yes. I want to sell them all."

"Very well, sir. Let me just repeat that order to you, if I may. You would like to sell one hundred fifty Morson Grayhead April fifty-five puts, correct?"

"Correct."

"Was that a market order, Mr. Josephs? Or would you prefer a limit order?"

"Market. Sell them at the market. Just sell them all."

"Very well. I look forward to seeing you."

Warren didn't bother answering. He hung up the phone, dropping his head with his hand still resting on the receiver. He stood motionless, realizing the absurdity of what he had just agreed to. He didn't have time to drive to White Plains. As it was, Warren knew he'd be lucky to make it to the estate.

For a brief, fleeting moment, Warren actually thought he *could* do it. But reminiscent of that split second following a cut that you know is going to bleed—that nanosecond of hope as you stare at the dry and lifeless slice—once the blood starts to flow you realize just how foolish your hopes had been. It took about two seconds before Warren realized that his blood was flowing, hemorrhaging all around him, all over him, mucking up everything he'd waited all these years to enjoy. His mind turned in a vicious torrent, collapsing on his very sanity.

Warren thought he might go mad. All his work . . . his waiting. And for what? To come up empty-handed? Warren would *never* let that happen. But where was he going to get six hundred thousand dollars? A little whisper kept warning him that it could be a trap. The police obviously knew who he was.

That meant that they had his social security number and date of birth. Shit, he thought, they probably know what cereal I eat. It couldn't be that hard to find someone's brokerage account. Warren didn't know and damn well wasn't going to try to find out. There was just no way he could take the chance. His well-rehearsed plan lay in shambles before him now. Somehow, in a matter of two hours, his purpose—his reason for living—had fallen from victory to a desperate attempt to remain free.

Warren watched Scotty lying in a heap inside the Volvo and berated himself for ever letting him out of his sight. Warren's lips quivered with rage; the very sight of his moronic lackey evoked a murderous rage, the likes of which even *he* had never felt. If that overgrown piece of shit hadn't taken Valerie, none of this would be an issue right now. No one would care if he casually drove down to White Plains to sign Rheinhoffer's godforsaken piece of paper. Time wouldn't be an issue. He'd have all day, just as he'd planned. God, did Warren *hate* Scotty! From his point of view, the mindless simpleton had ruined Warren's whole miserable life. It was at that moment that Warren made up his mind. If it was the last thing he ever did, Warren would see to it that Scotty Himmerton never saw the light of another morning.

He walked back to the car, putting it into drive.

Scotty began, "Did you find who—"

"*Shut up!*" Warren gripped the steering wheel, his knuckles white with fury. He pounded it with his right fist. "Shhhit!"

Scotty pushed himself back against the passenger-side door, scared to death of the animal Warren had become. He had never seen him like this before. Scotty remained silent, afraid to open his mouth.

"Think. Think," Warren repeated again and again to himself. "There's got to be another way. Just think."

Warren sat now, wondering what the chances were that the authorities were using Rheinhoffer to set a trap for him. It made sense that the office manager would have to sign off on all money transfers. That much rang true. But still, something wasn't right. The crap about being out the rest of the week, and only being able to get the LOA authorized today? He knew that had to be bullshit. Brokerage firms had to be able to function in an office manager's absence. Do they really have to wait until he comes back? That couldn't be the case. There had to be someone else available to authorize these, and similar, requests. Warren wished he knew more about the back-office mechanics of Wall Street's ways.

There was one way to find out. He turned to Scotty. "Stay here. I'll be right back." Warren walked back to the phone and called the Thompson McElvay office again. "Hi. What is Mr. Rheinhoffer's secretary's name?" he asked the receptionist in a low, disguised voice. Once he had her name, he hung up, waited a few moments, and dialed the 800 number again. "Yes, could I speak with Linda Forrantino, please?"

JAKE PULLED UP to the main entrance of Northern Westchester County Hospital at 11:33 A.M., taking his FIRE MARSHAL medallion out of his glove compartment and tossing it haphazardly on the dashboard. He slammed his door, locked his car, and jogged through the hospital's front entrance. Almost as an afterthought, he stopped, stepped back outside, and eyed a row of red and yellow rosebushes lining the front of the building. He jogged down the steps and strode over to them, stopping long enough to pick a long-stemmed beauty resting up against the brick wall. Jake broke off the thorns as he whipped himself back up the steps via the wrought-iron handrail, stopping at the information counter just long enough to get Valerie's room number.

"Take the elevator to the third floor," the woman said in a calm, disinterested voice, completely unaware of the gravity of the moment. "When you get off, go left. It will be a few doors down on your right."

"Thanks," Jake said on the fly, pushing the UP button incessantly upon reaching the elevator. It seemed to take hours. Jake tapped his foot in staccato-like fashion, watching the illuminated numbers above the two doors move in exasperating slow motion, as if they were purposely making him wait.

Once off the elevator, he turned left as instructed and slowed his gait. He immediately saw a uniformed New York state trooper sitting in a chair outside a room halfway down the corridor. The trooper may well have been reading a newspaper, but his antennae were clearly functioning. Jake noticed the trooper glance up at him, and walked quickly but casually in his direction. He watched as the trooper laid down his newspaper and stood.

"May I help you, sir?" the trooper asked, standing now directly in front of Valerie's door.

"Yes," Jake said, reaching back with his right hand to retrieve his wallet. Jake noticed the cop place his hand near his weapon. The movement was slight, but it caught Jake's attention nonetheless. "I am Chief Fire Marshal Jake Ferguson. I need to speak with Ms. Medforth," he said, placing the stem of the rose in his mouth while removing his ID.

The trooper studied the photo, glanced up at Jake, back down at the photograph in his hand, and finally handed it back to him. Most investigators don't show up for an interview with a rose in their hands, and Jake could see the questions forming in the trooper's eyes.

"She's a friend," he said, sliding his leather ID holder back into a pants pocket before pulling the rose from his mouth.

The trooper nodded with understanding. "She may be sleeping. She was pretty well banged up when she got here."

"I understand. Thank you for your diligence."

Jake took a long, deep breath, his emotions alternating surreally between a childish giddiness and a killer's instinct for revenge. He could see the door was open a crack and placed the rose behind his back before slowly pushing it open, peeking his head inside.

There were two beds in the room, but one was empty. Valerie's eyes were closed, her bruised and battered face lying still, propped up on a couple of uncomfortable, hospital-issue pillows. One of the nurses had set her bed at a slight incline, and Jake could easily make out the gauze bandages wrapped around the matted, dirty hair of her head. He turned, just enough to close the door quietly behind him, and edged his way slowly toward her, stopping at one point to study the intravenous tube inserted in the back of her left hand.

He wanted desperately to speak with her, to kiss her lips, but knew also that she alone had the information that might help him break the case. Time was so critical now. He wanted to let her sleep, but knew that Warren wouldn't wait. When this was all over, there would be plenty of time for intimacy. Right now, he had a madman to catch. Jake knew in his heart that Valerie would understand. He didn't know if the doctors had sedated her and hoped she would be coherent enough to talk. He stood by her side and watched her eyes flicker wildly beneath the thin skin of her lids. She had obviously gone through hell. Her face was scratched and bruised, and her wrists had been bandaged, though Jake could see that blood had begun to ooze to their surface. He coughed a couple of times, hoping she'd open her eyes.

She did, though it was hardly the serene acknowledgment of the safety of his presence he had envisioned. Instead, when they popped open, fear and dread filled her bulging, bloodshot orbs. Panic clearly enveloped her as she screamed something incoherent, causing Jake's heart to jump.

"Shhhh," Jake said, laying the rose on the bed as he leaned over her, wiping sweat from her brow with his handkerchief. "It's me, Val. Shhhh . . . everything's all right. It's only me."

The state trooper poked his head inside the room. "Everything okay?"

Jake looked up. "Yeah, I must've woken her from a bad dream."

Valerie's body remained rigid as the realization seeped in. The trooper disappeared once she relaxed, as she became aware that she was safe. "Oh, God, Jake," she said, reaching out to touch his cheek with her right hand. "I'm so glad to see you. Thank *God* it's over."

Jake knelt and kissed her nose lightly. "It's okay, Val. It's okay."

"Promise me you'll stay right here," she said.

Jake released the aluminum side bar and lowered it slowly to the floor. He sat down on the side of her bed, taking her right hand into his. "Valerie, I need your help now," he said, gazing into her troubled eyes. "I can't stay here very long. I'm sorry, Val. I really am. But the men that did this to you are still on the loose, and with your help, I think we can nail them." Jake squeezed her hand and raised it to his lips. "You understand that, right? They *must* be stopped."

Valerie closed her eyes. "I know, Jake, I know," she responded softly. "I just thought I would never see you again."

I just thought I would never see you again. Valerie's words melted into Jake's heart, seemingly healing a thousand wounds. "Well, you were wrong, weren't you?" he said with a smile. "You can't get rid of me that easily."

Valerie forced a weak and tired grin. "It's so good to hear your voice."

"Valerie," Jake began slowly. "I know this will be difficult . . . but I need to know what happened. Can you talk about it?"

She nodded. "What do you want to know?"

"Everything. Don't leave anything out. Tell me *everything.* Can you do that?"

"Yes," she mumbled. "It was so frightening."

"I can only imagine."

He hated to push her, but what choice did he have? If he could have played this out any other way, he would have given everything he owned to do so. But he couldn't. Jake needed Valerie's help, and he needed it right now. A part of him wanted to let her rest, to let her forget her ordeal. But he knew that was impossible.

"Unfortunately, time is critical, Val." Jake pulled out his tape recorder. "I hate to ask this of you, but can you tell me quickly? When this is over, I'll come back. I promise. We can spend as much time together as you want. But right now, you have to talk to me. Tell me everything you can remember, as quickly as you can. Warren's on the move. If we hurry, we can catch him."

"Where do you want me to start?"

"Tell me how they got you. From there, just walk me through what happened. If it's not important, I'll let you know, okay?"

"Okay." Valerie closed her eyes as she attempted to replay the horror of the past twenty-four hours in her mind. "I remember showering and getting dressed. I opened your door to see if the *Times* had arrived yet. It couldn't have been two seconds, Jake. I didn't have time to react. Next thing I know, I'm falling backwards."

Valerie spent the next fifteen minutes relaying the details of her ordeal to Jake. She explained that she must have hit her head and blacked out, her coming to and realizing that she was chained to a boiler, Warren's rage at discovering her in the basement, his rabid fury and vicious brutality. She told Jake how he had kicked her and explained that was one reason why she had bandages on her head. She described her perceptions of the Scotty/Warren relationship: how Scotty was clearly not all there, and how Warren was obviously manipulating him toward his own selfish ends.

"Is Scotty involved in the murders?"

Valerie shook her head slightly, wincing in pain. "I don't think so, Jake. He's too slow. He took me as a gift for Warren. Can you *believe* that? As much as I hate him, I honestly don't think he would hurt a fly."

"So, you're telling me your abduction wasn't part of a larger plan?"

"I can't imagine it, Jake. You should have seen how Warren flipped out when Scotty brought him down to see me. He went off the deep end. I mean . . . he went absolutely stark raving mad. He kept screaming, 'Do you know what you have done? Do you know what you've done?' I think he wanted to kill him."

"Was Scotty frightened?"

"Very. I actually watched him pee in his pants."

Jake felt his pager vibrate. He pressed a button and looked at the number on its screen. It was Ederling's car phone. "Stay with me, Val," he said, reaching for the phone at her side. He dialed the switchboard and got an outside line. "Yeah, Donny, it's me. What's up?"

"Jake, Rheinhoffer just called me. He says Warren called him to liquidate his puts. It's a long story, but the bottom line is Warren said he'd be coming to the office by one."

"Good. Rheinhoffer pulled it off."

"Seems so. I assume you want the place surrounded, right?"

Jake looked at Valerie and winked. "Give me the whole works, Don. I want a SWAT team surrounding that place. Take him down, but remember not to do it in the office. I promised Rheinhoffer."

"Will do. Meet you there?"

"Yeah, I'm with Valerie now. I'm on my way. I'll call you from the car."

"Jake, was Warren involved in the kidnapping?"

"Yep. I'll tell you all about it when I see you."

"How's she doin' by the way?"

"She's a little roughed up," Jake said, looking into Valerie's eyes. "But she'll be okay. Especially if we bag him. Okay . . . go. Keep me informed."

"Tell her I said hello."

"Will do."

"Ederling?" Valerie asked after Jake hung up.

"Yeah."

"He's a good man, Jake."

"I know. He wants me to say hello. Listen, Val, I think we've got Warren nailed." He sat back down on the bed and took her hand again. "I have to leave. You going to be all right?"

"Yeah, I'll be fine," Valerie said through a forced but sincere smile. "Just catch him, Jake."

"Don't worry about that, Val. We won't get this close and blow it." He leaned over and kissed her softly on the lips. "I'll be back. Promise."

Jake rose from her bed and turned to leave. "Oh . . . I almost forgot." He picked up the rose. "This is for you."

Valerie smiled. "Thank you, Jake."

"See ya."

"Jake," Valerie called out.

Jake turned. "Yeah?"

"Hurry. Please?"

He blew her a kiss and left the room.

THOMPSON MCELVAY'S WHITE Plains offices were on the ground floor of a posh, newly constructed office building. Art deco in style and tall by Westchester County standards, it rose eleven stories and dwarfed the nearby downtown shopping district. It was both stylish and modern, yet its neo-sophistication was reminiscent of the architectural style so prevalent in Western culture in the late 1920s and early 1930s.

Outside and to the left of its main entrance rose a large, marble statue of a winged woman playing a harp atop a sculpted granite base in a pastel-lit fountain pool. Those who cared knew it to be a Greek goddess, but few had yet figured out which one. Jets of water cascaded in curves of varying heights through small openings in the tops of her strings, sprinkling all who approached with a light, rainbow-filled mist that floated effortlessly through the warm, late-summer air. To the fountain's left sat a white Ford van with the words SIGNS BY VINCENT painted in bright green calligraphy on both sides.

Two plastic signs of varying sizes leaned against the outside of the van, both bearing the name of some phony real estate company, while inside sat six heavily armed men—bearing a likeness more to modern ninjas than highly trained state troopers. Each wore black leather, fingerless gloves; baggy, black paratrooper pants replete with zippers and pockets on both sides; shin-high, laced, black trooper boots; a black, bulletproof vest; and a black helmet to which was attached a tiny communications device, not unlike those worn by a telephone operator.

Beads of sweat formed in tiny pellets on their collective brows as they sat silently, facing one another like paratroopers waiting for a jump. A few leaned back against the van's warm steel, while others leaned forward, elbows on knees; each of them clutching his weapon of choice between his legs with increasingly dampening palms.

Regardless of the manner in which they tried to relax, each had locked in on his respective task, reviewing over and over again in his mind the events that were about to unfold. All held fully automatic assault rifles except the commanding officer, who clung calmly to his portable radio. Of the five men with rifles, four held M16s, while a hawk-eyed young corporal massaged his M14. The M16 relies on brute force and rapidity of discharge to achieve its well-deserved reputation. But the M14 is far more reliable should the need for better accuracy arise.

Other men and women of varying formality of dress leaned against walls reading newspapers or sat at various locations eating lunch. On a concrete bench two men in suits pretended to split a pastrami sandwich, while a woman in a chartreuse sundress with a large, beachlike purse sat Indian-style under a young sapling of an elm, pretending to read the latest Danielle Steel novel. By the fountain a young priest read Bible passages aloud, while a middle-aged woman eagerly handed out leaflets about the one, true Savior. They all shared two things in common: they were heavily armed, and they anxiously awaited the arrival of Mr. Warren Josephs, or Parks, or whatever the hell his real name was.

Inside the growing heat of the van, Don Ederling spoke quietly via a cellular phone to his boss. "We're good to go here, Jake. There's only one person missing."

"Good," Jake said, speaking over the siren blaring from his cruiser. "I'm just past the airport. I should be there in fifteen minutes."

"We'll be here."

"Tell me what you got, Donny."

"We have a SWAT team ready to roll in a van outside the main entrance, and another five plainclothes hanging around outside."

"What kind of van?"

"White. Some sign company."

"Anyone inside the office?"

"No."

"Good. Listen up. Warren may not be alone. He might have Scotty with him. Take them both if you can . . . not that I think you'll have much trouble.

But remember, Warren's the catch of the day. No matter what, Warren walks away in custody. Got it?"

"Got it."

"Okay. See you soon. What's your number?"

Ederling told him. "Jake," he added quickly.

"What?"

"You know how you don't like public preaching?" Ederling asked, looking into the eyes of the SWAT commander sitting across from him.

"Yeah?"

"Just don't roust the priest when you show up, okay?"

Jake chuckled. "I understand."

The SWAT commander looked at Ederling as he depressed the END key. "Not the religious type?"

Ederling pushed the antenna back down into the mobile unit and shoved it in a pocket. He shrugged. "In his own way."

The commander remained silent, opting instead for a slight nod. Ederling couldn't help but wonder just what that meant, but thought it best not to ask. "Okay. So you guys know the plan, right?" he asked no one in particular. Ederling felt foolish after he'd asked it, watching the six men stare at him silently. They were hardly a convivial bunch.

"Don't worry," the commander answered for his men. "We know the score. No one moves until he enters the building."

"Right. And we don't take him until he comes out. Oh . . . and something else. Jake just told me our man may have someone else with him. We'll want him, too, but Jake made it clear that if for any reason it comes down to a choice, Warren's the one. Under *no* circumstances does he walk away from here a free man."

The commander smiled wryly, looking around at his crew. "Unless they're driving an M1 tank, Mr. Ederling, I don't think either one of them will be walking away from here of his own accord."

Ederling smiled, clandestinely eyeing the men surrounding him with their hands wrapped around their automatic weapons, butt-end down on the ribbed, steel floor. He fidgeted with his hands. For a moment he thought of taking out his 9mm, if for no other reason than to show them he wasn't just some lowly civil servant—that he, too, carried a weapon. He laughed internally at the idea. The term *penis envy* entered his mind. Ederling felt woefully out of place, as if he were wearing a leisure suit at the school prom. Come on, Jake, he pleaded silently, save me here, pal.

Ederling, the SWAT commander, and his crew sat quiet and motionless in the growing heat of the van, listening to intermittent transmissions quietly squawk over the radio. They had discussed leaving the van running so as to have use of the air conditioner, but opted against it. They did not want to draw any more attention to themselves than absolutely necessary. After what seemed like a week, Jake finally called the van from a parking garage across the street. It was 12:31 P.M.

"Yeah," Ederling answered.

"Okay, Donny, I made it," Jake said. "I'm in the garage across the street. Any sign of him?"

"Not yet."

"Good. I'm going in to talk to Rheinhoffer for a minute. Page me if you see him coming."

"Don't be long, Jake. We're pushing the deadline."

"Don't worry."

This was Jake's case and he very much wanted to give the scene a once-over before it was too late. He strode casually up the granite steps to the fountain level, scanning all around him with eyes that hardly moved. He saw the van, the ranting priest and his forlorn companion, the two men on the bench, the woman under the tree, and a handful of other people in various modes of leisure, just hanging out, enjoying the warm rays of the mid-September sun. Jake thought he had a few colleagues spotted, but even *he* wasn't sure who was part of the team—and he knew what to look for. *That's good. Warren's hardly stupid.*

The tension, the hatred, the cold-blooded predator's desire for the kill—all of these emotions churned in a violent eddy through Jake's mind as he walked toward the building's front doors. He was completely numb to the fountain's refreshing, cool mist as it flirted across his face. He zipped up his windbreaker, just enough to keep it closed, fearing it might blow open in the breeze, offering a view of his gun. He pulled on the etched-steel doors and entered the air-conditioned lobby, not bothering to eye the plants, the marbled walls, or the statuary. Time was of the essence now. Jake wanted to get this part over with as quickly as possible and get the hell out of the way.

He opened the door to Thompson McElvay's office and stepped inside, announcing himself to the receptionist. "Have a seat, Mr. Ferguson. Mr. Rheinhoffer will be with you shortly."

Shortly's not good enough. "Tell him I need to see him immediately," Jake said to the young woman.

"Yes, sir."

Jake frowned slightly before sitting in a dark green, Georgian Revival, mahogany armchair. It looked ornate but was surprisingly comfortable. He didn't know much about furniture design, but still, it seemed to him a pretty good example of baroque run amok. He leaned forward, his hands clasped between his knees—body language for "I'm waiting."

Jake had no sooner begun to eye the office's rich woodwork and dark green carpet when from out of nowhere a tall, thin man with balding, silver hair suddenly stood in front of him. "Mr. Ferguson?"

"Yes." Jake stood. "Mr. Rheinhoffer?"

"Pleasure to meet you. If you'll follow me, sir, my office is this way."

Jake stood firm. "Do I have to pass by here when I leave?"

"From my office? Yes. Why?"

If Warren did show up to sign his papers, Jake could hardly afford to just walk right past him. The whole mission would be compromised. He much preferred a place out of the way, anyplace where he did not have to pass by this spot again. "Is there someplace else we can talk? Someplace that might have access to a back doorway?"

Jake's request was unexpected. Somehow Rheinhoffer hadn't pictured it this way. He was a little taken aback, though he certainly didn't show it. "Of course. The kitchen's this way. Follow me."

Jake followed his guide up three carpeted steps and down a back hallway, eventually coming upon a small, tiled room with a long table, a watercooler, refrigerator, coffeemaker, and other modern appliances found in most any office kitchen. "I can leave through there?" Jake asked, pointing to a door next to the watercooler.

"Yes. It will take you to the back stairs. Just follow them out to the door marked EXIT. You'll be at the other end of the lobby, the one I'm assuming you entered." Rheinhoffer was more than a little curious. "Why the cloak-and-dagger, Mr. Ferguson?"

Jake looked at his watch. "There's not much time remaining before one o'clock, Mr. Rheinhoffer. Unless Warren lied to us, he should be here any minute. He knows what I look like, and the last thing I want to do if he gets inside before I get out is to pass him as I leave."

Rheinhoffer nodded, indicating that Jake's logic made sense to him. "You know he's coming then?"

"That's our best guess. Would you pass on six hundred K?"

"Probably not." Rheinhoffer took a seat, motioning for Jake to do the same, and leaned forward, placing his forearms on top of the table. "I'm a little nervous about this, Mr. Ferguson. Not for my own safety, you understand. Hell, I was in the Marines for six years. I don't scare easily. But I must have your assurances that my employees will be safe. That is absolutely imperative."

Jake leaned toward him and spoke in soft tones. "Mr. Rheinhoffer, as far as we know, he is coming here for no other reason than to sign whatever papers you told him you needed." Jake smiled. "Nice job, by the way. Let me know if you're ever looking for work."

"Your people are all in place?"

"Yes," Jake said, nodding slightly.

"Not inside the office, right?"

"They've all been instructed to take him down outside. Trust me, Mr. Rheinhoffer, your people will only know what's happened through the grapevine. They won't see or hear a thing. Unless of course . . ."

Rheinhoffer frowned. "Unless what?"

"Oh, it's nothing, really," Jake said with a flip of a hand.

"I'm afraid that's not good enough, Mr. Ferguson. Unless what?"

"Well," Jake started, looking around to assure they were alone, "there is always an outside chance Mr. Josephs could be armed and may decide to go out in a blaze of glory. But even if he does, still, it will happen outside. It's just that . . . well . . . frankly, in that case your people will probably hear some shots. But I have to stress that the chances of an armed confrontation are highly unlikely, Mr. Rheinhoffer. We simply have too much firepower, and of course, the element of surprise. We'll have him down and surrounded in seconds. He won't even know what hit him."

Rheinhoffer stared at Jake. "So, you do this for a living, huh? Seems a touch more exciting than my job."

Jake smiled and leaned back. "I don't know. From what little I've learned in this case, it seems to me that you guys get your share of excitement. Anyway, believe it or not, this kind of thing is pretty rare. My job can be as boring as the next."

"Not today, huh?"

"No. Not today." Jake leaned forward, resting his elbows on his knees. "So . . . you up for this?"

"What? Mr. Josephs? Hell, I'm looking *forward* to it."

"Good. No heroics, right?"

Rheinhoffer chuckled lightly. "Mr. Ferguson, I'd love nothing more than to drop him myself, but I like to think that, at my age, I'm a tad smarter than that."

"How long will it take?"

"To sign the LOA?"

Jake nodded.

Rheinhoffer pursed his lips. "Four, maybe five minutes, max. We've already typed up a letter for him. All he has to do is fill in some specs and sign it. But you know how it goes. There'll be the usual pleasantries. He'll have to announce himself to the receptionist just like you did. I'll have to introduce myself. Then there's the formality of taking him back to the cage, having him read the LOA. You know? The usual."

"The cage?"

"Oh, I'm sorry. Every brokerage office has a cage. It's lingo from the old days when men on Wall Street sat behind wire-meshed cages wearing green eyeshades. It's where all the securities are held, checks delivered and picked up, that type of thing." Rheinhoffer smiled. "Although, if you were to ask my staff, they would probably tell you they sometimes feel like they are in a zoo."

Jake rose and stretched his back. "I know the feeling."

Rheinhoffer remained seated. "Don't we all."

"Okay," Jake began, staring at his host. "Before I go, tell me if anything has happened that's different. Has there been anything out of the ordinary? You know, things missing. Plants misplaced. People missing. Anything at all that has struck you as unusual."

"Plants out of place?" Rheinhoffer asked with raised brows.

Jake closed his eyes. "Anything."

Rheinhoffer looked to the ceiling. "Well, there was one thing, Mr. Ferguson. It could be nothing, but then again, maybe you should know about it."

Jake frowned. *A last-minute surprise.* Jake hated surprises. "What's that?" he asked, sitting back down.

Rheinhoffer picked up the phone on the kitchen table. "Linda, would you come back to the kitchen for a moment? Thanks."

Jake looked at his watch. It was almost 12:45. "What's up, Mr. Rheinhoffer? We're pushing our luck."

"It's my secretary. She got a call a short while ago from a man claiming to be a salesman with Bloomberg.

"Who's Bloomberg?"

"Not who. What. They're a financial services company. Stock and bond quotes, financial news, that kind of thing. Anyway, he told her that he spoke with me this morning and that I told him to call her and make an appointment for either Thursday or Friday."

Jake didn't like the sound of this. "And?" he asked slowly. "Did you?"

"Did I what?"

Jake took a breath. "Did you tell him to call her?"

"That's just it. I never had any such conversation."

Jake's heart sank as he stared into Rheinhoffer's eyes. This did not bode well. "You're absolutely sure?"

"Positive, Mr. Ferguson. The auditors are in this week. My *wife* hardly sees me when the auditors are here. I certainly wouldn't set up a meeting with some salesman. Not this week. Anyway, we already use Bloomberg."

Jake turned at the sound of Linda Forrantino's pumps clacking on the tile floor. Jake and Rheinhoffer rose as she approached. "Linda, I'd like you to meet Mr. Jake Ferguson. He is the fire marshal I told you about on the Josephs case."

"Oh, yes, nice to meet you," she said with a pleasant smile, extending a hand. Both men sat as she settled into a chair at the head of the table. "Linda, would you please tell Mr. Ferguson about the conversation you had with that Bloomberg salesman."

She looked at Jake and smiled. "Well, he was very nice, actually," she began, explaining in some detail her conversation with the caller. "He told me that he had spoken with Barry earlier this morning, and that he had told him to make an appointment through me for later in the week."

"Did that strike you as odd?" Jake asked.

"Yes, very. Barry usually leaves his calendar pretty clear when the auditors are here. I especially didn't think he wanted to see a salesman. Not during audit week." She paused and looked at Jake, almost as if worried that her words were not sitting well with him.

"Go on," Jake said.

"Well . . . he asked me if Barry was leaving town. The man said he thought Barry had mentioned something to him about being out of town the rest of the week and wanted to know if he'd gotten his dates mixed up."

Jake interrupted her. "He thought Mr. Rheinhoffer was leaving town?"

"Oh, yes, he seemed somewhat surprised to hear that Barry was going to be around. I explained that there must have been a misunderstanding, that he never leaves when the auditors are here."

Jake turned to Rheinhoffer, his face and tone of voice clearly more serious now. "What exactly did you tell him when you spoke to him, Mr. Rheinhoffer? I need to know exactly."

Rheinhoffer didn't seem to understand Jake's question. "I told you, I never spoke to the guy."

Jake waved a hand. "No, no, not the Bloomberg guy. Mr. Josephs."

Rheinhoffer looked to the ceiling again, reliving his conversation with Warren in his mind. "Oh . . . well, let's see. I told him he had to come in today. That I was leaving at three and would be gone for the rest of the week."

Jake turned to Forrantino. "And you told the caller that Mr. Rheinhoffer wasn't going anywhere? That he was going to be in all week?"

"Yes," she answered hesitantly. "Did I make a mistake?"

Jake ignored her question. "Mr. Rheinhoffer, how did this one-o'clock deadline come into play if you told him you were leaving at three?"

"He set it. That's what time he told me he could be here by."

Jake looked in Rheinhoffer's eyes. "All right, this is very important, sir."

Jake leaned forward while placing his arms on the table. "Can you tell me when it was that Mr. Josephs called to liquidate his puts?"

"Sure. I remember it clearly. I keep detailed records of all my phone conversations, Mr. Ferguson. You can't be too careful in this business, you know."

"What time was it?" Jake asked again, losing patience. Nightmare visions began flashing through his brain, little flits of fear traveling through its lobes at the worry that Warren had bested him. This whole dragnet was collapsing right under his nose, very likely to result in a colossal waste of time and resources.

"He called about eleven thirty-eight, and I don't think we hung up until around eleven-fifty. Something like that. I can check my logbook if you'd like."

"That won't be necessary," Jake said, turning to Forrantino. "Ms. Forrantino, what time was it when you received the call you just described? Can you remember?"

"Yes, I do. It was twelve-fourteen," she answered quickly.

"You sure?" Jake asked.

"Absolutely. I remember it because I had just come back to my desk after relieving our receptionist for a bathroom break. I glanced at the clock on my desk when I sat down. My phone rang as I was looking at it."

"But you must get dozens of calls in a day. How can you be sure that was the time this one came in?"

"Because it was weird," Forrantino said, flipping the palms of her hands up. "Like I said, I knew Barry would never set up a meeting with a salesman during an audit . . . or at least I thought so. It just struck me, I guess. The whole thing seemed so out of character for Barry. I kept watching the clock during the whole conversation."

Jake took a deep breath. Their story bothered him. "Okay, thanks. I guess that qualifies as out of the ordinary." He turned to Forrantino. "Anything else happen before or since that call?"

"How do you mean?"

"I mean, has anything else happened that struck you as odd?"

Forrantino looked at Rheinhoffer. "Yes. There was one other thing . . . I think."

Jake wasn't surprised.

"It's not that either one of these things really stood out," she began, "although the Bloomberg guy did, I guess. But it was the combination that I found odd."

"The combination?" Jake asked. "What combination?"

"Well, a man called . . . couldn't have been more than a half hour ago, maybe forty minutes."

"And?"

"Well, during that period I told you about when I was at our reception-ist's desk, she came back. I was standing up to give her back her chair and a call came in. She wasn't quite ready yet, so I took it."

Jake's eyes were fixated on Forrantino. "But with all the calls you answer every day, why is this one memorable?"

"Well, it was a man. He wanted to know the name of Barry's secretary. I just told him. I didn't bother explaining it was me. I knew if he called back, I'd already be at my desk."

"Is a request like that unique?" Jake asked.

Forrantino pursed her lips. "No, not really. It's certainly not unheard of. People will occasionally want to speak to me. Especially salesmen."

"She's a great gatekeeper," Rheinhoffer added.

Jake's heart sank. "How long after that did you get the call from this sup-posed salesman?"

"Very soon. A few minutes, I think. Like I said, I had just returned to my desk."

"Was it the same voice?"

Forrantino looked a bit confused.

"The man that wanted to know your name. Was his voice the same as the salesman's?"

She looked at her feet, hesitating for a moment, listening to the conversa-tions again in her mind. "No. Similar, maybe . . . though one seemed deeper. I guess I just ignored the similarity. I answer so many calls, Mr. Ferguson. I must've figured even if it was the same guy, he'd probably misplaced the name Barry gave him. It happens."

Jake turned to Rheinhoffer. "How long have you known about this, Mr. Rheinhoffer?"

Rheinhoffer looked at his secretary. "I was in a meeting with Stan, right? You didn't tell me until I got out. When was that? Twenty minutes ago, something like that?"

Forrantino nodded. "Give or take."

Jake hung his head, running his fingers through his hair. He exhaled deeply, knowing in his heart he'd been duped. *Dammit!* "Can I use your phone?" he asked, his voice beaten, his pace more leisurely, though in a dejected sort of way.

"Is there a problem, Mr. Ferguson?" Rheinhoffer asked.

Jake sat sideways on the table, speaking as he dialed. "You could say that."

Everyone in the van tensed as Ederling's phone rang. This was probably it. "Yeah," he answered on the first ring.

"Donny, it's me. Warren's not coming."

"Come again," Ederling said through squinting eyes.

"You heard me. The whole thing's a ruse. He's onto us. A hundred to one he doesn't show."

Ederling was incredulous. "But how? I mean—"

"Later. Meet me out back of the building." Jake rose and extended his hand to Mr. Rheinhoffer. Jake could see he was puzzled. "I'm afraid we've been had."

"I hope we didn't do something to screw this up," Rheinhoffer said.

"No, Mr. Rheinhoffer, you did an excellent job. Better than I would have anticipated. Same goes for you, Ms. Forrantino. But we're all learning the hard way that Mr. Josephs is no dummy. I'm afraid this just confirms it."

"So that's it?" Rheinhoffer asked, rising to his feet.

"Probably. I'll keep my team in place until three, but I'm pretty certain he's not going to show." Jake looked at his watch: 12:58 P.M. "Listen, I hate to seem rude, but obviously I have things to do. Thank you both very much for your time and effort. You've been a pleasure to work with. If for any reason he *should* show up, just follow the same procedures we've discussed. Nothing's changed in that regard."

"Gee, Mr. Ferguson," Rheinhoffer began, "I feel bad about this."

"Don't. There wasn't a damn thing you could do about it. You did the best you could and I mean that."

"Here, I'll show you out," Rheinhoffer said.

Jake smiled, fighting back his true disappointment. "Thanks, but that won't be necessary. I know the way."

JAKE STRODE SLOWLY out the building's front doors and walked around to the back, stopping to drop his head at the sight of Ederling standing by a Dumpster. Cooling droplets of water had somehow floated in the breeze behind the building. Jake was aware of them now as they played faintly around his face.

He approached Ederling slowly. "Fffuck," Jake said in disgust under his breath, taking off his windbreaker and holding it over his arm. He thought of tying it around his waist, but opted against it. He didn't want anything imped-ing his gun should its use still become necessary.

"What the hell happened?"

Jake felt sick as he relayed the events that had just taken place. He and Ederling played out what Rheinhoffer and Forrantino had told Jake and were both in agreement—it was a good bet Warren wasn't going to show.

"Son of a bitch!" Ederling boomed.

"I thought we had him, Donny. I was actually allowing myself to get pumped."

"What the hell are we going to do with all these people out there?"

"Come on," Jake said, walking toward the front of the building. He turned the corner and looked around as he walked over to the van. He rapped twice on the door, and stepped in when someone opened it. "Christ, it's an oven in here. Turn on the air-conditioning, for God's sakes."

The SWAT commander was not amused. "What the *hell* is going on, Mr. Ferguson?"

Jake explained, feeling embarrassment as he retold the story. It was hardly an ideal ending, but what could he do? Jake had acted on the best information he had available to him at the time and would have played it the same way a hundred times over.

"I'm sorry, gentlemen," he said, scanning the van, making contact with each man's eyes. "I know what a pain in the ass this has been." Jake turned to the commander. "We have to cover all the bases. Hang out here until three, then pack it up. I know why you're sitting here in this heat, and I thank you for your professionalism. But I think it's safe to throw on the air now. The chances that our boy's going to show are pretty slim at this point. But still, let's just play it safe. At least until three."

The commander was not used to taking orders from a fire marshal, but knew this was Jake's case. He was an ex-military man and understood the importance of chain of command. "We're here 'til three." He took out the keys to the van from a side pocket on his pants and tossed them to a colleague. "Jimmy, get the air on. We're going to be here awhile."

Jake looked at him, his eyes expressing profound disappointment. "I'm truly sorry about this, Commander."

"Hey, what are you going to do, right?" the commander said, letting Jake off the hook. "We all do the best we can with what we've got. You'll get him."

Jake rose, bending as he opened the door. "Not at this rate."

"Comfy, huh?" Ederling said as Jake met up with him outside the van.

Jake shook his head. "Yeah, I feel bad for those guys."

"Such a nice bunch, too."

Jake looked at Ederling. "Feeling a little out of your league, Donny?" Jake asked with a mischievous grin. "Did you show them your gun?"

"Fuck you."

Jake exhaled deeply, resting his hands on top of his head. He stood quietly for a moment, his eyes closed to the humiliation all around him. "Okay, so where does this leave us?"

"Out in the middle of a very large lake without an oar."

"Dammit!" Jake yelled. "All right, back to square one. Follow me to my car. We're wasting our time here."

Jake and Ederling sat dejected in the front seat of the Crown Victoria, scrutinizing each other with eyes that said it all. "Goddamnit!" Jake bellowed, slamming an open palm against the steering wheel. He closed his eyes and took a long, deep breath. "All right, Donny, we have a lot of thinking to do, and very little time in which to do it. Where does this asshole go from here?"

"I know this may sound crazy, Jake, but if it ain't here, then I think I know where."

"I got a theory, too. Let's hear yours."

Ederling turned sideways on the seat. "All right, since Valerie's escape, he's got to know we're onto him big time, right? He's got to assume she's already called you and fingered him as the same guy she saw in the bar."

Jake munched on a fingernail. "If he hasn't, he's a hell of a lot dumber than I thought."

"Okay, so Warren knows now his money's not accessible, and he also knows he's not leavin' the country. Not as a normal passenger anyway. And we know he's got Scotty with him, or at least he did the last time anyone saw him. Through this whole mess, we may not have figured out just what makes Lianne Rybeck tick, but we know one thing for sure. She loves that kid. Seems to me Warren's got a pretty powerful bargaining chip riding around with him."

"So, what are you telling me? You think he's headed for the estate?"

"You got a better idea?"

Jake turned the ignition. "No, I was thinking the same thing."

"Yeah, yeah . . . sure you were."

Jake smiled, laid an arm across the back of the seat, and glanced behind him, pulling his cruiser out of its spot. "I just hope we're not too late."

"You want to call her?"

Lianne Rybeck had hardly proven a model of cooperation. Jake dropped his head and stared at Ederling from the tops of his lids.

Ederling folded his arms. "I didn't think so."

IMMEDIATELY FOLLOWING HIS conversation with Linda Forrantino, Warren knew that a trip to Thompson McElvay's White Plains office was absolutely out of the question. Warren hung up and stared across the street at the trees bustling in a stiff, late-summer breeze. It *was* a trap. He knew now that son of a bitch Rheinhoffer wasn't going anywhere. As much as the thought of being set up sickened him, he had no other choice. He simply could not go. But as Warren thought about it, he realized it might actually work out well to his favor. He could use the ruse of his arrival at Thompson McElvay as a red herring, drawing the police far away from where the real action would be. If they were trying to draw him into their net, they would grow old waiting.

As painful as it was for Warren to admit, his plan had now officially fallen apart. There was no doubt in his mind the authorities were onto him and had smartly recruited Rheinhoffer to participate in the ploy. Oh, they're good, he thought. But he also knew that they had absolutely *no* idea whom they were dealing with. If the cops thought they were smart, he intuitively knew they hadn't seen smart. Go ahead and wait, assholes, he thought. I got business to attend to.

Warren hung his head. Something still didn't fit. The timeline was out of whack. Valerie had only escaped about an hour ago. That wasn't nearly enough time for the authorities to find his account, fill Rheinhoffer in on the case, and enlist his cooperation. And *that* could only mean one thing: Jake Ferguson et al had tagged him the killer long before Valerie ever entered the picture. For a moment he tried to think of how, but ditched the frustrating exercise in futility. He assumed it had to have been the evening at the bar. Though Warren still thought it a stretch. However they'd figured it out, it was definitely moot now. The only thing that mattered now was his survival.

But Warren wasn't ready to give it all up just yet—not by a long shot. Not after all these years. He had *earned* this, and no one, not some two-bit fire investigator or anyone else for that matter, was going to deprive him of his due. There was one last alternative, one he hadn't thought of until just now. He furled his brows as he pondered that it always seemed to come back to Lianne. Warren wondered when he was ever going to get that maddening bitch out of his life.

Lianne Rybeck might have a plane, and thus his ticket to freedom, but she also had something more important—millions of dollars in jewelry. Melt down the settings, and those precious little stones would not only be untraceable, but could yield Warren far more than any of his wasted Wall Street games. Lianne had more money than God. She would gladly give them up, especially if it meant getting back her son. Anyway, Warren wasn't greedy. He didn't want them all. Just a million or two.

When Warren first hatched the whole Morson Grayhead idea, two goals were foremost in his mind: to bring the firm to its knees, and to make a score large enough to start a new life. The former he had done. In fact, after Severin's suicide, he didn't think he could have done it much better. Bringing that pretentious windbag down to earth was a dream come true, and pinning it all on Lianne's useless moron of a son would simply have been icing on the cake. But now . . . all Warren wanted was to get out of the country . . . *and* his money. That much he'd earned. How he got it, from where it came, he really didn't care anymore. The only thing that bothered him was that he had not had time to figure this new angle out. His last one had been planned for years, and look at how that fell apart. But then again, Warren reminded himself, sometimes spontaneity is best.

Warren turned and stared through the Volvo's windshield at Scotty, slumping childlike in the front seat. The reflection from the rustling trees on the windshield danced across his face. Warren couldn't help but wonder what it was like in his simple little world. Not that Warren was sympathetic. On the contrary, the emotions he felt raging inside him now were anything but. More than his freedom, almost more than the money, what Warren really wanted was to see Scotty Himmerton's last breath of life. He only regretted that he would have to keep him alive long enough to fulfill his end of the deal. Warren feared that without Scotty, at least for now, Lianne might have been right. He might well spend the rest of his life in jail. And he would rather die than allow his incarceration to happen again.

But to Warren's way of thinking, he was only going to have to put up with this inane reality a little while longer. Once he delivered Scotty to Lianne, and once he heard her verbally instruct the pilot of the plane, they would both be as good as dead. As he stood staring at the Volvo, he smiled inwardly, wondering if this whole thing hadn't somehow actually worked out for the better. He would not only get his money, but also have the unplanned opportunity to take care of a few loose ends. The thought calmed Warren, the prospect of how much more peaceful his remaining life would be knowing both their stinking-rich mouths would be shut for eternity.

He walked quickly toward the car, opened the door, and scooted in. Scotty did not look at him, opting to stare outside the passenger-side window instead. Warren looked at his watch: 12:21 P.M. He put his keys in the ignition and pulled out onto the road. If he played his cards right, it would soon be over.

Chandler Boutet had pulled Sammy's Saab to the side of the road about an eighth of a mile from the Texaco station where Warren and Scotty now sat in the parked Volvo. He waited quietly behind the steering wheel, binoculars to his eyes, watching Warren walk back and forth intermittently from Scotty's car and the pay phone. Chan turned and glanced out the passenger-side window just long enough to see Sam jiggle his right arm and waist as he finished up a much needed piss. Chandler turned his attention to the gas station again, just as the Volvo was pulling out. He leaned over and wrapped twice on the window with his binoculars.

"They're mobile. Let's go," he said as Sam opened the door and slid in.

"*Man* . . . that felt good," Sam said. "My eyes were floating."

Chan looked behind him to his left before pulling slowly out onto the road, keeping a good quarter mile between the two cars. They followed the Volvo in silence for a while before Sam finally spoke.

"How long we gonna do this for, Chan?"

"As long as it takes."

Sam lit a cigarette, flipping out his match and pushing it through the partially opened window. "As long as it takes?" He looked at Chan. "As long as *what* takes?"

Chan was quiet. That was a good question. He wondered how he should answer it. He couldn't very well tell Sam, "As long as it takes to make sure this scumbag gets to the estate so I can be sure of his fate." Chan drove in silence, his mien pensive, almost withdrawn.

Sam didn't wait for a response. He wasn't trying to dig up the truth as much as he was trying to get a handle on what was *really* making his friend tick. "Look, Chan, you and I . . . we're pretty close, right?"

Chan glanced at Sam. "Of course. Why?"

"Because 'as long as it takes' doesn't work for me. I don't think you're telling me everything you know about this here little caper we've found ourselves on. And frankly, I think I have a right to know."

"How do you mean?" Chan asked the windshield.

"Well, for starters," Sam said, smoke wisping out of his mouth as he spoke, "you can fill me in on our objective. I mean, are we just going to follow this guy around until he drops? What's our goal here anyway? Seems to me a few things have changed since Dan. Don't you think?"

Chan remained quiet, thinking that perhaps Sam was right, that maybe he wasn't being fair to his friend. "Our goal *has* changed, Sammy."

"Gee . . . that's news to me. Care to fill me in?"

"How much of this shit do you really want to know?"

"Look, Chan, I'm not an idiot." Sam's voice was firm—the kind close friends can use with one another. "I know what's going on here, and I know what you and Lianne spoke about when you asked me to step outside the car."

"Okay. So?"

"So you want to get paid. Fine. Me? I don't give a *shit* about the money. I want to see this motherfucker fry." Sam turned to his friend. "How about you? Where do *your* priorities lie?"

Chan didn't say a word as he slowed at the intersection of Routes 137 and 121, stopping to look in both directions. He followed the Volvo right on 121 and realized they were heading toward the estate. He had some important decisions to make, and if Warren was heading to the estate, Chan had to make them quickly.

"Look, you're right, okay? I do know something you don't."

"No shit."

"It's not how it looks, though. The money's not what's keeping me quiet.

I just don't think making you privy to it is going to make your life any easier, Sam. That . . . and I did give my word."

"Your word? To whom?"

"Lianne Rybeck."

Sam rolled down his window, flicking his butt to the road. He rolled it back up and chuckled sarcastically to the windshield. Chan could tell that Sam was beginning to lose respect. "Look, I can't *make* you tell me. I don't even *want* to. If you don't want to bring me up to speed of your own accord, then I guess I don't want to know. It just seems to me that after what happened to Danny, maybe your loyalties would have changed somewhat. It's not exactly like we knew we were tracking a madman, Chan. I don't know about you, but I'm pretty pissed off at Mrs. Lianne Rybeck. And, if after all that's happened, you still feel you owe her, rather than Dan . . . then I can only guess she's paying you a shitload of dough. And that's a shame. Because that's not the Chandler Boutet I know. Then again, maybe I don't know you as well as I thought, huh?"

So, there it was—out in the open, painfully slashing at Chan's conscience. Sam's words tortured him, like bamboo shoved under his fingernails. He wondered if the money *had* contaminated his thinking, and if what Sammy had just said was true. Chan worried that perhaps somehow he had misplaced his loyalties. One of his two best friends in the world had been brutally murdered, leaving behind a loving, giving wife and two children most men would die for, and all Chan could think of was the cash. The reality of the moment stunned him. Chan wasn't sure who the hell he was anymore.

"How much is she paying to turn you like this?"

It was time to come clean, if it was even possible anymore. "A hundred K."

Sam sat stoically, quietly staring out the windshield. "I didn't know you were such a cheap date. You're selling Danny out for a lousy hundred large?"

"Now wait just a minute, Sam," Chan started, resenting his sudden sense of nakedness. "I don't appreciate—"

"No, *you* wait a minute! You're so worried about the goddamned money? Go ahead, take mine. I don't give a shit. But our best friend is lying toasted in a plastic bag somewhere, and you're dragging me all over kingdom come, keeping me in the dark like some kind of mushroom. And for what? So we can follow this asshole till hell freezes over? I don't think so, Chan. We're waiting for something, but only one of us knows what it is. Why don't you just let me off here. I'll see that this thing gets taken care of the right way. At least one of us hasn't been bought."

"Hey, fuck you, okay? No one's *bought* me, Sammy. *No one*. Understand?"

Sam remained silent.

Chan drove quietly for a few moments. "Do you know where we're headed?"

"I don't even know where the hell we are."

"They're going to the estate."

"So?"

"You know why?"

Sam eyed Chan's profile, dipping his head slightly as if to show he was not interested in games. "No, Chan, why?"

"Because Lianne Rybeck has set a trap for our man. She's going to kill him, Sammy. We've been following him to make sure he gets his ass on that estate. From there, she'll do the dirty work."

Sam closed his eyes and rubbed a temple. Chan had just said *checkmate* and the pawns had hardly been moved yet. "I'm missing something here. She's not doing this because you asked her to?"

"No way. It's a long story, but basically this is something she's needed to do for a very long time. I guess I just didn't feel like talking her out of it."

"Son of a bitch," Sam said in a bewildered tone of voice. "How long have you known about this?"

"Since yesterday."

"You mean, when you went to go see her?"

Chan nodded slightly. "Yes. Like you mentioned, I was none too happy when I burst into her room. But one thing led to another, and the next thing I know she's begging me for help."

"Obviously, she didn't know who she was talking to."

Chan gave him a glance. "Not so obvious."

"Did you help her?" Sam asked with some amazement. It would certainly be out of character for the law-and-order man he'd always known. "You're not taking part in this, are you?"

Chan wanted to make sure his ass was covered. This was exactly why he would have preferred to have kept this between him and Lianne. Two people can keep a secret only if one of them is dead. "No, I don't have anything to do with this, Sam. That's the God's honest truth. My only part is not calling the cops."

"And making sure he gets to the estate."

"Yes. But I've done nothing to force his choice. He's going there of his own accord."

Sam looked out his window. "I can't believe this."

The two drove in silence for a while. "Now you know."

"Yeah. Now I know," Sam said to his passenger-side window. He turned and spoke softly to his friend. "Listen . . . about what I said back there . . ."

"Forget it." Chan didn't blame him. Chan would have felt the same way. And besides, the two of them had been through hell the past two days. As with a married couple, things get said in the battle's pitch.

"So what's her plan?" Sam asked.

"I didn't ask. I do know that she's going to offer him use of the company plane, but that's about it."

Sam rubbed the back of his neck, staring out his window. "This is too much," he said with a weak chuckle. "So you're telling me that if we can make sure this asshole gets on the estate, he's as good as dead?"

Chan lifted a shoulder. "Don't know. Guess it depends on how good Lianne's plan is."

"Well?"

"Well what?"

"Is she good enough? Can she kill?"

Chan opted not to tell Sam that it wouldn't be her first time. "Yes, I think so."

"Well, shit . . . let's *carry* the bastard up there."

"He's just over the rise," Chan said, pointing up the road. "If I'm right, when we get up there, we'll see them stopped at the guardhouse."

Sam lit another cigarette. "What if she fucks it up? Then what do we do?"

Chan slowed the Saab to a crawl, pulling to the side of the road just prior to poking its grill over the crest of the hill. "That's not our worry now."

Chan put the Saab in park, opened his door, and stepped out. "What are you doing?" Sam asked, looking at Chan's jeans through the driver-side window.

"We're the only car for miles," Chan said. Sam stepped out and rested his left elbow on the roof, watching Chan start toward the top of the rise with binoculars in hand. "If he's watchful at all, he'll spot this baby coming up over the ridge in a heartbeat. I don't want to take the chance. Not when we're this close."

Sam followed behind him, jogging a couple of steps to catch up. Chan had already reached the top and was looking down the hill through his binoculars. From this vantage point he had a clear view of the guardhouse entrance and the last part of the drive before it dipped slightly on the approach to the estate's four-car garage and Chan's apartment. With the exception of parts of the first floor near the kitchen, much of the mansion itself was clearly visible, though the porticoed entrance and garage were completely blocked from his view.

"Are we going in?" Sam asked when he caught up with his friend.

Chan dropped the binoculars to his chest and eyed Sam quizzically. "Are you nuts? No way I'm going in there. This is about as close to this mess as I want to get."

"So, that's it? We're done?"

"Almost."

"What if she messes up?" Sam asked. "What if she can't pull it off and we see him leave again?"

"That's why we're staying right here until something happens."

"Give me a for instance."

"I don't know," Chan said, squinting through his binoculars again. "Cops come. We hear a shot. Someone comes or goes. We'll know it when we see it."

Scotty's red Volvo came clearly into view as it rose up the slight hill of the drive. Sam didn't need binoculars to make it out. "There they are!" Sam said, rubbing his hands together with excitement. "They're going in. Oh, *pleeease* make this happen." Sam turned to his friend. Though they were several hundred yards away, he still whispered. "Hey, Chan, is it wrong to pray for someone's death?"

Chan had already been there. "I've been asking myself the same thing."

ODDLY, NO GUARDS were on duty when Warren and Scotty pulled up to the Rybeck estate. In fact, not only was the main entrance unguarded, the gates to the mansion were flung wide open, as if welcoming them both home. Warren knew Lianne well enough to feel slightly on edge. In all the times he had entered these grounds, he had never just driven in. It made him wonder. It would be blip number one on his radar screen.

"Stay here," Warren said to Scotty as he pulled around, parking the Volvo under the portico roof. "I'll come get you when we're ready."

"Where's Valerie? You promised she'd be here."

Warren had already stepped outside the car and closed the door. He leaned his head through the open window. "I don't know. Just stay here. I'll come for you once your mother and I have talked."

Warren walked around the back of the car, stopping as Scotty opened his door and stepped out. "Scotty, what the hell did I just say to you? *Please*, just stay in the car. I'll come get you."

"Can I see my mom?"

"Yes, Scotty, you can see your mother . . . later. Right now, I want you to stay put."

The kitchen door was open, covered only by a turn-of-the-century screen door. Warren opened it, took one last look at Scotty sitting forlornly inside the Volvo, and stepped inside. The kitchen was empty. No one was preparing the evening meal, nor was anything cooking on the stove or in the oven. For the first time, it dawned on Warren that Lianne had most likely sent everyone away. Blip number two.

He walked quickly through the various rooms of the sprawling home, checking the formal dining room first, then the sitting room, the living room, the music room, and the solarium, before finally heading down the Victorian-tiled foyer toward the north wing. He stopped at the entrance to Severin's study, just long enough to poke his head in. Warren was preparing to move on when he caught a movement in the corner of his eye. Lianne was sitting in a large leather chair, the same one Ederling had sat in when Severin Rybeck had attempted to explain the concept of options to him and Jake.

"Well, well," Warren said, stepping slowly into the sunlit room. "Hello, Lianne. We finally meet again. It's been a long time."

Ice rattled against the sides of her glass as she whirled a half-finished lemonade on her knee with her left hand. Her right was stuck between the side of the chair and the seat cushion. Warren noticed her body tighten, but her right arm and hand remain still. Blip number three. "Not long enough," came her stone-cold retort.

Warren smiled and walked into the room, sitting on the far end of the sofa opposite her. He knew he needed to be very careful here. He had just walked into the lioness's den, and everything he had seen so far told him she did not plan on his walking out. "You didn't miss me? Not even a little?"

Lianne remained silent, staring at him with steely, frigid eyes.

"Bet you never found another man who could make you come the way I did, huh, Lianne? By the way, did you ever find another man?"

Lianne hated Warren more than words could describe. Her brow was stern, her glare viperous, burning laser-guided holes of spitting rage directly between Warren's eyes. "Where's Scotty?"

"He's here."

"*Where* is he?"

"I told him to wait in the car."

Her stare continued unabated as she nodded her head almost imperceptibly. "Here's how we're going to do this, Warren."

Warren sat forward, waving a hand in the air. "Wait, wait, wait," he said quickly as if she had somehow gotten it all mixed up. "*You* are not going to tell *me* how this thing goes down. Your darling little son still believes me. *I* call the shots from here on out."

"I don't think so, Warren."

Warren laughed out loud. "Lianne, I can still read you like a book," he said, chuckling. He mocked her now. "What? You gonna shoot me? Oh, *please.*

Don't you want to at least wait until I disown your precious one in front of your eyes? Those were your words, weren't they, Lianne? You kill me now, guess who he's going to blame?" He didn't bother telling her that right now, Scotty could probably go either way. "He will hate you for the rest of your life."

Warren was always in control. He always had all the answers. It was all Lianne could do not to fill him with lead as he sat. She took a sip of her lemonade and set the glass down on the end table beside her. "You're a disgrace to the human race, you know that? It makes me sick to even look at you."

Warren smirked, scratching his cheek as if she were boring him intensely. "Really? What exactly makes you say that, Lianne? Is it because I like money? I guess you're not guilty of that, right? No wait, I got it . . . it's because I don't want to work for it, right? Yeah, that must be it. So, tell me . . . what exactly did *you* do to earn yours? Plop out? Now, *that's* earning it, huh? Or is it because I go after what I want? Is that it? Of course, you don't do that either, do you? You know, Lianne, now that I think of it, you and I share a lot in common."

Lianne tried to block out his words, but they seared her eardrums nonetheless, every one of them piercing like an ice pick. She closed her eyes, tilting her head up slightly. Her immediate thought was to breathe deep. She needed to control her rage, at least for a little while longer, at least until Warren voluntarily walked out of Scotty's life. If she removed him from it forcibly, there was no telling what the fallout might be.

"Go ahead, Warren. You tell yourself whatever lies necessary so you can look in the mirror every morning. You and I both know you're a cold-blooded murderer."

The game was afoot. Warren smiled with glee at the prospect of taking Lianne on. "Yes, indeed, ladies and gentlemen," Warren said, clapping his hands together, "the truth comes out." He sat forward, scorching Lianne with a murderous stare, his voice suddenly turning deeper, more menacing. "Just whose *truth* do you listen to, Lianne? You can't possibly believe that. Do you *really* think that your burning Josephine alive was somehow different? Or is it just that you're rich, and I'm not. You know? Your motives always purer, seeing as how they're coated in gold?"

"How'd you find my son?"

"Scotty?" Warren asked with a wave of a hand. "Easy. I needed a little help once I got out of prison. I've had my eyes set on you long before I ever walked out of there. But I made some good friends. Helpful friends. Remember? I can be dashingly charismatic when I want to be—"

"What you mean to say is when there's something you *want.*"

Warren sat and stared at her with pursed lips. "Can't argue with you there." He smiled broadly. "So, anyway . . . a few of my friends set me up with a new identity, a new name, new papers . . . it's easier than you might think. One day, I booked a trip for you and Severin to Boulder. I booked two out, but three for the ride back. Guess who the third was?"

"What do you mean, *you* booked our trip?"

"That's my job, Lianne," Warren said with a smile. "When I do something, I do it right, remember? I told you I've been planning this."

The extent and scope of Warren's scheme seemed to grow before her eyes. They widened with the sudden realization that he had maniacally burrowed himself into the inner workings of the Rybecks' lives, going so far as to follow virtually every trip she and Severin had taken the past few years. "You work at Executive Travel?"

A broad Cheshire-cat grin grew on Warren's face. "Surprise."

Lianne dared not dwell on it too long. It was this very psychotic obsession that frightened her, even as she sat with her hand on a gun. "You do it right, huh? You seem to have screwed this one up pretty well."

Warren's eyes narrowed. "No, Lianne, *I* did not screw this one up. Your moronic son takes those honors."

She spoke calmly, her voice strained. "Warren, I would appreciate it if you would not call Scotty names. He does very well with the challenges God has given him. Or should I say, with those you and that bitch wife of yours gave him."

Warren remained silent for the longest time. "Ouch," he finally said, affecting a nonexistent emotional hurt. The word rolled slowly off his tongue.

"If you ask me, Warren, he's got more sense than you'll ever have."

"*Please* give me a break, Lianne," Warren said as she stared at him with the ire born of a mother's love. "Fine. He's a rocket scientist, okay?"

Lianne had had enough. "Get Scotty."

"Not so fast, Lianne. We have a few details to work out first."

"I said . . . get Scotty."

"And I said, not yet."

Lianne's spine tingled. "What? What do we need to work out?"

"First, I want to hear you speak with the pilot of the plane. And I want to be on the phone. I want to know this flight's for real."

"Fine. What else?"

Warren wagged a finger. The sooner she made that call, the closer he'd be to ridding her from his life. All he'd need then were the jewels. "First things first. Right now, we call the pilot."

"Where do you want to go?"

Warren smiled. "You must think I just fell off the turnip truck. Just tell him we'll be heading south. Plan on refueling in the Caribbean."

Lianne knew she would never get her son until she fulfilled this part of the bargain. The sooner she made the call, the sooner she could rid the world of Warren Parks. "Fine," Lianne said, reaching over to the phone on the end table.

"Where's another phone?"

Lianne pointed to Severin's desk and watched as Warren rose and took a seat in the leather-upholstered swivel chair. He listened intently with a hand over the receiver as Lianne spoke to the pilot in some detail. She explained that a friend of the family would be traveling to an as yet unknown destination, but that his flight plan should include refueling in the Caribbean. From there he was to take his guest wherever he was told.

Every plan has its weakness, and Warren knew this was his. There was no way he could be certain that she had not just spoken to an FBI agent. But if she had set a trap, he felt sure she would come clean once Warren told her that Scotty was also being sought by the law. An Achilles' heel is a wonderful thing, he thought. Far more useful than a nose ring.

"Scotty comes with me," he said immediately after she hung up.

Lianne shook her head vigorously. "Absolutely not. Leave him here or there will be no flight."

Warren leaned on the desk, staring at her in silence. "Lianne, don't be unreasonable. You can't expect me to get on that plane once I've given you everything you want. We can both come out winners here. Just use your head."

One of us will, she thought. Hell, it was all a charade anyway. Warren was never going to get close to that plane. "How do I know you won't kill him once I've given you everything *you* want?"

Warren walked back to the sofa, sat down, and scrunched his face, implying that her concerns were completely unfounded. "Why would I kill Scotty, Lianne? I don't give a *shit* about him, and you know it. All I want is to get him out of my life. You can have him, believe me. But there's another reason you should let him travel with me. Your rocket scientist there is in deep, deep trouble. You make him stay here, and I can promise you he's going to spend a good, long time in jail."

Lianne sat up, removing her hand from the gun concealed beneath the cushion. "So help me God, Warren, if you've gotten my boy into trouble . . ."

"Relax, Lianne. I didn't do shit. It's just that Einstein thought it would be sweet if he brought me home a surprise. It just so happens she already belonged to the fire marshal."

Warren's words paralyzed Lianne. He couldn't possibly be telling the truth. "What are you talking about? Don't you *dare* play games with me, Warren. Not now. Not when I hold your future in my hands."

"You don't believe me? Fine. Ask him yourself, Lianne. He kidnapped the goddamned fire marshal's girlfriend!"

"That Ferguson fellow?"

"Oh, I see you know him, too?" Warren sat back, nodding his head. "Yes, Lianne . . . that Ferguson fellow."

Lianne put her hands to her mouth. "Oh, my God. Did you put him up to that?"

"Right. I'm a hairsbreadth from doing my thing clean, and I'm going to tell him to kidnap Ferguson's girlfriend. Jesus Christ! I keep telling you, the kid's an idiot."

"Stop it!" she yelled, tears welling up in her eyes. "Just stop it!"

Lianne's pleas were still bouncing off the room's walls when Warren spoke. "Back to matters at hand. That flight's clean, right, Lianne?"

She nodded.

"If it's not, your boy's going down with me."

She stared at him. "I told you. It's clean, Warren. There's no trap."

"Good. Okay, there is one last thing."

Lianne was fuming now. She never thought she would have to harbor her son. But it didn't matter. She would worry about that *after* Warren lay lifeless on the floor. No one but her and Scotty knew Warren was here. Lianne would bury him under the rosebushes and no one would be the wiser for a long time—if ever. She thought it more than fitting that both animals that had ruined her life should meet their end at the scene of their crimes.

"Let me guess, Warren . . . you need some money, right?"

"I always liked that about you, Lianne. Always so perceptive. Rich . . . but perceptive." Warren scratched something off the palm of his hand, working it longer than Lianne thought she could stand.

"Goddamn you, Warren! Do you want money or not?"

"Yes and no," he said, looking up. He had almost forgotten how easily manipulated she could be. He felt emboldened, deciding now was his one chance. "I kind of had in mind more than just traveling cash."

"How much?"

"Two million."

Lianne didn't flinch. Warren was never going to spend a penny of her money anyway. "I have two hundred thousand in cash in the vault. I can wire the rest."

Warren knew this game. "You can't do that over the phone, Lianne. You and I both know you have to be there in person."

It was Lianne's turn to laugh. "Oh, Warren, how painfully naive you are," she said, enjoying now her opportunity to mock *him*. "Do you presume to think I can't? That I just call up the local branch and ask to speak to the manager? My family is one of the wealthiest in this country. I can do *anything* I want by phone. You see, Warren . . . the truly wealthy don't like to be made to leave their compounds. It's not safe, you know?"

Warren hated her pretentious manner, her holier-than-thou persona—the high and mighty with their inherited riches and imagined self-worth. It would please him beyond description to slit her neck from ear to ear. His mind would forever recall the memory, and he would relish the vision every time it did. But Lianne was right. Warren was naive when it came to the inner workings of the super-rich. Maybe she could wire him money via the phone, but then again, maybe not. The jewels he could see and touch. No thanks, Lianne, he thought. Warren thought it safer to settle for a bird in the hand.

"I was thinking more along the lines of some of your jewelry." He paused for a moment, watching for her reaction as he held out both his hands. "Now, don't go getting all worried, Lianne. I'm not going to clean you out. Just some of the bigger items. You know, enough to give me a steady start in my new home. Although, now that you mention you have it, I think I will take some cash as well."

Lianne feared this moment—the point in time when Warren would make her change her plans. He was always more clever than she. Lianne couldn't help but wonder if this was somehow part of a larger scheme. Retrieving her jewelry would require leaving the chair, and that would leave the gun unattended. She couldn't very well take it with her, but loathed leaving it for him to pick up. Her mind scrolled quickly through the various pros and cons, finally deciding to take a stand.

Lianne spoke defiantly. "I'm not lifting another finger until I see my son." She wrapped her arms around her chest. "I'm setting you up like a goddamned king, and I haven't even *seen* him yet. This is not a parasitic relationship, Warren. It's time for *you* to give something to *me.*"

"Symbiosis."

"What?"

"It's known as a symbiotic relationship: one where two parties feed off the other. I think that describes us well, don't you?"

Lianne shook her head. "Whatever, Warren. I don't give a shit what you call it. I just want to see my son, and I'm not moving until I do."

Warren studied her with stone-cut eyes. He stood silent for a moment, reflecting on his downside. He was going to need to bring Scotty in sooner or later, and besides, she would spoon-feed him those diamonds if he'd disown Scotty in her presence. "All right, Lianne," Warren said as he stood. "You want to see Scotty, I'll go get Scotty. I know how *special* he is to you." He turned the corner to the hall. "God only knows why," Lianne could hear him say through a laugh.

"HI, MOM," SCOTTY said with a large smile as he entered the study. She watched him look around the room and noticed his frown when he saw just the two of them. "Where's Valerie?"

Warren stood behind the sofa and rolled his eyes, fully aware of Lianne's movements and location in the room.

"Oh, Scotty!" Lianne said, rising to her feet for the first time. Her son's eyes were swollen, cuts and abrasions covered his face. There's something special about the love a parent feels for a child, genetic to the core—deeply rooted in origin—as primeval as the first lungfish to crawl from the water. Lianne was blinded now to all that surrounded her, her only concern the welfare of her son. Scotty seemed so sad, frightened really, not at all the person she had last seen.

"Oh, honey, I'm so happy to see you. Come here, darling. Mommy loves you so much." She opened her arms as she walked quickly toward him, lost in a mixture of bliss and horror at the pathetic sight of her only child. "My God, Scotty, what happened to you?"

"How are you?" Scotty asked, returning her hugs as he eyed the room over his mother's shoulder. "Where's Valerie, Mom?"

"Valerie?" Lianne asked as she released him, holding Scotty out in front of her by the shoulders. "Who's Valerie?"

As the two embraced, Warren had slid his way quietly to the far edge of the sofa, then pounced to Lianne's chair with catlike speed. He reached down between the cushions and stood now at the foot of the chair, pistol in his hand. "Okay, okay, enough of the crap," he said, brandishing his newly acquired weapon. "I don't have time for this bullshit. Let's get down to it, shall we, people?"

Lianne turned from Scotty's hug, dutifully standing in front of her son, arms extended behind her, as if penning him in. She stared down the gaping hole of the dull-matted, black-barreled Colt M1911 self-loading pistol with which, only moments ago, Lianne had planned to end Warren's life. She wasn't frightened—not for her own safety anyway. She had entered this day with a certain degree of finality, ready to welcome death as her friend. But if Warren had designs of murdering her son, he was going to have to blow her away to do it.

"So, that's it, Warren? It ends like this?"

"Lianne, I came here in good faith to make a swap. A swap we both agreed to. And what do I find in your chair? *This?*" Warren asked, holding the gun up sideways. "Let me guess. You didn't know it was there."

Lianne laughed. "Good faith? You came here in good *faith?* Don't forget, Warren . . . I can still read *you* like a book."

"Really? Well, then, why don't you tell me how this chapter ends."

Lianne held her hands out, waist high, trying to calm the situation. "Warren, there's still time to do this as we planned. You kill me now, you leave here penniless."

Warren sat on the edge of the oversize chair, aiming the gun at Lianne. "That is why you are going to get the cash and jewels . . . *now.*" There followed a lengthy silence as Lianne desperately tried to think events through in her mind, her deliberation finally interrupted by Warren's next command. "Come here, Scotty."

"No!" Lianne bellowed, holding him tightly behind her. "You stay right here, Scotty." She spoke in Warren's direction, but her words were clearly aimed at her son.

Warren spoke forcefully, slowly, emphasizing his desire. "Scotty . . . come here, now. I said *now*, Scotty."

Lianne was beyond tears. If it were a revolver Warren held, she would gladly have welcomed a game of Russian roulette. Winner takes all. She could feel Scotty move, taking a few steps back. She turned, facing her son, holding his cheeks in her hands. "Scotty, please don't. I'm begging you, honey! Please don't go to him."

"Don't worry, Mom."

"*Please* don't, Scotty."

"If I come over there," Scotty finally asked Warren, "do you promise not to hurt my mother?"

"Have I ever lied to you? I don't want to hurt anyone, Scotty. I just want to get my money and get the hell out of here. Who do you trust, Scotty? Me, or your mother? Remember, this isn't even my gun. This is your mother's gun, Scotty. She was going to kill me with it, weren't you, Lianne?"

"Don't listen to him, Scotty," Lianne begged. "He's lying to you. He's going to kill us both. Can't you see that? He's lying, Scotty."

"Go ahead, Scotty," Warren said with a smile. "Ask her. Ask her whose gun this is. Well? Go ahead. Ask her if she was planning on killing me."

Scotty's eyes gazed at his mother's. "Were you, Mom? Were you going to kill Warren?"

"Scotty . . . listen to me." Lianne's eyes begged her son to see the truth. "No, honey, I wasn't going to kill anyone. I promise," she lied, wiping the sides of his face with the backs of her hands. "I only had it for protection. Warren is not what he seems, honey. You *must* believe me."

With stealthlike movement, Warren had risen from the chair and walked the few steps toward his two captives. He grabbed Scotty by the arm with his right hand and whipped him viciously out from in front of Lianne, knocking her to the floor in the process. The power was all Warren's now. He was no longer interested in placating Scotty's childish needs. Nor was he interested in seeing this little dance through to its conclusion. His was a need driven by maniacal obsession. The only thing that mattered—the *only* thing of which Warren's mind could clearly think—was to get his hands on that money, the jewelry . . . *and* secure his freedom. Everything else was static.

"Warren, don't do that!" Scotty said, frightened, taking a step to help his mother. "Look what you did to my—"

"Shut up!" Warren boomed, slamming Scotty down into the chair. "Sit down and shut your *fucking* mouth! Do you understand me?"

"Scotty!" Lianne wailed. She rose to all fours, spittle drooling from the corner of her mouth. Rage and fury roared through her veins, sending her body into near convulsions. She rose to her feet, staring at Warren with bloodthirsty eyes. "You son of a bitch! You lay one hand on him and so help me God—"

"Careful, Lianne, careful." Warren had walked behind the chair. "Use your head."

"I will kill you," she said, possessed now of a hatred she had never before felt. She took two steps toward the chair. "I will kill you with my bare hands."

Warren grabbed Scotty by the hair, brutally shoving the Colt into his mouth, chipping his two front teeth. *"Careful, Lianne!* One more step, and I swear, I'll blow his brains out."

Lianne stopped.

"I see I have your attention now." Scotty struggled to breathe, but Warren only shoved the gun harder and deeper down his throat.

Lianne could hear her son choking, blood dripping from his chin. "Okay, okay," she said, raising her hands and taking a few steps back. "Okay, you win. Just *please* . . . *please* . . . remove the gun from his mouth."

It was Warren's turn for rage. He yanked Scotty's hair, keeping the Colt wedged firmly in place. "Not until I get what I want."

Lianne held her hands to her mouth, near panic at the sight of her son being held so brutally captive. "Oh, God!" she clamored, her hands ripping at her cheeks. "I'm begging you, Warren. Just take the gun out. I will get you anything you want."

Warren ripped the gun from Scotty's mouth, the barrel's sight slicing its roof. "All right! *There!* Happy, bitch?" He yanked Scotty's head back cruelly by his hair, the Colt planted firmly at the top of his skull. "Now, I'm not playing any more games. I said, get . . . the money."

Tears welled up in Lianne's eyes now. The sight of her son so tortured, so used and horrified, was more than she could stand. "It'll take me a little while," she said, the words shaking from her mouth.

"How long?"

"Fifteen minutes."

Warren looked at his watch. "You have ten. Go!"

Lianne stood motionless, trying to offer encouragement to her son with her eyes. "I love you, Scotty. It'll be okay, honey, I promise. Mommy will be right back."

"You have nine minutes," Warren said, watching Lianne run from the room. "Call the cops and I blow his brains out."

Scotty winced in pain, coughing up blood as Warren gripped his hair, pulling his scalp painfully with each jerk of his head. Warren watched him with contempt from behind, desperately fighting back his desire to pistol-whip him to death where he sat. Scotty's shoulders heaved up and down slightly. Warren could see that he was crying. "Stop crying!" he boomed.

"I thought," Scotty said through tears, sniffling out the words, "I thought you were my friend."

"You were wrong."

"But—"

Warren struck him fiercely on the side of the head, hitting him in the ear with the side of the gun. "Shut up! Just shut up! Shut the *fuck* up!"

Scotty was dazed and confused. What had he done to deserve such treatment? Somehow, in the back of his mind, he was aware that events were taking place of which he had no comprehension. Scotty held his right hand to his now bleeding ear. "Where's Valerie?"

It was all Warren could do not to rip Scotty's hair out by its roots. He stepped in front of the chair, leaned down, and shoved the Colt directly into his captive's Adam's apple. "She's not here, you fucking idiot! Haven't you figured that out yet? She's not here! She's never been here! And she is never going to come here!" Warren slashed the muzzle of the gun across Scotty's face several times, brutally slicing his skin with each swipe. "*Valerie! Valerie! Valerie!* If it wasn't for you and that goddamned bitch, I would be packing right now!"

When Warren had finished with his tirade, he raised the gun shoulder-height, as if he were going to swipe it across Scotty's face. Scotty's eyes were pools of fear. He raised his hands and ducked his head, desperately trying to avoid the blows he was certain were coming. He reached out blindly into the air, trying to grab the gun, Warren, anything that might prevent the beating. Warren smiled at Scotty's pathetic attempt at self-defense. He snatched one of Scotty's wrists and shoved two of his fingers in his mouth, seizing them in his jaws with animalistic might. Scotty screamed in pain as the metallic-like taste of blood spurt into Warren's mouth. He spit it back into Scotty's face.

"You useless piece of shit," Warren said, pushing Scotty back with his free hand.

Scotty held his fingers in his hand, grimacing as he squeezed, trying vainly to stanch the crimson flow. He whimpered now, completely defeated, totally at his captor's whim. Tears rolled down Scotty's cheeks as he sat, his whimper eventually amplifying into wails. He cried openly as a clear, reddish-hued bubble formed between his lips.

Scotty's childlike whimpering, his crying and screaming, nearly drove Warren over the edge. He wanted desperately to rid himself of this walking nightmare. He walked to the back of the chair and placed the barrel of the gun lightly into Scotty's bleeding ear. "Now . . . don't make me ask you again. I said . . . *shut up!*"

Warren paced back and forth behind the chair, killing time as he waited for what seemed an eternity for Lianne to return. Scotty never once thought to stand up to his tormentor. He was scared, confused, in pain, childlike in his thought processes. His only thoughts were the safety of his mother and that he had just lost his one true friend. No matter how much Warren apologized, Scotty didn't think he would ever be able to forgive Warren for this one.

"Your mother has one minute left," Warren said, looking at his watch. "Then, *you* can kiss your brainless ass good-bye."

"Please don't hurt her," Scotty said, realizing he had spoken. In Pavlovian fashion, he ducked with his hands over his head, protecting himself from the beating he was sure would follow. But nothing happened. In fact, Scotty thought he was aware now that Warren had stopped moving altogether. Scotty waited in a crouched position, thinking maybe Warren was just playing with him. Scotty finally looked up at the sound of heavy breathing emanating from the doorway. His mother stood gape-mouthed, staring at him in wretched disbelief. In her hands she held an inlaid, dark cherry, wooden chest a little larger than the average fishing tackle box.

"Well, it's about time. I was just preparing to blow your son's head off."

Lianne fought back a nauseous wrath as she beheld the frightful sight of her mutilated son pathetically slumped in the oversize chair. "What have you done to him?" she asked, looking up at Warren.

"He doesn't learn so well, Lianne. A little slow, I think."

"You *bastard!*"

"Yeah, yeah. Are those the jewels?" Warren asked, pointing toward the box with the gun.

Lianne dropped the chest at her feet. "You sick son of a bitch!"

Warren looked to the ceiling, then brought his eyes down on her with full force. "One more time. Are those the jewels?"

"Maybe."

"Maybe, Lianne? Maybe?" Warren walked directly behind Scotty and struck him brutally over the top of the head with the butt of his gun, the blow impacting with the thud of an egg splattering on a kitchen floor.

"*Stop it! Stop it!*" Lianne begged.

"I'd say you both have a little learning problem," Warren said, meeting her glare. "Here's the rules, okay, Lianne? I am going to beat this useless piece of shit to death unless you learn a little respect. Now . . . for the last time. Are those the jewels?"

"Yes! Yes! Stop! Please! In God's name, please, just *stop!*"

"Put the box in the middle of the floor and open it."

"Let Scotty go first," Lianne said, shaking her head.

Lianne watched in horror as Warren pistol-whipped Scotty again, several times in quick succession, blood running down his forehead and cheeks, not necessarily from these particular blows, but from the many that had gone before. "Man, what is it with you people?" Warren asked incredulously. "Is it the money? Is *that* what it is? No one can tell you stinkless shitbags what to do? Is that it? Now, I said, put the box in the middle of the floor!"

Lianne knelt down and picked up the jewels, carrying the glazed, heavy chest to the middle of the huge Turkish rug and setting it down. "There. Two hundred thousand and the jewels. Just like you asked. Now, I'm begging you, Warren, let Scotty go."

"Open it," Warren demanded.

Lianne did as she was told, her mind racing for a way out. She knew Warren planned to kill them both. If only there was some way . . .

Warren shooed Lianne away with the gun, walked over to the box, and looked down. It was perfect—better than he'd imagined. There were brooches and pendants, rings and necklaces, precious gems and glittering diamonds of every cut and size. Not to mention eight stacks of neatly wrapped greenbacks. All in all, there was enough there to make him a wealthy, happy man, for a long time. Warren chuckled. "Let him go? Let who go?"

"Warren, don't do this. *Please.* Let my son go. Just look at him. He needs a doctor."

"Oh, I get it," Warren said in mock realization. "You want me to let *Scotty* go."

Lianne stared at him. "We had a deal, Warren. I've upheld my end."

"You know, Lianne, it's a funny thing about deals." Warren raised the pistol to Lianne's chest. "They have this strange way of never really working out."

Lianne stared down the barrel of the gun. The opening seemed larger-than-life—as if she could slide her entire arm down it and rip its deadly bullets out by hand. She feigned fear now, peripherally watching Scotty quietly lumber from his chair, wobbling like a newborn calf as he stood. He may have lacked the intestinal fortitude to save himself, but gained it and then some at the sight of his mother's imminent demise. Warren was directly between the two of them, unaware that Scotty had risen to his feet. Blood trickled from his right ear, his eyes were nearly swollen shut, his mouth and nose bled openly, tiny droplets of shiny crimson dripping off his chin onto the imported rug.

Lianne knew Scotty had it in him. So smitten with a mother's undying love, she knew in her heart he could never let her down. "Please don't kill me," she said, trying desperately to keep Warren's attention just long enough for her son to jump him.

"Well, let's see . . . the plane, the cash, the jewels . . ." Warren rattled off, aiming the Colt with two hands directly at Lianne's torso. "You know? I think I have what I need, Lianne. You've been most accommodating. Kind of like the old days."

Lianne knew it was over. The hammer had not even made contact, and yet she could already hear the explosion, see the fiery blast, and feel the .45-caliber smash into her chest at two hundred and fifty meters per second. Hurry, Scotty! her mind screamed. Hurry!

"Say bye-bye, now, Lianne," Warren said, laughing as he pulled the trigger, gleefully anticipating the devastating vision to follow. But to his consternation and dismay, nothing happened. Not even a click.

Like all self-loading semiautomatics, unless the slide is pulled back, not only is the chamber not loaded, it isn't even cocked. In a moment of naked terror, Warren realized what he had forgotten to do. But it was too late. When you have trapped the enemy and stand with a heel on his throat, you had best make sure that foot doesn't slip. Lianne stood cringing, standing motionless with her head cocked slightly, her eyes closed to the end she was about to meet.

"Goddamnit!" Warren screamed, placing his hand on the slide at the very moment Scotty pounced on his back. Scotty wrapped his arms around Warren's chest, flinging Warren's arms down toward the carpet as he struggled madly now to cock the gun.

A second passed before Lianne realized she was still alive and thrust herself into the fray, leaping onto Warren with a full-lung scream, ripping at his eyes with her fingernails, viciously biting his nose with her teeth. Warren screamed in pain, flailing his head back and forth as he frantically attempted to pull back the Colt's slide. He fell backward, over Scotty, thumping painfully on top of the open jewelry case, Lianne following suit as if she were a Siamese twin.

Lianne lay on top of him, clawing wildly at his face and arms, piercing the air with maniacal screams. She released her clench on his nose in an effort to reach for the gun as Warren kicked a fading Scotty away with his feet.

"The gun, Scotty!" she screamed. "Get the gun!"

With an instantaneous snap, Warren slammed his forehead into Lianne's nose, sending her head reeling back in a burst of white heat and pain to the thalamus region of her brain. Warren thrust his pelvis, throwing his feet up over his head, flipping Lianne off him as he landed half sideways on his knees, in front of Scotty as he lay on the floor.

Heroically, Scotty rose wearily, swiping at his kneeling tormentor with his right hand. Warren rose to his feet, smashing Scotty savagely in the nose and mouth with his foot. Lianne screamed when she heard the unmistakable cocking of the slide, aware now that someone was soon going to die. She rose to her knees, desperately trying to shake off the fuzziness in her head, only to hear Warren thunder something unintelligible at her son. Lianne raised her head, shaking away cobwebs, watching as Warren stood over Scotty, pistol cocked, held out and downward with two hands, pointed directly at his chest.

The shot roared in a reverberating concussion back and forth across the room. *BOOM!*

"*Nooo!*" Lianne screamed as the first shot rang out with ear-deafening force.

"Take that, you motherfucking son of a bitch!" Warren yelled.

"Scotty!" Lianne screamed with her hands over her ears, her sanity ebbing away, sliding forever through a one-way door. "Oh, dear God! *Scotty!*"

"Here's another, you mindless bastard!" *BOOM!*

"*Scot-ty!*" Lianne screamed again.

Warren's rage was surpassed only by Lianne's as she heard him curse her son one last time. "This one's for Valerie, you idiotic, useless piece of shit!" *BOOM!*

The acrid smell of spent cordite permeated the air as Lianne's innermost fear played out demonically in front of her eyes. She rose in a psychotic rage, devoid of any and all thought or premeditation, reached over with both hands and swooped up a crystal lamp from the nearest table. Lianne swung it full force, cracking open the side of Warren's head, sending him flopping to the ground like so much Silly Putty.

Lianne dropped the lamp where she stood and ran to Scotty's side, slumping to her knees, ranting incoherently as her horrified eyes gazed at the beaten, lifeless corpse of her son lying motionless on the floor. A growing puddle of thick, flowing blood slowly gathered on the handsomely woven rug beneath him. "Scotty," Lianne blathered mindlessly as tears streamed openly down her face. "Oh, God!" she screamed to the ceiling, roaring to the heavens. "Oh, God!" The room echoed with her demented wails of grief. *"Aaagggghhh!"* Lianne screamed again and again, shaking her head wildly, unable to cope with the pain and grief of her loss.

It was not supposed to end this way. It just wasn't fair. Lianne couldn't help but wonder why it was Warren who always won. All her motherly love, all her years of paying and praying, caring and worrying, the endless, sleepless nights . . . and for what? For *this?* Everything she'd done to protect him, and still Scotty ended up with three slugs in his heart? It was more than Lianne could bear. She slid her hands under Scotty's wet, sticky torso and picked him up, bending him at the waist, hauntingly clinging to her life's only treasure, afraid that to release him would somehow bury her sanity forever. But it was too late. Lianne rocked Scotty back and forth, holding him tightly to her chest, praying that she might somehow squeeze his very essence into her soul, desperate to carry him once again in her womb as she had done so many years ago.

"My baby, my baby," Lianne whimpered repeatedly as bloody saliva dripped from her mouth. "Oh, my baby." She rocked him slowly, stroking his hair, wiping blood from his face with the corner of her blouse. She closed her eyes, her mind filling with thoughts of times gone by—of more peaceful days when Scotty was still a happy, vivacious little boy—a dry sponge soaking up all the world had to offer. Lianne's mournful repose was not to last long, however, for it was soon disturbed by the sound of Warren's moans as he groggily awoke from his sudden, unplanned nap.

Lianne was on autopilot—her living death wish now forcibly shoved into the frontal regions of her brain. She walked to the lamp and picked it up, took three steps in Warren's direction, and stood over him like the conquering foe she was. Lianne was staring at him when he opened his eyes. "Hello, Warren," he could hear her say. "You're mine now. You don't know what pain is . . . yet." Then she smashed the lamp down onto his face with brutal force, blackening out his light of day yet again.

A PHOENIX RISES

Book VI

J AKE HAD ALREADY killed the siren on his cruiser as he and Ederling came barreling up Route 121 from Upper Hook Road. They both spotted the Saab parked to the side of the road before Chan and Sam heard the roar of the engine or noticed the wigwags flashing alternately on the grill of the car.

"You see that, Jake?" Ederling asked as they sped toward the hill.

"Yeah."

Both men eyeballed the car as they approached, hypersensitive now to anything out of the ordinary. "Jake! Two men!"

"I see 'em! I see 'em!"

Jake reached behind him and pulled out his .357, while Ederling readied his 9mm. They sped up the hill, screeching to a halt at a thirty-five-degree angle in front of the Saab. Chan and Sam were jolted into action by the sudden, unannounced appearance of the law and had both taken refuge behind different tree trunks a few yards into the woods, just off the side of the road.

"The woods, Jake! The woods!" Ederling said as he prepared to exit the vehicle. He had rolled down his window and jumped from the cruiser first, standing behind his open door, his gun pointed at the trees.

Jake jammed his cruiser into park and followed suit, opening his door and standing on the running board, his arms lying over the roof of the car, also aiming his weapon into the woods beyond. Twice in his career he had been in situations where he had drawn his weapon and was required by law to announce himself. He hated the thought of yelling, "Fire Marshal, freeze!" He'd done it the first time, several years ago, but his suspect only laughed at him before taking off on foot. Jake thought it comparable to yelling, "Dog-catcher! Come out with your hands up!"

Too much was at stake now; too many lost lives, unanswered questions, and too much uncertainty to mess around. "Police!" he yelled. "Put your weapons down and come out with your hands up!"

Both men noticed Chan haltingly poke his .45 out skyward from behind the tree. "We can explain!" he yelled. "Don't shoot!"

"Hands up, gentlemen!" Ederling ordered.

Chan and Sam stepped slowly out from behind their respective sanctuaries, arms held high above their heads. "That's it," Jake said, egging them along. "Slow now. Keep your hands up where we can see them." The two men walked slowly toward the road, Chan's binoculars dangling at his chest. Jake came around the cruiser, closing in on their marks, his .357 held firmly out with two hands. He realized now that neither of them was Warren. In fact, Jake realized he had never seen either of them before. "On your stomachs!" he ordered them. "*Now!*"

The two men dropped to their knees as Jake walked to Chan's side, grabbing his binoculars from around his neck. He flung them to the dirt and maintained his vigilance on the two captives.

"Hands behind your heads!" Ederling barked.

Ederling stood, legs spread at shoulder distance, his 9mm pointed directly at Sam's head, while Jake holstered his weapon and straddled Chan on his knees, bringing his arms around to his sides, cuffing them one at a time. "Stay put," he said, rising to his feet. He removed his weapon again and covered for Ederling as he performed the same task on Sam. Feeling somewhat safer, Jake and Ederling holstered their weapons, jerking both captives up to their feet via firm grips at the armpits.

"It's not him," Ederling said.

"I know," Jake responded.

"We're cool, man," Chan said. "We're on your side."

"Who the fuck are you guys?" Jake asked, pulling Chan to the side of his cruiser. "And what are you doing out here spying on the Rybeck estate?"

Ederling moved Sam to the opposite end of the car. "Do you have to keep these things on?" Chan asked, poking his manacled hands out from behind his back. "Trust me, you're going to need us."

"Right," Jake said. "First, I want some explanations, gentlemen."

The last time Chan had worn handcuffs was in training at the Federal Law Enforcement Training Center, or FLETC, in Glance, Georgia. He'd forgotten the claustrophobic inability to move freely, the mind's yanking at the chains, even though it knows the cause is lost. "I know what it looks like, but we're—"

"Quiet," Jake interrupted. "I'll do the talking."

Chan closed his mouth, sighing deeply as he let his shoulders sink.

"You," Jake said, standing in front of Chan. "What's your name?"

"Chandler Boutet."

Jake looked at Ederling. "Did you say Chandler Boutet?"

"That's right."

"Severin Rybeck's limousine driver?"

"*Ex*–limousine driver."

Jake smirked. "Whatever. You know, your name just keeps popping up. You sure get around, Mr. Boutet. For a while there I thought there was a good chance you were roasted to a crisp in your Jeep down in Jersey."

Chan hung his head. "No. That was my best friend."

"I'll bet." Jake looked in Sam's direction. "You, Mr. Talkative over there. What's your name?" Jake asked.

"Sam Broadman."

Jake's sixth sense was beginning to tell him that both these men were okay. But still, he wanted more facts. "Okay, guys, someone's got some talking to do. Who wants to start?"

Chan and Sam looked at each other. Chan took the honors. "Look, I know what you're thinking. We both know what you're thinking. We've got cops' minds. We both spent twenty years in the Secret Service. I know what *I'd* be thinking if I drove upon you two out here spying on Lianne's place."

"Lianne, huh?" Jake asked. "First-name basis?"

"What's your name?" Chan asked. Jake told him. "Mr. Ferguson, I worked there for five years."

"Okay, so you say you're ex–Secret Service," Jake responded. "How do I know you're not yankin' me?"

Chan motioned to the Saab with a nod of his head. "In the car. There's a green knapsack on the backseat. Inside you'll find my commission book."

That sounded legitimate to Jake. He knew that all federal law-enforcement agents carry commission books, basically an official form of ID, with a badge number, photo, and a list of authorized activities its holder is sanctioned to carry out. He also knew that if his captive was on the up-and-up and had indeed left the Service, the word RETIRED would be stamped in bold red across his book.

Jake eyed Chan, eventually walking to the Saab and rummaging through the knapsack. He quickly found Chan's book and opened it, pursing his lips as he eyed the word RETIRED stamped at an angle in large, red, block letters on the page opposite his photo. He carried it back to the cruiser and looked up at Chan, then down at the photo, checking to make sure it was the man standing in front of him. Jake closed it and held it in his hands. "All right. So you're for real. You mind telling me just what the hell you're doing out here?"

"The same thing you are, I would imagine. We're following Warren Parks."

Jake stared at him, his eyes narrowing in skepticism. "Just for the sake of argument, let's say I believe you. What the hell are *you* following him for?"

"Because that's what Lianne hired me to do."

Jake and Ederling traded glances. "What do you mean that's what Lianne hired you to do?"

"Just what I said." Chan shrugged his shoulders. "Lianne asked me to follow him and record his every move. Who he met. Where he went. You know? The usual surveillance crap."

"She's been paying you to follow Warren?"

"Yes."

Jake's anger was hard to squelch. "You mean to tell me you've known where this son of a bitch has been the whole time?"

"Now wait a minute, Mr. Ferguson. It's not quite that simple. I guess the best answer I can give you is yes . . . and no. I mean, we didn't exactly know *who* he was when this whole thing started. We didn't piece it together even *after* he torched Dan."

Jake tilted his head. "Dan?"

"Yeah, Dan Shackling. He was Sammy's and my best friend. His death . . . you know? The way he died and all . . . it's been a real difficult thing for us to accept. Especially for Sammy over there." Chan dropped his voice. "He watched him burn. I think it's going to leave its mark."

So that's whose ring it was. DS. Dan Shackling. At least Jake was getting some pieces of the puzzle. "Okay, so Lianne hired you to watch Warren. Who are these other guys? Who the hell was this Shackling guy and your friend over there?"

"You ever sit on a stakeout before, Mr. Ferguson?" Chan asked.

"Yes."

"Alone?"

"No."

"I rest my case. I needed help, so I called the two men I trusted most. Both of them are ex-Service."

Jake turned to Sam. "You," he hollered in Sam's direction. "You ex-Service, too?"

Sam nodded.

"You got ID?" Jake asked.

Sam nodded again, motioning with his head toward his Saab. "Glove compartment."

"Check it, Donny."

Ederling did, walking Sam's book over to Jake once he'd retrieved it. "He's good."

Jake looked at it, checking its photo against Broadman's face. "So, where's Warren?" Jake asked.

Chan thought of filling Jake in on the whole story, but opted against it. He could only hope that Sam would do the same. "In the estate."

They were so close Jake could taste it. "Donny," he said with a flip of his head as he stepped back onto the dirt shoulder of the road. "Come here a sec."

The two men huddled on the side of the road, discussing the various ramifications of releasing their prisoners, and whether they even had enough to hold them. Even if they didn't, Jake still had half a mind to handcuff them both to their bumper until this whole thing had reached some kind of resolution.

"What do you think?" Jake asked.

"They appear to be clean, Jake. There's no law against following someone."

Jake rubbed his hand over his mouth. "Okay, tell you what. Go to the cruiser and run them through the computer. Let's just make sure they're clean. If we don't get a hit, we let them go."

"Works for me."

Chan watched Ederling as he walked toward the cruiser. "You checking the computer?" he asked Jake as he approached.

"Yes. Something to hide?"

"You're wasting your time. We're both clean as soap."

"Good. Then you won't mind the wait." Jake stood on the shoulder of the road as Ederling slid into the cruiser to run their names through NCIC. Chan interrupted Jake's thoughts. "Look, Mr. Ferguson, I know it isn't my place to tell you how to run your investigation. But if you ask me, you and your partner here are wasting your time. Warren's up there right now, and God only knows what's going on in that house."

"What makes you say that?"

"It's a long story, believe me. But my bet is Lianne is going to try and kill him. Now . . . you can either keep screwin' around with Sammy and me here, or you can let us go. Like I said, you're going to need our help."

Jake was unconvinced. "Really?" he asked sarcastically.

"Yes, *really*," Chan answered with equal sarcasm. "Let me ask you something, Mr. Ferguson. When was the last time you fired your weapon?"

Jake hesitated. It had been longer than he wanted to admit. "Irrelevant."

"Where?" Chan asked. "On the range?"

"Yes."

Chan shook his head. "Ever fire it on duty? Even once?"

Jake saw where this line of questioning was headed. "Listen, I don't have to—"

"Answer my question, Mr. Ferguson. Have you ever fired your weapon on duty?"

If these two men were ex-Service, Jake knew he could not hold a candle to them relative to firearms training. "No," he said abruptly, painfully aware of his sudden feelings of inadequacy.

"You probably only fire it a half dozen times a year, right? Just enough to keep your license? Care to guess how many rounds I've fired, Mr. Ferguson? Take a wild stab."

Say what you will, Mr. Boutet. Last I checked, it was I who placed cuffs on you. "I'm not interested."

Chan was clearly frustrated now. *"Bullshit*, you're not interested! You and your partner there are going to go up there with about as much firearms experience as your average priest. In the Service, we needed to qualify every month. Every *month*, Mr. Ferguson. Together, Sammy and I have fired well over a quarter million rounds. That's two hundred and fifty thousand rounds for Christ sake! We can help you, man. Don't just shut us out. Let's work together."

Ederling came back from his computer check, announcing that they were both clean.

"All right," Jake said, taking out his handcuff key. "You're clean."

"I already told you that."

Jake eyed Chan. "It's always wise to make sure."

"Well, now you know."

Jake took a few steps toward Chan. "Yes, now I know." Jake had no sooner removed his keys, when all four of them heard three gunshots echo over the glassy surface of the Cross River Reservoir. Jake stopped and looked at Ederling. "Jesus Christ. Was that what I think it was?"

"Of course it was!" Chan yelled. "Come on! Come on!" he urged, turning himself around with his hands stuck out behind his back. "Hurry it up, will ya?"

Jake and Ederling unlocked both men almost simultaneously. Jake had to think quickly. He hated to bring these two men along, given their civilian status. But on the other hand, they were hardly rookies. And the mansion was huge, impossible for two men to cover adequately. It was executive decision time—the kind that can cost you your job. Jake squatted, his head drooped practically between his legs.

"Jake, we have to move, man," Ederling said.

"What about the guards?" Jake asked. "Surely they heard it. I'm afraid we're going to be walking into a friggin' shooting gallery, with no one knowing who the bad guys are."

"There *are* no guards," Chan said. "And anyway, even if there were, what's our alternative? Sit here?"

"He's right, Jake," Ederling said.

"I know, I know." Jake looked up at Chan. "What do you mean, there's no guards?"

"Just what I said. Sammy and I just watched them drive in. Gate's open. No one stopped them."

"How do you explain that?"

"I don't know," Chan said, losing patience. "Maybe Lianne sent them away. Who knows, and who the fuck cares? So, what's it gonna be, Mr. Ferguson? You know you need our help."

Jake didn't know these two men from a hole in the ground. They were both armed, and the last thing he needed to worry about now was looking over his shoulder. They were both an unknown—yet another variable in an already complex equation. Every bit of law enforcement training he'd received told him to handcuff Boutet and Broadman to a tree until this thing was over. But, when it was all said and done, Jake was a fire marshal, not a cop. The overwhelming preponderance of training he'd received involved fire, not incarceration and shoot-outs. If he'd been a cop, he might have decided differently. But for Jake, it was the two men's Secret Service commission books that tipped the scales.

Jake took one long breath and made his decision. "Your weapons legal?" he asked Chan and Sam.

"Yes," they answered in unison.

"Extra ammo?"

They both nodded.

Jake hoped he was making the right decision. "All right, you're coming in with us," he finally said. "Here's what we're going to do. Don and I are the first line of defense, got it? Neither of you are law enforcement officers, so we have to be very careful how we approach this." Jake turned to Ederling. "Donny, give Sam your radio." He turned to Sam. "Mr. Broadman, you hang at the gate. Anyone tries to get in or out, report in immediately. I'm calling for backup. I'll let them know to look for you." Then Jake turned to Chan. "Mr. Boutet, you come with Donny and me. I want you to guard the front entrance to the house. Anyone runs up that driveway or across that lawn, take cover and scream bloody murder." He looked into each man's eyes. "Questions?"

Everyone shook his head.

"Okay, let's go. We'll take my car."

The four men piled into Jake's cruiser as he turned the ignition and squealed up the remainder of the hill then down the incline. He radioed for backup, slowing as he came to the gates. Jake stopped and opened his door, placing one foot on the drive as he looked around. Ederling did the same. Sam got out of the car, shoving his 9mm Glock in the small of his pants. It caught Jake's attention. A Glock is not your average handgun.

Jake felt it only prudent to check for guards first, before entering the grounds. The last thing he needed was a shoot-out before even reaching the estate. "Hello!" he called out, listening for a response.

He and Ederling looked at one another over the roof of the car. "Nothing," Ederling said.

Jake looked at his partner. "They must be gone."

Ederling eyed the wide-open gates. "Maybe, but you think they'd just leave them like that?"

"Something's wrong," Jake said.

"No shit," Chan added from the backseat as Jake ducked and slid back in, closing the door after him.

"Hey," Jake said, only half tongue in cheek. "Quiet in back."

Jake pumped Chan for specifics of the inside of the mansion as they rode up the incline of the drive. It was surprising what he and Ederling learned in the minute or so it took them to make the trip. Jake looped around and up, eventually coming over the rise, heading down toward Chan's apartment.

Ederling immediately noticed the HIMRTON license plate on the Volvo. "See the plate, Jake?"

"Yep," Jake answered, whipping out a three-point turn, backing his cruiser up to Scotty's grill.

Chan got out and looked up the drive. "I'll be somewhere between here and the front."

Jake hated to waste the man's talents, just leaving him out in front like that. He was obviously trained and probably knew the Rybeck home better than anyone. But there was no other choice. Jake simply could not take the chance. "Focus on the front," he told Chan. "You hang back here and someone could get out the front door undetected."

"Don, this way," Jake said, pistol-arm bent, cocking the .357 skyward. Ederling followed in similar fashion as the two men entered the kitchen. Besides the door they had just opened, three others led out of the kitchen. One was to Jake's left, apparently accessing the back stairs, the same ones Lianne had taken when she came down a few morning's ago to solicit Chan's help in tracking Warren. The other was on the right to the far left of the wall, while the third was to Ederling's immediate right.

Jake took a few quick strides to the door leading to the back steps, pushing it open with his free hand, peering up the stairs. Satisfied that no one waited on the steps or the upstairs landing, Jake nodded for Donny to take his closest door, while he moved quickly to the one farthest away. They both stood by their respective doors as Jake raised the thumb and two fingers of his left hand. He dropped his thumb first, then a finger at a time. As the third digit fell, they both pushed their way out, Jake ending up in the foyer, Donny in the formal dining room.

Jake remembered what Chan had told him on the way up the driveway. "If you enter from the kitchen, there are two doors leading out to the main sections of the house. One leads to the formal dining room, the other to the foyer heading to the north wing." Jake crouched with his pistol held out in front of him, moving it quickly back and forth, sweeping his surroundings behind the safety of his deadly rounds. Nothing. He turned to his right to see Donny, but Chan had been right. He and Ederling were now separated. Jake found himself staring at an ornately decorated wall with a thick, hand-carved ceiling molding. On it hung two huge oil paintings.

The faint smell of spent cordite hung in the air, though it was impossible for Jake to tell from which direction it came. Someone had fired a gun near this spot. He stopped, sniffing the air, as if an animal in the wild. There was something else, something he had smelled a thousand times before. He sniffed, stopped, and sniffed again. Unless Jake was seriously mistaken, he thought he could smell gasoline. He knew that to head left would take him deeper into the bowels of the mansion. But he hesitated doing that without Donny at his side—or at the very least, making him aware of his whereabouts. He thought of using his radio, but opted for silence instead.

Jake walked slowly a few steps to his right and looked down a long, shiny, black-and-white-marble-tiled hall. Against the stair wall stood a walnut, inlaid checkered game board. His eyes scanned the hall to his left and in front of him as he slowly made his way toward the front door. Flecks of dust danced in the air, illuminated by rays of sun as they cascaded through the beveled, crystal windowpanes lining the height of both sides of one of the mansion's back doors. Jake hugged the wall to his right with his back, extending his gun farther up the stairs with each step. When he was almost at the base of the winding, walnut stairs, he turned, dropped to one knee, and shoved his Smith & Wesson up toward the landing. There was nothing. No movement, no sound, and more importantly, no smell.

As Jake stood now facing the steps, he felt emboldened by his discovery. Whatever it was he had smelled, it was definitely *not* coming from this section of the mansion. The vicinity in which Ederling toiled was now to Jake's left. He walked quickly toward the doorway leading to the sitting room and whispered, "Donny. Donny. You there?" He almost wet his pants as Ederling poked his head out from the doorway, practically sticking it in Jake's face.

"Jesus Christ, Don," Jake whispered. "You scared the living shit out of me."

"I heard someone out here. You're lucky I didn't blow you away."

Jake looked at him. "Funny." He took Ederling by the arm and pulled him back into the room. "Listen, when I came into the foyer, I could smell cordite and gasoline. As I came down this way, the smell got weaker and weaker. Whatever's going on, it's not happening here. Follow me."

Ederling grabbed his arm. "Where the hell is everyone? You think Lianne sent them all away?"

"I don't know, but I haven't heard a peep. You?"

"Nada."

"Come on."

Ederling followed Jake as they quietly made their way back down the hall to the corner where the oil paintings hung. Jake put a finger to his mouth, pointing down the adjoining hall with his gun. "Smell it?" he whispered.

Ederling nodded. Neither man spoke as they worked their way slowly down the corridor, the unmistakable smell of explosives and gasoline growing with every step. This part of the foyer was dimmer than the rest. The walls were a dark mahogany, each section ornately carved with scenes from the hunt: foxes, horses, dogs, and men with rifles adorned each panel, the burgundy, gold, and green embroidered runner only adding to the effect.

Jake stood with his back to a pack of dogs as Ederling leaned against a terrified fox. They scooted slowly down the hall, each man with his back to a wall, each scanning behind and in front of them. Jake could see a set of open double-hung, wooden doors, to the left of which sun filtered through from a set of windows against the west side of the house. An open door only a few feet from Jake threw a patch of sun against a painting of two mounted riders atop huge, Secretariat-like thoroughbreds.

Jake motioned for Ederling to skip across the rays flowing through the doorway so he might enter from the opposite side. Ederling made the trip quickly, quietly taking two large strides on the runner, placing his back on Jake's side of the wall to the right side of the door. Jake motioned to Ederling with his forefinger, pushing his hand down, then pointed to himself, pushing his thumb up. Ederling knew immediately what it meant. He was to turn toward the room kneeling down, while Jake would turn in standing up. Jake's left shoulder was inches from the open doorway. He pointed to his nose, pretending to sniff, signifying that he thought the smell emanated from this room. Ederling nodded in agreement.

Sweat dripped down Jake's ribs as he envisioned what awaited them on the other side. He had practiced something similar to this a few times on the range, but only the *real* thing makes you better. As he had in the kitchen, Jake held up his thumb and two fingers. He slowly initiated a finger count, turning his body toward the cavernous room when his third digit fell. He held his gun in both hands, extending it fully outward. His arms moved deliberately, back and forth, up and down, covering every inch with his muzzle and eyes in a matter of seconds. Jake could feel Ederling's shoulder and arm rub against his leg as Ederling crouched, doing likewise.

"Jesus Christ," Jake said.

Ederling stood and turned toward Jake. He holstered his gun. "Oh, boy," he said slowly. "I got a bad feeling about this one."

Lianne sat on a cast-iron radiator, her back against the far wall, her right hand buried in Warren's hair. He lay half on his side, half on his knees, obviously alive, but clearly in pain. In surreal fashion, Jake watched her slam his head down into the sharp metal edge. Her misplaced smile said it all. "Mr. Ferguson. Mr. Ederling," she said, beaming, as if delighted they had come to visit. "How sweet of you both to come. Warren and I were just talking about you, weren't we, Warren?" She whipped his head again against the radiator when he did not respond, the very sound giving Jake a headache. "Weren't we, Warren?" she asked again.

Jake heard a grunt.

"Good boy. He's a slow learner, I'm afraid," Lianne said as if apologizing for Warren's behavior.

Jake placed his gun in his holster, stepping timidly deeper into the room. He was acutely aware of the thick fumes hanging in the air and immediately took a defensive mind-set. Formulated for high combustibility, few things burn like gasoline. Only as he approached did he notice that Lianne held a crystal cigarette lighter in her left hand. Jake looked at Warren, noticing that he was drenched from head to toe. Fluid dripped from his nose and chin, as if he had just dunked his head into a pool. A red, two-gallon gasoline container lay empty on its side to Lianne's left. Jake could only assume she had doused Warren with its contents. Jake had to agree with Ederling. This one looked very, very bad.

"Lianne, please don't do this," Jake said. "Don't let it end this way."

"There's orange juice and milk in the fridge," she said politely. "Please, help yourselves."

Jake had already called for police backup, but he hadn't counted on this. The slightest miscalculation on Lianne's part, and he wouldn't need cops, he'd need firefighters. He turned toward Ederling. "Call an ambulance, and get the fire department out here, now." Jake took a few more tentative steps into the room as Ederling left. As he approached the back of the leather sofa, a beaten, broken body came into view, lying lifeless on the floor in a glistening pool of blood. Jake had never seen Scotty, but knew immediately that it was him. Who else could it be?

Jake spoke softly, respectfully, as if truly empathetic to her loss. In reality, Scotty was the man who had kidnapped Valerie. Jake hardly felt remorse. Still, he had a role to play, and it appeared to him there was precious little room for a second take. "Is that Scotty, Lianne?" he asked, feigning sympathy as he pointed toward the body.

"Please help me," Warren moaned. *"Please?"*

Warren tried to move, but Lianne slammed his head again, looking down as she reprimanded him. "Warren, I told you not to talk. We've already had this discussion. Don't make me have to use this," she said, brandishing the lighter in front of his face. "I promise, you won't like it."

Warren cried openly, his body shaking with fear. Jake couldn't quite figure what was keeping him in one spot. *Why is Warren allowing her to punish him this way? There must be something I'm missing.* He gazed at Warren more carefully, finally noticing that Lianne had tied his hands and feet together with a braided curtain rope. She had also strung it through the radiator. Jake knew that Lianne was well past gone as he watched her every move. He was torn. A part of him really didn't care if she touched a flame to Warren's dripping wet body. Jake's darker side told him it would be pleasurable to watch Warren writhe in pain. His logical, professional side told him otherwise.

"Is that Scotty, Lianne?" Jake asked again.

"You know," she said, looking around the room, "I always felt this room could use some flowers. It seems so stark, so bereft of life. Don't you think, Mr. Ferguson?"

Jake realized there would be no pushing her. This was one act in which he definitely had to follow her lead. "Yes," Jake said, looking around. "Flowers would be nice."

"Maybe some azaleas?"

"Or marigolds. I know you like those."

"You know, you're right," Lianne said, raising her eyes to meet Jake's. "Marigolds would be perfect in this room."

Jake walked around the sofa, kneeling as he felt for Scotty's pulse.

"Oh, he's dead, Mr. Ferguson. Yes. I'm afraid my Scotty is dead. Isn't that right, Warren? . . . Warren? Isn't that right?" He nodded vigorously when Lianne asked him again.

Warren was begging for his life now, not at all the man Jake had expected to meet. "Please stop her. Please," he pleaded, his last word seemingly bouncing out of his mouth between sobs.

"Quiet!" Lianne boomed, slamming his head once again against the radiator.

Jake eyed the crystal lighter Lianne held in the palm of her hand. It seemed overly large, at least four inches tall, with a small, silver flint on top. Occasionally, she would hold it up just right, allowing the sun's rays to project an incongruous, bright rainbow across the fresco paintings on the study's ceiling.

"Lianne," Jake said as he stood. "What do you say you give me the lighter?"

He could see from this vantage point that a pool of gasoline had formed around Warren's body. As Jake studied the unfolding events in front of him, he became far more concerned about the fumes than he was about the liquid. They were strong, and Jake knew Lianne was completely unaware of the peril in which she had placed herself. The average person is dangerously ignorant of gasoline's extraordinarily explosive characteristics, erroneously assuming that the liquid itself must be ignited to make it burn.

Jake felt certain Lianne was no different, certain that she mistakenly believed she would actually have to touch a flame to Warren before she could witness her desired result. But Jake knew better, years on the job and dozens of unexpected deaths and maimings telling him otherwise. The air was heavy with potentially deadly vapors, and Jake found himself maintaining a healthy distance from them both. He eyed the empty gasoline container on the floor again, making a mental note of its volume. Two gallons of gasoline is a lot of fuel, especially in an enclosed room. Jake knew that if Lianne sparked that flint, she and Warren would both go up like a roll of toilet paper heaped atop a winter night's fire. And that would be one party Jake would just as soon not attend.

"Why would I do that, Mr. Ferguson?" Lianne asked, responding to Jake's request.

"Because, Lianne . . . it's the right thing to do. Killing Warren will not bring back your son. And it will only land you in jail."

Lianne laughed aloud. "Jail? *Jail?* Oh, Mr. Ferguson, you make me laugh. You can't be serious. You hear that, Warren?" she asked, looking down upon her helpless captive. "Mr. Ferguson says I'm going to jail." She raised her eyes to Jake's. "Do you honestly think I care what happens to me now? I care about one thing, Mr. Ferguson, and one thing only: ridding the world of this pathetic excuse of a human being. No . . . I'm afraid you will need to find a better deterrent than jail. I'm going to take out Warren here the same way I did his wife. In a painful ball of flame." She looked down at the sobbing wretch whose life she literally held in her hands. "Isn't that right, Warren?"

So much made sense now for Jake. *Lianne had killed Josephine. Of course! Why didn't I see it before?* It explained so much—the fires, the blackmail, maybe even the rapes. "I don't believe you," he said, stalling for time.

"Really?" Lianne made a move with the lighter. "Watch me."

"Okay, okay," Jake said, holding out his hands, taking a few steps back. "I was wrong. I believe you."

Lianne sat up straight, as if satisfied that she had regained Jake's respect. "Good," she said, adjusting her shoulders.

Lianne was clearly bent on making this thing happen. Jake was reaching now, desperately searching for a way to prevent, even just stall, the inevitable; perhaps a comment, an observation, anything that might make her change her mind, at least until the fire department could arrive. But how do you reason with someone who's lost their mind? Jake realized now that even if his backup arrived that very instant, it would prove useless. Shooting Lianne was out of the question. He couldn't risk a muzzle's spark igniting the whole room, thus causing the very thing he was trying to prevent. And even if that weren't a concern, what it boiled down to was this—Jake simply wasn't willing to take one more life to save Warren's. He just wasn't worth it.

Jake tried to reason with her. "Lianne, listen to me carefully now. Can you smell those fumes?"

Lianne closed her eyes and inhaled. "Beautiful, aren't they?"

"Not really, Lianne. You strike that lighter, and you will go up in a ball of flame."

Lianne frowned. "What do you mean?"

"Gasoline doesn't burn, Lianne. It's the *fumes* that burn."

"Right," she said in taunting disbelief. "Anything to haul him in alive, right, Mr. Ferguson? Please . . . please tell me why you care."

The fumes were making Jake nauseous. He had half a mind to go ahead and let her immolate them both. "I don't. But two wrongs do not make a right, Lianne. If you murder Warren, then you will have proven yourself no better than he."

"Find another sucker, Mr. Ferguson. I'm not buying today."

"I'm dead serious, Lianne. Please. Do not do this."

"So am I, Mr. Ferguson. Anyway, even if you're right—"

"Oh, I'm right, Lianne. Count on it."

Lianne paused. "As I was saying . . . *even* if you're right, I really don't give a damn."

Jake had witnessed too many horrors of the beast. "You will when your skin starts to melt."

"We'll see."

Fight fire with fire. Jake couldn't see another alternative. "Okay, you want to burn to death, be my guest. But first, Lianne, let me ask you one question."

She raised an eyebrow. Lianne was listening.

"If it's true that all you really want is to rid the world of Warren's presence, then why is he still alive? Why haven't you already struck the flint and been done with it?"

"Not that it's any of your business, Mr. Ferguson, but I had only just sat down when you and Mr. Ederling arrived. Warren here didn't go get the gasoline himself. And he sure as hell didn't tie himself up. Isn't that so, Warren?" Lianne motioned toward Scotty's body with the lighter. "My precious baby has only been dead a few minutes. Had you given me one more, I think it safe to say that you would never have met your nemesis alive." She smiled. "See? Things are looking up for you already. It must be your lucky day, Mr. Ferguson."

Ederling came back into the room, walking slowly to his boss's side so as not to startle Lianne. "Everyone's on the way," he whispered.

"Good."

Ederling leaned toward Jake's ear. "Listen, Jake, I don't know about you, but I say we just let her fry the son of a bitch. I mean, do we really care if she kills him or not?"

Jake closed his eyes and rubbed the back of his neck. "You think I haven't thought of that, Donny?"

"Well?"

Jake turned toward his friend, speaking in hushed tones. "I can't let that happen, Don. I just can't."

"Why not? Jesus, Jake, it'd be justice if ever there was such a thing."

"It's not that."

"Then what? You can't tell me you give a *shit* about this guy."

There wasn't time to explain. Not now. Later maybe, but not when Lianne held a ticking time bomb in her hands. "Look at me, Don," Jake said, staring into Ederling's eyes. "That will *not* happen. Not on my watch."

Lianne was saying something to Warren, completely oblivious to the conversation taking place in front of her. The two men whispered anyway. "You ask me, I say fuck 'em both," Ederling said.

Jake's eyes were cast in stone. "I said . . . *no.*"

Ederling squinted, wondering what the hell made Jake tick. "All right, all right," he said, putting his arms out. "Just thought I'd throw it out."

"Trust me."

Ederling sighed deeply. The whole thing didn't make sense anymore. "Okay, you're the boss. So how do you want to handle this?"

Jake turned a bit, just enough to hide his face from Lianne. "Let's approach her from two sides. If we can stall her long enough, we can get the fire boys in here, and they can hit them both with foam."

It all seemed a waste of time to Ederling. "Okay. Let's do it."

Jake and Ederling separated slowly, Jake going left, Ederling right. "Have a plan, do you, Mr. Ferguson?" Lianne asked.

Jake was a little surprised. He would have bet Lianne had paid them no attention whatsoever. He couldn't help but wonder if indeed she hadn't really snapped. She certainly had her faculties about her when it counted. "No plan, Lianne. We just want to talk."

Lianne looked to her right, speaking to Jake. "Talk? About what? How you're going to try to save Warren, here? Don't even *think* of it, Mr. Ferguson. The one man in this room who deserved to be saved is dead. And now, Warren is going to die, too."

"Don't do this, Lianne," Jake pleaded again. "You have no idea what will happen to you."

"Warren," Lianne began, "tell the nice fire marshal how you burned all those helpless victims. Then let's see if he still feels like saving you."

Jake did have a case to close. *I might as well take advantage of it.* "Did you commit the Morson Grayhead murders, Warren?"

Warren rocked back and forth, as if kneeling in prayer to the radiator. "Oh, God. Oh, God," he mumbled with nerve-racking frequency.

"Warren?" Lianne asked, pulling at his hair. "Answer the question."

"Yes, yes!" Warren shouted. "I murdered every one of the sniveling little bitches."

"Why?" Jake asked.

"Why?" Warren strained his neck to look up. He spoke to the wall. "Because it was time, Mr. Ferguson. Time for me to cleanse my past and start anew. Time to finish what Lianne started a long, long time ago. Finish the sacrifice to the demons of my world."

"Enough!" Lianne shouted. "Enough games. I think the time has come for Mr. Parks here to die."

"No one's going to die, Mrs. Rybeck," Ederling said.

Lianne's head snapped left, catching Ederling's last words. He had moved closer than she had thought, and was beginning to feel a loss of control over the situation. "That's enough, gentlemen," she said, holding the lighter to Warren's head. "I suggest you both leave the estate."

"It's not that simple anymore, Lianne," Jake said. "I think you know that."

She turned to him as Jake took a few slow steps toward her, Ederling being more aggressive in his pursuit, taking advantage of Lianne's distracted glare.

"Warren, these men are trying to save you. Isn't that nice?" Warren whimpered incoherently. From his angle, Jake could see that he had soiled his pants. "Do you think you deserve to be saved?" she asked him. "Do you, Warren?" Warren nodded his head vigorously up and down. Lianne looked to Jake and smiled, wearing an almost embarrassed grin. "Pay him no heed, Mr. Ferguson. I'm afraid he has a vested interest."

Ederling took a long stride toward her.

"Stop!" she boomed, placing her thumb on the flint.

Jake grimaced. Ederling was in danger now. If she struck the lighter, all three of them would go up. "Careful, Donny," Jake said. He could almost hear Warren's screams now. *Just one flick* . . . Jake tried desperately not to envision it.

"Lianne! *Stop!*" he yelled.

"Mr. Ferguson, I am bored with your games. For the last time, I suggest you leave the room."

"We can't do that, Lianne," Jake said, his tone of voice growing more firm. "Lianne, listen to me, now. *Please* don't strike that lighter. I will say it again. You have no idea what will happen if you do."

"Mr. Ferguson, your lies are falling on deaf ears." Lianne held the lighter away from her body, as if pointing it at Jake. "See? I can press this flint and nothing will happen."

"*Please!*" Warren screamed. "*Don't!*"

"*Nooo!*" Jake and Ederling yelled in unison, subconsciously stepping back.

But Lianne would have none of it. There was no way she would allow Jake and his partner to free Warren through their childish lies. This was her crowning moment of glory. Lianne would *never* let it slip away.

"Enough!" Lianne ordered. "See? Watch," she said confidently, placing her thumb to the lighter's flint. "We both know nothing's going to—"

"*Lianne!*" Jake screamed again. "*Nooo!*" he roared, instinctively stepping back as he watched her thumb depress.

With a momentary shock a blinding ball of flame exploded in the room, hurling great waves of heat out and away from the wall. Though it seemed longer to Jake, in reality not more than a second passed before Warren began screaming in agonizing pain, the flames licking every inch of his body, ravenously devouring the fuel he had become.

As the initial wave subsided, Jake and Ederling jumped toward the inferno, both men shielding their faces with their arms. Jake had been truthful. The searing ball of flame had fully engulfed Lianne, setting her hair and clothing on fire. In a scene reminiscent of the self-immolating monk in the streets of Saigon during the Vietnam War, Lianne remained eerily still for a moment, apparently unfazed by the painful wounds being inflicted upon her. Jake and Ederling stood, mouths open, in absolute awe of the Kafkaesque scene unfolding in front of their eyes.

Perhaps Lianne had truly not believed Jake, or perhaps she really *did* think it was a death she could face. But she was very, very wrong. Jake knew that the body—and the mind—will *always* choose another way to die, *any* other means than those wrought by the hideous claws of the beast. Why else would people actually jump from a burning building? Because they think they will live? Never. It's just better than the alternative.

Lianne seemed almost stunned that she was, in fact, on fire. She was burning, but primarily because she was in the fire's perimeter, not because she was covered in gas. There was still time. She could still be saved, though her remaining days would probably be a living hell. And though it may have seemed like an eternity to Jake and Ederling, a few ticks of the clock were all it took for Lianne to loose her placid demeanor. Jake's spine froze stiff as the air in the room exploded in a series of mind-searing screams emanating from deep within her lungs.

Ederling made a move to grab her by the arm as Jake ripped down a drape, but the heat was too intense. More than once Ederling was thwarted in his attempt. Lianne stood, flailing her arms, her entire body now fully engulfed in flame. She had apparently been sitting on the Colt. Her skin began dripping from her hands as she miraculously, almost unbelievably, lifted it to her mouth.

"She's got a gun!" Ederling screamed.

Jake and Ederling both rolled toward the wall as Lianne pulled the Colt's trigger, spraying the scorched wall behind her in an explosive circle of red and gray. The concussive force of the shot stunned both men as it echoed off the walls of the room. Warren bounced pathetically in a ball on the ground, screaming in unimaginable pain, unable to move but a few feet in any direction from the radiator, tethered as he was to its base. Jake pushed his body back from the heat, yanking a huge, velvet curtain to the ground with one final tug. He gathered it in his hands and attempted to throw it over Warren, but it was no use. The flames were too large, the heat too intense.

With a smaller flame, and under different circumstances, Jake could have wrapped him in the curtain, rolling him back and forth over the floor. But the flames that swallowed Warren had long tentacles, spanning several feet in each direction. Jake's job was further complicated because Warren was tied practically in a ball, thus rendering Jake's rolling him impossible even if he *could* get to him.

Jake could do nothing but listen to Warren's screams, watching in horror as the velvet curtain melted over his dripping skin. A few moments passed, and then . . . mercifully, there was silence. The only noise left for Jake to hear was the pounding of his heart and the crackling of the flames as they began their inexorable climb up the mansion's west wall.

A professional who deals with fire just can't watch a body burn—whether it's dead or not. Out of sheer reflex, Ederling stepped to the far side of the radiator, ripped down the other curtain, reached over, and grabbed Lianne's left arm with it, dragging her away from the heat. He wrapped it around her and patted her aggressively, smothering the hungry flames, all the while pushing back vomit as the horrid smell of burning flesh and hair hit his nostrils.

The fire was clearly gaining the upper hand just as Chan appeared in the doorway. He had apparently heard the shot. "Jesus Christ!" he screamed. "What the fuck happened?"

Thick black smoke filled the room as flames simultaneously rolled over the ceiling and took to the rug below, crawling along its surface like a serpent on the hunt. "Chandler, help me here, will you?" Jake asked hurriedly, picking Scotty up by the arms. Chan joined him from the foyer. "Get his legs," Jake said.

Together they carried him to the foyer. Scotty's back had been blown completely away. Jake thought he could see an occasional glimpse of sunlight through the three tennis-ball-size holes in his chest as they waddled him away, depositing him halfway down the hall in the direction of the sun's rays shining from beyond. They stepped to one side as Ederling dragged Lianne past them by her scarred and bleeding arms.

Ederling coughed a few times as the three men stood and gazed at one another, the popping and crackling of the flames clearly audible in the otherwise still and quiet house. Jake leaned back against the wall and closed his eyes, raising his head toward the ceiling. Bedford's Volunteer Fire Department was quite a distance from the estate, and though Jake listened intently for sirens, he could hear none. He figured it could be a while longer before he did. Even his backup had yet to arrive, though that did not surprise Jake. The West View Estate was hardly on the beaten path. Smoke billowed out of the room as the three men caught their breath in the relative safety of the foyer.

"Anyone feel like filling me in here?" Chan asked.

Jake and Ederling looked at each other. *You wouldn't believe us if we tried.*

It doesn't take long for a room fire aided by two gallons of gasoline to get serious. "Jake, we should get out of here," Ederling said.

Jake shook his head. "What a shame, Donny."

"I know."

Chan looked back and forth between the two men as flames began licking at the plaster ceiling in the hallway. He was visibly agitated by the growing inferno in the adjacent room. "How long you guys gonna stand around out here?"

Jake knew fire better than anyone. He knew they were safe. At least for a while. "Chandler, meet us outside."

"You guys going to be all right?" Chan asked. Jake and Ederling both nodded. "Okay, you don't have to twist my arm. I wouldn't stay long if I were you."

Jake exhaled deeply, watching Chan jog down the foyer, exiting via the first kitchen door. Jake nodded toward the two lifeless bodies lying just a few feet away. "Don, we can't very well leave without them. You get Lianne. I'll get Scotty."

If Jake were a cop, or virtually anyone else for that matter, he would probably have let them burn inside the study. After all, they *were* dead. But no one—breathing or otherwise—was going to serve as further fuel for the beast. Not in Jake's presence.

The two men grabbed their charges by the wrists, dragging them slowly down the hall toward the kitchen doors. Blood dripped from Scotty's and Lianne's wounds, the heels of their shoes painting macabre, swaggering lines of crimson as Jake and Ederling worked their way down the foyer, through the kitchen, out to the fresh air of the driveway beyond. Initially, they laid them just beyond the door, but realized that soon enough the firefighters would need to use that entrance.

Each man caught his breath before dragging them farther away, down to the safety of the cobblestone drive in front of Chan's apartment—in the end as it had been in the beginning, mother and son journeying together into the great unknown.

JAKE FIGURED A good ten minutes had passed before he could hear the wailing of sirens roaring up Route 121. He and Ederling stood on the front lawn, watching as windows blew out from the intense heat inside the study. Flames roared through the opening, gorging themselves on the open-ended supply of air. Ederling turned at the unmistakable roar of diesel engines as a small cadre of fire apparatus finally made the loop over the hill to the Rybeck home. Two police cruisers followed behind them.

Other than in training videos and various demonstrations the two men had witnessed over the years, neither had ever been given the opportunity to watch a real, unplanned fire grow from scratch *and* witness the arrival of the first engines on the scene. They stood back, observing with exhausted interest as the engine company hooked up hose lines and the ladder's driver set his truck.

Jake smiled as he read the motto on the ladder's side door: FIND 'EM HOT AND LEAVE 'EM WET. He wondered just what it was about firefighters that intrigued him so. Maybe it was their sense of humor in the face of unrelenting danger, or their unwavering need to assist a total stranger at the risk of life and limb. Or maybe . . . maybe it was Poughkeepsie. Whatever it was, it only grew with each passing case. Jake looked skyward as white smoke began to spew from the windows of the Rybeck home, wafting up in huge, rolling balls—the unmistakable sign that for the millionth time, someone was putting the wet stuff on the red stuff.

Ederling was similarly fixated on the unfolding scene in front of them. He turned to his friend. "Mind if I ask you a question, Jake?"

Jake found himself fascinated by the actions of the senior officer at the scene. He didn't bother returning the stare. "Shoot."

"You know in the study there, when I was thinking we should just let Lianne roast the bastard?"

"Yeah. What about it?"

"You were pretty adamant about not letting that happen. I guess I just don't understand why you cared."

Jake turned toward him, gazing into Ederling's puzzled eyes. This case had changed both of them. In a million years Jake could not imagine that his best friend would ever have suggested such an unthinkable outcome. But Jake understood. It wasn't as though the thought hadn't crossed *his* mind. But Jake didn't care anymore. The moment had finally arrived. It was time to come clean.

The floor was Jake's now. "You know how I seem to hate this job sometimes? Especially the roasts?"

"We all hate the roasts, Jake."

Jake smiled in reluctant agreement. "I know, I know. But not like me. Even *you* have to admit that."

"I can't argue with you there."

"Ever wonder why?"

"No, not really." Ederling had never thought there was actually a reason. He just figured it was part of who Jake was, never realizing it was actually part of whom Jake had become.

"Well, there's a reason for it."

Ederling thought it odd how you can know someone for years—be closer than brothers—and never really *know* what makes him tick. People seldom give it all up, even to a spouse. He widened his eyes, raising his eyebrows to signify he was listening.

"When I was five, Donny, I started a fire by mistake. It was cold, and I lit a pile of cardboard boxes in the back stairwell of an old apartment building across the street from where I lived. I was just a kid, Don. We were fuckin' around. Shit, I wasn't thinking. I didn't have a clue what I was doing. I just thought some flames would be fun to watch."

Ederling was trying to follow this through to its natural conclusion. "Were you alone?"

Jake turned as the captain on the scene yelled some orders. "No," he began, returning his gaze to Ederling's eyes. "I was with a friend, but he died of cancer a few years back. Anyway, needless to say, the whole thing got way out of hand. Like idiots, rather than running for help, we tried to throw snow on it. I had no idea how quickly fire can spread. Before I knew it, the whole rear stairwell was in flames. I panicked. I ran, Don. I ran home."

"Okay, so you started a fire as a kid. That's a big boat, Jake."

"No, Donny," Jake said, wiping sweat-matted hair from his forehead. "This boat is pretty small."

Ederling cocked his head. "How small?"

"Small."

Things made sense now. Ederling already knew the rest. "Someone died, didn't they?"

Jake closed his eyes, the sounds of the screaming, burning man jumping from that window still clear in his ears. "Yes," he said softly. "I watched him jump, Don. From my bedroom window. I watched him screaming, hanging out the window, crying for help. He was screaming, Donny."

Finally, Ederling felt as though he understood the secret behind it all. The great and talented fire marshal was doing a job he hated as a payback to society. "Is *that* why you do this?"

Jake exhaled, nodding. "Yeah, even after all this time. It's probably still the only reason. It's about the only thing that enables me to live with myself."

Ederling felt sympathy for his friend. What a living hell his life must have been, keeping such a horrible secret for so many years. "I'm sorry, Jake."

Jake waved him off. "Don't feel sorry. Just understand why I couldn't let Lianne burn Warren. I just couldn't stand to hear those screams again, Don. I wasn't sure I could take it."

Ederling shook his head, rubbing the stubble of his face. "But you did. Take it, I mean."

So, it's out. Somehow, the purge made Jake feel better. "Yeah. I took it."

"Hey, come on, buddy," Ederling said, placing a hand on Jake's shoulder.

"That was a long time ago. You're still the best there is. No one even comes close. We both know that. Shit, *everyone* knows that. I think you've suffered enough, don't you?"

Jake pursed his lips. "Not like that man in the window."

Ederling was quiet for a while, returning his attention to the organized chaos playing out in front of them. "You must've gone through hell."

There's an understatement. "That's one secret that stays just between us. Got it?"

"What secret?"

Jake turned to Ederling with a smile.

Ederling returned the look, smiling back in turn. "Listen, why don't you come over for a steak and beer tonight. Let's celebrate wrapping this thing up. I doubt we'll ever have another one quite like this."

Jake wiped his hair again. "Hardly the ending I'd like to see on every case."

"We did what we could, Jake."

"I know." Jake glanced down at his filthy, soiled clothes. "Listen, thanks for the invite, but if it's all the same with you, I'll take a rain check. I think I'm going to go home and shower. Right now, there's someone else I'd rather see."

"Val?"

"Yeah." Jake looked into his friend's eyes. "I think I'm in love, Don."

"Oh, come on," Ederling said with a friendly punch to the arm. "Love, shmove. Now, deese steaks. Deese ain't what yous call your regular slabs a meat, dere. We gets dat . . . ah . . . grill ting goin'. Dis here could be one of dem dere special nights."

Jake looked at his friend and laughed. "It'll be special, all right."

"You dog," Ederling responded with a smile.

Jake smiled back and took a long, deep breath. It was time for Act 2 in the life of Jacob Ferguson. "Yep," Jake said as he exhaled, "and I still got a few new tricks to learn."

AFTER JAKE HAD finished recalling his horrible memories of Poughkeepsie and declined his partner's dinner offer, both men stood silent
for some time. What Jake had not told Ederling, in fact, what he didn't really
understand himself, was that from the moment he had watched that man
jump to his death in a ball of flames, Jake's future had been preordained.
True, Poughkeepsie had been a living nightmare for him. But as horrible as
the events of that evening so many years ago had become, the second Jake's
immature eyes saw his helpless victim thump to the concrete below, there
would never be a career choice for Jacob Ferguson. Like so many before
him, he had succumbed to the seductive nature of fire.

For the beast is not only a living, breathing animal. It is a siren's song—so
deadly yet so very mesmerizing, a temptation few humans can ignore. Who
doesn't gather to watch a building burn or become lost in the hypnotic dance of
a burning fireplace? What Jake never fully realized was that he was no different.
He had just been touched too intimately at too impressionable an age.

Inexplicably, there exists an allure between humans and the deadly flame.
Something primordial—a love-hate relationship seeded in our deepest roots.
Human beings are the only species on earth that will stand and watch fire, and
certainly the only ones who will start it. All others run. So what is it, exactly,
that makes a child want to become a firefighter? Is it to save lives? Maybe. But
one can do that in plenty of other professions. No, a child becomes a firefighter
for one reason . . . and one reason only. The seductive lure of the *fire*.

Hell.

For mortal men there is but one hell, and that is the folly and wickedness and spite of his fellows; but once his life is over, there's an end to it: his annihilation is final and entire, of him nothing survives.

—MARQUIS DE SADE
(1740–1814)